PACIFIC CLIPPER

Also by Richard Doyle

DELUGE
IMPERIAL 109
HAVANA SPECIAL

PACIFIC CLIPPER

Richard Doyle

Arlington Books
King St. St James's
London

To Sally with love

PACIFIC CLIPPER
First published 1987 by
Arlington Books (Publishers) Ltd
15–17 King Street, St James's
London SW1

© Richard Doyle 1986

Typeset by Inforum Ltd, Portsmouth
Printed and bound by
Billing & Sons Limited, Worcester

British Library Cataloguing In Publication Data
Doyle, Richard, 1948–
Pacific clipper.
I. Title
823'.914[F]   PR6054.09/

ISBN 0–85140–617–3

ACKNOWLEDGEMENTS

This book would have been impossible without the generous cooperation of many people.

Especial thanks is owed to Pan American World Airways Inc. whose illustrious history forms the background to this tale. Ann Whyte of the Research Department and Librarian Liwa Chiu provided a wealth of details on the pre-WWII trans-Pacific Clipper service and allowed me unrestricted use of their records and library.

The Boeing Company remains justifiably proud of their magnificent B314 Flying Boats. Marilyn A. Phipps of the Historical Services Department was unstinting with her help, producing manuals, photographs and much other technical information.

Cindy Lilles, Public Relations Director at the Manila Hotel and Tanya R. Bova of the Royal Hawaiian were of enormous assistance recapturing the flavour of a great era of luxury travel.

Finally my largest debt is to Captain William B. Masland and the late Captain J.C. Kelly Rogers, Masters of Flying Boats, from whom I gained valuable insight into the pioneering days of air flight. Both gave freely of their time and personal papers and I could not be more grateful.

> *And they were stronger hands than mine*
> *That digged the Ruby from the earth —*
> *More cunning brains that made it worth*
> *The large desire of a king*
> *And stouter hearts that through the brine*
> *Went down the perfect Pearl to bring.*
>
> *Rudyard Kipling*

Prologue

HONGKONG BRITISH CROWN COLONY TUESDAY DEC-
EMBER 2nd 1941. *The priest was scared.* It was barely dawn, the
twisting streets surrounding the cheap hotel were still half dark and
choked with the mist which at this season creeps down from the green
peaks to infiltrate the city. Impossible to see more than a dozen feet in
places, but already the first risers were stirring, he had heard a
rickshaw rattle past not two minutes ago. In a short while it would be
too dangerous, he must leave now and trust to the mist to shake off
pursuit. Last night the *Shi-sign* had been found chalked above the gate,
proof their spies must have located him. For some reason they had not
attacked in the darkness. Perhaps it had been an added refinement of
their cruelty to let him suffer in sleepless fear. One thing was certain:
to remain longer was death.

The damp air struck chill as he slipped out into the little square,
clutching under his coat the heavy silver crucifix, and the fog caught in
his throat so that he stifled a cough. The vicinity was empty, no sign
for once of the beggars who had haunted his movements these days
past. *Spies and fifth columnists!* They were everywhere, watching,
waiting, ready to strike at the appointed signal. While the authorities
slept and the Colony lay officially at peace a secret invasion had
already begun.

He started across the square, nervously glancing over his shoulder.
The stones were slippery with moisture and the fronts of the buildings
opposite loomed distortedly through shifting veils of fog. Only the
trickle of water in the gutters and the muffled sound of his own
footfalls broke the blanketing silence. With every second that passed
he expected to hear shouts of alarm. He had almost reached the far side
when suddenly from somewhere close by a prayer gong began to peal
out, the swelling notes echoing relentlessly on his heels.

Instantly he broke into a run making for the nearest alley, a crooked
defile shouldered on either side by the overhanging upper stories of
rotting tenements, its surface pitted and garbage-strewn. The priest's
feet slipped and slithered in the reeking central gulley. He was

short-winded and out of condition, soon his breath became laboured, pain stabbed at his side. Chest heaving, he stopped to listen. No sounds of pursuit. The prayer gong had ceased its mournful peal. Had he panicked for nothing?

Cautiously he walked on a few yards further regaining his breath, then abruptly halted again. Something, he could not be sure what, had caused his fears to return. He crouched tensely. The mist was swirling thicker than ever, coils of vapour writhed into fantastic forms in the watery light. In vain the priest's eyes strove to pierce the murk, every sense alert for a hint of danger.

A cock crowed making him start, the raucous cries ringing out over the rooftops. In one of the shuttered houses a child was sobbing and its mother called to it sleepily in Cantonese. A dog barked and was answered by another. Nothing he could fix on as wrong, yet even so instinct cried a warning.

Then he heard it again: a tapping, faint, irregular but unmistakable, the touch of wood on stone. It was drawing closer, approaching up the alley. The hair at the nape of his neck pricked and he froze listening. *Something, someone* was advancing on him unseen in the fog. Uncertainly the priest began to retreat, backing down the way he had come. The noise followed after at the same unhurried pace.

A paralysing sense of dread overcame his exhausted brain. The sounds were growing louder, whoever it was must be gaining on him. He tried to mumble a prayer but the words would not form. Every nerve in his body shrieked at him to run, but his limbs seemed powerless to obey. Shrinking up against a wall he remained transfixed, his gaze locked upon the fog bank which concealed the oncoming figure.

Slowly a dark shape materialised out of the mist. Hooded and cloaked in black, feet bound with rags, it groped its way blindly forward. A short staff rapped against the stones, sweeping the path ahead for obstacles. The priest stared mesmerized. On the figure came, limping up the alley. Three yards off it checked and stood swaying.

The spell which had gripped the priest snapped. Stepping out from the wall he confronted the menacing presence, "What do you want?" he cried hoarsely, his voice flattened and muffled in the fog. "*Nay wun mee-ye? Nay sing mee-ye?* What do you want and who are you?"

The beggar's face beneath the hood was invisible. He stood four-square across the alley grasping his staff. Terror flowed from him like a tangible force.

"Who are you? What do you want with me?" The priest's voice cracked as the fear hit him anew. "Why do your people hunt me? I am

8

a man of God!" Pulling the long crucifix out from under his coat he brandished it before him. "A man of God!"

The beggar let out a low hiss. Suddenly he whirled, his staff lashing out like a striking snake. With a scream the priest jerked back. The crucifix flew from his grasp and a bolt of searing agony shot through his arm from wrist to shoulder as the beggar's staff slammed into his hand, shattering the carpal and metacarpal bones. Gasping with pain he staggered against the wall.

Quick as a cat, the beggar followed up the attack, stepping in close, his staff a blur. So fluid were his movements, so swift yet unhurried, it was hard to separate the blows, one flowing from another in ruthless precision. Striking aside the priest's feeble attempt at a guard, he jabbed the tip of the staff savagely into the base of his throat choking off his cries. Reversing the direction of the thrust he brought it scraping down the breastbone forcing him to his knees.

Throwing back his hood the beggar stood over his helpless foe. A black cloth bound his head leaving only a narrow slit through which his eyes surveyed the priest dispassionately, doubled up and retching in the filth of the alley. Gripping his staff with both hands he pulled it sharply apart. With a click and a ring of steel a sword blade slid into view, gleaming palely in the dim light.

The beggar thrust the scabbard section of the staff into a belt at his waist and shifted his stance sideways on to his victim's bowed shoulders. Calmly he raised the sword above his head in a two-handed grip. Not a soul peered from the shuttered windows round about. There was a soft, snapping sound as the honed blade did its work, followed by the thump of the severed head. A jet of scarlet squirted from the stump of neck as the still-living heart pumped out its contents in failing pulses and the trunk slumped forward into a spreading pool of blood.

There were voices now in the fog and footsteps audible, approaching up the alley. The beggar's movements continued unhurried. He gathered up the mutilated head and wrapped it in his cloak. Stooping briefly to wipe his sword blade clean he resheathed with a click and pulled forward his hood. Once more he was the simple figure of a blind man pathetically fumbling his way through the back streets. Beneath his mask though his teeth bared in a smile of satisfaction: the killing had been childishly easy; if all Westerners were the same his Emperor's victory would be great indeed.

The tapping of his staff faded away into the mist. Behind in the alley he left the corpse of the first American casualty of the war that was about to begin.

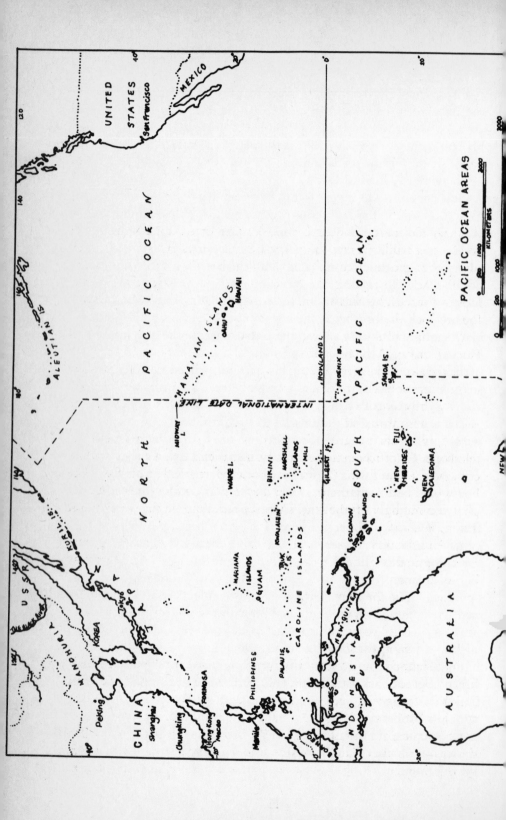

PACIFIC OCEAN AREAS

I

A sound of distant thunder rolled across Kowloon Bay. The army was conducting artillery practice again in the hills. In the belfry of the clock tower over the deserted railway station a shadow stirred. Dressed in coolie black the Japanese lay prone on his belly, swordstaff thrust loosely through his waistband, a powerful telescope to his eye. It was four o'clock, he had been waiting two hours.

With sharp blasts of its whistle a launch sporting the blue pennant of Pan American Airways pulled away from the junks and sampans clustered along the Victoria quays and went cutting across the harbour in the afternoon sun, making for the Kowloon shore. It slowed briefly to cross the wake of a top-heavy green ferry, then settled on course for Kai Tak aerodrome at the base of the peninsula.

Observing its progress the Japanese frowned and adjusted his telescope. An officer in the stern came into focus, tall, wearing a white cap and dark uniform. Canvas mailsacks were piled at his feet. The box would be among them. He let the telescope traverse left. The sun glinted blindingly off the huge flying boat resting on the water at Kai Tak. *The Pacific Clipper.*

Oi! But she was enormous. Truly *Amerika* must be a land of giants. Even so, he thought defiantly, we shall humble them. And softly he began to sing:

> *The Emperor's reign will last*
> *for a thousand and then eight thousand generations.*
> *Until pebbles become mighty rocks*
> *covered with moss.*

In the launch Munro settled the cardboard box on the bench beside him and gazed back astern. Ships of every shape and size jostled in the harbour: freighters, junks, tramps, ferries, warships, *walla-wallas*. Shirtless coolies padded back and forth along gangplanks like trails of ants, bent beneath monstrous burdens. From the red brick of the naval dockyard on the island's western slopes, Hongkong's waterfront swung round in a long shallow crescent to the banks and office blocks

11

of Victoria and the festering slums of Wanchai, all dominated by the mountainous Peak behind. It was, he thought, a hell-hole.

An ancient RAF torpedo bomber touched down returning from patrol as they approached the marine terminal. Otherwise there was little sign of activity. With Japanese forces controlling the surrounding territory, civilian flying had all but ceased over the mainland, although the Nationalist Chinese still ran a skeleton service up to the capital at Chungking for those willing to brave the nightfighters.

Like an ocean liner the Clipper towered over the seaplane dock, the Stars and Stripes emblazoned on her burnished duraluminum hull. It made Munro feel good just to look at her. The Chinese launch crew circled smartly under the tail and cut the engine. Picking up the box, he stepped ashore, broad-shouldered, agile and very tough. Deep set steel grey eyes and wiry black hair. Beneath the port wing the flying boat's main passenger hatch to the lower deck stood open. Tossing a casual salute to the turbaned Sikh soldier on guard, he ducked inside.

"Wipe your feet, darn you!" came an irate shout. O'Byrne the purser bustled up in a white mess jacket, "Can't you see the carpet's just been cleaned?"

"Sorry Pat," Munro laughed and clapped a hand briefly on his shoulder. The lower deck was O'Byrne's personal domain. He was one of those scrawny shrivelled-up Irishmen and you couldn't guess his age within ten years. They were standing in the main lounge, the largest of the eight passenger cabins. It was luxuriously furnished with upholstered armchairs and tables of polished black walnut. A squad of locally employed Chinese were at work with dusters and carpet sweepers. Munro wondered fleetingly what they made of it all. Right now upwards of thirty thousand of their compatriots slept homeless on the streets and the dead-trucks went round each morning to collect the corpses for burning.

"What's that you got there?" O'Byrne eyed the box under the First Officer's arm.

"A parcel for the Skipper. It came over with the mail. There's some galley stuff in the launch, the boys'll bring it aboard." Moving forward through to the spiral staircase by the galley, Munro climbed to the upper deck.

To the crew's way of thinking the flight deck was the Clipper's most impressive feature. The spacious high-ceilinged cabin, fully the size of the downstairs lounge, was lined with dark green mohair and carpeted and sound-proofed throughout to the same standard as the passenger level. There were separate stations for six officers simultaneously on duty, each with their own instruments, and the twin

12

pilots' seats up in the nose could be curtained-off for night flying.

"What's this? I didn't order anything sent out," Ross said when Munro dumped the box in front of him on the long chart table. He and Kurt Thyssen, the navigation officer, were going over the flight plan for tomorrow's trip to Manila. Fifty years old, he was senior captain on the line, with a face tanned and creased like a piece of worn leather and eyes red-rimmed from countless hours squinting into the slipstream of open cockpits.

"It's addressed to you. Some Chinese left it at the mail counter across the way. Want to open it up and see what's inside? It must weigh all of twenty pounds."

"Maybe it's Bishop Buchan," suggested Stewart Whitely with a chuckle from the radio desk behind.

"Who the hell asked *your* opinion?" Ross growled across the cabin and Whitely cringed. He was close to Ross in age and one of the top radio operators in the business, but he had never overcome his awe of captains. Ross was crusty at best and today he was in particularly vile humour.

"Pass the thing here, I'll open it," said Thyssen, whose North German forebears had bequeathed him his stiff blond hair and pale eyes.

Ross's scowl deepened, "Godammit, you mind your own business too." He studied the handwritten label. "*Mister*," on the big Clippers, as aboard ship, the first officer was '*Mister*' to his captain, "Mister, gimme that pocket knife from my desk."

A hatch opened in the starboard bulkhead to the rear affording a glimpse of a narrow walkway, brightly lit and crammed with ducts and piping, that ran inside the thickness of the wing; a huge man in white overalls stepped through. "Hi fellers." Even on the Clipper's lofty flight deck, Ed Crow the chief engineer, seemed to be half-crouching and there was Choctaw Indian blood staring out from the flat, proud, dead-pan features with the copper-bronze tint to them.

"Early for Christmas, huh?" he remarked casually inspecting the box.

Outside on the hull they could hear sounds of the launch crew loading mail bags down into the main hold behind them through the roof hatch.

"For Christsakes don't you start," Ross regarded him irritably. Impatiently he sawed through the string and lifted off the lid. The others leaned forward to see as he tugged away the brown paper wrapping.

"Oh God," Ross breathed suddenly, "Oh Jesus God *no!*"

13

The head grinned up at them hideously, mouth agape, eyes open and staring in the agonised rictus of death.

Through his telescope the Japanese in the clock tower observed a police car drive onto the dock. Two uniformed officers descended. *Yoi! The arrow had found its mark.*

"Inspector Playfair, Special Branch, British Hongkong Police," the senior of the two men introduced himself on the flight deck, "and my assistant Lieutenant Harris." He was the image of the British colonial officer, thin, sharp-featured with a trim moustache. The lieutenant was young and pink-faced. Like the rest of British military personnel out East both wore shorts and knee length socks. Munro could never get used to that. The crew had been joined in the control cabin by the Chief's relief, Chuck Driscoll, a stocky young man whose passion was football.

Ross responded with a sullen grunt. At first he had refused to call in the police. "Hell Skipper, what else can we do?" Munro had demanded, "Throw the thing in the harbour and pretend it never happened? This is *murder*, for Christsakes!"

With cloths from the galley Playfair and the lieutenant lifted the head carefully out of the box. Stewart Whitely gagged and made hurriedly for the washroom. Munro forced himself to look: a European, middle-aged to elderly, drained of blood the skin was waxy smooth and white as marble.

"I take it none of you know him?" said Playfair, observing their expressions.

Ross shook his head, answering for them all.

"There's this, sir," Lieutenant Harris had found a piece of card in the bottom of the box. He brought it out, holding it by the edges as he had been taught so as not to spoil the fingerprints. Only something told Munro the people behind this weren't going to be caught by their fingerprints. The card was smeared with dried blood but the writing was legible, a single word: MILI.

"*Mili*, now who or what would *Mili* be?" Playfair wondered aloud. He turned the card over. On the reverse was a scrawled ideogram.

With a groan Ross flopped down at his desk, shoulders hunched. Chief Crow regarded him impassively for a moment then turned away. Through the window above the chart table Munro watched the driver of the police car questioning the launch crew down on the dock.

14

The sun was sinking, the prop blades striking long shadows across the wing. The inboard set had just been replaced, they had become pitted with corrosion. The salt spray did that landing and taking off. *Mili*, did the word touch a faint chord of memory? He could not be sure. "Inspector, what the hell's behind this – is it the Japs?"

"I was hoping you people might have the answer to that," Playfair said, handing the card back to Harris. "Tell me, Captain Ross, what *exactly* do you know about Bishop Buchan?"

Ross stared blankly in front of him. He seemed not to have heard the question and it was Munro who answered. "Not a lot. He was an American who spent most of his life out here in China. He died a few months ago in Peking, some people blame the Japs for that. We're flying the body home to the States." The rest of the crew looked on stony-faced. Coffins were bad medicine.

"The Japs agreed to release the Bishop's body," Thyssen pointed out, "why should they want to interfere now?" He was leaning against the back of one of the pilot's seats, his uniform cap tilted carefully over one eye in a manner that never failed to irritate Munro.

"Why indeed," Playfair agreed, "I wonder, might I see the coffin for a minute?"

"It's not aboard, they're scheduled to deliver tomorrow morning with two cases of his private papers."

"Ah, so it's at the Consulate still?" The Inspector sounded disappointed, "Well, in that case perhaps you can let me have a complete list of passengers and crew for tomorrow's flight?" He glanced round the circle of faces. Stewart Whitely had returned looking pale. O'Byrne was on the stairs following proceedings pop-eyed.

"For a passenger list you'll have to contact Alan Bond, our operations manager over in Victoria, but I can give you a crew roster, sure. Aside from the seven of us here, there are two up at the maintenance depot drawing spares and three off-duty."

"*Twelve* of you? Isn't that a large crew for a civilian plane?"

"We're a big plane, the biggest in the world," Munro ignored the innuendo. "Some of our flights run twenty hours at a stretch so we operate a watch system like at sea. The captain has four pilot officers under him to share flying duties and the engineer and radio officer each have a relief. Pat here has two to help him on the passenger deck."

Ross came to all of a sudden, "*Scott*, where is she?" he demanded abruptly.

The others blinked at him, "Sally went off-duty midday, Skipper," Thyssen reminded him, "with Shapiro and Fry. You gave them a twelve hour liberty."

Munro caught Inspector Playfair's inquiring look, "Sally Scott is our stewardess. This is her first time in the Colony." He might have added Scott was also the first ever female flight crew on the Company's books and Ross had raised hell when he learned she was to join them. "Shapiro and Fry are third and fourth pilot officers."

"Does anybody have an idea where they might have gone?" Playfair was looking at Chuck Driscoll as he spoke but the youth shook his head unhappily. "We'd better take their descriptions then." Harris flipped open a notebook and stood, pencil poised.

"Aged twenty-two, short blond hair, blue eyes, five foot five, one hundred and twenty pounds," Thyssen supplied the details promptly.

Stewart Whitely sniffed, "I'll bet you know what size brassiere she takes too."

Thyssen reddened, "What the hell's that supposed to mean?"

"Nothing. You know." There was a crackle of static from the radio-telephone. Whitely flicked a switch and picked up his earphones. "Message for you, Inspector," he began jotting on a pad. "Major Slater from the US Consulate will meet you at the Hotel Asia in forty-five minutes."

"Ruddy idiots," Playfair muttered irritably, "I've told them not to send messages like that over the air in clear." He turned to Ross, "Captain, I must ask you to accompany me back to Victoria."

Ross darkened, "What the hell for?" he rasped.

"Because, Captain," Playfair replied quietly, "the murdered man's body was discovered there a short while ago – he was to have been one of your passengers tomorrow."

There was silence. Ross's fists were clenched white at the knuckles. The crew glanced at one another uncertainly, trying to avert their eyes from the ghastly object on the table. Driscoll was as pale as Whitely. Only the Chief seemed unmoved, but he was watching Ross.

"Godammit no!" Ross growled at length, "I don't care who the guy was, I'm not leaving the ship." He scowled sullenly first at Playfair then at Munro, "*Mister*, I'm sending you."

"Aye, aye sir," Munro's face was set. If he were captain he would want to sort this business out himself, not leave it to his officers. Command responsibility they called it. Playfair gave a shrug.

"Skipper, how about me going ashore with them to try find Scott?" Thyssen suggested eagerly, straightening his uniform, "I know the places Shapiro hangs out. Most likely they'll be at Yung Kee's or Jimmy's . . ."

Ross silenced him with a look, "Shut up. We've enough fools missing without you. Mister, go with the Inspector. Report straight back to me when you're through."

"Aye, aye sir," Munro replied again, very formal. He stared Ross directly in the eye, "I'll check it out."

"And you can tell those bastards from the Consulate I'm not holding the ship for them, understand? I don't give a damn who their orders come from." Munro turned to go. Deep down in Ross's gaze he had seen something that made him sick in his gut and somehow ashamed too.

Fear. Ross was afraid.

Nor was that all. He was waiting below in the lounge for Playfair when Driscoll appeared still looking strained. "Max," he whispered urgently, "about Scott and the others . . ."

"What about them? If you know where they are why didn't you say so earlier, for Christsakes?"

The young engineer bit his lip. "I think they went to *Macao*."

Up in the clock tower the Japanese made out the two figures leaving the flying boat. He tracked the vehicle across the airfield to the main gate before intervening buildings obstructed his view. He shut the telescope with a snap. Simple to guess their destination.

There was a whirr of machinery behind him and the clang of the bell reverberated in his ears. Five o'clock. *The hour of the Cock*. Gripping his swordstaff, he ran lightly down the stairs to ground level. The station yard was deserted. Once trains had set out from here for Europe, but now the line was cut at the border and the carriages stood empty. Easily evading the security patrol, he slipped out through a picket gate and was lost among the crowds.

It was the rush hour. In Kowloon traffic had backed up along Nathan Road as far as Yaumatei. Rivers of people swarmed the streets, spilling off the sidewalks into the roadway, dodging between the cars and trolley-buses. The police driver switched on his siren and yelled at the rickshaws and cyclists. In the back of the ancient Humber the two men sat silent. Playfair seemed preoccupied and Munro had his own worries. Jesus, *Macao*! Some people kept their brains in their asses. The gaming tables of the neighbouring Portuguese colony were strictly off-limits. Pan Am crews were forbidden to stray from British territory, anyone who did was putting his career on the line.

It was to be expected of Shapiro: a debonair batchelor with a taste for the fast life. And Chris Fry, the junior officer on board and at

17

twenty the youngest, was a mere boy. Scott was different.

When the Clipper's crew learned a stewardess was being assigned them, they had a mental image of the girl – attractive, charming to passengers, suitably impressed by the experienced men on the flight deck. Sally Scott was pretty alright, a blond-haired tomboy whose cool blue eyes had won round even a determined woman-hater like O'Byrne. She also had a pilot's licence and as many hours logged as Shapiro. From day one she had demanded equal treatment and gotten it. She made no secret of her ambition to command a Clipper. Munro admired her guts.

Only now it looked as if she had screwed up.

They reached the vehicle ferry for the Island and the Humber was waved to the head of the queue. Munro got out and leaned on the rail as they chugged across the harbour. If Ross learned of this escapade he'd have both men grounded and Scott out on her ear.

He sighed and flicked the butt of his cigarette into the waves. He had been trying not to think about the Skipper.

Ross was a legend among pilots, one of the original pioneer heroes. He had flown Neuports in France against Richthofen and bi-planes through the Andes mountains. He had survived forced landings in the desert and crashes on the polar ice cap. He was one of the breed which numbered Lindbergh, Willie Post and Rickenbacker.

Only now he was afraid.

Munro knew, though pilots seldom spoke of it, that there came a stage in the life of every flier when self-doubt began to creep in. When a man no longer had faith in his judgement. When he found himself checking the instruments twice, then again. When he started flunking landings or putting back for no good reason. As if his natural instinct for caution had become a cancerous growth betraying him into acts of cowardice. No one could predict the onset of the disease or help the victim. He had to fight it through on his own. Most succeeded and found new strength in doing so. A few did not.

Ross could go either way.

They drove off again onto land past the towering facade of the Hongkong and Shanghai Bank and turned eastward along Des Voeux Road. The traffic stream was heavier still on this side. Clerks and secretaries streamed from dense-packed office blocks. By the cricket ground a bomb shelter was being dug. It looked insubstantial. A scandal over defence contract profiteering was currently rocking the Colony.

"Where are we headed?" he asked Playfair. "*Wanchai,*" came the clipped reply and his spirits sank a further notch. The island's notorious waterfront district was a warren of bars and brothels and opium dens where every variety of vice flourished in its most sordid form. Human life came cheap in the Wanchai.

The Humber swung inland and straightaway began to climb, its engine grinding in low gear as it crawled through the teeming streets. On Hongkong Island the city rises steeply within a stone's throw of the shore, the buildings piled tier on tier laddered back against the slope.

An outsize wooden tooth with bloodied root hung above the spot where a sidewalk dentist plied his trade in the open air, flanked by a fortune teller's booth and a drugstore displaying dried sea horses and cages of writhing snakes. Many of the alleys were cut with flights of steps, narrowed by street stalls and restaurants. Munro's nostrils twitched to the scent of spicy foods. Once he glimpsed the interior of a duck seller's with row upon row of dripping birds hanging by their necks.

Famished children dressed in rags beseeched every passer-by, "*Kumshaw! Kumshaw!*" Grandmothers squatted in the gutters, mending stockings for a living. On they went, following one road after another, threading their way between the slums, lurching and bumping, till at last the car rounded a corner and halted in a tiny square perched on a terraced outcrop of the slope.

Playfair indicated a gabled roof and red neon sign twisted into Chinese characters, "The Hotel Asia – this is where your man was last seen alive."

The hotel smelt of opium and fear.

On the wall behind the small reception desk hung a faded portrait of Generalissimo Chiang K'ai-shek. They went through a bead screen into the bar. Its windows were curtained, glass-topped tables round a small dance floor, muted lights and swatches of tinsel for decoration. A massive chrome jukebox took up most of one corner.

The girls stood around the walls, eyes cast down, nervously awaiting their turn to be questioned. Chinese, Filipinas, half breed Portuguese, one or two pure white Russians. They were young – some very young – and mostly pretty, Munro noted.

Playfair had taken over an office at the rear. Waiting for them was a Chinese in a high-collared yellow uniform with black leather belt and holster strap, like the Generalissimo in the picture outside.

"Have a seat, Munro," Playfair indicated a hard wooden chair in front of the desk. "This is Colonel Huang who is cooperating in the investigation." The Chinese nodded briefly without smiling. In his cap he wore the blue and white enamel badge of the Kuomintang Army.

"What do you make of that?" Playfair handed him the card which had come with the box.

"It was sent to the plane, *heya*?" Huang's English was halting. "Mili? That means nothing to me."

"Look on the back."

Huang did so and stiffened, "*Ai-yah, the Shi-sign!*"

"Precisely," the Inspector agreed grimly. He turned back to Munro, "Major Slater from the Consulate should be with us shortly. You've met before of course?"

"Not that I recall." From the window of the office Munro could see across the bay towards the hills of the New Territories standing dark against a sky aflame with purple and gold. Beyond lay China and a continent at war. What was the *Shi-sign*? He was damned if he was going to ask.

"Slater flew in last night from Chungking," said Playfair. "He's been handling the Buchan negotiations on behalf of your government. That's why I thought you might know him."

"Well I don't." Any minute now, Munro was thinking, he'll be calling me 'old boy'. Huang was following the exchange with eyes like black pebbles.

"Quite, just thought you might," Playfair took up a notepad. "Is this your first trip to the Colony?"

"I've been flying this route almost a year," Munro was willing to bet the Inspector knew that, "not always Hongkong, we alternate Singapore."

"And how about Captain Ross?"

"He was with the Atlantic Division until very recently, the New York–Lisbon run. He transferred out at the end of last month and took command of the ship in 'Frisco. He's an old China hand though, flew a lot of the original surveys for the routes out of Hawaii."

The Inspector studied his notes frowning, "According to our information Captain Ross last visited these parts in 1937 when he was involved in planning Amelia Earhart's round the world flight, the flight on which she vanished."

Overhead the floorboards creaked as someone moved around upstairs. "If it's information on the Skipper you want, ask him not me," Munro said curtly. It was news to him Ross had known Earhart, certainly he never mentioned her.

Playfair remained unruffled, "Just trying to get the full picture, old boy." Munro felt the barest flicker of satisfaction. There was a knock outside at the door. Major Slater had arrived from the Consulate.

He was not alone. Two men were ushered into the room. One was a gaunt individual with a pasty complexion and thin sandy hair. He was dressed in an ill-fitting suit and clerical collar. Nervous perspiration beaded his skin.

Major Slater wore his civilian clothes like a uniform. Pressed linen suit and polished shoes. He had a hard boney face and abrasive manners. On his right hand was a Marine Corps ring. He greeted Playfair and Huang without ceremony and scowled at Munro. "Who the hell said to bring him in?"

Playfair's moustache twitched. "In view of the connection with the Clipper it seemed logical. I would remind you this is British Crown territory and I am in charge of the investigation."

"*Bullshit!* This is an American operation and I say who gets to be in on it," Slater retorted bluntly. "You've had that from the Governor's office." He jerked a thumb to introduce his companion. "This is Reverend Jordan, Bishop Buchan's closest associate during the final days in Peking. Right, let's be getting on with it then, Playfair. What is there for us to see?"

The Inspector flushed. "The body is upstairs," he said tightly.

"Playfair is Special Branch, that's the political wing of the British police," Slater muttered to Munro as they climbed the hotel's rickety stairs, "and Huang is Chinese counter-espionage. I don't know what your role is in this, Munro, but if it's anything I ought to be aware of now's the time to sing out."

"I haven't a goddam clue what any of this is about," Munro hissed back.

"Then I hope to hell you've had the sense to keep your mouth shut, buster, that's all."

The room into which Playfair led them was lit by an oil lamp. The shutters were closed but Munro guessed it too faced out across the harbour. The paint was peeling off the ceiling. There was a washstand with a cracked mirror over it, an empty clothes press and a wide, hard bed. On the floor stood an enamel spitoon.

The Inspector drew back the sheet. It was not a pretty sight. An attempt had been made to bind the neck with cheesecloth but nothing could disguise the corpse's mutilated state: they had been forced to wedge the head in place with cushions.

"According to the surgeon's report," Playfair said, "death was instantaneous and resulted from a heavy blow to the nape of the neck with a sharp-bladed weapon, severing the cervical vertebrae. In plain language the fellow was beheaded as we can all see for ourselves, probably using a sword. His other injuries are broken bones in the right wrist and some minor cuts and bruising. Anyone care to put a name to him?"

"Okay, Playfair, cut the chat," Slater answered harshly. "You know darn well who he is, same as we do: Morris Oliver, Bishop Buchan's former deputy in Canton. Correct, Jordan?"

The white-faced priest was dabbing at his mouth with a handkerchief, plainly distressed. "I'm sorry," he apologised weakly. "Yes, it's Morris, Morris Oliver. Oh God! *Why*? *Why him*? He was such a simple, good man." His voice became a sob.

"You say he was Buchan's deputy?" asked Playfair after a pause, "Is that why he was booked on the Clipper?" He shot a glance across at Munro.

Jordan nodded, "Morris had known Buchan longer than any of us. He was based in Canton till the Japanese forced him out. I hadn't seen him in almost two years. He was supposed to meet us last night at the airport . . ."

"Had he received any specific threats in recent weeks?" Playfair had his notebook out again.

"How in hell is he supposed to be able to answer that?" Slater interrupted angrily, "He's just told you he only flew in last night with me. Jesus, you Limies burn me up! Your people were meant to be watching this end."

Playfair's jaw tightened. "We might have done more if we'd been kept fully informed – as you agreed."

"Yeah? And what's that supposed to mean?" Slater's eyebrows which were ginger in colour and bushy, met in a line across the bridge of his nose.

Playfair produced the card from the plane, "Does the name Mili convey anything to you?"

"*Mili!*" Slater snatched it, "Shit! This was sent to Ross?"

"In the box with Reverend Oliver's head. Tell us please about Mili."

"Why ask me?"

"I'm asking everyone . . . and you seemed to recognise the name."

The two stood glaring at one another. "Well I don't. Are you calling me a liar?" Slater spat.

You bet we are, you bastard, Munro thought watching him. The whole set up stank. A man was dead, murdered, and here they were playing games.

Playfair controlled his temper, "Try the other side, perhaps that will jog your memory."

Slater flipped the card over in his fingers. "An ideogram. What's it mean?"

"Colonel?"

The Chinaman's pebble eyes surveyed them each in turn. In the lamplight his skin was yellow as soap. "The *Shi-sign*," he said quietly. "It was found upon the hotel gate last night."

"Talk English for Christsakes," Slater said, "what's the *Shi-sign*?"

Huang regarded him unblinkingly, "Japanese character for *Yon*, the number Four, can represent also *Shi – Death*. The *Shi-sign – Death Warning* is an ancient symbol of terror used by our deadliest foes from across Eastern Sea." His voice grew harsh, "*Kokuryu-kai*! The priest was murdered by the Black Dragon!"

The room seemed suddenly very still. All attention was riveted on the Colonel, "*Kokuryu-kai*. Black Dragon. I'll be a son of a bitch!" Slater swore softly, "Some fuck-up this has turned into!"

Inspector Playfair drew the sheet back over the body. "You never warned us this operation involved the Black Dragon," he complained to Slater. "The Governor gave express orders there was to be no provocation to the Japanese."

"Quit fretting about provocation," Slater told him grimly. "When the Japs are ready to go to war they'll make their own provocation and you people had better believe that." Leaving the Inspector bristling he turned to Huang, "Okay Colonel, suppose we accept the Dragons are behind this, why pick on *Oliver* for Christsakes? What was he to them?"

Munro interrupted, "Would you gents mind telling me who exactly these Black Dragon are?"

Slater flashed him a scowl, "A secret Japanese political cult dedicated to the expansion of the Empire. Tokyo's answer to the Nazi party. Its agents are among the best trained in the hemisphere, fanatics, ruthless. This is none of your business, Munro. I don't know what the hell you're doing here," he added irritably.

"Why not try asking the guys who put that package with the mail?" Munro retorted, the lines round his mouth drawn tight, "If there's a threat to the Clipper I want to hear about it."

Huang regarded the shrouded figure on the bed. "*Ai-yah*, he will not be the last victim. If Black Dragon are moving openly to attack, general war cannot be far distant."

He spoke calmly. Munro felt his mouth go dry. Maybe war really was coming, the way the newspapers and radio kept saying which, even so, you never quite believed, probably because you didn't want

23

to. Here now though in this squalid room, with a butchered corpse just starting to stink in the corner, it seemed very close indeed.

"What I don't get," Slater was saying, "is what Oliver was doing? He wired Jordan he would be at Kai Tak to meet us from Chungking. If he was in trouble why didn't he go to the authorities?"

"Reverend Oliver was a frequent visitor to this part of the Colony," Playfair informed him. "He undertook missionary work among the girls of Wanchai."

"I read you," Slater's mouth twisted, "Missionary work, eh? That's a new name for it. Do you suppose he had the girls sing hymns while they worked him over?"

Reverend Jordan pursed his lips. Playfair's manner became rigid. "As it happens the interest was entirely genuine," he replied freezingly. "Oliver made no attempt to preach morality to the girls, he recognised they had to live. He used to listen to their problems and help where he could."

"I am certain Morris's actions would have been perfectly sincere," Jordan chimed in.

"Reconstructing his last movements," Playfair continued, smoothing his moustache, "it seems Oliver arrived here yesterday evening at around seven. He locked himself in this room and wasn't seen again until his headless body was discovered in an alley off the square early this morning. We suspect he knew he was being hunted and dared not leave the hotel to seek help."

Outside now it was nearly dark. The British had decreed another blackout practice tonight. Away in the distance Munro could hear the popping of firecrackers exploding at a Chinese wedding festival in defiance of the regulations. This was how it must have been for the dead man during the last night of his life, sitting up here with only the lamp for company, *listening, waiting* . . . He stopped to examine more closely a dog-eared photograph wedged into the mirror frame.

"He hid up till first light then tried to make a run for it," Slater muttered. "Poor bastard, at least it was quick. What's that you've found there, Munro?"

The photograph showed a group of four men, all in late middle age, picnicking on a carved stone bridge. In the centre, holding down her skirts against the wind, was a girl with reckless eyes in a pale fine-boned face and a cloud of blowing hair.

"That's Bishop Buchan with the cane. I recognise him from the newspapers," Munro said, "and Oliver beside him."

"It must have been taken in Peking when they were both there in 1937," said Jordan peering over his shoulder. "On the far left is Father

24

Carmichael, now in the Philippine Islands, and the fourth," his voice quavered, "is Dr. Ronald Currie. *Was* I should say, he died two months ago of enteric fever. I don't know who the girl is."

Neither it seemed did anyone else.

Playfair suggested they return to the office. "It would help if we could dispatch the body off to the morgue before the blackout closes down. Munro, would you mind seeing to the lamp?"

No one was anxious to linger at the bedside. Huang led the way out. "Will you be wanting to ship Reverend Oliver home on the Clipper with the Bishop?" Playfair inquired of Jordan in the doorway, "It'll be a while, I'm afraid, before the body can be released. There has to be an inquest."

"No way," Slater answered for the priest with decision, "the plane leaves as scheduled. This changes nothing."

Munro was glad to hear it. He put out the lamp, plunging the room into darkness. As he headed towards the exit he reached out for the photograph and slipped it into a pocket. Playfair, holding the door for him, did not notice; the others were already in the passage.

Downstairs in the lobby were gathered the same frightened faces. Huang stalked up and down, regarding the girls contemptuously. Shit, I bet he enjoys this, Munro thought. He was sick of the whole rotten business. "Inspector, do you need me any more?"

"No, I don't think we need detain you," Playfair dismissed him. "I take it you're stopping at the Peninsula Hotel with the rest of the crew? Of course mum's the word on everything this evening."

Munro nodded. He was turning away when Slater caught him by the arm. "Okay, pilot," he snarled in an undertone, "I got you figured. Fancy yourself a tough guy, huh? Well get this: for the next seven days you're *mine*, understand? Till we hit 'Frisco I own that plane of yours and every son of a bitch aboard. This operation's big, the biggest most likely you'll ever meet. Screw up and I'll have your ass in a vice and that's a promise!"

Munro shook his hand off, feeling the rage tight in his chest, the sudden urge to violence, the streak of savagery few suspected he possessed, but which ran in him never far below the surface and twice had almost cost a life. The last time when he'd been fouled in the ring at Annapolis. He'd never boxed again after that night.

"I take my orders from Ross. You have any complaints, see him."

"Yeah? I may just do that," Slater retorted. "You can tell him I'll be over later."

Uncertain whether to regard this as a promise or a threat Munro

25

took his leave. The police Humber was waiting outside in the square and he rode back alone.

*   *   *

HIROSHIMA BAY. JAPAN. 5.30 pm. A winter's evening was closing in and flurries of snow were sweeping the chill waters of the naval anchorage. Barely visible in the gloom, the ponderous slate-grey bulk of the great battleship loomed like an armoured steel mountain rising from the depths. Thirty thousand tons, sixteen inch cannon, home to two thousand men, she was *Nagato*, flagship of the Combined Fleet.

At his desk in the day cabin beneath the bridge, a tall balding officer in the dark blue uniform of a Rear Admiral sat writing on a message pad: Matome Ugaki, fifty-one years old, authority on naval strategy and Chief of Staff to the legendary Yamamoto.

'*Niitaka yama nobore ichi-ni-rei-ya*' – 'Climb Mount Niitaka 1208' Laying down his pen he pressed a bell to summon a signal ensign. "Get this off immediately in the new flag officer's code to the *Kido Butai*."

Kido Butai – the Strike Force. It was a solemn moment in the nation's destiny. Even now, unbeknown to the world, a thousand sea miles north of Midway six of the Imperial Navy's latest carriers escorted by the battleships *Hiei* and *Kirishima* together with a supporting armada of heavy cruisers, destroyers, submarines and supply ships were plunging eastwards across the Pacific towards the American bases in the Hawaiian Islands. By this signal, under the authority of General Staff Order No. 12, the hour of attack was confirmed – dawn of December 8th.

The count-down to war had begun. There would be no turning back.

II

"The sun in the east is red with the blood of war and from the sea a dragon rises."

Forty miles south west of Hongkong across the Pearl River estuary in Portuguese Macao, the last notes of the Angelus were fading on the air. Along the esplanade couples strolled arm in arm admiring the sunset and watching the fishing junks leaning their batwinged sails into the wind as they headed up for the inner harbour. In a sooth-sayer's booth near Kun Yam temple a slim, straight-backed Chinese girl was hearing the future told.

"Your journey will be arduous, dangers lie ahead, beware of treachery . . ." the seer peered into the bowl of water. He was from Turkestan, a lizard-like man with a soft, scented beard. Beside him slumped in a wooden chair, an elderly female assistant breathed heavily, her eyes closed in trance. She it was had the power to summon the spirit whose message the man interpreted from images in the water. Yu-Ling herself could discern nothing in the bowl, which did not necessarily make the seer a liar.

"You will have help however; I see a friend, a man," the seer was interrupted by a sudden snort from the old woman. She had woken and was blinking about her owlishly. The spirit had departed as they were apt to do just when the story became interesting. Smiling, the seer put aside the bowl and began discussing Yu-Ling's horoscope. "Born in the former Imperial city of Peking at the hour of the Tiger under the twelfth moon of the year of the Dog. A propitious combination: the yin and the yang balanced, the elements fire, water, wood and metal all present and your name, *Jade Years*, chosen to represent the earth quality," his shiny domed head nodded approvingly. "We are now in the eleventh moon of the year of the Snake, a harmonious period for you both in year and month. You show wisdom in selecting this moment to travel."

Yu-Ling listened attentively. Seventeen years old, she was as delicately pretty as her name, her chin firm, her ebony black hair brushing her shoulders and cut straight across a high forehead. At the convent school here in Macao the sisters had frowned on fortune tellers, but like all civilised persons Yu-Ling knew the *fung-sui* were born with extraordinary powers and it was only sensible to consult them.

The seer was summing up. "You are about to embark upon a perilous journey. War and other dangers beset the way, thieves and false friends will seek to lure you astray. Nevertheless you have chosen rightly I judge, for greater perils still threaten if you remain and the time is favourable for the undertaking. The stars smile upon you and applaud your courage. Be steadfast in your intentions. Good fortune awaits if you pass this test."

Yu-Ling's brow furrowed as she considered his words. Certainly it was true dangers surrounded them in Macao. Blue shirts, Tao Tai, Red Pang Triad, Japanese Kempeitai. So many enemies, so few friends to trust. Last month their gardener's body had been taken from a well. He had been thrown down alive. The horror was with her still.

By a foodstall in the street outside a scrawny-tough, one-eyed Taiwanese in black pyjama garb spat into the gutter and kicked a colleague squatting on his heels. "Get up, motherless lump of dog-dung," he hissed. "Must my one eye do the work of four while you snore in the dust? Here comes the fornicating princess again."

"Is she truly a princess, One-eyed Tok?" His companion scrambled to his feet. "Is that why the Eastern Sea Devils want her, *heya*?"

"*Dew neh loh moh* on your princess! Am I a *fung-sui*? How should I know what they want? Now make haste or we'll lose her in this fornicating crowd."

With a heavy heart Yu-Ling retraced her steps through the busy cobbled streets. Winding uphill her way brought her out beneath the ruined baroque facade of Sao Paulo church, its stonework carved by Japanese Christians three centuries past. Beyond, the city's lights sparkled like jewels against the darkening hills of China across the water. For several minutes she paused here, gazing over the rooftops, savouring for the last time the scents and sounds of home. From the convent below rose the chanting of the nuns at prayer, bringing tears to her eyes.

Under a street lamp on the far side of the square a trio of acrobats were performing on a pole for coppers. The two Taiwanese mingled with spectators observing the girl covertly. "*Ai-yah*, One-eyed Tok," growled the shorter as they moved off again, "princess or not, she's made for pillowing and her golden gully will be sweet as honey. Whoever takes her maidenhead will be at one with the gods."

28

Slipping expertly through the crowds in the dusk, they trailed her round under the walls of the ancient Monte fortress into the quieter streets of the residential district.

"*Ho*, good, she goes home," One-eyed Tok grunted at last. "I wonder if that lying *fung-sui* saw her true fate in the water?".

Approaching a single storey villa, four wings surrounding a garden, Yu-Ling entered by a side gate and crossed the courtyard to the hall. Inside, divans covered with Mongolian rugs stood against the whitewashed walls and a Wei dynasty Buddha faced two blue porcelain phoenixes. A wizened amah was waiting for her.

"*Ai-yah*, Yu-Ling, what did he say, the *fung-sui* man? Is the date propitious? Will you travel safely, you and Honourable Uncle? Will your *joss* be good and, please all gods, do you return soon?"

"So many questions, Ah-May," the girl chided her gently. "He said much, he said little. It is their way."

"*Ai-yah!*" the old woman clutched her to her withered bosom and wailed, "*Ai-yah, Yu-Ling, Yu-Ling*! My old eyes shall never see your pretty face again!"

"Hush, hush, Ah-May," Yu-Ling comforted her with little pats. "It is not for long we shall be gone. It is only a journey till times are better." Holding the old amah tight she bit back her own tears. "No, no. No more weeping or you will disturb Honourable Uncle. Has he woken yet from his nap, *heya*?"

"He rang for you not ten minutes past. Eeee, Yu-Ling, will they cure his sickness, the *quai loh* foreign devil doctors?"

"We must hope so, Ah-May, they are clever, very clever. Now have you food ready? We should eat before we depart. Off with you then, quick, quick!"

"Yu-Ling, always quick-quick," shaking her grey head dolefully the old servant shuffled off toward the kitchen. The girl cast a fond glance after her then ran lightly to her uncle's study.

The door stood ajar and a lamp burned within but the room was unoccupied. Stripped of its rare scrolls and ivories, the nephrite carvings and other treasures put away for safekeeping, it seemed dismally bare. Yu-Ling was about to go out again when she saw the red lacquer casket on an opium table in the centre. Inlaid upon the lid was a gilded dragon breathing fire. *So he has done it*, she thought and her heart began to pound. *He has opened the vault!*

From outside came a noise of engines. A pair of white uniformed motorcyclists of the Portuguese police had swung their machines in at the upper end of the street. Crossing to the window the girl watched as they approached, the long yellow beams of their headlamps probing

29

the shadows. For a moment she fancied they were slowing and her body tensed. She could feel the heavy throb of the motors and see the tommy guns slung on the men's backs. Then they rolled on by to disappear in the direction of the Praia Grande.

That is the third time, she thought, *three times is a threat*.

"They have gone, the *ch'aai-yan*?" The gentle voice behind made her start.

"Yes, Honourable Uncle, they went down towards the water." She turned back to the room. The old man was clothed like a mandarin in a long wide-sleeved silk gown. He was spectrally thin, his beard silver white in the lamplight. The two faced one another across the table on which reposed the casket.

"Will they arrest us when we seek to leave?" Away in the distance she could still discern the engines' receding growl.

"They would rather see us gone, Third Niece," her uncle answered gravely. He had been her father in all but name since the fourth year of her life. "The Portuguese fear for Macao while we remain, so sought after have we become, and this with us." His hands with their long curving nails gestured lightly over the red box.

The girl's glance followed the movement and she shivered, hating the casket for what it was said to contain. Hating and fearing it too for the shadow it cast over their lives.

"And these *quai loh* foreigners from the Land of the Golden Mountains, can we trust them? What if they betray us?" she cried nervously, the seer's warning ringing in her brain.

"*T'ung t'ien yu ming*," the old man's voice remained calm. "Listen to heaven and follow fate. The gods grant us no other road. Only the barbarians from the Golden Country have power to protect us now. We must trust to the bargain."

"*A bargain on the devil-box*!" Yu-Ling trembled afresh, "All gods preserve us! Not even the Dragon-Empress herself dared that!"

HONGKONG. The blackout was producing chaos. Cars and trucks struggled through the darkened streets, the beams of their papered-over headlamps reduced to feeble orange glows. It was seven p.m. when the police Humber finally dropped Munro off at the Peninsula.

The ornate lobby was ablaze with light and crowded with officers from all three services, their uniforms contrasting with the evening dresses of the ladies. Beneath the gilded ceiling waiters in soft slippers moved nimbly among the tables balancing trays of cocktails. The Hotel Asia seemed a world away.

The first people he noticed as he came through the heavily draped doors were Chief Crow and Driscoll drinking beers at a table to the left of the entrance. An unspoken rule reserved the right of the lobby for old friends, engaged or married couples, while the left side was for single men and women "looking for dalliance" as the hotel delicately put it.

Both men spotted him in the same instant and jumped up. "Hey, Max, over here buddy!"

Several ladies turned their heads as Munro moved easily through the throng. "Any word on Scott and the others?"

The Chief shook his head, "Nope, not a thing so far. How was it your end?"

"Messy. Is Ross around?"

"Skipper's in the bar, least he was a while ago." The Chief turned to his young assistant, "Chuck, go see if he's there still and on your way back check the desk for messages."

"What happened after I left the ship?" Munro asked as he and the Chief sat down and pulled their chairs close.

"That limey lieutenant took statements. There wasn't a lot anyone could tell him. Ross put Thyssen on security watch for the night, he has to sleep aboard and Tad Gotto stays to cook his supper."

"That's kinda rough on Tad." Tad Gotto was the Hawaiian junior steward, a popular member of the crew.

"O'Byrne's keeping him company. He went back out to Kai Tak with their gear."

A white-coated waiter approached the table. The Chief waved him away and lowered his voice, "Max, Ross knows where Scott's gotten to, I told him. Okay, Okay," he said placatingly, "it ain't my job, only Ross and I go back a long way together. Believe me, this business could really cut him up."

"How did he react?"

"Like you'd expect. He called the Consulate, not a lot more he could do. They picked a bad time to break the rules. Let's just hope they make it back safe."

"Chief, what is it bugs Ross about Scott? He hasn't let up on the girl since she stepped aboard. Hell, she has more spunk than half the guys I could name and she can fly. She'd make first rate flight crew if only he'd give her a break."

"It's her flying that's the trouble," the Chief murmured and then broke off as Chuck Driscoll reappeared in the lobby.

"Skipper's in the bar, Max. He wants you to join him there."

"What d'you say we all step round to Jimmy's afterwards for a bite?" the Chief suggested as Munro stood up. "We can talk easier there."

"Great idea," he nodded. Jimmy's Diner, up the Nathan Road, was run by a former US Navy CPO and his Cantonese wife. You could order a hamburger or steak and fries with ice cream to follow and real American coffee. It was a favourite haunt of the Chief's where he would consume prodigious quantities of beer without apparent effect. "I'll check with Ross and join you there, okay?"

"Sure, Max, see you later."

As the two engineers strolled away in the direction of the doors, the waiter clearing the tables nearby abandoned his task and hurried through to the rear. "*Ai-yah*, get out of my way, dunghead!" he cursed one of his compatriots by the service exit.

"Dunghead yourself, Third Table-waiter Chan. Where are you going at this time and in the fornicating blackout, *heya*?"

"*Dew neh loh moh chow hi*, I'm off to tumble your wife. Mind your own fornicating business!" he spat rudely and darted into the night.

The Peninsula's bar was solid and old fashioned, its mahogany-panelled walls hung with portraits of past British governors. Munro found Ross drinking gimlets in the company of a sandy-haired American in hornrims.

"This is Bob Cashin of *Time-Life*," Ross introduced him, "one of our passengers tomorrow. He flew down from Chungking last night."

It crossed Munro's mind that a lot of people seemed to have made that particular trip. "How was it?" he asked.

"Scary as hell!" Cashin grinned boyishly, "We took off in a storm to fool the nightfighters and flew most of the way at tree level. I never thought we'd make it, but those pilots are a fine bunch."

"They should be, a thousand a month basic plus two hundred dollars each round trip, the Chinese are paying them now, I hear," Ross sniffed. He swallowed a gulp of his cocktail and changed the subject. "So tell us, Bob, what's the outlook? Will it be war this side of Christmas?"

"God alone knows," the journalist replied, "or maybe God and the Japanese High Command. The diplomats are still talking in Washington. So long as the talks don't break down we're safe, I presume. The British have beefed up their fleet at Singapore. According to the radio they've sent out some of their heaviest units. With our own Navy in Hawaii that may deter the Japs."

"So it looks like peace then?" Ross said hopefully. "For the present anyway?"

They were interrupted by the arrival of Alan Bond, Pan Am's local manager, at the head of a group of business-suited Chinese. Munro stiffened abruptly: following behind was Colonel Huang.

Bond was a tall, harassed man with nervous hands. Even in peacetime running an airline out of China called for exceptional qualities; now with war closing in it was a nightmare.

"Gentlemen, I'd like to have you meet His Excellency Minister Soong of the National Government of China, who will be travelling with you tomorrow. Minister, Captain Ross who commands the aircraft and First Officer Maxwell Munro."

Ross and Munro shook hands. The Minister was suave and sleek. He had the soft, pudgy grip of a child and expensive dental work. The others of his entourage followed suit. Colonel Huang remained aloof, eyes watchful. He must have left Wanchai moments after the Humber.

"And this is Mr. Bob Cashin," Bond continued.

"But of course, Mr. Cashin is an old friend," the Minister beamed. His English was excellent, the accent Ivy League. "Good to see you again, Bob. I was sad to learn you were departing our country. Happily I can now look forward to your company on the trip."

"Same here, Minister," Cashin agreed. Munro saw him nod coldly in Huang's direction and receive a stony glare in return. Soong meanwhile was disposed to be chatty.

"You might like an interview with me for your magazine as we travel? Readers in America would enjoy that I should think. Doubtless you have heard how I successfully concluded negotiations with the Japanese for the release of Bishop Buchan's remains?"

"You always did have excellent contacts with the Co-Prosperity Sphere, Minister." The journalist's reply drew shocked hisses from Soong's underlings. It was tantamount to accusing the Minister of collaboration.

Soong's grin became fixed. "Very amusing, Bob, but they are our enemies and soon, I think, yours too, the *dwarf bandits*." He used a popular Chinese epithet.

"Better than the red kind, eh Minister?"

Soong's smile vanished completely. Colonel Huang whispered something in his ear. Alan Bond threw the two pilots a long-suffering look as the party moved on.

"*Dew neh loh moh*, a piss on you and all your generations," Cashin muttered under his breath, watching them go. "T. Hollington Soong,

Vice-Minister for Economic Affairs, direct descendant of Confucius and the most corrupt politician on the Asian continent. It's thanks to him I'm being railroaded out of this country."

"How's that?" Munro asked.

The journalist made a wry face. "An article I wrote last month on Chennault's Flying Tigers and the P–40 pursuit planes being sent out by the US government for the defence of Chungking. In it I mentioned how Hollington Soong – he's westernised his name like many American educated Chinese – was siphoning off sixteen thousand dollars personal commission on each plane. He complained to the Embassy, stories of that kind aren't what the administration is looking for, so all of a sudden I'm being recalled. Now the skunk has the nerve to suggest I write him up again!"

"Hell of a way to fight a war," Ross said.

"The war is a joke, a joke in bad taste. Thirty percent of Chinese soldiers die before they even reach the front line – of disease, starvation and brutality, which suits the officers who pocket their wages. There are no doctors or trucks, if you're wounded you die. All the Kuomintang top brass like Soong traffic regularly with the Japanese. Most of China's military supplies are brought in through Jap lines, bartered for tungsten and tin. The famous Burmah road is a propaganda myth to attract more western aid for the benefit of Soong and his cronies.

"Meanwhile the peasant pays forty-three separate taxes, always in advance and figured in grain because the government doesn't want its own depreciated currency back. When the total exceeds what his land can produce, he has to sell out to speculators for a few cents an acre. He'll sell his wife and children too if they're lucky, otherwise they'll starve. Later the same speculators will offer him back his own grain at a sixtyfold price increase. Top of the whole dungheap is Hollington Soong."

Flushing, Cashin stopped. "I'm sorry, I didn't mean to deliver a lecture. It's just that it gets to you after a while," he said simply.

The other two listened sympathetically. They had heard the stories before; everyone had. "The Japs are to blame for most of it," Ross said bitterly. "Remember Nanking? Two hundred thousand murdered, goddam butchers!"

Cashin nodded, "The declared motto of the Imperial Army is *Senko Seisaku*, the Three Alls – Kill all, Burn all, Destroy all." His mouth hardened, "In which they are no different from the armies of Chiang K'ai-shek or any of the other warlords in China – with one exception."

He paused. "What's that?" Munro asked, though both he and Ross had guessed the answer.

"*The Reds.*"

The clock over the bar read seven thirty. Tossing off his drink Cashin slipped down from his stool. "Promised the boys at the Press Club I'd stop by for a farewell dinner. I'll see you both on the Clipper tomorrow."

For a minute after he had gone the pilots sat without speaking, then abruptly Ross picked up his glass and led the way to a corner where they could talk without being overheard.

"Shapiro took Fry and Scott over to Macao with him this afternoon. Some joker in a private plane offered them a ride."

Munro nodded. "The Chief says the Consulate are looking for them."

"Of all the boneheaded, idiotic . . .!" Ross cursed, "I'm putting Shapiro and Fry both down for transfer and I'm recommending Scott for discharge when we dock at San Francisco. They should have figured the consequences before they broke regulations!"

He paused. Munro made no comment. "What's wrong, lost your tongue?" Ross rasped.

Munro shrugged. "First we have to find them."

"By Christ, Mister, don't try to tell me my job! You think I'm doing this because I want to get rid of the girl? Well you're damn right, I do. There's no place for a woman in the cockpit, never will be."

Outside in the lobby the babble and chatter was increasing in volume. There was a burst of braying laughter. "Jackasses!" Ross glowered, "One of these days the bombs are going to start dropping, I hope they laugh then. Okay, Mister, let's have your report. I want chapter and verse. Just who was this passenger got himself killed?"

Munro recounted events at the Hotel Asia, omitting only the removal of the photograph. That was nothing to do with Ross. "Slater said to tell you he would be over later."

"Slater's a bastard, always was," Ross declared flatly. "If I'd known he was involved I'd never have accepted command." He brooded a minute. "Did he discuss the cargo at all?"

"The Bishop's coffin you mean?" Munro had been wondering when that would come up, "No. Should he have done?"

"Maybe, maybe not," Ross shied away from the subject. He was fiddling with a pack of cigarettes.

"Slater spoke as if you had known each other a while."

"I was under him once before, in '37," a distant look came into Ross's eyes, "he was a bastard then too. If it hadn't been for him . . ."

He broke off suddenly, glaring at his first officer with hostile suspicion. "*What the hell is this*, Mister, *a goddam interrogation?* Mind your own bloody business! Now get out of here!"

Son of a bitch, Munro shook his head as he left the bar, he had touched on a raw nerve there.

Collecting his key from the desk, he took the elevator up to his room on the fourth floor. The bed had been turned down neatly and blackout drapes drawn over the french windows to the balcony. On the side table lay the copy of *Moby Dick* he'd been carrying for two trips now. A rummage through his suitcase produced the travelling photograph frame his sister had once given him. From underneath a picture of her and the kids he extracted a colour portrait of a girl with ivory white skin and a fiery mane of hair. Her laughing eyes challenged him boldly. Across the bottom corner was a scrawl: '*Mad, bad and dangerous to know! Max, my darling – G.*'

The words rang empty now. Time had drained them of sentiment leaving only a bitter residue of resentment. He should have thrown the damn thing away, cleared her out of his life completely. An affair like that lasted a man a long time, too long. It left him dead inside.

For some moments he studied the photograph, reliving memories, testing the old wounds. Rousing himself at length, he carried the picture to the lamp and compared it with the one found at Wanchai. The definition of the latter was poor but even so, and allowing for a difference of age when the shots were taken, there could be no doubt they were of the same person.

Which might be a coincidence. Only Munro didn't believe in that kind of coincidence.

Four floors below the street was quiet. Occasional pedestrians stumbled by in the darkness but the hotel entrance this side was shut and most were sticking to the main avenues. His swordstaff slung at his back the Japanese slid from the cover of a parked truck and flattened himself against the wall. Clothed entirely in black: hood, mask, loose-fitting jacket and leggings, split-toed *tabi*, hands and face smeared with charcoal, he blended invisibly into the shadows.

Motionless he stood listening. He could freeze all night if need be without moving a muscle, just one part of his perpetual training. His mind's antennae raked the darkness, alert for signals of hostile presence – *haragei*, the sixth sense perception of danger, refined in him to a degree no westerner would have believed possible.

Nothing, all was clear. His glance strayed upward briefly, targeting again the American's window in the dimness above. From a pouch he took a coil of thin cord plaited from human hair, silky supple and strong as steel wire, attached to one end was a triangular padded hook. Whirling a length deftly, with a flick of the wrist he sent it flying up to catch in the railings of a second floor balcony.

Up in the bedroom Munro shivered involuntarily. He slipped both photographs back in the frame and moved to the window, trying to shake off a sense of unease. Fumbling with the drapes, he unfastened the catch and stepped out onto the balcony for a breath of air. The night was warm with a smell of rain on the breeze and the throb of music rising from the dance band. Away to his left the harbour glittered blackly and the dark hump of the Peak was flecked here and there with points of light. So much for the regulations.

The vague disquiet persisted. He had an uncanny sense of being watched from close at hand. Leaning over the parapet he peered into the gloom, wishing he had a flash. Not a thing to be seen but the feeling of danger grew and his scalp pricked warningly.

A gust of wind stirred the curtains behind. "Hey, up there!" broke an angry shout, "Put out that light!" From the corner of the street below a beam probed upwards. Munro jerked round hastily to obey. As he did so he caught a sharp hiss of fury in the darkness close by and his heart leapt pounding in his chest.

The figure was formless, a shadow against the night, crouched ready to spring not six feet away on the parapet of the neighbouring balcony. He must have stared right at it a second ago and still not seen. The eyes pierced his own and locked; flat, implacable, dead as stones.

All this Munro had only the briefest instant to register. There were barked orders below and sounds of booted feet. A second torch joined the first, sweeping the wall with its beam. He blinked dazzled for a moment and then gaped in sudden amazement.

The parapet was bare. The black figure had vanished as soundlessly as if it had never been.

MACAO. In the mirrored and chandelier-lit main salon of the Estoril Casino a fat, bald Chinese with the face of a Buddha sat at the head of a table ringed with players. One hand held an ivory wand, before him on the green baize gleamed a heap of ivory buttons. A bell rang, last bets were closed. Slowly, deliberately, the Buddha began to count, four at a time, with his slender baton. A chorus of excitement arose as he reached the end: three buttons remained over; three was the winning number.

37

This was *fan-tan*.

"Three again! Son of a gun, this has to be my night!" Half way along the table Tony Shapiro exulted as he raked yet more silver *patacas* towards the already large pile before him. "Okay sugars, this time we're shooting for two."

"Eee! Number two, he bets on two!" The little bevy of sing-song girls squealed delightedly and clapped their brittle hands, "All gods bring luck!" Beside him Sally Scott nudged his elbow, "We gotta go, Tony, if we want to make that ferry."

"Sure, sure, just another coupla minutes," Shapiro promised impatiently, his handsome Latin features tight with concentration. Across the table a White Russian with a pearl pin in his tie, was betting on one. The bell rang again and everyone leaned forward eagerly to watch the Buddha make his count. There was breathless suspense for a moment then the girls erupted again. *Two it was*! Such *joss* the American was having!

Scott groaned inwardly. Nine o'clock was fast approaching, the last ferry back to Hongkong was due to depart in little more than fifteen minutes. If they failed to catch it they would be stuck in Macao for the night.

"It's a cinch," Shapiro had assured her and Chris Fry, the tall shy Texas boy, as he explained the plan. "Forty minutes after we come off duty the Sikorsky will have us in Macao. Lunch, chicken *biri-biri* with some *vinho verde*, a quick trip round the sights, then we hit the tables. The ferry back gets us in just after midnight. No one will miss us and we'll have a ball!"

And Scott had been grateful to be asked along, to be treated like one of the boys.

Macao's sleepy Mediterranean atmosphere had been delightful. The green and ochre plastered walls of the old buildings reminded her of a Riviera town set down amid the colour and hubbub of the Orient. Their tour of the city colony had taken in Sao Paulo, the shrine of the Goddess A-Ma and for good measure the Boundary Gate to the mainland where steel-helmeted negro troops from Portuguese Africa stood guard opposite a sullen detachment of the Imperial Army of Nippon.

It was the men's first glimpse of the soldiers they might one day be called upon to fight and they were disappointed. The Japanese looked small and puny in their ill-fitting uniforms. Several wore spectacles and the rifles they carried were too big for them. Shapiro was scathing, "Shit, who'd be scared of them?"

Fortified by this discovery, they had made for the casino.

A silver chalice containing a fresh supply of ivory buttons was being placed before the Buddha. "Tony, for Godsakes!" Scott pleaded.

"She's right, we don't have much time," Chris Fry too was growing anxious. A doe-eyed Eurasian beauty with iridescent nail polish and an enticingly voluptuous figure stroked his arm soothingly. Beside these exotic creatures Scott felt out of place in her uniform, even if they did rent by the hour. How could men be such idiots?

Across the table the Russian with the tie pin was pocketing his remaining money. "You too are travelling to Hongkong tonight? I have a taxi ordered and should be happy to offer you a lift to the ferry." Observing the Americans' surprise, he bowed with a click of the heels, "Prince Cherkassy, passenger on tomorrow's Clipper."

Shapiro lit up, "Gee, that's mighty kind of you, sir." Scott was doubtful. The Russian was in his fifties, solidly built with a square hard face, a lipless mouth and brutal eyes.

But Shapiro was kissing the girls goodbye and distributing handfuls of shiny *patacas*. Outside by the front steps an ancient Chevrolet stood waiting. Scott stifled her disgust as the Prince settled himself beside her on the rear seat. His silk shirt was yellowing, she noted, and frayed at the cuffs.

"You were fortunate at the tables tonight," he remarked enviously to Shapiro when the car was in motion.

"Yes sir, around two hundred US I figure, only it's all in Portuguese."

"Kurt Thyssen will change it for you," said Chris cheerfully. "If you're desperate that is."

"You're kidding, at his lousy rates that'd be like throwing it away."

"And you, young lady," the Prince turned to Scott, "were you a winner also?"

Scott shook her head, "I quit when I was down ten bucks, I'm not much keen on gambling." To her relief there was the wharf ahead with the ferry alongside, an ancient top-heavy two-decker flying the red ensign.

"A game of poker would pass the journey," the Russian suggested as they climbed aboard watched by armed police. The bridgehouse was laced with barbed wire and a bored British Tommy in battle kit lounged outside the upper first class saloon.

"Count me out, fellers," Scott said, "I'm going to lean on the rail and watch us leave."

"*Senores e Senoras, attençao*," a loudspeaker blared overhead. The gangway was about to be raised and a few latecomers were sprinting along the quay. With a quick patter of feet a Chinese girl came darting up from below. She was a slip of a thing, graceful in a flowered *cheong-sam*.

Scott watched her turn to help an elderly mandarin in button cap and gown up the steps. With agitated gestures the old man motioned her to precede him into the saloon. Bringing up the rear a black clad coolie, one eye milky from cataracts, dumped suitcases inside the door and scuttled away.

The shriek of the boat's whistle split the air and the engines began to throb as the gangway was swung inboard. More blasts on the whistle followed, warps were cast off and minutes later they were under way and moving slowly downstream, the glittering waterfront sliding by astern. Leaving the dark mass of mainland China to starboard, the ferry rounded the headland and the beam of Guia lighthouse flashed out overhead as they entered the Sea of Nine Islands.

The night was overcast, neither moon nor stars visible. A breeze off the sea brought a light drizzle and soon the passengers were seeking shelter in the saloon. Left alone on the upper deck the sentry retreated aft into the lee of the wind. Propping his rifle against a bulkhead, he began to roll a cigarette. In the distance the lights of Macao twinkled peacefully.

All at once his spine arched back like a bow in a spasm of agony and his hands flew to his neck to claw desperately at the steel noose which had clamped about his throat. Helpless to cry out, for a brief terrible space he fought violently for life, blood spattering the deck as he tore his own flesh in a frantic bid for air.

Satisfied his victim was dead, One-eyed Tok unwound the thin strangling chain and eased the soldier's body forward onto the rail. "*All gods piss! Give me a hand with the fornicator!*" he hissed. His partner seized the legs and together they heaved the corpse up and over the side. The splash was lost in the churning wake and the rain sluiced the blood from the scuppers.

III

In a small dusty room over a back alley restaurant in Kowloon's Walled City, Colonel Huang sat round a table with five of the most powerful men in the Colony. Not even the British Governor in his mansion wielded such authority over life and death. Roughly dressed, scarcely better than common coolies; one man in his seventies, the others ranged from forty up; brutal, determined, ruthless – they were the Khans of the Red Pang Triad.

"We live in difficult times. Civilised people should stand together. Old Friends should support one another, *heya*?" Huang phrased his words carefully. To Chinese the term 'Old Friend' signified a relationship of mutual trust, an alliance of interests extending back over years, sometimes over generations.

"*Fornicate times!*" It was the youngest of the five, Lim Ta-Wei, Tiger Lim, hatchet-faced boss of the Colony's waterfront extortion rackets, who answered scowling in gutter Cantonese. "We of Honourable Red Pang do not forget friends, or enemies – ever. You should know that, Huang Ko-Fang."

"The assistance of the Honoured Society in the common struggle against the Sea Devils is acknowledged by the Kuomintang, all favours shall be repaid at war's end." Huang waited a moment, "Yet even now the struggle enters a new and critical phase."

There was silence. Five pairs of eyes regarded him with cold hostility. Over against the door squatted two brawny streetfighters, both deaf and dumb, and therefore employed at all such meetings. Others guarded the stairs. The Walled City outside was an enclave of lawlessness, a no-man's-land neither Chinese nor British where only the triads ruled. "The Eastern Sea Devils who seek the subjugation of our country are the enemies of all patriotic persons," he added pointedly.

"Piss on your patriotism!" Tiger Lim exploded with sudden vehemence, "Favours repaid, *heya*? And who warned Sea Devils are watching house of dogmeat Mandarin? Yet now what we learn?" his

41

voice rose to a screech, "Only he guards one richest treasure all China for thieving Minister Soong take Golden Country! You not tell that, *Old Friend*!"

"You were well rewarded for your part. It is unmannerly to suggest Old Friends cheat," Huang replied coldly.

"And is fornicating unmannerly conceal truth from Old Friends!" Tiger Lim shot back. The other Khans were growling in agreement and Huang cursed to himself. He had warned Hollington Soong of the danger this might happen. There was loss of face involved now and that they dared not risk, not with a triad as jealous and powerful as this one.

Leaning forward a trifle he said, "This affair is being controlled by the barbarian *quai loh* from the Golden Country, not by our own people. It is possible an adjustment could be made." He saw the flicker of greed in their eyes and concealed a smile.

"*Eee*, the Old Buddha's Birthstone!" Pockmark Wong sucked in his cheeks and whistled, "For years they said it was a legend. How came Mandarin by it?"

"A ruby, big as a turtle's egg. She wore it between her breasts. When she died the eunuchs stole it."

"I heard it was a diamond, pink like the dawn. Also all who look on it are cursed."

"*Aiee*, but she is dead and the Dragon Throne empty. The curse may be lifted."

Huang sat listening with contempt, knowing he could turn their avarice to his advantage. "Accursed or not, be assured Minister Soong will negotiate a generous settlement," he remarked after a pause.

"Where Minister tonight?" a harsh voice demanded from the end seat, "Why he not come himself if matter urgent as you say?" All heads turned to the weather-beaten old man with the razor-slit eyes, who until now had taken no part in the proceedings. Huang stiffened warily. High Khan and ruler of the Section 14–K Triad, Kao Kang was the ranking gang leader present, an illiterate Haklo peasant, vindictive, cruel and mortally suspicious. Without his assent there would be no deal with the Pang, whatever the inducements.

"Tonight he eats at Government House. The British seek support from the Generalissimo's armies against the Sea Devils."

"Generalissimo agree, you think?" the old bandit snapped in his execrable accent.

Huang shrugged, "Am I a politician?"

Tiger Lim scratched his nose with a hand scarred and calloused from a hundred fights. One finger glittered with a diamond set in gold. "Some say *quai loh* Americans buy Colony from British, make present Chiang K'ai-shek."

"Piss on that!" another Khan on his left said scornfully. "The mother-defilers wouldn't sell a single *mou* of their stinking empire for all the gold of Eunuch Tung."

"*Ai-yah*, better the Sea Devils than the dog-dung British!" snarled Pockmark Wong. "Leave triads alone to run affairs."

Yes, and pay you to bring in the opium which destroys our people, Huang reminded himself bitterly. Oh, they are clever the Sea Devils and they understand us too which is worse. It was close in the shuttered room and he could feel the sweat beading his brow. "*Aiee*, are your memories so short? Have you forgotten what their armies did in Nanking and Shanghai, *heya*? Even now agents of the Black Dragon are at work among us." He was watching Kao Kang as he spoke.

The gang leader's lips drew back exposing the stumps of blackened teeth. "We hear Dragons' quarrel is with *quai loh* foreign devils from Golden Mountain, your friends, *heya*? What to us if the fornicators kill each other?" He laughed mirthlessly and the other Khans chuckled.

"The enemy of my enemy is my friend," Huang quoted, feeling his temper slipping. Curse these foul bandits! They were worse even than barbarians. "Enough of this fencing! Where does the Red Pang stand, with Japan or the Middle Kingdom?"

"*Ai-yah*, the Red Pang stands for the Red Pang." Kao Kang's eyes glowed hot with anger as he hawked and spat over his shoulder onto the floor. Jerking his head at Tiger Lim he said in Haklo dialect which he knew the Colonel did not understand. "Show this turd-eating northerner what the partisans sent us."

Lim lifted a cloth swathed bundle onto the table and pushed it across to Huang. A nauseating stench filled the room as the coverings fell away revealing a charred leather dispatch case. Bright scratches on the metal showed where the lock had been forced. Striving to ignore the odour of burnt flesh, Huang raised the flap. The documents inside were scorched dark brown and brittle but the writing was legible – just. His heart leapt at the sight of the chrysanthemum seal.

Glancing up he met Kao Kang's gaze. "*Aiee*, good," the old Khan cackled. "You speak Sea Devil tongue? *Quai loh* pay plenty money, *heya*?"

Huang nodded without speaking and lowered his eyes again to read. *Ai-yah*, if the British should come by these, or the Americans! His blood ran cold. He saw now the bargain they must make. *It was one they could not afford to keep.*

"The Khans want *what*? The devil-box! The Empress's jewel! Are they out of their fornicating minds?"

The moon shone on the blacked-out facade of Government House. Puffing a cigar, Hollington Soong sprawled in the rear seat of his ministerial limousine parked in the driveway. Huang's urgent summons had brought him out from dinner.

"*Ai-yah* listen! Four nights ago a Japanese aircraft crashed in the mountains in Kwangtung province. On board was a courier with secret despatches for the 23rd Army. The Sea Devils sent bombers to destroy the wreckage but partisans recovered the plans even so. Now the Pang have them."

"Plans, what plans?"

"*Higashi no kaze ame – East Wind Rain.*"

The Minister choked on his cigar, "*Oh ko*, are you positive? When, by the Gods?"

"A week at most. Tokyo will give the final word."

"Within a week!" Soong screeched in panic. "*Dew neh loh moh* on the Sea Devils!" With an effort he controlled himself. "*Ai-yah*, and the filthy Khans have proof, *heya*?"

"I saw the papers myself. They were genuine. The Pang gives us till midnight to agree to their terms or they go to the British." Huang motioned towards the portico.

Hollington Soong swore fluently, "We must radio Chungking at once. The Generalissimo has to be informed."

"*Oh ko*, Minister, there is another way, *heya*? Contact the Sea Devils . . ."

"*We'll meet again, don't know where, don't know when
but I know we'll meet again some sunny day.*"

The jukebox was pounding out the tune for the fourth straight time in a row, Driscoll had taken a fancy to it. Dinner was finished, he and Davey Klein were dancing with a couple of bobbed-haired sing-song girls while Munro, Stewart Whitely and the Chief sat with their jackets off conferring over coffee and beers. They were the only customers left. Jimmy himself, a bull-necked veteran of the Spanish war, was doing his accounts in a corner.

"Bucktoothed murdering savages!" Whitely banged his glass down with tipsy belligerence, "The sooner we declare war the better, I say. Roosevelt ought to send the fleet into Tokyo Bay and blast the place."

He seldom drank, but tonight the slaying of the priest had affected him badly.

"No use pussyfooting around negotiating. Force is the only thing those yellow-bellies understand. Right, Chief?"

The engineer was studying the swaying rump of the waitress whose thigh-slit red *cheong-sam* fitted her as sleekly as a second skin. With a sigh he transferred his attention. "Sounds to me like war began already," he rumbled.

Munro put a match to a cigarette, grey eyes regarding him steadily through the smoke. The Indian's face was impassive as carved wood. Whitely tittered uncertainly.

"What's funny? You think the Japs killed this guy Oliver on account of they didn't like his sermons? The fighting's started and in my book that's war."

"*. . . till the blue skies*
drive the dark clouds far away."

In the background Vera Lynn had reached the end of the first verse again. The Chief took a swig of his beer and belched softly, "First thing the Japs'll do when the gloves are off is take Guam, it stands to reason. Leaving Manila an' points west out on a limb. They'll have to develop a new route down through New Guinea and the Solomons – and there's no one knows that area like Ross. I'll wager a month's pay it's why he was sent out."

And Ross had served under Slater in the past, back in 1937. Munro hadn't mentioned that.

"You must have been hoping for the captaincy yourself, Max," Whitely spooned more sugar into his cup. "You had your Master's ticket and everything. Fact is, you'd probably have gotten it by now if you hadn't slugged that passenger on Wake. The Company had to pay out money there."

"The son of a bitch was drunk and abusing a woman, he deserved everything he got," Munro's reply was curt. All the same there was truth in what Stewart said. He had been stuck at First Officer six years now.

"Boy, you should have heard Thyssen laugh when Ross was transferred," Whitely continued unabashed. "That guy has it in for you, Max. He reckons now he has a chance to steal the captaincy over your head. He's passed his Master's too, remember."

"Maybe so, but he doesn't have my seniority," Munro could have bitten his tongue off as he spoke. Damn Whitely and his infernal gossip!

"Sure, but Thyssen kisses ass and they like that Stateside. Now he's out to do a hatchet job on the Skipper. He's told me confidentially he's keeping a diary on everything Ross does."

"Shit, that's sneaky even for Thyssen," muttered the Chief.

"He keeps notes on you too, Max, and he's in with all the Company brass."

But Munro was not to be drawn further, "Good luck to him then," he said crisply, ending the conversation. He signalled the waitress to bring the check. "Time we were shifting back to the hotel."

There remained one question he wanted to ask and he waited till Stewart went in search of a lavatory. "Chief, you were Pacific Division in '37 weren't you? Do you recall the Earhart flight?"

The Chief gave him a speculative look over the rim of his glass, "Sure, I recall it. Why?"

"Because according to the police here the Skipper was involved," and Munro repeated what Playfair had said. "Is that what you meant when we were talking about Scott earlier? She reminds him of Earhart?"

"They could be sisters, but it's more than that."

Munro hitched his chair forward and took a drag of his cigarette, "Chief, Earhart's last flight was a round-the-world stunt, pioneering a new route across the South Pacific to Hawaii. In July '37 she took off from Lae, New Guinea headed for Howland Island in mid-Pacific. She never made it. The story was she ran out of fuel and went down somewhere in the Marshalls. That's about all I know. Where does Ross fit in?"

The Chief swigged some beer thoughtfully. "I was based at Pearl that year, running overhauls on the Martin-130's. Ross came through in May, I think it was, or early June. According to him he had been hired to advise Earhart on the final stage of the route. The Navy were shipping him out to Howland to be on hand when she reached there. The Navy were giving Earhart a lot of help, he said.

"Did Ross think the Government was backing the flight?"

"If so he wasn't saying. I didn't run into him again till six months afterwards, in a San Francisco bar, drunk. Of course I asked him about the flight, it was still news then, but he didn't want to talk. In the end he lost his temper and told me to get the hell out and leave him alone."

Same as in the bar of the Peninsula tonight, Munro thought. "Chief, Earhart's route took her close to the Japanese Mandate; the region's always been forbidden territory. There were rumours that might have had something to do with her disappearance."

"After what happened today I'm certain of it."

"On account of the murder?"

"On account of *Mili*. Hell, Max, surely you recognise that name?"

And then with a sudden flash of clarity, Munro realised why it had sounded familiar.

". . . *but I know we'll meet again some sunny day.*"

The music ceased and twisting his head Munro saw skinny Davey Klein, the Clipper's junior radio operator, standing by the jukebox searching in his pockets for change. "Hey, Davey," he called, "how's about playing something different?"

"But it's a keen tune, you said so."

"Doesn't mean I want to learn the darn thing!"

With a grunt the Chief heaved his great bulk out of his seat. "Gotta take a leak," he announced. He moved off leaving Munro alone at the table finishing his cigarette. The waitress in the red *cheong-sam* came and perched on a chair beside him.

"Max, you airplane captain, *heya*?" she purred squeezing his hand, "Plis, wen fly you take me? Make good for you, number one jig-jig all China, no?" She was young, eighteen, soft pleading eyes and a willow body and once last trip he had taken her to bed.

"Plis," she nestled against him, "plis, take Wei-Wei wen fly. Bling lotta money for you. Sell club Manila. Pay plenty dollar Chinese girl, make you one rich fella, *heya*? Plis, Max, no make stop here for bloody shit Japanese come, plis!"

He put a comforting arm around her. "Wei-Wei, you're safe here. This place is lousy with troops; the Japs will never dare start anything." He was trying to convince himself as much as her but the girl only gazed at him wordlessly and the guilt twisted inside him.

"Listen, kid, we'll be back in a month. If things look rough then maybe I can . . ." He broke off suddenly, "Jesus Christ, Wei-Wei!" He made a grab for her as she tried too late to jerk away. Something tumbled to the floor. His wallet. "What is this, a shakedown? I never figured you for a thief!"

"Max, plis! Me no thief, promise!" The girl's features crumpled, "One fren' mine big trouble . . ." Tears began spilling down her cheeks.

"Cut it out!" he told her harshly. "Godammit, Wei-Wei, if you're in a mess why don't you come and ask me straight instead of sneaking my wallet?" He let the girl go and picked it up from the floor, "Here," peeling off a red hundred dollar note, he stuffed it into her fist, "now beat it. Go on, scram!"

The girl stared down at the note in dumb bewilderment. "*Aiee*, Max," she sighed as she turned to go, "better maybe you no come back. Plenty bad peoples Hongkong, Black Dragon, *heya*?" she drew a slim finger across her throat, "Today kill one American fella."

"The Black Dragon!" Munro caught her by the wrist, pulling her back, "Wei-Wei, what the hell do you know about those bastards?"

Terror showed in the girl's face, "Ssh, no speak that name," she begged, "very, very bad peoples, many spy." Her voice sank to a frantic whisper, "You fly Golden Country, no come back. *East wind rain, heya?*" Snatching her arm free she darted away.

A shadow fell across the table. He looked up sharply. Ross was standing there, glowering down at him. Munro hadn't heard him come in, for a big man he could move very quietly when he chose.

"On your feet, Mister, and round up the others. We're sleeping aboard tonight, all of us."

Barely had the Americans gone when Wei-Wei slipped out the rear of the restaurant wearing cheap cotton pants and shirt, her red *cheong-sam* clutched in a paper bag. The narrow back alley was pitch dark and her wooden sandals clattered on the stone as she felt her way up towards the main road. *Aiee, this hateful blackout!* She was very much afraid.

Nathan Road was easier. She crossed and entered a twisting side street heading for Yaumatei Ferry. Fewer people here but twice, three times she had to step over prostrate bodies. Asleep? Dead? Impossible to tell; each day the trucks took away more corpses. *Joss.*

Two cyclists pedalled by. She shrank into a doorway. *Holy Virgin protect me, hide me from the Dragons.* By year end the Japanese would be in the Colony, Deng Min-Ta had warned. Bald-head Deng, her uncle's fourth cousin and oh so secret sympathiser of the puppet regime in Nanking. "Wise to collaborate, *heya?* Do as the Dragons ask?"

She pressed on, tripping and stumbling in her haste. From somewhere up ahead her ears caught the tap of a beggar's staff. *Quai loh* law forbade begging, whoring too. Stupid, how else were people to live? Voices sounded behind and her heart began to thud. Was she being followed? *Oh, oh, terrible to have betrayed the Black Dragon!*

The tapping grew louder. The street seemed suddenly deserted. Trembling, she stood for a moment in the blackness listening, sensing stealthy feet in the alleys. Abruptly her nerve broke and with a whimper she turned to flee.

The next instant a cloth bag descended over her head and she was pulled struggling behind a wall. "*Ai-yah,* Wei-Wei Chu," a Taiwanese accent grated, "did you think to escape us? Where were you going?"

"*Aiee,* I was coming to you," she gasped half suffocated, "I was coming, Lords, I swear!"

"Liar!" The grip on her arms tightened viciously, "You were

48

running away. Do you take us for fools, *heya*? The photograph, did you bring it?"

"I tried, I tried, Lords, but I couldn't. It was impossible. That's the truth, by the Virgin!"

The hood was ripped away. She was being held by two men. One was Table-waiter Chan from the Peninsula. A third man faced her, lithe, powerful, masked in black. A blade gleamed in his hand. The girl's legs buckled with fear.

"Search her!"

Cotton tore. In seconds she was naked, her garments shreds. "Nothing! Not a fornicating thing!"

"Listen, whore," one of the Taiwanese spat, grabbing her by the hair, "we were in the kitchens, we watched you with the American. What you say to him, *heya*? What you tell him?"

"I told him nothing, *ahh*!" A hand slapped her brutally across the mouth, "I . . . told . . . him . . . *East wind rain*!" Urine coursed hotly down her thighs as her bladder voided uncontrollably. Sobbing she slumped in her captors' grip.

"*WAAA*!" a furious rasp broke from the beggar, "*Higashi no kaze ame! I-ye*!" With sudden appalling ferocity he struck. The Taiwanese sprang aside as the two handed blow split the air with a hiss. Wei-Wei felt a pain, sharper than anything imaginable, pierce her shoulder and slice down, down, burning like ice, through her breast and belly to her pelvis. So this is death, she thought despairingly as she fell.

ELEVEN PM. On the Macao ferry a bell clanged. "Fornicate the gods," One-eyed Tok growled to himself on the lower deck as the chimes died away. "We shall be in British waters soon. What do the Sea Devils wait for?" Scratching his piles he peered into the darkness to port.

The rain had ceased and the vessel was steaming through a light swell. Little moonlight penetrated the overcast, but somewhere not far ahead lay Lantao Island and the seaward boundary of the British Colony. On the deck above Yu-Ling stood by the rail.

A figure brushed against her making her start. "Oh, I'm sorry," a voice apologised. "I didn't see you there for a moment. Sure is black out here."

Squinting in the darkness Yu-Ling recognised the fair-haired American girl from the saloon. "Yes, it is very dark," she replied shyly.

"Oh, you speak English!" Surprise and pleasure sounded in the other girl's voice.

49

"A little only, at school I learn . . . I learned," Yu-Ling corrected herself blushing. "Please to excuse my error." She had been working so hard to improve her grammar.

"You speak just fine," Scott assured her, "heaps better than . .. " A sudden blast on the boat's whistle swamped her words. The deck heeled sharply and they grabbed at the rail for support as the bow swung round and the engines slowed. "Say, what gives?" she cried above the din, "We seem to be stopping."

A searchlight flashed on from the bridge. The beam swept the surface of the water and fastened on the hull of an ocean-going junk lying fifty yards off. Its sail was down, collapsed in folds upon the deck and Yu-Ling could see the captain by the tiller, hurling abuse at the dog-dung *quai loh* who had run down his ship. "I think," she told Scott, "that one from his crew is lost in the waters."

The gap between the two vessels narrowed as the junk drifted nearer. A British officer with a megaphone shouted peremptorily at the Chinese captain to put up his helm. "*Ai-yah*! Put up your own helm, motherless whores! Do you own the seas?" With a defiant yell the junk's master deliberately turned his bows in towards the ferry. There came a growl of powerful diesels and the water under its stern began to froth white. "Hallo, the bugger's motorized!" Scott heard a passenger exclaim.

The ferry's own engines throbbed in a hasty effort to claw away but the junk was very close now, almost alongside starboard. Screams broke out among the passengers as they saw its decks were no longer deserted. Brandishing guns and knives, men were pouring up through the hatches and out from under the sail where they had lain concealed. "Christ!" somebody shouted aghast, "They're pirates!"

Pirates! Stark terror erupted at the cry. Shrieking men and women fled the rails in panic. Caught in a stampede, Yu-Ling and Scott were knocked to the deck.

With a jarring crash the ships came together and rolled there, grinding horribly. Hooks and grapnels thudded home among the timbers, lashing the junk to the ferry's side, and a savage cheer went up from the attackers as they swarmed aboard on the lower deck. Simultaneously the ferry's lights flashed on along her length.

The first blast of the boat's whistle sent One-eyed Tok and his accomplice swiftly to the upper deck. Crouching by the rear bulkhead of the first class saloon, they drew from their shirts egg-shaped sulphur bombs and lighting the fuses tossed them spluttering through the ventilation scuttles. A series of crackling explosions sounded on the inside.

50

In the saloon surprise was total. Within seconds the cabin was engulfed in smoke. Ears ringing from the blasts, Chris Fry stumbled from the card table. Panicky figures blundered against him and poisonous fumes burned his throat. Consumed by the fear of being trapped, somehow he found the door and shoved his way through into the open air to collapse on deck.

A man burst out of the smoke waving a pole. With a shock he realised it was not a pole, but a rifle with a foot long bayonet and threw himself flat. A swirling mob charged over him as he tried to rise. Bullets zipped overhead and ricocheted angrily off metal fittings. Crawling into the cover of a ventilator he lay prone and prayed.

Behind him Shapiro staggered out of the saloon gagging from the sulphur. Instinctively he cast round for a weapon. Clipped to a lifeboat davit close by was an iron crank handle for the winding gear. As he snatched it up he heard Scott's voice screaming.

"Scott!" With a shout he plunged forward through the mob. She was by the companionway, struggling with two coolies who had seized a young Chinese girl. Shapiro swung his davit handle and it came down crack on top of the nearest coolie's shaven skull with a force that jarred his arm. Blood spurted and the man dropped like a sack.

One-eyed Tok reacted with frightening speed. Loosing the girl he whirled to meet the attack, in one hand a knife, in the other the thin steel chain he had used to throttle the soldier. Easily dodging the American's first clumsy blow, he feinted to one side with the knife to throw him off balance. As Shapiro swung at him again he crouched low and with a flick of the wrist sent the chain snaking out to hook around his opponent's forearm.

Shapiro felt the links bite into his flesh and tried to pull back. Too late. Before he could recover he was jerked off his feet and helplessly snared.

Gripping his knife hard, Tok moved in for the kill. He had never thought to cut a white man's throat, serve this fornicator right for interfering. *Ai-yah*, dead all men were the same.

Fear knotted in Shapiro's belly as he floundered on his back, fighting to free himself from the chain. He saw the killer glare in the man's face and the blade glinting in towards him and tensed for the thrust . . .

It never came. A shot cracked in his ear and the pull on the chain slackened. He rolled sideways and scrambled up, panting. The coolie was writhing in the scuppers by the rail. Standing over him, re-loading a little silver-plated derringer, was the White Russian Prince Cherkassy.

51

An Englishman had joined Chris behind the ventilator. "Can you swim, Yank? Because if these bastards take us, that's what you'll be doing." Yelling like fiends the pirates were rampaging through the ship. A band armed with pistols and rifles were preparing to rush the bridge. Suddenly a deafening boom rocked the night.

"Jesus! What was that?" Away in the direction of Lantao a red light winked. A shell screeched overhead to burst with an ear splitting crash in the sea a hundred yards astern. "It's the British Navy!" Chris cried, "There's a gunboat coming up. Wow, not before time!"

The panic was on the other side now. Whistles shrilled urgently on the junk as the pirates scrambled madly to get back aboard. The crew were hacking at the cables binding them to the ferry. Pursued by jeers from the passengers, several of the attackers flung themselves bodily over the rails. One fell into the water to be cut screaming to pieces by the prop.

The gunboat's white bow wave was coming up fast. Its shells were still falling short of the junk which had pulled free from the ferry's side and was making away astern.

"Aw heck!" exclaimed Chris as the gunboat ceased firing and slackened speed to come alongside. "they're letting them escape!"

"Under orders not to risk an encounter in Nip waters," said the Englishman disgustedly. "Here, take a look at this," he was examining a rifle dropped by one of the pirates. Like the weapon Chris had dodged moments ago, it had a viciously long bayonet. "Arisaka 6.5 millimetre Mauser action," he worked the bolt, flicking out an empty shell. "Standard issue to the Imperial Army. I wouldn't mind betting the yellow-bellies are behind this."

Shapiro helped the girl Yu-Ling to her feet. Order was slowly returning aboard the ferry. People were picking themselves up off the deck, moving to the rails to cheer the warship.

Then came a sudden cry from astern.

Surrounded by a crowd of tormentors, One-eyed Tok lay doubled-up in agony in a pool of his own blood. Hate filled faces leered down at him spitting and hooting. *"Ai-yah, filthy pirate, kick him!"*

"Give him one for me!"

"Aiee, kill the swine!"

The pain in his gut was like burning knives and he prayed for death, cursing the cowards who had fled leaving him to fall alive into the hands of his enemies. The mob gave back as a tall figure loomed up, the White Russian, "Ach, so this scum still lives, does he?"

Tok grimaced, *"Fornicate you and all your line,"* he gasped painfully, knowing what was to come. The Russian's expression was brutal. Seizing the injured man in his powerful arms, he lifted him up and flung him over the rail into the sea.

The crowd roared. Scott hid her face. Chris and Shapiro turned away sickened.

IV

At Kai Tak security had been tightened. Soldiers stood about cradling weapons and a sergeant shone a flash in the crew's faces before waving them through the gates. Down by the seaplane dock there was an armoured car lurking and another identity check before they were allowed onto the pier where the Clipper was berthed.

Stewart Whitely shivered in spite of the warm night as they humped their flight bags from the taxis. Visions of that nightmare severed head swam before his eyes. He wished he hadn't drunk so much. Were they pulling out tonight? How about Scott and the others, surely Ross couldn't just abandon them?

Ross wasn't answering questions.

The airliner was fully blacked out, water gurgling quietly along the hull and the huge fuselage looming in the darkness. O'Byrne let them in, "There's a couple of guys waiting. Dunno who they are. Second Officer's with 'em. What's it all about?"

Slater was being shown round the passenger deck by Kurt Thyssen. He greeted them impatiently, "What kept you, for Christsakes? I don't have all night." With him was another man, a European in his forties, slight, sunburned, with a lean hawk's face.

Ross scowled at Thyssen. "Who the hell asked you to give tours? This isn't a goddam pleasure yacht." He led the way to the upper level. The flight deck portholes were shuttered too and the cockpit section in the nose curtained off. Green shaded lamps, the thick carpeting and leather seats made the long cabin inviting by night. There was a book open on the chart table: Dale Carnegie's *How to Make Friends and Influence People*. Thyssen was a sucker for self-improvement.

"Okay Slater, you've gotten us all here, where's the cargo?" Ross demanded.

"How d'you think we came over, walking on the water?" Slater's voice was metallic. "There's a Royal Navy launch docked in back of us. The cargo's being off-loaded now. This here's Dr. Latouche, from Paris. He'll be overseeing the technical side."

Technical side, what technical side? the Clipper's crew wanted to ask. Ross ignored him and stuck a cigarette in his mouth. He jerked his chin at Munro, "You're in charge, Mister." By the rules cargo handling was the first officer's responsibility, just as navigation was Thyssen's.

"Aye aye, sir." Munro turned to Slater, "Do you have the configuration details; dimensions and weights for each item?"

"Yeah, Latouche has all that stuff. Right Doc?"

From an inside pocket the Frenchman produced a waybill. "I think this tells you what you need, if there is anything else please ask." His voice was pleasant and he had a way of looking you straight in the face when he spoke.

"No, I guess it's all here," Munro studied the flimsy which listed one casket, property of the US Government, contents *'human remains'*, and two trunks of papers. "Any special instructions?"

Everyone looked to the doctor. "The two sealed trunks require handling with the utmost caution. In no circumstances should they be opened or interfered with. Those employed loading must wear gloves – any skin contact is to be avoided."

The crew paled. *Gloves, skin contact – Christ, what was in those trunks?*

"Lower away, easy now." Held in the glare of flashlights, the dully gleaming metal case descended slowly through the cargo hatch between the wings suspended from the slings of the flying boat's in-built crane. On top of the hull Davey Klein and Chuck Driscoll steadied the load, relaying instructions from Munro inside the hold, out to the port wing where the Chief stood at the winch controls. Also present was Latouche, his quick gaze alert to every detail. As instructed, all were wearing gloves.

"Another foot . . . steady . . . a bit more. *Okay*, that's it!" The cable slackened and the young officers climbed down to aid Munro. Situated immediately aft of the control cabin, the cavernous main hold was stacked high already with freight. Wire cages against the bulkheads held bundles of express and diplomatic mail and the deck space was piled with canvas sacks. Hatches either side gave into additional holds located within the thick wing stubs. At the far end, opposite the door to the control cabin, another hatch led to the crew's rest quarters.

"Trust Shapiro and Chris to miss out on this," Davey groused as together they manhandled the cumbersome object over to the space they had cleared and lashed it down firmly. "What you got here, Doc? Feels like it's full of bricks."

"*Gold bricks* most like," Chuck grunted. The Doctor did not reply. Kneeling, he conducted a careful examination. The others too studied it. Externally, there was little to remark: a four foot by three, square-ended grey steel footlocker, fastened at the side with heavy duty brass padlocks. Stencilled on the lid was the number 92, no other markings.

"If it's alright by you, Doctor," Munro said, "we'll put the next one over against the starboard bulkhead and the coffin opposite the water tank. It's a question of distributing the weight evenly."

Leaving them to carry on, he returned to the control cabin. Alan Bond had arrived and was talking to Ross up in the cockpit. Stewart Whitely was on the radiophone to the tower. "How do you expect us to load cargo without lights?" Munro heard him saying. The British were taking their blackout seriously. Sounds below told where O'Byrne and Gotto were busy making up beds.

The hatch to the port wing walkway closed behind him on a spring as he stepped through into the wing. Inside, a narrow lighted tunnel smelling of oil and gasoline with a lattice aluminum decking, bored through a mass of metal piping, control cables and multi-coloured electric wiring. It was cramped for a large man and he crouched low to guard his head as he made his way along to the inboard engine nacelle.

There was more space here. Two men could stand to work side by side in comparative comfort. It was one of the miracles of the giant Clippers that all four engines were accessible during flight and if necessary could be stripped down completely for repair from within the wing. On several occasions crews had had cause to bless this facility.

In either side of the nacelle, trap doors opened outwards on chains to form working platforms. Munro climbed out onto one and stood erect.

"That you, Max?" The night was black as the inside of a coal bunker. The military had refused permission to use the Clipper's roof-mounted searchlight. Munro could just make out the bulky figure of the Chief on top of the wing beside the derrick. He clambered up beside him.

"How goes it out here?"

"Peachy. If you strain real hard you can see six inches in front of your face. Some clown will fall in the drink before this is through. I just hope it ain't me."

There were dim shapes moving on the pier below the fifteen foot propellors and they could hear Thyssen talking. Then Slater's voice volleyed up impatiently, "Hey, Injun! Cut the pow-wow. The sooner this stuff's aboard, the sooner we can all pack up."

"Asshole!" the Chief muttered and flipped the cable release on the derrick. "Mind your heads!" he sang and the men below scattered cursing as the hook plummeted into their midst.

Munro climbed back down onto the nacelle and descended the ladder to the dock. Slater was chewing irritably on a cigar. "If that guy were in my outfit he'd be on a charge," he scowled.

"You ought to report him, Max," Kurt Thyssen chimed in. "This is Government business, doesn't he realise that?"

"I guess not, why don't you get up there and tell him?" Munro shone his flashlight on the rest of the cargo. The second trunk was identical to the first. The coffin sat apart, a brass plaque gleaming on its teakwood lid. "Okay, let's get the slings on."

Unnoticed amid the operation, a dark-skinned, muscular youth with jet black hair slipped quietly out through the main hatch. Tad Gotto, the junior steward. Showing his pass to the soldiers on the dock, he hurried up the path to the Marine Terminal building.

"Whatsamatter, you deaf or somethin'?" he demanded, pushing past the night clerk who finally responded to his knocking. "Gimme the laundry key will you. I gotta full crew sleeping aboard tonight."

Behind the passenger lounge were airline offices and storerooms. Gotto opened up the linen cupboard and made a pile of sheets and towels. The clerk leaned in the doorway watching. He was Eurasian, sly with grey flecked dark hair and upward slanting eyes. "There was a guy here this evening asking for you," he said.

"Oh yeah, who?" Gotto was counting the sheets.

"Said his name didn't matter, just he wanted to see you. I think he was from Taiwan," the clerk added carefully.

Gotto stiffened, "I dunno anyone from there."

"*Liar*," the clerk retorted, smirking, "you know plenty, important people, people from across the Eastern Sea, *neh*?" He sniggered. The next instant he was slammed up against the wall, choking, with Gotto's hands at his throat.

"You call me a liar, you dirty goddam bastard?" Gotto shook him so his teeth rattled in his head, "What d'you mean, huh? What you tryin' to pin on me?"

"*Aiee*, nothing, nothing!" the clerk squealed. "It was only a joke!" Gotto's grip tightened savagely.

"Shut up! Shut up you son of a bitch or I'll bust you in the mouth! *Wakarimasu*?"

"*Hai*, yes understood," the clerk answered weakly.

Gotto banged the outer door behind him. Carrying the load of linen he started back down the path. By the steps he stopped. A metallic gleam had caught his attention among the whitewashed rocks that lined the way. Bending, he examined the object in his fingers: a gilt enamelled button, it bore the device of the chrysanthemum flower. Heart pounding, his hand closed round it.

The Bishop's coffin was the last to be swung aboard. They had taken down the derrick and Munro was checking the wing for scrapes when a car rolled to a halt at the head of the pier. Footsteps sounded on the planking. Peering into the darkness he recognised Inspector Playfair. "Ah Munro, I've some colleagues of yours here. A Royal Navy patrol took them off the Macao ferry an hour ago."

Munro saw a head of tousled blond hair behind him and heaved a sigh of relief, "Godammit Scott," he said, "you people sure picked a time to go missing. Are you okay?"

"Yes, we're all fine," she nodded wearily. "I guess we blew it, huh Max?"

Somebody else was trying to push past from the rear. "Mr. Slater! Mr. Slater!"

"Oh shit!" Slater muttered.

It was Reverend Jordan.

"Mr. Slater," the priest stammered, "they just told me at the Consulate you're loading Bishop Buchan's coffin tonight. I protest, you had no right to move it without my permission. I had a press conference arranged for tomorrow, photographers . . ."

"Sure I know, Reverend," Slater cut him short, "change of plan. Relax, he's being taken good care of. Check for yourself if you want."

He led the way inside the hatch. The rest of the party followed. Munro found himself alone on the jetty with Playfair. "Your friends had a lucky escape," the Inspector commented, "their ferry was attacked by river pirates. If the Navy hadn't been on hand they might not be alive to tell the tale."

"*Pirates? Jesus!* Do they still operate in these waters?"

"Yes and they're growing bolder. Whether there's any connection with the murder we're not yet certain. Speaking of which, do you remember that snapshot you turned up at the Hotel Asia?"

"I remember. What about it?"

"After you left, Reverend Jordan asked if he might have it – as a memento of his friend. Only trouble was the thing had gone, vanished. We none of us could find it anywhere." There was a pause. Munro said nothing. "Strange, wouldn't you agree?"

"So is murder. You think I took it?"

"It seems somebody did," Playfair remarked drily. "No, what puzzles me is the motive. Except for the girl we had identified everyone in it. Perhaps it's a case of 'cherchez la femme', eh?"

A knife twisted in Munro's gut. *Damn Georgiana!* Why had he taken the photograph? He sure as hell didn't want her back in his life.

The interrogation was interrupted. Slater had returned, Jordan with him. "What are you doing out here, Playfair?" he said rudely, "This is none of your affair."

The Englishman's jaw jutted, "As it happens murder is very much my affair."

"Then it's me you speak to, not Munro, and right now I'm busy." Hands on hips Slater faced him aggressively but the Inspector stood his ground.

"You'll be interested to learn we've managed to clear up one point. *Mili*. It's an island in the Pacific, an atoll I think you call it, one of the Gilbert group."

"The Marshalls," Munro corrected him, too tired all at once to care. "It's in the Marshall Islands, not the Gilberts."

"You knew this all along?"

"No, I'd forgotten, It came back to me this evening." Overhead Munro could hear a plane. He glanced up but the sky was obscured by a raft of cloud. What was it Wei-Wei had said? *East wind rain*? But these clouds were travelling south.

Slater gave a snort. "So it's an island. Big deal. Where does that get us, Playfair?"

"I'm not certain at present but I intend to find out," Playfair said firmly. "I don't like strangers conducting their private wars on my patch, not even our so-called allies." Saluting curtly with his swagger stick, he walked off up the jetty.

Slater stared after him, fists balled at his sides. "Two-faced limey son of a bitch! I had the Governor on earlier, Playfair's been squealing to have the flight held. Well screw him!" He swivelled back to Munro, eyes glittering, "*Okay, feller, talk fast: what do you know about Mili?*"

Three am. The hour of the Tiger. The sentries were changing. Soundlessly the Japanese emerged from a culvert near the water's edge and flitted wraith-like across a patch of open ground to the shadow of an unfinished sandbag gun emplacement. Senses cued for danger, he

59

crouched motionless. Dogs were barking but they were far away. A few yards in front a small stone jetty loomed, sounds made by the water indicated boats moored alongside. Lifting his head he tested the air, concentrating on the inside of his nostrils below his eyes. The rancid white man smell came plain to him. A soldier was down there.

Silent on the fabric soles of his *tabi* he crept closer, crouching low, using the higher ground behind for cover. The soldier was visible now, silhouetted against the night sky, sitting on an oil drum at the head of the jetty, rifle propped nearby. Noiselessly the Japanese stole to within a sword's length and sank into a pool of shadow, waiting, still as death.

A minute ticked by. The moon shone briefly out then vanished again behind a cloud. With a creak of webbing the soldier yawned and stood up, reaching for his rifle. Before he could touch it the Japanese sprang on him from behind. One hand hooked out and round striking for the unprotected throat with the bony edge of the wrist. Simultaneously the other fist smashed with pile-driving force into the man's right kidney.

Choking with pain and terror, diaphragm nerves paralysed by the throat strike, the soldier clawed mutely at the arm clamped about his neck like a rigid iron bar. He was helpless as a child against the vicious strength of his attacker. The relentless grip tightened, an enormous force pressed his head forward and he went limp as the carotid artery collapsed, starving the brain of blood.

Counting ten heartbeats, the Japanese maintained the stranglehold till he was certain the man was unconscious. Squeezing the stomach to force out the air and prevent a death-rattle, he lowered him to the ground. The entire attack, carried out in complete silence, had lasted no more than fifteen seconds.

There was an open launch and two or three oared craft tied up to the jetty. Lifting the weighty body in his arms he carried it up a little way and slid it into the water face down, wedging the head under the launch's bow. The rifle went in beside it. One more enemy dead. *Karma*. Everything would point to an accident.

He turned his attention to the boats.

Two were clinker built rowboats too bulky for his purpose but the third, a flat-bottomed punt with a low freeboard, was ideal. He snapped its chain with a tool from his sack and climbed aboard. Lying prone on his belly he began paddling softly with his hands in the direction of the Clipper pier.

Munro awoke with a taste of danger in his mouth. Tense in his bunk he lay listening. All was quiet, the waves lapping gently against the hull outside. The luminous dial of his watch showed a quarter after three, half the night to go. Sitting up on an elbow he felt beneath his pillow, the photographs were safe.

It was airless in the cabin. He was sharing the upper deck quarters with Ross, snoring underneath him, and the Chief and Thyssen opposite. The rest were down below on the passenger deck. It was seldom they all slept aboard like this. Lifting a corner of the window shade, he peered out. The harbour was tranquil. Still he felt uneasy. Maybe he would fetch a glass of water from the galley, it would be an excuse to check the ship. He reached for his pants.

There was a degree of light in the hold next door from the navigation astrodome in the overhead hatch. Nothing looked to have been disturbed. The metal trunks were still in place. Munro stepped round the mail bags and ran his flashlight over them. Drops of water glistened on the lid of the Bishop's coffin, it must have gotten splashed crossing the harbour. He was about to check more closely when out of the corner of his eye he saw the door to the control cabin opening stealthily.

In two strides he was across the hold and ripping back the hatch, flash levelled. The figure outside gave a gasp of fright and recoiled, arms raised against the light. "*Who the hell . . . ?*" Munro snarled, then let out a sigh of exasperation, "Godammit, Tad! What are you doing prowling about this time of night?"

"Gee, Mr. Munro," Gotto gulped shaken, "I thought I heard a noise up here."

"I wanted a drink. Sorry if I woke you." They were standing in the hatch, the instrument dials in the cabin beyond reflecting the light like ranks of eyes.

"A glass of iced water? Wait here, sir. I'll bring one right away."

"Thanks, but don't worry, I can get it myself."

"It's no trouble, sir," Gotto insisted starting back below. Munro followed him down anyway. In the chrome fitted galley the steward poured him a glass from the cooler, "Those crates up there, Mr. Munro, you reckon there's really papers inside?"

"That's what the manifest says. Try not to worry about it, Tad. Get some sack instead."

Everyone was spooked tonight. Returning to the upper deck Munro switched on the lamp over the chart table. The maps were stored in lockers underneath. It took him only a moment to locate the one he wanted. Spreading it out he reached for the measuring dividers.

Minutes later he straightened up again puzzled. Frowning, he replaced the chart and doused the light again. Nothing made sense.

Mili . . . Ross . . . Earhart . . . The figures just didn't add up.

Across the water in a Kuomintang owned mansion on the Peak, a telephone shrilled.

"*Wey?*" a voice answered guardedly in Cantonese.

"Tell your masters we accept. Meet as arranged. Be on time, *wakarimasu?*"

"Understood." Colonel Huang replaced the receiver thoughtfully and looked at Hollington Soong, who reclined on a sofa opposite. "The Sea Devils' High Command approves the plan. Everything is set."

The Minister made a worried grimace, "*Aiee*, Huang Ko-Fang, I do not like it. I accept no responsibility."

"You would prefer to surrender the Manchu jewel to the Red Pang, *heya?*" Huang's tone was sardonic.

"No, no," Soong replied hastily, "that is out of the question, the Generalissimo himself forbids it. The Pang's terms are impossible, impossible," he repeated. "And yet we must have the papers . . ."

He motioned to his secretary, a spectacled and intense young man working at the desk, "Simon, pour me another Scotch please, then you may go to bed, we have an early start. And on your way up check all is well with the Chen's, *heya?* No, Colonel," he turned back to Huang, "do not misunderstand me, I was simply wondering if another appeal to the High Khan's patriotic sense . . ." he gestured airily, " . . . we would pay any reasonable price."

Huang regarded him stonily, "The Pang will not bargain. They have made that clear. They will settle for the jewel and the jewel only."

There was a short silence. The secretary bowed and bade both men goodnight. Soong drank deeply from his glass. "What of the British then?" he asked as the door closed.

"The *quai loh* will know nothing, we have chosen a remote spot to make the exchange." Huang permitted himself a brief smile, "As it happens, the village where Tiger Lim was born."

Hollington Soong's jowls quivered, "Great gods protect us," he muttered. "If the Red Pang should ever learn of this treachery our lives will not be worth the flicker of a candle's flame."

*   *   *

The ether trembled. In the Japanese Empire the time was 4:26 am. From the lattice mast of the MKY Radio tower a coded high frequency transmission was being beamed westwards round the world. Tokyo was speaking with Berlin. War was fast approaching and the *Gaimusho*, the Foreign Ministry, had an urgent dispatch for Ambassador Oshima in the Axis capital.

Ten thousand miles away on the rock–bound New England coast at Winter Harbour, Maine, an array of lofty aerials at a secret US Navy monitoring station plucked the message from the wave-bands and a warning lamp glowed in an underground receiving room as the spools of recording machines sprang suddenly to life.

The dispatch was not long. No more than a quarter of an hour elapsed before the duty shift had it transcribed and punched onto a teletype tape. A landline connection was dialled and the coded text fed through the transmitter.

In Washington DC another teleprinter, located in Room 1649 on the first deck of the Navy Department Building on Constitution Avenue, began to chatter in response, spewing out a copy of the intercept on yellow paper at a rate of sixty words per minute. The watch officer, a junior lieutenant of OP–20–GY, the Navy's cryptoanalytic section, ripped the page off the printer and logged the time, 2:44 pm, fourteen hours behind Tokyo on a bright but chilly afternoon.

Taking his seat at a nearby desk, the lieutenant switched on an elaborate apparatus resembling a pair of typewriters connected to a wooden cabinet looped with complex electrical circuitry. From experience he recognised the indicators on the message as CA-PURPLE, the highest Japanese security classification for a Chief of Mission dispatch. Methodically he typed out the letter groups of the coded intercept on the keyboard. In the cabinet beside him electrical relays hummed and flickered. Slowly, at a rate this time of five words to the minute, a plain text copy appeared on the printer.

Still in Japanese, the decoded message was passed next door to the translation section. When an English version had been finally agreed, fourteen copies were made. Two were retained for departmental files, the remaining twelve were placed in brown manila folders inside padlocked leather pouches for delivery by armed couriers.

At 4:36 pm, the first of these pouches was handed in at the White House basement mailroom to the President's naval aide, who signed for it. Exactly seven minutes later this officer was shown into the second floor study by an usher. The President was at his desk; one of his personal advisors, a tall silver-haired Southerner of patrician bearing, pacing the carpet. The aide would later testify that both men seemed to have been expecting him. Saluting, he wished them good

63

afternoon and unlocking the pouch with his personal key, placed the intercept in its folder before Franklin Delano Roosevelt.

"How much time is left to us, Kim?"

The tall man scanned the pages: '. . . *say very secretly to Herr Hitler . . . extreme danger war may suddenly break out . . . may come quicker than anyone dreams.. . .*' He closed the file and passed it back. "A week at most, Mr. President, less if the intelligence reports are correct. I doubt if even the Emperor could stop the militarists now."

The President returned the manila folder to the Naval officer who locked it away again, saluted crisply and withdrew. So jealously guarded was this secret ability to read the enemy's diplomatic codes, not even the White House was permitted to retain copies.

"Kim, I'm concerned for Major Slater's operation," the President continued when the door had shut again, "and particularly after this news from Hongkong. If Tokyo has learned of our plans they may go to any lengths to stop us."

The man called Kim resumed his pacing. "The picture is confused, Mr. President, but Slater's report indicates strong probability of Black Dragon involvement." Briefly he sketched out the details. "The British authorities in Hongkong are unhappy," he concluded in his soft drawl, "they're threatening to hold the plane for inquiries."

"I have Prime Minister Churchill's personal assurance their people will not interfere. I think we may rely on that."

"I hope so, Mr. President. Unfortunately there is another aspect to the problem – Mili atoll."

"*Mili!*" the President's head jerked up in surprise, "But that was years ago. Surely there can be no link?"

"Only two men know the full story of Mili: Slater is one, the other's a Pan Am pilot named Ross, now in command of the Pacific Clipper in Hongkong."

Stretching, a Scots terrier got up from its basket and wandered over to the President's wheelchair. He stroked its ears absently. "You know, Kim, in the light of the risks involved I'd like to turn this whole project over to the military from Manila on."

"Use one of MacArthur's bombers? He'll not thank you for that."

"True, and I can't blame him. He needs everything he has down there to defend the Philippines. But I'm thinking of Guam, the island's defenceless, ringed by Jap bases. It wouldn't be the first time a civilian plane has gone missing in those waters."

"I'll see Slater is informed of the switch. You'll tell General Marshall yourself?"

The President nodded, "George knows how I want this played."

The interview over, the other man paused for a moment to gaze out from the long windows behind the desk. Across the bare lawns the slim shaft of Washington's Memorial stood straight and clean in the watery December sun.

"Kim," the President's voice was gentle. Their youth had been spent together at Groton and Harvard, "Kim, where is Georgiana now?"

A shadow came into his friend's face, "Manila, still in Manila, drat the girl! I wired her to come home but she takes no notice of me anymore." He snorted irritably, unable to disguise the vastness of his concern.

The President's eyes clouded. He pushed his wheelchair back from the desk a little. "Kim," he said soberly, "she may have left it too late."

The tall man looked at him and his hands trembled. She was his only daughter.

V

WEDNESDAY DECEMBER 3rd. Dawn found the Crown Colony misty and overcast. Above the rugged hills of the New Territories a small plane droned, the British morning patrol flight out of Kai Tak. Half way up a pinewood slope near Castle Peak, Colonel Huang heard the sound as he paused to regain his breath and checked his watch. *Ai-yah*, almost six, he would have to hurry if he were to make the rendezvous. Behind him the road wound eastwards through the hills to Fanling and the border, while away to the west gleamed the waters of Deep Bay. Moving cautiously between the dripping trees, he reached the crest and peered down into the valley.

Yes, there was the village, less than half a mile away on a shoulder of the hill, its walls and roofs emerging from a sea of fog. A cart track threaded out through a patchwork of lawn-sized fields to connect with the main road. Passing directly below Huang, it crossed a stream on a narrow bridge of stone.

He focused his binoculars on the village and whistled softly. *Aiee*, it was a fortress, complete with massive outer walls of stone and gate towers. No wonder Tiger Lim had wanted such a place at his back. It must have been built as a defence against pirates before the British came. Life was stirring among the houses, the cooking fires were alight and he could hear the bark of chow dogs. But the paddies were empty still. He turned his attention to the bridge where the exchange was due to take place.

From the road came the sound of a vehicle.

It was a van. As it drew into sight Huang saw it was an old Post Office van and mentally congratulated Tiger Lim on his craftiness. Any hijacker would hesitate before attacking a government vehicle. It reached the bridge and halted. A Chinese got out. He walked up and down, peering over the parapet, then went back to speak to someone inside the cab. Two more men descended. Huang strained through his field glasses but recongnised none of them. Surely they had to be the Pang? Then a fourth man emerged and he breathed a sigh of relief. It was Lim.

Oh ko, where were the Sea Devils?

The group on the bridge were displaying signs of nervousness. Tiger Lim climbed back into the driver's seat and sat there with the engine running while his henchmen paced the approaches, pistols drawn. Finally Lim lost patience. He tooted the horn; the others scrambled in. With a grind of gears the van rolled forward off the bridge and down towards the village.

Fornicate the gods! What were the Sea Devils waiting for? Huang flung aside his binoculars and cast about the valley anxiously. Once the Pang reached the security of the fortress village it would take an army to fetch them out.

A scream rent the air, a stark, paralysing yell torn from the throats of men at the extremity of agony and terror. Cursing, Huang jerked the glasses up again. *Ai-yah!* The van was burning!

Fifty yards from the bridge at a bend in the track it was stopped with a front wheel in the ditch and smoke belching from the cab. As he watched a long, hot crocodile of flame spouted from the concealment of the culvert and licked greedily at the stricken vehicle. Huang's breath hissed between his teeth.

A door of the cab swung open and a figure stumbled out, a human torch. It made five yards then fell. Through his glasses Huang could spot the soldiers moving in closer. The weapon operator with the heavy tank on his back and the long hose-connected nozzle was squirting short jets of flame around the sides and rear. Now the whole van was enveloped in fire. The hiss and crackle was audible up on the ridge. The terrible shrieking had ceased, the gangsters must all be dead. With a boom the gas tank exploded and the blazing wreck toppled over into the ditch.

Huang shut up his field glasses and put them away. Clever, very clever of the Sea Devils. They must have sent the flame-thrower team in from the sea. Nothing could possibly have survived its intense heat. A burnt out van was much less suspicious than one blown apart by a bomb or riddled with bullets.

Tiger Lim had died hard. *Joss.* It was not the Chinese way to shrink like a woman at the sound of an enemy's scream.

Yu-Ling awoke trembling in a strange bed. Where was she? In her dream she had been running from the pirates again. A ship's hooter was sounding outside in the distance. Of course. Relief flowed through her: British Hongkong, Minister Soong's foreign-style mansion on the Peak. It had been too dark when they arrived to see anything. Leaping out, she flung open the shutters.

The view across the harbour made her blink. *Ai-yah*, so this was the Empire! There must be hundreds of junks out there, ships, tugs, ferries, more than she could count. Macao seemed a village by comparison.

Memories of last night sent another shiver down her spine. Truly the enemy would stop at nothing. The pirates were in the pay of the Japanese, Colonel Huang had said so in the car on the way here. He frightened her that one. The great Minister Hollington Soong, on the other hand, had been friendly, pleased to see them. There was a young male secretary with him, another nice person with a westernized name, Simon Ho.

She washed swiftly and dressed. Foreign-devil bathrooms were strange – no chamber pot to save the urine so precious for the flowers. The stolid bodyguard on duty in the hall watched her slip quietly into the next door room. Her uncle lay as she had left him, his beard combed down over his chest, the devil box, swathed in yellow silk, secure in the crook of his arm. He turned his head at her approach.

"*Tso sun*, good morning, Third Niece. You have slept soundly after the hazards of our journey?"

"*Tso sun*, Honourable Uncle. Like the little death. And you?"

"I too have rested. Should I be rising?"

"Soon. It is early yet, there is no need of hurry." Kneeling beside the bed, Yu-Ling poured his medicine and helped him drink it from the spoon. "Give me your hands," she commanded. Tenderly she massaged the stiff joints and rubbed salve into them.

Rising at length, she went out into the hall and addressed the guard. "Please call a servant. My uncle, Honourable Professor Chen, requires *cha* to drink." The man ignored her. He was Chinese dressed western style, small porcine eyes and a barrel chest. She repeated her request stubbornly and he turned his back with a contemptuous snort.

"*Ai-yah!* Are you deaf? Fetch a servant!" the Minister appeared in the doorway behind them. "What are you, a barbarian from the Outer Provinces? Are your ears filled with dung?" he screeched. "The Princess wants a servant. Find one!"

The man blenched and fled. "Useless pig!" Soong spat after him. He glanced at Yu-Ling, "Pretty, very pretty, little Jade Years," he commented, eyeing the fit of her *cheong-sam*. "Now hurry along, you and your uncle must be ready to leave one hour from now. Golden Country *quai loh* do not like to be kept waiting."

Yu-Ling returned to her own room and shut the door.

The day was still overcast around seven thirty when Munro headed up to the marine terminal for breakfast. Aboard the aircraft O'Byrne had Scott and Gotto at work already, setting the lower deck straight. Groundcrew in white coveralls were manhandling fuel hoses from a tanker truck on the dock and the smell of avgas hung in the air.

"Stay off the bacon," the Chief advised in the dining room. Munro ordered scrambled eggs with coffee and grabbed a paper. '*Pirate attack on Macao ferry*', screamed the headlines, '*Four dead, eleven injured, British soldier missing.*' There was no mention of Morris Oliver's death.

Shapiro entered with Fry. "Say, what's this about a passenger getting killed yesterday?"

"We're late. Get on and eat," Munro told him without looking up.

Thyssen's pale eyes narrowed spitefully, "I just hope Ross throws the book at you guys, leading Scott into trouble like that."

Shapiro flushed, "Hell, she's not a kid for Christsakes."

Ross put in an appearance, tired-eyed and impatient to be off. He gulped some coffee and ordered everybody peremptorily out into the operations office for a flight briefing. 'Not you two, Fry and Shapiro. You can get back aboard and stand guard over the cargo. And God help you if anything happens to it because you'll stop here till the Japs come!'

The Pan American operations office was furnished with a teleprinter and a wall map of the Pacific. A jovial RAF meteorologist was waiting for them. "Right ho, chaps," he stepped out in front of a chart board bearing faded notices of army gunnery practice and the dangers of overflying Japanese territory. "I'll start with the current situation: seven tenths cloud with a ceiling at two thousand; winds fresh, eighteen knots from the south east. As of this moment the skies are clear over Manila, you'll be glad to hear, but there's low stratus reported extending to within an estimated three hundred miles of the Luzon coast. Be prepared for patches of turbulence, your passengers won't thank you for spilt soup!" None of the crew smiled. Weathermen were all the same with their jokes. They didn't have to fly through the stuff.

"Turning now to the upper air maps . . ." The fliers gathered round to study the charts. "There are indications of a depression building between latitude 15 and the Marshalls, perhaps headed for New Guinea," he tapped the map. "I'm afraid I can't be any more specific, our Nip friends aren't being very co-operative with their met. reports these days."

Again Munro recalled Wei-Wei's warning about the winds.

Working together from the charts they drew up a three dimensional

69

plot determining the safest, most efficient speed, track and altitude for each sector of the route and prepared estimates of fuel consumption.

"Sixteen fifty gallons it is," Chief Crow heaved himself from his seat, "If anyone wants me I'll be down on the ship." Munro referred briefly to his slide rule and entered the figure on the weight report. Ninety-nine hundred pounds, almost four and a half tons of fuel the Clipper would be hauling aloft and this was a short flight, on later stages up to sixteen tons of gasoline would swell her tanks.

With a pencil Ross made a mark against where two lines met on the Clipper's track. The Point of No Return. The allotted flight time to Manila was a fraction under six hours with two hours additional fuel as a safety margin. Till the aircraft reached the spot Ross had marked, they would retain the option of putting back to the Colony. Once past it and return against the winds became a mathematical impossibility.

Alan Bond entered wearing his usual harassed air. "All set?" he said to Ross, "How does the weather look?"

Ross glanced at him and scowled, "There's a low over Scarborough Reef, a typhoon heading up near Guam and it's an even chance Cavite will be socked in with cloud. Otherwise everything is dandy."

Bond handed Munro the passenger manifest. "Thirty-two today. We're about to start checking them through. There's one British VIP, Sir Ambrose Hope. He's a diplomat, one of their top experts on the East. I hope he doesn't give you any trouble. Minister Soong's party of course will be occupying the bridal suite."

Of course, Munro thought. The rearmost compartment in the Clipper's tail was fitted out as a luxury stateroom, the Chinese government would be paying a heavy premium to reserve it for Soong's use. And this in a land where a coolie's lifetime earnings did not even buy space sufficient for his grave.

A mile away across the harbour in Victoria the police Humber drew up on the raked gravel forecourt of Government House. "Morning Inspector," a uniformed equerry was waiting under the portico, "His Excellency is expecting you." Playfair followed him inside the lofty hall, shoes echoing on the marble floor.

The french windows of the Governor's private study opened onto a garden terrace. There were blue Chinese carpets on the floor and Chinnery drawings on the walls. The Governor sat behind a Chippendale desk, elegant and detached. Eton and the Rifle Brigade. He motioned Playfair to a seat. "Sir Ambrose is present as you requested. There's not a lot of time. I suggest we keep this as short as possible."

The gentleman in the other chair nodded. Sir Ambrose Hope had the aristocratic features of a Scottish laird and wise melancholy eyes. Playfair knew his story: a diplomat who had lived in the Orient most of his working life and loved its people. Now, unaccountably, the government was sending him to Russia, his wife had died, he was beginning to drink.

A security risk, one they had to take.

Quickly, concisely Playfair began to speak. The men's faces were taut by the time he finished. "Have you discussed your suspicions with the Americans?" the Governor clipped.

"No sir, I wanted your approval first."

"The orders from London are clear: there is to be no interference on our part."

"I understand that, sir."

"This killing yesterday, what's Slater's opinion?"

"He thinks it's a ploy, Tokyo trying to rattle us, frighten us into stopping the cargo leaving."

"And you don't agree?"

"Not if the Dragons are involved, no sir."

The Governor turned to Sir Ambrose, "As our oriental expert what do you say to that?"

"*Kokuryu-kai*," Sir Ambrose smoothed his white hair thoughtfully, "the name derives from the Black River on the Manchurian frontier, synonymous therefore with Imperial expansion. Perhaps as many as a hundred thousand adherents mainly in the armed forces, fanatic militarists, super-patriots. Four years ago they gunned down half the Japanese cabinet for 'pacifist attitudes'. I agree with the Inspector, if they are determined to recover the cargo they will go to any lengths."

"And do we know what makes this cargo so important?"

With a key from his pocket Playfair unlocked his briefcase and extracted a two page typed document bearing red SECRET stamps and security codings. "This signal came in overnight from Joint Intelligence, Singapore. It's a report on the man travelling with Major Slater under the name of Dr. Marcel Latouche. *I think you'll agree it makes frightening reading.*"

MANILA–GUAM–WAKE–MIDWAY–HONOLULU–
SAN FRANCISCO the sign read. "Thank you, Mr. Cashin. Here are your baggage receipts and hotel vouchers for the voyage." The time was now eight fifteen. Alan Bond was personally manning the Pan American ticket counter in the passenger terminal. The importance of this flight had been made very clear to him. "This is Miss Scott, the

flight stewardess, who will be helping take care of you."

"Oh hi. Say is it okay if I keep my typewriter? I plan doing some work on the trip if it won't bother anyone."

"Certainly, sir, that'll be no problem," Scott assured him with a smile, blond hair neatly brushed, trim and fresh in a clean uniform. "Please check with Security Control, then take a seat in the lounge. We shall be boarding in thirty minutes."

The journalist moved away from the counter and his place was taken by a florid-faced Englishman in a monogrammed blazer. "Hugh Gordon Smythe . . . British subject . . . aged forty-nine . . . wife Cynthia, maiden name Wilson," he slapped down a pair of blue and gold passports. Bond flicked the pages, checking the US visas.

"Thank you, Mr. Smythe, may I introduce . . ."

The dried-up woman with him interrupted. "Gordon Smythe," she corrected sharply, "the name is Gordon Smythe."

"Of course, I'm so sorry, Mrs. Gordon Smythe," Bond pencilled an adjustment to the manifest. "Is that a camera I see you have there? I'm afraid it has to be placed under seal for the flight, military regulations you understand."

"Ridiculous!" the Englishwoman sniffed, surrendering it to Scott. "Anyone would think we were spies. Felicity!" she called impatiently to a large fair girl dawdling behind with some army officers, "Stop chattering and come and show your passport. You're holding us all up."

"Coming, Mummy," her daughter cried. "Goodbye, you darling boys!" she flung her arms around the young men, kissing them, and came bouncing breathlessly over. "Gosh, isn't she a marvellous plane! Can I sit next to the captain at lunch? He's not married is he?"

"No, Ma'am, the captain's not married," Scott struggled not to laugh. Boy, wait till the guys got a load of this baby.

The next passenger at the counter was a woman, tall, narrow faced, with upswept hair and the ravaged remains of what must have been considerable beauty. "Mrs. Maria Bianchi, American citizen travelling to Honolulu." Her voice was a pleasing contralto with a slight Eurasian accent.

"Nice to have you with us, Mrs. Bianchi," Bond scanned her passport, noting that she was forty-six, born in Shanghai, China and had acquired citizenship six years ago. She was smartly dressed in a tailored suit of yellow linen and there was a diamond on her finger that would have paid his salary for a year. He had an impression of a business-like woman, well able to look after herself and underneath, a strong sensuality.

72

"Scott," he said thoughtfully as she walked away, "that woman has something, what is it?"

Scott grinned, "A past, Mr. Bond, I'd say she has a past."

Flash bulbs popped by the entrance doors and a buzz of interest ran through the hall. Bond looked relieved, "This must be the Soong party. Good, I expected them to be late. I'd better let Ross know," he lifted the desk telephone.

Scott made no response. Amongst the Chinese approaching she had just recognised the old mandarin and his niece from the ferry.

The mechanics had finished fuelling and test run the engines. Down on the Clipper Munro was making his pre-flight inspection: trim tabs, elevator hinges, pitot tube, the list covered forty items plus. Small details, but all potential killers.

Which was why he was taking his time, inspecting by the book. Because of the men he had once known, classmates, companions from early days aloft – names now blank on the roll. Men whose lives had been cut short by mountain peaks that should not have been there, by fire, ice, engines or instruments that had failed them under pressure or a single moment's carelessness. Flying was too deadly a business to be taken casually.

Inside on the passenger deck Tad Gotto was supervising the stowing of baggage in the special overhead holds above the after cabins. Munro went past him, through the luxury rear suites and out into the tail cone beyond the bulkhead to check the control cables to the rudders and ailerons. Returning along the promenade passage to the main lounge, he met Slater and Dr. Latouche coming aboard with Jordan in tow.

"No problems?" Slater gave him a curt nod. "Good, let's take a look."

They mounted the stairs to the flight deck. Shapiro and Fry jumped to their feet as they entered the hold. "Report to the Skipper up at the office," Munro told them, "I'll be following in a couple of minutes."

The metal cases were untouched. Latouche knelt beside them. From a bag he was carrying he took a pair of gloves. "Okay, outside everyone," Slater ordered brusquely, "you too, Reverend, you can have your turn with the Bishop later."

"But surely . . ." the priest started to protest, then subsided meekly before the ice of Slater's stare.

Munro stood his ground for a moment. "I have to secure those lashings again when you're through."

73

"Do what the hell you like, this won't take long," Slater shut the hatch firmly in his face.

Munro left the aircraft seething. Sonofabitching government agents giving orders, taking over the ship! Christ, no wonder Ross was sour.

Eight thirty-five. The minutes were slipping by towards take-off. The departure lounge was filling rapidly: a party of British military bound for Singapore, two Swedes with the Red Cross, a wealthy Eurasian merchant, several English families with children, a civil engineer from Ohio. Scott welcomed them smiling brightly.

"Yes sir, that's correct, we stop the night in Manila, accommodation has been reserved." Was it for this she had joined the Company? The rest of the crew were busy drawing up flight plans and checking the ship while she was stuck here playing nursemaid to idiot passengers. Even Tad Gotto had more responsibility.

Well you're wasting your time worrying about it, girl, she reminded herself bitterly, because Ross is going to have you fired for sure.

A new figure approached the counter. She glanced up and repressed a shudder, Prince Cherkassy in his shabby-smart planter's suit, travelling on a Portuguese passport. A gleam came into his eyes as he recognised her, "Ach, so you have recovered from our little adventure last night?"

By daylight, Scott saw his face bore marks of extensive surgery. The skin across the left side was stretched tight like a mask and puckered with scar tissue where they had rebuilt the jaw. Whatever had caused the disfigurement, he must have been lucky to escape with his life.

"You're looking pale, are you feeling alright?" Bond asked as the Prince departed with his tickets.

"It's that guy, he gave me the creeps, that's all," she forced a smile. "How are we doing on the list?"

"Only one left now, Sir Ambrose Hope. I hope to God he's not going to hold us up." Bond glanced anxiously at the clock.

"I don't care who the hell he is!" Ross spluttered, his heavy face red, "If the guy can't make the gangway on time, tough, he stays behind!" The briefing was over, he had scrawled his signature to the completed flight plan and the crew were waiting in the office for the boarding bell.

Alan Bond sighed, "I don't like it either, but this is a British colony and he's one of their people. We have to hold till he gets here."

"No, godammit! It's a trick by the Brits to keep us back."

Outside on the apron an RAF plane was warming up and the noise rattled the windows. "Ross, be reasonable, no one's trying to pull anything. Sir Ambrose is on his way, he's running late that's all. Anyway," Bond added tactlessly, "I've checked with Slater and he agrees we have no choice."

The name stung Ross, "Screw Slater! Screw the pair of you and your damned orders! I'm responsible for the safety of the aircraft and its passengers. Three hours delay here and we can't land at Cavite after dusk on account of the minefield, we'll have to postpone a whole day. And one man's died already in this murdering Colony!" He glared round him at the crew, "You men start getting your gear together."

Godsakes Ross, Munro wanted to tell him, back off. You can't fight the whole world. Thyssen was sitting there looking smug, this would make a great entry in the creep's little book.

The telephone squawked suddenly. Bond snatched it up on the first ring and listened for a moment. "Well, thank God for that. Okay, carry on." He put the receiver down and smiled tightly, "Looks like we can all relax, Sir Ambrose just arrived." There were murmurs of relief.

"*God damn you all!*" Ross breathed.

A sharp-eyed Chinese photographer was working the passenger lounge. It was usual for the local press to cover Clipper departures and he received scant attention. Spying Yu-Ling, he levelled his camera. She blushed and dropped her head, but he only grinned and triggered the flash anyway, making her blush even more.

"You are not afraid, Third Niece?" her uncle patted her hand. They were sitting by a window watching the great airliner being readied down on the water.

"N . . no, Honourable Uncle," she whispered, awed by her surroundings; so many *quai loh* with their loud voices. "Only sad a little," she confessed.

The old Mandarin nodded gently, "It is indeed bitterness to forsake one's homeland." He sighed, his eyes clouding, "You were too young to recall the day we fled Peking. How beautiful the world was that morning, bright and clear, the roofs of the Forbidden City shining in the sun. Children were flying kites with little flutes in them and their song poured down from the sky like silver rain."

Opposite on a sofa Minister Soong frowned, "Simon, explain please to Honourable Professor Chen such talk is unwise," Yu-Ling heard him say to his secretary. Feng, the Minister's burly Chungking bodyguard, sat sullenly beside them.

A bell sounded two strokes. "Ooh, look at those gorgeous men!" a girl exclaimed as the crew appeared outside the windows, filing down the path to the dock. Among them Yu-Ling recognised another of the Americans from last night. He was young and, merciful gods, how tall! Were they all giants in the Golden Country? People were collecting their hand baggage and crowding towards the exit. With a beating heart she helped her uncle to his feet.

A fire tender had drawn up on the dock and the beaching team were standing by to cast off as Ross led the way down to the ship. Out on the water the service launch was returning from its search of the take-off run.

With a drilled economy of movement the crew took their stations. Kurt Thyssen dumped the ship's briefcase on the navigation table and extracted his charts. Stewart Whitely turned on the goose-neck lamp at the radio desk and began flicking switches and adjusting dials like a musician tuning for a concert. Up in the cockpit Ross and Munro settled into the pilots' seats, loosening their ties.

"Check list," Ross reached for the printed card.

"*Vacuum valves?*"

"*On.*"

"*Gyro compass?*"

"*Uncaged.*"

"*Altimeter?*"

"*Set, thirty − zero − two.*"

"*Trim tabs?*"

"*In neutral.*"

"*Cowl flaps open left and right?*" Both men glanced from their side windows.

"*Propellers?*"

"*Low pitch.*" Munro could hear the sounds of the first passengers boarding below. The accumulated tensions of the past twenty-four hours were slowly ebbing from his body as the familiar routine took over. Soon now they would be airborne.

Wide eyed with excitement, Yu-Ling allowed herself to be handed down from the broad sponson into the saloon. Her first glimpse inside the plane took her breath away; it was grander even than the mansion.

Marvelling, she followed the others aft through a succession of plushly furnished cabins.

"Here we are, Excellency, the Honeymoon Suite," the white jacketed steward opened a door at the end of the passage. The compartment inside was fitted out like a western-style drawing room. There was a settee and a pair of armchairs, a writing desk, even a low table with fresh flowers.

"Your own private washroom of course," O'Byrne indicated another door. "Anything you need, just press this bell. If you'll please take your seats, we shall be taking off in just a few minutes."

As Sir Ambrose Hope stepped onto the gangway he checked suddenly. "Something the matter, sir?" Scott asked.

"No, no. I . . ." The diplomat passed a hand across his brow. "I thought I recognised someone – from the past." He shook his head, "But it can't be."

He was staring after Maria Bianchi.

"Whitely, how about the radios and D/F?"

"All check out, Skipper. Launch reports water clear."

"Secure doors and hatches."

"Upper deck hatches secure."

"Nacelle hatches secure, sir."

"Lower deck hatches secured, Captain," Chris Fry's voice from the bottom of the stairs. Only the bow hatch now remained where Shapiro stood. Munro could see his upper half leaning out to talk to the men on the dockside.

"Prepare to start engines."

"Aye aye, sir," the Chief responded. His post was the nerve centre of the ship; ranged before him instruments monitored every aspect of the engines' performance. His big hands moved deftly over the control levers. Main fuel valves on. Engine selector and fire bottles set. Mixture control on Full Rich. *"Ready on engine two."*

At a nod from Ross, Munro reached for the master ignition on the overhead panel. Ross eased the throttles open a crack with his left hand and pressed the starter button and booster. There was a splutter from the port inboard engine as the blades began to turn. It coughed once or twice then settled down to a steady rumble. Suddenly the ship which had been lying inert and dead in the water was a living thing again. The crew felt their spirits lift.

"Stand by to cast off."

Up in the nose hatch Shapiro waved an arm across his chest and waited for the boss of the beaching party to acknowledge. The wind whipped his hair, making speech impossible against the shriek of the props. Unhitching the bow warp, he cast it clear and twisted round to give the thumbs up to the bridge. Freed from her moorings, the huge flying boat began moving ponderously away from the dock.

On the shore a crowd of spectators waved farewell. The Chinese with the camera snapped a last shot and walked quickly back into the ticket hall. There was a telephone booth near the main doors. Entering, he dialled a number and waited impatiently for the connection.

"*Wey?*"

"*Ai-yah*, I'm at Kai Tak. Tell the Dragons the American plane is leaving now. Yes, by the gods, our man is safe on board. The dog dung *quai loh* suspect nothing."

He hung up. Someone was rattling the doors of the booth. "Wait your fornicating turn!" he snarled rudely, backing out. Instantly two men fell on him from either side, pinning his arms, "*Aie!* What the . . ." the words died in his throat as he met the icy stare of Inspector Playfair.

"So, my little yellow friend," the Englishman said bleakly, "tell us who you've just been calling."

"*Close bow hatch.*"

Rocking lightly on the swell in mid harbour the Clipper turned slowly into the wind. Shapiro waved farewell to the launch and pulling the hatch shut behind him, dropped down into the wedge-shaped anchor room. Nautical equipment was stored here, boat hooks, canvas buckets and the heavy steel anchor. A watertight door in the bulkhead opposite gave onto the passenger deck and to his right was another hatch used for loading cargo. Climbing a vertical ladder to a trap in the ceiling, Shapiro crawled out through an opening on the bridge between the pilots' positions. "*All bow hatches secure, sir.*"

Stewart Whitely held the R/T microphone to his lips, "*Kai Tak control from Clipper. Request Take-Off clearance.*"

"*Roger Clipper,*" a clipped English voice replied, "*you are cleared to depart. Wind south fourteen knots. Good luck.*"

"*Flaps ten degrees.*" Ross had both hands on the yoke with the aircraft's nose aimed straight for the mouth of Lyemun Channel. Smoothly Munro opened up the throttles. The full-throated bellow of the engines echoed out over the water as the Clipper surged forward, a white wake trailing from her stern.

"*Fifty knots. Sixty. Sixty-five.*" On the instrument panels needles measuring air speed, rpm, cylinder temperature, fuel and oil pressures were swinging round their dials. They were on the step now, sixty-two thousand pounds of men and machinery thundering across the harbour, engines straining beneath the power, the lower deck port-holes blotted out by curtains of spray.

"*Seventy knots. Eighty!*" Now they were skimming the surface. The Chief's eyes were glued to his gauges. Up in the cockpit Munro had one hand on the throttles ready to yank them back at a sign of trouble.

At one hundred and five knots Ross pulled back slowly on the yoke. The drumming under the hull ceased and smoothly, majestically the great plane lifted into the air. In the rear cabin Yu-Ling gripped her seat as the needlepoints of spray obscuring her window cut off suddenly and she spied the waves sinking away beneath them. Up, up they rose till the ships at the wharves were no bigger than toys and the city colony lay spread out below backed by the brown hills of China.

At the sight of those hills a lump came into Yu-Ling's throat and a tear stole down her cheeks. Silently she bade farewell to China, the Middle Kingdom, the centre of the world, her home.

VI

The Clipper passed the Point of No Return shortly after noon, cruising smoothly on autopilot at three and a half thousand feet in broken overcast with Munro and Shapiro at the controls. Ross was at his own table writing up the log. Earlier attempts to gain height had been blocked by turbulence. The winds, which had been south-easterly on take-off, had backed soon after leaving Hongkong. Now they were blowing on the tail and Chris Fry was on his way aft to take a drift reading.

Carrying the long drift sight, he let himself into the hold. The metal crates were lashed down firmly by their handles. Chris eyed them, wondering what they really contained: bullion according to Chuck Driscoll who had helped load them. There had to be some reason for all the drama. Stepping round the coffin, he went through into the crew quarters beyond.

It was empty, the berths stripped off and piled with the crew's flight bags. Squeezing past the bunks, Chris unclipped a panel in the portside wall at floor level opening to the interior of the wing behind the auxiliary cargo hold. The low space was crammed with life vests and emergency equipment.

A numbing blast from the slipstream engulfed him as he crawled inside and unfastened a hatch in the floor. Through patches of cloud the South China Sea was visible far below, dotted with white caps. He was glad he wasn't a sailor. Carefully he secured the Gatty drift sight to its mount and reached for the rack of drift bombs, thin-walled glass flasks filled with aluminum powder. He enjoyed this part.

He waited until a good wide gap came in the clouds, held the flask over the hatch and dropped it out. It fell away cleanly, shrinking to an invisible dot, then abruptly an iridescent splash leapt into being on the ocean's surface as it burst on the water. Seen through the drift sight it made a clear reference point. Chris adjusted the focus bars and read off the angle.

He was about to close the hatch when his attention was caught. The cloud had closed in again but through it he had a momentary sighting of something below, a shadow, blurred by the haze, but unmistakably the silhouette of another aircraft on a parallel course. He leaned out for a clearer glimpse but the mystery ship had vanished. A Navy plane out from Luzon? Or British RAF escorting them? Surely they would have been warned?

"It looked big, whatever it was," he reported when he returned to the control cabin with his readings, "a four-engined job."

"Probably a Navy PBY," Ross grunted from his desk at the rear, "did you see any markings?"

"Sorry sir, none I could make out."

"Anyway a PBY has twin engines," Thyssen said.

"Think I don't know that, damn you? So maybe it's an Army B–17. Klein, raise Manila, ask are there any military flights in our vicinity." Davey had taken over from Stewart Whitely on radio watch.

At the engineer's station Chief Crow stretched his back and yawned, "Five bucks says it's a Jap."

There were no takers and minutes later Manila confirmed no US aircraft near their track.

'*Grand Hotel of the Air*' was a frequent press description of the Boeing Clippers and the atmosphere of the lower deck during flight reminded Scott of the lobby of some swank place like the Pen or Honolulu's Royal Hawaiian. It was not just the decor, the muted colours and soft lights. There was the same brittle conversation, the same well-heeled people lounging at ease, smoking and drinking cocktails. It made her long to be up on the flight deck.

She was in the bow cabin supervising luncheon. Seating here was reserved during the day for off-duty crew. The walls were covered in a lighter shade of the green mohair on the upper deck with bronze lacquered fittings and tan upholstery. It was here that the bar was located and at midday space along one entire wall was given over to an elaborate hot and cold buffet.

"Hi, Scott, what you got for us?" Munro appeared as she was serving two children from the next cabin.

"Oh hi there, Max. Lobster mayonnaise, roast duck and asparagus on toast, with Black Forest gâteau and Peach Melba to follow. Mind you don't spill that now, kids," she said to the boys and they trotted off, gaping at Munro in his uniform. "So is the Skipper coming down?"

"Are you kidding?" They both laughed, Ross's dislike of flight

81

socialising was legendary. "He'd rather starve. O'Byrne's taking him up a tray and I've been ordered to stand in."

Several passengers entered, among them Bob Cashin the journalist. "Some spread you people provide for your guests, Munro, I'm putting on weight already. Say, I want you to meet a friend from Chungking days, Sir Ambrose Hope of His Majesty's Embassy."

Munro shook hands. Sir Ambrose had an easy manner, it would be hard not to like him. They moved to the bar. "Another Clipper Cocktail? Certainly, Sir Ambrose, glad you enjoy them," Scott fixed the drink, White Label rum and French vermouth shaken with grenadine, and presented it to him.

"Thank you very much, my dear. Allow me to drink to your lovely blue eyes."

She laughed, colouring. The old man was charming, he must have been dangerous once.

The main saloon was crowded to capacity and noisy as a fashionable restaurant. Silver and glass gleamed against crisp damask linen. O'Byrne showed Munro and the two men briskly to the big centre table. The only other ship's officer present was Stewart Whitely with a party of British military. There was no sign of Slater or Dr. Latouche or any of the Chinese. They must have opted for the second seating.

"May we join you, gentlemen?"

Reverend Jordan was indicating two empty seats. With him was a fellow American, Mr. Wirth, affable and overweight. "Call me Eddie, I'm with Lend-Lease. Pleased to meet you all," he beamed, seating himself opposite Munro. "Plane sure is full today, people getting out while they can. I guess it means the peace talks are running out of gas, huh?"

"That depends if you're an optimist or a pessimist," said Cashin. "What's your opinion, Sir Ambrose?"

"Of the Washington peace talks?" the diplomat cocked an eyebrow, "An exercise in futility in my view."

"How so, Sir Ambrose?" Munro asked.

O'Byrne came up with the wine list. "Thank you, I'll stick to cocktails." Sir Ambrose turned back to Munro. "Because neither side can afford concessions. American public opinion demands a Japanese withdrawal from China as a precondition to lifting the western oil embargo. Tokyo is desperate for fuel but withdrawal would entail too great a loss of face and precipitate a coup by the militarists. Extending the war to seize the South-East Asian oil fields is the only course left to them."

The aircraft trembled in an airpocket. Near the after door at a table

82

for three, Cynthia Gordon Smythe picked resentfully at her food. "It's insulting the way they're treating us. We should have been invited to sit at the Captain's table."

"My dear, it's a buffet not a formal luncheon, people can sit where they choose. Besides it's only the First Officer, not the Captain," her husband sought to pacify her.

"That's not the point, Sir Ambrose is there. You should have made it clear who we are. Now we shall be given second placing right through the voyage."

The plane shuddered again, setting the wine glasses tinkling. "Oh God," she moaned, "don't say it's going to be rough. Felicity, run and fetch me my pills!"

The weather was deteriorating. Through the thickening overcast those on the flight deck could discern ominous thunderheads rearing like a mountainous barrier across their path. Rain lashed the windshield in intermittent squalls, drumming on the hull. Ross had returned to his seat in the cockpit and switched off the autopilot to fly the ship on manual. Even so the turbulence increased. "To hell with it," he growled at length, banking them away towards the south. "No point fighting our way through. Give me a course to take us round the edge."

Down in the dining saloon Munro was only half attending to the conversation. He had sensed the Clipper come round onto her new heading and guessed the reason. Instinctively he was busy calculating the implications: one hundred miles perhaps added to the route but the winds would be even more on their tail. A small increase in power should make up the difference easily, there was plenty of fuel in reserve. Of course it all depended how wide the front was.

Abruptly, something Cashin was saying to Jordan made him prick his ears. "Reverend, by any chance did you know a priest in Hong-kong called Oliver? He ran a mission in Wanchai, I believe."

"*Morris Oliver?*" Jordan's tongue flicked over his lips, his eyes met Munro's for an instant then slid away. "Yes, he is an old friend, we are colleagues in the same order."

"Oh, then I don't mean to upset you, only there was a rumour yesterday in the Colony he had been killed, murdered by the Japs."

A shocked hush descended round the table as every gaze turned to Jordan. The priest's pallid skin glistened sweatily. "I'm sure that must be a mistake, I was with Morris myself last night."

The silence hung. Cashin's stare was unblinking behind his glasses. "Yes, I guess it must have been a mistake," he said quietly. Slowly they all relaxed.

Munro wouldn't have believed a priest could lie that well.

Three compartments down, in G cabin, Prince Cherkassy finished his martini and pressed the steward call-button. Opposite him, on a blue upholstered seat piped with rose-coloured suede to match the carpet, Mrs. Bianchi sat reading a paper by the window. The Prince surveyed her appreciatively, everything about her he noted, clothes, jewellery, shoes, was well chosen and expensive.

"Would you care, Madam, to join me in a drink?" he suggested.

She lowered her newspaper and regarded him coolly. Her eyes were dark and attractively tilted, the cheekbones hinting at Slavic blood. "Thank you, a gimlet please."

Tad Gotto bowed and hurried away. The Prince glanced at the discarded paper, "The news from Europe is interesting?"

"Hitler's armies are at the gates of Moscow, but the winter is the coldest for a hundred years. Perhaps it will save Russia yet."

"That I doubt, these Germans are tougher than Napoleon's troops," said the Prince. "Moscow will fall and with it the regime of Joseph Stalin." He changed the subject, "You are travelling through to California?"

"No, as far as Honolulu only. And you?"

"I shall spend Christmas on the West Coast, I do not like the winter either you see. After that my plans are uncertain, I may visit Europe in the spring."

A flicker of sarcastic amusement showed in the woman's eyes, "If Moscow falls, you mean. Do your kind really believe the Nazis will restore your estates?"

The Prince shrugged, "Certainly the *Bolshevists* will not."

"*Chen Yu-Ling*," Simon Ho whispered nervously, "your uncle, the Honourable Professor, does not look well."

The girl bit her lip and nodded. Wrapped in a travelling rug in one of the rear suite's big armchairs, the old Mandarin was deathly pale, his face drawn with pain. "I am worried this journey will be too much for him. His medicine does not seem to help."

Unfolding a pocket handkerchief, Simon Ho wiped his brow. He glanced around the cabin. Bodyguard Feng dozed in another armchair, over at the writing desk in the corner Hollington Soong was working on some papers. "I will speak to the Minister, perhaps we should summon Dr. Latouche."

84

The Frenchman sniffed the bottle of medicine Yu-Ling showed him and tasted a drop on his finger. "*Alors, petite,* how often does he take this?"

"Three times daily, but if he wakes in the night or is in pain then I give him more."

"Try not to do that if possible." Replacing the cap, Latouche felt gently for the pulse in the Chinaman's thin wrist.

"It is nothing, I am only tired a little," the Mandarin protested weakly. "Tell them, Third Niece, it will pass."

"Rest will help. I suggest we have a bed made up."

Slater had accompanied the doctor. "We could look after that thing for him," he pointed to the cloth wrapped box.

"*No!*" the old man came suddenly alive. He clutched at the casket, glaring about him in fright, "*No, it is not for you, not yet!*" he quavered fiercely. "*We have a bargain!*"

Despite the turnaway, weather conditions continued to worsen. The forty ton flying boat swayed and rocked in the stormy air and Munro saw several diners leaving for their seats.

"Brandy," Sir Ambrose declared emphatically, "it settles the stomach." He signalled O'Byrne, "Who'll join me? You, Munro?"

"Afraid not, Sir Ambrose, I'm due back on duty." Munro's head was tilted listening to the beat of the engines, it was fractionally ragged, one prop must be running out of sync.

On the flight deck Ross confirmed his fears. "Cylinder head temperatures on number four went haywire a few minutes back. I've eased off the juice while the Chief takes a look. It's a bitch, just when we need the extra power!"

Two o'clock and Stewart Whitely had also returned to the flight deck. At the radio desk Davey Klein was straining to copy a weather report against a background of heavy static from the storm. "Seems like Cavite's open still," he said at last, slipping off his earphones thankfully, "for the present that is."

"What's our latest position?"

"Three hundred miles east of Lingayen, maybe closer. Kurt doesn't trust his sightings. Figure another two hours anyway."

They changed seats. "That static makes my ears ache to hell," Davey was complaining, "and there's some station keeps blasting away in code on the lower marine frequencies. I think I got a call sign

JCS Yokohama. See what you can make of it."

Up in the cockpit Ross and Munro sat hunched over their controls like wrestlers. The ship was flying parallel to an immense barrier of cloud stretching to the horizon, a seemingly limitless mass of towering cliffs and escarpments piled one upon another, backed by mountainous thunderheads. The Clipper's altitude was now eight thousand feet but the summits of those clouds, by Munro's estimate, must be three times that and more, twenty five thousand feet, five miles above the ocean's surface. All the malevolent energy of the storm was visible in the writhings of great dirty white columns of vapour, big as hills, churning against one another like a restless sea, their dark interiors streaked here and there with lurid fire.

The barrier lay between them and Manila, pass it somehow they must.

A cleft appeared in the cloud wall, a cavernous valley winding back into unknown depths. Ross slid open his side window and regarded it, scowling. "*Chief*, how are those temperature readings?" he bawled above the slipstream.

"Number four's still running a fever. At a guess it's a sticking inlet valve, but this ain't no time to break her down unless we have to."

Ross shut the window again, "Okay, hold onto your seats, we're going in."

Light rain hissed on the windshield as they entered between the cliff faces. At first the way seemed no bumpier than before. Peering up from his own window, Munro could see the cloud masses rearing up on either side to stupendous heights and above it all, incredibly, a tiny strip of blue sky. Ross had eased the throttles back till their airspeed was a crawling one hundred and twenty knots and was concentrating on his instruments.

The drumming of the rain increased in violence, blotting out forward vision. Dribbles of water trickled from the sills of the cockpit windows. No one spoke. They climbed steadily to nine thousand feet without incident. Over the interphone they heard Davey Klein reporting to Whitely from the anchor room that the trailing antenna was safely reeled in. A sharp downdraught dropped them two hundred feet but Ross was ready, he wound back on the stabilizer and levelled off. "That was just an opener," quipped Shapiro.

In the next instant, as if the storm had heard, the flying boat shook, so savagely for a moment Munro thought it must be a mid-air collision, and began to fall again sickeningly.

"*Give me low pitch!*" Ross yelled to the Chief, struggling to control the bucking yoke with both hands while the seat belts jerked tight against their weightlessness, "*And full power!*"

Munro rammed the throttles forward against the stops, no time now to worry about the effect on the sick engine. The altimeter in front of him had gone mad. Ross had the aircraft standing on her tail under maximum power, yet according to the instruments they were actually *descending* at an appalling eighteen hundred feet a minute.

They passed seven thousand feet without a pause, the engines screaming vainly against the downdraught. At this speed they would run out of height altogether in less than four minutes. Lightning seared the clouds. Dazzling fire filled the cabin and thunderous detonations bellowed in their ears. The instrument panels danced on their shock-proof mountings as the plane juddered afresh. Munro's eyes were glued to the dials, unbelievably the altimeter had reversed itself and was winding back.

Ross pushed the yoke forward as far as it would go and held it there, shoving the nose hard down in a power-dive attitude but the Clipper went on soaring up relentlessly while the gravity pinned them into the seat cushions.

"*Skipper! We're losing number four!*" the Chief's voice cut urgently through the noise of the elements, "*Oil pressure's gone, she must've swallowed a valve!*"

"*Jesus Christ, Chief!*" They were up to nine thousand, being battered from all points by violent air currents, "I need that engine, you gotta hold it somehow!"

"*It's no go, Skipper, she's off the gauge. She'll catch if we don't kill her!*"

Ross let out a stream of profanity but the threat of fire was too deadly to be ignored. "Alright, feather the bitch!" he shouted without relaxing his hold on the yoke.

Munro pulled back on the throttle lever for number four. He reached up to flip the ignition switch on the upper panel. Behind them the Chief shut the Fuel Cutoff and whacked the big red feathering button. Slowly the fifteen foot blades of the starboard outer prop ceased to revolve. Leaving Driscoll to mind his station, the Chief disappeared into the wing.

Mercifully the rate of ascent had eased. At nine thousand two hundred they levelled off and began drifting downward. The air grew momentarily calmer. Ross relaxed his grip on the controls long enough to light a cigarette. "Fuck of a time to lose a motor," he commented tersely.

Munro did not speak. It was tempting fate to suggest the storm might have finished with them. Nor had it. A scant minute later there came a second jarring bump and once more they were plunging downwards with nerve-rending velocity. At seventy-nine hundred feet they bottomed out. This time there was no compensating uplift, only a third descent, steeper than before.

"*Number three is heading for the red!*" Now suddenly disaster loomed in earnest. Already they were down below seven thousand. With a second engine throttled back the plane began dropping as if the ocean were reeling them in on a line.

Using the interphone Munro rang through to the outboard nacelle and got the Chief. "Looks like the bitch has blown a front cylinder plug!" the engineer yelled down the line, "Goddam oil all over! I'll have to break down the fire wall. Let you know soon as I figure the damage."

At four thousand feet the ocean became visible in patches, storm-tossed and ugly. Ross was fighting for every foot of altitude, with Munro bracing on the port rudder to counteract the ship's terrific yaw. But each pocket and squall drove them inexorably lower. Stewart Whitely was on the emergency frequency to Manila, a Navy PBY was being dispatched to rendezvous their position.

The interphone rasped again with the Chief's voice, "It's the plugs for sure, some saphead mechanic left 'em loose and we lost compression."

"Will she restart okay?"

"How can I tell, for Christsakes? She's lost enough oil to float the Pacific Fleet. Send Chuck out here and watch those other head temperatures – unless you want to join the fishes!"

"Kurt, what's our fuel situation?" Ross called over his shoulder. "How much can we dump?"

"We're fat. We can lose five hundred gallons, no sweat."

Five hundred gallons, three thousand pounds, nearly a ton and half off the flying boat's burden. If they jettisoned the mail and freight as well as the passengers' baggage they could lighten the load by another six thousand, four tons in all. Enough perhaps to stay aloft, even on two engines.

Stewart Whitely dashed their hopes. There was heavy static all around, discharging fuel in present conditions would incur grave risk of fire.

The altimeter was showing two thousand six hundred and falling, with indicated air speed down to eighty-five knots.

One and a half engines out of commission, nearly forty percent of their power gone and the strain on the remainder correspondingly increased. *If the trouble should spread. . . .*

"Hell, it's only three hundred miles to the coast," Shapiro remarked with forced cheerfulness. "We can taxi in from here."

"Mister," Ross said quietly, "I want you to go below and have O'Byrne and the stewards get the passengers into life jackets in case we decide to ditch. Then you can start preparing to jettison cargo: baggage first, freight next, mail last of all, you know the drill."

"Aye, aye sir," Munro hesitated a moment, "how about the special cargo?"

"You can *start* with that, by God!"

Sally Scott was by the ladies' powder room cleaning up after a sick child when she saw Munro coming down the after passage with his long stride. "Hi, what's the score?" she said valiantly, brushing back a strand of blond hair. She caught the look in his eye and was instantly serious, "How bad are we?"

"Right now, hanging on by our teeth." He gave her the facts straight without trying to play down the danger. "The Chief doesn't know yet if the dead prop can be restarted. We're going to try lightening ship but if another engine goes on us or this weather doesn't let up, there's a chance we'll have to ditch. Help the passengers into life jackets and Pat will assign them to rafts. Try to minimise the emergency if you can, stress this is only a precaution when an engine quits. Tell them there are Navy float planes coming out to meet us and they'll be able to land alongside if necessary."

"Sure, Max," Scott's glance strayed briefly to the window and he knew she wasn't fooled. The seas below were running twenty foot crests, ditching in that lot would be like flying smack into Diamond Head. The PBYs would be lucky to find the wreckage, let alone pick up survivors. All she said though was, "Max, our Wright Cyclones are twin fourteen cylinders. If two are down that's fifty-six plugs. *Nobody forgets to tighten fifty-six plugs.*"

Munro nodded grimly, the same thought had occurred to him.

From a porthole by the radio desk Stewart Whitely willed the blades of the dead propeller back into life. The cloudbase was above them now, grey and forbidding as the ocean beneath but faintly lighter towards the west, lending just a hope the storm might be clearing. *Oh God, let it be so*, he prayed silently, the thought of ditching making his bowels churn.

A fresh barrage of static crackled in his earphones. Twisting the receiver dial to try a lower frequency, he got a strong morse signal. That must be Driscoll's station, JCS Yokohama. Out of habit Whitely jotted down the letters. It was all in code groupings military style. The repeat-back was very faint and verbatim, letter for letter, as if the receiving station were re-transmitting the message for copying.

He was puzzling over this when he heard Thyssen's cry.

Slater and Latouche had a small cabin to themselves next to the rear suite. They listened tensely as Munro spelt out the position. Latouche was first to speak, "*Eh bien*, it seems we have no choice. There are certain precautions however . . ." he began unbuckling his seat belt.

Slater's eyebrows twitched violently, "*Dump the cases*? Are you out of your skull?" he exploded in disbelief. "That cargo's beyond your authority, Munro. Lay a finger on it and I'll see you never fly anything again bigger than a box kite! Godammit, where's Ross? I should have guessed he'd foul up somehow!" Ripping off his belt, he made for the cabin door.

Munro stepped back into the passage and stood blocking his path, "Ross has his hands full flying the ship. I don't care what you've got in those trunks, they're going over the side – unless you figure on swimming home."

"Don't give me that bunk, these birds float. What's wrong, you scared of getting your feet wet?" Slater attempted to push past. They jostled stupidly for a moment, then broke apart. "*Shit*, Munro, you're really something, ain't you?" Pulling a letter from his pocket, he brandished it in the pilot's face. "Here, read this. It's from your company president, Juan Tripp, and if that don't grab you, the one underneath is signed by the Secretary of War!"

At that moment all hell broke loose. Without warning the aircraft lurched savagely, flinging all three men off their feet, and went into a screaming dive towards the ocean.

Up on the flight deck Shapiro clung to his seat appalled. Before him on the engineer's panel temperature gauges quivered in the red as Ross applied full emergency power in a desperate effort to pull them out of the spin. Through the portholes the ocean's surface loomed gigantic, rushing nearer by the second. They were below the thousand foot mark and still falling and Shapiro was actually bracing himself for the crash when the controls at last began to respond and they flattened out, a mere four hundred feet above the wave tops.

The mad howl of the engines eased and there was a pounding of feet on the stairs as Munro came running up from below minus his cap. "What the hell happened?" he asked, gazing at their shaken faces. Following close behind him, Slater and Latouche paused at the top step.

"*Goddam crazy idiots!*" Ross raged, craning to see out the windshield, "Pissing yellow bastards!"

"What's up, Skipper?" Munro repeated, slipping back into his seat.

"That fucking Jap plane, it just flew right at us, for Christsakes!"

They all stared from the windows. The storm now showed definite signs of breaking up with shafts of sunlight striking through the clouds in the distance. There was no sign of the other plane.

"You sure it was a Jap?" asked Slater.

"Son of a bitch wore the Red Sun, didn't it? Christ, it only missed us by a length!" Ross had throttled back as much as he dared and was holding them level at four hundred. "Shapiro, how are those gauges reading?"

"Number three is boiling, oil temperature is off the dial!"

"I'm going to dump that fuel, we'll have to chance the static," Ross reached down for the valve handle on the floor beside his seat.

"*Jesus! Here it comes again!*"

Every gaze snapped round in time to spot the Jap plane drop neatly out of the cloud two thousand yards ahead to starboard on a right angle bearing to their track. It was a four engined flying boat, big as the Clipper almost, painted blue with wing floats not seawings. They could see the blood red emblem and the glassed-over gun turrets at the nose and tail and atop the hull.

They watched it draw level with their course, then swing deliberately in towards them. "What the hell do the bastards think they're playing at?" Shapiro muttered nervously.

"*Whitely, get onto Manila! Tell 'em we need help!*" Ross slammed open the throttles and the engines bellowed forth as he hauled back on the yoke, clawing for height. But the Japanese plane was bearing in on them very fast now, head on and growing larger with every second, the nose gunner in his dark helmet clearly visible crouched behind his weapon.

With a sick clutch of fear in their guts they tensed, waiting for the red wink from the cannon's mouth.

The two planes were closing at a combined speed of around three hundred knots with the Boeing shaking beneath the strain of trying to make height on two good engines and sixty thousand gross weight. This was playing chicken with a vengeance and for a petrifying instant Munro thought they had left it too late as the monstrous blue snout of the Jap ship seemed to fill the windshield. Then miraculously its keel roared past overhead. Ross had pushed the stick forward to drop the nose and peel away to safety. The crew let out a long breath of relief. But the encounter had cost them a precious hundred and eighty feet.

"Navy says the PBYs can be with us in forty minutes," called Whitely from the radio desk.

"Piss on that, the yellow-bellies will have us in the drink next time round!"

"I didn't know they even had planes this big."

"I'll burn their asses in Manila," Slater swore. "There was supposed to be an escort to meet us two hours out."

Even as he spoke there came a cry from Chris Fry in the hold where he was standing look-out from the astrodome. The attacker was lining up for another pass.

There was a commotion on the stairs. Reverend Jordan was trying to slip past. Slater caught him by the arm, "Where d'you think you going, Reverend?"

The priest gaped at him, pale and shaking, "*The coffin! The Bishop's coffin!* They said you're going to throw it overboard!" Pulling free from Slater's grasp, he made a dash for the hold and slammed the hatch behind him.

The Japanese plane was overhauling them fast. Reaching for the interphone, Munro punched the button to call number four nacelle. "Chief, we got company, Japs. Looks like they're aiming to force us down. How soon can you give us power on that engine?"

"Figured something must be up," the Chief hollered back, "that last flip nearly had me out the hatch. I'm coming through to crank her now."

Blackened with oil he emerged from the wing. They waited tensely while the controls were set for restarting. "*Ignition on,*" Munro's hand was already at the switch. The engine hiccoughed angrily and back-fired, spurting tongues of flame from the air scoops.

"Start, you bitch, go on *start*, for God's sake!"

"*Give her more boost!*"

For several agonising moments it seemed the motor would refuse to catch. Then to the crew's relief, the blades whirred into life.

"Okay, run her up gently to full throttle," the Chief released the feathering button and made for the wing hatch again, "and we'll see if we can't do the same job on its buddy."

The effect on the Clipper's performance was dramatic. With three engines on full power their speed surged to a hundred knots and the nose began to climb.

"Skipper, you still want to jettison fuel?"

No response. Munro glanced across quickly. Ross was taut in his seat, hanging on to the controls grimly.

"*Three o'clock high, Skipper! He's starting his run!*"

Still no acknowledgement from Ross. He was staring fixedly ahead, body rigid. What was he waiting for? Either he was long on nerve or . . . *Jesus Christ*! The man had gone into shock! Urgently Munro hauled back on his own yoke. The deck angled sharply, vibrating with the strain as the flying boat clawed skywards. If only they could reach the cloud cover . . . but the Jap pilot had the edge on them still.

And Ross was frozen at the controls, paralysed by his own fear.

The Japanese ship came tearing in for the kill. They could see the deadly fat-bellied silhouette growing larger and larger as it bore down on them, turrets manned. Would it let go with the guns this time? Back in the cabin Stewart Whitely was praying aloud.

"*Skipper*!" Munro strove to pierce Ross's trance. "Skipper, we can't trade height and we can't outrun him. We've got to get smart before he starts shooting!' The sweat was breaking out on his palms. No time to wait any longer. He scanned the instruments. They had the power, if they could just break past . . .

He eased the column forward a trifle and their speed picked up as the ship levelled off. They waited, all eyes glued to their attacker. The port wing dipped as he banked the Clipper into a turn. Less than a thousand yards. Every nerve was strained to snapping.

Now! With the enemy plane almost on them he stamped hard on the rudder. A shudder ran through the ship and the horizon slewed. There was a momentary glimpse of the red sun insignia flashing past the windows as they side-slipped cleanly without losing altitude. A burst of triumph came over Munro, the huge airliner had handled just like a fighter. Outmanoeuvred completely, the Japanese pilot had overshot his target in the dive. By the time he pulled out and regained height they would be safely in the clouds.

As if they had all been holding their breath everybody on the deck began talking at once. "Boy, oh boy, we ran right round them! The bastards will never catch us now!" Shapiro crowed. Stewart was white with relief. Even Slater had a smile. With a groan Ross seemed to come to. He stared at Munro.

In the midst of the noise Chris Fry's voice became audible, "*Hey*, somebody give me a hand in here!" he shouted from the hold, "There's a guy trying to cut loose the coffin!"

It took a while to convince Reverend Jordan the emergency was ended. "Crazy mutt," Slater snorted as the priest was finally persuaded to return to his seat, "for two bits I'd throw him and his bishop to the sharks."

The storm's strength had abated for good. Before long they were flying in clear skies with an escort of twin-engined Navy PBYs and no further sign of their attacker. The mountains of Luzon appeared rugged in the distance as they approached the lush green coast. Manila Bay came in sight with the warships of the Asiatic Fleet lying at anchor and at four forty-six pm, an hour behind schedule, the Clipper's keel settled smoothly on the water at Cavite Naval Station.

VII

IT WAS THE BLUE HOUR IN MANILA. Across the city bells were chiming, summoning the faithful to Mass. As the sun slid down in flaming splendour behind Corregidor and the purple mountains of Bataan, a cooling breeze sprang up off the sea. Driven from their lairs by the clamour of the bells, flocks of bats flapped from the ancient Spanish steeples, wheeling above the river where sugar barges drifted downstream between the scented gardens of moss-grown palaces. Lights sparkled in the dusk along the boulevards and down in *Intramuros* the cobbled streets echoed to the rattle of horse carriages and the throb of Latin music.

Along Dewey Boulevard stately mansions lined the shining crescent of the bay. Slender native outriggers glided seawards, their sails ablaze beneath a sky shot with crimson and gold. The air was warm with scents of copra, mangoes, sampaguita blossoms and jasmine. It was the time of the *paseo*, the evening parade. Pretty señoritas with flowers in their hair strolled the parks with their duenas, fluttering their eyes at slim-hipped young men. In plaza cafés elegant couples bowed to friends with old-world courtesy. Beneath the palm trees lovers sighed.

Grandest of the great mansions fronting the bay, Queen of the Golden Mile, the immense green-roofed Manila Hotel stood like a palace amid the tropical lushness of its gardens. Kings and presidents had graced the terraces, film stars and tycoons made it their home. The balls given in the Sea Pavilion were legendary.

The Clipper passengers would stop here. Naturally.

In the white-pillared lobby smiling brown waiters darted among the planters of bamboo and fan palms with trays of gimlets. Groups of all nationalities sat drinking at the little rattan tables. Dutch, British, French, Indian, Javanese, Spanish, Chinese, Americans and the infinitely varied mestizo faces of the interbred Filipinos.

Before the marble portico doormen in immaculate white uniforms, caps and gloves stood to attention as the twin standards of the United

95

States and the Commonwealth were lowered on the penthouse roof, fluttering in the sultry twilight. The flags' presence was symbolic, the hotel was home to General Douglas MacArthur, Commander-in-Chief of Fil-American forces in the Islands.

With a spurt of gravel a yellow Cadillac roadster swung in at the driveway and pulled up beneath the overhang. Porters hastened forward to open the car door. There was a flash of pale thigh and up on the terrace some young man whistled involuntarily.

The driver was a redhead, American and stunning.

Indifferent to stares, she breezed through the lobby in a Schiaparelli sundress. A bellhop followed at her heels laden with golf clubs. By the private elevator a security guard snapped to attention. A buzz of interested comment broke out as the doors closed behind her.

So that was the Delahaye heiress. The papers had said she was back in town. In a chair beneath the palms near the double grand stairway Ruth Simms flicked the pages of Vogue idly. Nearby several other ladies were glaring jealously in the direction of the elevator. Entry was the most sought-after privilege in the capital – it led directly to the MacArthur penthouse.

Good luck to the girl, she deserved it. Ruth didn't care. Manila meant nothing to her any more. She only wanted out. For herself and her family.

A waiter approached. She shook her head. More cars were arriving. The bar was filling up for the evening. A bunch of Air Corps men went through, laughing and cracking jokes. How young they seemed, how unafraid.

At last a sunburnt man in a dusty civilian suit appeared hurrying towards her. Ruth sprang up, dropping her magazine. "Eliot! Eliot! Did you get them? Did you get our tickets?"

"Relax, honey," he gave a quick kiss to the faded fair hair, "I have 'em right here in my pocket. Everything's confirmed, we leave Friday morning."

"Oh, Eliot, thank God!" his wife's worn looks dissolved in relief. "*Friday*? But I thought . . ."

"Now, Ruthie, I told you relax, stop fretting yourself. The flight's been put back on account of engine trouble, that's all. They promised me at Pan Am we'd be away Friday."

There was a troubled look in his eyes. He was keeping something back, she could tell, and she felt the fear rise choking in her throat again, "Eliot, what is it? What's the matter? Tell me!" she begged.

His mouth tightened. "There's nothing the matter, it's all okay," he said sharply. "Get a hold of yourself, for God's sake."

"I'm sorry," her hands twisted helplessly, "it's not just us, it's the kids I'm scared for," she trembled. "If war comes . . . think of them caught in the bombing . . . like those newsreel pictures. I get nightmares about it."

"I know, honey, but don't you worry, there'll be no bombs in Kansas, Missouri." Putting an arm around her shoulders, he steered her gently towards the exit. "C'mon, time we were heading back. We've a lot of goodbyes to say."

The lobby and bar were packed. Bob Cashin checked them both, then tried the Champagne Room. Finally he located Sir Ambrose in a corner of the smoking lounge drinking cocktails with Hollington Soong. Capiz shell lamps, delicate as Tiffany glass, filled the lounge with a soft glow. Both men were wearing white tuxedos. Simon Ho was with them.

"The Minister and I are invited to dine at Malacañang Palace with President Quezon," Sir Ambrose told him. "I understand General MacArthur will be present."

"That kind of invitation I could do with. You going too, Simon?"

The young man started at the mention of his name, "N. .no, I am to stay here with Honourable Chen."

"Fine, maybe we can get together for a drink after dinner, then?"

"My secretary has much work to do this evening, Bob. Indeed, I was not aware that you and he had met," Soong said smoothly. He selected an oval cigarette from a gold case and waited for Ho to light it for him.

There was an awkward silence. Sir Ambrose intervened tactfully to change the subject, "And how is Professor Chen?" he inquired of Soong. "Recovered after the flight, I hope."

"Quite recovered, thank you. Doctor Latouche is with him and he is resting. Of course these journeys are hard on old people."

Sir Ambrose frowned thoughtfully, "I am trying to remember, Professor Chen is the celebrated archaeologist, is he not? The man responsible for excavating the Eastern Tombs of the Manchu Emperors?"

"I believe that *was* his speciality. But of course he has been retired now for many years." Soong's tone was dismissive.

"Let me see, the excavations were conducted in 1928 or thereabouts. It was said though that the tombs had been extensively looted before that."

The Minister gestured impatiently, he was wearing jewelled sleeve-links, "It is possible, one hears of such things."

"The Eastern Tombs, sure I remember," said Cashin. "More than fifty million US dollars the haul was put at: gold, jade, ropes of pearls . . ." He grinned mischievously, "They say some of those pearls wound up round the neck of Madame Chiang Kai-shek."

The Minister set down his glass. "That is insulting," he said frigidly. "It is also a lie." Rising, he bowed stiffly to Sir Ambrose. Simon Ho hastened after him as he swept out.

"You shouldn't tease them like that, Bob," Sir Ambrose's eyes twinkled. "You know how they hate to lose face."

"Hell, it gets my goat when I think of the way his kind have plundered China. The country would be better off under the Nazis – at least they're efficient."

A bunch of young, sharkskin-suited Filipinos sauntered past, chattering. Taking off his hornrims, Cashin began polishing them on a napkin, "I stopped by the cable office tonight to wire off a story on the flight. Figured it would make good reading, *American aircraft buzzed by Jap warplane*. What I hadn't bargained on was a couple of goons stepping up and confiscating my copy right under my nose."

Sir Ambrose looked up, an eyebrow cocked, "Army Intelligence?"

"Acting on the orders of the General, so they said." The journalist replaced his spectacles, "I don't like censorship, it just makes me more determined to get to the bottom of their game." He paused, eyes suddenly shrewd, "Hollington Soong just gave me an idea where to start."

Upstairs in the Manila's guest rooms, American efficiency blended discreetly with oriental tradition. Beds were four posters, carved from native mahogany and hung with filmy mosquito nets. Each room had its own balcony with louvred shutters to catch the breeze and overhangs for protection against monsoon rains. There were tapestries from Mindanao on the walls, antique ceramics and wicker chairs. Floors were polished mahogany again and windows set with capiz shell to soften the glare of tropic suns.

Maria Bianchi, in a silk-embroidered Chinese robe, was seated at her mirror. Beside her on a rosewood dressing table inlaid with mother-of-pearl stood a vase of pink roses and a photograph of a little boy. She was reading a message from the Prince: *I should be most honoured by your company at dinner tonight.*

There was hotel notepaper in a drawer. Taking a pen she wrote in clear bold script, *Thank you, I am already engaged for this evening. M.B.*

"Return this to His Highness," she handed the envelope with a peso to the boy, "and please tell the desk I am expecting a visitor, a gentleman. He is to be shown straight up."

The boy grasped the coin and hurried away. Maria returned to her mirror.

Half an hour later she was dressed and ready when the tap at her door came.

"Mrs. Bianchi. Welcome to Manila!"

"Thank you Mr. Breen. Come in please. It's good of you to see me at this hour."

"Not at all, Ma'am, delighted to be of service. You are a valued customer of the firm."

"I'm glad you think so." She shut the door. A delicate lattice screen separated bedroom and sitting area. She motioned him to a seat, "Tell me, is everything arranged?"

"Yes Ma'am," the tubby little lawyer beamed happily, "the child was brought down from school last night and we have organised for him to stay until departure with the same family he spends vacations."

"He is well, he is happy?" she interrupted eagerly, perching on the edge of a chair and smoothing her skirt. "He was not upset to leave his friends?"

"Happy as could be when I saw him in my office. We've had him fitted out with some clothes for the trip. Jefferson High are expecting him at the start of the year, they've had a check for a term's fees in advance. It's all in the accounts here," he patted the file he had brought.

"Good, good. Leave them there on the desk, I will study them tonight. Ah, how I look forward to seeing him, it has been so long." She clasped her hands and her chest heaved in her low-cut gown, "And now to other business; the money has been transferred as I ordered?"

"Yes indeed, Ma'am," tugging his gaze from the diamond brooch at her breast, the lawyer fumbled in the file, "this confirmation came through yesterday. The last remittance has been credited to your new account in Honolulu, three hundred and seventy one thousand dollars." Perspiration beaded his head, "If I may say so, Ma'am, you are a wealthy woman."

Dusk had fallen by the time the crew reached the hotel. Tree frogs piped in the gardens and the terraces were floodlit. Munro drew a room on the third floor. As always the clothes he kept here were hanging ready, his riding boots freshly polished. Dumping his bag, he grabbed a towel and swimming trunks and headed back downstairs.

"*Red sails in the sunset* . . ." humming, he made his way round to the hotel garage. The last streaks were dying in the sky over the bay. The evening air was hot and damp, thick with exotic scents and from *Intramuros* came the musical chant of bells. Manila was his favourite city anywhere. He loved the gaiety of the people, their machismo and warmth, the exquisite courtesy of the Spanish grandees, the savage, primitive beauty of the tropical jungle. So different from barren, overcrowded Hongkong.

That was why he had the car.

He had bought it last trip from a departing Army officer, a big open Pontiac with whitewall tyres, wide running-boards and deep leather seats. Now it lived in the Manila's garage and was a source of much pride.

"Hi, Emilio, how's she running?"

The little Filipino mechanic looked up from under the hood, his brown face splitting in a wide grin, "Evenin', Mr. Munro sir, I hear de plane go over, figure you be comin' round soon. She running jus' fine, smooth as silk. I change all de plugs like you say an' check de timin' too."

"Great. Did you manage to trace that whine in top? Chief Crow says it's the magneto."

The technical discussion occupied some minutes. "You wanna take her out now, Mr. Munro?" Emilio suggested.

He shook his head, "No, I'm bushed, we had a tough flight up. Tomorrow morning though, first thing, okay?" There was nothing to beat the dawn cool of the islands.

He was about to turn away when he noticed the yellow Cadillac, "Nice. Who's is it?"

The mechanic nodded, "Dat one belong to Don César de Santa Cruz. He len' it some girl he got stayin' de hotel."

The Santa Cruz family were part of the Manila oligarchy. Munro had met some of them. Old Spanish and rich. Very rich. Gold mines and sugar.

"Lucky girl," he said.

"*Qué pasa?*"

They both spun round sharply. The speaker had come in the main doors. A burly figure in tan police uniform with captain's bars. Pitted skin and sunglasses. A *mestizo*, a half-caste.

"You Munro?" the tone was curt.

"That's right. What can I do for you?"

"Santos, I'm in charge of the detail guarding the hotel."

Munro felt a jolt of surprise, "Guard detail? Since when, for Christsakes?"

"As of tonight." The sunglasses surveyed him coolly, weighing him up, "I heard you kept a car here, that it?"

"Yes, Emilio takes care of her for me. It's all cleared through the hotel if you want to check."

"I already did." Again the sunglasses. "Figuring on going out somewhere tonight?"

Munro's temper began to rise, "Why, do I need your permission?" They faced each other for a moment. He shrugged, "So long, Emilio. Tomorrow morning, okay?"

"Sure thing, Mr. Munro, I have her ready."

He nodded to Santos, "See you around."

"*Sin duda*," Santos smiled thinly. "Without doubt."

Munro could feel the sunglasses on his back as he left.

The pool was deserted, its surface milky smooth in the dusk. He shucked his uniform in an empty changing-room, stuffing his wallet under a locker for safety. The coolness of the water was bliss against his skin. Invigorated, he set himself to twenty lengths Australian crawl. Fast. Eight kicks to a stroke. Driving the tension from his body with the punishing rhythm.

Breathing hard, he rested against the stone edging. The world was warm and peaceful. Fire flies flickered in the darkness, a woman was laughing up on one of the balconies and from the hotel came the tinkle of a piano.

Cops. Guard details. Why? There was no danger here, this was American territory.

That goddam cargo. An hour ago at Cavite, Navy Intelligence had debriefed them. Listened to their account of the flight and the Jap plane. Listened and ordered them to forget it.

"It never happened. Discussion of the matter is prohibited, even among yourselves. Your flight logs will omit all reference to hostile aircraft, understood? This is a political decision, gentlemen, and it comes right from the top. From General MacArthur."

The crew had gaped at one another as the words sank home. The attack on the Clipper was being dismissed. There would be no protest at the outrage. No threat of retaliation. *Officially it had never even happened.*

Then there was Ross.

101

Neither of them had mentioned those seconds in the cockpit as the Jap plane tore down. The rest of the crew hadn't seen and Ross had made a faultless landing at Cavite. The stress had been enormous. Anyone could be forgiven for losing their nerve momentarily.

Anyone but the Master of a Clipper.

Abruptly he shivered and stared into the shadows. The terrace was empty, yet there was a sense of unease, of being watched. He shook it off and climbed out of the pool.

The changing-rooms were in darkness. He had left the lights on. Puzzled, he tried the switch. No use, the fuse must have blown. The corner of a bench caught against his knee as he groped his way inside, making him curse. Where had he left his clothes?

Faint light filtered through a window in the rear wall and the blackness became marginally less intense as his eyes adjusted. This was the wrong row of lockers. His was the second, about half way down. Dripping, he turned to retrace his steps . . .

A movement. More felt than heard. A stirring of the air as someone, something glided past the bottom of the row in the direction of the door.

With four long strides he spun round the end of the lockers. A figure loomed before him, hooded in black. There was a hiss of fury and barely in time he jerked back as a fist arced out of the darkness and the locker wall shattered into matchwood.

In the instant he knew he was fighting for his life.

He struck out and felt his knuckles connect with a body of rock hard muscle. *Jesus!* It was like punching a sack of cement! The response was a hammer-blow to the chest that drove the air from his lungs. Before he could recover another caught him on the left shoulder. The pain was excruciating, his entire arm went limp for a moment as if the bone were broken.

Another furious crash and again wood splintered beside him in the dark. A hand clutched at his hair, trapping him in a murderous embrace. Desperately Munro brought up a knee. It drew a grunt of surprise and the grip slackened momentarily. Tearing himself free, stepped in low and put every ounce of weight into a savage uppercut with his right. His trademark in the ring. The impact jarred his shoulder and this time he felt the crunch of bone beneath his fist.

The black figure reeled back with a crash against the lockers. The punch would have knocked most men out cold and he must have taken it on the point of the jaw. Two of Munro's bouts in the ring had been ended just so.

But no! Incredibly his opponent was still on his feet, shrugging off

102

the blow as if it had hardly touched him. He must be built like a steer to take such punishment. There was a blur in the blackness and Munro flung himself aside to avoid a kick that split a panel section from top to bottom.

A stab of fear ran through him. He had to break out fast. His left arm was still numb and just one of those plank-smashing strikes to a vital organ would spell massive injury, probably death. He threw one last punch blind in the darkness, hit something soft, knew it was not enough to do real damage, lowered his head and charged.

Caught by surprise, his attacker's breath exploded in a gasp as Munro's forehead butted him squarely in the chest. He went down backwards, and Munro leapt past him to the end of the row. Ignoring the pain in his bruised shoulder, he grasped the top edge of the nearside lockers and heaved. It rocked ponderously. *Come on, you bastard! Fall!* He could hear the intruder scrambling for his feet. He swung again with all his weight. The unit tottered and Munro jumped clear as the heavy lockers crashed over.

He stumbled through the door and slammed it shut behind him. No lock and he'd never hold it alone. But there were hurried footsteps on the paving now. People had heard the noise. "What's going on there?" An American accent. Santos. And someone else with him, Tad Gotto. How in hell did they come to be here? Both stared at him, panting in his wet swimming shorts.

"Golly, Mr. Munro, what's up? You okay, sir?"

"A thief, godammit! I got a thief in here. Call hotel security. Hurry, man!" Already he could hear scraping sounds from inside, a thud as the lockers were pushed away.

"A thief? He was after the . . .?" Santos choked off his words, but not before Munro read his meaning. *The photograph.* Jesus, him too! *Why?*

The night erupted. Wood shattered, glass splintered in fragments. The window! Cursing himself for a fool, Munro burst back into the locker room, the others at his heels. Where the window had been at the rear there was a gaping hole onto the gardens.

The thief was gone.

Heart pounding, he felt beneath the locker where he had left his wallet. It was still there.

The photographs were safe.

Upstairs on the third floor Sally Scott brushed out her blond curls and slipped into her newly pressed evening frock. Knocking at Munro's

103

door and getting no reply, she went down the corridor to O'Byrne's room. The purser was in his shirt sleeves sorting tickets.

"Run these vouchers up to the Chinese party for me, there's a good lass," he said to her, "the Minister's taken rooms on the fourth floor."

The silent Chinese bodyguard answered the door upstairs. Cropped black hair and muscles straining the sleeves of his suit. He showed her into the drawing room of a palatial corner suite with french windows to a balcony. The Minister was sitting eating rice cakes and arguing with Simon Ho in Cantonese.

"Yes, what is it? What do you want?" he demanded impatiently.

She explained about the vouchers, "Every passenger has one for each meal, you just hand it to the waiter when he brings the check. The only thing not covered is liquor, the Company doesn't pay for that."

"Yes, yes, that will do, thank you," Soong waved her away with his mouth full. The window behind opened and the Professor entered on the arm of his niece. Yu-Ling's *cheong-sam* was pale pink and she looked as pretty as a flower. Hollington Soong smiled at her lasciviously. Truly she was most temptingly beautiful.

Scott handed the vouchers to Simon Ho, "There are enough here to last you through tomorrow. If it turns out we're stopping longer I'll bring you some more."

"What is that you say? We are to stop longer? How much longer?" Soong interrupted with a sharpness that made her jump.

"Sir, I have no information at all on our departure," Scott told him honestly. "I doubt anyone does till the engineers report tomorrow. The Company will do its best to avoid delay, naturally."

The Minister had gone grey in the face. "There can be no more delay!" he shrilled. "Every day lost is disastrous. I have business of the utmost urgency in Washington. It is vital, *vital*, I reach there before next week."

"I'll be sure to tell Captain Ross that, sir." VIPs always thought the world was run for their benefit. The mechanics would fix the plane as quick as they could no matter who was on board.

The bodyguard let her out again. As she passed down the corridor on her way to the lift a door opened a crack. Reverend Jordan's head poked out for an instant, then it slammed shut again.

There was still no answer from Munro's room and no sign of him or Tad downstairs. The evening was hotting up; the lobby full of guests in tuxedos and pretty gowns.

Near the bar she bumped into Prince Cherkassy. "Miss Scott, I have been searching for you. Dine with me tonight, please." It was almost an order.

"I'm sorry, your Highness, but I'm on duty this evening," she squeezed a semblance of regret into her voice.

"Tomorrow then. You are on duty tomorrow night?"

" 'Fraid so, your Highness, guess it'll have to wait till the end of the trip. Excuse me." She slipped away with a smile, revolted by him.

Glancing into the Jungle Bar, she spotted the Chief among the palm fronds. Chuck was with him and Davey Klein. They hailed her over. "Have a drink, Scott, what'll it be?"

"Thanks guys, lime soda – lots of ice."

For a moment the buzz of conversation around the bar seemed to skip a beat. She saw the Chief stiffen and looked round. A girl had entered behind her. A redhead. She was holding the skirts of a black silk evening gown and her skin was pure alabaster. It was the most beautiful dress Scott had ever seen and the girl so astonishingly lovely there was a sense of shock somehow, like seeing a rare creature for the first time. The crowd near the bar parted as she glided through. Then all at once she stopped, a smile lighting up her face. "Why, *Chief*! Hell, this is a surprise!"

The Chief sucked in a deep breath and let it out slowly. "Hi, Georgiana," he said, "long time no see."

Munro's bruises were stiffening by the time he reached his room. He ran a tub and relaxed, soaking his limbs. In the mirror panelling of the bathroom a red weal throbbed on the bunched muscles of his shoulder. Maybe tomorrow he'd treat himself to a massage.

Then he remembered the masseurs here were all Japanese.

He dried and put on a clean uniform. Before leaving he undid the shutters to check the balcony. Nothing outside except the strains of the band playing on the Lunetta, the piping of the tree frogs and across the park the glimmering lights of *Intramuros*, the Walled City.

But the fear was here. He could sense it like an evil stench on the wind. *They* were nearby, watching, waiting. One of them had attacked him tonight. *Kokuryu-kai . . . Black Dragon*.

He bolted the shutters again and shut the windows. He was on the point of going out when he noticed the photo frame was missing.

They had been here too.

An idea came to him swiftly. He glanced at his watch; half past seven. Two minutes later he was stepping out of the elevator downstairs in the lobby. Over at the reception desk a Filipino sugar baron was complaining because he couldn't have his usual suite and a uniformed courier was emptying the mailbox.

105

"Give me a stamp for the US, will you?" Munro asked the clerk on duty.

The mailman shut the box with a clang and locked it. "Here, bud, one more for you," Munro handed over the envelope and saw it placed in the mail sack. It was addressed to himself in San Francisco. For the remainder of the trip the photograph would ride the Clipper's mail hold in complete security.

"I never thought it would be your flight, Chief," said Georgiana. "Guess I should have known." Her eyes were green like the sea off a reef. They matched the emeralds of her necklace. She was about twenty-six, Scott decided. At her back was a panther-like Spaniard, lithe, arrogant, as darkly handsome as she was pale.

"So is *he* here too?" she heard Georgiana ask.

"Max? Yeah, he's still the First."

"Same old outfit, huh?" Her voice was a soft, rich drawl that sounded as if she laughed easily.

"We got one new recruit; Sally Scott, Miss Delahaye," the Chief introduced them, "Scott joined the crew last month."

The extraordinary green eyes widened, "I didn't realise Pan Am had put stewardesses on the Clippers. Must be exciting."

"Not enough for Scott," the Chief answered before she could reply, "she wants to be pilot."

"They're teaching you to fly?"

"It's not necessary, I already have my licence."

"*You pilot the Clipper?*" A new respect showed in the girl's face.

Scott shook her head, still awed by her beauty, "I'd like to, sure, but so far the Company won't play."

"Probably scared you'll take over a man's job," Georgiana said.

"It seems you have done that already, *si?*" the Spaniard put in. He wore a white mess jacket with a red cummerbund; a clothes horse but no cissy.

Georgiana laughed, "This is César, he believes in the old-fashioned role for women. I give him a lot of trouble."

The Spaniard's eyes were black and deep against his olive skin. He was young, in his twenties, and frighteningly attractive. He answered abruptly, "You make trouble for yourself not me. Unfortunately we do not have time to discuss that now or we shall be late for the party."

A little wrinkle of annoyance appeared on Georgiana's brow. "Some party, with more of your aunts waiting to give me the once over!" she retorted. "Well, buy me some cigarettes then, wasn't that

106

what we came for? I must have cigarettes if I'm to get through the evening."

"I have them here, *querida*," he held up two flat boxes.

But Georgiana was talking to Scott again, "I started to learn to fly once. I had my first lesson from Amelia Earhart."

The circle around her went suddenly quiet. "You knew Amelia?" the Chief said after a moment.

"No," she shook her head and the flaming hair rippled on her bare shoulders, "not really. Dad once did some business with her husband and he asked her to take me up."

Her voice trailed off. Her gaze was fixed over their shoulders at someone who had just entered.

It was Munro.

At the sight of Georgiana he stopped dead for a moment. The colour drained from his face and every line in it went taut. On one cheekbone a livid bruise stood out like a brand.

"Dixie!" he said chokingly, "How in hell did you get here?"

"Hallo, Max," her voice was icy sweet but her whole body had stiffened. "I notice your manners haven't changed. Nice to see you again. It's been almost three years hasn't it?"

"Something like that. What brought you here?"

"I've been playing a tournament, staying with the MacArthurs. Aren't you pleased to see me?"

"Delirious. How long are you staying?"

Georgiana's eyes became innocently wide, "Why darling, till the flight leaves of course. I'm going to be one of your passengers again, just like old times. Oh, by the way, you haven't met César have you? César de Santa Cruz. We're travelling together." She paused, watching him carefully as she delivered the final punch, *"We're going to be married."*

VIII

INTRAMUROS – *THE WALLED CITY*. Slowly, ponderously the military truck ground along the ancient cobblestones. On the roof of the closed body a circular radio antenna rotated back and forth – a sightless eye probing the airwaves. Inside technicians recruited by the Counter Intelligence Corps listened for sounds of illicit transmitters. Reaching the gates of the Puerto Real it braked and halted.

From a slit window in the medieval wall the Japanese watched and swore softly as the antenna settled on a bearing.

A taxi forced its way through the arches, honking at the horse carriages and pedestrians streaming in and out. Many passers-by wore carnival dress for the feast-day coming. From his window the Japanese could hear trams clanking past down on the boulevard. Still the truck did not move.

By the Amida Buddha, if those fool monks were transmitting!

At last the driver came to life again. With a clash of gears the truck lurched off in the direction of the bay. Pulling a painted animal mask over his face, the Japanese ran down the steps of the turret and slipped out into the street.

The night was warm and music spilled from the cafés and squares of the old city. Dark-eyed señoritas swung by on the arms of jealous escorts, old ladies in lace mantillas, shrill-voiced urchins running barefoot, Chinese flower girls, limping beggars, hawkers, whores, soldiers. Anonymous among the throng, the Japanese moved sure-footed, past the governor's palace into a maze of narrow alleys, the map memorized in his head as sure to him as a guide.

Anger burned in his heart. Anger with himself for permitting the American pilot to escape. He had been tired, *i-ye*, but that was no excuse! No, something else, the American had been *aware*, had felt his presence before even he entered the locker room.

Haragei – the sixth sense.

Kerosene lamps flickered on street-corner fruit stalls. *Calesas* rattled past, high-wheeled gigs drawn by trotting ponies. Behind the great

Romanesque church of San Agustin he ducked through a barred gate into a dingy courtyard spattered with bird droppings. A stone passage beyond ended in a locked iron door.

"*Higashi no kaze ame!* East wind rain!"

"*Nishi no kaze hare!* West wind clear!"

Bolts scraped and the door swung open. In the gloom a figure in the saffron robe of a Buddhist monk stood holding a drawn sword.

"Remove your mask."

"*I-ye!* Do not give me orders! I am from the *Kokuryu-kai!* I have the passwords, take me to your Commander."

Another yellow garbed priest stepped from the shadows. The points of their swords touched the visitor's throat. "The mask, dog!"

"*WAAA! Shimai!*" There was a blur in the darkness and a clash of wood as the staff swept the blades aside. Before the first guard could move a foot pinned his knee against the doorframe and a paralysing grip fastened on his left shoulder. He screamed once as the joint gave and slid to the ground senseless. His companion let out a cry of rage. Lifting his sword for a two-handed sweep, he rushed forward, murder in his eyes. The Japanese dived under the blow, staff lunging. There was a whistling snap and the tip shot out to smash into the guard's throat. In terrible pain the man reeled away. With a contemptuous snort the Japanese strode through into the hall beyond.

Lit by candles, it was furnished as a temple. Stone floors and shadowy frescoes. At the far end incense smoked before a statue of the god in stone. A brass bell hung in a nearby corner, but of human occupation there was no sign. Warily, still clutching his sword-staff, he stepped toward the idol.

A soft footfall jerked him round suddenly. Three men were approaching from the rear. Two were dressed the same as the guards, the third was older, his tonsured hair was grey, his robe crimson. All three bowed low.

"Respectful greetings, *Osho-san*," the Japanese responded, bowing in turn.

"Welcome," the man's voice was melodious, "please forgive your reception by these miserable guards, they were uncertain whom to expect."

"I most humbly apologise, *Osho-san*, for my impatience in striking them."

"It is nothing, they were fools," the chief monk cast a casual glance towards where the injured guards lay groaning. "*Aie*, we were warned you were good, but not this good. *Iai-jutsu*, the killing draw; never have I witnessed such speed."

109

"You do me too much honour," again the Japanese bowed.

"Your mission honours us all. Come, your journey has been wearying. A bath has been prepared, afterwards food, wine and we talk, *neh*?"

"First I have urgent news. Tonight we received the signal: in four days Imperial forces strike against the West. *Tenno Heika banzai!*"

Porcelain *sake* cups clinked in a toast. The two sat on their knees at a low table in a side chamber. The Japanese had removed his mask. His features were strong and clear in the lamplight.

"The *Amerikans* are suspicious. They have detector vans sweeping the city for your transmitter."

"They suspect nothing. It is routine, the vans follow a similar pattern each night, beginning and ending always at the same time. Fools, *neh*?"

"Perhaps," anger flitted momentarily across the other's face. "*I-ye*, today they outwitted us and now the *gaijin* are alert to our plans."

"*Karma*. Fortune favoured the enemy. Possibly our airmen were not sufficiently resolute. They will be punished."

"And now? What is our next move? Does the High Command have orders for us? Or are they too occupied with the great plan?" the Japanese spoke bitterly.

"Enough," the *Osho-san* admonished him. "This mission is constantly on their minds. We must wait to see what steps the *Amerikans* take now. The aircraft is being watched continually. If it or the cargo are moved we shall know at once. Meanwhile the *Bund* are learning what they can. They have highly placed agents here and understand the urgency. This man they have given you, he is reliable, *neh*?"

"For a *gaijin*, yes." The Japanese narrowed his eyes, "He has not yet been put to the test."

"And this photograph?" the *Osho-san* inquired. "Explain please its importance." He listened gravely while the other told him. "Stupidity. How was this permitted?"

"Apologies, lord. The *gaijin* police arrived before the priest's room could be searched."

"Your apology is unnecessary. No blame attaches to you. Nevertheless it must be recovered. Quickly. Its existence imperils everything."

"We are certain one of the *Amerikans* has it. For what reason is unclear." The Japanese passed a hand across his bruised jaw, "And he is wary as a snow leopard with young."

With a soft knock monks entered bearing steaming bowls of food. Soup, noodles, tempura. "Even so," the *Osho-san* said when they were alone once more, "the photograph must be destroyed, *neh*? No matter who stands in the way."

They began to eat.

MANILA HOTEL PAVILION
CARNIVAL NIGHT SPECIAL
DANCE TO THE MUSIC OF TIRSO LOPEZ
CABARET STARRING FAMOUS SINGER AND ARTISTE LOLA MONTEZ

EIGHT PM. A huge moon bathed the gardens in silver. Beneath a domed ceiling on marble columns open to the tropic breeze, couples danced against a background of whispering palm trees and the murmur of waves on the seawall. Diamonds, champagne, Kleig lights, two orchestras. Tuxedos, mess-jackets, and gowns sparkling with jewels whirled across the floor. At candle-lit tables wine flowed.

The Manila's nightclub was one of the legends of the East.

"Golly, I'm exhausted!" Felicity Gordon Smythe fanned her chest with a menu at her parents' table after an energetic dance with Chris Fry. "And famished," she added, seizing a handful of crisp-fried anchovies from a bowl. "Mmm, the food here is scrumptious!"

Mr. Wirth was sitting with them, "Try these garlic shrimps," he said, leaning across to peer down the front of her dress.

"Chris won't like that!" the girl shrieked. Chris Fry blushed scarlet. Felicity's mother looked pained.

Prince Cherkassy came into view, following a waiter to a table by the dance floor. Observing fellow passengers, he bowed slightly. Mrs. Gordon Smythe snatched the opening at once. "Oh, Your Highness, won't you please join us for a drink?"

The Prince regarded them with dislike. He detested all British and these seemed worse than most, but the daughter had a certain brazen attractiveness about her. "Thank you, most kind," he said coolly, taking a seat.

A fresh bottle was popped, "Health," he raised his glass.

"Cheers."

"Bottoms up!"

"Mr. Wirth has been telling us the most interesting things about this flight," Felicity's mother gushed. "He says the Clipper is carrying a secret cargo. That's why the Japanese flew so close to us today. Is that true, do you know, Mr. Fry?"

" 'Fraid I'm not the man to ask about the cargo, Ma'am. That's the First's responsibility."

"Keeping it under your hat, eh?" Gordon Smythe grunted. "Good lad."

His wife looked put out. "Well I don't call it very helpful, I must say. Who knows what those dreadful Japanese might not have done?"

Felicity nudged Chris playfully, "What is this cargo? Are we flying with the crown jewels on board."

"Honest, honey, I don't know and that's the truth."

"I'll bet Mr. Wirth knows. Don't you, Mr. Wirth?"

"Yes, do tell us, Mr. Wirth."

"Well," Eddie smirked at the attention, "confidentially, I've heard this Bishop Buchan business is a blind. There's a secret American ground force fighting alongside Chiang K'ai Shek's men in China. Plague has broken out in the ranks and bodies are being flown home in sealed boxes for post-mortem examinations by Army doctors. That's why Latouche is aboard – he's a specialist in Oriental diseases."

"Pshaw!" The Prince gave a snort. "Believe that and you will believe anything." His eyes drilled into the Lend-Lease man. "Health," draining his glass he rose and left.

The music had changed to a samba. Scott was dancing with Stewart Whitely. One thing about being the only girl on the team, you got plenty of floor practice. She was wearing her one silk dress and it looked good on her, she knew, white against her tanned skin and fair hair. Out here blondes were at a premium.

Yes, but some of the women had fabulous gowns new every night. And the rocks they wore! Look at that kid over there, the lithe dark girl with the Navy lieutenant, she couldn't be more than seventeen and dripping rubies.

Stewart was chattering away in her ear, he was a poor dancer but he made up for it with gossip.

"Some surprise I'll say Georgiana showing up like this and as a passenger too. I wonder how old Max is feeling, they were a hot item once."

"When was that, Stewart?" Scott steered them out of the path of another couple. Through the pack she glimpsed Shapiro partnering a nurse from Sternberg with a smile like a Kolynos toothpaste ad.

"Three, maybe four years back. Lasted quite a while. They met when she was playing the international circuit."

"Of course, Georgiana Delahaye," Scott realised where she had heard the name now, "she's the lady golf champion. So what happened?"

"Max never let on. One day she just wasn't around any more."

"She's certainly a beauty."

"Rich too, her old man's a senator and a big wheel in Washington, so they say," Stewart gave a chuckle.

"What's so funny?"

"Kurt Thyssen once tried to kid Max about her. I forget what it was he said exactly, but Max belted him. Knocked him down flat right in the lobby of the Royal Hawaiian. So it's a sore subject okay."

Over at the crew table under the pillars Munro was watching the dancers, trying to keep his mind off Georgiana. Many of Manila's prettiest debutantes were present tonight, bare-armed, gazelle-like creatures with liquid eyes and opal skin. Curious how the combination of Malay and Spanish blood resulted in such beauty.

Maybe that was what he needed, a woman.

Scott was looking pretty. He could see Kurt Thyssen following her around the floor with his eyes. They had finished eating and the Chief was starting on the cold beers. Chuck and Davey Klein had retired to the bar with some Air Corps buddies, Shapiro was dancing, Chris Fry also. Ross and Tad Gotto had not put in an appearance.

He wondered where they were.

"*Buenos noches*, Munro?"

Captain Santos had come up behind them. He had taken off his sunglasses and there was a girl with him. He gestured to the empty seats, "May we join you?"

They all stood up. The girl was slim and feline with sluttish, insolent eyes and sleek, black hair and her silver lamé dress clung tight about the hips. There wasn't a lot to the dress. Her figure was perfect.

She held out a hand with long scarlet nails, "*Encantado*, I am Lola Montez, I have heard much of you, Mr. Max Munro," she purred huskily.

"Oh, who from?" he said, on guard.

She grinned slyly, displaying small sharp teeth in a full scarlet mouth. She was heavily made-up, but it looked good in this light. Very good. He caught a whiff of her perfume.

"Colonel Nieto is always talking about you."

"You know Manuel Nieto?" Munro relaxed. Nieto was a Filipino and a close friend, an aide to President Quezon. He concentrated on her, "Montez, that's Spanish?"

113

"Portuguese. From Goa, but I was born in Singapore."

They sat down. "Cigarette?" he proffered a pack. She reached in her purse and came up with a long holder. Kurt Thyssen leaned forward with a lighter.

"*Muchas gracias.*"

Santos had taken a chair on Munro's right. "Still no trace of that guy who attacked you," he muttered in a voice no one else could catch.

Munro nodded without speaking. He had held off telling the others till he saw Ross.

"Mr. Slater was very concerned when I reported it to him, he wants to talk later."

"He knows where to find me then."

"Don't be a *fool!*" Suddenly Santos's whisper became a lash. "Whatever you've gotten your hands on somebody wants it bad enough to kill you! Let me have it now before you wind up dead!"

"Is that a threat?" Munro hissed back. Was Santos trying to scare him or was he playing some private game? And why had he brought the girl over?

One way to find out. He touched her arm, "Miss Montez, do you care to dance?"

On the other side of the floor Maria Bianchi and Mr. Breen had ordered grilled lobster. They were discussing the sale of certain bonds Maria had brought with her.

"I want you to sell tomorrow morning at the best price offered. Cash. Immediate settlement."

"You understand the discount on Chinese securities, even government stock, is extremely high. I doubt we shall obtain twenty five per cent of face value."

"Thirty per cent," Maria told him decisively, "after expenses, of which you will keep five. With the US government guaranteeing fresh loans to China, you should be able to find buyers without difficulty." At twenty five per cent net she was still doubling her money.

Mr. Breen did some quick mental arithmetic on a hundred and twenty thousand dollars worth of bonds and made his commission six thousand bucks, more if he could screw the discount down a point or two.

"I don't think you ever told me the exact nature of your business in Shanghai, Madam Bianchi. Was it bond trading?"

The woman's eyes transfixed him with a basilisk stare. "I don't like questions about my private affairs, Mr. Breen. *I'll thank you to remember that.*"

Back in the Jungle Bar, Chuck and Davey Klein had teamed up with a bunch of Air Corp men from Clark Field and were rolling dice for rounds of cocktails.

"Heard you people had some trouble with the Yellow-bellies on the way in today," a tow-headed captain grinned, throwing back a Blue Lagoon.

"Who told you that," Chuck said surprised.

The captain shrugged, "It's common knowledge, I guess."

"Takes place all the time," a pilot said. "We run into Japs most days, but the brass try to keep the lid on it."

"You think they mean business?" Davey asked.

"Hell no!" there were laughs. "Just let the bastards try. Man, the stuff we got coming in here now, we'll blast them right outta the sky!"

"Say, you heard the new joke about the Japs?" said another officer. "Every generation they're growing smaller; soon they won't be able to squat."

There was more laughter. The captain thumped the bar, "Hey, let's have another round, Sidecars this time."

"Naw, Pink Squirrels."

"White Ladies."

"Loser decides. Where're those dice?"

"Which outfit you guys with?" asked Chuck.

"Twenty-seventh Bombardment Group. B–17s," the captain said proudly. "Yessir, when the rest of our ships are delivered next month we'll knock hell out of the Nips, you watch."

"Sure be a relief," Davey said fervently. "This afternoon they were all set to knock hell out of us."

Up in his room Ross poured another slug of whisky into his glass from the Haig and Haig pinchbottle he had ordered up and added some ice. The bottle was going down fast, it was almost half empty. He had better go easy. Not that he was drunk. It surprised him how much it seemed to take these days.

He gulped a mouthful anyway and took a bite of the cold toasted cheese-on-rye that had come with it. The rest of the crew would be eating downstairs in the Pavilion, wondering where he had gotten to.

If they cared at all. Most probably none of them did. Well, fuck them, it was none of their damn business.

He looked in the drawer again.

Most places they put a Gideon Bible by the bed. Not this time. Not for him. Instead there was a book: AMELIA EARHART – LAST FLIGHT.

Bastards!

1937 July 2nd. Daybreak. Howland Island. A wet mist rolling off the sea. Parties of seamen shooing Gooney birds from the runway. In the prefabricated control hut a group of men clustering anxiously round the radio.

"KHAQQ Earhart to Howland . . . We must be on you but cannot see you . . . gas running low . . . unable to reach you by radio . . . flying at altitude 1000 feet . . ." The woman's voice sounding high-pitched and alarmed.

At a nod from an officer the operator switched to transmit. "Howland to KHAQQ. Please maintain transmission so we can get a fix."

Static crackled emptily in the loudspeakers.

Outside on the rough coral strip the wind was freshening, whipping away the smoke from the stack of the Navy cutter anchored inshore. "So what's gone wrong, Captain?" Slater gripped his arm.

Over to the north west massive storm clouds had risen to 10,000 feet. "The front's cut her off, Major. Her RDF is out. She hasn't a hope in hell of a visual sighting."

"Keep your voice down, godammit. Her course is secret."

"Major, you heard what she said. She's running low on fuel. We gotta get search ships out – fast!"

"And blow the whole mission? Not yet, dammit. Not yet!"

Ross buried his head in his hands and wept.

There were other parties that night.

The walled and moated gardens of the sprawling mansion in the exclusive Santa Mesa district were hung with Chinese lanterns. Private police guarded the gates. Beneath the portico chauffeurs from the limousines parked in the driveway played dominoes. Inside, two dozen guests sat down to dinner.

In the darkness of the veranda beyond the fly-screens a man crouched patiently. By day he was a humble gardener, by night a lieutenant in the *joho kyoku* – Japanese Naval Intelligence.

Watch, listen, report – for two years his mission had been the same.

Soon, soon his hour would come. *Higashi no kaze ame.*

The Delahaye girl was behaving badly, Ruth could see.

"War with Japan by Christmas, I had it from one of MacArthur's people yesterday," the Dutchman said. "Your President Roosevelt has it planned to take care of the unemployment."

"Aw, c'mon," Georgiana riposted briskly. "He promised in the election no American boys would fight in a foreign war."

"War by Christmas," Van Cleef repeated firmly, stabbing the table with a finger. "Maybe sooner even." He was in his fifties, lean and fit still.

"Well, me I am for it," said César. "It is time we taught the yellow-bellies a lesson."

"How d'you know they won't teach *us* a lesson?" Georgiana suggested. The men exchanged superior glances. The idea, trust a woman. "Well, how do you?" she demanded angrily, tossing her head.

The other women watched her critically. They were Spanish, friends and relatives of the Santa Cruz family, which was why she was here, to be introduced. And observed. Ruth Simms could tell she was making a very bad impression. Manila society was conservative. Girls were expected to be quiet and virtuous, not appear at dinner parties in strapless dresses and argue with the men.

The men were loving it which was making the women even more jealous. César too.

"Of course César knows these things," an old crow in a black lace mantilla over a high silver comb rebuked her with pursed lips. "He is in the military reserve, an officer."

Georgiana was not deterred. "He's never been to China though, he's never seen the Japanese fighting. Have you, César?"

César's eyes darkened broodingly in his long handsome face. "That is of no consequence," he said impatiently. "And I tell you this, if war comes . . ."

"Stop it!" Ruth Simms cried suddenly. "Stop it! Stop it!"

The others at the table looked at her. She glared at them frantically, "War, war, war! Can't you talk about anything else?"

"*Bravo*, Ruth," Conchita de Santa Cruz, her plump, pretty hostess, agreed. "Everywhere, at every party it is the same nowadays, the men speak of nothing but war. We women are sick of such talk."

Her husband held up his hands, "It is my fault. A thousand apologies. Let us agree no more talk of war tonight."

Barefoot waiters in white coats entered bearing bowls of fruit in hot coconut milk. "You are leaving on the Clipper, Friday?" the Dutchman asked Eliot Simms. "Very wise. Myself also, affairs permitting."

"I heard the plane had trouble on the way from Hongkong," someone else said. "The Japs tried to force it down."

Conchita glanced hastily at Ruth, "*Nombre de Dios*! That is not true, is it?"

"Even the Nips wouldn't attack a civilian plane."

"What about the one that disappeared in '38, the *China Clipper*?"

Ruth Simms felt her head swimming. With a murmured excuse she slipped from her seat.

"Ruth," Conchita followed her into the hall, shutting the door. "You are feeling ill? A *migrano*? Let me send for Doctor Vargas."

"No please, Conchita. I shall be fine, I just need a breath of fresh air. I'll look in on the kids a minute, then come back."

"The men with their stupid talk, showing off before that girl. What does César want with such a one? She dresses like a street walker! Stay out as long as you want, Ruth. Kiss the children for me."

Wearily Ruth pulled herself together. Conchita and Ramon were wonderful, having them to stay in their house and treating them like their own family.

If only she could rid herself of the terror.

The two girls were sound asleep, sheets thrown back in the heat, arms wrapped tight about a favourite toy. Gently, without waking either, Ruth tucked them in and kissed the damp blond curls. Paula the oldest had only lately recovered from malaria. It was on account of her they had delayed their departure.

Softly she opened the door of the next room. The boy's eyes gazed up at her. "Can't you sleep, Ricky?"

The dark head shook, "I was thinking about the flight. Mamma is coming too, isn't she?"

"Of course she is, darling, she'll be there to meet you at the hotel," Ruth whispered as she kissed his forehead. "You're going to be very happy together." He was a sweet boy. What kind of mother was it who never saw her son and communicated only through lawyers? "Off you go to sleep now."

She closed the door.

The boy lay in bed, listening to the murmur of voices down the passage. Suppose his mother had forgotten him though? The thought worried him. It had been almost two years. He had changed a lot in two years. Suppose she didn't *love* him anymore?

On an impulse he slipped out of bed. Unfastening the window, he scrambled through down onto the terrace. The night was warm and scented. Cicadas and tree frogs shrilled in the darkness. Over by the

118

kitchens he could hear the servants clattering dishes. Carefully he picked his way round the house to the verandah.

Light poured from the windows of the dining room. He stood on a chair and peeped in at the party.

A hand touched his leg. He jerked round with a gasp nearly falling from his perch.

"*Ishido*! Gee, you gave me a fright. What are you doing out here?"

"*Ssh*, same like you. Watch people, *neh*?"

The boy nodded. It sounded reasonable to him. Together they turned back to the window.

"Wow, Ishido, the lady with the red hair, she sure is beautiful. She looks like a film star, huh?"

The gardener's white teeth gleamed in the darkness. "*Ah so*," he breathed. "*Ah so, desku*."

IX

NINE PM. Across the city bars and cafés were filled with people crowding in for the start of the fiesta. On the Calle Real two young men finished their meal at a *sushi* counter and stepped out into the street.

"Tad, I have to go round to my uncle's *dojo*," the taller of the two said on the bustling sidewalk. "Why don't you come along, huh?"

"Gee, Mish, I'd like to but I oughta be getting back to the hotel."

"C'mon, it's on your way. You'll meet some real interesting guys."

Gotto wavered. Mitsuji Hata was twenty, American born like himself and a student at the university. They had met six months back at the *jai alai* stadium on one of Tad's early trips out. He'd mentioned the *dojo* before, but this was the first time he had asked Tad along. "Sure, why not. I can always catch a cab afterwards."

They walked down as far as San Agustin then took a small turning to the left. Crumbling Spanish houses overhung the street. A pretty girl was leaning from a shell window flirting with boys below. Tad saw her throw a flower down to them. Mitsuji stopped before a door and knocked. It opened. There was a muttered exchange of Japanese then he beckoned Tad to follow.

The building was an old warehouse with stone pillars and groined archways. In silence they climbed to a landing giving onto a passage. Through the soles of his shoes Tad was aware of vibrations jarring the heavy timbers. Faint sounds reached him muffled by the walls, thuddings on the floor, the clack-clack of wood on wood. Evoking in his mind subconscious images of a buried past.

Mitsuji paused before another door set flush in the wall. "There's a class in session. We can watch from the gallery so long as we're quiet."

The sounds of combat ceased as the youths entered the *dojo*. It was a long room like a gymnasium with a high ceiling, constructed entirely of perfectly fitted honey-coloured planks. Racks of practice staffs lined the walls. Six figures in padded protective armour and face-guards were bowing to an iron-haired man, who sat arms folded on a dais beside a small *Shinto* shrine. Across his knees lay a three foot wooden *bokken*.

"My uncle," Mitsuji whispered proudly.

More figures filed in below. All but one wore yellow robes beneath their armour. The last, with his back to them, was simply dressed in black cotton leggings and belted jacket. They bowed deeply to the *sensei* then to one another and took up positions, hands gripping the hilts of their *bokken*.

"*HAI!*" Without a shred of warning two rushed on the black.

Bokken clashed. Harsh cries echoed round the *dojo* and bare feet thumped on the boards. The ferocity of the assault was shocking. Blows rained down with blinding speed slashing, slicing, cutting, chopping in blurred sequence, faster than the eye could follow. His *bokken* whistling in fluid arcs, the black parried strike after strike, now lunging, now sweeping vertically, leaping and whirling with breathtaking agility. An assailant reeled away, disabled by a hit to the throat. Instantly another sprang forward to take his place.

"Incredible, huh?" Mitsuji's eyes were shining. "This is real combat fighting. See how he goes for the vital points: throat, wrist, groin, the inside of the arm. With a *samurai katana* any of those strokes would kill in seconds."

"Who is he?" Tad gasped in admiration.

"A *sensei*, a master." More shouts rang out below. "Those cries are *ki-ai*, release of spirit energy at the instant of cutting."

Something in his manner made Tad concentrate, "Where's he from?"

"He's a visitor. From home, *neh?*" his friend shot him a quick glance.

"From Japan? I thought all those guys were sent back months ago."

"*Aiee*, you're one of us too, remember." Below the black had disposed of two more attackers without slackening pace.

"I'm not. I'm . . ."

"An American?" Mitsuji finished for him sharply. "How much longer you gonna kid yourself, Tadeo Gotto? Look in a mirror sometime. You're Japanese, with a Japanese name – that's what your Yankee friends will say when war comes."

"It's a damn lie! And if there is a war I'll be in it – fighting for America."

"Fool! You'll be in jail," Mitsuji whispered back fiercely above the clash of *bokken*. "We know for sure they have plans to round up every *nisei* in the country." He gripped Tad's hand on the rail of the gallery, "Listen, big things are happening. Japan's gonna smash the Yankees

121

soon. Manila, Hawaii, the whole Pacific will be ours!"

Tad shook him off incredulous. "Never!" his voice was a shout.

Down on the floor the black dealt the last of his armoured opponents a slashing blow across the face guard. He lowered his *bokken*. Chest heaving, he bowed to the *sensei* and turned. His gaze met Tad's.

The youth quailed.

Alone on the rear terrace of the Manila Hotel, Bob Cashin threw his cigarette away in a stone urn. Checking to make sure he was not being watched, he slipped quietly down the steps into the gardens. It was four years since he had been here last but the gate in the wall was where he remembered. It was unlocked and he let himself through.

Turning to his left, he picked his way along the park wall till he came to an alley leading down to the water. In the darkness it smelt of fish and rotting mud. A faded sign loomed up LEGASPI LANDING.

There were cars here and radio music coming from a wooden shack hung out over the water on stilts. Voices mingled with the chink of glasses. Checking behind once more, he pushed through the bead curtain.

The smoke inside made his eyes water. Filipino fishermen crowded the bar, grimy men in singlets drinking San Miguels with Dobie gin chasers. No sense of hostility, this place was fashionable with the smart crowd. Late at night, not now. He was the only foreigner present.

He sought an empty table in a corner. A plump whore slouched over. "Hi, Joe, wanna drink?"

He nodded, "A beer."

"One beer, one whisky!" A waiter slapped down the glasses. The girl drained hers at a gulp and signalled for another. "Me Suzie, ten dollar quick time. Drink then go in back, okay Joe?"

"Uh uh, sorry darling, not tonight."

"Make special price for you, five dollar," the girl persisted. She was around fourteen, young even by Manila standards, a brown-skinned Visayan with gold earrings. "Okay t'ree dollar, Joe. Go now, huh?" Her voice became a whine, "*Please* Mister, or boss t'row me out."

Cashin sighed; it was the oldest shakedown in the business. For the sake of peace he passed over a few notes. As the whore slunk off he saw the bead curtain part again and Simon Ho entered.

With a nervous glance around the Chinese sat down at the table. "I cannot stay long or I shall be missed," he whispered.

They waited silent while fresh beers were brought. "So what's the story, Simon?" Cashin kept his voice low.

The young man shivered, "I do not know. What story? I should not be here, it is too dangerous. I am being watched."

"Don't tell me you and Hollington Soong are flying halfway round the world just to bring home Bishop Buchan?"

"The Minister will gain much face politically." Ho's English was nearly as good as his master's.

"What's the true reason? What's behind it all?"

"One cannot be sure, there has been no word officially."

"Unofficially then, what have you heard?" Cashin pressed him, but the Chinese made no reply. His fingers shook as he lit himself a cigarette.

"Would it have to do with the Manchu Tombs?"

Ho's mouth went slack, "*The Tombs*! What have you heard?"

"I know about the treasure, how it had accumulated since the foundation of the dynasty only to be looted during the bandit years."

"Not all was stolen." Ho's voice was low, "The thieves were afraid to enter the deepest vaults, they were left untouched. And afterwards there was a restoration."

"A restoration carried out by Professor Chen, now travelling with us."

"Honourable Chen, yes. He was chosen by the last of the Emperors, the puppet P'u Yi. He had married into the Yellow Banner Manchu clan and so was acceptable. His niece, Chen Yu-Ling, would be a princess but for the Revolution."

"A princess, a *Manchu* princess?"

"So they say. It means nothing now."

"She's pretty."

"Yes, the Minister thinks so too."

"Is that why she and the old man are flying with you?"

"He is very sick. Without medicines from your doctors he will soon die." Ho took a jerky pull on his cigarette and crushed it out, "I must get back before they miss me."

"Who, Soong? I thought you said he was dining at the Palace." Cashin leaned forward urgently, "Simon, quit stalling me for heaven's sakes and tell me what's going on. Why did the Japs try to turn back the plane?"

"You have heard about the Black Dragon killing in Hongkong yesterday? One of your countrymen, a priest. He was due to fly with us on the Clipper."

"Yes, but everyone denies it. Even that Jordan character said it wasn't true."

"Because they are frightened. Hollington Soong almost fainted when he was told. The Dragons terrify him. *They terrify us all.*"

Slowly, reluctantly Ho was beginning to talk. "For months Chungking has been petitioning Washington for fresh loans, the Government is desperate for aid. A short while ago in great secrecy a deal was struck."

Light dawned in Cashin's eyes, "*The loot from the Tombs*? No wonder the Black Dragon are interested."

"It is not only the Dragons." Ho's manner became agitated again. He glanced over his shoulder, "Bob, things are going to happen. Things that concern America!"

"What do you mean? What things?"

The bead curtain clicked. A pair of young Chinese entered the bar and began calling rowdily for drinks.

"What is going to happen?" Cashin repeated in an urgent undertone. Ho shook his head mutely. Either he did not know or was too scared to say.

"Simon, please," the journalist gripped his hand.

"*No!*" Ho shook free violently. His face was sweaty. "They would have me killed," he hissed. "East Wind Rain, tell your people that, do you understand? *East Wind Rain!*"

Upstairs in the hotel Yu-Ling knelt before a low table. On it a single lamp burned, the rest of the bedroom was in shadow. Carefully with a clean needle she coaxed the tiny opium pill into the bowl of the porcelain pipe.

"*Daw-tse*, thank you, Third Niece," Professor Chen accepted the pipe, holding it in his long, bony fingers while she applied the flame. The sweet heavy scent of the drug suffused the room.

Latouche coughed. "How many a day?" he asked.

The Professor inspected the bowl to satisfy himself it was smouldering properly, "Three, sometimes four," he answered with a ghost of a smile.

"And the medicine also."

The Professor lay back against the pillows. The silk-wrapped box was beneath his arm and a great stillness seemed to possess him. His eyes were shut, the thin lashes motionless, only his chest moved, drawing in the smoke. He might almost have been asleep. After a while he spoke, "When I was young I feared death. Now, as death itself stands waiting at my gate, I have discovered something that I fear more – emptiness, emptiness of the soul."

"And you find this relieves the pain?" the Doctor gestured towards Yu-Ling still on her knees at the table. She watched him covertly. Perhaps he disapproved of the black smoke like so many *quai loh*.

Her knees felt cramped but she put the pain from her mind. Pain and tears were the way of life for a girl. Through the open window she could hear dance music. She wished they could have eaten downstairs in the hotel and seen the western ladies in their gowns. Tomorrow though Minister Soong had promised to take her to a ball at the Presidential Palace. "And you shall dance with me, eh, little Jade Years?" he had pinched her cheek slyly. *Oh ko*, she knew what Minister Soong wanted.

Her uncle was speaking again, "The landscape of my mind is peopled with spirits, for a while the opium puts faces to them. Perhaps it is the only form of after-life: the friends we have forgotten living on in our dreams."

The Doctor leaned forward, eyes deep in the lean face, the fingers of his hands pressed together, "Does the Duke of Chou live on in your dreams?"

Yu-Ling tensed. All her life she had been forbidden to utter that name.

"The Duke?" the Professor's breathing quickened a little. "Alas I was a disappointment to him, I fear. He wanted his life's work to continue, but it was not to be."

"They were hard times after the revolution," the Doctor's voice returned gently, "and you were not to blame he was betrayed."

All gods protect us! He knows everything! Yu-Ling thought.

Her uncle drew on the pipe again, deeper, "I warned him not to trust the Empress, but he refused to heed me. She promised to grant safe conduct from the palace and the Duke believed her." His voice dropped so that his niece and the Doctor had to strain to catch his words, "But he had his revenge, the devil-box betrayed her in the end as he foretold."

As it betrays us all! Yu-Ling wanted to cry.

The bedroom door opened suddenly. The ugly face of bodyguard Feng glared in on them, "*Ai-yah*, where is that fornicator Ho?"

Sweet Georgia Brown! In the Pavilion the evening was hotting up. The band was pounding away with a wickedly fast rhythm, the brass section on their feet, horns sounding out like cannon. Munro tightened his arm round Lola Montez's slender, surprisingly muscular waist.

Sweet Georgia Brown! She pressed herself against him at the turn. He felt the warmth of her breasts and hips and his loins stirred. The tip of her tongue began tracing a moist trail of tiny kisses under his jaw.

One part of him was repelled by this sluttish, glittering woman, the other part wanted her – badly.

Yes, but what did *she* want?

Across the floor Scott felt Thyssen's hold on her tighten again as they danced and resignedly pushed him back. He made her skin crawl, she had to force herself to grant him one turn an evening. Right now he was trying to impress her talking about the parking lot he owned – ". . . showing a fair profit now. I'm after a garage next with a Chevrolet agency." The music slowed. Thank God it was over.

"Sally, one more. Just one, please."

"Honest, Kurt, I'm whacked. I'm going to go powder my nose and sit it out for a while."

She collected her purse from the table. Munro and his girl were still dancing. Boy, their third spin together and she's really giving him the treatment.

Thyssen was waiting for her by the pillars.

"Kurt, no!" she said fiercely as he tried to grab her.

"Please, I've something for you," he drew her behind a huge planter filled with feathery bamboo. "I want you to have this, Sally," he pressed a flat package into her hand.

"What is it?"

"It's for you. Go ahead, open it."

Reluctantly she undid the wrapping. Inside was a slim leather case. She pressed the catch. "Oh God," she groaned.

"Pretty huh? It's brand new. Look at the back, I had them put your initials on."

"*A gold watch*! Kurt, I can't take this."

"Sure you can. It's for you, a present," his voice became throaty, "I thought maybe tomorrow evening we could have dinner, I know a place in the old city . . ."

She pushed the box back into his hands, "No, Kurt."

His eyes popped, "What d'you mean? Don't you like it or something?"

"I'm sorry," she said firmly, "it's a lovely gift and I'm very touched, but no, I can't accept."

He stared at her, mouth open, "But you've got to take it!"

"I'm sorry, Kurt, but the answer's no. I told you already, I've a boyfriend back in the States. Now please, stand out of my way."

"You don't understand, I got money, this is nothing, you wait," he

126

grabbed her wrist. A middle-aged Filipino couple passing by eyed them disapprovingly.

"Let go of me," she snapped, jerking her arm free. "Save your dumb gifts for someone else."

"Sally, wait, listen to me," he pleaded, still trying to thrust the box on her, "I really care about you . . ."

"Kurt Thyssen, for the last time," she rounded on him furiously, "get off my back! You're a married man and even if you weren't, even if you were the last guy on earth, I still wouldn't touch you!"

"Max, it is time to prepare for my act," Lola drew apart from him with a little sigh of reluctance. "Afterwards," she murmured softly, "afterwards we dance again, *si?*"

"Yeah, let's do that," he heard himself say. She squeezed his hand briefly and slipped away behind the band.

Back at the table the Chief was sitting alone with a small dark handsome Filipino in a white sharkskin suit and correspondent shoes.

"Max, *amigo, mabuhay!* Welcome back! We were just watching you dancing there with the lovely Lola."

Munro grinned, "She says she's a good friend of yours, Manuel."

"Yes, that is true," Colonel Nieto nodded. "I introduced her to the President last week and so she is grateful to me."

"How about the President? Is he grateful too?"

"I think so, at least he has invited her out to Pasay."

Munro sat down and took a cooling drink of scotch and soda. The President had a private hideaway villa out at Pasay for music and parties with discreet company. Nieto had taken him along a couple of times.

"By the way, Max," the Colonel was saying, "Chief Crow says you're staying over till Friday, are you free to play polo tomorrow for the Scouts?"

"You bet," Munro brightened at once. He had joined the Manila Polo Club on his first tour out east and played whenever he got the chance.

"*Excellente*, with the army on stand-by we are short of half our players. Tomorrow afternoon then, four o'clock. I will organise mounts. *Adios.*"

So the Philippine Army was on stand-by alert. The authorities were taking the current crisis more seriously than they were letting on.

The Chief regarded him impassively with his flat eyes. He was on his eighth beer and still as sober as a judge. "You know we darn near took a duck in the ocean today," he said casually after a moment.

"Not according to the authorities."

"You want to hear a crazy theory?"

"Shoot."

"Ever feel you were being used for livebait?"

"Something like that did cross my mind."

"It's an even bet those trunks of Slater's are full of rocks."

"He's flying with us, don't forget."

"So maybe they haven't told him either."

"Jesus, that's one hell of a way to start a war!"

Fool the Japs with a fake cargo, pack it aboard the Clipper, let them shoot it down!

Insane! Fifty innocent lives! No one could be that cold blooded, not even to start a war!

What were fifty lives against millions in a war?

There was a loud flourish from the band. It was time for the cabaret. Clutching their drinks, Chuck and Davey Klein came hurrying back from the bar with their friends.

The first act was a team of Oriental acrobats, shirtless men with glistening torsos who leapt and bounced and tossed one another in the air and, for a finale, somersaulted through blazing hoops. A pair of flamenco dancers followed, graceful and intense, heels clicking, skirts shaking to guitar and castanets.

"Where's Lola Montez?" demanded Davey as they clapped.

"Say, you guys still be around Sunday?" said the Air Corps captain. "We're throwing a party here, gonna be the best show this side of Minsky's."

Chuck shook his head. "We'll be on Midway Island."

The lights dimmed. Into the spot trained on the stage stepped the leader of the orchestra, microphone in hand, "Ladies and gentlemen, *Señores e Señoras*, the moment you have all been waiting – a big hand please for – LOLA MONTEZ!"

The drums rolled. There was a prolonged burst of applause. With a glitter of silver Lola stepped into the circle of light. She bowed to her audience and lifted her head. An expectant hush fell.

"A man without a woman is like a ship without a sail,
is like a boat without a rudder, is like a kite without a tail . . ."

"Wow, what a dame!" Davey whispered, "Max ought to be here to listen to this. Where is he, Chief?"

The gardens were quiet and still. Munro had come outside to think. Without intending to, he found himself heading back towards the pool.

It was deserted.

A shoe crunched on a gravel path. In the moonlight he glimpsed a figure slipping away under the trees. A European, tall and gaunt, Reverend Jordan. What the hell was he up to?

Stepping softly across the grass, he set off in pursuit.

The park around the hotel merged on the east side into a golf course laid out over what had once been the moat girdling *Intramuros*. Jordan was evidently in a hurry, he did not bother to look behind to see if he were being followed. A fruit bat brushed Munro's hair as they crossed the eighteenth green and ahead of them loomed the massive walls of the medieval city.

Jordan was twenty yards in front. He seemed to hesitate for a minute as if uncertain which direction to take. Almost as a signal a bell began to peal from one of the city churches. Jordan stiffened at the sound and started forward again, heading for the Puerto Real. Soon he was mingling with the traffic at the gate.

Munro quickened his pace to close the gap. He reached the gate to find a bullock cart laden with tobacco bales blocking the way. By the time he had struggled past the priest was nowhere to be seen.

He stopped a passer-by, "*Por favor, amigo*, which bells are those I can hear?"

"They are the bells of San Agustin ringing for the Fiesta."

"*Muchas gracias.*"

"*De nada, señor.*"

Once *Intramuros* had been the fortress city of Spain's eastern empire. As early as the sixteenth century it had held palaces, barracks, and a university. Baroque mansions looked down on cobbled streets that had once echoed to the tramp of conquistadors. Arched doorways displayed the mouldering arms of long-dead grandees. In Fort Santiago there were garroting posts and flooded dungeons. Even now the inhabitants remained largely Spanish, the traffic horse drawn. To enter *Intramuros* was to step back into the days of the Inquisition.

The crowds were thick in the square before the church. Chinese lions, carved in stone, guarded the gates to the courtyard. Munro, peering this way and that for a glimpse of Jordan, found himself carried through in the squash. As he struggled to extricate himself a roar went up from the throats around him. Preceded by flaring torches, a lifesize effigy of the Holy Virgin was approaching up the Calle Real.

Nuts to this. He hadn't come here to take part in a pageant. But a troop of Filipina nuns had him boxed in and his elbowings drew only benign smiles as the chanting mass of humanity moved inexorably toward the great carved doors.

He craned his neck, seeking a means of escape. The cortège had reached the courtyard gates. Worshippers were pouring up behind, filling the square, clambering over the courtyard wall. No hope of getting out that way.

His gaze fixed on a figure on the wall and he felt his stomach contract.

Crouched against one of the pillars, a man in dark coolie pants and shirt was scanning the crowd in the glare of the torches. A cat's head mask hid his face but as Munro's eyes met his and locked, he *knew*.

Kokuryu-kai! Black Dragon!

The perfect stalking ground: one quick thrust with a knife from behind and the killer would be lost in the crowd before anyone realised his victim was dead.

Only who was the quarry? Himself or Reverend Jordan?

Where was Jordan?

With a quick jump the Japanese sprang down from his perch and was lost to view. Shouldering the nuns aside, Munro plunged after him.

The Virgin entered the courtyard and the bells overhead broke into a wild carillon. Flanked by priests, a bishop dressed in purple and gold appeared on the steps. He raised his crook and from inside the church came the deep-throated chords of the organ. The crowd surged forward singing. Caught in the stampede Munro was swept backwards. He stumbled on the steps and almost lost his footing. The Japanese had disappeared. The crush tightened, funnelling him through the doors. Angry and helpless Munro let himself be carried inside.

Chandeliers lit with flickering tapers hung from a *trompe l'oeil* ceiling and the air was thick with the reek of dripping tallow. Borne now on the shoulders of choristers, the Madonna processed solemnly up to the high altar while her adorers spilled in through the great doors, filling the nave and aisles. Pushing and squeezing Munro managed to force his way across to the right hand section of the congregation. The bells had fallen silent. Around him worshippers were dropping to their knees. In vain he tried to spot the cat's head mask.

Chanting priests weaved back and forth before the gilded altar while acolytes swung fuming censors and rang bells to drive away evil spirits. The congregation rose to murmur the responses. Munro cursed his height. He stood out too easily among the slightly built Filipinos.

Sweet strains of an anthem filled the church. His eyes rose to the choir loft and the darkness of the bell tower.

There on the ladder! Tucked up under the trap to the belfry next to the dangling ropes, the masked figure stared back at him menacingly.

Beside him a plump mestiza family in their Sunday best clutched their rosaries and crossed themselves. "*Perdoneme*," he whispered, "Excuse me please." They glared at him as he squeezed in front. "*Perdoneme, perdoneme*," slowly, with difficulty he passed along the line towards the north aisle.

The pillars along the aisles were hung with images of martyred saints. Beneath the arches he glanced up. The Japanese was still in position. Keeping himself hidden, Munro crossed the aisle and moved down towards the rear of the nave. There was less crush here out of view of the high altar. The side chapels with their votive candles were almost empty.

Standing beneath the vaulting of the tower he stared up, shading his eyes against the big chandelier. Dimly far above he could make out the belfry platform and the twisting ladder clinging to the sides of the tower. Was he gone? *No. A movement.* Slipping downwards to the choir loft.

Looped back against the end wall were the pulleys for the bells. An old man in a brocade vest stared mouth agape as Munro ripped the nearest free and shook it loose.

Without stopping to look round he heaved downward. The rope gave elastically but no sound came. It jerked back against his grip and hung shivering. Again he pulled with no result. By now the Japanese would be alerted. Munro racked his brain, trying to recall the chiming mechanism. Rhythm, that was the key. Let the rope run free at the end of the pull, catch the tail again as it rose.

One . . . two . . . BOING! The first note rolled from the tower. *BOING! BOING!* The sound swelled majestically, reverberating through the church. Munro could see the Japanese gazing at him dumbstruck. *BOING! BOING!* Now people were rushing round him. Hands clawed at the bell rope. A babble of angry voices, Spanish, English, Tagalog, assailed him. A monk in a black habit was shaking

131

him by the shoulders, shouting to know what he was doing.

"Look!" He pointed upward at the still transfixed figure in the mask. "A spy! A spy for the Japanese! A murderer!"

"*Nombre de Dios!* A murderer here in the house of God?"

"He killed a priest! An American!"

The cries ran through the emotion-charged throng.

"*Murderer!*"

"*Spy!*"

"*Priestkiller!*"

In moments a baying mob had gathered beneath the bell tower. The Japanese was staring above him now as if gauging his chances of escape through the belfry and out over the roof. Abruptly he seemed to change his mind and with startling speed came swarming down the ladder to the level of the choir loft.

A yell went up. "Spy! Murderer! Stop him!"

A group of men were already scaling the spiral stairs to the loft. Others rushed to follow their lead. Munro tried to shout a warning that the man was dangerous, a killer, but no one was listening now, they had scented blood. The mob roared as they saw their prey was trapped.

"Catch him! Catch him!"

"Drag him down!"

"*Diabolo, diabolo!*"

The Japanese gained the wooden parapet of the loft. Others were closing in on him now from the direction of the choir stalls, cutting off any hope of retreat. Still there was no trace of fear in his bearing. With a throat-scraping yell he raised his staff. A gleaming blade appeared in his hand. The leading men on the stairs stopped short in terror. Panicking, they began tumbling backwards.

The Japanese paid them no heed. Leaping onto the stair rail, he tensed himself. Six feet away and a little below, a massive chandelier hung on its chain. With the agility of an acrobat he sprang outwards. Screams erupted below and the mob scattered as the chandelier slewed wildly overhead, showering lighted tapers on them. Timing himself exactly, the Japanese released his hold at the end of the swing and dropped to the ground.

With perfect balance he landed on his feet, arms spread. The blade sang as he whirled about. Worshippers fled shrieking behind the pillars. The mask was gone, fallen in his leap. Munro saw cropped hair, flattened cheekbones, eyes like slits of hate, teeth bared in an animal snarl. Then the Japanese was gone, racing through the door into the hot night.

132

Munro ran after him.

The square outside seemed strangely calm after the violence in the church. Spectators of the parade were drifting home. A gang of kids frolicked on the courtyard wall. From a sidewalk café came strains of a guitar. There was no trace of the Japanese, he could have disappeared down any one of a dozen alleys.

A lamp on the corner cast a pool of yellow light on the stone paving. A gaunt figure stood underneath. *Jordan.*

X

Ribbons of glowing headlamps coruscated on Dewey Boulevard's Golden Mile.

"But, Mr. Munro, I still do not understand, why should the Japanese pursue you? What possible threat could you be to them?"

Munro and Jordan had hailed a cab to take them back to the hotel.

"Unless . . ." the priest continued hesitantly. "You remember a photograph you found? In Hongkong, in . . . that room. A picture of Morris and some others in Peking?"

Munro tensed in the rear of the cab. "I understand that went missing."

"Yes. Please do not be offended, but Inspector Playfair suggested perhaps you might have taken it for some reason."

The cab swayed as they turned off the boulevard. The royal palms lining the hotel driveway gleamed silver in the lamplight. Another car was following. "A tourist snapshot? Why should that matter to them?"

The priest shook his head in the dark. "I only wish I had examined it more closely. Perhaps if I were to have another chance . . ."

They pulled up at the steps. A uniformed porter opened the cab door. As Munro paid off the driver he heard angry voices. A limousine had drawn in behind and a girl was storming out up the steps. A red-head in a strapless gown.

Georgiana.

"Dammit, César! I refuse to spend my evenings being insulted by those witches you call your aunts!"

"Georgiana, I warned you that dress was unsuitable. The women of my family are old fashioned in these matters. You are to be my wife, remember? Certain standards are expected."

"I'm wearing black aren't I? Who the hell gave them the right to criticise the way I dress?"

At the sight of Jordan and Munro the two checked. "Max," Georgiana laid a hand on his arm, "take me inside and buy me a big drink, darling, I'm dying of thirst."

"Miss Delahaye, Reverend Jordan," Munro's attention sharpened as he made the introductions. "The Reverend was a close associate of Bishop Buchan," he explained to Georgiana.

"In that case I'm very glad to meet you, Reverend. My father, Senator Delahaye, was a great admirer of the Bishop's."

Jordan swayed on his feet. Clearly he recognised her from the photo and was badly shocked. Gulping, he said, "I . . . fancy we may have met before. You . . . you were in China, were you not, with your father in 1937?"

"Oh really? I'm sorry, I have a hopeless memory for names. Was that in Peking? We visited there together."

"I believe so, yes," Jordan wiped his brow. "And now please, if you will excuse me . . ." he hurried away down the lobby.

"Poor man, he doesn't look well," Georgiana turned back to Munro. "Was he captured by the Japanese too?"

"You don't remember meeting him or another priest called Oliver?"

"Oliver? I'm not sure, yes I think so maybe. But Max darling, it was five years ago nearly. Before I met you even."

César was standing by scowling and smoking a cigarette. Throwing it down he interrupted curtly, "Georgiana, I am going home. I am sorry you find my family boring, let us hope they do not feel the same for you. *Buenas noches.*" He stalked away to his car.

"Arrogant Spanish prig!" Georgiana stamped her foot. "How dare he? I don't care what his family think about me!" She squeezed Munro's arm. "Max, listen to that music. Remember our dances together here?" Her green eyes mocked him, "Don't tell me you've forgotten already, darling."

He shook his head, "Sorry, honeybee, I'm tied up. Maybe some other time."

Her gaze widened. "Why, darling," she laughed lightly, "you didn't think that was an invitation?" Her expression became one of tender concern, "Max, you're not being bitter and jealous, are you? I mean you surely don't imagine there's anything still between us? They were good times we had together but all that's over now, we agreed, right?"

"Sure, we agreed," he said, trying to match her lightness, but failing and feeling confused and angry inside himself because of it.

"I'm so glad, because now we can be friends, can't we? *Real* friends, with no silly jealousy like before," she said, piercingly sweet. "And I just know you're going to like César and be friends with both of us.

135

He's so good to me. Look!" she showed him her hand with the ring and the diamonds flashed under the chandeliers like ice as she waved him goodnight.

God damn all women! he thought angrily, viciously, as he watched her walk away, long-leggedly desirable in the black dress, the slim bare white back an insolent challenge to every male in the lobby. The frustration was burning in his gut like an ulcer and this was only the start of the trip. There was a whole week more of it to come.

He collected his key from the desk. The clerk passed him an envelope with his name on it. Inside was a gold embossed invitation to a carnival gala and fireworks at the Presidential Palace tomorrow evening. There was a note attached from Nieto: *Max, forgot to give you this earlier, hope you can make it. Hasta la vista.* That was decent of Manuel.

As he waited for the elevator there was a bustle of excitement among the other guests. General MacArthur was returning to his penthouse. Munro watched the imperious figure in the gold braided cap stride through the lobby with his wife. Jean MacArthur looked a million dollars. Among the entourage were Hollington Soong and Sir Ambrose Hope.

Upstairs he rapped on Tad Gotto's door. No response. Frowning, he went to his own room.

The searchers had been ruthless. Every drawer was up-ended, the contents scattered, even the lining of his suitcase ripped out.

"About goddam time you showed up!"

He whirled, fists balled. In the window to the balcony stood Slater.

"Jesus Christ! Did your goons do this? What the fuck d'you think you're playing at?"

"What do *I* think I'm playing at? Shit, that's rich. Some cheek you got, Munro."

"Son of a bitch!" Munro stared furiously round the wrecked room, "My suitcase, the bastards shredded it! You'd better have a warrant for this, Slater."

"I'll show you a warrant," Slater's voice was granite-edged, "a warrant for your arrest. Now hand it over."

"What, for Christsakes?"

"*The photograph*, the one you stole in Hongkong," Slater spat. He kicked at the scattered clothing on the floor irritably. "Okay, pilot, quit stalling, we know all about the girl. Your former cutie pie, Miss Delahaye, the girl in the picture no less."

"Leave her out of this, damn you!"

"You brought her into it, not us. Senator Delahaye . . ." Slater

136

checked himself, "The Senator doesn't want the Japs after his daughter."

Why should they be? Munro thought of the envelope he had put into the mail. He wasn't ready to confess yet. There were too many questions to be answered first.

Slater was moving about the room, searching still, checking behind mirrors, lifting rugs. He rifled the pages of a flight manual and tossed it in a corner. "Alright, flyboy, I won't tell you again. Hand the bastard thing over."

"I haven't got it, damn you. Now get the hell out of here!"

"I will, with the photograph. Jesus, do we have to search you too?"

"*I haven't got it!*" The anger was building up inside him like steam in a boiler and his fists were itching to let fly.

They heard the elevator clang. Scott appeared in the doorway carrying her shoes. "These things have been pinching me all evening," she smiled. She saw the upturned drawers and her brow wrinkled, "Boy, Max, what happened to your room?"

Then the screams began in the garden.

"Gee, I sure have enjoyed tonight."

"Mmm, me too."

Beneath a tulip tree Chris Fry tightened his arm round Felicity Gordon Smythe's waist and pulled her close for another kiss. Her lips felt full and slightly wet. Tentatively he let his tongue seek hers. She responded with an eagerness that made his head spin. He brought his hand up to squeeze her breast.

"No, no, that's enough!" she giggled, pulling away.

"Aw, honey. One more kiss, huh? Promise I'll be good."

"You'll have to catch me first!" Laughing, Felicity made a dash for the terrace steps. Suddenly she halted, swaying. Her hands flew to her mouth, she let out a piercing shriek.

The body lay face down in the shadow of the balustrade, dark stains seeping onto the stone.

"Okay, clear back there!" Santos ordered the ring of onlookers, "*Nombre de Dios*, Constable, have some men cordon the area off! And fetch lights!" He turned to Chris Fry and the shaken English girl, "Was it you found him?"

Fry nodded in the darkness, one arm around Felicity, "Yes, sir, we were uh . . . taking a walk . . . we came up the steps and . . . and there he was."

"See anyone else? Anyone else at all?"

"No, sir."

"Senorita?"

Felicity shook her head wordlessly.

More people were crowding up to see and being kept back by the police. The night manager appeared, wringing his hands, pleading with everyone to leave. Two constables pushed through with flashlights. Carefully the body was turned on its back. "Jesus," Munro heard Slater say, "he must have fallen from a balcony."

It was Simon Ho.

"*Ai-yah*, is he dead?" Hollington Soong asked anxiously.

Insects whirled in the flashlight beams as Latouche closed the eyelids gently, "*Oui, il est mort*. Poor young man, there is nothing I can do."

Munro gazed up at the lighted windows of the fourth floor corner suite. Fifty, sixty feet. A hell of a drop anyway. "Someone must have heard, surely?"

"Do not ask me, I was dining at Malacañang Palace." Soong held a hurried exchange with his bodyguard. The man replied in terse grunts. "Feng here was guarding the Chens. Simon was supposed to stay too, but it seems he went out drinking. No one knew he had returned."

"He tipped over drunk?" Slater muttered. "How long ago, Doc?"

"Half an hour perhaps. Not long. He is quite warm still."

A dark uniform loomed up. Thyssen. With him was the Chief, all the crew were here. "I called Sol Boden," he said to Munro.

Sol Boden was Pan Am's general manager in Manila. That was bright of Thyssen to think of calling him. It would look good in any report.

"How about Ross?"

Thyssen shrugged, "He's in his room," he said contemptuously. "With a bottle." There was thinly veiled satisfaction in his voice. The mean-minded bastard saw promotion staring him in the face.

"Let me through, dammit!" Someone was trying to get past the police line. Bob Cashin.

The journalist came stumbling into the lights, spectacles awry. "Oh my God," he gasped, halting shocked at the sight of the bloodied body, "*Simon!*" He gaped round at them, "When . . . How . . . how did it happen? I was with him not an hour ago."

"You were together with him?" Soong rounded on him in the darkness, "Where?"

"At Legaspi Landing."

"*Heya?*"

"It's a bar," Santos told him, "a bar down by the water."

"You had a meeting with him there, a secret meeting?"

"We had a drink together. It wasn't secret."

"*Ai-yah*, what did you speak about? Spies!"

Everyone was concentrating on the journalist now.

"Many things. China, the war, why the Japanese . . ."

"Spies! *Communists!*"

"Simon Ho wasn't a communist! He wanted a decent government for his country, not corrupt warlords like the Kuomintang!"

"How many drinks did you have?" Slater interrupted.

"Drinks? I had two beers. Simon barely touched his."

"What happened afterwards?"

"Afterwards . . . afterwards Simon went back to the hotel."

"Alone?"

"Yes, we thought it best to split up. I walked down to the road and caught a cab to the Main Post Office. I wanted to send a cable, try and beat the censors, but it was closed."

Feng and Hollington Soong exchanged another burst of rapid-fire Chinese. "What time was this?" Santos demanded.

"Ten thirty, eleven. Half an hour ago. How can he be dead?"

"*Joss.*" Back in the suite, Hollington Soong shivered, pouring himself a large brandy from the sideboard and gulping it. "*Joss*. Gods are gods and they decide when we are to die."

Yu-Ling was stunned.. "But it cannot be!" she cried, clutching her hands to her breast. "Tell me it is not true," she blinked back tears.

"*Ai-yah*, of course it is true. He was stupid, degenerate, drinking with spies," Soong snapped crossly.

"I do not understand, what is this talk of spies? He was a good man, *heya?*" she searched Latouche's face, wishing she could read the expressions of *quai loh.*

Gently the Frenchman took her hand in his, "Yes, *petite*," he said quietly, calmingly, "he was a good man but now he is dead. *Joss*, as the Minister says. Try not to be afraid, you are safe here with us."

Joss, Yu-Ling, thought sadly as she crept away to her foreign-devil room with its strange bed and oh so clean and spotless bathroom. *Joss*. Poor Simon Ho, so quiet, so kind. Death was everywhere. In her mind she heard the words of the *fung-sui:*

Beware of treachery . . . thieves . . . and false friends . . ."

Ai-yah.

139

Munro went back to his room in sober mood. The lights were on still. Reclining on the bed in a coral silk robe and negligé, was Georgiana.

He let out his breath slowly, "Dixie, what the blazes are you doing here?"

She pouted, "I dropped in to wish you goodnight. Don't say you're cross, darling."

She was barefoot, her toenails painted. He had forgotten how long her legs looked.

"I like your calling clothes," he said with sarcasm.

"Dear Max, so stiff and correct," she stretched languidly. "Though I must say," she added with a glance round, "you leave your room in an awful mess."

"Sorry if my habits offend you," he picked up a couple of shirts moodily and threw them in a drawer.

Georgiana watched him, smiling like a cat, "Did you know I had a visit earlier from your Major Slater? He spun me an extraordinary tale, all about my photograph being mixed up in a murder in Hongkong and how you had stolen it. Is it true? Do tell me."

"Slater should mind his own damn business!" Reluctantly, Munro gave her the facts.

"Darling, you mean you snatched the photograph just for old times sake? How terribly romantic. Let me see it."

He shook his head, "I got rid of the thing." He didn't say how.

"That's too bad." Swinging her legs down, she slipped off the bed. "I guess Slater's interested on account of Dad."

"Your father? You mean Slater works for Kim?"

"That's what he said. You know Dad, he has more spies on his payroll than Himmler."

"A regular one man Klu Klux Klan," Munro agreed sourly. He was trying not to think about her body, the way her breasts moved under the gown.

"He always liked you though." Stepping close, she put her arms on his shoulders, "You're not very gallant, darling. Aren't you going to kiss me?"

Her lips were parted expectantly. He could smell the familiar perfume in her hair and the fear of old ghosts knotted in his stomach as her green eyes stared darkening into his own. His arms seemed to slip around her waist of their own accord and he felt the warmth of her flesh beneath the flimsy silk.

No, he wanted to say, no this is all wrong, but the words did not

140

seem to come. His mouth covered hers, crushing her lips fiercely against his own. "Oh, Max," she shivered and tightened her arms. His hands caressed her flanks, sliding up inside the robe to cup her breast. The nipple was hard with desire.

With a sudden laugh she jerked free, "Uh uh, that's enough, Max. I have a fiancé, remember."

He stared at her, breathing hard. "You bitch!" he swore softly. "You cunning little bitch!"

"I've a fiancé remember." Her parting laugh still taunted him as mechanically he collected up his belongings and chucked them in the closet. Goddam all women! Well, he wouldn't fall for that again. She could save her tricks for her Spanish fancy boy.

He showered and put on a bath robe, then picked up the telephone, "I want an alarm call for tomorrow, six thirty."

"Si, senor. Buenas noches."

A mosquito net enclosed the bed in a muslin tent. He was about to get in when there came a soft tap at the door. Hell, now what? Irritably he flung it open.

A silver lamé dress shimmered in the passage. Lola Montez.

He awoke with a start in the darkness. The fan was clicking overhead. Stretching out a hand he felt for the girl. The love-making had done him good. A fierce, hot, biting, writhing, sweating, primitive battle.

The bed was empty.

He peered through the mosquito net. Naked, she was stooped over the pile of clothes on the chair, feeling through the pockets of his uniform.

He switched on the lamp and she jumped back blinking in the light. "*Madre mia*, you startled me. I was looking for a cigarette."

"Try these!" he tossed her the packet from the bedside table. She caught them against her breasts.

"Please, I did not mean you any harm, I swear."

"Shut up!" he told her harshly, climbing out of bed. "Who sent you?"

"No one, I . . . I need money . . . I didn't think you would notice," she stammered.

He hit her. Once. Not hard, with the open palm. She began to cry.

"Now tell me the truth. Who sent you, Santos?"

She bit her sluttish lip and nodded. Santos, he thought, my old pal

141

Captain Santos. Whose side was he on?

He picked up the silver gown and threw it at her. "Scram, darling!"

TWO AM. The darkest part of the night. Invisible in the angle of a wall where the shadows lay deepest, the Japanese crouched, ears tuned to the minutest noise, mouth open slightly to increase the hearing range. About him all was still, only the tree frogs kept up their musical piping. Deliberately he concentrated on the sound, imprinting the pattern on his mind so that the slightest alteration in rhythm would act as a warning.

An iron drain pipe ran to the roof of the side wing. Gripping with hands and feet he swarmed upwards, noiseless as a climbing snake and deadlier, his ink black clothes and hood blending with the darkness.

Reaching the gutter he froze, motionless against the wall, *haragei* probing the shadows. Somewhere down in the gardens a bird shrieked once and was silent. Uncoiling his grapnel one-handed, he sent the cloth-wrapped hook flying up to lodge on the parapet of the corner tower. Fifty feet above the ground he pushed out with his feet, supported only by the slim cord of plaited hair, and swung across the gap to the penthouse balcony.

He landed noiselessly, ducking out of sight below the stone balustrade. A curved blade slid into his hand ready. No room here for swordplay. Not a sound disturbed the stillness. His eyes scanned the darkened balcony. *The doors here lead to the General's formal dining room,* they had told him, *his Gold Room, he calls it.*

Cautiously he tried the nearest handles. *Doors inside the penthouse are never locked. There are no guards, not even a dog.* A draught of cold air struck him as he eased the metal framed door open. *I-ye!* He had been warned too about the air conditioning, even so the temperature drop made him shiver momentarily.

It was darker inside. The long table stretched away into blackness flanked by chairs. Faint outlines of gilt framed mirrors and oil paintings. He wedged the door ajar as an escape route and waited a minute to adjust his eyes. Then soundlessly he crept inwards.

The air conditioning hummed in his ears as he entered the reception hall. Glass cases gleamed before the elevator. *MacArthur's gold Field Marshall's baton, his medals and stars are displayed in this room.*

Excitement gripped him. This was the heart of the enemy's headquarters. He fought it down and paused to reorientate. Opposite to the right lay the main drawing room. To the left was the General's

142

library. Ahead, down a corridor running the length of the apartment, were the seven family bedrooms.

You will find your victim in the fourth sleeping chamber.

One door was not quite shut. A faint glow came from within. Stealthily the Japanese put an eye to the crack. Inside a boy lay asleep, a night-light candle guttering in a saucer of water. He watched for several moments, then silently moved on.

The fourth chamber.

He thrust the knife back in his sash. *It is of the utmost importance there be no trace of a killing.* He would use a pillow. Pressed down over a sleeping victim's mouth it brought unconsciousness within seconds, death in little more.

Gently he turned the handle. The door swung open.

Then it came.

He froze, muscles tensed, adrenalin coursing in his veins, frantically straining his ears to isolate the sound from the background hum of machinery. *I-ye*, there it was again! A whistle. Faint, far off, high-pitched beyond the range of normal human hearing. The recall signal.

By the Buddha! So close. Another minute and the mission would be accomplished. And yet his discipline did not falter even for a moment. Leaving the door, he ran fleet-footed and silent back to the balcony, hooked his cord to the stone balustrade and launched himself downwards into the night.

Scott stirred. Someone was calling her name, "Mis' Scott! Mis' Scott!"

"Tad! Is that you?" Throwing off the sheet, she pulled on a dressing gown over her pyjamas and unlocked the door. The young steward slipped quickly inside. "For God's sake, where have you been?"

"Hush, not so loud, Mis' Scott," he whispered urgently, "I was scared, there's things going on, bad things. I think maybe you the only one trust me."

"Tad, don't be silly, we all . . ." she broke off. Footsteps were coming up the passage. Men, several of them, bearing something heavy. There was a murmur of voices as they tramped past the door. She recognised Jordan's among them, he sounded angry. They faded off down the passage and the elevator clanged shut.

Gotto cracked the door open a fraction and peered out. "It's okay," he whispered, "they gone."

"Who were they? What was it they were carrying?"

143

"Major Slater an' a bunch of soldiers. They're bringing out the coffin."

"The coffin! You mean Jordan has it here? In the hotel?"

"Yeah, only now I hear 'em say they taking it out to Clark Field."

Scott stared at him in the darkness, "*Tad, what is this all about?*"

★   ★   ★

Hongkong. Shamshuipo Police Station. Three a.m.

"*Ai-yah, dunk the fornicator again!*"

"No, wait . . . ARGH!!"

The prisoner's scream choked off abruptly as the two Chinese constables forced his head down into the tub. The water frothed and bubbled. He struggled frantically for several seconds, then went limp. Colonel Huang stood by impassively. Inspector Playfair sat at a desk watching with an expression of distate. They were questioning the man taken at Kai Tak.

At a signal from the Colonel the constables hauled the prisoner up again coughing. He collapsed to the floor, stomach heaving, liquid gushing from mouth and nose.

"*Oh ko,*" Huang stared down at him scornfully, "answer quickly, *heya*, why were you at the airport?"

The naked man sucked air into his lungs in long whooping gasps, "I . . . I told you . . . to check on the cargo . . ."

"That is not all. There was another reason, *heya*? You had an agent aboard the Clipper."

"AIEE! Yes, an agent."

"Whose? The Sea Devils'?"

The prisoner nodded weakly from the pools on the floor.

"His name, dunghead!"

"I wasn't told, by the gods!"

"Stinking liar! You were sent to watch him safe aboard. His name – before we drown you in your own vomit!"

"I wasn't told, I swear it! Just to report if anyone was stopped . . . AARGH!"

"That'll do, Colonel," Playfair interrupted. "Bring him over here," he snapped to the constables. Groaning, the man was dragged to a hard chair in front of the desk. Playfair turned a lamp on his dripping face. "Now, we'll leave the airport for a minute, I want to talk about the priest. The priest, eh?" he rapped. The man's eyes gazed at him dulled with the extremity of exhaustion. "The *quai loh* murdered here two nights ago. Why was he killed?"

144

". . . *Kokuryu-kai* . . . they ordered it."

"Why? For what reason?"

A pause. "The plan . . . in danger."

"What plan?"

A feeble shake of the head.

"How was it in danger then?"

"He . . . he knew . . ."

"What? Who?" Playfair's voice sharpened. "The Jap agent?"

Silence.

"*Ai-yah*, throw some water over the fornicator!"

A pail was brought. The prisoner remained unconscious. Playfair felt his pulse. "Damn!" he snapped, frustrated. "Just as we were getting somewhere."

"He is faking!" Huang clicked his fingers. Another bucket of water was thrown over the man.

"It's no use. Take him back to the cells," Playfair dismissed them. "Have the doctor attend to him. I don't want the bugger dying on us."

He watched the limp body dragged out and yawned wearily, "Tough little bastard but he knows something alright. We'll start again in the morning, Colonel."

"*Ai-yah*," Huang's eyes were like chips of obsidian glass, "tomorrow he will break!"

An hour later the station was quiet. In the detention block at the rear the sergeant on night duty dozed at his desk. "*Oh ko*, wake up, dog." The sergeant's eyes jerked open. A Chinese stood before him dressed like a sweeper. "See!"

The sergeant shivered nervously as he recognised the chrysanthemum button in the man's palm. As arranged there was no one else present on the wing. Without speaking, he selected a key from the chain at his waist and unlocked one of the steel cell doors.

The figure on the plank bed inside shrank back against the wall as they entered. "Ssh, we are friends, *heya*?" the sergeant hissed. A gasp of hope broke from the drenched prisoner, a gasp which changed suddenly to a whimper of fear as he was seized in an iron grip. Brutal fingers clasped his jaw, prising it open, and a hard pellet of glass was forced between his lips.

"*Ai-yah*, hold him tight!" the cleaner spat, clamping his mouth shut again with both hands to crush the capsule. "Fornicating poison takes time to work!"

145

XI

THURSDAY DECEMBER 4th. Dawn was stealing into the sky over Luzon. In the pale grey of the heavens the stars were fading and a rosy satin flush stained the eastern horizon. Slowly the flaming disc rose above the mist-shrouded mountains. It touched with fire the jungle-covered ridges and the terraced rice paddies and sent warm shafts of light sliding down the green valleys. Splashes of crimson and gold tinged the palm thickets and dense groves of mahogany and bamboo. On the primitive grass air strip the fighter planes glistened with dew.

The calm was illusory. In a radar hut atop a nearby hill, specialists on watch anxiously studied a pattern of white blips that pulsed on their screens, growing stronger with each sweep of the circling beam. Unidentified aircraft heading in from across the South China Sea. An officer dialled Fighter Control at Nichols Field, ninety miles to the rear, and spoke urgently to the duty commander. Even as he did so alarm klaxons were shattering the peace outside.

Within minutes the early morning air was vibrating to the splutter of Allison radials and blue exhaust fumes were drifting across the dispersal as the Kittyhawks taxied out, the downdraught of their props blasting dust over the crouching ground crews. The earth shook beneath the roar of noise as pilot after pilot gunned his motor then launched his stubby craft screaming up the strip. The young sun glinting redly on their wings, the metal specks wheeled away towards the northern horizon.

In vain. Already the radar trace was fading. From thirty thousand feet the intruders had spotted the fighters scrambling to intercept them and were turning back. By the time the Americans reached their position the skies would be empty.

SIX AM. In the shadow of Bataan's jungle-matted volcanoes an ancient Ford car bucketed slowly along a rutted track in the direction

146

of Manila. The scenery was brilliantly exotic: towering mahogany trees, tortured banyans hung with liana vines, forests of bamboo, acacia, coconut palm, yellow Spanish Flag and spear-bladed *alang* grass, waterfalls cascading through canyon walls in misty rainbows. The two men in the back seat lost in thought. They were Americans, priests from the Maryknoll Mission at Bagnac.

"What's this place, Pilar?" asked the junior of the two, a husky young man in glasses, as they entered a native *barrio*.

"No, sah, Pilar coupla mile up. We hit de highway den, go quicker," the driver tooted his horn impatiently at a buffalo cart.

"Phew, sure is hot already," the priest removed his glasses for a moment to mop his face.

The older man was gazing out of the window still. "See that?" he pointed. "The opposition's here too." Beneath a giant rubber tree shading the crossroads stood a figure in the unmistakable saffron robe of a Buddhist monk.

His companion nodded, "They're everywhere nowadays, in the towns, up in the hills, all over. Walsh writes from Zamboanga more come in on every steamer."

"That's the first one I remember carrying a staff."

Jolting on out of the village, the Ford was waved down at a bend by a band of workmen. The driver spoke to them in Tagalog. "Dey say big tree down, block de road," he announced, putting the car into reverse and turning off onto a narrow side track, "dis way take us roun'."

"There was another of those monks with them," muttered the old man half to himself.

The new track was thickly overgrown. After a while the passengers became concerned, "Vicente, you think those guys knew where they were sending us?" Just then the car stopped, they had reached a stream among the trees. The driver swore. He was preparing to back up again when there came a cry from the rear. Out of the bush had emerged more of the yellow monks.

"Hey! What d'you think you're doing?" the young man shouted as they were dragged from the vehicle, "Take your filthy hands off! I'm Dr. Bell of the Bagnac Mission and this is Father Carmichael . . . *Oh my God!*" Vicente staggered round the front of the car, blood welling up between his fingers as he clutched at his belly in agony. A foot long shaft of steel impaled him through the back like a monstrous skewer. His legs buckled and he crumpled tiredly to the ground. Grinning, his killer tugged the blade free.

"*Vicente!*" With a cry the priest tore himself free from his attackers.

147

Before he could reach the dead man a savage blow from behind smashed him to his knees. Sick and dizzy, he struggled to rise. Another of the monks clubbed him brutally across the face.

"*Shimai*! Enough!" a voice commanded in Japanese. At once rough hands seized the semi-conscious Americans and dragging them to a nearby clearing in the bush spread-eagled them on their backs across a fallen trunk.

"Dr. Bell," the leader smiled grimly down. His shaven skull gave him an air of grotesque cruelty. His sword glittered in the sun as he tapped the blade lightly against his victim's arm. "Dr. Bell, where is coffin?"

"Coffin? What coffin? You savages, you murdered . . . *Aargh*!" The priest thrashed in pain. With shocked disbelief he gazed at his right hand, the fingers bloody stumps severed at the knuckles. The men pinning him chuckled.

"Coffin of Bishop Buchan, *neh*? Last night take from hotel, *neh*? Where?"

"Please . . . Jordan has the coffin . . . I don't know anything . . ." Another shriek. The left hand this time.

The leader placed the dripping point on the American's cheek just below the eye. "Better you tell, Yank," he said seriously. "Where is coffin?"

"Please," the priest whimpered, "please, I don't understand . . . Why are you doing this . . . why . . .?"

The monk sighed, disappointed. He pressed the blade forward.

Screams filled the clearing.

In the Manila Hotel the day's work was beginning. With a jaunty smile a young thin-faced Chinese sauntered in at the staff entrance. "So sorry, bus delayed, army convoy."

"Charlie Wu, six minutes late," the clerk grunted sourly. "Fined two pesos."

Ai-yah, go fornicate in your mother's dung! the youth said to himself sullenly. His heart froze in his chest as the half-caste Police Captain appeared behind the clerk. "Wu," the man grunted, studying the card, "Chinese, huh? What section?"

Wu gawped at him. "He works in the laundry," the clerk said. The cop stared at the youth for a moment, his gaze chilling behind the dark glasses, then with a jerk of the head dismissed him.

Aiee, that was a near one, Wu trembled as he made for the wash-house. Fornicate all blackface barbarians! He changed into his

148

white jacket and rode the service lift to the fourth floor with a hamper of clean linen. Nodding casually to the guard on duty in the passage, he carried his burden to the houseboy's pantry.

It was empty. Good. On a shelf lay the bundle of morning newspapers for the guest rooms. He dumped the hamper and began leafing swiftly through them. It took him only a moment to find the one he sought, a popular Chinese language daily. With a fountain pen he drew a neat ring in red ink around a paragraph in the classified section.

Oh ko, he chuckled happily as he replaced the paper in the pile and let himself out. How the Northerners would curse and fart when they read the greetings from the Red Pang!

On the same floor Yu-Ling awoke and opened her shutters. Sun streamed in and a murmur of waves on the salt breeze. The bay was smooth and bright as glass. On the horizon two ragged volcanic peaks rose from a sea of smoking mist.

Hail Mary, Mother of God, pray for us now and at the hour of our death. Poor Simon Ho. Terrible to die so suddenly, so far from home. *Joss.* Gods are gods, she thought sadly. Last night she had burned incense in the suite and hung a mirror on the door to turn away the dead man's spirit should it try to return. *Hail Mary Mother and Joseph, bless Honourable Uncle and make him well*, she prayed fervently, afraid suddenly for the future.

She bathed and dressed quickly, then knelt on the floor with her yarrow stalks. Perhaps the oracle held an answer.

Dividing the forty-nine stalks at random into two bundles, she picked one from the right hand pile. Turning to the second pile, she proceeded to discard stalks, four at a time, till only one remained which she added to that in her hand. Then she did likewise to the first pile and this time was left with three stalks, making a total of five which she placed separately.

Continuing the selection twice more with the discarded stalks yielded two handfuls of eight each. She now had the first line of her oracle: 5–8–8–; a *yang* line.

Six times in all she repeated the process till the oracle was complete. It had five *yang* lines and one *yin*. On consulting her chart she read this was the tenth hexagram of *Lü*, known as The Treading, composed of the trigrams *Ch'ien*, Heaven and *Tui*, the Lake.

"*He treads on the tail of the Tiger, but it bites him not.*"

149

SEVEN AM. The Pontiac was waiting by the front steps as Munro came down in britches and riding boots. The hotel mechanic was running a wash leather over the windshield.

"She's looking great, Emilio," he slipped him ten pesos. "Here, treat your girl at the carnival tonight." He was climbing in when a shout stopped him.

"Munro, wait a minute!" It was Bob Cashin tumbling down the steps, bow tie askew, "Are you off somewhere? When can we talk?"

"I'm driving out to the polo club for some ball practice. Come along for the ride if you want."

"Thanks," the journalist scrambled in next to him. With a wave to Emilio, Munro pressed the starter. As they swept out of the driveway he had a momentary glimpse in the rear view mirror of a uniformed figure watching from the portico. Sunglasses. Captain Santos.

Mansions in secluded gardens and stately villas lined the long seafront. The High Commissioner's Residence, the Army and Navy Club, the Moorish castle of an eccentric millionaire, embassies and consulates, their white stucco facades gazing serenely out across the bay towards Corregidor.

"Simon Ho wasn't drunk last night," Cashin yelled above the engine as they sped along the boulevard. "And he wasn't a communist, whatever Hollington Soong claims."

"You think someone pushed him off that balcony?"

"I don't know but I'll tell you this, he was scared half out of his mind."

"Scared of who – the Japs?" A carriage swerved across the road and Munro slammed his fist on the horn.

"According to Simon, the Chinese are flying their gold reserves out to the States to help finance the war. Is that true? Is that why the Japs tried to stop the plane yesterday?"

Munro ducked the questions. Journalists were all the same when they got the scent of a story. Like terriers after a rat.

They left the suburbs, accelerating out on the Makati road heading for the polo club. As they entered the first *barrio* Munro glanced back. A motor cycle had tucked in behind and was trailing along in his dusty wake making no attempt to pass. The rider wore goggles and a leather helmet over some kind of yellow habit. Each time Munro looked he was still there.

Breakfast at the hotel was served outside on the terrace. It had rained during the night and the gardens smelled clean and newly washed.

The vivid green foliage was splashed with riotous colour, pools of water lilies sparkled in beds of lush ferns and huge iridescent butterflies fluttered amongst cascading blossoms.

At the crew table Ross and Munro were absent. Tad Gotto had eaten earlier and left. Stewart Whitely sat with a copy of the Manila *Daily News*, "Just look at that," he exclaimed disgustedly, "not a mention of the accident here last night."

"The hotel probably fixed to have it played down, bad for business," Shapiro scooped at a fresh papaya. He was wearing slacks and a Hawaiian shirt.

"If it was an accident," Stewart hinted darkly.

"The medics said so, didn't they?"

"Some coincidence then."

"Wonder what the Skipper means to do."

Thyssen gave a sniff, "When he sobers up."

There was an embarrassed silence. The junior crew members avoided his eye. Thyssen scowled, "No need to look so darn shocked, we all know he was soused last night."

The Chief raised his head from his plate, "You spoken to Ross?" he asked in his bearlike rumble.

Thyssen went pink at the neck, "No."

"Seen the First then?"

"You know darn well I haven't. I mean he ain't here, is he?"

"Then keep your big yap shut," the Chief told him bluntly.

In a corner of the terrace Reverend Jordan was breakfasting with the Gordon Smythes. Conversation was largely taken up by Cynthia, furious not to have received an invitation to the Presidential gala.

"It's an insult, they say the Chinese party have all been asked!"

"My dear, Hollington Soong is a government minister," her husband pointed out. He wore a blue blazer with a gold embroidered crest and a silk cravat. "Anyway after what happened last night I hardly think it likely they will accept."

"That's entirely by the way," his wife snapped. "You must get onto the Consulate at once and have our names added to the list." She looked up, "Ah, here's Mr. Wirth."

"Morning folks, Felicity," the Lend-Lease man greeted them, beaming. "How you keeping, Reverend? Say, I didn't know we shared a hobby." The priest blinked at him. "I mean photography," he pointed to the camera in its case by Jordan's elbow, "Leica, huh? Sure wish I could afford one of those." He stretched out a hand.

"Please do not touch!" Jordan said sharply, moving it out of reach.

"Gee, I'm sorry, I was only interested," Wirth looked hurt. The man was staring at him like a thief. "You're mighty lucky having a Leica," he said lamely.

The Priest's fingers gripped the leather case. "I am sorry, it . . . it was a gift . . . from the Bishop," he stammered, getting awkwardly to his feet. "Please excuse me."

Scott had finished her breakfast and was throwing fruit to some of the half-tame monkeys that roamed the park when Ross finally showed up.

"Hi, Skipper," she greeted him with a sunny smile, "you want some coffee? There's fresh in the pot here." His appearance shocked her. Ross's face was grey and haggard with fatigue. He looked as if he'd been on an all night jag and she could almost smell the liquor on him.

He gave her a barely civil grunt of acknowledgement, "Where the hell's the First?"

"Max drove up to the Polo Club for some practice before the match," Stewart Whitely volunteered. "Said to tell you he'd go on to Cavite afterwards."

Ross glared. His eyes were sunken and suspicious as if he guessed the unspoken accusation now in all their minds. "Then the rest of you get moving too. I want all systems aboard checked through. We're pulling out of here as of midnight tonight."

Their jaws dropped. "Gee, Skipper," Shapiro gaped at him, "but I thought we had today free. Chris and I were planning a picnic with our girls up at Lake Taal."

Ross ignored him. "We leave in fifteen minutes. Whitely, you and Klein be sure to bring your logbooks. The Navy want to hear about those signals you picked up."

"Yessir," Stewart responded, jumping to his feet.

"Thyssen, wait behind. I want a word with you."

Kurt paled, "Skipper," he spluttered, "what I said, I . . ."

But Ross wasn't attending. Scott had got up with the others. He waved her back, "Not you," he said curtly, "you're not needed."

She was bewildered, "But, Skipper, Pat will want . . ."

He turned on her crushingly, "O'Byrne can manage, he has Gotto to help him. So far as I'm concerned, Miss Scott, *you're just a passenger on this voyage.*"

152

Slater and Sir Ambrose Hope were breakfasting in the Champagne Room. Alone. Theirs was the only occupied table. The waiters understood they were on no account to be disturbed.

"This is all Playfair was able to come up with?" Slater was sifting through a file. "Gordon Smythe – suspected tax evasion. Prince Cherkassy – nothing known; Captain Ross . . ." He looked up, "Not a goddam thing to go on."

"Nevertheless, someone among them . . ." Sir Ambrose let the suggestion hang.

"Let's get this straight," Slater sprinkled sugar on his grapefruit and began to eat. "You're saying British Intelligence think the Axis have a man aboard the Clipper, correct?"

"A man – or a woman," Sir Ambrose wiped his moustache carefully. He liked to start the day properly with Scot's porridge oats and bacon and eggs, washed down with a jug of Buck's Fizz. "Three days ago, Major, London intercepted a signal from the *joho kyoku* in Tokyo to Ampt V1 of the RSHA, Berlin."

"So the Nazis and the Yellow-bellies are allies, what else is new?"

From a locked dispatch case on the floor beside him, Sir Ambrose extracted a brown folder. "This is a translation of the intercept. It confirms that an agent recruited through the *German-Amerika Bund* recently underwent training at the spy-school in Shanghai for a special mission during the first week of December."

Slater scanned the contents of the folder, "There's no mention of the Clipper."

"The message is flagged for the attention of the Director of SS Technical Research," the old man watched him closely. He was taking a risk, breaching security to obtain the American's cooperation, "It all fits, Major."

Slater stared at the flimsy again, "Maybe, maybe not," he passed it back and shrugged. "It's unimportant anyway; the cargo was flown out of here last night on an Army bomber."

In silence Sir Ambrose reached for the jug to pour himself another glass of champagne and orange juice. Through the windows he could hear the splashing of swimmers in the pool. Overhead the fans whirred creaking. "There's still Latouche, Major," he said quietly. He saw Slater's expression freeze and knew that he had touched the mark, "We've read his file, we know all about him. *And so do the Nazis!*"

Down by the swimming pool Tad Gotto dipped a finger in the water as he passed. Pity there wasn't time to take a swim. He hurried towards the locker room. Sounds of hammering within. Workmen were busy already, repairing last night's damage.

"Think I left my shorts in here. Okay if I take a look?" he asked the Filipino foreman.

One of the locker units was too badly beaten up to be fixed. Tad stood back to let the men carry it outside. A couple of others were in a mess too with fist-sized holes smashed in the wood. He measured a panel against his thumb and whistled softly, it must be all of an inch thick. Munro had said his attacker was unarmed, what kind of a guy could punch through solid mahogany?

Down the far end they were replacing the window. The intruder had flung a stool through it to make his escape. Afterwards the cops had searched the gardens, they hadn't found a footprint even.

He stepped closer, broken glass crunching under his shoes. Suddenly his gaze sharpened. Threads of cloth had snagged on the bottom of the frame. Carefully he picked them out. Coarse black cotton.

Behind him, an ill-tempered voice shouted to the workmen in Spanish. Wrapping his find quickly in a handkerchief, Tad turned to leave.

"*Nombre de Dios*! What are you doing in here?" Captain Santos snarled at him. "Get out, little snooper, or you'll be in trouble, *comprende*?"

Upstairs in his bedroom Hollington Soong was having a massage when Feng burst in without knocking. "*Aiee*, see this!" he thrust the newspaper under Soong's nose.

The Minister gasped, clutching a towel round his pudgy body. "Out! Out! Get out of here, whore, we want to be alone!" he pushed the pretty little masseuse into the passage. "*The Pang*! All gods bear witness, that fornicator Huang, he swore to me on his ancestors the Pang would never discover, *never*!"

"*Oh ko*, we must tell the *quai loh*, demand protection, *heya*?"

"*Dew neh loh moh*, don't be a fool!" Soong shouted back. All gods curse filthy murdering gangsters! He had almost burst a vein at the sight of the red-ringed message. *Hollington Soong will pay, he and all his generations*! No appeal, no mercy, only the inevitability of death as certain as a court sentence. *He and all his generations*. Everyone of his blood, from the littlest child to the greybeard on his deathbed, the innocent along with the guilty, strangled, knifed, poisoned. Then at last they would come for him and his line would be ended for ever.

Ai-yah, the Devil-Box!

In the penthouse the telephone rang.

"I'll take it in the library." Pushing back her hair, Georgiana came in from the main terrace of the palatial MacArthur residence. She wore green beach pyjamas and the polished floor was cool under her bare feet.

"Georgiana?" It was Colonel Nieto speaking, "*Querida*, you owe me one, as you say in your country."

"Manuel, you're a darling! You fixed it?"

"Yes, it is all arranged. Your Maxwell Munro will be playing today for the Scouts."

"Bless you, Manuel, you've earned yourself a great big kiss."

Replacing the receiver, she dialled the number of the Santa Cruz mansion in Malate.

"*César darling*, such lovely flowers and after the way I behaved last night! You are adorable . . . No, truly you are . . . Well, it's sweet of you to say so and I promise to be good in future. Listen, darling, I was going to ask, are you playing polo this afternoon against the Scouts . . .?"

Humming a little tune, she went skipping back out through the dining room onto the family terrace. Beneath an awning sat a petite vivacious woman, dark-haired in a white dress and native sandals, Jean MacArthur.

"Georgie, honey," she smiled. "You're looking mischievous. What have you been up to?"

At the polo club a score of ponies were being exercised in the cool of the morning. Munro parked the Pontiac beneath a giant rubber tree that shaded the entrance to the stables and went to find a groom.

They led out the Gypsy for him, a flea-bitten grey who looked nothing beside the prize arabs but had the cleanest legs that ever a pony owned. Munro patted his neck and took him for a short canter round the pitch, then settled down with a stick and a practice ball to get his eye in.

Forehand, backhand, off-side, near-side, under-the-neck. Up and down the short green turf they chased, the pony's hooves drumming in the dew, the ball smacking sweetly against his stick.

Livebait! What better target to tempt an enemy than a cargo of bullion? And the Japanese had taken the hook. Could Simon Ho have been murdered because he had guessed the truth?

His shoulder was stiff and sore still from the battering last night. It hurt like hell on the follow through. Exercise would put that right. He swung again, driving the ball towards the far goal posts. The Gypsy snorted and pricked his ears, responsive to the slightest pressure of his calves.

The journalist was guessing. He hadn't seen the cargo. For Christsakes what was in those crates? It sure as hell wasn't bullion.

He walked the pony back on a loose rein and watched to make sure they gave him a good rub down before rejoining Cashin at the car.

The day was growing hot already as he turned the Pontiac's nose homeward again and the jungle beside the road steamed in the sun. Natives in bright loincloths worked the sugarcane fields, swinging *bolo* knives. Traffic was light up here still, creaking bullock carts and the occasional military truck roaring past in a cloud of dust.

"Bob, do you think Soong knows more than he's telling?"

"I'd bet on it. Simon claimed he had done some kind of deal with the Japs, he thought it involved the Chens."

"A Kuomintang minister working for the Japs?"

"That wouldn't bother Soong. The Chinese have a different attitude towards treason. But my guess is he's playing his own game."

They were approaching the brow of a hill. Ahead lay a double chicane bend then the road opened out again into a long straight between coconut groves. As they crested the rise a figure in yellow waved from a bank. The first of the bends was coming up, Munro dropped a gear and spun the wheel over. The Pontiac took the corner with a squeal of rubber and he caught her smartly as the rear end broke away.

He jabbed the throttle and the revolutions climbed. The car steadied as he lined up for the next curve. A cyclist swerved to avoid them as they rocketed past close to the ditch. Hard over again. Another squeal of protest from the tyres. Catch her once more. The last corner flashed by and the road lay open ahead, straight between ditches and empty for a mile, the palms overhead waving in the breeze. Exhilarated, he pushed the speed up. Seventy, seventy-five, eighty . . .

Maybe it was a flash of colour that alerted him. A glint of yellow in a thorn thicket to the left that caught his eye scant seconds before the trap sprung.

"*Get down!*" There was no time to brake. With a bang like a cannon shell the windshield exploded in a million fragments. There was a monstrous twang. The Pontiac rocked and something struck Munro across the shoulders. He wrenched at the wheel, rubber screeching as the tyres skidded out of control.

156

The ditches either side would stop a tank. He pumped the brakes as the car slewed terrifyingly towards the nearside with the back wheels locked and sliding. The windshield was gone, the glass shattered and the frame smashed back flat. Gritting his teeth, he steered into the skid. He heard a tyre go and they bucketed furiously among some loose scree on the road edge. For what seemed an eternity the car careered along on the lip of the ditch, then somehow miraculously he had control again and they were slowing.

"*Jee-sus!* What in the world was that?" Cashin gasped shakily, poking his head out from under the dash as they pulled up. "Did we hit something?"

Munro wiped the dirt and glass from his face with a sleeve. There was blood on his hands from a dozen scratches. He stared back over his shoulder. The thicket behind was obscured by a cloud of dust. Scrambling away up the hill was a yellow figure.

"What the hell happened?" Cashin repeated, straightening his glasses. "One moment we were driving along an empty road and the next, *boom*, all of a sudden I'm under the seat!"

Munro switched off the engine and climbed out. Stiffly he walked back towards the scene of the accident. In the dirt lay a twisted length of steel cable. He pulled it out. One end was frayed where it had snapped, the other attached to the trunk of a tree four feet from the ground. The rest would be in the far ditch.

"What have you found?" Cashin came up.

Munro showed him, "Quarter inch cable, probably a stay from a pylon. Some joker hacked it down and strung a length across the road. Impossible to see almost. Darn near took our heads off."

He looked up. The yellow figure had vanished. Along the road was coming a military convoy. He stepped out to flag down the lead truck.

Cashin was staring mesmerised at the killer wire. "Sweet Jesus Christ," he croaked hoarsely, "which one of us were they trying to get?"

XII

It was going to be another hot day. After breakfast Ruth Simms decided to postpone the rest of her packing and take the children to the beach. It would be their last chance, poor little things.

They set off through the lush gardens Teresita, the *yaya*, carrying the basket with the towels, the children clutching buckets and shrimping nets. The air was steamy, scented with frangipani and magnolia. Ricky plucked three dew-beaded pink orchids, gave one each to the girls and put the other behind his ear. Ruth and Teresita laughed as they watched them run across the grass.

A reek of woodsmoke reached them. Round a clump of green banana plants they encountered the gardener. "Hi, Ishido!" Ricky shouted, but the little Japanese vanished into a stand of bamboo.

"Where's the bonfire?" said Paula, the older of the two girls. "Oh, it's next door."

The smoke was curling up from the neighbouring compound. Peering through a gap in the fence, they saw flames crackling merrily in an incinerator.

"Gee whizz, look at all the papers those men are throwing on," Ricky whispered, "boxes and boxes. What are they doing it for, Mrs. Simms?"

"I'm not sure. Who lives there, Teresita, do you know?"

The *yaya*'s round Visayan face broke out in smiles. "Very nice people," she said earnestly, "Japanese, from Embassy in town."

Ruth felt suddenly sick.

"Now don't fret yourself about what Ross said. Sure he doesn't mean the half of it. You'll see."

So Pat O'Byrne had counselled Scott after she left the terrace.

"But Pat, what can I do? He's determined to throw me off the ship. When we get back to the States I'm finished with the Company."

"Listen to the girl! D'you think the management are a bunch of idjits? They know Ross and the other old-timers can't abide females on their flights. It's me they'll want to hear from," the Irishman's eyes twinkled, "and I shall tell 'em straight, you're the best thing that's happened to this ship since she was launched."

"Oh Pat, that's not true, but you are kind."

A party of passengers passed them in the lobby with smiles. "See that?" Pat jerked his head. "You're good for business, girl, and that's what counts with the bosses. They'll tell Ross to go to blazes. And so they should," he added, pursing his lips, "the way he's behaving hisself just now."

Scott's brow furrowed again, "It's not only me, Pat, is it? He's in trouble, I wish there was something we could do to help."

The airport bus drew up outside with a beep of its horn. They watched Ross climb in, carrying his flight bag. He must have vacated his room already. The Steward shook his head with a sigh, "He's not a man to take help from anyone, that's his problem."

Damage to the Pontiac was superficial, a front tyre shredded and the interior full of smashed glass from the windshield. Even so it was after nine by the time the wheel had been changed and Munro and Cashin were on their way again.

Back at the hotel garage, the car's battered appearance caused comment. "Do what you can, Emilio," Munro told the dismayed mechanic. "The windshield surround is shot to hell. I'll speak with Chief Crow and see if we can have the workshops at Cavite make us a replacement."

"*Madre mia*! You lucky you ain't dead, Mr. Munro, never mind de car! Okay, leave with me, I fix up."

They washed off the blood and grime and went to report the incident. Slater was not to be found but Captain Santos was in the manager's office. He listened to their story sceptically. "Did you see anyone?"

"Only the joker in yellow on top of the hill. The convoy commander had a platoon search the bush but by then the Japs had scrammed."

"What makes you so certain they were Japanese?"

"For Christsakes, who else?"

"*Guerilleros* perhaps, there are still a few left who are impatient for freedom. Or it may have been children playing a game."

"*Children!*" Munro exploded, "Godammit, we could've been killed."

The policeman shrugged, "I will check it out anyway." He unclipped a gold Parker pen from his shirt pocket, "Call me on this number if anything else occurs. I will speak to Major Slater myself. In the meantime nothing has happened, *entendido?*"

"To hell with that bastard," Cashin said as they left the office. "I want to locate the hotel doctor, it could be he has more information on Simon's death."

If someone else hadn't gotten to him already, Munro thought. He nodded grimly, "I still have a hunch Oliver is the key to all this somehow. If we knew why he was murdered. . ."

"Any of the newspaper offices will have files on Bishop Buchan, there might be a mention of Oliver. I'll see what I can dig up."

Minutes later Munro was in a cab on his way out to Cavite.

Which of us were they trying to get?

Cashin, because of something Simon Ho had told him? Or Munro himself because . . .? Because of what? The photograph?

Maybe Bob would find the answer.

Yu-Ling stood with Latouche on the shaded balcony of the Soong suite, gazing out over the bay. "*Alors*, the island there that you can see is Corregidor, the American fortress guarding the bay, and beyond, those are the mountains of Bataan."

"How beautiful they seem, all purple and blue in the distance. There were no mountains in Macao, how I wish . . ." she sighed.

"What do you wish, *Mademoiselle?*"

"To stay a little while and climb the mountains," she laughed gaily for a moment then her face clouded, "but that is impossible I know."

As if in answer the window frames rattled and a dull boom echoed across the bay. Yu-Ling shivered, "*Ai-yah*, war is coming."

"Do not be afraid," the Doctor said softly. "It is only a practice still."

She looked up into his face, her dark eyes round, a child seeking reassurance, "The soldiers from the Golden Country, they will protect us against the Sea Devils, the Japanese, *heya?*"

He touched the soot black hair, moved by her trust, "With their lives, *petite*, with their lives," he answered, his spirit twisting inside him, knowing the Americans must kill her, himself, the old man, all three, rather than see them taken alive by the enemy.

In the drawing-room behind Professor Chen sat inscribing his journal. It was his custom each day to record thoughts and impressions of the previous twenty-four hours.

It is my intention to set down a record of the great jewel, the Empress's

Birthstone, lest the time come when memory of these matters grows dim. Something of the legend my third niece, Chen Yu-Ling, already knows; this then is the full story.

He paused to rest his brush hand and examine his work, taking pleasure in the blackness of the characters against the parchment.

The Duke of Chou, my father-in-law, was one of the true savants of his age. His fame was spread through many countries and he travelled far, even as a young man to the land of the Golden Mountain.

It was the encouragement of friends in the Golden Country that persuaded him finally to undertake his long planned expedition to the deserts of Siankiang. Since then many others have searched for the legendary 'living metal' without success. They believed that vast mines, once owned by the great Genghis Khan, lay hidden beneath the sands.

Though the Duke discouraged such speculation, he did not feel the time was yet right to lay his discoveries before the world. Unfortunately for him however news of his work had arleady reached the ears of the Dragon Empress.

The air throbbed again to a distant concussion. With a sigh the Professor laid down his brush. Guns, guns everywhere.

Flight list in hand, Scott knocked at Bob Cashin's door. She was checking personally with all the passengers in the hotel to make sure they understood the new departure arrangements. Ross's bark might be worse than his bite, she wasn't sure about that, but if somebody got left behind there would be hell to pay.

The door opened, "Hi, come on in," the journalist said. He was in shirtsleeves. "I'm just on the phone, I won't be a minute."

"No, lady," he went on, picking up the receiver again, "I'm not sick, I only want to speak with the doctor for a few minutes. What's that? Yeah, half an hour is fine. Where is that again?" He scribbled on a pad, "Okay thanks, 'bye."

"Sorry," he turned back smiling. "What can I do for you?"

Scott told him about the change to the schedule, "Our new departure time is midnight. The bus will leave the hotel at ten pm or if you prefer a taxi we ask you to check in at the Cavite terminal by eleven."

"We're leaving *tonight*?" the journalist blinked through his glasses at her. "This section isn't normally a night hop, is it?"

"No, that's true," Scott conceded, "I guess the Skipper feels he can make up lost time this way."

"So what time do we hit Guam then?"

"Approximately ten am depending on the winds. We'll know more when we have the flight plan."

Cashin was looking at her shrewdly, "This switch, does it have any connection with the attack on the plane yesterday?"

"No. At least I don't think so. I understand the Navy will be giving us an escort, though."

"None of the papers carried the story this morning, did you notice?" he scratched his head, frowning. "Sure is turning out one heck of a trip."

You could say that again, Scott thought to himself as she went next door to Reverend Jordan's room.

There was no answer to her knock and she was moving on to try the Soong suite when the door opened a crack. "Oh good morning, Reverend," she said turning back with a smile, "sorry to bother you but there's been a change to the schedule."

Wordlessly the priest stood aside to allow her into the room. He seemed ill-at-ease. A shabby, black bag lay on the bed, spartan amid the luxurious furnishings. It looked as if he were packed ready to leave anyway. "You don't have to check out till after dinner," she said, guessing probably everything the man owned in the world was inside that cheap bag, "the rooms are reserved through tonight."

He stared intently at her with his pale eyes. "I shall not be travelling with you," he interrupted her all at once. "I have decided to return to China."

"Oh, but I thought you and Major Slater . . ."

"Major Slater and I have parted company," a hard edge came into Jordan's voice, "last night he and his men came to take the Bishop's coffin away. They will not even tell me where it has been sent." He shrugged his gaunt shoulders, "They began by deceiving me, now they no longer trust me. I shall go back to China where at least I am needed."

He seemed less angry than lonely and afraid. Scott pitied him.

She let herself out and was moving on towards the Soong suite when the elevator clanged and Slater himself came hurrying up the passage at a near run. Without sparing her a glance, he rattled impatiently at Jordan's door. "Reverend, you in there, godammit?"

"Ye'll appreciate, Mr. Cashin, everything I'm telling you is speculative, highly speculative."

"Doctor Mackenzie, if I understand you right, you're suggesting Simon Ho was murdered."

The hotel medic was a dry-mannered Scotsman in his fifties with crinkly, grey hair. There was a print of Edinburgh Castle above the

162

examination couch and a faint smell of antiseptic.

Mackenzie took a pipe from a wooden rack on his desk and began to fill it, "Murder now, that's for a court to decide. And in any case you'd need a deal more evidence than I've found."

"You said an injury . . ."

"I'd hardly call it an injury. A wee bruise to the side of the neck. It might mean nothing at all."

"This bruising then, it couldn't have been caused by the fall?"

The doctor tamped down the tobacco in the pipe bowl and applied a match. "I assume, Mr. Cashin, you're familiar with the term strangulation?" The journalist nodded. "Three different methods," Mackenzie tapped them off on his fingers. "Pulmonary – choking of the air passage, Sanguinary – cutting of the blood supply, Nervous – caused by massive shock to amongst others, the Vagus Nerve."

Cashin was leaning forward intently, a frown of concentration on his boyish face. Through the open window came shouts of children playing by the swimming pool.

Mackenzie continued, "The Vagus Nerve runs down from the *medulla oblongata* to the sinus node of the right auricle. In other words, linking the brainstem and the heart." He paused and touched the left side of his neck, "It passes here alongside the trachea close to the surface. A very vulnerable spot as ye can imagine."

Cashin felt his throat go dry. "You've mentioned this to the authorities?"

The Scotsman took a long draw at his pipe. "I'd be wasting my breath," he said tersely. "Before you came in there was a call from the hospital morgue. The body was removed twenty minutes ago for cremation."

"The body's been cremated already? On whose orders?"

"Aye well, it's my understanding instructions were given by Minister Soong."

Scott had finished her list. There were no messages for her at the desk. Oh well, maybe she would take the chance to buy some Christmas presents in town, then cool off with a swim.

She fetched her purse from her room and returned to the lobby to come face to face with Georgiana, stepping out of the MacArthur elevator.

"Oh hi, Sally. I was hoping to run into you."

"Morning, Miss Delahaye." Her beauty was stunning by day as well. Lovely clothes again and a vast straw hat.

163

"I'd like to talk. Could we go somewhere?" She saw the purse. "Or were you just leaving?"

"I was going downtown, nothing that can't wait though."

"I have things to get too. Suppose we share a cab or a *calesa*? César has the car, I'm afraid."

"A *calesa* would be great, I love those horses."

"*Oi*! See, the Yankee red-hair!"

For as long as anyone could remember an elderly Japanese had run a flower stall under the trees by the entrance to the hotel driveway. His unfailing politeness made him a popular figure with guests.

"Quick," he hissed to the two small boys watering the plants, "one of you follow that *calesa*. Don't lose it on your life. The other find the *Osho-san* and warn him. *Isogi! Isogi!*"

"*Wakarimasu!*" the boys leapt onto bicycles. Pedalling hard the elder sped away for the Isabella Gate to *Intramuros* while his brother tucked in behind the blue painted horse carriage.

It was very pleasant in the *calesa*. A little awning shaded the girls from the sun. The driver tapped the horse's flank with his whip and they swayed along at a trot. Garish jitney buses weaved among the traffic honking furiously. On the tree-lined avenues the crowds were polyglot: Filipinos, Americans, Chinese, Spanish nuns, Moros in turbans and loose pants, old colonials in pith helmets, servicemen in uniform.

"*Mango, papaya – qué bonitos!*" At every corner vendors squatted on brightly coloured mats before mounds of ripening fruit. Crossing the river, there were rafts of green coconuts being guided downstream with the current, rice barges, houseboats and white painted inter-island steamers tied up at the piers.

"Have you seen Max this morning?" Georgiana asked.

"He went riding before I was up."

Georgiana tilted down the brim of her hat. Her skin was a perfect creamy white. She must burn easily in the sun. "He and I used to go together; I guess you know that?"

"It's been mentioned."

"I'll bet it was Stewart told you," Georgiana laughed lightly, "he's a regular gossip column." She shot Scott a quick look. "Did he also say why we split up?"

Scott shook her head, "I don't think he knows. Should he?"

"No, not really," Georgiana fanned herself. The shadow of the hat hid the expression in her eyes. "Matter of fact I'm not exactly certain myself."

The bells on the harness jingled as they rattled over the tramlines in the roadway. A heavily laden cart crossed ahead of them pulled by two patient wide-horned water buffalo.

"Do you find him attractive?" Georgiana asked suddenly.

"Who, Max?" Scott felt herself colouring. She wasn't sure where this conversation was leading. "Well, yes," she said reluctantly, "most women do I should think."

Georgiana nodded, "I used to reckon it was the uniform." She laughed again. Then abruptly she said, "Max is a very determined man, as you've probably realised."

"That can be a good thing in a pilot."

"Is that what you want to be too, a pilot?"

"I *am* a pilot. I'd like to captain a Clipper one day."

"That's important to you? More so than being a man's wife or the mother of his children?"

"I'm not sure," Scott answered slowly, "I suppose I hope I can be both one day. Amelia Earhart . . ." she stopped.

"Yes, Amelia," the other girl flashed a sad smile, "look where it got her."

Out at the Navy Yard the sun was scorching, heat bouncing off the whitewashed buildings like the walls of an oven. Sailors and Filipino dock workers swarmed everywhere preparing vessels for sea. Munro had the cab drive him down past the Marine barracks and the stuccoed Spanish Commandancia. Alongside the jetty a destroyer was taking on fuel. Further out three submarines clustered round a depot ship. A bat-winged PBY Catalina float plane had just touched down in a cloud of spray and was taxiing to its mooring. It looked like the rest of the fleet was at sea.

Security guards were on duty at the two hundred foot wide main doors of the giant Pan Am hangar. Inside, the Clipper lay hauled from the water, her huge burnished hull ablaze under the arc lamps. Beneath the wings, three-storey mobile work platforms swarmed with white clad mechanics. Compressed air tools stuttered, winch motors whined, an entire engine was being swung into position on the starboard wing.

The old familiar airplane smell caught his nostrils as he stepped through the hatch. Pat O'Byrne was whistling in the galley. There were canvas sheets down to protect the carpeting and stores piled in the main lounge. Oxygen bottles had been dumped in the passage. Automatically he checked the inspection tags, his pilot's training taking charge again, noting details, scanning for defects. It was good to be back aboard.

Up on the flight deck the radio was playing light music softly. The only person in the control cabin was Chief Crow, leaning on the desk of the engineer's station in oil-stained overalls, studying a manual. He eyed Munro's scratched face with interest, "Trouble on the road?"

"You could call it that." Briefly Munro gave him the details of the incident. The Chief listened in silence.

"What'd the cops say?"

"Santos reckons it could've been kids."

"Helluva game for kids!" The engineer rubbed thoughtfully at the oil on his hands with a piece of cotton waste. "Guess it's as well we're pulling out tonight," he said finally.

Munro's attention focused, "What d'you mean, we're pulling out tonight? Who said so?"

"Ross. He's decided on a night flip over to Guam," the Chief told him in his leisurely way. "He and Thyssen are up with Sol now clearing it."

Feet thumped overhead as someone clambered across the fuselage. In the background a woman was crooning on the radio. Munro shed his jacket and slung it over the back of the co-pilot's seat. "Where's everyone else gotten to?"

"Stewards are both below, Chuck is topsides with the maintenance crews, Chris went up to collect the mail."

The mail. Amongst it would be the photograph. Had he done the right thing consigning it to the sacks? Too late now to change his mind.

"The military sent for Stewart and Davey to go across to Corregidor. Something to do with those Jap transmissions they picked up on the trip yesterday."

Munro nodded. There was rumoured to be some kind of top secret army listening post on the island. Stewart would be in his element.

"How about the special cargo?"

"That's another thing, the cargo's gone. Word is the Navy flew it out last night."

"*The cargo's gone!*" Surprise hit him, mingled with relief. Maybe now the Japs would let them alone. Maybe they would even lose Slater. His eyes narrowed, "Chief, how was the Skipper this morning?"

Crow shrugged and stared at the rows of dials above his desk as if

166

trying to conjure up Ross's image in their glass, "Like anyone else with a head on."

"It showed, huh? Did the rest of the crew notice?"

"Couldn't hardly fail to with Kurt there to point it out."

The crooning on the radio stopped and a voice came on inviting listeners to identify the singer. Chuck Driscoll stuck his head through the starboard wing hatch. "Hi, Max," he said with a grin. "Chief, you want them to start connecting up the fuel lines to Number Four?"

The big chart of the North Pacific had been left open on the navigation table. On an impulse Munro pulled out Thyssen's instruments and began reading off distances with ruler and dividers. "Chief," he said when Chuck had gone, "did you ever work on the Lockheed Electra, the 10–E?"

"*The Earhart ship*? Sure, I've had experience of Electras. Why?"

"What was the cruising speed, approximately? Can you remember?"

"One fifty knots or thereabouts."

Munro frowned. "That's what I thought but the distances don't add up." He pointed with the end of the dividers, "Lae to Howland, twenty-five hundred and fifty miles. Earhart took off with fuel for over four thousand. When she went off the air twenty-four and a half hours later she still had six hours flying time left."

"Six hours, nine hundred miles, assuming no head winds. Where would that put her?"

Taking Howland as centre, Munro described a circle with the dividers. When he straightened up they both whistled.

The line ran directly through Mili atoll.

The interphone on the desk buzzed sharply. The Chief picked it up, "Crow. Yeah, he's here. Who wants him?" He passed the receiver across, "For you, Sol Boden."

Munro took the instrument, "Sol?"

"Max, can you come up to the office right away?" the manager's voice sounded anxious.

"Sure. Something wrong?"

"You'll find out. Just get on up here," the phone went click.

The Pan American offices at Cavite were similar to those at Kai Tak, an imposing ticket hall and departure lounge for passengers and behind, a series of cramped rooms in which the work was done.

Sol Boden's was on the first floor. It faced the bay, but the breeze was minimal and a creaking fan on the ceiling only stirred the tired air without cooling it.

167

Sol was a square, scowling man with sweat rings on his shirt, perpetually overworked. He waved Munro to a sagging wicker chair. "You want a cold beer?" he opened the door of a battered fridge and brought out two bottles.

On top of a filing cabinet was a scale model of a fancy steam yacht. Trim and white hulled with teak upperworks, around two hundred feet overall Munro estimated, "Pretty."

"The *Southern Cross*, she used to belong to some Wall Street czar. The company bought her last year and sent her down to New Guinea. She'll act as a floating base camp and hotel for when we open up a route to Australia."

"Good idea," Munro nodded thoughtfully. The Chief had said there would be a new route soon. It looked like his predictions were right.

Sol levered the caps off the beers and passed one across. "I had Ross in here just now," he said, resuming his seat.

Munro put the neck of the bottle to his lips and let the cool liquid run down his throat, "I hear he aims to pull out of here tonight."

Sol made a wry face. "Him and Slater cooked that up between them. Slater even persuaded the military to turn off that goddam minefield. The man's got clout alright," he added grudgingly.

"He's got clout," Munro agreed, taking another slug. There was a strained pause. Sol was looking unhappy, maybe he had gotten wind of Ross's drinking.

"That Jap ship yesterday," Sol continued, then hesitated again.

"I thought there wasn't supposed to be one, *officially*."

Sol scowled into his beer, "Yeah, well unofficially Navy Intelligence are querying your description. They say the Japs couldn't build a ship that big."

"Tell that to Tokyo."

Another pause. Outside in the bay a boat's siren went *whoop whoop whoop*. With a grunt Sol swivelled his chair round to stare out the window. "Max," he said abruptly over his shoulder, "Ross wants you to transfer out of the Clipper. As of now."

Munro sat very still.

Sol swung back, his gaze stark. "Well," he demanded peremptorily, "ain't you going to say something?"

"Did he give a reason?"

"Yeah, he gave a reason," Sol said violently, "the best goddam reason in the book – he said you lost your nerve and panicked when the Japs bounced you off the coast yesterday. Claims if he hadn't been there you'd have ditched. *And Kurt Thyssen confirms it!*"

168

Down in the Clipper Pat O'Byrne stuck his head out of the galley. "The idjits left the demerara off the canteen order again," he shouted to Tad Gotto polishing silver in the saloon. "Get on up to the stores and see what they're about."

"Aye aye, sir," Tad assented cheerfully, reaching for his cap.

He walked briskly up through the streets in the bright sun. Navy men in whites swarmed everywhere and the yard bustled with activity. Trucks ground by towards the quays laden with munitions. Near the machine shops gangs of Filipino workers were bringing out torpedoes, slim evil-looking things. Tad shuddered.

Approaching the Commissary he heard a whistle and his name hissed urgently. In a bus shelter on the corner Mitsuji stood signing to him. Tad hesitated. Reluctantly he hurried over.

"Godsakes Mish, you've no business on the base!"

"I had to see you. Look I'm sorry about last night."

A shore patrol jeep went by. Tad glanced round nervously. "I told you, I don't want anything to do with your friends."

"It's not for my friends, it's for me," the youth sounded desperate. "Tad, I've got family back in Japan. They'll be in big trouble if I don't help."

Tad chewed his lip, his round face twisted with anxiety. "Geez Mish, you're talking about *treason*. We're both Americans!"

"Are we just?" Mitsuji's tone was bitter. "I used to be a cadet in the ROTC. Last month they pushed me out, said they didn't want any damn Japs around. You'll see, your job will go the same way before long."

"That's not true. They wouldn't do that."

"Fool! There's a war coming. It'll be the colour of your skin that counts then." He gripped Tad's arm, "Listen I'm not asking anything vital, just a sneak at the cargo manifest . . ."

They were getting ready to load the mail. From the window of Sol's office Munro watched the coloured canvas bags being trolleyed down to the hangar escorted by Shapiro and Fry.

Jesus Christ, Ross! Ross and Thyssen! No prizes for guessing how Kurt had been persuaded to go along. With Munro out of the way he would be First Officer with an inside track to a captaincy when Ross finally cracked.

Son of a bitch, what was Ross playing at?

169

"Godammit, are you going to sit there and tell me you believe this crap?" he had sworn at Sol.

"No, but . . ."

"But what? You've known me ten years. You've flown with me. Do you think it was me chickened out?"

"Christ, Max, I don't know what to think. If it had been anyone else saying it I'd have kicked them out on their ass, but for godsakes this was *Ross!*"

Yes, he thought bitterly, this was Ross. Ross the senior captain on the line. Ross the legend. Who would believe *his* nerve had gone.

At stake was Munro's whole career.

Out in the bay a flock of gulls wheeled and dipped screeching around a refuse barge. A submarine was moving slowly seawards on the surface. Sol Boden's craggy features tightened. "Jesus, I hate this kind of business!" he said savagely.

"Listen, Sol, before this goes in the logs I want Ross in here. I want to hear him make these charges to my face."

Sol massaged his jaw uncomfortably, "Suppose I marked you down as taken sick? Ross would agree to that. Then you could rest up here for a week and I promise to give you your old slot on the next ship in."

"*Bullshit!*" Munro's fist slammed the desk. "That's no bargain, Sol, and you darn well know it. If I walk away from this I'm through, I'll never make Master."

Master of Ocean Flying Boats – the most prestigious and demanding rank of any airline in the world.

There were only twelve of the giant Boeing Clippers in existence and three of these were loaned to the British for their trans-Atlantic service. Competition for a left hand seat was ruthless. Popular legend held it was easier to make the bridge of a Navy battleship.

Munro had sweated a dozen years for his chance. It was almost within his grasp, he was just one step away.

Now Ross was about to dash his hopes for ever!

By Christ, he wasn't going to let him.

When the *Osho-san* learned of the failed attack on Munro's car his fury was vast. "*Bakamono!*" he cursed the monks. "Fools, outcasts, cowards! Four of you against two unarmed Yankees and you let them escape!"

"So sorry, Lord. We were interrupted, a convoy of soldiers . . ." the leader of the assassination squad grovelled on the floor of the temple.

"*Shimai! Ikinasai ima!*"

"*Hai, Osho-san.*" The monks fled.

The *Osho-san* paced the dais, breathing deeply. *Karma.* Nothing to be gained by wrath. He considered the implications. At his back coils of scented smoke wreathed the statue of the god.

Another yellow clad figure entered and bowed before his leader. "*Nan ja?*"

"Forgive me, *Osho-san*, there is a message from Kiro the flower seller. The Yankee woman has left the hotel. She and another are headed for *Intramuros* in a horse carriage."

"*Ah, so desku?*" the *Osho-san*'s eyes gleamed. "Good, send word to the Captain. This time there is to be no failure."

XIII

CORREGIDOR – THE ROCK. Engines idling, the sleek PT boat nosed into North Dock. "Thanks for the ride, boys!" Stewart Whitely and Davey Klein waved to the men on the bridge as they stepped ashore, exhilarated after the fast run across the bay.

So this was the Rock.

Ringed by sheer cliffs, the island fortress lay astride the entrance to Manila Bay guarding the approaches from the sea. From its volcanic slopes massive siege cannon leered across the waters. Mortar pits spotted the thick bush and beneath Malinta Hill an underground defence complex capable of supporting seven thousand men had been blasted into solid rock.

Corregidor was impregnable, the Gibraltar of the East.

A jeep screeched to a halt on the dock. "Hi, you the folks from Pan American?" a young seaman hailed them. "Hop aboard."

They climbed in, clutching the log books they had brought. The driver spun the wheel and they shot off in a cloud of dust. "Where are you taking us?" Stewart yelled, clinging to his seat.

"Monkey Point, the Navy tunnel."

"What happens there?"

"Search me, bud, ain't never been inside. It's all top secret."

They bumped over a light railway line. "Looks like you're putting in a lot of work round here," Davey said. Down along the shoreline men stripped to the waist were stringing barbed wire and digging foxholes, hammering away at the rock with Barco drills.

"Oh, them," the sailor snorted, "that's the Army. What the hell they gotta be scared of?"

"A war maybe," said Stewart and the seaman grinned.

A slip road brought them to a gate in a high wire fence. The sign read UNITED STATES NAVY 16TH NAVAL DISTRICT COMMUNICATIONS SECURITY SECTION. Radio masts were outlined against the sky. Armed guards checked their identities and waved them through. The jeep drove into the compound and halted outside the entrance to a tunnel

172

screened from the road by palm trees. "This is it, fellers."

". . . and these sets are where we monitor submarine transmissions," the Lieutenant on watch explained. "As you gentlemen most probably know, submerged subs can only receive signals in the low frequency range."

Bored into the hillside for a depth of fifty yards, the neon-lit tunnel was walled and roofed in smooth concrete. Powerful radio gear, tabulators, machine printers and direction-finding equipment lined the sides. Ventilator fans hummed continuously.

"Yes, we've seen your transmitting tower at Cavite," Stewart nodded. He and Davey gazed fascinated at the sophisticated technology. Both had pledged never to reveal details of what they might learn here.

"We're part of the Mid-Pacific Strategic Direction-Finder Net, all our bearings are plotted on the main board and radioed to Pearl." The Lieutenant was in his forties, spectacled and balding. On duty under him were two dozen clerks and technical experts including one, Stewart noticed, from the British Royal Navy.

"Did you pick up JCS Yokohama yesterday same as us, Lieutenant?" he asked.

"We identified Yokohama, no problem. What interests us is this *repeat-back* you heard."

"It was pretty faint, but I'll swear it was verbatim, another station copying the first, letter for letter."

"How come you people didn't catch the signal here, sir?" asked Davey, "These receivers are a heck of a sight more sensitive than anything we have."

"We did for a while but we had problems with interference. Your set was several thousand feet higher, don't forget. That helps a lot. Also the same storm which masked us may have boosted your reception."

A yeoman clerk stood at the big chart, marking up changes with coloured pins. "Blue for American naval units, black for British, orange for Japanese," the Lieutenant explained.

"Is that your job here, keeping track of the Jap navy?"

"Much of it," the Lieutenant answered elliptically. "Is it possible what you heard was a re-broadcast, say by a convoy flagship, for copying by other vessels with antennae too small to receive the original JCS signal?"

"It's possible," Stewart frowned, trying to recall. Then his face

173

cleared, "Of course, I get it," he exclaimed excitedly, "*low frequency transmissions*! A re-broadcast by the flagship for submarines scouting ahead of the fleet."

The Lieutenant grinned, "Now if we could check your logbooks maybe we can deduce a position from them."

Together they went to work with charts and compass bearings. "Exactly as we thought," he straightened his back finally, "slap in the middle between the Aleutians and Midway."

He moved to the map. Stewart followed his glance. In the empty quarter of the northern Pacific, far from any shipping lanes, were a pair of lonely orange markers.

"Yes, we've been monitoring them for a couple of days," the Lieutenant said quietly, "we think they may be *carriers*."

Out at Cavite the work went on.

"That's the lot," Chris Fry called up to Shapiro as he shoved the last of the mail sacks through the cargo hatch under the port wing. Moving out of the way of the mechanics on the platform, he slid nimbly to the ground by the escape rail and entered through the main hatch.

"Anyone seen Max?" he asked cheerfully on the flight deck. "We got some mail to stow for him."

Nobody spoke. Ross was at his desk with Thyssen seated opposite. Standing over them, clutching a wrench, was the Chief. All three were tight-lipped with anger.

Chris halted uncertainly, "Sorry to butt in, Skipper, I'm looking for the First."

Three sets of eyes turned on him chillingly. "Munro's ashore. Now scram," the Chief growled.

"Uh sure, Chief, you don't happen to know when . . ."

The engineer cut him short, "Beat it, son, unless you want a busted head."

Chris gulped, "Yessir." Hastily he ducked past them into the main hold.

"You weren't *here*," Ross said as the hatch closed. "You and Driscoll were both in the wings, so was Shapiro. You didn't *see*!"

"No one saw except the Skipper and me," Kurt Thyssen backed him up. "Stewart was on the horn trying to raise help and Chris was back in the hold."

"I didn't have to be here," the Chief returned, massively unmoved, "to know Max ain't chicken."

174

A white icecap of anger rolled down over Ross's eyes, "Are you calling me a liar, dammit?"

The silence hung. Ross went purple. "You can't let him get away with this, Skipper," Thyssen muttered.

"Kurt," the Chief jerked his head at the stairs, "suppose you take a walk, huh?"

The Second Officer's jaw dropped. "Godammit, Crow," Ross gritted, "who the hell d'you think you are giving orders?"

"Kurt," the Chief repeated in the same voice, ominous as the rumble before an earthquake, "get below." Thyssen hesitated for a second, looked at Ross, then turned sulkily for the stairs.

The Chief put the wrench in a pocket of his overalls and sat down in the vacated seat. His flat deadpan eyes regarded Ross unwinkingly. "*You're drunked.*" It was a statement. "I known you a long time, Ross, longer than anyone else aboard, but this the first time I ever known you drunked in command.

"Sol must have seen it too," he continued while Ross stared at him speechless. "Course there's no call for you to worry about that, ain't nobody going to believe it. Ross, the Senior Captain on the line, Ross drunked, ha," he shook his head. "Same way nobody's going to believe Max Munro is chicken either."

Ross's hands tightened about the perspex ruler on the desk. Behind them in the hold they could hear the thumps of the mail sacks being stowed.

"Max Munro is the best darn pilot I ever flew with. He's even as good as you used to be, Ross. He ain't no crazy hell-for-leather stuntman either, I'd fly with him anywhere. And he sure as hell ain't yellow."

"Well, I say he is and it's my word counts!" Ross flared, stung at last.

"If it comes down to an enquiry," the Chief explained patiently, "it'll be your word, yours an' Thyssen's, against the rest of us. But it won't come to that because you can't afford an inquiry."

"The hell I can't!"

Somewhere outside a power drill began to whine naggingly. The Chief heaved a sigh, "You can't afford an inquiry the way you're drinking nowadays. If it comes to an inquiry you're finished. If you keep drinking like you are you're finished too." He paused, "Skipper, I don't know what your trouble is and I ain't asking but I'm offering to help – any ways I can."

Ross was staring at him, his face livid, the lines like knife cuts. "Son of a bitch! You too," he hissed. "*You too. All of you!*"

175

Down below Kurt Thyssen stood in the passage, one hand on the stair rail. There was a thin smile on his lips as he listened. Things were turning out just dandy. By the end of this trip he'd be rid of Munro, either Ross would bust him or more probably Max would transfer of his own accord. Leaving himself as the only logical candidate for First. As for Ross, he smirked, six months he gave the old man, six months maximum, before he cracked up. Permanently.

In six months, Kurt reckoned, six months *conservatively*, he would be Skipper.

Then Sally would want to know him. By God yes.

He glanced round. Tad Gotto was standing in the entrance to the galley, watching him. "What are you staring at, you damned Nip?" he said, flushing. "Haven't you any work to do?"

In the Manila Hotel Maria Bianchi was on the telephone to Mr. Breen, "Good morning, have you sold the bonds?"

"Yes, I took thirty percent. I had a heck of a time getting it, but . . ."

"But you managed nevertheless, good," Maria cut him short. "Thirty percent of one hundred and twenty thousand is thirty-six thousand dollars."

"Less my commission," the lawyer put in hastily, "we agreed five percent, remember?"

"Which comes to six thousand dollars, leaving a balance of thirty thousand due to me. I will stop by your office this afternoon. Please have everything ready. I shall require cash."

"*Cash!*" There was a squawk from the other end of the line, "Thirty thousand bucks! You can't walk around with that in your purse. We'll give you a bank draft."

"Cash," Maria told him coolly, "American dollars, large denominations. We'll count them together." She replaced the receiver.

Lifting it again she dialled the desk, "Please order me a car with a driver for this afternoon. A driver with reliable local knowledge."

"*Olé, the red is down!*" The crowd went wild. The tiered benches of Manila's La Loma Cockpit were packed with fans, screaming, yelling, gesticulating. The *kristos* were standing on their seats shouting the odds, sealing bets in a blur of hand signals. In the caged sand arena a green-tailed cock strutted round a bundle of quivering feathers.

"*Matyeryebyets!*" Down at the front row section reserved for moneyed patrons Prince Cherkassy cursed. He had five hundred pesos riding on this bout.

A fresh roar went up from the crowd. The *sentenciador* had declared the green the victor. Fuming, Cherkassy peeled some notes from a roll of bills and tossed them to a bookmaker's olive-skinned urchin on the bench behind. The next bout had a *bulik*, a pie-bald. Maybe his luck would change.

It was sweltering in the stadium. He mopped his face and squinted round behind at the benches. Every tier was jammed. Filipinos, Spaniards, mestizos, shirt-sleeved clerks, peasants from the *barrios*, tattooed natives from the jungles of Luzon. Cockfighting was the national passion.

The next pair were brought into the arena by their trainers and the crowd's interest quickened. One was a big cross-breed out of a professional stable with pie-bald tail feathers, the other was smaller, a spirited yellow and white native. Steel spurs, razor sharp, were strapped to their right legs. The birds rolled their eyes fiercely, puffing up their chests and ruffling their gaudy neck feathers into fighting crowns.

"See his leg scales," a mestizo with a mouthful of gold teeth jabbered excitedly examining the big pie-bald through the bars, "and that plumage, not a chink anywhere." He yelled to a *kristo*, "Hey, five hundred! Five hundred at five to two!" The bookmaker acknowledged the bet with the briefest of nods, memorizing it and the odds instantly, laying the sum off within seconds with other punters.

"Five to two, *ya está*!" the mestizo cackled gleefully, hearing the odds shorten.

Cherkassy's eyes narrowed as he studied the cocks, reckoning them up for strength, speed and stamina. Behind them the *kristos* were calling four to one against the pie-bald's opponent. "A thousand!" he shouted suddenly. "A thousand on the yellow, by Christ!"

The mestizo gasped, "The yellow! Have you gone mad, Señor? It's a chick beside the *bulik*!"

"Size! Size means nothing. It's speed and courage that count. Yes, the yellow's got guts. See the way it holds its comb."

"A hundred pesos says you're wrong, Señor."

"Done, by Christ, and another hundred says the yellow kills!"

Excitement gripped the fans as the birds were teased. The trainer of the yellow put his hand over the cock's head, pulling it back against its side. Instinctively the pie-bald pecked at the exposed neck. Then it was the turn of the yellow. The ritual was repeated. Now both would fight to the death.

The *sentenciador* gave the signal. With a flutter of feathers the gamecocks flew at one another. Instantly the crowd was on its feet screaming in a dozen dialects, urging the birds on.

"See, the *bulik* has made the first strike!"

The two cocks broke apart momentarily. The yellow's comb was torn and there were flecks of blood on the clean sand of the arena. A fresh clamour of betting broke out.

Again the birds clashed, leaping and pecking, neck feathers stiff, wings outspread, whirling to stab with the terrible spurs. Cries of admiration and dismay greeted each blow.

"*Olé*," the mestizo exploded suddenly, "the yellow is down! I warned you, Señor."

"That cheat of a trainer, he squeezed as he let go! Wait, the yellow is up again! It was only a fall."

The shouting redoubled as the birds flew at one another again. Cherkassy hammered on the bars of the grill, cursing fluently in three tongues. The *kristos* were offering six to one now against the smaller bird.

"Yes, yes! Another thousand on the yellow!" he yelled, beside himself with frenzy. He got a wave from the *kristo*. As he turned back a great roar erupted round the stadium, the pie-bald was down.

"*Madre mia*," the mestizo gasped in disbelief, "the big bird is finished."

Trailing blood, the *bulik* fluttered across the sand arena, pursued by the yellow. The spectators were howling for the kill, the betting frantic.

Cherkassy gripped the bars, intoxicated by the tension. Another leap and clash of wings. A glint of spurs. "*Matyeryebyets!*" he exclaimed with a shout. The crowd exploded afresh. The yellow was down again, gored mortally in the throat.

The *sentenciador* picked up the dying bird and held it for the *bulik* to administer the two pecks to the corpse required by tradition before a victor could be declared. The crowd whistled and stamped their feet.

"*Madra mia*," the mestizo gasped again weakly, "what a bout! You were right, Señor, the yellow had courage but the *bulik* was too much for him."

Sweating, his chest hurting, Cherkassy counted out his losses with shaking hands. Twenty-two hundred pesos. A thousand American. *Mother of God*. If only that cursed *bulik* had stayed down he'd have cleared his debts for the entire week.

Abruptly he stiffened. Across the arena a figure in dark glasses was observing him.

A sneer touched Captain Santos' lips as he saw the Russian turn ill-temperedly away to lose himself in the crowd. Serve him right, only a fool would have backed the yellow cock.

Interest was building for the next fight. More spectators crowded into the stands as fresh birds were brought on. *Kristos* began shouting the odds. The clean-cut plain clothes man from the American Counter Intelligence Corps tapped him on the arm, "Hey, our target's moving." Santos switched his gaze back to the upper tier. A Japanese in a cheap straw hat was making for the stairs. Ishido. The gardener from the Santa Cruz mansion.

"You got all the exits covered?"

"*Si*, of course."

"Okay let's move."

The two officers sauntered round behind the stands and joined the stream of people pushing through the main gate. Ouside, a lively mob thronged the plaza. Foodsellers had set up their stalls under the acacia trees and groups of slick-haired youths were bantering with the senoritas.

"There he is. Over by the old dame selling lottery tickets."

"*Si, si*. I have him too," Santos fingered his whistle.

"Hold it! Wait for his contact to show."

The gardener was hovering among the stalls. He haggled over a twist of sunflower seeds and drifted slowly across the plaza cracking them in his teeth to join the queue at the drinking fountain. Santos and the young American followed, keeping their distance in the crowd. The Japanese drank and turned away wiping his mouth. Out of an alley close by stepped a saffron robed monk. He gave a covert signal.

"Looks like this could be it," the CIC man muttered. "Everyone stay loose, give 'em time to make the drop."

They waited tense while Ishido and the monk edged closer. "Just a bit more an' we got the suckers cold," the American prayed.

WHEEEE!!! Suddenly Santos' whistle shrilled. People froze startled as police swarmed into the square. The monk and the Japanese whipped round. Quick as cats they fled in opposite directions.

"Jerk! You goddam jerk!" the CIC man cried with furious disbelief. "We almost had them!" Snatching a pistol from an underarm holster, he sprinted in pursuit.

Santos charged after him into the excited crowd, a squad of his men following. Feet pounding on the cobbles, they raced down the first side street scattering children at play in the gutter. At the bottom, more traders, water carriers, people swarming again. No sign of Ishido or the monk. They ran to the next corner. "I'll take the left!"

Santos gasped to the sweating American and they split among the maze of alleys.

Terror-stricken, Ishido tore through the jostling crowds, ruthlessly shoving people out of his way. *Curse the Amerikans! If it hadn't been for that whistle* . . . He squeezed against a wall to let a laden cart pass. Glancing back, he saw uniform caps still close behind and leaping a small stall, burst out of the alley into a road. Horns blared, cyclists collided swearing as he rushed headlong through the traffic.

He ducked into a street on the far side and fled on, dodging the drains, chest heaving, his mind full of obscenities. *Namu Amida Butsu, what stink-bellied spy had betrayed the meeting to the gaijin?*

Sweat pouring down his face, Santos chased across the road in pursuit. Peasants gawked at him as he barged through their midst knocking an old man screeching into the gutter. Santos paid no heed. He turned left, then right and found himself in a cobbled street. It gave onto a canal. Muddy water steamed in the noon sun, stinking of sewage. There was a small bridge ahead and a cluster of barges. On the far side he caught a flash of a straw hat disappearing down some steps under the arch.

Behind him he could hear the shouts of his men. Desperate now, he ran along the tow path, pain stabbing in his side, breathing laboured. He reached the bridge and flung himself over. The steps beyond were slimy with age, he almost fell. In the shadows a figure crouched cornered.

"*Oi! Higashi no kaze ame!*"

"*Nishi no kaze hare!*"

"*Aiee*, I thought for a moment you were one of the *Amerik* . . ."

A shot boomed like a cannon in the confined space, swallowing the gardener's words. He fell to the ground clawing at his chest. Deliberately Santos fired again. The body jerked and went limp. Already boots were clattering across the bridge above. Swearing savagely Santos pulled a knife from his pocket. Flipping open the blade, he tossed it down beside the corpse.

The CIC man panted up at last, "Jesus Christ, did you have to kill him? He's no use to us dead!"

Santos slumped against the brickwork, catching his breath. His heart felt weak. "*Madre mia*, it was him or me," he croaked.

Twenty minutes later a black police car was heading across Jones Bridge to *Intramuros*. Threading through the twisting back streets, it halted outside a dilapidated mews house.

"Wait here till I return," Santos ordered the driver.

"*Si, Capitan*," the man took a cheroot from his pocket and settled down in the seat. The Captain was visiting his mistress, he would be some time.

"Don't you ever knock?" Lola Montez demanded as he entered her room. She was in a black lace slip, brushing her tangled hair, lipstick smeared over her bitten-looking mouth.

"Shut up," Santos told her curtly. "Well, did you find it?"

"No," she answered sullenly.

"Nothing?" He grabbed her by the nape of the neck and shook her hard. "You were a long enough while at it for nothing."

"That's right, *hit me*," she flared bitterly. "He did, the American. He caught me searching his pockets."

Santos swore, "So you spent the night giving him his money's worth, whore!"

"Why not? He was good, better than you."

He struck out viciously, knocking her across the bed. "*Bastardo!*" she came at him with the hairbrush. He caught her arm easily and took it away.

Releasing her, he frowned at the clothes strewn around the room, "What's this, are you packing?"

She rubbed her wrist. "I'm leaving, I've had enough. There's a boat sailing at three for Batavia."

"What are you using for money?" he sneered.

"Everything I've got!"

Turning her back on him defiantly, she picked up the brush again. Santos watched for a moment, then began undoing his belt. "*Valgame Dios!* What the hell are you doing?" she spat, baring her teeth. "That is finished between us."

He laughed thinly as he pulled off his shirt, "Think of it as an exit tax."

Intramuros. The two girls had finished their shopping.

"Gee, I'm late for lunch already. César will be going wild. Honey," Georgiana appealed to Scott, "the restaurant is on the next block. Do you mind if the *calesa* drops me off first and goes on to the hotel?"

Across the road at a distance, a stolen Buick with heavy fenders was parked in the shade beneath the crumbling Spanish wall. Inside, a mean-faced Filipino sat fingering a switchblade knife. "*Pronto!*" he growled to his companion. "Here come the whores now."

The driver started the engine. They watched the two women climb into the *calesa*. It set off at a smart trot.

"*Bueno*, they're heading for the Calle Real. Turn left. We'll cut down past the Plaza Roma and catch them at the Luna intersection."

The Buick shot away tyres squealing on the cobbles. They rocked round a corner on two wheels and raced down the narrow medieval streets, the driver beating a tattoo on the horn as he swerved recklessly among bicycles and carts.

"There's the Luna, slow down!"

Brakes screeching, they slackened speed at the crossroads. Ahead, a tree-lined avenue bisected the city. A stream of brightly painted *calesas, carromatas* and *carretalas* trotted up and down.

"It had a pink shade. Quick, with the black pony coming now!"

"*Cabrón*, I only see one of the whores! What happened to the other?"

"*Madre mia*, too late to worry. One's enough!"

With a clash of gears the heavy Buick bounded forward. People scattered screaming suddenly as it roared towards the intersection. Ponies shied in fright and a jitney bus mounted the sidewalk. The driver had his foot hard down on the accelerator, gripping the wheel tight. The pink *calesa* was barely twenty yards away when the coachman saw the car coming and hauled frantically at his reins. The two Filipinos flung up their arms to shield their faces as the Buick's fender crashed into the *calesa* wheel. A shrill neigh burst from the horse as it came down in a tangle of harness and broken shafts. With an explosion of splintering wood the light carriage disintegrated, hurling its occupants into the roadway.

"*Ei ei, bravo!*" The youth with the switchblade cried gleefully, twisting round to look back as they sped on up the Luna. "That's settled the gringo whore."

Behind them, people were running towards the wreckage.

Manila had a tradition of a strong and independent press. At the *Herald* offices Cashin was welcomed as an old friend by the editor, irrepressible Carlos Romulo. He confirmed the news blackout.

"What could we do, Bob? It was a personal appeal from General MacArthur's press secretary. In the interests of national security we were asked to print nothing on the Clipper."

Cashin blinked behind his glasses, "Does that include the death of a passenger at the Manila Hotel last night?"

A telephone rang on Romulo's cluttered desk. He picked it up and held a brief conversation in Spanish and Tagalog. By the open window a cat dozed in the sun on a pile of papers.

Romulo put down the phone. "I called Army Headquarters; they said to drop it, he was a member of a Chinese delegation whose presence had to be kept secret. I agreed to play along." He shrugged, "It was only an accident."

"Suppose I told you there was more to it? Suppose I told you this morning an attempt was made to kill me?"

The little Filipino glanced at him shrewdly, "Are you serious, Bob? Do you know something?"

"Right now it's a crazy muddle but if I could use your files for the afternoon I might pull together a story – one you could even print."

Romulo spread his hands, "Be our guest. First though, we eat."

Lunch was at a popular open-air restaurant tucked away behind the fish market. Carlos insisted they sample *sinigang*, a tangy stew of prawns and fresh local vegetables soured with tamarind. Then ice cream served in the half shell of a young coconut so that scrapings of the sweet gelatinous meat were mixed with every delicious spoonful.

Sitting over tiny cups of strong black coffee the conversation became serious again.

"Carlos, what is the score? Why are the authorities so jittery?"

Romulo was playing with a toothpick. His twinkling eyes grew grave. "Let me tell you a story. Last month we had a blackout practice in Manila. You can imagine the kind of chaos it caused. My driver couldn't find me, there were no taxis, I had to walk home from the office. Under the Puerta Isabella I felt someone slap me on the back. I turned to look but could see nothing in the dark. On reaching the house though, I found a notice in Tagalog gummed to my jacket: Support the greater East Asian co-prosperity sphere."

"Here too, huh?" Cashin sucked in his breath, "I knew it'd been happening in Hongkong and Singapore."

"Yes, it is the same everywhere. A fifth column is being mobilised in our midst."

They went back to the office.

The library was down in the basement. The familiar musty smell of mouldering newsprint. The young Filipino in charge wore American sneakers, his accent pure as Broadway. "Sure, help yourself to the index, Mr. Cashin, and we'll fetch whatever you want from the stacks."

Cashin sat down at the table and began wading through a pile of dusty files. The papers were yellow and brittle with age. The earliest reference to the looting of the Manchu Tombs came in 1928. That summer relics had begun turning up for sale in Peking. Jade orbs the size of cantaloupes, amber tortoises symbols of longevity, even dew-drop pearls from Tz'u-hsi's Phoenix Crown . . .

Cashin chewed the top of his pen, making rapid shorthand notes. All the evidence pointed to authorized plunder by the Kuomintang military. Outraged, the Emperor had appealed to Chiang K'ai-shek for return of the scared treasures. In vain. There was too much booty involved.

Near the end of the the last file Cashin's attention was caught by a short paragraph. His interest quickened at the mention of Professor Chen. He stopped, puzzled, and read it again.

"Sir, sir!" Over at the counter the young librarian held up the telephone, "A call for you."

Cashin took the receiver, "Yes?"

"Bob? Carlos here. I thought maybe you should hear – there's been a *calesa* accident on Calle Real, a member of the Clipper's crew is in hospital."

XIV

BATAAN. THREE PM. A few acres of maize and cassava had been scraped from the bush along the road. Clay-pot stoves smoked outside thatched huts raised on stilts and pigs rooted in the open drains. Nervously the men of the *barrio* waited in the sun to be questioned while children pressed round the police truck as the canvas wrapped bodies were loaded in.

"Three in three days! Son of a bitch, what have the Japs got against missionaries?" Slater swore. The eighty degree forest heat was sweltering. He and Sir Ambrose were slumped in the front of a car under a big rubber tree with the doors open.

The Englishman mopped his face with a silk handkerchief, "And they were tortured, whoever killed them wanted information."

"*On what*? Neither of them knew a goddam thing about the mission. Unless maybe Jordan told them, huh, Jordan?" Slater swung round in his seat. The priest was sitting in the rear, his face ashen.

"I wrote Carmichael the same as Morris Oliver; that I would be passing through and hoped to see him, nothing more, nothing," Jordan's voice faltered. "*Oh God*, what have I done to bring death to my friends like this?" he broke into a sob.

A pot-bellied infant stared at the car, sucking a piece of fruit. Slater jerked his head to Sir Ambrose. Together they got out and walked over to the waiting natives.

There were three to four dozen. Sturdy, brown-skinned men, some in ragged shorts, others in bright coloured G-strings, many with long *bolo* knives at their waists. A little apart a plain clothes sergeant from the Counter-Intelligence Corps was questioning a yellow-robed Buddhist monk.

"Where did you pick this gook up, Bixell?"

"In the bush back of where we found the bodies, sir. Tried to run for it when he was seen."

The monk's gaze met theirs defiantly. Shaven head and upward slanting eyes. Slater glanced at Sir Ambrose. He nodded. "A Jap,"

185

Slater muttered. "Ask the headman if he's seen him before?"

The village headman was a barrel-chested elder sporting brass earrings and an Army fatigue cap. "*Hindi, hindi po!*" he shook his head violently at the question.

Slater brushed the flies away from his face. There was fear here, he could smell it. Was it the police, the white men and their guns or something else?

Shit, if the Japs can scare people like this right here in our own back yard the war's half lost before it's even begun.

From the step of a hut a hag with withered breasts shouted something.

"She say dis men pass 'long road all de time," the sergeant's Filipino interpreter translated, "village people no speak dem."

Slater's face closed, "Search the bastard."

The sergeant signed to his men. There was a cry from the monk. The skirts of his robe flew as he jerked free of their grasp. A constable screamed, clutching at his groin.

"Jesus, he's got a knife!"

The monk whirled, the blade flashing in the sun. With a yell he leapt a drainage ditch and tore for a defile between the huts. Two natives barred his path, *bolos* swinging. He whirled again to confront the sergeant and the barrel of a cocked .45 automatic. Other men came running up. Slater whipped a pistol from under his jacket. The monk was surrounded by an armed circle.

"Okay, Tojo, throw it down or we'll fill you full of holes!"

The monk's teeth bared. "*Tenno Heika banzai!*" Reversing the knife, with both hands he thrust the point up suddenly under the base of his chin. Blood spewed out in a stream and he pitched forward on his face in the dust.

They stared dumbly at the twitching body. A young constable turned away gagging. "Christ on a crutch!" Slater said dry-mouthed, "He didn't even blink, just skewered himself."

Sir Ambrose spoke. "The Japanese code of *bushido* teaches there is no greater shame for a soldier than to be made prisoner," he said quietly. "Death, even at his own hand, is preferable."

He saw the Americans gape at him. How naive they were, he thought, such concepts altogether outside their experience. Well, they would learn.

The sound of a vehicle made them glance up. A jeep had turned off the road and was bumping over the dirt space between the huts scattering livestock. It carried US Army plates. Out jumped a second lieutenant in tailored cKcs.

Slater's expression twisted, "Godammit, now what?"

"Major Slater?" The lieutenant was very young. He looked at the natives with their *bolos* and at the body in the dust oozing blood and went green.

"Okay, son, don't worry about him. You got something for me?"

The lieutenant pulled himself together with an effort, "Major, I have to ask you for identification please, sir."

Slater flipped his wallet open. "You from Headquarters? What's eating them?"

"Sir, I've an urgent message from General Sutherland. The bomber, the B–17 with your special cargo board – *she's missing, overdue.*"

Chic in a grey silk dress and matching hat, Maria Bianchi came out through the swing doors of an office on the Escolta and climbed into her waiting car. In her purse was thirty thousand dollars collected from Mr. Breen.

The Filipino driver squinted at the new address she gave him. "Sure dis de place you want, lady?" he asked troubled.

"You know the house?"

The man's brow furrowed, "Yeah, I knows it. Only I don't tink it de kinda place a lady wanna go."

"Nevertheless please take me there," she said firmly and settled herself in the seat.

They headed south towards Ermita. The driver was concentrating on the traffic. Sliding across to be out of view of his mirror, Maria opened her purse. With deft fingers she divided the bundle of notes. Two sets of five thousand dollars and one of ten thousand she sealed in separate envelopes, the remainder went into her wallet.

It was cooler in the suburbs. Tree-shaded avenues and opulent villas set among lush gardens. The car halted before elaborate wrought iron gates and the driver hooted the horn. A slouching gardener let them through and closed the gates again behind.

"Dis de one, lady. Casa Aurora."

The villa stood quiet, windows shuttered against the sun, bougainvillea trailing from balconies over the pink wash plaster. Maria rang the bell in the Spanish tiled porch. A maid in a candy pink dress opened the door.

"*Buenas tardes*, I have an appointment with Madame Aurora."

The hall inside was over-furnished, the air heavy with cloying scent. As Maria was led through she heard a scuffle of feet on the stairs and a trill of childish laughter.

187

The boudoir was pink too.

"A glass of champagne, Mrs. Bianchi?" Madame Aurora's tea gown rustled as she sank back onto the chaise longue.

"Thank you, nothing."

"*Bueno*." She dismissed the maid with a flick of the hand and smoothed her coiffured hair. Pinned to her chest was a triple bloom hibiscus. She was a mestiza, a formerly handsome woman run to fat. Her glance appraised Maria critically.

"So you have come for Teresita?"

"Yes. I trust she is ready."

"You will be taking her back to Shanghai?"

Maria evaded the question, "May I see her?"

"But of course, she has been wakened," the other woman's teeth showed briefly in a smile. "Such a sweet pretty child, Teresita. Clean, good-tempered, obedient . . ."

"So she should be at the price," Maria cut in.

". . . and most popular with our clients."

"The figure is too high."

Madame Aurora's tone sharpened, "Your agent agreed the money. You will not do better anywhere in Manila." A tap on the door interrupted them. "Ah, here she is now. *Adelante*. Come in, precious."

A girl entered cautiously, limbs trembling, dark eyes darting anxiously. A budding figure but the face of a child still. About eleven years old, Maria judged. Under the filmy shift she was naked.

The woman reached out and pulled her close. "My little Teresita, eh?" She pinched the girl's cheek, her voice sugar sweet, "She is like a daughter to me."

"I wish to speak to her," Maria said. "Alone."

The woman hesitated a moment, then motioned sulkily in the direction of the windows.

Maria led the girl out onto the terrace. It was bright and humming birds were feeding amongst the flowers.

"Teresita," she said gently, "when did you come here?"

The girl stared at the ground. "Holy Week," her voice was a whisper. "*Mia madre se muere*. My mother died."

"And are you happy?"

Teresita did not answer.

"Listen, there is a man, a *gringo*, comes here to see you sometimes. He has hurt his hand – like so," she demonstrated.

The girl flinched. A big tear was rolling down her cheek.

Maria squeezed her shoulders and kissed the dark hair softly, "Hush little one, do not be afraid. Everything will be alright."

Back inside the boudoir she snapped open her purse. "Five thousand dollars we agreed, Madame Aurora."

Out at the polo ground a loudspeaker blared –

"LADIES AND GENTLEMEN, THE FIRST MATCH TODAY IS BETWEEN COL-ONEL MANUEL NIETO'S ANGELS AND THE SULU SCOUTS LED BY CESAR DE SANTA CRUZ."

Champagne was being served on the members' terrace. Ladies in afternoon dresses twirled their parasols, flirting with escorts in crisp linen suits and Panama hats. Cavalry officers tapped polished boots discussing horse-flesh. The Manila Polo Club was among the most exclusive institutions in the Far East.

Down at the rails the ponies were under saddle. Munro patted the Gypsy on the neck and checked his girth. It was to be a four-chukka match, four players a side and eight mounts. Each chukka of seven and a half minutes with a three minute interval between. He would ride him in the first and again in the third, the most vital.

The groom handed him his whip and a mallet, a slim fifty-two inch shaft of spliced malacca cane with a narrow sycamore head and the old-fashioned Rugby handle that he still preferred to the fashionable Parada.

Nieto came bustling up and called him together with the rest of the Angels team: wealthy Luis Roxas from the National Bank and a lanky cavalryman from Fort Mckinley named Ritchie, whom Munro had played against but never partnered before.

"The good news first," Nieto told them, "two of the Scouts have dropped out so they are bringing on substitutes. The bad news is one of them is Van Cleef."

"The Dutchman! *Madre Mia!*" Roxas crossed himself in mock dismay, "Surely that one counts as two players."

Ritchie scratched his long chin with his whip, "What's his handicap now, seven?"

Munro's handicap was two, the same as Roxas. Nieto and Ritchie were both three.

"César is a three. How about the other substitute?" asked Roxas cheerfully. "Is he another Dutchman?"

Nieto became embarrassed suddenly. "Yes, the other substitute," he coughed. "Er, Max . . ."

But Munro was not listening. He was staring past them at the Scouts' team. So were Roxas and the American.

"*Nombre de Dios!*"

"Holy cow! Will you look at that!"

Prancing by the rail on a little Arab mare, a polo-mallet over her shoulder, was Georgiana.

"Max, believe me, I swear," the Colonel pleaded. "I did not know myself until a moment ago."

Munro turned back, his face stark, "It's your match, I don't care who plays." Jamming his helmet down on his head, he reached for the Gypsy's stirrup and swung himself into the saddle, "If you want to louse the game up that's your business."

The teams took positions for the throw-in. Ritchie and Roxas were playing forward, Nieto at Number Three and Munro back, defending the goal. On the opposing side César led the forwards, it would be up to Munro to mark him. Georgiana was half-back. Perfectly fitting English britches and the spill of flaming hair caught up severely under her helmet.

Two-faced bitch! She had set him up for a fool, she and her smart-ass boy friend. Don César de Santa Cruz with his Cadillac and his diamond rings. *You're not jealous, are you, Max? I do so want us to be friends.* The hell she did!

And tonight they were all flying back together on the Clipper like one big happy family.

Well maybe he'd be spared that at least.

"*Where are you going now?*" Sol had demanded as he left the office at Cavite.

"*To have it out with Ross. Where d'you think, for Christsakes?*"

"*Cool down, Max, you'll only make it worse. Stay away from the ship. Go take the afternoon off and let me work on him.*"

"*Jesus, Sol, Ross's nerve is shot. Whatever's back of this, it's breaking him apart.*"

"*Stay away from the ship, blast you, that's an order. Go play your match and I'll call you later.*"

The Gypsy danced nervously under him. "Steady, old fellow," he murmured, easing the reins. A horse responded to your mood, so too in a different way did an airplane.

The umpire threw the bamboo-root ball in on the half-way line. There was a click of sticks, a scuffling of hooves, then the Dutchman had it clear. Lofting his mallet, he smacked the ball hard up the field towards the Scouts' goal and took off after it like a rocket.

A roar went up from the crowd as Nieto and Roxas galloped madly after him. Munro wheeled back on the Gypsy to defend the goal. César was racing up on his left, screaming for the pass, with Georgiana on the Arab tearing in support. Without breaking stride the Dutchman hooked the ball across.

Munro put spurs to the Gypsy's flanks and the little grey streaked to intercept, his hooves drumming on the hard ground. César had eyes only for the goal now and they came up on his blind side. Stirrup to stirrup they raced for the ball, César sawing furiously at the reins to ride them off, both ponies shouldering for room and the goal wide open. At the very last second the Gypsy edged his nose in front. With a squeal of protest César's pony shortened stride and Munro took the stroke in a cloud of dust.

The backhand shot caught the Scouts wrong-footed. Nieto picked the pass up neatly, spinning his pony round the hooves of Georgiana's Arab and galloping off with it down the boundary. Seventy yards from the base line he passed across to Ritchie, who hit the ball home unopposed.

The crowd yelled. First blood to *los Angeles*.

César rode back to the line, his handsome face venomous.

The second chukka was a fast one. After their drubbing the Scouts were playing very seriously. They kept the ball in the Angels' half, pressing them hard. Munro's new mount was a big bay with strong quarters. He was sticking to César like glue and the Spaniard's temper was fraying.

Then Van Cleef won the ball out of a scrimmage. He smacked it up the pitch and both teams tore in pursuit with the umpires scuttling to get clear.

"Watch the goal!" Nieto yelled and Munro wrenched his pony round. The long bouncing drive had carried the ball out to the boundary. Georgiana was racing up on the far wing with no one to stop her.

"Georgiana!" the Dutchman shouted and cut the ball across.

Munro wheeled to intercept.

It was their first contact together. She was riding well, standing in her stirrups to take the stroke, long legs gripping her pony's flanks. He laced his whip across the bay and streaked to head her off.

Eighty yards from the posts they collided in a cloud of dust, hooking furiously at each other's sticks, the ponies squealing with excitement and rage. The bay laid his shoulder to her mare's quarters and shoved her aside just as César and Nieto came up together. Cursing and elbowing, they jabbed at the ball with shortened sticks, chopping at the ponies' legs. The dust rose chokingly and Munro felt a burning pain across his wrist as the Spaniard's whip slashed out.

The suddenness of it made him jerk the reins and the bay stumbled,

191

almost bringing them down. Georgiana seized her chance. Leaning forward she took a hurried swing. The stroke sliced and the ball shot away over the back line. A groan of disappointment went up from the crowd.

Munro reined in and an instant later was almost hurled to the ground by César cannoning into him from behind.

"Watch where you're going, godammit, the ball's out of play!"

The Spaniard's proud features were taut with fury, "And you, watch what you are doing! That was foul play of yours!"

"What the hell are you talking about?"

"You and Georgiana. She was following the ball and you deliberately rode across her. The umpire should have called a foul!"

"Jesus!" Munro wiped the sweat running down his face with the back of his hand. A smarting welt scored the wrist. "Listen, pal, this is a match. If you and Georgiana want to play patsy, fine, but get careless with that switch again and you'll regret it."

The Spaniard's eyes blazed, "*Bastardo*!" Munro saw his whip hand clench and tensed. "Stay away from her, American, I warn you!" he jerked his pony away.

Shit, Munro thought watching him go, that was all he needed to complete his troubles – a jealous fiancé.

Back at the Manila Hotel Latouche was offering to take Yu-Ling for a drive. "It is a pity, *n'est pas*," he said to her uncle, "for *la petite* to see nothing of this so beautiful city?"

"Indeed you are most thoughtful, my friend," the old man smiled. "I wonder," he glanced at Yu-Ling, who stood with her eyes demurely cast down, "would it please you to go with this western person, Third Niece?"

"As you wish, Honourable Uncle," she whispered.

"You would not be frightened, *heya*?"

"Oh no, Honourable Uncle, I not afraid!" she exclaimed hurriedly and flushed pink with embarrassment.

"I will take good care of her, *bien entendu*, Professor."

"Truly is it said, many pleading voices can melt metal," the Professor observed. "So be it, Third Niece, you shall go."

The girl gave them both an ecstatic look, "*Daw-tse*, Honourable Uncle, *daw-tse*!"

In Cantonese he said to her, "You will obey this barbarian doctor person in all matters and conduct yourself as befits the daughter of a Princess of the Yellow Banner."

Yu-Ling clapped her hands, "All gods bear witness, I shall be a true Manchu."

"*Alors*," Latouche announced as they set off in a *calesa*, "first I think we visit the Escolta to view the American shops, then a tour of the Walled City. How does that suit you, Mademoiselle?"

Yu-Ling nodded and gripped the side of the swaying carriage, too excited to speak. How wide and grand the avenues seemed after her native Macao. How shiny and powerful the cars of the Americans speeding by. The bells on the harness jingled as they rattled across the sluggish river and bold-eyed, dark-skinned youths on bicycles flashed grins at her and whistled.

CANADIAN PACIFIC, proclaimed a sign on the Escolta, EMPRESS OF BRITAIN 128 DAY WORLD CRUISE. At the Lyric theatre Heddy Lamarr was starring in *Ziegfeld Girl*. The store windows were crammed with a glittering display of Western goods: refrigerators, cameras, radiograms, canned food, THE NEW MIXMASTER – A MUST FOR EVERY HOME, Yu-Ling wondered what that could possibly be. Eyes popping, she held tight to the Doctor's arm as they strolled beneath the awnings.

She was more interested in the fashions. Could she ever wear such clothes? Perhaps you had to be taller. *Quai loh* women were veritable giants. How purposeful they seemed too, striding up and down in their big hats, swinging their arms, talking loudly. She was much struck by the sight of Eurasian and Chinese girls with Marcelled hair waves. *Ai-yah*, how daring! She would like to try that.

They stopped at a pharmacy. "I have to collect some things here," Latouche said. He held a long conversation with the man behind the counter. Yu-Ling studied the advertisements for face creams, wondering what he was buying.

"*Bon*," he said at last, collecting his purchases, "let us find a place to talk."

"This medicine, it will make Honourable Uncle well again?" Yu-Ling asked, biting her lip.

They were sitting in a little open-air café opposite San Agustin in *Intramuros*, drinking cups of frothy Spanish chocolate and watching the urchins playing at checkers on the pavement with bottle caps.

The Doctor composed his face carefully before answering. "No, *petite*, but it will make the pain easier to bear I hope," he said.

"But the doctors in the Golden Country, they can cure him, yes?"

He saw tears brimming in the brown eyes and sighed. Yet to lie to her was crueller still. "It is possible they can help him – a little," he told her gently, "but it will mean surgery, an operation and even so he cannot have many more years left to him.

A tear splashed over onto her cheek. She wiped it away and hid her head. The Doctor regarded her shaking shoulders silently for a minute then tenderly reached to cover her small hand with his own, "*Petite*, I did not say it will be at once. You will have a little time together yet."

The third chukka after the interval started badly for the Angels.

César's mount was an imported black gelding, Munro had the Gypsy again. Nieto won the ball at the throw-in but the Dutchman pinned him down and a scrimmage developed.

Twisting and turning they churned the ground, striving for the advantage, teeth flashing in dust-streaked faces. Then Roxas missed an easy stroke, the Dutchman swiped with his mallet and the ball rose whizzing through the air like a shell straight to César.

In an instant he had spun the gelding and was chasing off down the wing with it before Munro could block him. Right on the forty yard line he centered with a clean smacking shot that hopped and bounded across the hard ground. Ritchie and Van Cleef were neck and neck, fighting for the pass and Georgiana saw her chance again. Sweeping through from behind, she leaned forward on a loose rein and tipped the ball in to a burst of applause from the spectators on the rails.

One all.

One all and four minutes left. Both teams were putting their utmost into this chukka, whoever held the lead at the finish would have the match in their pocket.

Sticks clashed. The game was on again.

Back and forth the ball flew across the field with the ponies thundering in pursuit, their steel-shod hooves kicking up the dust. Ritchie almost fell on a turn and the umpires gave a penalty hit against the Scouts for crossing.

Then César made a shot from sixty yards that sent Munro scrambling for it frantically. He caught it right in the goal mouth and cleared with a splitting backhander that jarred his arm and simultaneously he felt the head of his mallet fly off.

"Take it, Luis!" he heard Nieto shout as the ball went slicing towards the boundary. Luis Roxas bolted up the pitch on his short-backed grey, the Dutchman after him. Munro pulled the Gypsy round and galloped for the rails where a groom was waving a fresh stick.

He snatched it up and dived back into the game.

Less than a minute to the bell.

Georgiana had the ball and hit it forward but her drive lacked power. Ritchie scooped it up short and a scrimmage formed on the half-way line. The melée broke apart and the Dutchman came out dribbling the ball, poised for a long shot up the field. Munro pressed his heels to the Gypsy's flanks and swooped down on him, his fresh stick lofted. With a smack that was heard in the stands he hit the ball full.

Another roar went up from the crowd. César was streaking up on his right but the goal was wide open, the enemy back nowhere to be seen. With seconds only left to play both men lashed their sweat-drenched mounts in a frantic race for the posts.

Forty yards from the goal. Thirty. Munro yelled in the Gypsy's ear, driving him on, too close now to use the whip. César was yelling too, sawing at the reins to ride him off. The ball was skipping towards the line, another second and it would be too late. Munro tightened his grip for the swing, but César was inching ahead . . .

Then the gelding screamed.

With a squeal of pain and terror that rang across the pitch the gelding fell at full gallop, pitching César over his neck. Munro felt the Gypsy stagger as the stricken beast's shoulder rammed them side-ways, and start to go down. He gave a desperate heave at the reins to miss the posts and jerked his feet from the stirrup. He hit the ground with a thump that knocked him breathless, rolling over in the dust.

Spitting out dirt from his mouth, he stumbled to his feet looking for César.

He was lying very still.

The time bell clanged urgently. People were running onto the pitch. Club officials, medics, stable-lads. The Gypsy scrambled upright quivering. His nostrils flared at the scent of blood. Tossing his head, he broke away.

Praying, Munro ran towards the inert figure on the ground.

The Spaniard lay face down, the splintered shaft of his mallet still hanging from a wrist by its thong. A few feet away the gelding twitched in spasm, near foreleg broken, the bone sticking through the skin.

The club doctor kneeled at César's side, feeling his head gently. His face was plastered with dust and there was blood on his britches. No injury though that Munro could see, it must be his mount's.

"*César!*" Georgiana leapt down off her horse and pushed through to his side. Her hair was tumbling down from under her helmet and her eyes were burning with anger and fright. "You damn crazy fool!" she cried at Munro. "You've killed him!"

Van Cleef caught her by the arms, "Calm yourself, Georgiana, he is only concussed I think." To Munro he said, "What happened? I did not see."

"He was riding me off, his horse tripped," Munro shrugged tiredly. "Maybe a stick hooked him. I don't know whose."

The Spaniard's eyes opened and he grimaced melodramatically.

The black gelding was struggling to rise. A club official came running out with a gun. Van Cleef took it. Moments later the sad flat whack of the shot echoed across the pitch.

"Stupid, stupid men!" Georgiana cried, dashing tears away with her sleeve and leaving streaks of dust on her white cheeks. "Stupid jealous idiots," she raged. "Showing off like a couple of children!"

Munro spun back stung. "*Isn't that just what you wanted?*" he spat savagely.

★ ★ ★

HONGKONG. Seven hundred and fifty miles across the South China Sea it was nearing five pm.

"*Ai-yah*, are your legs made of jelly, *heya*?" Colonel Huang goaded the rickshaw puller. "Speed up, I am in a hurry!"

Wheels rattled on the cobbled streets as the man laboured uphill towards the Peak. In the back Huang sat stiffly impatient despite the jolting. *Kokuryu-kai* had a spy on the Clipper, that much was known. If the dog-dung British hadn't let the prisoner be murdered under their noses they might have a name by now. *Dew neh loh moh chow hi* on all stupid *quai loh*! Imperative he wireless Chungking. The fornicators there would tell him what to do.

They climbed above the city. The rickshaw bowled along a twisting avenue past high walls spiked with broken glass. The puller drew up before tall gates, gasping, his ribs showing through his heaving chest. "Give me my money, I've earned it."

Huang threw him a half dollar and grudgingly added a three cent tip. He tugged the bell chain. There was no response. Frowning, he tried the gates. They were unlocked, the gardens empty. Lazy good for nothing servants, were they all asleep?

Suddenly he stopped short. In the driveway lay a dead bird. A cockerel. Head torn off, feathers drenched in blood. Tied to the legs was a scrap of silk. Imperial yellow. The mark of the Manchu. *The Red Pang had been here!*

He cocked his pistol, listening. All was quiet. Perhaps it was just a warning to frighten away the servants. Keeping to cover, he cut across the garden up towards the mansion. From the terrace there was a view to the hills of the New Territories. *Ai-yah*, that way the Sea Devils would come.

French windows stood ajar. Inside Chinese black lacquer mixed with ugly English reproductions. Nothing looked to have been disturbed. The stillness hung. Cautiously he went through to the stairs.

"*Wei*! Anyone here, *heya*?"

A floorboard creaked behind him. He spun at the sound. *Oh ko*!

From a door at the end of the hall burst a monster. A giant of a man, naked but for a loin string, garish tattoos covered every inch of his sweat-drenched body. A murderous hatchet swung from his fist and his eyes burned with a drug crazed blood lust that churned Huang's bowels.

"Death to the traitor! DEATH!" With a furious bellow the assassin rushed at him.

Jerking up the gun, Huang fired on reflex. Fired and missed and fired again. The bullet struck the giant in the stomach where a five-clawed dragon squirmed in red and green. He staggered and let out a roar of pain like a wounded beast.

And kept on coming!

Hum kar chan, it wasn't possible! Again and again the gun crashed out. Shot after shot tore home with no more effect than spit-balls. Slipping and lurching in his own blood the figure came on still.

"Death! Death! DEATH!"

Huang squeezed the trigger frantically. The hammer clicked on an empty chamber. With a shriek his nerve broke, he turned to flee.

A cry of manic triumph erupted from the dying killer's lips. With a last convulsive surge of strength he whirled the hatchet and brought it smashing down.

"DEATH!"

XV

CAVITE NAVAL YARD. With a clatter and a roar the Clipper's two inboard engines burst into life.

Slowly, with infinite care, tractors had manoeuvred the flying boat on its beaching trolley out of the hangar and down to the dockside. Stern first, steadied by restraining lines, the great hull had been floated off and the cradle withdrawn.

"*Ready on one,*" the Chief sang out.

In the right hand pilot's seat Kurt Thyssen reached for the overhead switches, "*Starting one.*"

"*Ready on four.*"

"*Starting four.*"

Launches fussing ahead of her, the Clipper moved slowly out into mid-harbour past the grey hulled Navy vessels lying at their buoys. Away in the distance across the great sweep of the bay Manila smouldered in a haze of heat.

"*Prepare for test run.*"

The roar of the outer starboard prop rose to a deafening scream as the revolutions climbed. Up in the bow hatch Shapiro blocked his ears and scanned the water ahead for debris. Blasting sheets of spray astern the Clipper swung into the wind. One after another the sixteen hundred horsepower Cyclones were run up to full-rated power.

"*All readings, check,*" the Chief scanned his dials.

"*Shut down one and four. Stand by to return to mooring,*" Ross ordered. Their speed fell away and the sound of the engines slackened as he eased back on the throttles.

"Mean bastard, the mechanics could have done all this," Shapiro grumbled to Chris as they stepped out onto the wooden jetty. "He's made us miss the polo. What d'you suppose is up between him and Max?"

Up on the flight deck the Chief completed his log unhurriedly and shut it away. Yawning, he stood up. "Figure I'll stop aboard this evening," he said.

Ross looked up from his desk at the rear, "Why, for Christsakes?" he snapped suspiciously.

"Precautions."

The wash of a passing vessel rocked the ship slightly. Ross shrugged, "Suit yourself."

"Fine, Chuck'll pick up my kit," the Chief opened the hatch to the starboard wing walkway and a smell of avgas and hot oil entered the cabin. "By the way, Ross," he added, looking back as he stepped through, "what I said earlier, about Munro. It still holds good."

"*Oi! The flying boat is ready!*"

Across the street from the Bachelor Officers' Quarters was a barber's shop run by a smiling nisei. The three pretty olive-skinned daughters he employed to cut hair made the establishment popular with servicemen from the yard.

"Yukio, Yukio," he beckoned urgently to the youngest from the window. "The monks must be warned. She has taken on extra fuel. Quick, fetch me a bird."

"*Kasikomarimasita.*"

Flashing a bright smile at her client, the girl hurried into the back. Her skirts fluttered round her legs as she shinned nimbly up a ladder and out through a trapdoor onto the roof. Hidden from view beneath straw matting was a wire-netting cage of cooing carrier pigeons. Reaching in, she drew one out and carried it downstairs to the old man and held it for him while he deftly attached a tiny message capsule to its leg.

"*Sayonara*, little bird," she whispered, releasing it in the back yard. The pigeon soared, circled briefly, then headed out across the bay in the direction of the city.

The Sternberg was the big hospital for US military out by Jones Bridge. Traffic was solid all along the Pasig River and it was after five by the time Bob Cashin's cab pulled up at the casualty entrance.

Almost the first person he saw was Sally Scott, chatting in the hall with a young intern. Her left arm was in a sling.

"Say, are you okay? What happened? I heard there'd been an accident."

"Why, Mr. Cashin," she looked surprised. "Sure, it's only a light sprain. They've just discharged me."

"My cab's waiting," Cashin said, "I'll take you back to the hotel."

199

A convoy of ambulances was drawn up in the parking area as they drove away. "Looks like they're shipping out non-urgent cases to make room for war casualties," Cashin said. He turned to Scott, "So tell me what happened?"

"Just a dumb accident. Two goons in a stolen motor shot the intersection onto Calle Real. I was lucky, the coachman's in quite a mess, poor guy." Scott was unpinning her sling as she spoke.

"Hey, should you be doing that?"

"Honest, it's okay," she straightened her arm to show him. "Look, I'd really appreciate it if the others didn't get to hear about this. Our Skipper's pretty strict, if he thinks I'm not fit he'll throw me off the flight."

"And you don't want to be trapped in Manila," Cashin nodded. "Sure, I understand."

The traffic had stalled. There was a Philippines Army convoy crossing the bridge ahead. "Draftees," the cab driver yawned picking his teeth idly while they waited for the road to clear. "Gov'ment call 'em up to fight de Japs," he chuckled at the absurdity of it. The young men in the trucks were singing. Was this how wars began? Scott wondered.

FIVE PM. Maria Bianchi entered the main gates of the US High Commission on Dewey Boulevard.

"Sorry, Ma'am," the marine sentry on duty inside told her, "the office is closed now."

"Mr. Collins of the passport section is expecting me."

He phoned through to check. She heard the glass inner doors open and glancing up met the gaze of Prince Cherkassy.

"Good afternoon, Madam," he bowed over her hand. "You are here to confirm your visa? But no, you are an American citizen, I think?"

She returned his stare coolly, "Yes, I am a citizen."

"But living in Shanghai?"

An impatient little frown cut her forehead, "Formerly I lived in Shanghai, now I am moving back to Honolulu."

"Oh, you were in Honolulu before?"

She did not answer. The marine put down the phone. "That's alright, Ma'am. Second floor, Mr. Collins will meet you at the elevator." He held the doors for her with a beam, "Did I hear you say you were from Shanghai? I've some buddies just in from there, the Fourth Marines."

Her heart missed a beat, "The Fourth Marines?"

"You didn't know? They pulled in from Shanghai yesterday."

She recovered herself, "No, I did not. I never met any Marines in Shanghai."

The Prince watched her thoughtfully through the doors as she tapped away down the corridor.

"Ten thousand dollars, Mr. Collins," Maria laid the bundles of notes on the desk. "Count them if you wish."

They were alone. The office door was locked. Everyone else on the floor had already left for the day.

"No, I'll take your word for it," Collins licked his lips greedily at the sight of the money piled before him. He was a thin man with greying hair and a mean mouth. Guiltily he scooped it out of sight into a drawer. The index finger of his left hand was missing. "Alright, let's get this over with. Give me the documents," he snapped nervously.

She handed him an envelope, "It's all here, birth certificate, father's passport, photograph."

"Good," he muttered. Switching on his desk lamp, he took a fresh US passport from his desk and began filling in the blanks. "Richard Anthony?" he glanced up. She nodded. Collins blotted the ink dry, chose a rubber stamp and wetted it on a pad.

"I had to have this specially made up, they changed the design last year. You don't know the trouble I've been to."

"You are being paid well enough for it. In three years you would not earn as much."

"I'm doing this *cheap*! Listen, if I'm caught I'm ruined," he said resentfully, pasting in the boy's photo. "It's not even necessary, I told you that in the beginning. They'd have given you a visa for him any day."

"It's necessary for me. I know what it means to be without papers. And he has the right. His father was a citizen and so am I now."

"Yes, but you weren't when he was born, you weren't even *married* then. Legally he's stateless. You should have waited." Collins slid the passport across the desk, "There, satisfied?"

Maria sat calmly in her seat, legs crossed. The passport lay untouched on the desk between them. "There is also the file," she said.

"Oh, yes," he affected surprise. A crafty smile lit up his face, "Almost forgot." He opened the drawer again and extracted a manila folder. Abruptly his face hardened, "I figure we should make a separate deal on this."

"No. We agreed – ten thousand to include the file!"

Collins' voice became a snarl, "Well, the deal's changed, lady. It's going to cost you the same again to have this lost."

"Impossible."

"The hell it is! Jesus, you must have been taking that much every week from your Shanghai operation. You'll pay alright," he slapped the file, "else this gets reopened and when Immigration learn how you made your dough they'll have you back in Shanghai on the next boat and the brat too. Citizen or no citizen!"

Maria's eyes became slivers of ice, "In which case the authorities here would learn of your taste for schoolgirls – and how you frequent a certain house in Ermita."

The man cringed, his face grey. "It's a lie, I was never . . ."

"Be quiet." Her voice slashed him. She stubbed out her cigarette, "Do you take me for a fool? I could have bought this," she indicated the passport contemptuously, "any time during the past four years for a quarter of the sum you demanded, but I had no intention of paying blackmail for the rest of my days. So I waited. I waited till I found someone as vulnerable as I was. *You!*"

"Damn you to hell!" Collins clutched his desk. "You have no proof."

"I have Teresita," Maria watched the name sink in.

The man gaped wordless.

"Yes, she is out of your reach now, at school – where she belongs."

"Please," the man begged. He seemed suddenly aged. She felt no pity for him, only a savage contempt.

"I have kept my side of the bargain. If you break yours, if so much as a breath of my past reaches my son, then I promise you, Mr. Collins, *I will bring your life crashing down in ruins!*"

The rear seat of the waiting car was piled with gaily-wrapped packages. "Quickly," she told the driver, "back to the Manila Hotel."

The sun was slipping down into the sea in fiery splendour as they sped along the boulevard and the Luneta was thronged with couples strolling in the languorous cool of late afternoon. It was done. The contents of Collins' file had been safely reduced to ash, Ricky's passport with the visa was secure in her purse and five thousand dollars had gone to the nuns for the care of little Teresita.

The hotel lobby was full of guests taking *merienda*. Waiters served delicious-looking sweet cakes sprinkled with coconut and there was the mouth-watering aroma of hot chocolate and fresh ground coffee.

The Gordon Smythes were sitting with Mr. Wirth. For once Cynthia was in a good humour; after much difficulty they had wheedled from the Consulate an invitation to the Presidential gala. She smiled as Maria was shown to a seat nearby. "Goodness, Mrs. Bianchi, you have been doing a lot of shopping!"

"Yes, isn't it wonderful," Maria beamed, handing a coin to the bellhop arranging her parcels. "My son is coming to join me. We've been parted for *so* long!"

As she spoke there was a cry from the steps. "Momma! Momma!" Ricky came running into the lobby, the Simms family trailing.

"*Ricky!*" Maria leapt up, scattering the boxes of presents. Tears pouring down her cheeks, she swept him into her arms and hugged him to her, "*Ricky!* Oh, my darling, my darling, at last!"

From a table under the palm trees, Prince Cherkassy observed the reunion with an enigmatic smile.

Its horn blasting lesser traffic aside, a military sedan swept through the gates of The House on the Wall – the exquisite eighteenth century building perched atop the ramparts of *Intramuros* that was Headquarters of the Philippine Department of Defence. Sentries snapped to attention as aides hurried Slater and Sir Ambrose Hope inside.

In an upstairs office cooled by whirling *punkah* fans a tall, dour brigadier general was waiting, Chief of Staff Richard K. Sutherland. His manner was tense.

"We came directly we got your message, General. What the hell's gone wrong?"

Sutherland told them bluntly, "The special cargo is missing. The B–17 flying it to Hawaii went off the air this morning. Efforts to re-establish contact have failed."

Sir Ambrose stood still for a second as if he had been dealt a physical blow. "Good God," he said quietly.

Through the slatted door they could hear Filipino clerks pecking away at typewriters. "Alright, give us the story," Slater gritted his teeth. "The President's gonna want to hear it."

"One thing first," Sir Ambrose interrupted. "Who made the decision to change the flight plan?"

Slater chewed his lip, "Washington – on my recommendation. After the Jap's stunt yesterday we figured it too dangerous to stick with the Guam route."

A balding Air Corps colonel drew down the big wall chart of the Mid-Pacific. "As you know, Major, the cargo was flown out from

Clark Field at 0200 hours this morning aboard a B–17 of the 19th Bombardment Group."

"You sent the Bishop's coffin along too?" Sir Ambrose said to Slater.

He shrugged, "It was the cover we agreed."

The colonel's finger traced along the map towards the lower left corner, "First stop was to be Lae, New Guinea . . ."

"New Guinea? The flight was via New Guinea?"

"Yes, sir, that's correct. Lae and Howland, then up through Wake and Midway to Pearl. There's no strip on Guam big enough to take the new bombers."

"Lae and Howland!" Sir Ambrose stared at them. "*The Earhart route*? You sent the cargo by the Earhart route? Good God, gentlemen," he said hoarsely, "*you need us now*."

Dusk was gathering in the room. Someone turned up the lights. Sutherland signed to the colonel to continue. "Flight time was estimated at nine hours forty minutes. The forecast was clear, with possible deterioration late in the day." He glanced up, "That was one reason why we decided to act quickly.

"Towards dawn the captain radioed the weather was slipping and he was encountering heavy turbulence. Over the next two hours contact worsened progressively and the last message, received at . . ." he checked his notes, ". . . 0916 hours, was garbled by static. It indicates they were flying parallel with the New Guinea coast approximately in the region of Hollandia."

"Since then nothing?" Slater said. The colonel shook his head mutely. "Jesus!"

"The Japanese?" Sir Ambrose queried.

The colonel shook his head again. "Their nearest base, here at Koror," he tapped the map, "is eight hundred miles away. So far as we know they don't have anything with the range."

"Was the bomber armed?"

"Yes, sir. As of last week all Army planes are on war footing."

There was silence in the room. Outside, bells were calling the Angelus. Slater's fists knotted. "I want to see General MacArthur," he said thinly. "*Now*."

High above Manila Bay the General was pacing his balcony, a jewelled cigarette holder clamped firmly between his teeth, his blue and gold West Point dressing gown streaming. Below the city sparkled with lights and a crimson glow suffused the sky as the sun dipped behind the purple mountains of Bataan.

Abruptly he swung, stabbing a finger at the group of waiting officers, "No, gentlemen, I will not risk another of my bombers on this enterprise. The Navy must take the task on now."

"Godammit, Doug, I can't spare any of my Catalinas either," peppery Admiral Hart, commander of the Asiatic Fleet, exploded. "Every plane I've got is in the air round the clock flying reconnaissance. You'll have to stick with the Air Corps!"

"I repeat, I cannot, *I will not* risk another bomber."

Slater cleared his throat, "General Mac Arthur, I have Presidential authority requiring that you make a B–17 available for this mission."

The General whirled on him, his anger icy. "Don't try to pull rank on me, Major," he snapped. "I decide when orders apply to me and I do not need the help of junior officers in that respect." He let the blistering rebuke sink in and continued, "For your information the President's message *requests* I give you such assistance as is in my power. It does not *require* me to turn over to you aircraft vitally needed for the defence of these islands."

Five stories below Colonel Nieto turned his Chevrolet into the hotel driveway and cut the engine. He placed a hand on his passenger's sleeve, "Max, do not blame yourself, it was an accident."

"Of course it was an accident," Munro opened the door to get out. "Did you think I was trying to kill him, for Christsakes?"

"No, no, of course not. It was the fault of Georgiana. I swear to you, Max, I did not know she was intending to play herself. Fortunately young César is not injured. My friend, I will see you later at the Palace. *Adios ko* – God be with you."

Son of a gun, Munro thought wearily as he walked up the steps in his dusty britches, a swell game that had turned out to be. A horse dead, a rider darn near killed, it had been more like a battle.

And all because of Georgiana.

"For the wind is in the palm-trees an' the temple bells they say . . ."

It was the blue hour again. Glasses were clinking in the bars. In the Champagne Room a piano tinkled and a baritone was singing:

"An' the dawn comes up like thunder outer China 'crost the Bay!"

He checked at the desk. Still no message from Sol. He went upstairs to his room, showered, wrapped a towel round his waist and stretched out on the bed. Maybe Ross had decided to pull out and leave him. But why? To cover for his own loss of nerve? No, there had to be more to it than that.

Mili. The answer had to be there. Mili meant Earhart and Earhart led to Slater.

Ross, Slater, Earhart.

He let it drop. Time to dress for the Palace Ball. His white tuxedo had come back from the valet freshly pressed. He was straightening his bow tie when the telephone buzzed.

"Max?" The voice was Sol's, "Is Ross there with you?"

"Ross? No, I thought he was still out at Cavite. Why?"

"Because he's needed here. Urgently. You'll have to stand in for him. Take the elevator to the penthouse and I'll meet you at the top in two minutes."

"What's up, for God's sake?"

"Godammit, just get here!"

He had never taken the private elevator before. It didn't seem so different from any other. At the top though it was like stepping into a museum. Swords and banners hung from the walls with oil portraits of MacArthur ancestors. Oriental screens and tapestries, Japanese vases, Chinese carpets and antique ceramics crowded the vast rooms.

The air conditioning was ferocious, he was glad of his jacket.

It wasn't Sol who met him but Georgiana, dressed for the evening in a low-cut gown and emerald choker, pale and damnably pretty. "Oh," she said taken aback. "I thought you were César. He's escorting me to the ball."

"He's up and around already?"

She made an impatient gesture, "He wasn't hurt, just stunned. They X-rayed him and let him go. If you're hoping he won't make the flight tonight, forget it – we'll both be there."

"You flatter yourself, Dixie. I don't give a monkey *who* rides in back so long as they pay the fare."

With a look of pure vitriol she turned on her heel and swept back into the drawing room.

Sol appeared, "Okay, Max, this way."

Proud, upright, thinning black hair, hawk-like features, General Douglas MacArthur dominated the penthouse library. His gaze narrowed piercingly, "We've met before."

"Yes, sir, at the Army and Navy Club in June," Munro was surprised. They had barely spoken together.

"General Sutherland, my Chief of Staff, and Colonel Willoughby, my G–2," the General indicated the officers gathered round the centre table. "Major Slater you know."

The walls of the room were lined with books, their spines gleaming in the lamplight. Ten thousand or more, titles like *Robert E. Lee* and *Clauswitz*, the General's famous military collection. Spread out on the table was a chart of New Guinea and the Solomons. Munro's pulse jumped a notch. He looked up and saw Slater smiling at him without humour, "That's right, pilot, you're going to fly us down to the swamps."

Munro stared at the map. New Guinea, the world's second largest island and the least explored. "You want us to fly down the Clipper and recover the special cargo?"

"Can you do it?" Again MacArthur's piercing gaze.

"Depends whereabouts the Fortress went down, sir. New Guinea's a big island."

The General gestured to his Intelligence officer, "Show him, Charles."

Colonel Willoughby leaned over the map, "Just before dusk a British survey plane spotted the wreckage here, on the Markham River west of Lae."

Lae, New Guinea. Amelia Earhart's last known stopping point. Munro shot a glance at Slater. "They're sure it's the Fortress?"

"It's confirmed. The Pan Am operator at Lae picked up a voice transmission from the crew. Seems one or more engines quit in the storm, they decided to ditch and wound up stranded in the swamps. The plane's a write-off but they're safe and the cargo is intact."

Of course, the *Southern Cross* was based at Lae. She would carry comprehensive radio and D/F gear.

"Do we have an exact position of the crash site?"

"Thirty, forty miles upriver from the town, judging from reports."

Munro nodded thoughtfully, "Their R/T set wouldn't reach much further at sea level." Then he frowned, "Flying you down to Lae is no problem. Ross knows the route. But a river landing's out. Not on that kind of water. Not unless you're figuring to write off another ship."

"Nobody expects you to," Slater said sourly. "There's an Australian military unit stationed in the town. They'll recover the cargo by launch. All you have to do is load it aboard."

Munro turned to MacArthur, "May I ask the General a question?"

"Fire ahead, son."

"Sir, wouldn't it be better to have the Air Corps or the Navy handle this? It will put us two days behind schedule and you're risking an expensive aircraft into the bargain."

He had expected a blast of anger but instead the General threw him a

207

quick grin, "In the normal course of events I would agree with you one hundred percent. This is no job for civilians. But I have to consider the effect upon the enemy. By weakening my strength at this moment in detaching yet another of my bomber fleet, I may actually be inviting an attack."

"I understand, sir."

"I was confident you would." Straightening up from the table, MacArthur clapped a vigorous hand to his shoulder, "Munro, at times of crisis such as these, we in the military look to our compatriots in Pan American as an Air Corps in reserve. I know you will not fail us."

It was Munro's first experience of MacArthur's infectious leadership. He found himself grinning back. "You can count on us, General. If the Australians recover the cargo tomorrow, we'll have it back here for you within twenty-four hours."

There was a silence. "Isn't that what's wanted?"

"Not quite, Max," Sol shook his head. "Our idea is the Clipper should fly straight on to Guam. The passengers will travel down to New Guinea with you. They can spend the night aboard the *Southern Cross*, it's what she's designed for."

The telephone rang.

Ross was on his way up.

"*You're insane, all of you*! Out of your fucking minds!"

MacArthur's eyes flashed ice, "Control yourself, Captain. I won't have such language used to me."

With an effort Ross got a hold on himself. "With respect, sir, you don't know what you're asking. New Guinea . . ." he took a breath, "New Guinea is the nearest place to hell on this earth. The terrain makes Bataan look like a meadow. It's got rain forest, swamps, mountain ranges, you name it. There's every kind of insect and disease, poisonous snakes, crocs . . . the weather changes from one minute to the next, it can rain as much as sixteen inches in a single day. If another storm blows up we could be socked in there for a week and if a typhoon hits we're finished."

"Hell, Captain," Sutherland interrupted sneering. "The Air Corps has been ferrying planes up through Port Moresby for the past nine months. They haven't lost one yet."

"Moresby is the capital. It's on the south coast and almost civilized by comparison with Lae. *Almost*. There you're talking about a prepared airfield with proper facilities. Lae is nothing but a godforsaken mining camp. No spares, no back-up, that was how . . ." he checked himself suddenly. Slater's eyebrows knotted.

"The *Southern Cross* is there," Sol put in. "She's fully equipped as a hotel and floating base."

Ross clenched his teeth, "General, believe me, New Guinea is just no place for a passenger plane."

MacArthur began to pace the room, his dressing gown with the varsity 'A' flapping about him. The others watched and waited. Abruptly he pivoted to face Munro, "Are *you* willing to make the trip – as captain if necessary?"

Munro swallowed. Ross was staring at him, so were the others. The expression on Ross's face made him sick. "Sir, I have no experience of conditions down there."

"That wasn't what I asked," the General waived the answer aside impatiently.

Oh Jesus, Munro thought. Hating himself, he nodded.

"Captain Ross," MacArthur rounded on him, cigarette holder jutting from between his teeth like a weapon. "This is an hour of emergency, vital national interests are at stake. In the name of the United States Government *I am ordering you* to make this flight."

The trapped-animal look was back in Ross's eyes again as he gazed at them. For what seemed an eternity they waited.

"Alright," he breathed. "Alright, curse you! If that's what you want, *we'll go!*"

The telephone shrilled again. Willoughby answered it. There was a pause while he listened, mouth drawn in a hard thin line. "I don't give a damn what the editors say, the story's embargoed at the highest level and we'll shut down any paper that prints it!"

He slammed the receiver down, "That was the Press Office, the newspapers have a lead on those missionaries."

Munro's eyes narrowed, "Missionaries?"

Slater told him. "There's been another killing. Two friends of Jordan's. Murdered by Buddhist monks working for the Japs."

Another killing! Munro felt the blood drain from his face, "*Buddhist monks?*"

"Yeah, guys with shaved heads in yellow robes."

Yellow monks. A figure waving from the hill this morning. A figure in yellow!

Then his attention zeroed. "The missionaries. What were their names?"

Slater stared at him, realisation dawning, "Bell, one was a Dr. Bell and the other was called Father Carmichael."

"Carmichael, the one from the photograph! Bishop Buchan, Oliv-

209

er, the man Jordan said was dead already . . .''

"Currie. His name was Currie."

"And now Carmichael. Georgiana is the only one left – and she's gone to the palace ball!''

Slater had blanched, "It's the gala night. Everyone's there. *Jordan's there!*''

XVI

MALACANANG. EIGHT PM. The breeze had dropped and the evening was warm and sultry. On the banks of the Pasig River beyond *Intramuros* the palace sparkled with lights. An envious crowd clung to the railings as long lines of gleaming limousines swept in at the gates. Liveried footmen held open the doors of the car bearing the blue and white flag of the Chinese delegation and Yu-Ling stepped out onto the red carpet. She was wearing her best, newest *cheong-sam* with a jade necklace and new silk stockings and her heart was bursting with excitement. *Oh ko*, never, never in a thousand years had she dreamed of an evening like this!

"Take my arm, little Jade Years," Hollington Soong wheezed, nudging her forward to join the receiving line, the Ambassador following with his number one wife, a haughty Szechuanese in stiff brocade. Inside the rococo palace Yu-Ling's eyes popped at the crystal chandeliers, the marble floors and gilded mirrors, the fabulous gowns and jewels and fans.

Manuel Quezon, the handsome, dapper President, was greeting his guests in the flower-filled hall. Yu-Ling approached nervously and dropped a low curtsy like the nuns had taught. The President's eyes twinkled as he raised her up. Colonel Nieto appeared to escort them through onto the terrace and Yu-Ling gasped afresh. The gardens glittered like some incredible stage set. Along the river banks torches flared, coloured lights twinkled in the trees and the dance floor under the stars was walled shoulder-high with shimmering ice to cool the revellers.

Hollington Soong saw the eager swell of her fresh young bosom and felt his secret sack jiggle. "Come," he said throatily, taking her hand in his and squeezing it, "let us go down *heya*?"

Dragons, tigers and ghouls mingled in the gardens. Many of the Filipino guests had equipped themselves with elaborate carnival masks. White gloved servants passed among the candle-lit tables under the trees with champagne and fresh squeezed *calamansi* juice and trays of *pika-pika* snacks, fried anchovies dipped in vinegar, tiny cakes of bean sprouts and shrimp, spiced Spanish pastries. Felicity Gordon Smythe pounced on them with a squeal of delight.

"Felicity, control yourself," her mother snapped. Her gimlet eyes were scanning the wealthy throng for someone she might recognise. Suddenly she brightened, "Why, Prince Cherkassy," she called. "How nice to see you."

The Prince inclined his head curtly. A small decoration gleamed in his lapel. "My regrets," he turned away.

Cynthia Gordon Smythe stared after him in astonishment. "*Well*, what an extraordinary way to behave!"

Georgiana squeezed César's arm. "Why didn't you tell me people would be wearing masks tonight?" she hissed as they made their entrance. "You know I love disguises."

"*Querida mia*, everyone would recognise you with your beautiful hair. It is I who should have a mask – to hide this," he touched the scratch on his forehead carefully.

She glanced at him sharply, "Remember what the doctor said, you're to take it easy tonight."

"Tcha! If I am fit enough to fly, I am fit enough to dance."

They drew abreast of an enormous eighteenth century mirror crowned with Conquistador arms. César squared his shoulders approvingly. Undoubtedly they were the handsomest couple present, he decided. "The emeralds, they look well on you, *querida*."

She touched a hand to her throat where the stones glowed against the whiteness of her skin. His family jewels.

BOOM! ZING! BOOM! TARRA! On the terrace the band struck up a march.

"Aha, that is the signal for the river parade," Colonel Nieto exclaimed. "The President will be viewing from the stand. Shall we make our way to the bank, Minister?"

As they moved down with the crowd Soong caught sight of Georgiana and César and beamed, "Miss Delahaye, what a pleasure. Does this mean General MacArthur too is honouring us with his presence?"

"Good evening, Minister. Yes, I guess the General and Jean will be along later. He was tied up when I left."

"Of course, of course, We servants of Government, our time is never our own. Permit me to present a fellow passenger travelling in my party. Miss Chen, Miss Delahaye."

Yu-Ling shook hands very shyly, awed by the American girl's tallness and beauty. Such flaming hair. And her skin, pale like ivory.

"Hi, call me Georgiana, do. How are you enjoying Manila?"

"Oh yes, very much, please. And tonight – wonderful, wonderful!" Yu-Ling blushed furiously and they all laughed, but kindly.

Burning flambeaux lined the river bank where the palace guests pressed forward to the water's edge. On the opposite shore the public park was dark with people come to watch the spectacle. A great cheer went up as Quezon stepped out onto the floodlit landing stage accompanied by the US High Commissioner.

A procession of brightly-lit sugar barges was rounding the bend in the river, the leading craft a mass of white lilies surrounding a life-size effigy of the Virgin and Child. A wave of applause broke from both banks and at the President's side the Cardinal Archbishop raised his hand in blessing.

Jangling their bells, the floats sailed past one after another, each a mountain of flowers and bobbing lanterns flickering on the water. Brown skinned youths and girls garlanded with hibiscus waved to the crowds, singing and banging tambourines.

Near to the Presidential party a formal group of Spaniards stood back from the edge. Ladies in mestiza dresses, butterfly sleeves framing the face and long sweeping skirts. "*Bueno*, my family!" César began steering Georgiana towards them.

She pulled away, "Darling look, the floats!" The señoras pursed their lips. Muttering, César followed her through the crush.

"*Isogi! Isogi!*"

"*Hai, tadachi ni.*"

The last of the barges had passed. Low in the water a small sampan slipped across the river with scarcely a ripple and glided into the shadow of the palace gardens. The four men aboard wore coolie black and their heads were shaven. They lay prone, paddling with their hands. The lights of the gala glittered in the distance. Noiselessly they worked the craft in beneath an overhanging tree.

A river boat chugged by in midstream with a fiesta party. Music and laughter floated over the water. Not a muscle moved aboard the sampan. There was a whispered command. Steel glinted briefly in the moonlight. Two figures sprang stealthily ashore and vanished cat-like among the bushes. In perfect stillness the others waited.

A bird hooted twice and was answered. One of the scouts returned momentarily. "Nothing. Not even a patrol. Fool barbarians are all over by the palace."

"*Yoi.*" The *Osho-san* gripped his swordstick. "Take the boat back," he ordered the remaining monk. "Wait across the river for our signal, *neh*? Two flashes then one."

"*Wakarimasu.*"

Speeding through the lights at the intersection, the CIC sedan carrying Slater and Munro screamed across Jones Bridge, a jeep load of Military Police behind. The river gleamed darkly to their right. Ahead blazed the lights of Malacañang, a mob of onlookers still milling about the gates.

"Christ, what is this, the Fourth of July?" Slater gripped the rear seat impatiently as the driver slowed. "Use your goddam horn!"

Gesticulating soldiers cleared a passage and waved them through. Skidding to a halt in front of the palace steps, they leapt out. "*This way, this way!*" gold-braided officers hurried them inside. Munro had fleeting impressions of sumptuous halls and Spanish Viceroys staring down from gilded frames. They ran through onto the terrace and scanned the torch-lit gardens. Jesus, there must be two or three hundred people down there.

A Presidential aide came panting up to Slater. "No damn Jap's gonna get in, Major. We've patrols out all round the walls."

"Fine. Now get those guests back inside the palace and we'll start searching the grounds."

"Impossible. The fireworks are about to begin."

"The hell they are!" Slater brushed him aside. He tore down the steps, Munro at his heels, the helmeted MPs following. Dodging past the tables and chairs, they raced for the river bank.

Craning his neck on the edge of the crowd, Munro searched for Jordan. Half the people were wearing masks. Then he glimpsed Hollington Soong. Shoving his way through, he broke the news. The Minister paled in the torch light and gibbered with fright. Munro left him to it, he'd recognized César. Georgiana was there too.

The Spaniard saw him and his face taughtened. "*Diablo!* What do you want?"

Tersely, Munro spelled out the position, "Get Georgiana away from here. Take her back to the palace and *stay with her*. Don't let her out of your sight."

César sucked in his breath with a hiss. He caught Georgiana by the arm and began speaking to her urgently. Munro turned away, the jealousy hitting him like a hammer.

But she wasn't his girl any more.

It was then he saw Jordan, disappearing into the trees.

"Don't be absurd, what possible danger can there be here?" Georgiana stamped her foot. She was refusing point blank to leave.

"*Querida*, please. Come to the palace, just as a precaution, *si*? Minister Soong has gone already."

"No!"

César's brow darkened, "Georgiana, stop behaving like a child! I *insist* you come away."

"Let me alone!" She snatched free angrily, "I'm fed up with being told what to do. You go to the palace if you like, *I'm* staying to watch the fireworks." Tossing her head, she flounced off into the crowd.

More guards had been drafted in and a cordon thrown round the palace. The crowd began moving back from the river shepherded by soldiers. Munro shouldered his way to the fringes. Jordan had vanished.

"Hey, bring that flashlight over here!" he shouted to an MP.

The man ran up. "Japs?"

"No. The priest!"

They plunged in under the trees, flashbeam dancing off the trunks.

"Jordan . . . *Jordan!*"

Running, they hit open grass again. The MP pulled up. "Must've lost him, sir. You sure he went this way?"

"Yes dammit!" To the left was a bank of shrubs. "We'll try that path. Quick!"

Bushes closed in on them as they raced along it, the MP leading. Away from the lighted area the gardens were black as hell. A branch whipped back in Munro's face. He stumbled, caught his foot in a root and fell heavily. Swearing, he picked himself up. One ankle was hurting like sin. Damn Jordan. Why hadn't the fool run for the palace?

With a whizzing sound something shot up into the night trailing red sparks. The fireworks had started. Ignoring the pain in his foot, he pressed on trying to catch up with the MP. Coloured stars were popping and spluttering across the sky. Suddenly a rattle of explosions echoed. Sharper. Louder. *Gunshots*. Ahead along the path.

Munro froze. Straining vainly for a glimpse of the flash, he crept forward cautiously, feeling his way. No more shots, no cries, nothing. His scalp pricked. He wished to God he had a weapon, the white tux made too good a target.

More fireworks soared skywards. Looming over the path was a large banyan tree, a mass of thick aerial roots descending from its branches.

His shoe knocked against something. A hollow sound. Metal. *A steel helmet.* His heart began to hammer.

There was a deafening bang and a rocket burst overhead in a shower of golden rain. With a cry Munro jerked back. In the sudden garish light the MP's face leered into his own, eyes starting from their sockets, blackened swollen tongue protruding hideously. Blood trickled from the folds of the neck where a wire noose held the sagging body grotesquely upright.

A twig cracked. He spun round. Poised above him a sword was etched bright against the sky. He lurched backwards as it sliced down in a hissing arc, feeling the wind of the blade against his skin. Cloth ripped as the razor edge tore his jacket. With a spit of fury the Japanese whirled for another stroke. Munro dodged under the banyan and the blade rang against the hard roots. Chips of wood flew as the swordsman followed him hacking and slashing furiously. Munro threw himself flat, his fingers clawing at the ground. It was moist and crumbly. Seizing a handful he twisted and flung it in his attacker's face. With a gasp the man staggered back. Munro caught the gleam of a shaven skull. *A monk!* He was scrabbling around blindly for a stick, a weapon of any kind, when his hand touched something cold and heavy. The MP's .45 automatic.

Snatching it up, he cocked the hammer and squeezed off a shot as the monk lunged again. A tongue of fire stabbed from the muzzle but the shot went wide. The pistol bucked in his grip as he fired a second time. A piercing shriek! Munro scrambled up. He could hear the Japanese thrashing among the bushes in the darkness. The impact of the heavy slug had blasted him off his feet. He sent a couple of shots ripping through the undergrowth. *More misses.* The skunk was getting away.

He followed in the direction of the sounds. Behind him in the park firecrackers banged and screeched and a succession of Roman candles lit up the sky. The vegetation parted. He was in a small clearing. Ahead, some kind of building. A summerhouse? Garden hut? The wounded Japanese was making for the entrance clutching his side. It was a clear ten yard shot, back at Annapolis Munro had averaged 87 out of 100 on the range with this same weapon. He took quick aim and pressed the trigger. A dull click. The clip was spent.

216

A trio of brilliant star bursts turned night into day. Every leaf and blade of grass stood out sharp in the harsh glare. Blinking, he saw a second figure step from behind the hut cradling a heavy Thompson sub-machine gun. Burly, uniformed. Captain Santos.

"Christsakes Captain, *shoot* the bastard! He's a Jap! He's killed an MP."

The police chief raised the machine-gun and swung round deliberately. *Away* from the Japanese. Munro stopped in his tracks, staring numbly into the yawning muzzle centred on his chest. He could see the bulge of the Cutts compensator on the barrel and the twenty round box magazine. No, it wasn't possible! Santos and the Japs. A load of things fell into place – the girl in his room, the wrecked Pontiac. His blood ran cold.

Another spectacular rocket soared heavenwards. "Santos, hold it! Don't be a fool. Slater's got men everywhere, the place is surrounded. Do a deal and you can save your skin yet!"

A vicious sneer twisted the police chief's features. "*Cabron*! I warned you not to interfere, now you know too much."

"*Wait!*" Munro was playing for time, trying to edge back towards cover. "The photograph! Don't you want the photograph?"

Santos checked. "You have it?" he snapped.

"Not on me, no. But I can tell you where it is."

"*Gringo liar*! Your room was searched. We would have found it."

Santos was steadying the gun to fire. Munro tensed, gauging the distance to the nearest trees. With these damn lights in the sky the Thompson would riddle him before he had gone five yards. There was a sudden whistling screech close by. Santos jerked out the way as a rogue rocket shot across the clearing trailing sparks and exploded against the roof of the summerhouse in a ball of white flames.

Snatching his chance, Munro broke for the bush. He hit a wall of foliage and dived in, flinging himself down. Behind, the Thompson cut loose with a deafening rattle. Bullets zapped through the leaves around him, ricocheting off branches as he hugged the earth. Using knees and elbows he wriggled deeper in. Another burst tore up the ground inches away and spurts of grit stung his skin.

A tree trunk. He crawled behind it and lay still. More shots sprayed the area as Santos fired wildly into the bushes. Less close this time. Then the shooting stopped. He waited, listening, not daring to move.

He let a couple of minutes pass. Still no shots. Was Santos waiting for him? He crawled on stealthily, forcing a way through the undergrowth. The path must be somewhere nearby. There were lights approaching now and men shouting. *Americans*. Christ, not before

217

time. A flash beam dazzled his eyes as he stumbled out into the open.

"Son of a bitch, Pilot," said a voice. "What the hell are you playing at?"

Another salvo of star shells burst over the gardens, flooding them with coloured light. Santos swore obscenely as he ran between the trees. God-cursed sky-rockets! He'd had the *gringo cold*. Now his cover was blown to pieces.

He saw torches jinking ahead and swung away. They were trying to trap him against the park wall. The river was close. If he could find a raft or a boat – make for the *kempe-tai* safe house in the Tondo.

He stopped among some oleanders to catch his breath. No sounds of pursuit. Had he thrown them off? A twig cracked and he froze straining to locate the source. *Mueran los gringos!* He snapped a fresh clip into the Thompson.

A whisper floated out of the gloom, "*Higashi no kaze ame.*"

"*Nishi no kaze hare.*" Lowering the gun he stepped cautiously out from the bushes. A dark figure moved to meet him, sword blade glinting. "*Diabolo!* You frightened me!"

"*Nan desu ka?* We heard shooting. What has happened, *neh?*"

"Those whore monks of yours. They killed a policeman and the *bastardo* Munro caught me with them."

"The *Amerikan?* He is dead, *neh?*"

"No, he escaped. Now the *gringos* are after me. You gotta get me away!"

A thunderflash exploded across the park, throwing up a fountain of sparks. Santos started. Another figure had appeared beside the Japanese. Faceless. Features masked by a grinning death's-head.

"*Nombre de Dios!* Is that you?"

"Who else, fool?" The voice was harsh, callous, inflexions distorted eerily by the mask. "The cargo. What news of the cargo?"

"*Ei*, the *gringos* have lost it. They flew it down to New Guinea last night in a bomber and it crashed in the swamps."

"*New Guinea?* You are positive?"

"Yes, yes. It's all over Headquarters, the search is top priority. General MacArthur's orders."

"And the Clipper has taken on extra fuel!"

The two figures conferred urgently in Japanese. Santos was glancing over his shoulder frantically. Sounds of the search were drawing closer again. "Listen, you've *got* to help me. It's your necks as well if I'm caught!"

"*Help you!*" The retort from the mask was chilling, scornful. "Bungling fool, you've endangered us all!"

The fireworks had finished. On the terrace the orchestra had taken over. Grand piano, trombones and the big sax pounding out their notes into the hot humid night. The younger guests flocked to the glistening ice walls of the dance floor.

On César's arm Georgiana swung into a tango. They had made up their quarrel. "Darling, I'm sorry. It was mean of me to spoil your last night at home."

"You see, *querida*, our customs are different here, old fashioned."

"I know, and that's what I love about Manila. It's just that sometimes . . ."

César's hand caressed her back as he guided her to the sensual rhythm of the music. "Georgiana," he chided gently, "I wonder, will you ever settle down?"

She pecked his ear, "Don't be silly."

A stir had broken out by the entrance. Couples were drawing back shocked. She saw Colonel Santos stagger onto the dance floor. His face was grey under the lights, eyes glazed. Swaying drunkenly he weaved among the dancers. A girl screamed. On her white gown was a bloody smear.

"*Qué pasa?*" César held Georgiana tight against the panicky rush for the exit. Up on the terrace the band played on oblivious. The Captain tottered to the edge of the floor. A bright scarlet trail mingled with the dripping ice as he dragged himself round the shimmering wall. Blood bubbled from between his lips and his hands clawed at the frozen surface. Very slowly his knees gave and he keeled forward on his face with a crash.

"Knifed through the lungs," Slater muttered. "Shit."

The Military Police had cleared the dance floor and thrown a sheet over the corpse. Munro turned his back on it. "The Japs got to him first."

Slater nodded tight-lipped. "He'd have blown their whole network. Christ knows how long the bastard's been working for them." He lit one of his cigars and chucked the match away angrily. "*Dammit*, he was right under our noses!"

A plain clothes CIC agent approached. "We've combed every foot of the grounds, Major. Not a smell of the Yellow-bellies. Reckon they must have made it across the river."

"What about the priest, Jordan?"

"No luck, sir. We're still looking."

"Goddamit, you've half the army here. The idiot must be some-where. *Find him!*"

The ball was breaking up. Munro joined César and Georgiana walking out to the front driveway. His tuxedo was a mess. He took off the jacket and slung it over his shoulder. No one felt much like talking.

The yellow Cadillac was parked by the statue of José Rizal, the Philippines national hero. César opened the passenger door. "*Ei!*" he started back. "Who is this?"

There was a whimper from the darkness inside. On the rear seat was a huddled figure. Munro glimpsed a pasty face. Reverend Jordan.

They helped him out. "Are you okay? What happened?"

Trembling violently, the priest pointed to the statue. Scratched in charcoal across the plinth was a number – Four.

The Shi-sign. Death.

ELEVEN PM. CAVITE. The sleek, black limousine purred through the sleeping dockyard to the seaplane terminal. Marine guards pre-sented arms. There was a flash of gold braid as General MacArthur descended. His wife, Jean, followed with Georgiana Delahaye.

The crew were assembled in the operations room when the General entered with Slater. "At ease," he tossed them a casual salute as he strode to the front. "Captain Ross, are your preparations complete?"

"Yes, sir." Ross had just signed the manifest. His voice was flat. "We can leave directly the passengers are aboard."

"Fine." The General turned to the rest of them, "I won't insult your intelligence, gentlemen, by pretending this is an ordinary flight. It is not. You are being dispatched on a mission vital to the security of our beloved country." His gaze surveyed the room swiftly, meeting each man's eyes in turn. "Military aircraft will fly with you through the night and into tomorrow. Major Slater has details. Any questions?"

There were none. He flashed a crisp smile. "Good luck to you all."

The first boarding bell rang. In the departure lounge César's mother dabbed at her eye with a lace handkerchief and embraced her son. Jean MacArthur kissed Georgiana fondly, "Goodbye darling, give my love to Kim. And César, you take care of her now."

Out in the harbour warships were sweeping the night with search beams. Sol Boden led the passengers down the jetty to the waiting Clipper. Bathed in the glare of docklamps, the huge airliner glittered against the blackness of the water, warm lights streaming from her portholes. Ricky clutched Maria's hand tight.

"Good evening, sir, madam," Ruth Simms bit back tears as Tad Gotto showed them to their sleeping quarters, she was so glad to be aboard at last. Beyond the main lounge the cabins had been transformed into snug bedchambers with two-tier curtained bunks each with its own window and electric light. Ricky and his mother were berthed across the passage. Soon all three children were scrambling on the beds.

Yu-Ling was sharing a small two berth cabin opposite the ladies' powder room with her uncle. Hollington Soong had reserved the rear suite's double bed for his sole use. The events at the ball had left the Chinese party shaken. Scott looked in to make sure they were okay. "You'll find seats forward for take off. We'll be leaving directly," she told them. "There's a call button by each bed, all you have to do is press it. Oh, and if you get hungry during the night, there'll be coffee and doughnuts in the galley."

"Please, what are doughnuts?" Yu-Ling asked.

"What are doughnuts? A kind of small sweet bun, with a hole in the middle," Scott laughed as she saw the bewilderment in the girl's face. "Tell you what, soon as we're in the air, I'll bring you one to try."

She moved back up the aircraft. The children's parents were trying to chivvy them off the beds. Prince Cherkassy was sharing a cabin with Slater. Reverend Jordan looked badly shocked still, he had declined a sedative from the doctor. She must remember to keep an eye on him. Further down she met Georgiana unpacking a négligé. "The ladies' rooms are aft when you want to change. And if you let me have your frock when you turn in, I'll hang it up where it won't get creased."

"Twenty five adults and three children all present and accounted for, Skipper," O'Byrne reported.

Up on the flight deck the crew were at their stations. Ross and Munro had gone through the pre-flight checks and were waiting for clearance from the shore.

"*Secure all doors and hatches*," Ross ordered. "*Prepare to cast off.*"

Through the windshield Munro could see the slick black waters streaked greasily with the lights spangling the Navy yard. A low moon hung behind clouds to the north west. The launches were moving back from the take-off area and away to starboard two PBY escort planes were standing by. Back of them in the aircraft were twenty-eight passengers, eleven tons of fuel, seventy odd thousand letters and an assortment of cargo including several cases of mangoes packed in dry ice for the hotels on Wake and Midway and a ball gown being returned to a New York couturier. Ahead lay twenty-two hundred miles, fifteen hours flying time, to Lae, New Guinea.

And Slater's cargo.

He cast a sideways glance at Ross. The skipper's face was impassive as his eyes ranged the glowing dials. His right hand gripped the throttle levers ready.

A green Very-light arced into the night.

"Control to Clipper, cleared for take-off. Winds southerly six knots."

"Prepare to start engines."

Sol Boden waved farewell as the Clipper pulled away from the dock. Out in mid-stream she paused, swinging into the wind and he caught the bellowing roar of the engines running up to full power. Ponderously the great plane began to surge forward, the shining wake astern lengthening as her speed built. Faster, faster, she was on the step now, skimming the surface, the thunder echoing round the harbour. Abruptly the foaming trail cut off and she lifted smoothly, heavily into the hot night.

"Flaps up five."

"Thirty inches and twenty-one hundred RPM."

"Course heading two ten degrees, Skipper."

"Roger, two ten it is."

A thousand feet above the bay the Clipper wheeled in the air. Below them Munro glimpsed the lights of the city strung along the shore like a brilliant map. The shimmering chains of the boulevards, the floodlit mansions, clustered *Intramuros*, the flickering pinpricks of fishermens' lamps out on the water.

Manila, he thought, Manila.

★　　★　　★

SUITLAND, MARYLAND. BUREAU OF THE CENSUS. For eight days now the Census Building had been under tight guard. Armed marines stood post outside every entrance. Inside, haggard from lack of sleep, staff worked flat out on twenty-four hour shifts, loading banks of IBM sorting machines with endless batches of punched cards, one for each of the hundred and ten million US citizens.

The project was colossal. In normal circumstances months would have been allotted. Now with every hour vital all other work of the Bureau had been shut down to concentrate resources on this one task.

So secret was the operation no record of it would ever be made. Acting on the direct orders of the President himself, government officials had sworn the Director and his department chiefs to vows of perpetual silence.

Using the censuses for the past two decade years, 1930 and 1940, teams of operators broke down the lists state by state. Clerks pored over endless screeds of printout. Comptometer girls sat in long rows, their fingers flickering at the keys of their machines.

As fast as one batch of cards was processed another took its place. The entire population was being sorted into broad racial groups: Whites, Negroes, Indians, Orientals.

Even before the last results had been fully collated, the millions of cards were being fed through the machines again. This time special parameters had been set up. Orientals were being sub-divided by nation of origin: China, Indo-Malaya, Japan.

Final tabulations began. The machines clattered again, throwing up lists of names across the nation.

Names and addresses of one hundred and twenty-six thousand, nine hundred and forty-seven Japanese–Americans resident in the USA.

Across the Potomac meanwhile, long black limousines had pulled up beneath the West Portico of the White House. The British Ambassador entered the President's study with Harry Hopkins and a small, quick-eyed Canadian millionaire whose code name was *Intrepid*, Co-ordinator of British Security, personal envoy of Winston Churchill.

They stayed for eighty minutes. It was three pm, still night half a world away in Manila, when they left the Oval study and the President turned to his sole remaining guest, "Well, Kim, how did we do?"

The tall man shook his head worriedly, "You promised them 'armed assistance'. That's war, isn't it? Can you swing the nation behind you in time?"

The President stared into the fire, "I have to, Kim. I have to."

XVII

FRIDAY DECEMBER 5th THREE PM. Ross was sweating. A sweat of fear.

The Clipper hung in the air, a speck of metal lost amid the immensity of mountains and sky.

Eight thousand feet below the forbidding coastline stretched unbroken as far as the eye could see, an endless barrier of razor-backed ridges and plunging valleys matted with dense rain forest rising to ramparts of shouldering peaks, their summits shrouded in cloud as if the land had not yet cooled.

New Guinea.

The sun slanting through the windshield made the cockpit warm. A bead of moisture gathered at his temple and began to trickle down the skin. He wiped it away. His hand was stiff from holding the yoke and he flexed it slowly before returning it to the metal. In front of him on the panel the instruments quivered faintly with the drone of the engines. He scanned them, hoping almost for a hint of malfunction, some reason to justify the terror that gnawed at him. Nothing; temperature, pressure, compass heading, altitude all normal. Every needle exactly as it should be. Beyond the windows the whirling arcs of the portside props glinted in the sunlight, cutting through the air in ceaseless rhythm, driving them remorselessly onwards at two and a half miles to the minute.

Still the fear persisted.

He glanced sideways across the cockpit. Shapiro sat in the co-pilot's seat, collar unbuttoned, tie off. His fingers tapped idly on the column of the yoke. Ross felt a sudden spasm of jealousy. What right had he to be so calm, so unafraid? What right had any of them?

Throughout the night he had stayed at the controls as they flew down over Mindanao and the Moluccas, the rest of the crew spelling each other in four hour watches while the passengers slept. At sixteen minutes past nine this morning, by Thyssen's calculations, they had crossed the Equator and turned east into the Bismarck Sea. The PBYs

224

which had escorted them from Cavite had waggled their wings in farewell and turned back. All day since then the Clipper had flown on up the coast alone – seven hundred miles of swamps and jungle, coiling rivers and mountains, always mountains.

The ship trembled in an air pocket. His hand stroked the stabiliser wheel and eased the throttle levers back a notch.

Shapiro looked up. "Want me to take over for a while, Skipper?" he offered.

Instant suspicion flared in Ross's fatigue-rimmed eyes, "Why, do you think I'm not fit to go on?" he snapped. He saw the young officer's face freeze and clenched his teeth, "Shut up and mind your own bloody business!" Reaching for the interphone, he flicked the button, "Purser? Send up more coffee to the bridge."

Downstairs on the passenger deck Tad Gotto returned to the galley, balancing a tray. "Air conditioning's packed up in the rear suite," he reported to Pat as he dumped dirty glasses in the sink. "Minister Soong says to have it fixed right away."

"He does, does he?" the Purser sniffed. "Stupid idjit's probably been playing with the settings. Did you check them?"

"Yes, Mr. O'Byrne, nut'in' doing."

"Okay, I'll ask the engineers to see to it when I take this coffee up."

Aft in the crew quarters Munro was woken by a tug on the shoulder. It was Chief Crow. "What time is it?" he yawned.

"Coming up six bells. Time you was showing a leg."

Munro sat up fully clothed. He had been sacked out for three hours between watches. Skinny Davey Klein was sprawled on another bunk deep into *This Above All*, the British best-seller explaining how they were going to win the war.

He reached for a cigarette. The Chief threw him a match.

"Thanks."

"Thanks nothing, they're Thyssen's."

"Who's up front now?"

"Shapiro."

"Shapiro and who? Not Fry?"

"No, Ross."

"Christ, still?"

The Chief shrugged. Except for visits to the washroom Ross hadn't left his seat since departing Cavite.

Munro lifted the blind shading the starboard porthole and peered out. Far below a line of surf fringed a narrow beach. Mountains ran right down into the sea from the clouds. God alone knew how high they were, over fifteen thousand feet according to reports.

"You gotta minute?" the Chief said casually. "There's something I'd like you to see."

Leaving Davey to his book, they went through into the hold. It was stacked high now with cargo, the couturier gown swinging from a hook in its protective case. The hatch through into the starboard auxiliary was open.

"The folks in the rear suite were complaining of too much heat," the Chief explained as they bent double to enter the wing stub. "When that happens it's usually the inlet shutter on the duct jammed open, so I checked here first."

Munro followed him, squeezing on all fours past the mail sacks and life rafts. Overhead was a mass of pipework and cabling. The vibration of the great engines only feet away made the metal panelling shake.

With difficulty the Chief twisted round in the confined space till he was propped on his back. "This is the heating duct," he shouted above the noise, tapping an aluminum pipe above him. "I was right, the shutter had jammed. It's free now. This here's what I wanted you to see though, the one behind the spar."

He shone his flash. Munro peered upwards, a standard one inch steel pipe, painted red, was visible against the roof.

"Know what that is?"

"Transfer line between the two wing tanks?"

"Nearly right," the Chief looked surprised. "It's the *cross feed* for the port motors. Means if either tank is dry we can run all four off the other. Okay, now feel along."

Munro ran his fingers over the length of the pipe. All at once he stopped.

"Found it, huh?"

Munro's mouth tightened as he felt the coin-sized dent where the line was crushed in, blocking it. "Accident or deliberate?"

The Chief snorted, "Your guess is good as mine."

"When was the line last checked?"

"Yesterday afternoon at Cavite. But it could have been missed, easy. The thing's damned near invisible unless you know where to look. I only found it just now by chance when I was pulling myself up from fixing the shutter." The Chief jerked a thumb over his shoulder, "The starboard tank's right behind us through that bulkhead. You can guess where we'd be now if the feed from that got blocked?"

"Both starboard motors out and no way of switching fuel to them."

"Leaving us only one way to go – down."

"*Son of a bitch!*" The muscles of Munro's lean face were taut. "I thought we finished with all this in Manila." He touched the damaged pipe again, "Isn't the system tested before take-off? How come the damage didn't show then?"

"Sure, but we only run it long enough to check the flow. There was probably enough gas in the pipe to work the meter for a couple of minutes."

They were both silent listening to the steady roar of the engines shaking the cramped wingspace.

"Chief, let's not kid ourselves, this was no accident. It's too careful and well concealed. Whoever did it knew exactly what he was about."

The engineer nodded, "Probably used the handle of a wrench levered against that spar. The bastard's only mistake was to knock the duct shutter as he was leaving. But for that we'd never have found it."

"We'd better check out the rest of the fuel system – *fast*."

"First we have to tell Ross."

Down in the main lounge on the lower deck the port window blinds had been drawn against the sun. People were chatting desultorily, reading books and magazines, staring out at the view. Prince Cherkassy was in a poker game with Mr. Simms and the Dutchman Van Cleef. Across the aisle a couple of Army men were watching the Delahaye girl and her fiancé, César de Santa Cruz, play backgammon.

". . . of course this part of New Guinea was until recently German territory."

Scott looked round in surprise. It was Cashin speaking. He and Sir Ambrose Hope were sitting at a card table with two oilmen.

He noticed her glance and smiled, "It's true, ask Sir Ambrose. Great Britain grabbed northern New Guinea as part of her spoils from the last war."

Sir Ambrose was fiddling with his tobacco pouch, "Australia actually," he murmured politely. "German New Guinea and the Bismarck Islands were awarded to Australia by the Treaty of Versailles."

"Still part of the Empire," Cashin said, winking at Scott.

The thought of landing on German soil, even former German soil, was somehow vaguely upsetting to her. "Are there still many Germans there?" she cast a look out the window at the green forest ridges sliding by below.

"Not now, m'dear. Most would have been interned at the outbreak of hostilities. A few traders and missionaries perhaps."

"Prospectors too, I guess," one of the oilmen, a Texan from Galveston working in Batavia, said. "There's gold down there."

"What about the natives, they friendly?" his buddy asked.

"In general, I believe, around the white settlements, but in the interior . . ." he shrugged. "It's fortunate the bomber crew came down near the coast."

The passengers had been told the reason for the detour was to pick up the crew of a downed bomber. Naturally no mention had been made of the cargo.

"Heck, I sure wouldn't like to spend a night out in that bush," said the Texan.

Counters clacked in the corner. "Georgiana, that is stupid. Play properly if you are going to play at all!" she heard César exclaim in sudden pique.

"Oh, very well," Georgiana's long white fingers moved deftly over the board. Her auburn hair was caught up in a knot at the back and the simple sports frock she wore somehow made all the other women look dowdy. There was a minute's tense concentration, then a burst of applause from the Army officers, "Hey, how about that? Well done, lady!" César got up and walked away tight-lipped.

Two cabins down Maria Bianchi and Ruth Simms were talking. "Never, I can never thank you enough."

"Really he was no trouble, we all of us loved having him. It's been swell for the girls to have a boy to play with."

"Ricky has been so happy with you. I wish . . . I wish it had been possible for me to have visited him. Two years, so long, so much too long! You cannot believe how I have pined for him."

"Yes, yes it must have been terrible for you." After some initial misgivings Ruth found she was growing to like Ricky's mother. Her presents to them had been truly generous. Also several things had been explained.

"They threatened to kidnap him if I didn't pay a ransom in advance. The gangsters in Shanghai are terrible. After my husband died I had to sell his business and of course when people know you are desperate they take advantage," Maria sighed and twisted the ring on her finger. "For two years they tried every trick to beat me down. I was in despair, I thought I'd never see my boy again, that he'd forget his mother . . ."

Ruth nodded sympathetically, "You must have been so worried, thank goodness it's all over now. What kind of business was your late husband in?"

Cursing as he bumped his head, Ross crawled backwards out from the wingspace and stood up, dark in the face. "A *bent pipe*, is that all you sent me in to look at?" he said scathingly. "Some mechanic's goof. What's the matter with you both?"

Munro and the Chief blinked at him.

"This was deliberate," the engineer answered quietly. "Like the plugs last time."

"You're telling me it's *sabotage*? We get fuel lines blocked all the time, that's why we carry engineers, for Christsakes!"

"Hell, Skipper, you know what that pipe could spell. After what happened last flight . . ."

"I know what it spells okay, Mister, it spells *fear*. You're scared!"

Munro almost hit him then.

"*I'm* scared," the Chief admitted frankly. "Scared to death of some joker cutting off our juice six thousand feet up. And this weren't no mechanic's goof, it's too darned neat for that. Someone's out to cripple us and I want that written into the log."

"Trying to cover yourself? Any blockage in the fuel lines should've been picked up on the pre-flight check and you know it. That's how it'll go in the log."

"*Is it what you're going to tell Slater too.*"

Ross whitened as if Munro had spat in his face. "What I tell Slater is my business," he grated. "Now get back to your stations, both of you. *That's an order.*"

In silence they returned to the control cabin. Whitely was taking a bearing on the RDF, rotating the aerial in the ceiling to obtain a signal. Munro remembered something. He stopped.

"Stewart, you still picking up those low frequency transmissions?"

The radio operator pushed back his headphones a moment, "There was a strong burst two hours ago. The bearing's shifted though, looks like whatever it is is moving south now."

A Jap raider heading to cut their course at Wake perhaps or Midway? Munro wondered as he tapped Shapiro on the shoulder to relieve him. Or was he growing paranoid? Almost certainly Whitely's signals had nothing to do with them. And yet after what they had just found anything seemed possible.

"Aircraft! Five o'clock ahead!" In the instant Munro grabbed the big binoculars from the pocket beside him and directed them out the starboard window at the twin dark specks rising through the haze. There was a tense pause as the others waited. He caught the flash of red, white and blue roundels and relaxed. "It's the Aussie escort."

Slowly the fighters climbed to join them. Antiquated single-engined bi-planes. The pilots waved cheerily from the open cockpits. "Crazy!" Chuck Driscoll shook his curly head in disbelief. "How they gonna protect us? It's all they can do to keep up."

Leaning between the pilot seats, Thyssen taped a small piece of paper to Ross's instrument panel. On it he had written the new compass course – 252 degrees. "We're through the straits, that's Finschhafen down there to starboard. You should see Lae coming up dead ahead in around fifteen minutes."

The white roofs of the settlement below slid away behind out of sight as Ross brought the Clipper round onto the new westerly heading. They were into the Solomon Sea now and entering the Huon Gulf. The sky was dotted with scattered cloud. Another chain of peaks became visible as a smoky smudge on the horizon, topped by columns of cumulus.

Stewart was talking with ground control. Munro could hear their voices crackling in his earphones, the twangy Australian accents of the airstrip radio and the sharper tones of the *Southern Seas* operator. Ross eased the yoke forward and his own wheel moved in unison. The altimeter began unwinding slowly as the nose dipped. A trickle of water ran up the windshield, flared by their slipstream.

"Lae reports winds south-east twelve to fourteen knots decreasing, visibility moderate, sea calm with slight swell, some rain showers. Altimeter setting twenty-nine ninety."

"Roger, Stewart, request guard boats to stand by. Our ETA twelve minutes," Munro had the flight manual open and was checking off details for the approach.

"The Markham River runs down one and a half miles west of the town. Single jetty, no rocks or coral, water shelving to four feet," he read out to Ross. "Low ground to north-east of strip, rising to timbered hills."

Ross did not reply. In silence the Clipper continued to descend.

"Honourable Uncle, please to wake up, *heya*?" Yu-Ling said gently. "I think soon we shall be landing." Down below in the rear suite the Seat Belt sign had come on. Carefully she helped fasten the Professor

230

in, then buckled her own belt about her.

"*Ai-yah*, so this is where the dunghead Americans have lost their bomber," Minister Soong clasped his fists as he stared out the window. "Filthy jungle. They have no right to bring us down here, none!"

He had been furiously upset ever since the news was broken to them at breakfast.

"*Another stop*! What do you mean, another stop?" he had screeched at the Purser. "Two days already we have lost on the journey and now you say we make an extra stop? And what is this?"

O'Byrne was handing round colourfully printed cards.

"We've crossed the Equator, Excellency. These are your official certificates, signed by the Captain."

Hollington Soong angrily tore them to shreds. "I don't want certificates, I want to get to America! America, do you understand? Not this . . . this *New Guinea*!"

Ranting and raving, he had stormed off to find Slater. Returning subdued he had gone into a huddle with Bodyguard Feng, agitatedly calculating how long it would now take them to reach the Golden Country. Several times Yu-Ling had caught the words *East Wind Rain*.

She thought they seemed frightened.

The plane circled over the gulf, losing height. Below the clouds a wide sluggish river cut through the jungle growth, its muddy waters pushing out into the blue-green of the sea like an enormous dirty tongue. Neat rows of houses came in sight, galvanized roofs winking in the sun, a strip of cleared ground with two aircraft standing by a hangar. The wing dipped further and Yu-Ling glimpsed boats drawn up along a muddy shoreline, a small jetty, moored at the end was a slim white ship like a seagull.

She felt her ears pop and chewed hard on the gum the steward had given her. They were circling round again, much lower this time. She could make out individual people, lots of them, like ants along the shore waving up at the plane. Now a great black shape, their shadow, was racing with them over the waves. A launch went by underneath so close she could see the brown backs of the men aboard. The sea was coming up. She clutched her seat. How fast they were going still. A sudden rush of spray blotted out the windows filling the cabin with a greenish light. With a long smooth surge the Pacific Clipper settled on the bay.

It was a perfect touch-down. That much you had to grant Ross.

"Well, the Yanks are here."

Tucked away on a small point beyond the airstrip commanding a view of the whole bay, a thatch-roofed native hut of sago palms hung out over the water's edge on stilts. From its platform a pair of white men studied the flying boat through binoculars.

"They ain't gonna be pleased," said the sergeant. He had a hard-bitten face under a slouch hat and his shorts were mud-caked.

"They can stuff themselves then. No one asked the bleeders down here."

They watched the Clipper cut her outboard engines and begin to taxi in towards the jetty. Already a small, excited crowd had gathered to greet her. "There goes the Pom Commissioner," snorted the lieutenant as a small car came rushing down the road from the town.

"He'll be wetting his pants. His radio's been burnin' up the air all morning."

"Better get on the horn m'self. Stay here an' keep watch." The lieutenant went inside the hut. Hammocks swung from the high rafters and weapons and stores were stacked against the walls. By a window at the rear stood a three unit teleradio. The aerial ran outside camouflaged up a hundred foot rain tree. He slipped on earphones and began tapping at the morse key.

There was a splash below as a muscular native, naked but for a small loin cloth, paddled his canoe in under the hut and made it fast to one of the supports. Shinning up the notched pole that served as a ladder, he saluted the sergeant.

"Yu lukim disfela, boss?" he held out a length of wood.

The sergeant turned it over in his hands frowning. A section of branch split lengthways, the underside scored with an irregular pattern of cuts. *"Where yu katchim, huh, Francis?"*

The native pointed behind him to the brown mouth of the river half a mile away. *"Long wata clos-tu."*

"Yu savvy fela mak im?"

The yokes of the black's eyes rolled as he shook his head, *"Fela mak dis wan bilong long-wei ples, mi no savvy dis pipal."*

The sergeant carried it inside. "Francis is back. More bloody message-sticks being floated down the river."

The lieutenant examined the stick carefully. Opening a drawer in the table, he took out two others. The markings on all three were similar.

"Can he tell us what it means?"

"He says no, but the bugger can guess alright, he's scared."

They stared out the window at the clouds lying heavy over the mountains. "Could be *Kukukuku* on the move again."

The sergeant spat sourly, "For sure something's buildin' up there."

The hatches opened and a wave of hot steamy air engulfed the decks bringing with it a mixed smell of salt water and mud. Up in the nose Shapiro was making fast the launch's tow line. The engines died and a clamour of voices became audible as a dozen canoes paddled vigorously out from the shore.

"Holy cow, get a load of this lot!" The men in the canoes were thick-set and swarthy, almost naked, with shocks of frizzy hair. Many had feathers or pigs' tusks through their hooked noses. Their women were bare-breasted in grass skirts. Ignoring angry shouts from the launch they swarmed eagerly around the plane.

The crew waved back enthusiastically, "They seem pretty friendly. How'd you fancy one of those babes?"

"One coconut, short time!"

"Yeah, and wind up in a pot!"

A second launch appeared and with difficulty forced a way through the mob. Husky young natives, lighter in colour than the men in the canoes, manoeuvred the flying boat towards the jetty where the yacht was berthed. Ross leaned from his window cursing them and vowing retribution if they scratched the hull.

"Careful now," Scott helped the Simms children out through the main hatch. "Mind your step on the planking." Held tight by their parents the two little girls skipped off up the jetty.

"One at a time please. Just follow the purser up to the gangway." After the long flight everybody was impatient to disembark. The dock was a mass of people, passengers, seamen, natives and Europeans from the town, all milling around excitedly.

"Yes, Minister, certainly, your baggage will be unloaded directly and brought up to the yacht for you." She pushed back a damp tendril of hair. Mrs. Gordon Smythe was looking outraged at the nakedness of the natives. Scott envied them. The heat and humidity were unbelievable.

Vivid green jungle steaming in the sun smothered the hills surrounding the bay, pressing down right to the water's edge, threatening to engulf the small township. No beach at all that she could see, only mud and mangroves and creeper-hung trees, with here and there splashes of brilliant colour. It looked primitive and beautiful and just a touch frightening.

Chris Fry flushed with embarrassment at a gaggle of excited young natives girls dancing about on long bare legs, their smooth, black skins bursting with health, pointed breasts thrusting disturbingly at him. Catching his stare they covered their mouths, giggling and laughing with a blatant sexuality that set his pulse racing.

"Boy, oh boy!" Shapiro gazed awestruck at the rakish lines of the vessel on which they were to stay, "Tonight I'm gonna feel like a millionaire."

The yacht was truly a beauty, spanking neat from stem to stern, decked and railed in solid teak, the blue Pan Am emblem showing on her funnel. Her deck awnings were spread and her brasswork shone so it hurt to look. The only other ship in the bay was a solitary rusting freighter anchored further out.

"C'mon, sailor," Chris tore his eyes away from the girls, "let's grab a cabin quick, unless you want to share with Thyssen.

The Clipper was drawn up under the stern of the yacht, secured by warps fore and aft, her hull protected by rubber fenders. Munro's shirt stuck to his back as he climbed the yacht's polished gangway after the Chief.

"Hi, I'm Kelly," a trim, sunburned man in his forties with a peaked cap greeted them at the top. "Skipper and base manager." He stuck out his hand beaming. "Welcome to New Guinea."

"Max Munro, first officer, and this is Chief Crow, our engineer. Looks like we brought the crowds out." Down at the foot of the gangway four Melanesian police in khaki shorts were struggling to hold people back.

"You can say that again. Your arrival is the biggest event here since the rainy season started."

"Ross said to tell you he'll be along in a while, he wants to finish writing up the log," Munro wiped the sweat from his face. "Say, is it always this hot?"

"Man, this is the cool of the day. You wait till tomorrow."

There was a splash from the dockside followed by loud cheers. A drunken miner had fallen in to the delight of his mates.

The Chief meanwhile was surveying the yacht's whitened decks and gleaming paintwork. "Fine vessel you got here," he grunted approvingly.

"Ain't she just?" the captain's blue eyes beamed with pride as he gazed over his ship. "You're our first passengers too. C'mon, I'll show you where to bunk, then give you the conducted tour."

He led the way aft. "How about the crew of the bomber, are they here now?" Munro asked him as they passed under the deck awning.

Kelly stopped, one hand on the rail of a companionway to the lower deck. His expression was troubled. "You'll hear the score on that in a minute."

The yacht was delightful. Yu-Ling had never enjoyed anything so much. She had a twin berth cabin next door to her uncle, with a porthole and a neat little handbasin hidden in a closet. She unpacked her travelling case and was hanging up her *cheong-sams* when there was a knock at the door and Scott entered.

"Miss Chen, would you mind if I shared with you tonight? It seems we're a little short on space."

"Oh, yes please, I most happy," Yu-Ling said blushing. Indeed she was happy. She very much liked this smiling American girl, always so kind and helpful. Hastily she moved her clothes from the bottom bunk. "You like this bed, yes?"

"Oh no, that's okay, you stay where you are. I'm just as happy up on top," Scott assured her. She crossed to the porthole and looked out, "That's good, we face seaward. Means we'll get the breeze. I wish it would rain though and clear the air."

There came a second tap at the door. Quieter and more discreet this time. It was Hollington Soong. "Ah, little Jade Years," he began throatily in Cantonese. Then he realised she was not alone and stopped abruptly, "I beg your pardon, Miss Scott, I did not realise you were in here."

"Why yes, Miss Chen and I are sharing tonight," she said brightly. "Is there something I can do for you, sir?"

He was visibly annoyed, "Miss Chen should have her own cabin. It is not right that she should be made to share with crew members."

Scott looked at Yu-Ling, "Would you really rather be by yourself? I promise I won't be offended if you say yes."

"No, no please," the girl stammered. "I like for you to stay."

The Minister stood for a moment in the doorway, swelling with anger. Turning on his heel he went out, slamming the door.

"Goodness," said Scott bewildered, "what was that about?"

Yu-Ling looked away. She was trembling. *Ai-yah*, she knew.

235

XVIII

"Lieutenant Jack Nash, Australian Imperial Force Commandos and our local Coastwatcher."

It was six pm. Dusk had fallen, the last flush of sunset was dying on the horizon. With doors and windows shuttered for security the skipper's cabin aboard the *Southern Cross* was stifling. Kelly mopped his face as he made the introductions. Present also were Ross, Munro, Slater and Sir Ambrose.

"Pleased to meet you, gents," the Australian was tanned and rugged-looking. There were tattoos on his brawny forearms and his faded khaki shirt bore neither insignia nor rank badges.

Ross scowled at him, "Coastwatcher, what's that for God's sake?"

"What it says, sport. A chain of observers spread out along the coast and islands. We keep an eye on things and report back what happens to Darwin."

"You mean you watch out for Japs?" Munro said.

"That's about the size of it."

"And do they come in here?"

"They take a look – *sometimes*."

"Okay, okay," Slater interrupted. "Cut the chat and let's get down to business. Where's the cargo from the bomber?"

"Well now, at a guess I'd say where it was before."

"Jesus Christ! You mean out in the swamps still?"

"That's right."

They stared at him. "And the crew?" Sir Ambrose asked.

"Same place."

There was a brief shocked silence. Ross's face was stark. Slater leaned forward, his gaze steely, "Orders were to recover cargo and crew, top priority. It's been twenty-four hours, you could've *walked* there by now. Who fouled up and how?"

"No one's fouled up, Major. I've had boat parties out searching the flamin' swamps all day since first light. We couldn't find the crash."

"Godammit, what d'you mean you can't find it? You had the

236

position last night, a plane from here spotted the wreckage on the river."

"The wreckage was *seen*, Major, late yesterday for about as long as a kangaroo's fart, through a gap in the clouds. No chance of a fix."

"Then why didn't you send up another plane, for Christsakes?"

"We did. The moment the weather lifted over the river valley. That was just two hours before you bleeders showed up." The Australian's expression hardened, "You can forget your orders, gents. This is New Guinea. Rivers change from one bleedin' day to the next, loop back, cut through bends, even the bloody natives get lost. The swamps are so thick we could be within pissing distance of the crash and still not see it."

"Shit," Ross swore sullenly. "I knew it would come to this. We'll be stuck down here for days. I *told* you, Slater!"

"Shut up," Slater did not bother to look at him. To Nash he said, "This plane, did it manage to locate the bomber?"

The Australian sat back and folded his arms. He nodded, "Clear over the other side of the swamp. We could've been searching till Christmas."

"How long to get up there?"

"By launch? Depends on the state of the river, sport. At a rough guess five hours."

There was a rumble of thunder from the hills. Rain spattered outside. Abruptly it changed to a violent downpour, hammering on the walls and roof with the noise of a waterfall. They could hear feet running for cover and the torrents swirling in the scuppers.

Slater swivelled to face the two airmen, his eyebrows quivering like a pair of insects attached to his skin, "What's to stop us using the Clipper to recover the cargo?"

They stared at him appalled. "You're out of your goddam mind!" Ross said instantly.

"Why the hell? We know where the bomber went down. We can locate it from the air and land on the river right beside the bastard. Makes sense to me."

"It would to a knucklehead! We're talking about forty-three tons of aircraft hitting the water at ninety knots. One rock and she'll rip open like a can of beans!"

"Godammit, I'm in charge of this mission. I can order you to take her in!"

The veins were darkening in Ross's face. His large hands clenched. "You've no power to make me risk my ship."

"How about you, Pilot? You go along with that?"

"All the way, Major. What you're asking is suicide."

"Christ you airline people, you're something else!" Slater turned tight-lipped to Nash, "We'll leave at first light regardless of the weather. Understood?"

The Australian nodded, "It's already fixed."

One point was bothering Munro. He looked at Kelly. "The radio, how come you didn't use their transmissions to get a cross-bearing on the crash site?"

"Because," the yacht's captain told him soberly, "we've had no radio contact with the crew since last night."

Down below on the cabin deck Kurt Thyssen finished shaving. Shaking out a few drops of cologne, he massaged his cheeks and ran a comb through his short blond hair. He checked his appearance in the washroom mirror. Pretty damn good. These silk shirts he'd gotten in Hongkong really showed off his tan.

A waste pipe gurgled nearby. From a small ventilation grill close to the ceiling came the sound of someone humming. The ladies powder room was the other side of the bulkhead. A sly look crossed his face. He carried the cork-topped stool over and climbed onto it. Peering through the slits in the vent he could see the Simms woman touching up her lipstick. Well, well, he thought, stepping down, this could make for interesting times.

The Chief sat down on his bunk and the springs creaked under his weight. "Not a *peep* out of them all day?"

"According to the yacht's radio operator the last message came through around twenty-two hundred. The crew had salvaged their emergency rations and were going to stick with the plane. The commander reckoned they could hold out several days if necessary."

"I don't like it."

"Nor do I, nor does anyone, for Christsakes!"

Munro and the Chief were dressing for dinner in their shared cabin. The engineer had the lower berth. He was too darn big to go elsewhere.

"Even if they changed their minds and decided to break out they'd have radioed in first."

"Unless the set packed up."

A mosquito that had gotten in through the screen whined near Munro's ear. He swatted it with a towel. Through the porthole they

238

could hear the waves slapping against the yacht's hull. "One of the crew has a busted leg," he said, pulling on a clean shirt.

"I thought no one was supposed to be hurt?"

"So did I. Seems we were wrong."

The Chief bent to lace up his other shoe. "I been doing some more thinking about the damage to that pipe."

"And?"

"Blocking the fuel line don't matter a damn. It only hurts us if the main feed seizes up. But the rest of the system is working fine, we proved that."

With another creak of springs the Chief stood up and reached into a trouser pocket, "Suppose though the Japs had a man on board, a man with one of these."

Munro took it, a spoked metal wheel of the kind made to fit on top of a tap. "A valve handle?"

The Chief nodded slowly, "Right. With one of these he could control any fuel line on the ship. Shut off the supply whenever it suited him. Like next time one of their planes jumps us for instance."

"Sure, it fits. *If there is an agent aboard.*"

They went up on deck. The yacht was bright with lights. People were strolling the rails in evening dress. A full tropic moon, striated with cloud, hung over the edge of the mountains like a silver face watching them. The rain had lessened the humidity but it was still very warm.

Sir Ambrose Hope was standing by the gangway in evening dress complete with red silk cummerbund. "Evening, gentlemen, I'm just waiting for the Major. We're dining ashore at the Commissioner's."

An idea came to Munro. There was something he wanted to find out. "Sir, could you do me a favour?"

"By all means, if it's in my power."

"Are you in contact with your people in Hongkong?"

"I can be. The Commission will have a radio transmitter."

"Could you get a message to Inspector Playfair asking him for any information he has on a Dr. Currie? He'll know who I mean."

The Englishman eyed him quizzically. "Ah, Major Slater mentioned that name – in Oliver's photograph wasn't he? So you think Jordan might still be at risk?"

"Him or Georgiana – Miss Delahaye. Maybe, I'm not sure but all four men are dead and there *has* to be a connection."

Sir Ambrose nodded, "I'll do my best then."

"Thanks, sir. I appreciate that."

Munro followed the Chief into the bar.

It was full of smoke and noise. Georgiana was sitting at a high stool. She had on some kind of slinky silk number and she wasn't wearing any stockings. When she saw them she smiled and the corners of her eyes crinkled up the way they did when she was having a good time.

"Hiya," she called gaily, "come and join the party."

They were all there, Bob Cashin, Kelly, Hollington Soong flashing his gold teeth, Feng silent and watchful, Dr. Latouche and the pretty little Chinese. Shapiro and Chris Fry were chatting up the Gordon Smythe girl. Mr. Wirth from Lend-Lease was holding forth to Van Cleef in a corner.

A cork popped behind the bar. César appeared panther-like at Georgiana's side, a hand toying possessively with the flaming hair cascading down her back. His white tux fitted without a crease and hostility smouldered in his dark Spanish eyes. "You will have a drink, si? Champagne, *Veuve Clicquot*," he snapped his fingers. He was the rich man's son again, arrogant, confident, showing off his woman.

Maybe they'd been to bed together, Munro told himself viciously, a hot wave of sexual jealousy spreading down through his belly into his thighs. He had a sickening picture of her lying with him, every defence down, every secret of that glorious white body open and revealed. Had she given him a good time? *Did she prefer it with him?*

He forced the images away and accepted the proffered glass.

The Chief shook his head, "Beer for me."

The barman was a little Filipino from Davos with a mouth crammed full of teeth. "I want to go swimming, but this guy says it's too dangerous," Georgiana told them. "Is that true, Max?"

Munro took a sip of the champagne, savouring the thin bubbles. It was very cold, just what he needed. "Bad sharks here?" he asked the man.

"*Si, señor, muy grandes*. At night they sleep under the boat. I have heard them."

"Nuts to that," a soldier on Georgiana's left objected. "Sharks don't sleep, not ever. Got no air bladder for buoyancy. They fall asleep they drown."

Kelly had been listening. "What he hears are crocs most likely. They're active at night."

"Crocodiles?" Georgiana turned her green eyes on him. Munro was conscious of her breasts moving against the thin dress. "I thought they were only in rivers?"

"No, there are salt-water breeds too. Smaller, but dangerous still."

César was studying Munro warily. He pointed to the Annapolis

240

class ring on his finger, "Georgiana tells me you boxed for the Navy?"

Munro's jaw hardened. "What else did she tell you about me?" he said deliberately and the Spaniard's handsome face set as if he'd been spat at.

"What is that supposed to mean?"

But Georgiana cut them short, "Darling, do shut up. Max hates to talk about the past – and so do I. Listen, there's the dinner gong."

"Good evening, Minister. I've put your party at the big table in the middle. Is everything okay with you downstairs?"

"Yes, yes, but *please*, what time do we depart tomorrow?"

"I'm sorry, sir, we have no information yet. As soon as we do I'll be sure to let you know. Enjoy your meal now."

Scott stood at the door to the dining saloon, checking off names as the passengers entered and dispensing anti-malarial tablets.

"Will you take some of these, Mrs. Gordon Smythe?"

"We have our own, thank you."

"A pill for you, Mr. Wirth?"

"Sure, I'll take one. Thanks, honey."

The yacht's saloon could seat fifty. Lamps glowed against the white panelling and the walls were hung with old sailing prints. Silver and fine crystal sparkled on spotless linen tablecloths. "Isn't this wonderful?" Ruth Simms sighed to her husband. "And to think we'll be home in just five or six more days."

"There's a rumour we may be delayed on account of these Air Corps men not having showed up yet."

"I don't mind, it will be nice for the kids to have a run ashore."

Native messboys in coloured sashes served iced soup. Prince Cherkassy was seated opposite, "These long flights must be difficult with children."

"Yes, poor dears but they've been so good. They're both tucked up in bed now and our good friend Mrs. Bianchi is reading to them. Her little boy used to live with us in Manila, you know."

"Ah, I was not aware of that. You are old friends then obviously?"

"No, we only met yesterday," Ruth explained. "They come from Shanghai. Maria was afraid Ricky might be kidnapped so she sent him away." She related the story.

"Indeed? Mrs. Bianchi must be grateful to you both. What kind of business did her husband leave her?"

"Do you know I asked her exactly that question and she acted like she hadn't heard me . . ."

241

"*It's humiliating!* Not once this voyage have we been given a decent table. Look at us now, stuck out on the edge of the room as if we were nobody!"

"My dear, we were offered the centre table . . ."

"With all the Chinese? It's bad enough having to sit in the same room let alone eat with them. *And for God's sake, Felicity, will you stop ogling those officers!*"

Hollington Soong was presiding over the centre table wearing a dinner suit. On his right Yu-Ling sat very straight in a pink cheong-sam, her hair tied back in a ribbon. A frown of concentration played over her pretty face. So many knives and forks and spoons. She had eaten Western style before, but, *oh ko*, never so formal as this!

"Evening, Minister. Hi, Miss Chen, mighty pretty dress that. Mind if I sit with you?" Cashin pulled back an empty chair.

"This is not your seat. See, the card it says . . ."

". . . Sir Ambrose Hope, sure I know, Minister. He's not here tonight though, he and Major Slater are dining out."

"*Ai-yah*," Bodyguard Feng had half risen, scowling, "shall I box the fornicator's ears?" he said rudely in Cantonese.

"Oh leave him be, Feng. Bob, do *you* know what is going on? How long we are to be delayed?"

Glasses clinked, plates clattered. Chicken à la King was followed by Baked Alaska. At the crew table Kelly had insisted Scott sit next to him. "Three months and two days since we sailed from Manila. You're the first white woman I've laid eyes on apart from nuns and even they were starting to look attractive."

"Aren't there any families in the town then?"

"Never were more than a handful and they shipped out to Australia last summer. Most of the men here are bachelors anyway, miners, prospectors, a few planters and traders, government officials. Rough diamonds, but a fine bunch when you get to know them."

"How about the airfield? Whose are those planes we saw as we came in?"

"That's Guinea Airways. They serve the goldfields at Bulolo and the big plantations up in the Central Highlands. Mine dredges, gasoline, pigs, cattle, you name it, they fly it. Most of the mining town of Wau across the mountains was brought in by air, even the galvanized roofs for the houses. Had to be, no way of getting it through the bush."

"And the gold comes out the same way?"

Kelly grinned, "Two million dollars worth a month! Sometimes I dream of chucking this in and taking off with a pan for the creeks."

Munro had been watching Georgiana across the room. She and César were sharing a table with Van Cleef and some army officers. She was talking gaily and tossing her hair. He pushed his plate away. "The strip here, it's where Amelia Earhart took off from?"

"Yeah, that's right. The plane was never seen again. You interested in her?"

Munro shrugged noncommitally, "I guess every flier is." Ross was down near the end of the table. He seemed not to have heard.

"Some people here reckon it was a spying mission. They say the Japs captured them."

"That's a load of bullshit," Thyssen snorted.

The Chief had forgotten his anti-malaria tablet. He swallowed it now with a gulp of water. "Since when were you the big expert, Kurt?" he rumbled.

"Heck, it's common knowledge. Noonan, her navigator, was on the bottle. He misread the RDF signal, overran the island and followed the reverse beam out to sea. Ask Whitely if you don't believe me."

The radio operator shrugged, "It's easy done, especially if you're flying dead-reckoning."

"Howland's another Wake, a pin-prick in the ocean, blink and you've missed it."

"Hell, I get worried sometimes looking out for Wake – even with Stewart and Thyssen aboard."

"Me, I get worried 'cause they're aboard."

"But when they found the beam signal fading why didn't they turn back and fly a search pattern until they picked it up again?" Chris Fry wanted to know.

"That's probably what they *did* do, only they turned the wrong way."

"Whichever way they're dead, poor fellers."

"*Shut up!*" Ross's voice cracked across the table like a whip suddenly. "Shut up, d'you hear! I won't have people saying that. She's not dead. *There's no proof!*"

Everybody stared at him. "Gee, Skipper, what d'you think happened then?" Shapiro asked unabashed. "Is she a prisoner of the Japs?"

"*No!*" The intensity in Ross's answer was shocking. His face had drained of colour and his hand shook as he reached for his whisky glass. "God damn you, just shut up about her!" he repeated thickly.

It wasn't anger only, Munro realised watching him. Ross was hiding something. What?

Under the table Hollington Soong squeezed Yu-Ling's knee. She started nervously dropping her spoon with a clatter.

"What exactly takes you to Washington, Minister, is it to ask for more aid?"

The men were talking politics again.

"And why not?" Soong guzzled a second helping of dessert. "We are fighting your war, after all. Without us Japan would have Asia at her feet by now. We ask only for the weapons. To quote Mr. Winston Churchill – *Give us the tools and we will finish the job.*" Gold teeth gleamed as he beamed round at his listeners.

Cashin assented thoughtfully. "What puzzles me though, Minister, is how your government intends paying. I understand Congress has rejected the idea of further credits."

"Oh, that is no problem," Soong said waving a hand airily. "Our funding at present is more than sufficient."

"Indeed?" Cashin came back quickly. "Would you care to comment then, on reports that China's remaining bullion reserves are being sent out of the country?"

Soong's jowls quivered. "Ridiculous," he spluttered. "There's not a word of truth in the story. Where did you hear such rumours?"

Cashin smiled thinly, "From an exceptionally reliable source, Minister, close to yourself in fact. Simon Ho told me – the night he died."

Simon Ho. Ai-yah! There were shocked gasps from the Chinese. Yu-Ling looked frightened. Soong gave a sharp hiss of anger, "That straw-head fool, what did he tell you?"

Behind his spectacles the journalist's eyes glittered. "He said the Clipper's holds are packed with treasure looted from the Manchu Tombs. But that's not the whole story, is it Minister? *Just what else did they find when they opened Tz'u-hsi's tomb?*"

Tz'u-hsi. The Dragon Empress. A shiver ran down Yu-Ling's spine.

The *Southern Cross's* junior watch officer entered the saloon. With an

244

air of excitement he made straight for Kelly.

"Yes, son, what is it?"

"Sir, we're picking up radio signals from inland – it's the bomber, *she's started transmitting again.*"

The yacht's radio station was on the bridge deck. Kelly led the way, Munro hurrying after. Stewart Whitely and Davey came with them. The operator on duty looked about seventeen but his equipment was first rate. Stewart gave a cluck of envy.

"What's the message, are they okay still? Tell them we're doing our best to reach them tomorrow."

The young operator shook his head frowning with concentration, one hand poised over his morse key, the other at the dials. "I dunno, sir. Can't make it out. They're just repeating the same group over and over."

He flipped a switch and the squeak-scratch of morse filled the cabin from a loudspeaker.

"*dit-dit-dit-dit-dah, dit-dit-dit-dit-dah, dit-dit-dit-dit-dah . . .*" Stewart was biting his lip. "Four, four, four . . ." The note faded out, swallowed in a mush of static. "Sounds like a homing signal."

"Are we sure it's the bomber?"

"There's no call sign but it's the right frequency and direction – so far as I can tell. Our RDF wasn't designed for this kind of close-range ground work."

"I thought they were sending voice before?" Munro said.

"They were at first but the signal was crummy. Then they managed to get the main set working. The last message yesterday came through clear as a bell."

That figured. The morse beam was narrower than voice, it would cut through static easier.

The youth's fingers tapped rapid fire on the key. "I keep calling but they don't respond."

He switched back to receive again and they all listened. Static crackled and buzzed, then through it suddenly they caught the click of morse again.

Dit-dit-dit-dit-dah, dit-dit-dit-dit-dah . . .

"Darn signal keeps fading out all the time," he muttered, twisting a dial. "Must be their batteries running down, else something's the matter with the set." The clicks grew louder momentarily, then died away altogether.

"Still the same . . . *four, four, four* . . . They must be trying to give us a fix."

"But why don't they answer to the call-back?"

"What d'you reckon, Stewart?"

Whitely shook his head, "Too slow and no rhythm. Whoever it is doesn't know his morse. What's happened to the trained operator?"

No one had an answer to that.

"Try contacting again, Sparks, real slow to give him a chance."

"Aye, aye, sir." The youth began tapping. This time even Munro could follow the letters, "PAN-AM BASE TO ONE VICTOR FOUR SIX QRK? QRK? QRK? – *Can you hear me? Can you hear me?*"

The loudspeaker stayed silent.

"PAN-AM BASE TO ONE VICTOR FOUR SIX. QRK? QRK? QRK?"

Again and again he repeated his plea. Vainly. Not a single click penetrated the hiss of atmospherics. "Looks like they've signed off."

"Keep trying. And call the airstrip, they may have taken a cross-bearing." Kelly glanced at Munro, "I guess we'd better get hold of Major Slater."

Out in the Clipper's starboard wing Chuck Driscoll lay jammed on his back beneath the fuel tank. A monkey wrench was clenched in his teeth and his hands were smeared with grease. For the past half hour he had been struggling to refit the selector valve.

Using the tip of a screwdriver he probed inside the filter unit for a tiny gauze strainer which had become dislodged when he tried to join up the inlet feed. With infinite patience he coaxed it into position. Taking the wrench from between his teeth, he applied his lips to the end of the feed pipe and sucked. The foul taste of avgas filled his mouth. He spat it out. Thank God for that. Now to recouple the drive shaft.

Carefully he slid the spindle home and fumbled on his tool tray for the locking nut. It slipped from his oily fingers and fell with a clink between the wing spars. *Damn!* He'd have to go fetch another.

He squirmed out from under the tank and made his way up the walkway to the control cabin. A stock of engineers' spares was kept in the main hold. Locating a replacement, he was heading back when he heard a hatch click. "That you, Chris?" he called. His stomach was rumbling hungrily. He sure hoped they'd saved dinner for him.

No answer. Maybe he had imagined it. Returning to the wing, he wriggled back under the tank and set to work on the valve again. He tightened the drive shaft and screwed down the cover, then began bolting the unit onto its mounting. Finally he tested the complete assembly. It was a good twenty minutes before he was through.

Packing up his tools, he dumped them in the hold. Still no sign of Chris, the skunk must have forgotten about him. He was changing out of his filthy overalls when something by the bulkhead caught his eye. An airmail envelope. Unopened. He picked it up and scratched his head, puzzled. San Francisco address, postmarked Manila. How had that gotten here?

He wrenched open the hatch to the nearest side hold. An avalanche of letters and packets cascaded out from the slashed mail sack inside.

"*Check the whole ship?*" Chris Fry exclaimed aghast. "Gee, Max, that'll take us hours!"

"I don't care if it takes all night," Munro answered him pitilessly. "Get cracking."

The rest of the crew stood round in the hold, shaken by the thought of an intruder. "Break out the manifests. I want a full inventory: mail, cargo, safety gear, cabin fittings, the lot."

"Hell, Max, one lousy mail sack," Thyssen protested. "Why the panic?"

"Don't argue. *Just do it.*"

O'Byrne and the stewards took the passenger cabins, the rest of them combed the upper deck and holds. Munro ducked inside the wing stub and crawled past the sacks. Kneeling, he examined the hatch in the floor. The latches were unfastened and there were scratch marks on the metal where someone had rammed a thin bladed tool up from below.

As he scrambled out again Kelly appeared carrying a dirty net bag of woven fibre. "Picked this up on the dock, a *bilum*, the locals all carry 'em."

Together they studied the mail sack. It had been slit clean up one seam. "Could be a native alright," Kelly muttered. "They're handy enough with knives, steal anything too."

"Whoever it was forced the underwing hatch and climbed up. Either he was dead lucky or he knew his way around."

"I'll get on to Nash, have some guards posted. Ross ought to hear about this, where is he?"

The Chief had come up behind them. "Guess I know where to find him," he sighed.

In the dripping blackness of the swamp death stalked.

Fireflies flickered among the bushes, the night throbbed with the singing of frogs and the shrill buzz of cicadas. A bird shrieked in the jaws of a snake setting off a cacophony of competing cries, repeated up and down the scale in demented chorus.

Sweating with fear the bombardier crouched in the life raft, listening.

A guttural croaking in the reeds sent a shiver through him. Croc. The brutes were everywhere, twenty-footers and bigger. They must have scented food. Gripping the paddle tightly, he edged closer to the bank.

He had to find the plane.

Were the natives still hunting him? All day he had dodged their canoes. Twenty hours now he had been hiding in this stinking swamp, exhausted and terrified, soaked by rain storms, his body a solid mass of pain from insects and the blistering sun. He couldn't take another night.

Were the others all dead? Curran, the radio operator, had been the first. They had heard his screams in the thorn trees. Fletcher had taken the flashlight and gone to help. That was the last he'd seen of either.

An eddy of breeze stirred the tall reeds. With it came a faint scent of woodsmoke. He tensed afresh. Was he near the plane again? In his panic flight last night he'd lost all sense of direction.

Cautiously, not daring to call out, he let the raft drift. The mosquitoes were gorging on his raw flesh but he forced himself to ignore them. The moon slid from behind a cloud. A short way off was the clump of kanaris where they'd set up camp? The plane would be on the far side.

All at once he made out the bomber's dorsal turret silhouetted against the night sky. Eagerly he dug the paddle into the water. The raft bumped the root of an overhanging tree startling a swamp hen from her nest. Cursing, he flattened himself in the boat till the squawks died away.

Quietly he manoeuvred alongside the tail aiming for the main hatch above the stabiliser. There was no light showing on board. No sound either. Even the frogs were silent. "Mac?" he called softly. "Anyone there?"

The raft rocked as he hauled himself up, stretching the cramped muscles of his legs. Awkwardly he clambered to the opening. The surface of the fuselage was slippery from rain. "Mac?" he called again, "Maconochie?" He poked his head inside the darkness of the hatch.

"*WAAAA!*" A shattering yell burst upon his consciousness even as the steel blade took him in the throat. Death came with lightning pain, the sword slicing through to sever the spinal cord. Knees buckling, his corpse fell backwards into blackness.

Below, the crocs moved in to feast.

XIX

The clouds had cleared. Stars were out and the bay was calm and beautiful under the moon, the water afire with phosphorescence where it lapped about the pilings. Music and laughter streamed from the bright lit yacht as the Chief and Chuck stepped down from the gangway.

"Kelly said to follow the rail tracks, they'll lead us straight to the strip," Chuck shone his flash on the steel lines running up the jetty.

"Let's hope they're not working tonight."

Lights in the township twinkled reassuringly. When they reached the wharf the tracks curved away to the left past a line of sheds where goods waggons stood in a siding. The rancid stink of copra caught in their throats. That must be what the freighter was loading.

Insects whined about their heads as they followed the railroad, treading on the ties. In minutes the shore was left behind and they were in thick brush either side of the track.

"Heck, how far did Kelly say it was?"

"About half a mile, no more. Gee, what was that?" Chuck ducked as a fruit bat swooped past on silent wings.

They walked on.

"Chief, you buy Kelly's theory?"

"That it was a native? You got a better one?"

"Nope. Only why would a savage steal letters he can't even read?"

There were lights now ahead and a mesh fence. They could hear a generator running and make out workshops and hangars. Looked like a bigger operation than Ross had let on. A native guard opened the gate and pointed them in the direction of the control block. The concrete between the buildings was wet still from the rain, pools of water glistening blackly in the flashlight. A plane loomed up parked on the apron, its engines protected by canvas hoods.

"Junkers Tri-motor," the Chief grunted. "Good kites. German."

The mosquitoes were savage. They lit cigarettes and wandered along the strip. It ran north-west from the sea and they could hear the

250

waves breaking. The air felt thick and heavy with more rain on the way.

"So this is where Earhart took off from," Driscoll said.

"Yeah," the Chief glanced over to the control tower. Lights were burning and there were vehicles parked outside. "Guess that's where Ross'll be if he's anywhere."

They were about fifty yards away when they heard the sound of an aircraft circling. The runway lights came on and looking up they saw the plane break from the overcast. It levelled off, red and green wing lights sinking to meet the white spots of the flarepath as the pilot eased his throttles and dropped the flaps. A brief squeal of scorched rubber from the wheels and it was down and rolling. Both engineers nodded approvingly. Smooth and very professional. They watched it taxi up and turn, motors shrieking. A two-seater Grumman amphibian. Just the job for this country.

Groundcrew placed chocks under the wheels and the noise fell off in a wail as the power was cut. The passenger was helped out. A white man, with one bag which he handled carefully. They caught a clear glimpse of his face under the lights. Dr. Latouche.

A car swept up. He was bundled in and driven away.

Chuck and the Chief exchanged glances. "What was all that about?"

"Search me. Fits though, he wasn't at dinner."

"Let's try the pilot, maybe we can get something outta him."

There was no trace of Ross in the control block. Out the back they met the Grumman pilot putting his gear in a jeep. A cheerful Australian with curly red hair and beard.

"Hi, we're from the Clipper. Saw you come in just now, neat piece of work."

"Gerry Spencer, Guinea Airways," he stuck out a hand. "Glad to meet you, fellers. Jump in and I'll stand you a beer in town."

They roared off out the main gates. Neat whitewashed bungalows lined the road, each with its own patch of well-tended garden. Ross's description didn't fit here either.

"See you got the doc back safe then," the Chief shouted as they rattled over the potholes.

"The doc? Oh, you mean the Frenchie. So that's what he is." Spencer spun the wheel, "Jeez, what's the story then? Some kinda epidemic upriver?"

"*Epidemic?*"

"Yeah, I flew him up to the edge of the swamps just before dusk. Spent three flamin' hours twiddlin' my thumbs while he took samples of the water."

"Say what he was looking for?"

"No. Just whatever it was he didn't find it."

They pulled up near the harbour outside a large ramshackle building. HOTEL CECIL proclaimed a sun-bleached sign over the porch. From within came sounds of boisterous drinking.

Someone thrust another warm beer into Chuck's hands. Who had bought the round he didn't know. Everyone at the bar seemed eager to stand them drinks. The place was seedy but comfortable, sagging cane chairs, radio crackling in the corner. A home from home for the expats in town – planters, prospectors, engineers with the big mining outfits, leathered diggers and several Guinea Airways people. Not many younger men, all off at the war presumably.

"Cheers, sport," a gnarled miner clinked glasses. "Name's Wade, Tom Wade. Good to see Yanks here. Always liked Yanks, fine blokes. Why ain't you in the bleedin' war though?"

"Hell, we don't want to spoil your fight."

The Australian tipped half a pint of beer down his throat and grinned. " 'Spose you've come to pick up those blokes went down in the swamps yesterday," he said, wiping his mouth. "Black Jack Nash and his mob were out searching for 'em today. Dint find 'em though. Poor bloody bastards, don't give much for their chances. *Kukukuku* been moving down into that area."

"*Kuk* – what?"

A burst of laughter drowned Chuck's words and sent the geckos on the ceiling scuttling. Another of the Guinea Airways boys was telling how an eight foot croc he had been flying out for a zoo had broken loose from its crate in mid-air.

Rain was drumming on the tin roof again, making the electricity flicker. "Were you around when Earhart came through Lae?" the Chief asked Spencer casually. He was propped against the bar, a head taller than anyone else in the room.

"You bet, mate. Watched her set off. She took the whole length of the strip getting that Lockheed into the air. Heck of a brave lady. Everyone was real cut up when she went missing. Wish I could've helped in the search but none of our ships here had the range."

"What d'you think happened?" Chuck said.

Spencer shrugged. "They claimed she ran out of fuel but that don't wash with me. I'd say the Japs got her."

"Meaning she wound up in the Mandate? But that would have put her way off course."

"Depends what her course was, don't it?"

They moved to a corner by the pool table and lit cigarettes. The Chief had brought a handful of beer mats from the bar. His big hands dealt two out on the faded baize. "Lae – Howland, a straight run of twenty-five hundred miles." Watching Spencer's expression deliberately he added a third off out to the left, making a triangle, "The Japanese Mandate. Let's get this right, you're saying Earhart *wasn't* headed for Howland Island?"

The Australian stared down at the table, "She was headed there alright, had to be. But there were some rum things about the set-up. Everybody here reckoned so."

"Like what for instance?"

"That ship of theirs, the Lockheed, she was carrying reconnaissance cameras."

"*Cameras*! You certain?"

"Saw 'em myself. A triple installation in the nose, real class job. I tell you she had government backing."

"Hold it," Chuck frowned. "You suggesting this was some kind of a spying mission they were on?"

The Australian tugged at his curly beard, "I dunno, lad. Not even sure I want to. If you're that interested try a bloke called Austin Fuller. He's an engineer, worked on the plane, helped prepare her for the flight."

"Where do we find him?" the Chief said.

Spencer nodded across the room, "Easy, here he comes now."

The Americans followed his gaze. A grizzled man in his fifties had just entered from the veranda.

With him was Ross.

NINE THIRTY PM. Out on the yacht Georgiana was dancing the *Suzy Q* with Tony Shapiro. They had set the phonograph up under the stern awning and clearing the deck chairs left space for a dozen couples. César was playing poker in the bar with Cherkassy and the oilmen, trying to keep an eye on her at the same time. It wasn't doing his game any good.

"Let's have another!" the Gordon Smythe girl shrieked as the record ran down. She was bursting out of the front of a too-tight frock. Eddie Wirth put on a *Cha-Cha* and swept her under the awning.

Yu-Ling swayed with Hollington Soong, forcing herself to endure his skin-crawling odiousness. His stomach was pressed against her and every few moments a hand would slide down to squeeze her rump.

253

"*Oh ko*, you dance well, little Jade Years. Yes, very well," he informed her smugly as the music ceased.

"Thank you, Honourable Minister, but please my feet are tired," she begged. "Could we rest a little?"

"Sit out? Pooh! Plenty of time to sit out later."

Across the saloon Scott saw a look of dismay cloud the girl's pretty face. Lecherous old goat. She moved smartly to cut in. "Oh, Minister, but you promised this one to me!"

Soong halted nonplussed, "Er, did I?"

"Yes, sir, right after dinner," she seized his arm. "I'm sure Miss Chen will excuse us, won't you, Miss Chen? Look, here's our Fourth Officer just back, he'll be happy to escort you, I know."

Beaming with relief, Yu-Ling gave her arm to Chris Fry. Scott stifled disgust as she submitted herself to the Minister's clammy embrace.

At the poker table César was down almost two hundred dollars to the Prince. "*Madre mia*, how can one concentrate with this noise?" he exclaimed testily as the cards were gathered in. "Gentlemen, excuse me, I am quitting."

"And me," one of the oilmen agreed. "This game's too rich for my money."

Cherkassy raised an eyebrow. "As you wish." He slipped the pile of notes smoothly into his wallet. Maria Bianchi was standing near the doors in a discreetly sensual dark dress. "Perhaps I shall take a turn on the dance floor."

The phonograph began belting out a jazz number. Catching sight of César, Georgiana spun over. "Darling, where've you been?" she kissed him breathlessly. "Let's dance!"

He shook her off irritably, "Pah, nigger music! You know I will not dance to that."

"César, c'mon, don't be so *boring*."

"I am not boring – and you have been out here long enough on your own. We are engaged to be married, remember?"

Georgiana stared at him uncertainly for a moment, then pouted, "Oh stuff, I'm having fun!" She flounced off.

Maria Bianchi had declined a dance. The Prince pressed a cocktail on her and they carried their glasses out to the starboard rail. "I hope this noise won't wake the children," she said frowning.

The Russians's lip curled, "Surely your boy is accustomed to the sound of dancing."

Her knuckles tightened on the rail, "What do you mean?"

"Come, do not play the innocent, Madam. Your business in Shanghai – a club was it not?"

"And if it was? That is no concern of yours."

There were footsteps on the companionway behind. Tad Gotto's head appeared briefly above deck, then ducked down again.

Cherkassy waited till the steward was out of earshot. "Perhaps not," he continued smoothly. "But our fellow passengers might be interested to know that the proprietress of Shanghai's *Red Lips* is travelling aboard."

Maria turned to face him, her mouth drawn thin and white. "I see," she snapped scornfully. "I have met your kind before. How much do you want?"

He smiled, "Not money, Madam."

"What then?"

Cherkassy told her.

She gasped and stepped back, a hand rising involuntarily to her breast, "My God, you cannot be serious!"

The Russian's laugh was chilling, "On the contrary, Madam. I was never more earnest in my life."

Aft in the saloon a glass fell with a smash. Maria stared at him, every muscle in her body wire-taut. The Prince took a step forward. Her eyes glittered defiantly. "*Stay away from me!*" she hissed.

Alone in the Clipper's hold, Munro stuffed a final fistful of mail into the replacement sack and cursed. Seventeen gone. Hell, that meant a load of paper work, special reports from himself, Ross and Kelly, endless queries from Head Office. Pan American didn't like to lose mail.

Only two of the sacks were tagged Manila–West Coast. And the thief had picked one. A *coincidence*? Nothing else had even been touched. The crew had covered the plane from top to bottom for no result. Munro had sent them back to the *Southern Cross* and stayed on checking.

He eyed the seal on the second sack. Tampering with US Mail was a federal offence. Too bad, he'd figure some kind of an excuse. Fetching a pair of wire-cutters from the Chief's box, he snipped the fastening and dumped out the contents.

There were a thousand envelopes, more. Rapidly he began to sort through, scanning for his own handwriting.

Twenty minutes later he had Oliver's photograph in his hand.

"*Faster!*" Felicity cried as Chris Fry twirled her round and back. Scott shook her head smiling at their hot flushed faces. Little Yu-Ling was safe now too, dancing with Bob Cashin. He was giving her a good time, teaching her the steps.

She watched Georgiana Delahaye saunter in from the bar, a long cigarette holder dangling from her fingers. The silk sash of her dress was knotted loosely on one hip and her gilt sandals had a two inch heel. Every male head turned to follow as she mooched round the saloon looking sulky and dangerous. Shapiro went over and said something, she shrugged him off. Maybe she'd had another row with her boyfriend. The lady sure was dynamite.

A tall figure entered from the deck. Max Munro, he must have finished on the Clipper at last. Scott saw his grey eyes flick over the party, summing it up, that way he had. Georgiana had turned her back, studiously ignoring him. She was by the phonograph flipping boredly through the records. Selecting one, she handed it to Davey Klein.

Hot jazz burst upon the night. Unhurried Max crossed the room and took her arm, "C'mon Dixie!"

"*Toe-heel, toe-heel, swing turn,*" Davey Klein chanted to the beat. "*Out in turn, arms cross, pull out* – Man, they're really cookin'!"

It was the *Lindy Hop*. Georgiana jitterbugging hard as she could go, haunches snapping, coppery hair wild. Round the edge people were crowding in to watch, clutching drinks, perspiring in the hot humid night, men's eyes locked on her body as the flimsy dress swirled. Davey tensed sweating as Munro caught her by the waist and spun her round. *Christ, what a figure!*

From the sidelines César glared murderously.

"Game for a hip throw?"

"Sure. Hold me tight!"

" *– toe-heel, toe-heel – UP!*"

A group of Army men urged them on. Hands clasping behind his neck she leapt for his hips, slim legs out straight. Everyone gasped. Her hair brushed the floor for an instant as he swung her down.

" *– and BREAK!*"

Straightening like a whip Munro whirled her upwards in a full circle. There was a flash of lace and long pale thighs as her skirts flew over her head and her toes in the gilded sandals touched the awning.

The Army men whistled and stamped. Davey let out a long breath, boy oh boy, some show that!

White with rage César turned on his heel and stormed for the bar. "*Valgame Dios*! Are all Yankee women whores?" he spat to the little Filipino. "Brandy, a double. *Pronto!*"

The music ended. People began drifting back inside. By the stern rail Georgiana leaned her head against Munro's chest. Neither spoke. The lights of the settlement twinkled peacefully ashore and the moon made a silver track on the water. His lips brushed her hair.

"Munro," a harsh voice interrupted. Slater, back from the Commissioner's. "Sorry to bust in, Miss Delahaye, but your boyfriend and I got business to discuss."

Georgiana straightened coldly. "You sure pick your moments, Major," she said. "See you around, Max."

They moved down the deck. Slater lit a cigar and tossed the match over the side in a glowing arc. "You don't waste time, do you, Pilot?" he sneered. "Well, try this for size. There was a signal waiting for me at the Commissioner's, from Hongkong forwarded via Manila. Remember your Chinese piece, Wei-Wei Chu? She was found dead two nights ago, murdered. *The Brits claim she was working for the Japs.*"

"Okay, everyone," Shapiro was shouting. "Let's finish up with a Conga. Hands on the hips of the person in front. C'mon, Miss Chen, it's easy anyone can do it. You too, Minister!"

Scott was on her way aft to join in when she bumped into Kurt Thyssen on the starboard deck.

"Sally, what's the matter between us?" he said huskily, pulling her into the shadows. "You've been avoiding me all evening." Crushing her suddenly in his arms, he kissed her hard on the mouth.

"What the hell's gotten into you, Kurt?" Scott tore her face away and struggled violently to break free. Stepping back, she landed a stinging slap on his face. "Keep your paws off me, you creep!"

"But Sally . . ."

"Get lost, Kurt!" She went on up the deck to the dancing, wiping her mouth where he'd kissed her.

"*One, two, three kick!*"

257

With Shapiro at the head, the column of dancers snaked through the saloon and out onto the portside deck. Behind him Yu-Ling, Hollington Soong, then Felicity, Chris Fry, Scott, Tad Gotto, Davey, Georgiana, Van Cleef – almost everyone still up.

"One, two, three, kick!"

Towards the tail the rhythm was slipping but nobody cared. Hands clapping, he led them past the lifeboats then twice round the foremast, faster and faster, trying to catch up with puffing Ed Wirth on the end. Helpless with laughter, they reeled back up the other side of the ship meeting Reverend Jordan on the way and flattening him against the rails. "Join on, Reverend!" someone yelled as they shot by.

With a final riotous circuit of the bar the dancers broke apart. Georgiana collapsed into a big armchair and kicked off her shoes, "Phew, I sure could do with a dip! I think I'll go get into my costume."

A stool rocked as César got up angrily. "*Madre mia*, stop showing off!" he scowled, his voice slurred. "All evening you have been making a fool of yourself!"

"*I've* been making a fool of myself? Just what do you mean by that?"

"You know very well. Dancing with crew members, flaunting yourself in front of all the ship!"

"Oh for goodness sakes," she fanned herself with a magazine. "We're not in Manila now!"

"As if that matters! Do you think it is pleasant for me to see my future wife behaving like a street harlot?"

"*Like a what . . .?*"

Georgiana stared at him incredulously, then burst into peals of mirth.

Munro strolled along the dock to the shore smoking a thoughtful cigarette. It had rained briefly, clearing the air, and water still dripped from the jacaranda trees. Frogs kept up a steady croaking chorus. In one of the bungalows someone was playing a piano, the notes trickling into the night.

He could hear a faint drone in the sky. A plane was passing over, flying very high. It was headed inland, not showing any lights.

Wei-Wei dead. Wei-Wei an enemy agent. Was it the photograph she'd been after that night at Jimmy's? Munro's hand went to his inner pocket – the envelope was still there.

East Wind Rain. She'd been trying to warn him of something. What?

He turned and began to retrace his steps. At the end of the jetty a couple of guards were patrolling by the Clipper. That was good to see. Further along, rows of lighted portholes gleamed aboard the yacht. The music had ceased, passengers were retiring to bed.

There was a muffled splash.

Voices shouted on the dock, raising the alarm.

Munro was already sprinting for the bows.

He ran to the spot where he thought he'd seen a figure fall, between the boat and the pier. Nothing. Ripples swirled darkly, gurgling among the pilings. The tide was running in.

The water heaved. A head broke the surface. Georgiana. She sank again immediately. Ripping off his jacket and shoes Munro plunged in, feeling for the body. It must have gone right down. He dived, groping helplessly in the inky water. His hand touched something. Hair? He grabbed and missed. Christ, where was she?

Lungs bursting, he surfaced, gulped a mouthful of air and dived again. For a seeming eternity he searched down in the silt and filth of the harbour till the pain in his chest drove him up.

Others were on the jetty now. The Chief and Chuck returning from the hotel. The big Indian was stripping off too. "Get lights down here, fast!" he bellowed at Chuck and heaved himself in.

"It's Georgiana, I can't find her!" Munro gasped, retching with the seawater he had swallowed. "She must be among the pilings." For the third time he plunged down, arms outstretched in the blackness, feeling for the slime-covered piers. God, how long was it already? He pulled himself under the jetty, stifling panic as the roof closed over.

Barnacles tore at his hands as he blundered in total darkness against the wooden posts. Still nothing. The force of the current was frightening. If it had swept her far under she hadn't a hope. Desperately he clawed along the rotting timbers, praying it was the right direction.

The Chief burst up from the bottom, blowing like a whale. Spotlights had come on and were sweeping the surface. Men were hurrying with flashes. "Shine your lights under that jetty," he shouted, treading water alongside the yacht. "The First's down there!"

The blood was roaring in Munro's ears. He had to get air. Hemmed in by the pilings, he flip-turned. Through the murk he could see a dim glow of light and propelled himself towards it. Something soft bumped against him. *A body.* He felt a limb and tugged but it wouldn't come. She was wedged up under the facing. The pain in his chest was like a vice now, his whole being screamed for oxygen. He had to free her this time or she was dead. Maybe was already? Strands of hair streamed against his face as he fought to get her loose. Material ripped,

259

he gave another frantic wrench and suddenly the limp body was in his arms. Darkness was coming over him, he was blacking out. With his last ounce of strength, he kicked for the surface.

"She has started breathing," Latouche said, "but keep working the lungs."

Georgiana lay face down on the jetty, her swimming costume in shreds. It seemed to have taken an age to bring her round. Munro pressed on the ribcage again, expelling air, conscious of the fragile woman's frame beneath his hands. She coughed up more water and moaned.

César elbowed his way through the circle of onlookers, distraught. "*Querida mia!*" he dropped in his knees and began massaging her hand frantically. "Doctor, she will be alright, yes?"

Latouche's sensitive fingers were at her wrist, taking its pulse, "We must get her to bed. She will be suffering from shock."

Georgiana's breathing was regular now. They stopped the artificial respiration and turned her over. The tattered satin of her costume slipped revealing a firm white breast, the nipple puckered darkly. César covered her quickly with his dinner jacket and turned unsteadily to Munro, "I do not understand. There was an accident?"

"Search me, chum. I was down here on the dock when she fell."

"She *fell* in?"

Munro wrung the water from his shirt. He shrugged, "Unless she was dumb enough to jump."

A stretcher party arrived from the yacht. Latouche had them lift her gently onto it. She was deathly pale still.

"My head hurts," she whispered. "What happened?"

Munro tucked the blanket round her gently, "You went swimming, Dixie. You're okay now."

She managed a weak smile, "Was it you saved me, Max? God, where would I be without you."

They carried the stretcher off. Munro went to retrieve his clothes from where he had dropped them. He picked up the jacket, then remembered. Quickly he checked the pocket.

The envelope had gone.

★ ★ ★

260

WASHINGTON. FRIDAY DECEMBER 5th. Ten hours behind New Guinea and half a world away, the translation section of OP–20–G was working overtime. For the past five days every listening station from Maine to Rio de Janeiro, from Dutch Harbour to Corregidor had been on round-the-clock watch of all Japanese voice newscasts.

Until further notice every single transmission from Tokyo was to be checked in its entirety. Checked for just four words: *Higashi no kaze ame*.

As the intercepts piled up at the rate of hundreds a day, weary foreign language experts laboured eighteen hour shifts, scrutinising each one for a buried reference to the code. The discarded teletype strips were fed through shredders and the bins taken out to be incinerated under armed guard.

So intense was the security there would be those who would subsequently maintain to their graves that the *winds execute* message was never in fact received. That it had never existed except in the imaginations of their accusers.

They had their reasons.

Higashi no kaze ame – East Wind Rain.

Armed Secret Service agents stood guard outside the big room on the White House second floor. Inside, portraits of past presidents stared down at the proceedings. Jefferson and Jackson on the west wall, Woodrow Wilson over the fireplace. Red damask curtains were drawn against the gloom of late afternoon and cigar smoke blued the air. Before each place on the octagonal mahogany table was a yellow legal pad and pencil.

The Cabinet was in session.

Secretary of State Cordell Hull, lanky and white-haired, a former backwoods circuit judge from the Tennessee mountains, was delivering his report on the talks with the Japanese peace envoys.

"Scoundrels and piss-ants, the worst people I ever saw! They don't mean business, Mr. President. With every hour that passes, I become more convinced they are not playing in the open," his high grating accents rasped round the table.

"Mr. President," Navy Secretary Frank Knox spluttered in his excitable manner, "we have very secret intelligence which mustn't go outside this room – *the Japanese Fleet is at sea!*"

The announcement electrified the meeting. There were shocked demands for more information. Where was the fleet headed? Who were the Japanese about to strike at?

261

The President's voice cut through the babble, "As of this moment we have no exact knowledge of their intentions. They could be aiming south to attack Singapore or the Philippines, or north for the Aleutians."

"It's south, Mr. President," Frank Knox interrupted again. "All the evidence points to them going south."

"It was my understanding we have no information yet with regard to direction."

"Yes, but we must conclude the fleet is moving *south*. It's the obvious course."

"They might be going *north*, we have no firm evidence to the contrary," the President persisted. He turned abruptly to the rest of the Cabinet. "I think we ought all to consider, suppose they attack Singapore? What should the United States do?"

One by one the vote went round the Cabinet table. It was a clear majority – if Singapore were attacked, the US should go to the support of the British.

"I confess I was mighty surprised, Kim," Roosevelt wheeled himself across to his desk. It was three pm and he was back in his oval study. "Even Frances Perkins was in favour."

The tall man frowned, "The Cabinet isn't Congress, Mr. President, or the country."

"I know, I know. We still need . . ." he weighed his words, "an *overt act*."

"You mean if they were to go for the Philippines?"

"Or another US possession." The President toyed thoughtfully with a model ship on his desk. His sinuses were giving him pain again and he was looking drawn. He changed the subject, "What's the latest on your Major Slater?"

"We won't know till tomorrow if they've recovered the cargo. Presuming success, the Clipper will fly directly on to Guam. From there it's four days to the West Coast."

"*Four* days?" the President mused. "Let's pray we can stall Tokyo that long."

XX

SATURDAY DECEMBER 6th.

. . . click . . . click-click . . . click . . .

Ricky woke hot. It was still dark. He kicked off the sheet and lay back, wondering what the time was. In the berth below Maria Bianchi stirred restlessly and turned over in her sleep.

. . . click-click . . . click . . . click . . .

The noise began again, metallic, faint and irregular, seeming to come from the deck overhead. It puzzled him. Quietly, so as not to disturb his mother, he clambered down the ladder to the floor and tip-toed over to the porthole. A streak of grey was stealing into the eastern sky but dawn was some way off. The bay was dead calm.

A solitary seagull flapped inland calling mournfully. The tapping, whatever it was, had ceased. Ricky yawned. He was about to get back into bed again when he thought he saw a momentary pin-point of light.

Blinking he rubbed the sleep from his eyes. Yes, definitely a light, flashing in the distance. It was too quick for a ship. He watched for a minute gripping the sill, wishing he could see better.

On-off . . . on-off . . . almost like a code. What was doing it? Straining in the darkness, he thought he could make out a shape on the water some way off. A sort of black hump on a raft.

The clicking overhead stopped. Ricky counted three more sets of flashes, then the signal ceased. As he watched the black shape seemed to slide below the surface and disappear. Nothing else disturbed the greyness of the dawn. Climbing back into his bunk, he lay down thoughtfully.

The last thing he remembered as he fell asleep was a door squeaking down the passage.

Ross too slept fitfully.

North-west from Howland. Forbidden territory. White blocks of cumulus

263

drifting against a wrinkled blue ocean. The steady hypnotic rhythm of the props. Six hours they had been flying now. Alone, himself and Slater.

"This is crazy, Major. We're two hundred miles inside the Mandate. If the Yellow-bellies spot us we've had it!"

"Keep on to the end of our range, damn you! We've got to find that plane before the Japs do."

"That's it isn't it? The bloody plane. That's all you care about!"

"Leave it out, Captain. You do your job, I'll do mine. What's this coming up now?"

Through the binoculars a greenish speck showed bright amid the blue.

"How the hell should I know! None of these charts match up. Could be Mili."

"Take her down. We'll check it out."

"Christsakes, what if it's a Jap base?"

"Dammit, I said take her down!"

The horizon tilted as they peeled off into a dive. Gradually the speck in the distance grew till they could make out a line of surf breaking on the reef. A coral islet, part of a larger atoll. Windswept palms, pale sands, a shelving beach.

"Not a thing. Must be uninhabited."

"Son of a gun, what's that?"

"Where?"

"Inside the reef. Look, there's something sunk in the water near the shore!"

Pulling back on the stick. Right rudder. Banking round in a tight turn for a second pass over the lagoon. Craning to see out. Hope and dread. Praying. Let it be, this time let it be!

"It's a plane! Jesus Christ, Ross, it's the Electra! It's them . . ."

The scene cut off like a cine-reel ending as he woke abruptly. He groped for the light switch. In his mouth was the sour taste of guilt.

FIVE AM. The sky was clear as steel and the sun spilled over the rim of the sea in a ball of liquid fire. Schools of iridescent flying fish skimmed the mirror surface of the bay. A few early pelicans flapped slowly off towards their feeding ground. Ashore, the mists were lifting from the jungled hills, cooking fires were alight in the native village, men were dragging down canoes to check their traps.

Munro came up on deck, dark hair wet from the shower. He had borrowed a bush shirt and canvas pants from Kelly. One of the yacht's tenders idled alongside, Slater in the bow, and Sir Ambrose was leaning over the rail in a paisley dressing down talking to him.

"Good morning, Munro," the old man turned. "Better weather for the search at least."

"Just so long as it holds, sir."

"By the way, I got that message of yours off last night. Playfair should have it this morning. Heaven knows when we can expect a reply. I asked them to wire every stop on the route to be safe."

"Thanks, sir. I've a hunch it just might be important."

Munro dropped down into the boat. Slater wore old Marine Corps fatigues and an officer's peaked cap. The bulge of a pistol was visible in one hip pocket. He gave a grunt, "Morning, *hero*." Jordan was with him, clutching his precious camera.

Munro ignored the crack. "Nothing further from the bomber?"

"No, and Kelly had his people listening all night."

"Looks bad for the crew then."

Slater shrugged and made no answer.

"What about the spotter plane?"

"The Brits said first light. It should be taking off now."

A Melanesian crewman stood at the tiller, ready to cast off. "Who else we waiting for?"

"Latouche – here he comes." The Doctor appeared at the steps. Slater bit back a curse. With him, kitted out in slacks and a pith helmet, was Georgiana. A purple bruise showed on one cheekbone, the only sign of injury from last night.

"Morning, Major," she said breezily, stepping into the stern. "Hi, Max, Reverend. Well, we all set?"

A slow smile creased Munro's eyes, "Welcome aboard, Dixie. I like the headgear."

Slater was fuming, "Hold it, lady!" he interrupted. "What d'you think you're playing at?"

Georgiana eyed him innocently, "Why, coming up the swamps to find Bishop Buchan. Isn't that the plan?"

"Are you nuts? We could be out on that son of a bitch river all day."

"I can handle it if you can, Major," a steely edge came into her voice, "and don't forget my father's footing the bill."

There was a loaded silence. "Aw hell," Slater gave in. "Have it your own way, but don't expect no pleasure trip."

So Kim *was* behind it. That figured, Munro thought.

The tender's engine throbbed and they pulled away from the yacht's side. A salt tang freshened their faces as they gathered speed past the bows of the Clipper. Looking back, Munro glimpsed Ross at the cockpit window. Neither waved.

Wading birds flew up from the mangroves as they entered the mouth of the Markham. The water here was a dirty brown with wide expanses of slimy mud and a stench of stagnant ooze. Two battered river launches were taking on supplies at a wooden landing stage. Slowing, the tender eased alongside and dropped them off.

"*Huri-up, you blak bastards!*" the hard-bitten sergeant bellowed at a file of native porters, fierce, hook-nosed men in scant bark G-strings. The launches were ungainly, flat-bottomed craft with a low freeboard and central deckhouse for the engine. Faded canvas canopies covered the sterns. Cases of C-rations and fresh water were being stowed under the bench seats.

"G'day, sports," Nash came striding up in shorts and heavy boots. His jaw dropped open, "Strewth, whatcha bring the sheila for?"

"She's from Washington," Slater told him curtly. "Now let's get this show moving."

"Gawd, Yanks!" Nash shook his head in disbelief. "Okay, you people hop aboard the front boat, my sergeant'll follow in the other." Aero-engines roared overhead, taking off from the Lae strip. "Search plane," he yelled above the din, "she'll call us up when she's over the crash."

They piled aboard and the barefoot crew cast off. Nash took the wheel amidships, a slouch hat crammed down over his eyes. Slung from one shoulder was a black machine gun with skeleton butt.

A smell of coffee brewing wafted back, the crew had a stove going in the deckhouse. It was nearly nine. The heat was fierce already, the sun a brilliant disc in the baking sky. The slow chugging of the launch seemed to generate no breeze, under the canopy the air was thick and muggy. Munro sprawled on a portside bench, Jordan slumped opposite, Latouche leaning against the stern, head tilted back, eyes closed. Slater was pacing up and down the deck like a caged animal. Only Georgiana seemed untroubled by the heat. She was up forward chatting to Nash at the wheel.

The cleared land and cocoa plantations were left behind and the river was cutting a broad tract through forest. Giant trees hung with lianas towered precipitously over the banks, their massive trunks coated with moss and parasitic plants, fern covered roots groping like tentacles for the water. Dense thickets of tangled black-green growth crowded the shore creating an impenetrable screen.

The river was sluggish with occasional swirls of current, its course meandering, looping endlessly back on itself in sweeping bends. The depth seemed to vary unpredictably from fathoms to scarcely a couple of feet and Nash kept a boy stationed in the prow with a sounding-pole. Occasionally rafts of vegetation and sunken logs came drifting downstream, but there was no sign of human life.

At times their progress was slowed to a crawl by sandbanks and mobs of wooded islands so that Nash and the sergeant had to steer the clumsy boats in and out among narrow channels searching for the main waterway. No sooner were they clear than a stuttering from one of the engines would cause a halt while silt was cleared from the intake filter.

There was a yell from one of the crew, a large snake had been spotted swimming for a patch of reeds. They watched the flat evil-looking head sliding through the water. Nash handed over the wheel and squatted on the seat next to Jordan. "How about the natives up country?" Munro asked him, "Any chance the bomber crew might have made it to a village?"

Under the brim of his hat the Australian's expression was hard to read. "They're not exactly friendly up there, sport. That's *Kukukuku* territory – bleedin' cannibals!"

Ahead in the middle of the river, just breaking the surface, a chain of sandbanks lay awash like a man's backbone running beneath the skin. They slowed and the boy at the wheel steered close into the starboard bank. It was dark under the curtain of trees. The throb of the launches' engines seemed muffled by the smothering forest.

The sounding-pole probed the weed-tangled surface as they crawled onwards. Clouds of insects whined amid the stifling stillness, but otherwise the immense jungle gave off no sound. Heavy foliage drooped motionless from the oppressive multitude of trees. Not a bird's call disturbed the silence.

The whites stared back uneasily at the fantastic and unstirring leaves. They sensed a brooding force within the jungle, a primeval malevolence resentful of their intrusion. The engine faltered a moment then picked up again. Simultaneously a cry rang from the darkness of the forest. A ghastly ululation that froze the blood, rising and falling discordantly only to end in a wail of infinite desolation.

"Wow, what was that?" Georgiana whispered shakily as they emerged into the sunlight again. The crew were cowering in the deckhouse, eyes rolling in fright. Munro gazed astern at the receding bank but the hideous sound was not repeated. It had been human though.

Nash had unslung his gun and was watching the trees. Slowly he relaxed, "I dunno, could be a warning, could be nothing to do with us."

"*Kukukuku?*" Munro suggested.

The Australian shrugged. "Hey, you black rascals, come outta there!" he yelled at the crew. "Back to work, *huri-up!*" Reluctantly they obeyed clutching their *parangs*.

"Sounded to me like someone with a knife in his belly," Slater muttered to himself.

Concern was clouding Latouche's face, "These *Kukukuku*, do they attack white men?"

"Normally no, Doc, but . . ."

"But what?" Munro said.

"There's something in the wind alright. We've seen the signs, message sticks coming down river, drumming in the night. Coupla weeks ago a missionary was axed to death. The planters are scared. Seems a new kind of cult has sprung up among the hill natives. They got some weird notion 'bout Jesus coming with a load of arms for them to drive out the whites."

"Are you saying there could be an uprising?" Jordan spoke for the first time. He was looking wretched in the heat, his clerical shirt drenched with sweat already.

Nash screwed up his face, "Anything's possible, Father. You see the black fella round the mission all smiles and singing hymns, you forget the beggar's dad was a head hunter. Murder and cannibalism are facts of life here. I've seen madness erupt out of thin air – when their blood's hot anything can trigger a slaughter."

"Like an aircraft crash landing in the swamps, is that what you're saying?"

"Too right, sport. Specially if it happened in *Kukukuku* territory."

Slater interrupted, "This drilling and waiting for weapons, are the Yellow-bellies involved?"

"That's the big one. We get reports of unidentified vessels off the coast, subs seen in the bays at night. I know blokes who reckon there are secret Jap colonies in the highlands."

"Cannibalism, race hatred and Japanese guns," Latouche murmured, "an explosive mixture. And the British outnumbered a thousand to one."

"With our boys in the middle," Georgiana said.

The river was changing. It had narrowed, the current moving fast between high, steep banks. Munro went forward to the prow. The lookout boy was scanning the water ahead, signalling directions with his arms to Nash steering. A broad-bladed *parang* was stuck through

268

the belt of his shorts and drops of spray glistened in his wiry hair.

Dark rocks slid by beneath the surface. They were approaching some rapids. Munro watched the broken water drawing nearer, foaming torrents sluicing over jagged outcrops. He glanced back at Nash. The Australian stood feet braced, a tattooed nude flexing on one bicep as he fought the wheel.

Spray shot past the bows, soaking them. The launch heeled as Nash swung her hard round, aiming for a narrow channel between the rocks. Plunging waves cascaded over giant boulders, battering the hull. The roar was deafening. They heeled again, the boat's engine straining against the churning current. Everyone grabbed for hand-holds and clung on as they shot out into clear water.

The sun beat down hotter than ever. Monotonously, they ploughed on northwards. The river broadened gradually until they were crossing a small lake. Startled by the launches, a flock of pygmy geese rose honking into the air. After the gloom of the forest the reed beds had a kind of desolate beauty. Away in the distance they could hear the steady drone of the spotter plane.

The launch party lay listless beneath the canopy. Ahead, the shoulders of the Bismarck Range were capped with ominous cloud. Conversation was desultory. The immensity of the hostile landscape, its heat, humidity, the sense of lurking danger seemed to lower their spirits.

Munro stripped off his shirt and stretched out forward trying to ignore the flies, when a shadow fell across his face. Georgiana, her legs long and straight in the slim-fitting pants.

She knelt beside him and traced the scratches on his skin softly with the tips of her fingers. "Did you get these saving me last night?"

He squinted down at his chest, "Yeah. Next time you go swimming, Dixie, do it in daylight."

"I owe you my life, Max," her voice was husky as she leaned over him. The top three buttons of her blouse were undone and she wasn't wearing much of anything underneath. "But for you I'd be dead."

"Thank the Doc too, it was him brought you round."

Her fingers continued their gentle caressing. "Whenever I'm in trouble somehow there you are. It's strange, isn't it, darling," she whispered, "how fate seems determined to throw us together."

Munro nodded, "Don't fret, honeybee, I won't show up on your wedding night."

She sat up straight with an angry jerk. "My God, Max Munro, you can be a sarcastic bastard when you try!" she hissed.

"I don't like playing games," Munro rolled over reaching for the cigarettes in his shirt pocket. "You didn't come on this trip just to thank me for fishing you out of the drink, so what do you want?"

She glared at him furiously, lips pursed. "Last night," she spat finally, "I want to know what happened – exactly."

His eyes narrowed, "You don't remember?"

"I'll tell you my side in a moment, first I want to hear what you saw."

Munro lit two cigarettes and passed her one, trying to recreate the scene in his mind. "I was down on the dock walking back to the yacht. There was a cry, I think, then I saw someone falling and the splash as you hit the water . . ."

"Was there anyone else about on the yacht when I fell?"

"There could have been, I wasn't watching. Why?"

She looked at him again, her eyes very bright, "Because I didn't fall, Max, *somebody pushed me.*"

The radio crackled in the deckhouse. Nash was talking to the search plane. "Beaut, I know the place, we'll head right for it."

The others sat up. "They've located the crash again in the swamps," he reported. "I'd put us about an hour away."

"Any word on survivors?"

"They couldn't see from the air but there's a native village close by, we may get some news from them."

He shouted to his sergeant in the launch behind. The river wound on deeper into the rain forest, its banks often lost in swampy pools beneath the trees. Patches of reed and waterweed threatened to block the channel. They had been going half an hour when the rain came. Fat, warm drops spattered on the canopy, changing abruptly to a solid downpour that blotted out the view.

At a walking pace they toiled on, the water swirling and gurgling in the scuppers. Nash was steering, straining to make out a course. Suddenly the man in the bows gave a cry. There was a whirring sound and a slim wooden shaft came clattering across the deck. A second arrow buried itself in the side of the deckhouse with a thunk, inches from Reverend Jordan's head. There were yells from the crew. Latouche pulled Georgiana down under a bench. More arrows skipped about the boat, plopping into the water as they sheltered under the seats. Cursing, Nash unshouldered his gun. Smoke spouted from the blunt muzzle. There was a quick rattle of shots like a car backfiring and brass shell cases tumbled from the breach as he let off a burst at the shore. Through the rain Munro had brief glimpses of black figures running in the shrub.

270

The crew were banging away with bolt-action rifles. Slater had his pistol out and cocked, searching for a target. Nash stopped momentarily to load a fresh magazine. All at once the launch shuddered violently beneath them and they ground to a halt. "*Shit*, that's all we bloody need!" he threw the engine into reverse, sounding the hooter to warn the second launch. The screw churned, kicking up a stench of river mud, but she stayed stuck fast.

Above the drumming of the rain came the sergeant's responding hail. He brought his launch up as near as he dared. The machine gun stuttered again as Nash emptied the second clip into the trees. The crew were jabbering excitedly still, but no more arrows fell. "Shut up you bleeders, they've cleared off! *Yu Francis, huri bringim rop.*" From under the forepeak they dragged a cable and ran aft with it along the streaming deck. The head boy coiled a length and balancing on the sternpost, flung it across the gap. A shout signalled it had been made fast.

The funnel belched smoke as both launches went astern, the rope straining. Still the mud maintained its grip. "We'll have to rock her off," Nash shouted to his passengers. Soaked to the skin, Munro and the others slithered back and forth across the stern to break the suction. The boat juddered, then they were sliding backwards through the water.

Slater picked up one of the arrows. It was light, tipped with bone. "Son of a bitch, I thought you said the bastards didn't attack whites," he said to Nash.

It sure was a mean mother of a river.

The rain had stopped and the air was hot and steamy. Nash left the main channel for a creek running deep into the swamp forest. Immense trees closed in, a dim greenish light filtering through the leafy veil. Long, moss-covered creepers hung down trailing into the water and huge cobwebs shimmered among the lower branches. The ponderous throbbing of the launch engines and the ripples of their wash served only to intensify the stillness.

Munro stood beside Nash at the wheel. "It's too bloody quiet," the Australian muttered. "We must be close to the village and we ain't seen a canoe or nothin'."

"How big's this village?"

"Thirty, forty families – 'bout as much as the land'll support. They live on fish and yams mainly, plus whatever they can get by raiding."

Slater joined them. "What's gotten into your boys?" he jerked his head aft to where the native crew were huddled together, peering into the gloom and whispering.

Nash glanced at them. "They get spooked easy," he said but his jauntiness was strained.

They pressed on slowly at half-speed, their bows nosing through the shadow-dappled water. Rounding one of the interminable bends, patches of cleared land appeared on the right hand bank. Latouche saw the village first. "Voilà!" he pointed ahead to where the creek divided on either side of a small island.

The launches glided in to a mud and shingle beach. Cutting the engine, Nash gave an order to let go the anchors. They stared uneasily at the settlement. It seemed lifeless. Nipa huts lined the shore built out on bamboo stilts, their dark doorways leering emptily. A low hill inland was crowned with what might be a meeting house. Abruptly Nash sounded the hooter. The harsh blares rang across the water and somewhere a startled bird screamed. Nothing stirred in the village.

"Where the heck is everybody?"

Nash shook his head, "No smoke, the cooking fires are out. No pigs or chickens around. They must've scarpered."

"Why? A raid by another tribe?"

"We'll soon find out." Nash reached for his gun and flung a leg over the side. "*Francis, Johnny, kom, yu-mi go luk-luk,*" he ordered. Slater and Munro grabbed a couple of *parangs* to follow. Jordan splashed into the knee-deep water after them.

Hefting the heavy bush knives they waded ashore and followed Nash up a causeway of spongy logs, slimy and treacherous with age, into the village. Piles of fish-heads and other refuse lay rotting in the sun. A communal firepit had been dug in the middle of a cleared area. Its ashes were cold. Round about stood a dozen or so rickety sago palm huts with broad-leaved roofs. Bleached crocodile skulls were pegged above the entrances. Nash pointed to the nearest, "*Lukim insait haus.*"

"*Yes, boss,*" Cocking their rifles nervously, the two blacks scaled the ladder and poked gingerly inside. "*Pipal ol go, no stap klos-tu!*"

It was the same in the others.

"The buggers have cleared out, taken their marys an' livestock with 'em," Nash said puzzled as they picked their way through the eerie quiet of the deserted village, half expecting an arrow in the back. "Why? Ain't been any fighting I can see. An' if there were a raiding party around they'd be safer on the bleedin' island."

A rough trail led out towards the jungle side of the island. "We'll check this for a way," Nash said. "Could be they've taken to the bush. Happens sometimes if they get scared."

The path was single file hemmed in by shoulder high *kunai* grass, its sword-edged blades tearing at their clothes as they passed. The sun was blazing down again, insects swarmed about them in the sticky heat. Slater wiped the sweat from his eyes and slashed irritably at the grass with his *parang*, "Shit, we're here to find the crash not look for goddam villagers."

There was a cry from up front. Nash and Johnny halted in shock, the others stumbling into them. In the centre of the track a swarming black cloud of flies buzzed greedily about a bamboo stake. Maggot-filled eye sockets stared sightlessly at them. *Jesus Christ!* Munro choked on the sickly-sweet smell of putrefaction. There was a retching sound from Jordan.

Borrowing a *parang* Nash advanced, waving off insects. Johnny and Francis whimpered uneasily. Partially rotted, the head was a ghastly spectacle. All the features were gone, eaten away, only the frizzy hair remained.

"It's a black," Nash coughed, reeling away. "Poor bleeder, but at least it ain't one of your fellers."

In minutes both launches were underway and moving out into midstream.

Georgiana passed Jordan a water-bottle. The priest drank deeply. "I . . . I'm sorry," he quavered, wiping his mouth.

Nash spun the wheel to avoid a mudbank. They were out beyond the island now, moving into an area of grass swamps. Munro lit cigarettes for them both. "Jesus," he breathed. "Is that a regular *Kukukuku* trick?"

The Coastwatcher scratched his leathery neck where an insect had stung him. "I ain't exactly sure," he said uncertainly. "Cannibals usually take the heads. They reckon by eating an enemy's brains they gain his strength."

Munro winced. He remembered the box on the chart table back in Hongkong. Terror-tactics again? But who was this directed at?

Were the Japanese behind both?

He glanced over his shoulder. Slater was out of earshot in the stern. "The Frenchman, Latouche," he muttered.

"What about him?"

"Last night he was flown up river. Our Chief Engineer spoke with the pilot."

Nash spat out a fleck of tobacco, "The Major fixed that one hisself with the Airways people. Weren't nothin' to do with me."

"They flew here, to the village?"

"No. Further back, where the creek joins the main river. Leastways that's what I heard. Some story about sampling the water coming down."

Turning casually, Munro studied the doctor talking with Jordan and Georgiana. What was his part in all this? The guy was so damn likeable it was hard to link him with anything sinister. And what the hell could be wrong with the water?

The land had flattened out into a dismal swamp stretching as far as the eye could see, a suppurating sore in the midst of the vast green hell. Winding among the maze of grass islets and choking reed beds the river split into a network of slimy waterways making it hard to discern a main channel. Stirred up by their passage biting swarms of mosquitoes seethed about them, hungry for exposed flesh.

Groups of crocs lurked on mudbanks, fat-bellied and hideous. At the launches' approach they slithered into the water only to disappear sinisterly. Nash put Johnny on the wheel and took station on top of the deckhouse, scanning the way ahead through binoculars. The water was shallow and turbid. Each time the sounding pole came out gaseous bubbles oozed slowly up from the liquescent mud. A stench of rottenness and decay hung over everything.

There was a roaring noise. The spotter plane was with them again, flying low so they could see the pilot. It headed out eastwards, circled, and flew back waggling its wings. "*Got her!*" Nash yelled, waving his arms. Jumping down heavily from the deckhouse, he grabbed the wheel from Johnny. "You can see the tail, over by those kanaris."

The engine vibrated as he opened up the throttle. Everyone was on their feet, gazing eagerly in the direction he pointed. Slater snatched the field glasses. Shading his eyes, Munro could distinguish the unmistakable silhouette of a B–17 tail assembly protruding from behind a thicket of tall trees.

MacArthur's bomber.

*   *   *

HONGKONG. The RAF had moored a barrage balloon adjacent to Shamshuipo police station on Kowloon. From his office window Inspector Playfair regarded the cumbersome blimp absently as it strained on its guy ropes in the breeze. Sir Ambrose Hope's signal of the previous night had reached his desk with the eleven am. tea round.

Currie. Dr. Ronald. He checked the name in the case file and

274

drummed his fingers on the desk. That photograph again. Had Munro turned it in?

He rang a bell and Lieutenant Harris appeared. "Job for you," Playfair told him gruffly, passing over the signal. "Get down to the Mission House and see what you can dig up. If that's no good try the Central Library and the American Consulate. There must be records of the chap somewhere."

"Yes sir," the boy hesitated. "Am I looking for anything special, sir?"

'Use your common sense, blast you. Who was he? Where did he work? Reverend Jordan said the fellow died of fever, see if there's confirmation of that. Now cut along."

Flushing, the lieutenant hurried off.

Currie – Oliver – the Black Dragon. What was the connection? Irritably, Playfair swung his chair to consult a wall chart. If the Japs intended action against the Clipper before it reached Pearl Harbour he had three days to find out.

Three days at most.

XXI

LAE. Thirty miles downstream in the galley of the Clipper, Tad Gotto took the chrysanthemum button from his breast pocket and studied it.

"*Gotto Tadeo, what is the supreme virtue in life?*"

"*The supreme virtue is Chu – duty to our benevolent Emperor.*"

"*Good. And the second virtue?*"

"*The second virtue is Ko – duty to our parents and ancestors.*"

"*And the third?*"

"*Nimmu is the third virtue – duty to our work.*"

He had only to shut his eyes and he was twelve years old again, back in the Shinto temple in Honolulu after school, sitting painfully on his ankles before the master's black kimono learning to be a good Japanese.

"*But I'm not Japanese, I'm an American. My father is American. An officer in the Navy. He provides for me and my mother. My duty is to him!*"

"*I-ye, shameful!*" the master's rod would crack across his shoulders. "*Gotto Tadeo, how dare you harbour disrespectful thoughts? You have a Japanese name, you are Japanese!*" And crack, crack, crack the rod would go again.

Tad bit his lip at the memory.

He checked the passage. Mr. O'Byrne must still be busy on the *Southern Cross* with the yacht's purser. Slipping the button back in his pocket, he nipped upstairs to the flight deck. Sally Scott and Shapiro were chatting in the cockpit, neither noticed him pass through.

In the crew quarters there were lockers for each of them. His was third along on the lower level. The button would be safe here till he could show it to the authorities back home in Hawaii.

If he showed it to them.

He must, he must.

Yes, but would they trust him – *a nisei*?

He opened the locker. Inside were a couple of magazines he was reading – and something else. Tad stared bewildered. Lying on top

276

was a bundle of letters. *Airmail letters.*

With a shaking hand he took them out. All had Manila stamps and were slit neatly open along the top.

Who had put them there?"

"What's that you got?"

The voice behind made him whirl. In the doorway was the Second Officer.

"No kidding, Scottie. You learnt to fly on skis?"

"You bet. It was February in Milwaukee, my first solo in an Avian Moth and snowing so thick I couldn't see a darn thing through the goggles."

"I lost track of the field my first time, had to land in a corn pasture."

Scott laughed. She was sitting in Ross's seat, her hands playing with the control yoke. The cockpit windows were open. Outside, rolls of rain cloud were sliding down towards the coast from the jungle clad hills. The atmosphere was hot and heavy. "Tony, how about running through the instruments again?"

"Boy, you're serious about this, aren't you?" Shapiro shifted the gum around his mouth and winked. "The Skipper'll do his nut if he catches us." He leaned across her in his rolled up shirt sleeves, "Driving this baby is a heap easier than you'd think. No need to worry about engine temperatures, fuel mixtures and that kind of stuff, the Chief handles it behind. Which leaves us free to concentrate."

"Okay, so let's imagine we're starting up. I'm First Pilot, I unlock the controls, open cowl flaps left and right and select low pitch."

"Set throttle to 600 rpm and notify Engineer to start engines."

"Secure all hatches. Ignition on."

"Check. Ignition on," Shapiro stretched up to tap the master switch on the overhead panel.

"Throttles 1000. Start and boost!"

"And away she goes!"

There was an interruption behind. The door from the main hold flew open and Thyssen burst through, dragging Tad Gotto.

"Look what this thieving Jap had hidden in his locker!" he brandished the letters. "I caught him red-handed."

Scott and Shapiro came down from the cockpit. "Here, see for yourself," Thyssen tossed them onto the chart table dramatically. Gotto stood looking dazed and lost like a small boy.

Shapiro flipped through the envelopes, "It's the missing mail alright." He glanced worriedly at the steward, "I guess we have to tell the Skipper."

"Hold it a second," Scott cut in, "I want to hear what Tad's got to say."

"Gee, Miss Scott, you gotta believe me, I dunno nothing 'bout this. I went to my locker jus' now and the letters was inside. Somebody put 'em there."

"Sure, somebody put them there," Thyssen's pale lips curled in a sneer. "You last night, when you stole them."

"It ain't true! Miss Scott, tell 'em it ain't true! You know I'm no thief." His brown eyes turned on her, pleading.

"Steady, Tad, of course I believe you. For Godsakes," she rounded angrily on Thyssen, "Why the heck would anyone want to steal a bunch of letters?"

"He's a yellow-bellied Jap and he's working for them, that's why."

"That ain't true. I'm American born same as you!"

Thyssen snorted contemptuously, "Try telling that to the cops, slant-eyes."

"Cut it out, Kurt! You haven't a damn bit of proof."

"Cool it, both of you. This isn't getting us anywhere," Shapiro put a hand on Scott's arm. "Let the Skipper sort it out, huh?"

One of the wing hatches clicked open and the massive figure of the Chief stepped into the cabin in his overalls. He surveyed them weightily, "Sort what out?"

"Chief, I'm glad you're here," Thyssen got in quickly, "just look what's turned up in this man's locker."

"Don't listen to him, Chief, he's fingering Tad for a Jap spy."

The Chief heard them out a minute, frowning. Then he jerked his head in the direction of the hold, "Let's go take a look at the lockers."

In the crew quarters Tad's possessions were strewn over one of the bunks. "You did this?" the Chief asked Kurt.

"Yeah, that's right. I wanted to see what else he'd got hidden."

"Anyone could have stashed the letters," Scott interjected. "It's no reason to pick on Tad."

The Chief nodded, he squeezed the youth's shoulder reassuringly. Casually, he stirred the gear on the bunk with a finger; a biking magazine and two comic books, a pack of jelly beans, a comb. "How'd the letters get here, son?"

Tad shook his head. "I dunno, sir. It ain't nothin' to do with me, honest."

"Okay folks, party's over. I'll speak to Ross," the Chief rumbled. "You can put your stuff back, Tad."

"I'm Second Officer, it should be me makes the report," Thyssen protested, stiffening.

The Chief fixed him with an eye, "I said *I'll* tell Ross."

"I saw a submarine this morning."

Ricky stood under a breadfruit tree on the edge of the market and scuffed dirt with his shoe. The Prince said nothing, he was examining a piece of native carving.

"A submarine," Ricky repeated, "it was winking its lights."

The excursion had been announced after breakfast on the yacht. A trip ashore to visit the settlement. About half the passengers had signed up including Ricky and his mother. They had seen the Commissioner's bungalow, the botanical garden and the sports grounds. Now, trailed by a mob of inquisitive piccaninnies, they were strolling in the busy market, bargaining for curios and snapping photographs.

The prince put down the carving and wiped away a bead of sweat. The day was hot and thunderous with intermittent bursts of rain. "So, you saw a submarine?" he said deliberately, taking hold of the boy's hand. "Come, let us go for a walk and you can tell me."

A few crowded stalls away, Maria Bianchi watched Ruth Simms fixing a ribbon on her younger daughter's sun-hat and felt a surge of envy. How uncomplicated the woman's life must be. She loved her husband, she loved her children, she was going home. Simple. That was how Maria intended to make her own life.

But first there was the matter of the Russian.

Natives plucked at the tourists' clothes clamouring for their attention. Eddie Wirth had paid a dollar for a pink shell necklace. A woman waved a garishly painted mask in Eliot Simms' face. "Spooky, huh? How'd you fancy wearing one of these for Hallowe'en?"

Maria glanced at the haunting image and shuddered, "Horrible. In Shanghai the Chinese made masks for the New Year, but they were beautiful."

"Each to his own taste, I guess. Me, I like these primitive crafts. Say, how much d'you want, lady?" he asked a wizened grandmother with empty breasts and teeth reddened by betel nut.

Leaving them to haggle, Maria moved on, picking her way round patches of mud. The market was bustling and colourful, baskets of sweet potatoes, tobacco leaves, squealing pigs strapped to poles, carved canoe paddles and displays of superb bird feathers. Vendors squatted on the ground shouting at buyers in pidgin, some old, some young, their skins ranging from pale coffee to deep blue-black, tattooed and scarred in intricate tribal patterns. Eyes met hers boldly, a dignified people despite their nakedness.

The sun shafted through a break in the clouds, glaringly hot. Maria put up her parasol and waved the flies away. A frown creased her forehead. The Russian. This morning he had repeated his ultimatum. Everything she had striven for, the whole new life she had planned and constructed for herself and Ricky was at risk because of this one man.

The Madame of the Red Lips Club. No! She had put that behind her. Forever.

Where was Ricky?

The two Simms girls were by their mother watching a boy split jelly-nuts with his *parang*. Ricky had been with them. Where was he now? In a sudden access of alarm she stared around the sea of brown bodies.

"Maria, what is it? What's wrong?"

"Ricky! Have you see him?"

"No, I thought he was with you . . ."

Not stopping to listen, Maria started back the way they had come. "*Mem, Mem,*" eager hands grabbed at her as she pushed through the crowd, "*Mem, Mem, you buyim kau-kau here!*" She shook them off, pleading vainly, "My little boy, have you seen my little boy?" Faces gaped uncomprehending.

A figure loomed up suddenly in her path. A linen suit and silver-topped cane. "My dear Madam, what is the trouble?" the voice steadied her.

"Oh Sir Ambrose, please help me. Ricky's lost!"

"Lost? Nonsense, m'dear. I saw the lad by the road a moment ago. We'll soon find him." Taking her arm, he steered her through the crowd, "He was with that Russian fellow, Cherkassy."

"Prince Cherkassy!" Undisguised horror sounded in Maria's voice. Breaking free, she ran out from the market. A jeep shot past in a cloud of dust. Choking, she scanned the shore. Down by the water a man was leading a small child by the hand.

"Ricky!" Maria screamed. "*Ricky!*"

The boy heard her and waved. He said something to his companion, who turned to look. They began walking slowly back. The Prince was smiling.

Maria clenched her teeth, murder in her heart.

Yu-Ling leaned on the *Southern Cross*'s deserted port rail and gazed longingly at the green mountains. She wished she could have gone ashore too but Minister Soong had forbidden it flatly. "Leave the ship? *Ai-yah*, what for? There is nothing to see only blackface savages and *quai loh*. Much better that you stay here and look after me. My poor head aches, I could not sleep a wink last night for worry, perhaps a massage would help, *heya*?" Feigning excuses Yu-Ling had fled on deck. *Oh ko*, if old uncle should die who will protect me from such people?

With a faint toot a small steam engine came fussing down past the rows of neat white bungalows, pulling a line of wagons. Yu-Ling watched it clank onto the jetty where a crane was unloading into lighters. Funny little town. She wandered round the deck to starboard only to see Hollington Soong coming up the companionway from below with Bodyguard Feng. Hastily she ducked behind a ventilator. They passed by heading towards the radio office, the Minister talking volubly. "We must get word to Chungking, further delay here may be fatal!" he sounded very concerned.

Yu-Ling put the matter out of her mind. Finding a quiet spot in the stern she settled down in a deck-chair with her English Grammar.

Bob Cashin had dropped out of the tour ashore early on. Hell, this place was the pits and he had better things to do, like trying for a snoop at the Clipper's cargo holds. Maybe find out if the Chinese really did have treasure aboard. His shirt sticking damply to his back, he walked up the jetty past the yacht to where the flying boat was moored. A native constable stopped him at the gangway.

"Pass, suh."

"That's okay, buddy, I'm a passenger."

"Sorry, suh. Orders, pass only."

Cashin gave up. It was too hot to argue. He made for the yacht and a cool drink.

Melanesian crewmen in white shorts were polishing the brasswork on deck. In the saloon César de Santa Cruz sat alone at the bar looking moody.

Cashin took a stool and wiped his face with a handkerchief. "Man, it's hotter than hell out there," he told the barman. "Gimme the coldest San Mig you got and one for my friend here."

César tapped a cigarette on a slim gold case. It was engraved with a map of the Philippines, the principal towns marked by rubies. His handsome features were morose and sulky. The barman set two long glasses of iced beer before them and Cashin drank thirstily. "Hear your fiancée went upriver with Major Slater's party," he remarked.

César assented with a barely civil grunt.

"Latouche and the Reverend too, as well as Max Munro. Odd party for a rescue mission, kinda makes you wonder what they expect to find."

César stiffened, his mouth hard, "I regret I cannot help you, Georgiana did not confide in me."

The radio behind the bar was playing soft music from Honolulu. Cashin took another drink of his beer. "That was one lucky escape she had last night."

"Lucky, *si*."

Cashin observed his reaction shrewdly. "Any idea how she came to fall?" he said probing further.

"From playing the fool, what else? You saw her dancing and drinking," César's eyes smouldered resentfully. "Like a *gringo* whore!"

"I guess everybody was kinda merry last night," Cashin agreed. "She led us all round the ship in a Conga, I remember that much."

"She said she was going to take a swim to cool off. I told her not to be crazy, that the harbour was full of sharks." César shrugged, "She would not listen."

"And where were you when she fell?"

The Spaniard glared at him suspiciously. "Me? Here, in the saloon," he answered curtly. "*Por qué?*"

Below deck Scott checked her watch, a good half hour till the shore party was due back. Taking a towel and her washbag from the cabin, she slipped along to the ladies' bathroom. Gee, poor Tad, she thought stepping into the shower, that scene on the Clipper had really shaken him up. It was no joke being a nisei just now.

She turned on the taps.

The door of the men's room clicked as Kurt Thyssen let himself in and fastened the catch. He took off his shoes and moved the stool quietly into position beneath the ventilator. Craning his neck, he peered through the grill.

A white towel lay on the mat. He could see Sally's ankles and the shadow of her body behind the plastic curtain. Suds were running down her firm calves. She must have soaped and be rinsing off. Kurt leered, wetting his lips, watching her outline move under the stream of water. Shit, some figure!

The noise of the water ceased, she'd shut off the taps. The curtain jerked. Was she getting out? A hand emerged and fumbled for her washbag on the floor. There was a chink in the curtain now allowing him a tantalising glimpse of pink-tinged flank as she stretched up. Boy, was this giving him a hard-on! She'd die if she knew he'd seen. Serve the frigid bitch right.

Scott took a last rinse under the cold tap, gasping with pleasure as her skin tightened. She shook the water from her curls and ran a comb through. Swell to be fresh again after the sticky heat.

She pulled back the curtain . . .

"*Hey, how much longer you gonna be in there?*"

Kurt jumped down from the stool sweating as the doorknob rattled again. He splashed some water hurriedly on his face and unlocked the door. The Chief barged in scowling.

"Shift your ass, Kurt, since when you had a monopoly on the can?"

"Hell, can't a guy wash in peace? What's eating you anyway?"

"I'll tell you, I've just seen Kelly – they've lost radio contact with Max's launch!"

"Gawd save us!" Nash whistled.

Munro stared through the binoculars. Her back broken, the bomber lay marooned in the swamp like the corpse of some giant prehistoric beast. The pilot must have brought her in as low as he dared, holding her up till the very last moment of the stall. The impact of the crash and the careering slide through the reed beds had torn away the port engines and the crippled fuselage had come to rest canted over at an angle, starboard wing submerged in the mud. Atop the hull the plexiglass dome of the upper turret stood empty. No movement, no sign of survivors, nothing.

They had anchored off a patch of swamp forest within hailing distance of the wreck. On Slater's orders a bucket had been put over the side and the contents taken to the deckhouse. Latouche was in there. After an interval of ten minutes he reappeared, "*D'accord*, it is safe to proceed."

Safe from what? Munro wondered. Useless to ask.

The water round the plane was thick with weed. Nash had a dinghy lowered. He and Munro took the oars, Slater and the doctor sat in the stern.

"Main entrance hatch is behind the starboard wing."

"Right you are, sport, we'll take her round."

There was a swirl in the water as they passed under the rearing tail and the boat rocked. Stirred by something large, a cloud of mud rose to the surface. "Croc," Nash grinned. "A whoppa."

283

The damage looked less severe this side. Some crumpling to the nose and bright gashes scraped in the hull. Beneath the cockpit window was a painted nude and the name *Fast Lady*. To the right of the stabilizer the main hatch gaped open. "*Easy*," Nash brought the boat alongside and stood up.

Slater caught him back, "Hold it, buster, the Doc and I go first, you two stay put." Gripping the sill he climbed up, helping Latouche after him. They disappeared inside leaving Munro and Nash to wait in the insect-laden heat. The reed beds were quiet. High overhead a pair of vultures rode the thermals watchfully. "Bleedin' buzzards," the Australian spat into the water.

After a moment Slater emerged, "Pilot, get in here."

The interior of the bomber stank of mud. A yellow life preserver bobbed on the floor in a foot of water. Stooping, Munro made his way forwards along a narrow catwalk past the waist gunners' positions. It was a while since he had been in a military aircraft, he had forgotten how spartan they were. No fittings, just the bare frames and stringers. Where the belly turret had been was a gaping hole. It must have been torn off in the landing. He stepped carefully over to join the other two in the radio room. Space to stand upright here and the overhead hatch was open.

Lashed against a bulkhead lay the teakwood coffin. There was no sign of the padlocked boxes.

"The cargo's gone, Pilot. So's the crew," Slater told him tersely. "Only the bastard bishop's left. You're a goddam flier, what do you make of it?"

Broken glass crunched underfoot as Munro squeezed down through the cockpit into the crushed nose. The bombardier's window was shattered and the front three feet of the fuselage telescoped. Over everything clung a coating of silver, glistening like hoar-frost in the sun. He drew a finger through it. Aluminium dust from the drift bombs. They would have been stored by the navigator's position.

No one had been down here since she struck, that was certain.

He clambered up to the cockpit again to check around. Both pilots' parachutes missing, survival kits too. And no sign of the inflatable dinghy these birds carried in the stern. It didn't take a genius to figure the answer. One point puzzled him though, someone had removed the firing pins from all the .50 calibre machine guns. Why?

A sound behind jerked him round. A figure stood in the hatchway, slender, face shadowed in the dim light. Georgiana. "Dammit, how'd you get here?"

"The sergeant rowed me over with Jordan. Everyone else is searching ashore."

"So you just thought you'd take a look around, huh?" Munro said cynically, dusting the glass off his hands, "Where do you fit into all this, Dixie? What did you mean back there when you said someone pushed you last night?"

Her slim shoulders shrugged beneath the blouse. "I saw you on the jetty and leaned out to call down. I'm not so dumb as to go swimming alone – or to dive off the dock side of a ship. There was a sudden shove at my back and that's all till I came to with you pumping me out."

"Who else was on deck at the time?"

She gestured impatiently, "You think I haven't been trying to remember? Anyone could've stepped out from one of the saloons."

Through an open side window Munro watched a chain of bubbles rise to the surface beneath the port wing. Another lurking croc? And still no word of the crew. He pushed the thought away and concentrated. "Why should someone want to kill you?"

"I'm not sure, Max," she caught her lip between her teeth, "but someone does . . ."

Traversing the gloomy bomb bay with its empty racks, they returned to the radio room. Jordan was fussing over the coffin, rubbing dirt off the polished wood. Munro flicked the switches on the big transmitter. The needles trembled a fraction then fell back. The barest dribble of power left on the batteries now.

Georgiana toyed with the earphones. All at once she stiffened, "Max, what's this?" She held up a scratch pad, the kind every operator kept handy for jotting messages. Munro's heart skipped a beat. On it was a pencilled scrawl. Ideograms. Japanese characters.

That transmission last night. The signal none of them could read . . .

"HEY, GENTS!" There was a hail outside. The sergeant had returned in the dinghy.

Tearing the sheet from the pad, Munro stuck it in his pocket. "C'mon, we'd better show this to Slater."

Hustling Jordan with them they sloshed back along the cramped circular tunnel to the hatch. Down in the boat the sergeant's face was glum. "We've found yer mates, sir. Poor bloody bleeders!"

"Man that is born of a woman hath but a short time to live, and is full of

misery. He cometh up, and is cut down, like a flower; he fleeth as it were a shadow . . ."

Slater took the lighted branch from Nash and thrust it in beneath the bodies. The fuel-drenched pyre caught with a rush, the crackling of the wood drowning out Jordan's monotone. A vulture flapped heavily away as oily smoke obscured the trees.

Munro and Georgiana held handkerchiefs to their faces. The stench had been bad enough back at the village, here in the bush it was overpowering. They had found two corpses swollen and stinking in the sun and pieces of another.

Slater turned away. In his hand were three dog-tags, all they had managed to collect. His mouth twisted, "Bastard savages, I'd wipe the sons of bitches out! These were kids, Munro, I briefed them myself in Manila, their commander was just twenty-four years old."

"What makes you so certain it was natives?" Munro thrust the sheet of Japanese characters at him, "We picked up this by the radio."

Slater's face paled under the peaked cap, "Yellow-bellies? *Out here?*"

"Either that or the Air Corps' running language courses."

Scavenging crabs scuttled for their burrows as they tracked back past stands of tall bamboo. A rough path slashed through the bush brought them to the clearing. A giant kanari, its trunk swollen with a spongy covering of rain-soaked moss, leaned at an impossible angle supported by a cradle of vines. Draped from its branches, shroud-like, was a parachute. Gear from the plane littered the area. Field packs, emergency rations, items of clothing. By the ashes of a smudge fire ants seethed over an open corned beef can.

"*Francis, Johnny, huri-up bringim out disfela!*" Nash yelled from the entrance of a makeshift shelter. Munro could see the sinister shapes of the grey steel footlockers from Hongkong. Latouche was bent over them, wearing gloves, his black bag open. At his direction they began dragging out the first.

Other boys spread the parachute over the rocks, piling things into it. Little heaps of belongings, a pair of socks, the wrapper of a Hershey bar, pathetic reminders of the young men who had died here. Georgiana's mouth trembled. "God what a waste," she muttered.

Slater stuck the chewed stub of a cigar between his teeth and lit it. "Godammit, Pilot," he growled, "it don't make sense though. If the Japs murdered our guys why the hell didn't they take the cargo?"

Munro's grip tightened on the handle of his *parang*, "Maybe they're coming back for it. *Maybe they're still in the area.*"

Forty feet overhead among the foliage, a yellow hunting wasp hovered an instant, attracted by beads of perspiration starting from a strip of unprotected skin. Steadying, it folded its wings and settled, antennae quivering eagerly, vicious sting protruding like a needle.

Motionless upon the bough, the Japanese regarded the glistening insect as it crawled across his wrist, willing himself not to flinch. It was almost as long as his thumb. He blew carefully. The wasp trembled irritably and arched its abdomen. Forcing himself to relax he blew again, directing the stream of air at its legs. The wasp resisted for a moment, then abruptly shot away.

He switched his attention back to the camp. The priest was still muttering over the bodies. *Karma*. The *Amerikans* were dead, their souls in the dark valley waiting to be reborn. If barbarians had souls. Below he could hear the red-headed whore talking with the flier who had fought him in Manila. *Hai*, he had a debt to settle there.

Shifting the angle of his vision, he scanned the swamp. Clumps of forest floated in the heat-haze like islands in a green sea. In the distance, lowering over the plain, mountain ridges dark with suffocating jungle. His heart ached for the pure slopes of *Fuji-san* in the Land of the Gods. Curse this vile country so far from home. Where were his own people? Since sunrise he had been watching for them.

Now the *gaijin* were here.

He must act alone.

Stealthily he inched along the branch to the main trunk. Strapped to his hands were articulated steel claws, light and razor-sharp, that dug into the bark to give him the freedom of a cat. Unseen, unheard, he dropped to the ground among the ferns.

The green fastness screened him like night. Paralleling the path, he pushed through the luxuriant growth, using the *ko ashi* technique to minimise the sounds of his passage. Lifting the knee high, pointing the toe down to penetrate the leaves at each step, like a crane picking its way in the marshes. A blessing on his masters for the long years of training.

Near the shore he sensed men approaching and sank back invisible among the vegetation. Two of the blackface savages were returning to the camp. One carried a coil of rope. He passed so close the Japanese could have reached out and strangled him. The acrid smell of their bodies lingered in his nostrils.

Water lapped in the bamboo. Parting the stems he peered out. The bomber's wreck was hidden by a bend in the channel. The *gaijin* had brought their boats into the shallows for loading and moored them to the buttress roots of a huge fig. He counted two more savages in the bow of the nearest. The other seemed deserted.

A pale green lizard clung to a leaf, regarding him with lidless eyes. Tail lashing it scuttled for cover as he flitted for the tree.

Shadow-still he stood pressed against the trunk. No alarm from the boats, but time was against him. The assault must be swift and deadly. With a light spring he began to climb, steel spikes gripping the smooth bark. Effortlessly he swarmed into the branches towards the point he had marked, a thick bough projecting out over the water. The woolly pates of the two blacks were directly below him. Balancing, he removed the left hand claw and from the pouch at his waist selected a tiny needle-pointed dart.

Banzai!

With a grunt of pain the first black lurched from the side, blood streaking his neck where the throwing knife had embedded in the flesh. His companion whirled in terror, clutching his *parang*. An instant later he was a corpse, his spine shattered in two places as the Japanese plummeted down upon him from the forest canopy.

The injured black had fallen to the deck, limbs threshing convulsively as the poison raged in his veins. Stooping swiftly, the Japanese snapped the man's neck with a dry crack and jerked his weapon free. Quickly he heaved both bodies over the side.

He snatched up the *parang* and streaked for the deckhouse. Hacking gashes in the spare fuel cans he tipped them into the bilges. A half minute's frenzied work left the engine a tangled mess of cut leads and severed pipework bleeding diesel.

A rapid check of the shore from the portholes. Still clear but he could feel the *gaijin* close now. He ran to the stern and jumped across onto the other boat. In the deckhouse here he found a radio. He had guessed they would have one. A blow from the *parang* finished it instantly. He turned his attention to the engine.

By the Amida Buddha! The crash of the shot, deafening as a cannon in the low cabin, boomed in his ears and a white-hot blast seared his shoulder as he flung himself aside. It was *haragei* that saved him. The sixth sense warning of attack that triggered his reactions a microsecond from death.

Framed in the doorway of the deckhouse the sergeant worked the rifle bolt frantically to eject the spent cartridge for a second shot. In a killing fury the Japanese lunged at him, right arm rigid as a spear. The steel claw on his hand slammed into the man's abdomen beneath the sternum, ripping upwards through the spongy tissue of the lungs.

Crimson blood sprayed the deck and the man was hurled back, flesh hanging in tatters, organs spilling from the gaping wound.

Tenchu! Punishment of Heaven! The Japanese sprang past the corpse. The injury to his shoulder was trivial. He banished it from his mind. The boats were disabled. Only one task left.

Splashing ashore, he raced crouching through the bush to where he had concealed the life raft.

XXII

Nash pounded down the track, unslinging the Sten gun as he ran. Throwing himself down in the reeds, he worked through on his belly to the water's edge. *Jesus wept*! Between him and the launches, bobbing face down in the weed, was one of the boys he had left on board.

Johnny wormed up behind him with a rifle. "Cover me," Nash ordered harshly. Jumping to his feet, he sprinted through the shallows to the nearest launch. There was blood on the deck and a *parang* lying in the scuppers. The deckhouse was a shambles. He swore viciously.

On the second boat he found his sergeant's body. Flies were buzzing over the spilled entrails. Christ Almighty, bastards! He felt his stomach heave and lurched to the rail. Bastards, bastards!

There was a hail from the shore. The square-jawed flier Munro was wading out. "What gives?" he vaulted easily aboard. Then he saw the gutted body and stopped, "Oh shit!"

"Bastards," Nash repeated again thickly. "He had a wife an' kids back in Brisbane. What the bloody hell am I gonna tell them?" There was no response from the tall American. He had picked up the sergeant's rifle. Nash nodded. He looked like he could handle a gun.

"See anyone?"

"No, but it ain't natives, that's a cert. They went for the engines, cut the fuel lines. Both boats. Which means unless we can bodge a repair somehow, we're stuck out here."

"*Esi!*"

Reverend Jordan clasped his camera strap nervously as Francis shipped oars and let the dinghy drift in towards the bomber. Squatting in the bows, Munro cocked his rifle scanning the derelict for any movement. All was still. "Okay, bring us alongside," he ordered quietly.

Slimy water slopped against the hull as they manoeuvred under the stern. There was an outside chance the radio batteries had enough juice left in them to send an SOS. It was about their only hope unless Nash succeeded in fixing an engine on one of the launches.

Get help or get out. They had to do one or the other. Fast. Otherwise . . .

"It's a right bleedin' pisser, Major. The Nips'll hold us till nightfall then move in."

"Nightfall be damned! They're just waiting for more of their buddies to arrive. How about that spotter plane? Any chance it'll come looking for us?"

A roll of thunder from the hills had answered Slater's question. The weather was closing in again.

"Cover me from the boat." Munro hauled himself up, noticing for the first time the dry rust-coloured stains on the sill. Men had died here too. Warily he stepped inside the fuselage.

Half a minute later he had seen all he needed to.

The radio cabin was a chaos of smashed dials and valves. Someone had taken an engineer's hammer to the main transmitter and the auxiliary. The generator was wrecked too. Only the coffin lay untouched amid the debris.

Were the killers still aboard?

Finger on the trigger, he picked his way forward through the bomb bay to the cockpit. There were smeared tracks on the floor that might have been anyone's but nothing had been disturbed and the glassed-in dorsal gun turret stood empty. The bomber had an eerie feel to it now that made his scalp prick.

The nose was clear too.

Breathing easier he started back. No sense hanging around. He was crossing the bomb bay catwalk again when he heard feet shuffling in the radio cabin.

The bay rear hatch was a narrow V-shaped aperture. He took it at a run, poised to squeeeze off a shot as he burst through. Inside the cabin a figure sprang away from the coffin in alarm.

"Christsakes, Reverend, I almost shot your ears off! Leave that thing. We're getting out of here before the Japs come back."

"No!" the priest clenched his fists. His face was flushed and sweating, sandy hair awry, chin jutting doggedly, "I can't, I won't abandon him, not . . . not after all that's happened," he cried thinly. And disregarding Munro he began single-handedly dragging the coffin aft towards the rear hatch.

Son of a bitch, Munro shook his head. You had to admire the guy's perseverance. He just never gave up. "Okay, Reverend," he sighed, "we'll do it your way. Only hurry, I'll lift the head, you take the feet."

Francis rolled his eyes in alarm as they hauled it to the hatch. With his help they lowered it into the stern of the dinghy and began pulling for the shore.

As they rounded the tail again something orange was bobbing in the reeds. The life raft.

Nash stuck an oil-streaked face out from behind the engine. "Alright, crank the bleeder," he grunted. Two of his boys flung their weight against the handle. The engine turned, coughed, spun a few times gathering speed, then died away. "Bugger!" Nash said. Everyone's spirits fell.

"Two thirty," Slater muttered chomping on his cigar, "three and a half hours till dusk. If the Yellow-bellies don't get here first." He scowled at the coffin next to the canvas-wrapped remains of their three dead, "That damn bishop, thought we'd gotten shot of him at least. Why the hell d'you have to bring him along?"

Munro didn't answer. It had begun to rain. Not in torrents as before, but a steady continuous downpour, swallowing up the swamps in a grey mist. They had piled everything aboard the second launch for relief of some kind from the elements and insects, and mounted guard to wait.

To wait for what?

Then it came to him. Part of the answer at least. "A stowaway, it had to be a stowaway."

"What are you jawing about?" Slater snapped.

"The Japs. They had a man aboard the bomber, must've sneaked him on before it took off from Clark base. Probably hidden in a wheel housing."

"Bullshit, that's impossible. Security round the ship was tighter than a fly's asshole."

"It wasn't tight *enough*, Major. Use your head, dammit, nothing else fits. Those were his transmissions we heard last night. No way could the Japs have located the crash that fast."

"One Jap didn't wipe out an entire bomber crew on his own, for Christsakes!"

"He could have done easy, if he caught them separated – like with the sergeant just now. And we only found three bodies, crocs maybe had the others or the swamps. But he's here alright and now he's gunning for us. You and your goddam security," Munro's voice was contemptuous. "Face facts, Major, Tokyo's had this mission of yours all sewn up from the start."

292

Slater's eyes glittered like ice in a frozen sea. "Is that so, pilot?" he grated. "Well the word is they got help on the inside – some dirty bastard selling out his country. Maybe it's *you*!"

Munro hit him.

Slater was ready for it. He sidestepped fast, blocking with his left arm and swinging in with a murderous right hook low to the belly. He was mean and tough and he knew all the tricks, but he hadn't counted on Munro's speed. There was a big hole open in his guard and Munro snapped through a straight left like a hammer.

Slater fell back against the deckhouse with a crash, blood trickling down his lip. He blinked dazedly for a moment as if in disbelief. "Son of a bitch, I'm gonna teach you a lesson, flyboy!" he scrambled to his feet again.

"*Stop it*!" Georgiana yelled pushing between them. "Stop it this instant, the pair of you! As if we hadn't enough to worry about without fighting one another."

"Outta my way, lady. I'm gonna break your boyfriend in two!"

"Knock it off, Major," she stormed, tossing her hair furiously. "You too, Max! God, men are stupid! If you're going to behave like kids go fight it out in the swamps!"

Breathing heavily the two backed off slowly. The native boys were watching open-mouthed. "We'll settle this later, Pilot," Slater spat a mouthful of blood over the side. "Without any skirts around for you to hide behind."

"Any time you like, Major," Munro told him.

From the deckhouse came Nash's voice again, "*Givim full wantaim moa*!"

"*Yes, boss*." The boys swung the engine. Miraculously this time the spluttering sound sustained and settled down to a steady rumbling rhythm. Nash emerged wiping oil off his hands. "Beaut, let's get outta this mud-pit."

At a snail's pace they chugged downstream through the rain. Francis stood in the bows probing the viscous mud with the sounding pole, rainwater sluicing down his back and shoulders. Without the other launch to tow them off they couldn't afford to go aground.

"How long for the return trip?" Munro joined Nash at the wheel.

"Current's with us now. Three hours, less mebbe. If the engine holds."

If the engine held. If the Japs did not come. If, if . . .

Minutes ticked past. The crash site was left behind. On the launch crept, still painfully slow. Nash was having trouble finding the main channel amid the network of waterways. At times progress came to a complete halt while he and Francis scanned the reeds through field glasses. Once too they thought they heard the drone of the spotter plane overhead but the cloud cover was total. Not until a break in the rain did they manage to locate the creek leading to the village.

"Phew, never thought I'd be so pissing glad to see this joint," Nash muttered as the nipa huts slid into view.

Munro had taken up the binoculars. "Still deserted."

"Yeah, they'll have left it for good. Bush'll swallow the place, in a couple of months you won't even know it was there."

The engine was labouring under the increased speed and starting to run ragged. "It's that bleedin' pump drive. I had to bodge the beggar with parts from the other boat. Take the wheel for a minute, sport," the Coastwatcher ducked below. There was some banging and swearing and the power picked up again. "Thanks," he reappeared.

"Just so long as it gets us home."

"We'll hit the main river in a bit. Should be plain sailing then."

The forest pressed in on them. Huge trees crowding the banks, the fronds of their branches meeting above the creek in a dim green tunnel. The native crew were congregated forward, talking in low monosyllables and watching the jungle nervously. Slater was astern under the canopy. Jordan had collapsed by the coffin exhausted.

Nash pushed back his hat and wiped sweat from his brow. He gave a sideways glance at the two steel footlockers hidden beneath a tarpaulin. "Whatever you people got in those bleeders, I hope to hell it's worth it!" he muttered angrily. "My sergeant's *dead*! He was a good bloke, a mate. So are two of my crew. All because some Yank bomber goes down in the swamps. And you're not even in the bleedin' war yet!"

"Take it easy, chum. There were six of our boys on that ship, remember."

A chain of islets loomed ahead. The Australian's shoulder muscles bunched as he swung the wheel over. "You was asking 'bout the Frenchie earlier. Well, I'll tell you something, it was me turned up those bodies in the bush. Only the ways he acts you'd think I'd found a bomb. Yelling at everyone to keep off, keep off while he checks."

"Checks what, for God's sake?"

"Search me, sport, because they sure weren't breathing. Major made the rest of us wait in the camp. Five minutes later the Frenchie comes out with his bag an' nods to him. '*Alright*,' he says, '*no danger*.' "

The tattoo on Nash's bicep flexed as he gripped the wheel spokes fiercely, "No danger, my bloody oath! What did they die from, Yank? *What's it all about, hey?*"

Then the engine gave out.

Powerless the launch drifted into the reeds under the lea of the nearest islet. Slater appeared at the deckhouse, "Now what? Can't you keep this rust-bucket moving, Aussie?"

Up in the bow Francis had looped a mooring rope round a stem of a giant overhanging banyan. "*Im bugarup tru, boss?*"

"*Nogat bugarup. Me fix olsem before!*" Nash yelled irately, pushing Slater out of the way. "*Yu, Johnny no stap klos-tu, go lukluk.*"

The two blacks climbed ashore and disappeared into the bush with their *parangs*. Still swearing to himself Nash dropped down into the engine well. "Give you a hand?" Munro offered, "I can use a wrench."

"Thanks, sport, it's most likely the bleedin' fuel pump again."

The engine well under the deckhouse was more cramped even than the Clipper's nacelles. Stripped to the waist the two sweated in a pool of spilt diesel to decouple the pump from the shaft. They were still at it when Francis reappeared in the hatchway.

"*Boss, bot kum.*"

"A boat? What kinda boat, for Gawd's sake?" Cursing fluently Nash squeezed from behind the engine block and went outside. Munro followed him. Georgiana was standing on the roof of the deckhouse gazing downstream. They were at the mouth of the creek where it joined the main river. Several more half-submerged islets, some no more than clumps of vegetation swirled by the current, lay between them and the opposite bank.

Everyone listened intently. Above the murmur of the river came the faint throb of engines.

"Must be a launch down on the main channel," Nash muttered. "Maybe someone sent a rescue party after us."

He didn't sound very convinced.

"I see it!" Georgiana called from the roof, pointing.

Grabbing the binoculars Nash scrambled up beside her. The others saw him stiffen suddenly, "Well, I'll be a jackaroo . . .!"

"What d'you see?" Slater snapped at him.

"*Japs!*"

"Jesus Christ!"

The growl of the approaching engine grew steadily louder. Scanning the river with the naked eye Munro made out a dark shape low in the water moving in towards the mouth of the creek.

"Inflatable assault boat," Slater muttered, "six man squad, light arms, marines or paratroops probably."

Johnny tapped his arm and pointed silently. Munro followed his gaze and his mouth tightened. A second assault craft had come into view following the first.

Nash jumped down to the deck. "We're sitting ducks out here!" he volleyed orders at the crew. Splashing over the side with ropes they began urgently hauling the launch deeper under the trees.

"Pilot, give a help with this cargo, damn you!" Slater rasped. Together with Latouche they manhandled the footlockers down into the deckhouse. "Doc, you stay here with me and keep your head down," Slater commanded drawing his pistol. "You too, Reverend." Jordan gaped at him. He was crouched by the coffin staring about wildly. "Godammit, let the Bishop alone, he ain't gonna come to any harm now!" Seizing him by the collar Slater hustled the priest through the hatch.

"*Get guns, run huri-up!*" Bare feet thumped on the deck, Nash's boys were taking up positions with their rifles. Munro pushed the coffin under one of the benches for cover and flung himself down behind the rail with the Lee Enfield. There was a clinking of cartridge cases as Nash ran crouching from man to man, distributing ammunition. "Here, take these, sport," he threw Munro a pouch.

A slim figure dropped down beside him. Georgiana had joined them. "What the heck d'you think you're doin', Miss?" Nash tried to thrust her away. "Get back in the deckhouse before your head's blown off!"

"I don't scare easy," she drawled. "I'll take my chances out here!"

There wasn't time to argue. The two boats had entered the creek, drawing closer at a steady ten knots, the men crouched aboard clearly visible with their weapons. A vicious looking machine gun projected from each bow. The lead helmsman was standing up in the stern searching for the best channel. "If the bleeder steers for the starboard bank we've had it," Nash hissed.

Munro threw a glance at Georgiana. She was prone on the deck legs splayed, peering over the side at the approaching boats. She tossed him a quick grin back. "Give 'em hell, Max."

He adjusted his sight till the bead centred on the helmsman's khaki chest. The range was less than two hundred yards. The Jap's face stared unseeing into his own, beardless, in his twenties. Odds of two to one and the Japanese had machine guns. He cranked down the elevation a fraction and took up the slack on the trigger.

The boat slowed to let the other draw alongside and guttural commands floated across the water. An NCO was indicating with his arm. There was a short pause, then a surge of foam under the sterns as both craft swung round together their bows pointed towards the islet.

Range one fifty. Breech bolts snicked along the launch's deck. "Steady, let 'em get closer," Nash ordered tersely.

From the deckhouse behind a sudden scream shattered the silence. Jordan's voice high-pitched with terror. It choked off abruptly. Too late! Aboard the assault boats there were sharp cries. The Japanese had seen the launch.

"*Fire!*" Nash yelled. Munro squeezed the trigger. BLAM! BLAM-BLAM! BLAM! All the guns went off together in a tearing volley. The recoil thumped against his cheek, there was a deafening rattle from the Sten gun and he saw the helmsman spin round throwing up his arms and fall into the water with a splash. He knocked the bolt up, jerked it back flipping out the empty shell, and slammed it forward again. Memories of the range at Annapolis. *Load and lock. Ten rounds rapid fire prone. Shoot!* Nash's weapon rattled again in his ear. Georgiana was crouching on his left, blocking her ears against the noise. He fired, worked the bolt, rammed in another bullet and fired again.

Load and lock! Load and lock! Burnt powder stung in his nostrils, his ears sang from the blasts. Impossible to miss at this range, every shot was telling. The boat was a shambles of dead and wounded men. He shifted target. The second craft was circling out of control, a figure slumped over the tiller.

RAT-A-TAT! Flame spurted from the muzzle of the machine gun and bullets smacked into the trees. The Jap gunner was firing high. Munro sighted quickly and let off a shot. Nash was swearing savagely at his side, the Sten had jammed on him. Another burst from the machine gun, lower this time, splinters flew from the rail and something zinged overhead with a banshee screech.

He snapped the bolt open again. Out of ammo, shit. He flipped the mag free, slotted in another five round clip and banged it home. The first boat lay dead in the water still but the second was ploughing desperately away upriver, the Japs on board blazing back at them with everything they had.

With a savage wrench Nash cleared the blocked feed and rammed home a fresh magazine. Ignoring the bullets splashing into the leaves he sprang to his feet, ripping short bursts into the fleeing craft.

Caught in the storm of fire the assault boat seemed to shiver in mid-stream and swerve back drunkenly towards the islet. "Keep shooting," Nash called thickly. "Don't let any of the bleeders get away." Munro put his last two rounds into the stricken craft. With a

297

sudden lurch it struck on a submerged rock and overturned in a welter of spray. A couple of bodies bobbed in the water for a moment then sank out of sight.

"*Cease firing!*" Nash shouted. "*Johnny, Francis, katchim disfela bot,*" he pointed to the nearer inflatable. "*Fetchim pipal hia, you savvy?*"

"*Yes boss, katch-im prisner.*" Drawing *parangs* the two blacks leapt into the water. The rest of the crew were jabbering excitedly.

Munro sat on the deck and lit a cigarette, inhaling the smoke deep into his lungs. He felt drained. It had been a massacre, the Japs hadn't stood a chance. But then neither had the bomber crew – or Reverend Oliver or the missionaries on Bataan.

Christ, where did it all stop?

Slater emerged from the deckhouse, reloading his pistol. We sure nailed the shitheads this time," his teeth bared wolfishly, "paid our boys back."

Nash scowled at him, "What was all that noise back there? Almost loused things up."

Slater shrugged, "Dumb priest panicked and started screaming to get out, I had to slug him. He'll be okay, the doc's fixing him now."

Nobody else had been even scratched.

Francis and Johnny came wading back through the shallows to the launch, "*Lukim prisner, boss!*" they chorused displaying their trophies with huge betelnut smiles.

Georgiana caught her breath. Slater's eyes bulged. "Oh shit . . ."

Dangling from their hands by the hair were two freshly severed heads.

FOUR THIRTY PM. South at Lae the heat had gone out of the day. In his cabin aboard the *Southern Cross* Professor Chen was inscribing his diary.

Last night, he wrote, *they were frightening the child again with mention of Tz'u-hsi. The Dragon Empress is in her grave half a century yet her name still conjures dread. Rightly so, but in the end she too was mortal. The great jewel, the object of her greed, became the instrument of her downfall. Justly therefore do we speak of the 'devil-box'.*

But to continue with the legend. In spite of all my urgings the Duke of Chou determined to obey the edict of Tz'u-hsi and returned to Peking. This was the time of the great disturbances of the I Ho Ch'uan, known to Westerners as The Boxer Rebellion. Gangs of youths from the outer provinces were pouring into the city, red sashes bound about their brows, chanting their cry – 'Uphold the great Pure Dynasty! Exterminate the Barbarian!'

On the night of the Duke's arrival the Eastern Cathedral was torched and the flames spread to the merchants' quarter. Great was the destruction and looting among the furriers, the jewellers and silk traders. Gaining his house with difficulty, the Duke ordered the servants to barricade all entrances and mount guard. He was about to retire when there came a pounding on the doors. A eunuch from the Palace was outside with an urgent summons from the Empress Dowager.

Carried in his sedan chair and escorted by a troop of Manchu bannermen, the Duke followed the messenger through the riot-torn streets. The lurid glow from the flames lit up the sky and the air was thick with smoke. At the Gate of Heavenly Peace the guards were more numerous than ever he remembered. Passing through, they traversed the moat to enter the Forbidden City beneath the four great towers that loom above the Gate of the Zenith.

Here in the Great Within all was serene and calm. The Grand Eunuch himself waited to conduct the Duke across the lantern lit marble courtyards, past the Dragon Pavement Terrace on which stands the Throne Hall of Supreme Harmony, past the secondary throne halls and the Treasure Houses, the Chapel of Imperial Ancestors and the Chamber of Diligent Government, to the Dragon Throne.

Ladies-in-waiting twittered like birds behind the ebony columns as the Duke was ushered into the Imperial presence and performed the k'ou-t'ou, the three protestations and the nine knockings, in symbol of submission. From beneath a brocade state parasol adorned with peacock feathers the Dowager Empress surveyed him haughtily. At her side was the Viceroy Jung-Lu.

"Humblest greetings, Queen of Heaven."

"Ha! So you have deigned to come at last!"

The Old Buddha was by this time in her sixty-sixth year. The beauty of her youth had fled, but not her temper. Clapping her hands, she dismissed all her attendants save Jung-Lu.

Now Jung-Lu, the Viceroy of Chihli, was Tz'u-hsi's favourite, a cunning man of great cruelty hated throughout the Celestial Kingdom. Therefore the Duke began to be afraid.

The Empress signed him to approach the throne, 'We wish to see for ourselves this great marvel you have discovered.'

The lamps were dimmed. Kneeling, the Duke drew forth from his robe the casket he had brought and the accursed radiance of the living metal blazed forth like an evil planet in the darkness . . .

With a sigh the Professor laid down his brush and flexed his bony fingers wearily. "Honourable Uncle, please not to tire yourself, heya?" Yu-Ling begged him. "The quai loh doctor said to sleep this afternoon."

"In a little while, child," he stroked her dark hair softly as she knelt at his side. Dear Third Niece so sweet, so pretty. Sad she had never known her grandfather.

He took up the brush again.

As soon as Tz'u-hsi laid eyes upon the wonder the Duke had brought, her greed was all-consuming. She began to question him eagerly seeking to know in what quantities it was to be found and where. When the Duke replied that only a few ounces had so far been extracted she became angered. "Do you take us for fools? You had armies of miners and foreign devils delving in the deserts of Sinkiang!"

"Nevertheless, what your Majesty holds in her hands is the fruit of ten years work."

"By the gods he lies!" Jung-Lu interrupted. "He thinks to keep the secret to himself. They say the magic metal cures all sickness and restores the old to youth. To deny such a gift to your Majesty is treason. I say summon the eunuchs!"

At the thought of her lost youth denied her the Empress's rage became truly terrible. "Take him away," she commanded furiously, clapping her hands. "If he will not reveal the source let him be subjected to the Death of a Thousand Cuts!"

"I was promised Imperial safe-conduct!" the Duke cried as the guards rushed in.

Jung-Lu smiled cruelly, "Safe-conduct does not apply to traitors."

Then did the Duke understand the faithlessness of his enemies, how they had plotted to betray him from the beginning.

Beneath the stern awning Hollington Soong licked the last drop of strawberry ice-cream from his spoon and smacked his lips, *Oh ko*, truly American desserts were delicious.

He wiped his fingers fastidiously and stood up patting his sleek belly. The yacht was quiet, some passengers had gone ashore, others were resting still. From the dock came the squeal of a derrick at work. Another coastal steamer had dropped anchor during the afternoon and her cargo of fifty-gallon drums was being lightered ashore.

Now was the time, by all gods.

Slipping below, he tapped softly on Professor Chen's cabin door. It was opened by Yu-Ling. Inside the old man lay on his bunk, eyes closed, hands clasping the silk-swathed bundle. "*Ai-yah*, Chen Yu-Ling, how is he?"

"Honourable uncle is sleeping now. Please not to disturb him, *heya*?"

Soong smiled unctuously. "I will stay with him, little Jade Years.

You may go on deck, to walk in the fresh air," he pinched her cheek.

The girl hesitated for a moment, then nodded dutifully. Collecting her small purse, she let herself silently out. Soong waited for the patter of her footsteps to disappear.

The portholes were shut and the scent of opium hung heavy in the cabin. He bent over the bunk. The mandarin's eyes were closed, the movements of his chest barely perceptible. His skin was translucent, parchment thin; the hands skeletal, the curling nail on the little finger almost two inches in length. Very gently Soong parted the folds of silk. He caught his breath greedily as he felt the lacquered casket beneath. Heart thumping he eased it out. The thing was heavier than he had expected. On the lid a gilded five-clawed dragon writhed like fire. Soong's mouth drooled. The seal of the Manchu throne.

He tried the catch. Locked. Curse the gods! He glanced around for something to force it.

"All crows under heaven are black but I had not taken you for a thief, Honourable Minister Soong," from the bunk Professor Chen was regarding him balefully.

"*Ai-yah*, old fool!" Soong raged, thrusting the box roughly back at him. "Enough of this game. Open the fornicator before I take a knife to it!"

The mandarin's hands trembled as they clutched the casket once more but his voice remained steady, "I will not open the lock and you dare not try to make me."

"Not dare, by the gods! *Dew neh loh moh*, I'll smash it to a thousand pieces!"

"Then will you die as assuredly as the sun rises," the old man replied unmoved. "Your orders are to deliver the casket unharmed and unopened. Disobey, place but a scratch upon the lock and your life is forfeit to the executioner."

Soong gaped, "What do you know of my orders, eh? Manchu liar!" But he was shocked, the Generalissimo had threatened just that.

The mandarin's thin fingers traced the inlaid dragon. "Even in your remotest dreams you would never guess what this contains. Bless the gods for your ignorance." His voice grew sharper, "Sea Devils, Red Pang, *quai-loh* Americans, all will kill to preserve the secret. Once the devil-box is opened the slaughter will not stop."

And Soong believed him. *Ai-yah*, the Kuomintang would slit his secret sack and feed the contents to the fishes if he betrayed them. The Red Pang had sworn death if he didn't.

Either way he was trapped.

He let himself out. In the passage Bob Cashin stood listening suspiciously. Pushing past the Minister tight lipped he jerked the cabin door back for a second to look inside.

"*Dew neh loh moh*, what are you doing? This is none of your business!" Soong snarled.

The journalist shut the door again. "Making damn sure he's still alive," he snapped. "Or have you forgotten about Simon Ho in Manila?"

"Simon? *Ai-yah*, that was an accident, he was drunk . . ."

"He was *murdered*!" The intensity of Cashin's voice was shocking, Soong stepped back a pace in alarm. "He was dead before they threw him off that balcony, afterwards you ordered his body cremated to destroy the evidence."

"Lies, filthy lies! You have no proof . . ."

"East Wind Rain!" Cashin cut him short. "Is that why he was killed? Or was it because of the jewel?"

The Minister clutched at the wall for support. "*Oh'ko*, I don't know what you mean," he gasped.

"Bullshit!" Cashin's teeth were clenched. "What's inside that casket the Professor guards so carefully? The robbers didn't loot everything from the Manchu Tombs, did they? What became of the Empress's Birthstone, the richest jewel in the world? It was set in a precious metal unknown anywhere else on earth – *a silver that glowed in the dark*!"

302

XXIII

"Depth twelve metres, *Captain-sama*."

A scant three miles out to sea the submarine levelled off beneath the surface. Eleven hundred tons of hidden menace, screws barely turning to maintain trim, ventilation system shut down for silent running, crew at battle stations tense and sweating in their clammy steel coffin.

"*Perisukopu!*"

Hoist cables whined as the gleaming oiled column slid from its well in the cramped, dimly-lit control room. Flipping down the handles her Commander stooped to the eyepiece for a 360 degree sweep of the horizon. No patrols, good. He switched the magnification to high and focused on the harbour. "*Ah so desku*," he breathed.

"The *Amerikan* plane, is it still there, *Captain-san?*" his First Lieutenant asked eagerly.

The bullet-headed Commander gave a grunt of assent. "Radio operator," he called brusquely over his shoulder, "still no message from the assault party?"

"Nothing, *Captain-sama*."

The Commander hissed again. Twelve men lost and the enemy probably alerted into the bargain. Devil take the Black Dragon and their secret mission! "*Perisukopu!*" he barked stepping back as the 'scope slithered down into its well again. "Descend to twenty metres."

"*Hai, Captain-sama*." Air blasted from the regulator tank and the deck tilted slightly. The depth gauge needles crept round their dials. "Twenty metres."

"Ahead slow. We will close to one thousand metres range."

The whirr of the electric motors filled the control room as the submarine's speed picked up. The Lieutenant's mouth pursed, he glanced at his wristwatch, "It is still light, *Captain-san, gaijin* aircraft could spot us."

"*Karma*, we must trust to the silt from the river to shield us. My orders are clear – the flying boat cannot be permitted to leave. We are

303

authorised to use all necessary measures short of outright war . . ."

High above the water a black-feathered pelican folded its wings and plummeted seawards in a power dive. Vanishing with a burst of spray it bobbed up again triumphant, a wriggling fish in its beak.

"Boy, did you see that? Those birds never miss," Chuck Driscoll applauded from the jetty. It was five fifteen. He and Davey Klein were returning with Scott from a visit to the settlement.

Davey shook his head, "All that diving, it damages their brains. They finish up blind."

"Oh that's horrible," Scott said. "It's not true, is it?"

"You bet, Kelly told me."

Fuel drums jarred and banged against one another as native coolies loaded them onto flat-bed waggons drawn by a squat loco. Chuck sniffed the air, "Avgas, they must be hauling it up to the strip."

Beyond the yacht the mechanics had finished their overhaul of the flying boat and canvas cowls shrouded the four engines against salt corrosion. A jeep came rumbling up the planking towards them. "Say, it's Kurt and the Skipper. Wonder where they're off to?"

"Maybe there's been some news of Max."

Catching sight of the three, Ross braked. His uniform cap was pushed back on his head and his face was set grimly. "We're looking for Tad Gotto, any of you know where he is?" he demanded peremptorily.

"Shucks, Skipper, I'm not sure. We just got back from town," Chuck said.

"Well, start looking. I'm placing him under arrest."

"But Skipper," Scott was stunned, "I don't understand. Why?"

A muscle twitched spasmodically in Ross's jaw, his eyes were bleak, "Because he's a Japanese spy, that's why, Miss Scott!"

"*Tad?*" Clattering down the yacht's forward companionway Scott burst into the crew's messroom. Three Melanesian sailors blinked up at her. "Sorry, have any of you seen Tad Gotto?"

"No, ma'am," they chorused.

She ran upstairs to the main deck and bumped into Kelly hurrying down from the bridge, four armed seamen at his back. "Sally, what in tarnation's going on? I just saw Ross, he's spouting some crazy story about one of your stewards working for the Japs."

"Oh God, Kelly," she gasped, tears of rage in her eyes, "I don't know what it's all about, except Ross is way off beam. Tad's no spy, I'll swear!"

The yacht skipper looked unhappy, "Hell, we've been told to bring the guy in – at gunpoint if necessary."

"Don't, please!" Scott begged him. "Let us handle it. If Tad sees a load of strangers coming after him, he'll just panic."

"I'm sorry, honey," Kelly made a stern face, "but right now I guess we can't afford to take a chance." He nodded to his men, "Okay, boys, spread out and start searching. Don't use more force than you have to."

They moved off as Chuck and Davey came pounding up. "He's not topside, Sally, we've checked all over."

"We've got to find him. If we let him hide or run away, Ross'll take it as proof he's guilty."

A hooter brayed out in the bay. The copra ship had weighed anchor and was preparing to put to sea. They saw her signal angrily again as a tug towing lighters cut across her track. "Sapheads, they'll be in trouble if they don't watch out," Chuck snorted.

"Guys, we must *think*. Where would he run if he was scared?"

"The Clipper maybe?"

"It's worth a try. C'mon!"

Georgiana had taken off her boot. Stripping away the sock, she rolled up her slacks and stuck out her foot. "This had better work, Max," she wriggled her toes.

"Relax, Dixie, it will." Munro leaned forward on the bench opposite and took her foot in his hand, conscious for a moment of the long full womanly line of the calf, the pale satiny-smooth skin. Drawing deep on his cigarette till the tip was glowing red he touched it to the leech.

"Ugh," Georgiana exclaimed in disgust as the squirming blob of jelly dropped off leaving a stream of blood. "Heck, I'm leaking to death!"

"The leech injects an anti-coagulant into the wound to promote bleeding," Doctor Latouche told her applying disinfectant. "*Interéssant, n'est pas?*"

Restless, Munro moved away forward to the prow. The engine had been holding up well. With the current behind her the launch was splashing along making better than twelve knots. There was a tang of salt in the air now, they were nearly at the coast. Another quarter hour according to Nash.

Suddenly he gripped the rail.

Beyond the distant trees a lightning flash of fire stabbed upwards, stark against the gathering dusk, and a plume of dark smoke shot into the sky, swelling and climbing like a monstrous bloom. Seconds later came the thunder-clap of sound, racing out across the flat ground.

Rolling out over the gulf the Grumman amphibian levelled off and settled smoothly onto the airstrip. The pilot eased off the throttle and steadied her with the brakes as he let the tail sink. Taxiing over to the tower he cut the motor.

Chewing a fresh stick of gum the Chief strolled across the apron to meet him. "Hi, how'd it go?" he drawled.

The curly-haired Australian recognised him and beamed, "Spotted one launch just a mile or so up river as I was coming in. Should be droppin' her hook about now. Dunno who's aboard, darn radio went u/s on me."

"Sounds like some of them stayed with the bomber then?"

"Search me, mate. Weather over the swamps is still thicker'n pigshit. Don't worry about your mates though," he clapped the engineer on the shoulder, "Jack Nash is a flamin' good bloke, knows this country blindfold."

The Chief squinted up at the sky. The sun was setting already behind the mountains, throwing long shadows across the strip. "He'll need to, ain't much time left till dusk."

A window opened in the tower and a man leaned out. "Hey, Gerry," he shouted to the pilot, "cut the chatter an' bring us your log book, I'm pissin' for a beer!"

"Gotta go, mate, so long," Spencer said to the Chief. "Oh by the way," he turned back for a moment, "Amelia Earhart, d'you get anything out of Austin Fuller?"

A distant expression crossed the big Indian's face. "Yeah," he nodded pensively, "you were right, an interesting guy."

As he walked back past the hangars along the track leading to the railroad a vehicle overtook him and pulled up sharply. "They said you'd come out here," Ross scowled from the driver seat of the jeep. "What're you doing, godammit?"

"The spotter plane was up again. Figured I'd see what news of Max."

"Munro!" Ross spat the name as if it were a dirty word. "You'd think he was captain the way you people run around after him." With a visible effort he controlled his temper and jerked a head at Kurt,

306

"Thyssen here just gave me the story on catching Gotto with the stolen mail."

"Telling tales outta school, huh Kurt?" the Chief said contemptuously, his black eyes flat. "Might've guessed, it's about your goddam speed."

The Second Officer flushed darkly, "I did my *duty*. That man's a Jap spy, for Christsakes!"

"Bullshit!"

"That's enough. Kurt was right to tell me," Ross's voice was raw-edged. "I suppose you were waiting to warn your precious Max Munro first!"

The Chief shrugged unmoved, "Mail's his baby, ain't it?"

"And a fine job he's made of it!" Suspicion and jealousy twisted Ross's features. "Munro had the ship searched after the break-in, how come he didn't turn up the missing mail then?"

"I wouldn't know. You suggesting he had a hand in stealing it?"

"*What if I am?*" Ross bared his teeth, "I'm not the only one, Slater reckons so too. That's why he's taken Munro up the swamps with him, to keep an eye on the bastard."

An open truck roared past, Spencer the pilot waving to them. The Chief shook his head slowly, sadly, "You're crazy, Ross. I dunno what Slater's got over you, 'cept it's mixed up with Earhart – an' Mili."

"Mili!" The colour was draining from Ross's face like the tide running out from a beach, "Mili's nothing to do with this, damn you. Earhart was never on Mili, she couldn't have been!"

"That's a lie, Ross. I spoke to Austin Fuller, they switched her engines. She reached Mili, then what? Did she die there?"

"*She's not dead!*" Ross's voice was almost a scream.

The air shook suddenly.

Like a monstrous drumbeat the thud of an explosion echoed out across the land. Unmistakable. Ominous. The three Americans froze. "Hell, what was that?" Thyssen gasped.

"It came from the ocean."

"Jesus Christ, look!" Grey-faced, Ross was staring in the direction of the jetty.

Belching into the sky was a dense column of black smoke.

Aboard the yacht, returning passengers stepped aside in surprise as Scott and the two men rushed down the gangway. They were tearing towards the flying boat at the end of the jetty when there were sudden shouts followed by a deep reverberating clang. One of the fuel lighters had collided with a moored barge.

"Dumb idiots!" Chuck jerked up short, "I said that would happen."

They stopped to watch a moment. The tug was going astern, foam threshing under its counter. Her skipper had his wheel hard over and was swinging outwards to haul the lighter clear. It didn't look like there had been any great damage, Scott thought.

It was her last coherent thought for several moments.

A flash of vivid light stabbed the dusk. She felt a burning wind sear her skin like the sudden opening of a furnace door and a violent blow drove the breath from her lungs, sending her staggering. With an ear-stunning blast the lighter disintegrated. A monstrous cone of fire, white-hot shot through with yellow, orange and flaring red, erupted from the torn hull in a hideous gusher of blazing kerosene.

Clouds of dense smoke boiled skywards. Lesser blasts rocked the bay as more barrels of fuel exploded sending up fresh spouts of fire. Fanned by an onshore wind a shower of incandescent sparks rolled across the jetty. Above the roar of flames came the screams of men burning alive.

Ashore and on the yacht alarm bells began pealing urgently. Scott saw the loco driver leap from his cab and join the native coolies fleeing for their skins. A brawny Australian foreman caught him by the scruff of the neck. "Get these waggons moving, you pissing coward, before the whole lot go up!" he yelled kicking him back aboard. The half dozen loaded freight cars were packed with enough fuel to destroy the entire jetty. Burning embers were hissing down into the water on every side. For a dreadful moment it looked as though they had left it too late. "Jeez, we'd better scram from here before we fry!" Davey cried to the others. Then with a lurch the bogies began to roll. Slowly with shrieks of its whistle the loco steamed backwards out of danger, the waggons rattling behind.

Up on the yacht fire parties were dragging hoses into the bows. A jet arced out towards the inferno on the water but its stream fell short. Stumbling in the smoke after the others Scott glanced back and gasped all of a sudden, "Oh my God, look!"

Where the train had pulled out, a stack of unloaded drums remained on the jetty. Below in the water blazing droplets from the blast had ignited patches of spilled fuel. Before their eyes a tongue of fire was licking up the wooden pilings only yards from where the Clipper was berthed.

Scott cast round frantically for a fire bucket, anything to fight the flames. There were shouts behind, others had seen the danger too. The blaze was spreading greedily among the tar covered timbers. It only needed one fuel drum to catch to turn the entire end of the jetty into a massive conflagration.

If the flames reached the flying boat she would burn like a torch.

Suddenly they saw the plane's main hatch burst open and a figure emerge clasping a bulky extinguisher. Leaping across the sponson onto the jetty he ran towards the fuel stack heedless of the appalling risk. Yanking the trigger he turned a stream of high pressure foam against the fires below.

"It's Tad!"

"Jesus, give him a hand *quick*!"

Eyes stinging in the smoke they raced for the plane. Blessing her emergency training, Scott flung herself through the lounge, grabbed a fire bottle from under the stairs and tore out again to join Tad beating back the blaze. Moments later Chuck and Davey came rushing up with the big CO_2 gas extinguishers from the hold.

Lit by the flickering glow of the burning vessels smoke and sparks were pouring from the pilings under their feet. The crackle of the fire as it spread among the timbers was frightening. If the fuel went up none of them would stand a chance. But more men threw themselves into the fray beside the four Americans. A bucket chain was organised. Slowly between them they smothered the flames out.

"Keep damping these timbers down or the bleeders'll catch again!" shouted the foreman who had saved the train. "And shift this sodding fuel out of the way!" Teams of willing hands began rolling the drums back up towards the shore.

"Gee, Tad, that was close!" Scott panted wiping the soot from her smut-streaked face as they lugged their empty fire bottles away. "If it hadn't been for you we'd have lost the ship!"

But the young steward wasn't attending. He gripped her shoulder. "We ain't clear yet, Mis' Scott. That other stuff, it's comin' closer!"

Scott stared past the flying boat's lofty tail and felt a wave of dismay. Out on the water the lake of burning fuel from the ruptured drums was spreading and drifting in towards the jetty. In a matter of minutes the Clipper would be cut off where she lay.

"We gotta have help!" Chuck yelled as they ran back down the jetty. "A boat to tow her out!"

Kelly appeared out of the smoke. "Slip the moorings!" he shouted. "I'll fetch some men, we'll pull her up under the yacht and train the hoses on her!"

"*No!*" Scott clutched his arm, "There isn't time. Chuck and I'll start the engines and taxi out!"

"You crazy? You're none of you pilots!"

"I can handle a plane on the water – if Chuck can give me power."

"Jeez, Scott, I . . ."

"We can't let her burn, for Godsakes!"

Chuck gulped. "Okay. You're right, Scott, it's our only chance!"

Kelly looked from one to the other. "I guess you know what you're doing," he said crisply. "Leave the warps to me then."

Feet skidding on the wet sea-wing, the four ducked through the hatch and hurled themselves upstairs to the flight deck. "Gotta check the batteries first!" Chuck called darting through into the hold. Her heart racing Scott slid into Ross's seat and unlocked the controls. One of the starboard side windows was cracked from the blast, no other apparent damage that she could see. Beyond though the wall of flames danced on the water terrifyingly close.

The lights flicked on as Chuck came running back. "Okay, you got juice for the starters."

"Hey, we forgot the engine hoods!" Scott yelled.

"Leave it to us, we'll get 'em," Davey shouted. "C'mon, Tad!" The wing hatches slammed behind them.

The instrument panels were coming alive now. Chuck was throwing switches at the engineer's station – master battery, carburettor air, autosyn dyn. Gas and oil both sufficient. Mixture control on Full Rich. No time for frills like checking water indicators or testing thermocouples.

"Inboard motors only," Scott was calling. "Start with Number Two, I'll need to swing her out past the yacht."

"Gotcha!" Chuck set the selector valves.

There were thumping sounds on the starboard wing. Tad was out on the inboard nacelle struggling to cut away the canvas hood. Scott cranked Ross's seat closer to the yoke, her eyes roaming the instruments before her. Props in low pitch. Throttles 600. Test flaps full range. All the First Officer's tasks to shoulder as well as the Captain's. Vacuum valves, trim tabs, limit lights. Golly, would she remember everything Shapiro had shown her? No time now for mistakes.

The boys were still wrestling with the hoods. What was taking them so long? How much nearer were the flames?

More hoses in action aboard the yacht now. The dazzling glare of a million candle-power searchlight swept the jetty cutting the smoke. Scott could see passengers being hurried ashore down the gangway. A burst of determination seized her; here at last was a chance to prove herself instead of acting nursemaid.

Tad's hood was dropping away. Davey was through on the port wing too and squeezing back through the engine hatch. Praying all systems were functioning, she stretched up for the ignition panel.

"*Start Two!*"

"*Aye aye, ready on Two!*" Chuck worked the priming pump.

"*Ignition on!*" Scott pressed the overhead button. "*Start and boost!*"

There was a splutter from the port inner motor as the prop broke into life. It spun a few times fitfully then subsided again. "Christsakes," Scott cried punching the starter again. "Give me more prime! I'm losing it!"

"I'm trying! I'm trying!" Chuck yelled back, working the pump frantically. "Leave the throttles alone or you'll starve it more . . .!"

"Gawd save us," Nash muttered, "what was it, a bleedin' air raid?"

As the launch steamed round the headland Munro stared through the binoculars stunned. At first sight the whole harbour seemed ablaze. Locked together in a ring of fire three craft were burning like torches, smoke boiling up hundreds of feet into the air punctured by spurts of flame from exploding fuel drums.

Where in all that inferno was the Clipper?

Then he saw her. Through the smoke the flying boat's hull was just visible beyond the *Southern Cross*. Christ, she hadn't a prayer, the flames were already leaping under her tail. Any moment now she'd catch.

"Oh, Max," Georgiana's fingers tightened on his arm. "There must be some way to save her! They can't just let her burn!"

The flames were drawing closer. Munro couldn't bear to watch any more. Sick in his gut he was turning away when there was a sudden excited scream from Georgiana, "*Max*, there are men on the wings! They're trying to start the engines!"

"What?" He snatched the glasses back from her. "You're right, by God!" His heart gave a leap, someone was cutting away the starboard engine hoods. He could make out figures in the cockpit too. One propeller began turning then stopped. "*Christ, get the pressure up, you fools!*" he shouted desperately. the motor was swinging again, more strongly this time . . . now a second one . . . both inner props were spinning . . . the ship was under power! Frantic with anxiety he watched the flying boat's nose emerge from the smoke, creeping out past the stern of the yacht. But Jesus, the flames had her boxed in, impossible for anything to break past.

No! There was a gap now! The wash of the props was sweeping the fires aside. She was swinging, a wing dipped dangerously but the pilot caught her smartly. Not Ross at the controls surely, too hesitant, but someone aboard who knew what they were doing. The bows were pointing directly at them, all at once he caught a glint of gold hair in the cockpit. "It's Scott, by God!" he cried.

"There's a row-boat heading out from the shore!" Davey Klein yelled up the stairs, "Looks like the Skipper aboard!"

Engines idling the Clipper swung slowly into the wind. Out in the bow hatch Tad waved both arms above his head. Exultant, Scott eased the throttles. "Anchor's holding," she called. "Stop engines."

"Roger, stopping both."

Chuck set the mixture controls to Fuel Cutoff and flipped the master battery switch. As the sound of the Cyclones died away Scott turned to grin at him, her face aglow with triumph, "Boy, oh boy, we did it, Chuck. We did it!"

He shook his head, "I just sat here pulling knobs, it's you deserve a medal."

"I'll settle for pilot's wings," Scott smiled, but then her expression went grave. Through the cabin portholes she had glimpsed the ships still blazing by the jetty, "Those poor guys on the tug, they never stood a chance."

There were footsteps on the stairs and Ross appeared in the cabin.

Chuck saw him first, "Why, Skipper . .. "

Ross seemed not to hear. Purple at the neck, his gaze was riveted on Scott. She had twisted round in the cockpit seat, one hand still gripping the throttle levers defiantly, her face pale, the earphone set crammed down over her blond curls. Wordless they stared at one another.

Ross's mouth opened but no sounds came. Uttering a sudden strangled sob he pitched forward and slumped to the deck with a crash.

"*Alors*, It is not serious, I think," Latouche reported back to the control cabin. "Exhaustion, strain from overwork. I have given him a sedative."

Slater snorted, "Exhaustion my ass, too much booze more like."

"Are you saying he'll be okay to fly again, Doctor?" Muddied and sweat-stained from the swamps, Munro sat at Ross's desk, Slater opposite, the ship's log open between them. The rest of the crew were ranged about the cabin and stairs. Whitely and the Chief at their stations, Scott perched on the chart table, Kurt Thyssen lounging studiously apart in the cockpit. It was six pm. Night had fallen with tropical swiftness. Across the bay patches of flame still burned on the water as fire-fighting teams mopped up.

The Frenchman shrugged, "When he has rested, perhaps."

That wasn't good enough. Munro eyed him straight, "In your professional opinion, as of this moment is Captain Ross fit to command the aircraft?"

They all waited for the doctor's answer. He hesitated, "At present, no."

The crew breathed easier. Now everyone knew where they stood.

Munro glanced at the bulkhead chronometer and noted the time in the log. Depriving a flying boat Master of his ship was no light step, it had to be done by the book. "Then as First Officer I am assuming command during the Captain's incapacity as provided by Company Regulations." He caught a flush of jealousy on Kurt Thyssen's face.

Slater rose to his feet. "Don't go getting too big for your boots, Pilot," he sneered. "Ross ain't sick. Couple of hours sack and he'll be back in the saddle. So far as I'm concerned he remains in charge."

Munro shut the logbook with a snap. "Better see that cargo of yours stowed aboard, Major," he said. "We'll be pulling out of here in two hours and I'd sure hate to leave you behind."

Across the bay the *Southern Cross* was alive with rumours. "*Aiee*, they are saying the Clipper is badly burned, Honourable Uncle!" Yu-Ling reported anxiously to the Professor, returning from a trip on deck. "Also there has been a great battle on the river between *quai-loh* and the Sea Devils with many killed!"

The Professor had been reading through his diary. He smoothed his silver beard tranquilly. "*Joss*. Truly does Sun Tzu say war is like fire; those who take up weapons are consumed by them."

"*Joss*," she agreed crossing to the porthole. "All gods preserve us from the Sea Devils." Peering out she could see lifeboats still searching the water for survivors of the blaze. *Joss*, she thought again.

She poured her uncle a cup of *cha* and helped him drink it. Then she went back out into the corridor. *Ai-yah*, she could hear *quai-loh* voices quarrelling in one of the cabins. One was the beautiful red-hair Miss Delahaye . . .

"Oh stop being such a fool, César. You don't *own* me, for God-sakes!"

"*Madre mia, es fantastico*! I am a fool to complain because my *novia*, my bride, disappears all day with her *gringo* lover like a whore!"

There was a ringing slap followed at once by a spit of rage. "*Ei*, I do it again. *Puta*! Whore!"

Yu-Ling was still listening spell-bound when a hand squeezed her rump from behind. She jerked round. Bodyguard Feng leered at her in his tight fitting suit. "*Ai-yah*, let me alone, pig!" Furiously she pulled away. "How dare you touch me?"

He chuckled, "Oh, oh, so the little Princess is a virgin, *heya*?"

Her nails clawed at his face. "*Hum kar chan*! May your whole family perish!"

He caught her hands easily. "*Ai-yah*, you'll have a Tortoise Head at your Jade Gate soon, little Princess," he jeered. "Honourable Minister Soong has plans for you, you're to be his *tse-mui*, his new concubine." He saw the expression of horror on her face and released her with a cruel laugh, "Go fasten the blind in the Manchu's cabin, the ship is being darkened in case of attack!"

An armed seaman checked Munro's identity as he came up the yacht's gangway with the Chief. Not a light was showing anywhere. Hoses and pumping gear still littered the decks and there was a pervasive smell of scorched timber and paintwork. The flames had come pretty close.

Kelly met them on the bridge. "Hi, how's Ross?"

"Still out for the count. What about our gas, will the Aussies let us refuel?"

The yacht skipper nodded, "Anything to get the Clipper out of here, they reckon that's what the Japs are after. Right now you're about as popular as a skunk at a corn roast. Someone claims to have seen a torpedo track in the water just before the explosion, the whole town's blacked-out and there's a Royal Navy destroyer making flank speed up from Darwin."

"Can't say I blame 'em," the Chief rumbled glancing across the water to where the tug's upperworks projected above the surface.

"Nor me. And if I were you I wouldn't waste time high-tailing it. How much gas do you need, Chief?"

Munro answered for him, "Full tanks."

Surprise showed fleetingly in both their faces. "A full load, that's sixteen and a half tons, Max," the Chief said. "We can make Guam on nine, easy."

314

"I know, dammit." Munro was weary. "Forget about the weight, I want the ship fuelled with every gallon she'll hold, okay?"

There was a short pause. The Chief shrugged impassively, "Sure, Max, anything you say. Full tanks it is."

Munro took a coded signal form from an inside pocket. "Kelly, when we're airborne, not before, I'd like this sent to Sol Boden in Manila. He'll know what to do."

"I get you, leave it with me."

Munro went below to wash.

The electric bulbs had been removed in the corridors but a strip of light showed under his cabin door. He turned the handle softly. It wasn't locked. Inside Georgiana was rummaging through the closet.

She jerked back startled, "Dammit, Max, you scared me half to death."

"I don't knock on my own door. Anyway how come you're in here, Dixie?"

A lock of hair slipped forward, shadowing her face. She pushed it back. It was another sticky night and she'd changed into a plain linen dress that looked simple in the way only expensive clothes did. "If you must know I was hoping to find that snapshot."

"The one of you? Well, you're out of luck, it's gone."

"Gone? You mean lost?"

"I mean *stolen*. Somebody on the dock sneaked it out of my jacket while I was diving after you."

"*Damn!*" she bit her lip.

Munro gave her a hard look. "Dixie, level with me. Are you snooping for Slater?

"Of course not," she made an irritated gesture, "But someone *did* push me in, whatever people think. If I could find the snapshot it might give a clue why."

He gripped her arm. "Four men from that photograph are dead already; last night you damn near joined them. What the hell the game is I don't know, but the prize is Slater's cargo – the cargo he's bringing home for Kim. *Dixie, we have to find out what's inside those footlockers!*"

The brass dinner gong boomed up on deck. Georgiana shivered and drew close to him suddenly. "Max, we daren't. Whatever it is, it's too terrible! Even Dad was scared." Her lips were cold as they pressed against his for an instant. Then she was gone.

It was dark as hell when Munro returned on deck again, shaved and changed, the mud of the swamps scoured off in the shower. Rafts of

315

cu-nim were edging out from the mountains obscuring the moon. Good, all the better for the plan he had in mind.

He could hear the passengers at dinner amidships as he groped round towards the gangway. Sensible of Pat to get a good meal inside them before the flight. Tomorrow they were in for a shock.

He caught a whiff of cigar smoke. In the shadow of the darkened fantail two people were whispering. A woman's voice, *"Ssh, don't worry, I can handle Max Munro. No problem."*

It was Georgiana. And the man with her was Slater.

EIGHT PM. The moon gleamed fitfully between banks of cloud and up in the settlement a stray light glimmered like a firefly against the inky backdrop of the mountains. Diesels idling softly, the submarine rode hull-down on the oily swell, deck awash, ripples of phosphorescence splashing her gun mounting, blacked-out conning tower invisible in the darkness.

"*Captain-sama!*" a look-out's urgent cry alerted the bridge. "Something moving by the dock!"

Even as he spoke from the hostile shore a green rocket soared up into the night.

The Commander focused his binoculars rapidly. His breath hissed, "*Oi*, the *gaijin* aircraft is starting her run!"

The moon came out briefly and the Japanese saw the flying boat swing into the wind and steady herself.

"We could man the gun, *Captain-san*? Finish her off with shellfire, *neh*?" the Lieutenant suggested eagerly.

"Fool! You want to start a war, *neh*?"

The man quailed. "So sorry, *Captain-san*," he stammered, "I only thought . . . the torpedo . . ."

"*I-ye*, don't think! Torpedoing the fuel barge was a gamble, not to be taken twice. Not till we receive the final signal, *higashi no kaze ame*! Send for the radio operator; Tokyo must be warned."

Engines bellowing under full power the flying boat reared up on the bow wave, the water rushing under her hull, the silvery trail of her wake streaming behind. Faster and faster she skimmed the surface. The foaming track cut off as she lifted into the air.

Higashi no kaze ame. East Wind Rain.

XXIV

A star glittered.

Blue-bright and cold. A brilliant jewel against the black velvet of the night revealed for a moment by a gap in the clouds. Sirius, the dog-star, first charted millenia ago by Pharonic priests to predict the Nile flood, now a beacon to guide voyagers across the featureless Pacific.

Perched on a ladder in the perspex astrodome Kurt Thyssen squinted through the eyepiece of his sextant, willing the dancing prick of light to steady itself in the bubble horizon as he adjusted the micrometer. Up front Munro had the ship on manual holding her rock level for the sighting. The star centred for an instant and he tripped the tumbler switch. A good one. He breathed again.

Over the next half minute he took four more readings. Satisfied, he shifted round to search for Betelgeuse.

The altimeter quivered at seven thousand feet.

Munro reached out to tap the dial with a finger. The radium tipped needle stayed obstinately put and he felt a momentary irritation with himself. Trying to second-guess your instruments was the kind of dumb trick that got rapped knuckles at flying school. A Clipper captain should set a better example. Over in the starboard pilot's seat Chris Fry was humming cheerfully, his thoughts most probably on his new girlfriend. He was too young to concern himself with the habits of captains.

He lifted his gaze. The cockpit was darkened, screened off by curtains from the cabin behind, and the luminous dials cast a faint reflection of his face in the glass of the windshield. Beyond, the blackness was stygian. If he twisted to the side and craned his neck he might catch the flickering tongue of an engine exhaust flame beneath the port wing, otherwise nothing.

Indicated airspeed read one sixty-five knots. The time was coming

317

up for twenty-two fifteen, a quarter past ten. Assuming no head winds, that put Lae some three hundred and forty miles in their rear. By rights then they should be safely through the straits and out into the Bismarck Sea.

Kurt would have the exact position soon. Creep he might be, but he was one hell of a fine navigator, Munro had to give him that. Without Kurt he would never have considered a passage like this at night.

And the worst, the most difficult section was to come.

He hadn't told the rest yet. Not even the Chief. If what he feared was true it was the only way.

Aft at the radio desk Stewart sat in a pool of light cast by the angle lamp, the hiss of the ether singing in his earphones as he listened to Madang up the coast chatting away in cipher to Lae. His hand crouched over the key longing to cut in with a QRK – *Can you hear me?* Even if only to let them take a bearing, but Munro had ordained radio silence. Sadly he switched down to 1500 kcs and Hawaiian music filtered through the loudspeaker.

"What's that, KGMB Honolulu?" Shapiro was sprawled in one of the rear seats. "Late, aren't they? It's three am over there."

"Air Corps must have a flight coming in from the mainland," Davey Klein told him. "They keep KGMB playing right through the night when there's military planes up for them to home in on."

"Swell, how come they don't do the same for us?"

"Cause we know how to navigate, stupid. Army guys get lost if they can't see the ground."

Over at the engineer's station the Chief was logging the cylinder head temperature. He looked up. "Be kinda helpful for the Japs too," he remarked.

Kurt Thyssen had completed his final observation. Zipping the Bausch and Lomb sextant into its soft leather case, he slipped the instrument carefully inside a pocket before climbing down. Without it they were, quite literally, lost.

He stretched his stiffened limbs in the darkened hold. A faint glow showed round the rim of the hatch to the crew quarters where Ross was laid up. That knucklehead Munro had ordered the whole ship blacked out, portholes sealed, even had the fuses taken out from the nav light circuits. Whatever had happened back there in the New Guinea swamps it had sure put the wind up the bastard. He'd taken one hell of a risk flying out tonight.

Thyssen smiled thinly to himself as he recalled the pre take-off flight

318

briefing round the chart table. "Max, it's lunacy. The straits are only fifty miles wide, they're hard enough to locate in daylight. And you've seen what those mountains are like."

"The cloud won't thicken up for another couple of hours yet, that should see us through. And the peaks on New Britain don't run over six thousand. I don't anticipate any trouble."

"The Bismarcks rise above *sixteen* thousand on the western side. With the load of fuel you're carrying you'll never make that. I want to log a formal objection."

"Your protest is noted. Now get the hell to work!"

Dumb asshole, Kurt snorted to himself. Now he was covered either way and Munro would catch shit when the brass back stateside found out. Which Kurt would see they did.

The ship shuddered in an air pocket. Kurt started. Out of the corner of his eye he had seen a figure move. Across the hold by the water tank where Slater's cargo and the coffin were stowed. A stab of fear shot through him. Shaking, he edged away, groping with a hand for the light switch by the main hatch. He snapped it on and felt a wave of relief. That darn ballgown! Swinging from a hook with the motion of the plane it had looked just like a man in the darkness.

Turning out the light again, he went through to the control cabin.

Munro switched on the autopilot.

He sat for a moment watching the instruments while he adjusted the settings, the yoke moving robot-like at the behest of the gyros. Then he pressed the button on the intercom, "Shapiro, spell me a while. I want a talk with Kurt."

"Aye aye, Max."

The cabin seemed very bright after the dimmed cockpit. Kurt was hunched over the chart table with protractor and parallel ruler. A separate panel of instruments was set in the bulkhead beneath the window, compass, chronometer, airspeed indicator and altimeter. Alongside was a shelf of books – *Star Almanac, Sight Reduction Tables, Pacific Navigator*. Kurt drew a careful line with a pencil and reached for a plastic disk computer.

"How are we doing?"

Kurt straightened up. "Five point zero six south, one forty-six point five five east. Approximately one hundred and twenty miles due east of Madang." He consulted the computer again, "In the last fifty-three minutes we've covered one hundred and seventy-four miles, so I'd say we're picking up a twelve knot tail wind."

319

"That's pretty good, Kurt," Munro studied the neat lines on the chart. Plotting a position accurately to within half a degree from star sights shot from a fast moving aeroplane was no mean accomplishment. "Now I want a change of course ninety degrees east."

Thyssen's jaw dropped, "Christsakes, you'll take us clear out over the Mandate!"

"Is that a fact?" Munro picked up the interphone, "Galley? My compliments to Major Slater, ask him to please come up to the flight deck."

"Twenty dollars then, agreed?" Van Cleef said.

"That war's declared before we reach San Francisco? Sure, I'll take you on, bud," one of the oilmen nodded. "That's war with Japan, right? We're not talking about the Krauts."

"No, no, America and Japan only, no one else."

"How about the British, shouldn't they be in on this too?" Bob Cashin grinned mischievously at Sir Ambrose Hope across the poker table.

"I feel certain if the United States were to be attacked Mr. Churchill would offer speedy aid," the diplomat responded with a twinkle in his eye. There was general laughter in the lounge. It was the only cabin not made up into bunks for the night and half a dozen late sitters were gathered round the big centre table while the stewards kept them supplied with coffee and drinks from the galley.

"Well, I'm with you," an Army officer told Van Cleef. "Hell, those buck-toothed bastards knocked off one of our bombers so I heard. The American public ain't gonna stand for our boys being killed."

"Didn't matter any when they sank that Navy gunboat, the *Panay*," the oilman cut the cards and shuffled. "We should've slapped the sons of bitches down then. Most probably this won't even come out. Roosevelt's got it all planned, he'll go to war when he's good and ready, not before."

Opposite him Prince Cherkassy waited impatiently for the fresh hand to be dealt. He was wearing his pearl pin and the luck was with him this evening, he had won more than two hundred dollars. "The Japanese are fools to attack America or England, they should make war against the Bolsheviks instead."

"Amen to that," said the oilman. "Stalin's a dirty crook same as Hitler. Let 'em finish each other off, I say."

Cashin observed Sir Ambrose wince a little at this description of his country's ally but hold his tongue. A new figure entered the lounge

320

from the direction of the stern, Reverend Jordan.

"Hi there, Father, you coming to join us?" Cashin welcomed him.

The priest glanced about uncertainly, "No, thank you, I was looking for one of the stewards. I, I wondered what time we will be landing tomorrow at Guam."

"Soon after breakfast, I think. I did hear someone say eight o'clock."

"If indeed Guam is where we are headed," said Van Cleef.

Everyone looked at him.

"What d'you mean? Where else would we be going? You think they're taking us back to Manila?" Cashin asked.

The white-blond Dutchman nodded towards the compass repeater that together with a chronometer was fixed to the forward bulkhead for the information of passengers. "At the moment we are travelling in the direction of neither. Unless I am mistaken our captain is making for the Marshall Islands."

"The way I see it we got no other choice."

They were seated round the captain's desk at the rear of the cabin. Slater chewing a cigar, the Chief in shirt sleeves, Kurt with his charts spread out. Munro was doing the talking. "Whatever cover this mission of yours once had, Major, it's blown so far as Tokyo's concerned."

"So what are you suggesting?" Slater snapped aggressively. "That we run like hell?"

"Question is where though? We got three possible routes." The others leaned forward to see as Munro tapped the chart. "One, we can head back up the way we came to Manila. With luck the Air Corps might arrange some kind of escort tomorrow morning out of Mindanao."

"I wouldn't bet on it," Slater grunted. "The way MacArthur acts you'd think he paid for those goddam bombers out of his own pocket."

"Sets us back a leg, even supposin' we do make Manila," the Chief observed frowning. "An' gives the Yellow-bellies more time to act."

"That's just what I figure," Munro agreed. "We're back where we started only worse off. Okay, option two is to head as planned for Guam. What's our current ETA, Kurt?"

"Seven thirty am. Or it was until you made that course change," Kurt added pointedly.

Slater was instantly suspicious, "What course change, for Christ-sakes? Who authorised it?"

Munro ignored the question. "Guam's exactly where the Japs expect us to make for. They'll have us pinned down from the moment we arrive. No way can we get off again without them knowing. They'd pick us off at their leisure anywhere they want on route to Wake."

There was silence, everyone remembering the flying boat that had jumped them over the South China Sea. This time it would be for real with the guns firing.

"What's your alternative then?" Slater asked harshly.

Munro drew the chart towards him. "Simple," he said quietly. "Fly directly to Wake Island."

Another trough of rough air made the fuselage creak. Tad Gotto came up from the galley in a white mess jacket, balancing a tray. "Coffee, Mister Munro sir? An' them's your favourite sandwiches, ham'n mustard."

"Thanks, Tad." Munro took one. He hadn't realised how hungry he was. "Everything okay below?"

"Yessir, mos' passengers gone off to their bunks now," Tad moved away.

"Are you out of your fucking skull?" Kurt Thyssen spoke first in a savage whisper. "Wake's three thousand miles away. We'll never make it!"

"Two thousand six hundred and fifty, only just further than Honolulu to 'Frisco," Munro swigged his coffee. "I checked before take off. We can do it on our heads."

"An unscheduled flight across the heart of the Japanese Mandate!" Kurt was staring at the chart in disbelief. "With no weather, no one aboard with route experience! It's madness, I tell you."

Munro opened the desk drawer and brought out a folder. "I've a complete route plan here with weather input from Guam, Wake and the British Gilberts. Kelly and I put it together while we were fuelling. There's a trough of low pressure moving north into the Mandate from the Equator, but it shouldn't bother us any. Otherwise all indications are good."

Slater cut in, "What d'you say, Injun? Can it be done?"

The Chief's eyes were very flat, "Let's hear the plan, Max."

Was Kurt right? Were the risks too great? In normal circumstances no sane captain would consider such a course of action for even a moment. But the Pacific stood poised on the brink of all-out war, he must weigh the threat with no margin for error.

322

He drew the chart towards him. "The most dangerous section of the trip over the central Mandate will be covered at night. First light should see us across the Equator approaching latitude 10, approximately three hundred miles north west of Truk."

"*Truk?*" Slater's manner sharpened perceptibly, "Did you say Truk, for Christsakes?"

"North west of Truk on the edge of the Mandate," Munro caught the Chief's eye for a moment and drew an imperceptible nod. "At which point," he continued, "we're only four hours flight time from Guam. No problem obtaining a radio fix of our position and in the event of mechanical failure we can still divert.

"By then we'll have burned off forty percent of our fuel load enabling us to cruise at a high altitude as we pass well to the north east of the Marshalls."

The Marshalls. Their eyes were drawn to the scattered group of dots on the map. Atolls with outlandish names – Jaluit, Kwajalein, Bikini, *Mili*.

"What's your opinion, Navigator?"

Thyssen shrugged. "He's the skipper now, it's up to him if he wants to risk the lives of everyone aboard," he replied bitterly. In fact the more he considered it the cleverer the plan was; he could have kicked himself for not having the idea first. Luckily it didn't look like the Major would go for it. Better play safe even so.

"I don't say it's impossible," he admitted grudgingly. "Everything depends on the weather. We're talking about running down a *sandbank* in a million square miles of empty ocean. An error of half a degree and we won't even see the place. If we hit cloud tomorrow and I can't get a sun fix we're sunk, Major."

"The last report from Guam weather was clear skies and Wake's RDF has better than a thousand mile's range," Munro said. "Ask Stewart."

"In *good conditions*. What if an electrical storm knocks out the reception? Ask him that! Or suppose we lose an engine in the night, any speed reduction and dawn will see us over Truk lagoon slap in the centre of the Mandate!"

"He's right," Slater shook his head decisively. "It's too risky. If the Yellow-bellies caught us over the Mandate they'd have the perfect excuse for forcing us down. We'd be playing straight into their hands." He stubbed out his cigar in the ashtray and stood up. "We'll stick with the original plan."

Munro remained where he was. "If the weather outlook deteriorates I'll consider aborting to Guam, but until then we make for Wake Island."

"Jesus, Pilot, you ain't got the first idea what you're proposing. Truk's a no-go zone, crawling with Japs. The lagoon there's tagged as a major fleet base. The slant-eyes fire on anything that moves!"

"*Is that what happened to Earhart?*"

Everyone stiffened waiting.

Slater's knuckes whitened on the back of the seat rest. "I guess you didn't hear me correct, flyboy," he gritted. "I said we're sticking with the original plan. That means Guam, okay?"

"Wrong, Major, you were summoned here for information only. As ship's captain I decide our course."

"*Ross* is captain still, you're in *temporary* command!" Slater's voice was raw. "Godammit, you've no authority for this, Munro!"

"It's you who have no authority here, Major. Now please leave the bridge, you're impeding the running of the ship."

"The hell I will! Get Manila on that radio, we'll sort this out at the top!"

"Request denied! The ship is on radio silence, there'll be no communication with anywhere till we reach Wake Island." Munro got to his feet, "Mister Thyssen, escort the Major below!"

Kurt pursed his lips with sly satisfaction. Munro was playing right into his hands.

Down in the galley Scott heated up some hot chocolate on the electric ring for the two little Simms girls. It was nearly twelve, Pat O'Byrne was snatching some rest leaving herself and Tad to mind the passengers. Acting nursemaid didn't bother Scott any more though. The guys had been treating her different since the fire. Munro had promised her a spell on the flight deck tomorrow.

She poured the drink into mugs and carried them aft through the lounge and down the draped corridor. Most of the passengers in the rear section of the Clipper were in their bunks already or preparing for bed. As she passed G cabin she glimpsed a coral négligé through the curtains, the Delahaye girl locked in an embrace with her Spanish fiancé. So they had made it up again. There had been some sparring between them earlier. César de Santa Cruz hadn't appreciated his future wife spending all day with Max Munro. She wondered how Max felt about it.

"Here you are now. Careful, mind you don't spill any."

"Gee, great!" The girls were sitting up in their bunks wearing cotton nightdresses, their hair in plaits. Comic books and jig-saw puzzles strewed the blankets.

324

Ruth Simms thanked her wearily, "I'm sorry, they just don't seem to sleep on airplanes."

"Oh they're cute, no bother at all," Scott tugged the older one's plait playfully. "You know I've got a kid brother about your age."

The girl glanced up, a dark moustache round her mouth. "Does he live in Kansas City?"

"No, in San Diego, but he likes chocolate too."

She collected back the mugs and kissed the girls goodnight. Out in the corridor Eddie Wirth was rattling the door of the rear washroom. "Some guy must've died in there or something," he complained. "Twenty minutes I've been waiting to use the john."

Scott tapped on the door, "Are you okay in there?" There was no response from inside. She tried the handle. It was locked. "The purser has a master key, I'll go fetch him," she said, worried. "Maybe it would be better if you used the washroom in the bow, sir."

"Lord save us, now what?" Pat exclaimed crossly when he heard. "Some idjit drunk most like. Let's hope it's nothing worse." Together they returned with the key.

The door was locked no longer. The compartment empty.

Scott wrinkled her brow, perplexed. "Pat, I swear . . . Mr. Wirth was here too . . ."

"Aye, well whoever it was is gone now," Pat snorted looking round inside. "Embarrassed to death by all the knocking I shouldn't wonder. Or maybe he had someone else in with him, I've known that happen before," he added darkly.

Tad had accompanied them. He sniffed at a small scent bottle somebody had left on the washstand. *Eau de Cologne.* Which of the passengers wore that? Nearby was a small metal washer of the kind used all over the ship. He picked it up thoughtfully.

Scott went back to the galley. As she passed the stairs she met Major Slater coming down from the flight deck. His face was thunderous. Without a word he brushed past her towards his cabin.

MIDNIGHT. The flying boat droned on through the darkness. The stars had gone, swallowed up by a spread of cloud. Swathes of rain slewed intermittently across the windshield. Thyssen was in the captain's seat, easing them upwards above a patch of turbulence. Munro cracked open the starboard engineer's hatch and a blast of noise struck him as he stepped inside the wing.

Howling draughts swept down the lighted tunnel that always stank of oil and avgas. Bent double he made his way out past the inboard engine towards the tip of the wing, steadying himself as the plane yawed in the bumpy air. Crouched in the far nacelle he found the Chief manipulating a wrench among a tangle of pipework.

"Trouble?" he yelled above the din.

"Naw," the Indian shook his head, "just slackening off the oil feed to the prop hub a touch." He tinkered a few moments more, then reached out a grease-blackened paw for the interphone on the bulkhead. "*How's the reading now? Fine, okay.*"

He replaced the receiver with a grunt and tossed the wrench back in the tool box. "You went out on a limb tonight, feller."

"You figure that too, huh?"

"Yup, an' I ain't the only one," the Chief searched in his overalls for some cotton waste to wipe his hands. "Rest of the crew reckon the same. You better be sure what you're doing, Max, 'cause otherwise that guy Slater's gonna have your hide."

"Too late to change things now, I'll just have to take whatever comes."

"Yeah," the Chief nodded philosophically, "I guess you will." In the lamplight his Choctaw face had a metallic sheen to it. "Did you stop to think how Ross'll react tomorrow when he finds we're headed for the Marshalls?"

The glass eye of the tuning dial glowed green and a chorus of atmospherics set Davey Klein's ears singing. He turned down the volume and switched to 6210 kcs, scanning the airwaves for contact. At night the wireless operator was the ship's eyes and ears, so Stewart Whitely claimed. Mouth too, he might have added, except Max Munro had ordered the transmitter key locked down.

A stream of high speed morse crackled briefly through the interference and was gone again before he could get a bearing. A military station in the Philippines or a Jap base in the Mandate below? No way of telling the range even.

The stillness of the ether troubled him. Normally the night was alive with ships and vessels calling one another, transmitting weather or position reports, or simply bored operators signalling across the empty void, seeking a human contact. Now suddenly the world had gone silent, as if a deadening hand had fallen over the ocean, blotting out all traffic.

He switched down to the lower marine band. Silence there too. Perhaps the range was too great, or perhaps the carriers had turned back.

From Tokyo to Singapore, from Hongkong to Hawaii the threat of war hung over the Pacific like a pall.

A heavier jounce than usual rattled the lower deck. "Mommy," Ricky called softly across the cabin, "can I come in your bed with you?"

"Ssh, yes, if you're very good and quiet."

Parting the curtains round his mother's bunk, the boy crawled in and burrowed under the blankets beside her. Maria folded her arms round him and held him close. "There, happy now?" she kissed his cheek. "Go to sleep then."

He snuggled up tight against her, secure in the warmth of her love. Worming under the pillow his fingers touched something hard and cold. "What's this?" he whispered.

Maria started. Her hand moved swiftly to push his away. "Not something for boys to play with."

"It's a pistol, isn't it? Why do you sleep with a pistol under your pillow?"

"Ssh, because back in Shanghai there used to be robbers."

"Are there robbers here too on the plane?"

"No, it's just a habit now." Sitting up on an elbow Maris reached down for her vanity case and slipped the little automatic inside.

Ricky lay quiet for a while. Presently he said, "Uncle Sergei has a gun too."

He felt his mother stiffen. "Uncle Sergei, who is he?"

"*You* know. The Russian next door, Prince . . . Prince . . ." He was not in the least awed by titles. Shanghai had been full of impoverished aristocrats, grand-dukes driving taxi-cabs and princesses dancing cabaret, but he found the name hard to pronounce.

"He killed a pirate with his gun, he told me today when we were walking by the market. And when I said about seeing a submarine he *believed* me."

Maria gripped him fiercely, "What else did he say?"

"That . . . that he knew us before . . . in Shanghai," Ricky's voice quavered not understanding as he sensed his mother's anger. "He wants to be good friends."

"*Shut up!*" Maria hissed suddenly, shaking him hard by the shoulders. "Shut up! We're not friends of his, d'you hear? He's trying to trick you. You're not to speak to him again, ever!"

Ricky began to sob.

327

THREE AM. The passenger deck was still. The cardplayers had departed finally to their bunks. Above the steady drum of the engines came only the hissing of the air vents. Down in the galley Tad Gotto was alone on duty. Scott had ended her watch at two. Slipping a small flashlight and screwdriver from the tool drawer into his pocket, he set off up the dimmed corridor towards the tail of the aircraft.

The rear wash-room was empty. He hung an Out of Order sign on the handle, let himself in and locked the bolt. Good. He looked round. The compartment was lined in gold embroidered fabric with panel trimming of lacquered bronze aluminum. There was a standard automatic toilet as well as a urinal and on the opposite wall were double wash basins with mirrors above and lockers for stewards' supplies beneath. Blackout cloth had been taped over the porthole.

He checked both lockers swiftly. Nothing, just the usual stocks of soap, towels and toilet paper. Taking out his screwdriver he turned his attention to the walls. The access panel behind the toilet came away easily, to his disappointment the space behind was empty. The same went for the urinal and the perspex splash-back to the basins.

Suppose he was wrong after all?

Stretching up to the ventilator he unscrewed the metal grills of the cold air and heat inlets, using the torch to peer into the ducts behind. Again nothing. He tried the steward's call button panel and unclipped the ceiling light fitting.

Nothing, not a solitary damn thing.

Suppressing his irritation, he checked round again. The mirrors? No, too large to be moved alone. He ran his hands carefully over the walls but the fabric was intact, nothing had been slipped behind.

That washer though.

He glanced up at the ceiling.

An idea came to him. Packing up his tools, he unlocked the door again and took down the Out of Order sign. A few feet away outside the rear suite a vertical aluminum ladder was clamped to the starboard wall. Glancing round briefly to make sure the corridor was still empty, Tad climbed up and pushed open the hatch above.

The space inside ran the width of the ship. This was the baggage hold where passengers' luggage was stowed during flight together with inflatable life rafts and other emergency equipment. It could also be reached from the upper deck via the crew quarters.

Shutting the hatch after him, Tad snapped on his flash and played the beam over the stacked cases and bags. Eerie shadows flickered against the walls. He shivered, there was no heat up here and the roar of the engines echoed boomingly.

He put on the main light.

Abruptly he stiffened. The hold had not been swept out. In the dust on the floor was the clear impression of a footprint. Not a western shoe – a split-toed sole. A *tabi*.

The enemy had been here.

Tad stared at it for a long moment, wondering what to do. Then switching off the light, he returned to the passenger deck.

★　　★　　★

Around the world in Cheltenham, Maryland at the US Navy's Intercept Station M, a special team of qualified *katakana* operators were monitoring Tokyo news and weather broadcasts. Shortly before dawn a routine meteorological report came through on 12,275 kilocycles. With the recording spools spinning an Assistant Warrant Officer began copying the Japanese telegraphic code. One section rang a warning bell in his memory: *Higashi no kaze ame*.

Quicky he referred to his watch supervisor's classified orders. The words checked.

Without delay he punched the intercept onto a teletype tape and dialled the direct landline connection with the Navy Department Building in Washington that went through to OP–20–G.

Satisfied, he entered the message in his log sheet and telephoned his supervisor to report.

XXV

SUNDAY DECEMBER 7TH HONGKONG. High point of every
Sunday morning in the Crown Colony was Church Parade at St.
John's Cathedral, Victoria. The congregation of British expatriates
and their families, swelled by officers from the garrison, had just
launched into the hymn '*Oh God our help in ages past*'. The GOC was
present with many of his staff and unmarried girls darted appraising
glances over their hymn books at the smartly turned out young
subalterns.

As the second verse began, a major in the Royal Scots hastened up
the centre aisle and whispered urgently to General Maltby in the front
pew. A ripple of consternation went round the cathedral as the
General was seen to leave his place and stride out followed by his
senior officers. Before the service had ended rumours were flying – the
Japanese were massing on the border, the Defence Council was in
session at Government House.

An hour later the rumble of trucks again filled the streets. Orders
had gone out from Fortress HQ for all troops of the garrison to take up
forward battle positions.

The police moved in on the Mission House at midday. Manoeuv-
ring through the narrow streets of the Chinese quarter, trucks dis-
gorged squads of men to positions at every intersection. Boots rang on
the cobblestones as barbed wire barricades were dragged across
roadways, sealing off all adjacent blocks. "*Auso! Auso!*" constables
hammered on tenement doors flushing out the inhabitants. Teams of
Special Branch officers set to work, checking identities, holding
suspects for interrogation.

By one o'clock the whole quarter was humming like a hive. Angry
crowds jostled impatiently at the barriers, choking traffic, screeching
raucous abuse at the khaki-uniformed Cantonese. "*Ai-yah*, motherless turds, get out the way!" Inspector Playfair's driver hawked and
spat out the car window as he forced a passage honking the horn.

"*Dew neh loh moh*, get out yourself!" an old woman with a basket of

330

dried fish spat back shrilly. "All gods fornicate police pigs stopping innocent people!"

"In your ear, old mother!" the driver cursed her. They reached the barrier and a sergeant waved them through. Beyond the cordon were more police and the riot squad with their wicker shields and long batons, waiting in case of trouble. A dozen quaking coolies were being paraded before a hooded figure in a truck. Playfair saw him nod once and a man was dragged off screaming. Informers – he didn't like it but how else were they to deal with these peasants?

On the corner of a waste lot stood a modern two storey brick building, its walls blackened by smoke. A fire crew were packing up their tender outside. "Stop here," he told the driver.

The interior of the Mission House was a gutted mess of burnt wood and ash, sodden with water from the fire hoses. The upper floor had collapsed but the main roof had held somehow though the beams were half charred. A constable led him through to a basement storeroom beneath the ruined stairs where they had found the body.

The stench of blood was enough to make a man vomit.

Even Playfair felt his throat tighten, and he had witnessed some messy things in his time.

The place was splattered like a slaughterhouse. Walls, floor, ceiling even. Sprawled in a dark pool in the middle of the room, wrists bound at the back with wire, was the body of Lieutenant Harris.

Daubed on the wall above was a crude ideogram:

Yon – the *Shi-sign* – Death.

*   *   *

The Clipper was flying blind.

The crew stared from the windows till their eyes ached. Beyond the glass lay a world of nothingness, an opaque screen without beginning or end. Swirls of moist grey-white vapour pressed about the plane, dampening out the sound of the engines, smothering any glimpse of ocean or sky.

It had been this way since dawn.

The aircraft's nose was dipping. Scott's grip tightened on the control yoke in sudden alarm. Were they heading for the water? Exerting self control, she forced her gaze back to the cockpit instrument panel. With visibility zero and no horizon to judge by, the senses could play strange tricks. "*Watch your dials, only your dials. Don't trust*

331

what your head tells you." They had dinned that into her on the blind flying course and Munro had repeated it when he surrendered the seat to her, "Keep your eyes on the gyro horizon, the ASI and Rate of Climb. Trust 'em, they'll tell you the truth!"

Beads of moisture trickled down the windshield. The cabin lights were switched on, anxiously she studied the green lit dials. The indicator plane of the artificial horizon was precisely centred, vertical speed showed zero. Straight and level flight. Another false alarm, she thought rubbing her eyes. The tiredness didn't help. With Ross sick they were short-handed, no one had gotten more than four hours sleep since New Guinea. Yes, but you're on the flight deck now, girl, she reminded herself, and that's all that matters.

She glanced at the altimeter, eight thousand one hundred. A tight frown crossed her brow. The extra hundred annoyed her, it was sloppy flying. With her right hand she stroked the stabilizer wheel forward a trifle. Reaching out with her left, she pulled the throttles back to match. At once the dull beat of the engines quickened slightly and the needle of the vertical speed indicator dipped. Tony Shapiro looked across at her from the left hand seat and smiled briefly without comment. This was her watch.

She waited while the altimeter slowly unwound and eased the controls again to level off at exactly eight thousand feet. Lifting her eyes to the windshield a moment she suppressed a sigh. Still the same blank cloud.

How much longer could they go on this way?

At first, when darkness began to give way to dawn, five hours ago now, they had sought to break through the cloud tops. Munro had taken the flying boat up to almost fifteen thousand feet before worsening turbulence had forced him back down to calmer altitudes again. And still no glimpse of the sun.

They needed the sun to locate Wake.

Over by the chart table behind, Kurt Thyssen sneaked a sideways look at Scott's neat blond head and swore to himself. Stuck-up little bitch, she hadn't glanced in his direction once, hadn't noticed him even. Hell, what was she doing up here anyway? Ross was right, women didn't belong on the flight deck.

"For Godsakes," he threw his pencil down exasperated, "how's a guy supposed to navigate when he can't see a damn thing? I'm plotting a line here that's no better than guesswork. We could be anywhere within two hundred miles either side." He glared towards the rear of the cabin where Munro sat at the skipper's desk writing up the log, "This idiotic plan of yours has gone far enough!"

Munro came forward. "Let's have a look at the chart."

"Here, see," Kurt showed him, "this is our track plotted through the night when I had star angles to work on. By six am, just before the cloud closed in, we were a hundred and fifty miles south east of Truk still. That last plot showed increased drift of four degrees to starboard. Continuing the line by dead reckoning and allowing for the same degree of drift, puts us here," he made a small cross on the chart, "on the edge of the Marshalls, seven hundred miles approximately south east of Guam."

Munro took up a pair of dividers and coolly measured the distances. It was as Kurt had said. "So what's bugging you then? You worried the drift angle could've changed?"

"Christsakes! An error factor like that, do I have to spell out what it means? It's almost five hours since the last star fix. The wind could've shifted round and be blowing right on our nose!"

"You've had your drift sights to work on and Stewart's been taking bearings on the Guam beacon, hasn't he?"

"That's bullshit, Max, you know darn well radio isn't accurate at range. And with no cross bearing we could be anywhere along the beam line." Kurt raised his voice deliberately for the rest of the cabin to hear, "Right now we could be heading off into the Marshalls!"

"So what are you suggesting, Kurt?"

"It's obvious, isn't it? Abandon this crazy idea. Turn about and make for Guam while we can still pick up the beam signal. You said yourself last night we wouldn't have no other choice if we hit cloud in the morning."

The cabin had gone quiet. The rest of the crew were hanging on every word.

"Chief, what's our fuel situation?" Munro asked.

The Indian consulted his gauges. He was still in overalls. He had been on duty all night without a break and it didn't bother him. "Twenty-one hundred gallons," he said indifferently. "Averaging one eighty-seven point five gallons per hour, one eight-nine this last sixty minutes."

So even allowing for a possible deterioration there was still fuel left for another ten hours flying. And the most likely estimate put Wake a thousand miles east, six to seven hours flight time at least – if the figures were right.

He turned to Whitely, "Stewart, how much longer d'you think we'll be able to go on picking up the Guam beacon?"

"Well," Whitely hesitated, chewing his lip, "it's getting very faint already . . . if reception holds as present, I guess maybe one more hour."

333

"And the beacon on Wake has a range of eight hundred miles, correct?"

"In good conditions, yes, but six or seven is more likely and even that's pushing it."

"You're going out to the limit, Max, and it's too risky, I tell you," Kurt said urgently.

Munro glanced towards the bulkhead clock. The hands read ten fifty-five. "We'll hang on one more hour. I'll review the situation again at midday. Till then we continue as planned."

The discussion was closed. Kurt clenched his lips furious.

"Gee," Shapiro whispered to Scott, "old Max sounds pretty darn confident, sure hope he knows what he's doing."

Behind them at the radio desk, Stewart Whitely was listening into his earphones again, his attention suddenly concentrated. A signal was coming through on the 96 metre band. High speed morse – QRK? QRK? QRK? *Do you read me? Do you read me?* – KHAZA KHAZA – QRK? QRK? – KHAZA.

The Clipper's call sign.

In his mind Ross was back at the atoll.

Hunched beneath the blankets in his bunk in the crew quarters aft, he lay drifting between sleep and wakefulness.

. . . full left rudder, yoke forward, banking round in a tight turn to starboard, the wing dipping as they came in for a pass at low level. Throttling back over the water . . . lower still . . . lower. Yes, there it was again, clear against the sandy bottom of the lagoon, the outline of an airplane!

"Twin engines, it's the Lockheed, Ross, the Electra! It's Earhart's ship, we've found them, by Christ!"

Amelia, Amelia! Staring down at the wreck, trembling with relief so much he could hardly manage the controls. Amelia, is it really you?

But then the fear hitting him again. Suppose it was a trap? Suppose the Japs were here already?

Slater still gabbling away excitedly, leaning out the starboard window with the binoculars, "Tail's bust off but the cabin's still above the waterline and the nose look's like it's intact, no obvious damage anyway. The main hatch may be open, I can't tell from this height."

"I'll take us round again. Keep your eyes peeled for Japs."

"Screw the Japs, forget about them, blast you! It's Earhart and Noonan we've come to find."

Still no sign of life from the downed plane as they made their third pass over the lagoon, full flaps and engines throttled back again, almost on stalling speed.

"Where in hell have they gotten to?" Slater pulling his head back in from the window. "One of them must've made it ashore, we picked up their SOS. So why did they cease transmission? The radio wouldn't have given out already, would it?"

"How should I know? Maybe the batteries got wet in the crash or something. Listen, Major, we're running low on gas ourselves."

"Shut up. Circle round, I want to take a look at the rest of the place. Maybe they're holed up somewhere hurt."

Gulls and gooney birds fluttering up as their shadow skimmed the scrub. "Godammit, Major, there's no one there, I tell you, the place is empty! We're too late, the Japs beat us to it!"

And then Slater's sudden cry, "Look over there, what's that? Jesus, I can see smoke! It's a native village, they're signalling to us!"

Outriggers drawn up on the foreshore. Palm huts and brown figures running along the sand, waving their arms at the great silver bird. But no white faces. As Christ is my witness, no white faces!

"Ross, you've got to set us down!"

"It's not possible, for God's sake, there isn't anywhere! You saw what happened to the other plane!"

"Bullshit, you can land this thing on a pin, if you have to! Try that beach again, we'll make it!"

But the fear was all round him now, suffocating him, squeezing out the courage like a strangling snake. The hands clamped to the yoke weren't his any more. "It's no good, it's no good! We're too late! I'm taking us up . . ."

He awoke, tears streaming down his face.

KHAZA KHAZA QRK? QRK? QRK? *Do you read me? Do you read me?* KMGB.

"It's Guam's call sign, Max, they're very insistent. You want me to acknowledge or not?"

Munro thought for a moment. Kelly was supposed to have warned all stations they'd be observing radio silence. This could be a fake, a ploy by the enemy to trick them into revealing their position. It might also be genuine – and vital.

He decided to take the risk. "Okay, acknowledge but keep it brief as you can."

Stewart's fingers tapped a staccato rhythm on the bakelite key – KHAZA KHAZA – *Reading you, go ahead* – The response was immediate. A sharp blast of high speed morse rattling in the earphones like automatic fire. Jotting down the letters on his pad, he sent a single curt *Received* and reached for the company code book.

He passed the decode up to Munro, "What now, Max?"

Munro read the signal and shrugged, "Take it down to him, I guess."

The message was in cipher. It was addressed to Major Slater.

Down on the main deck the passengers whiled away the journey reading books and magazines, playing cards and gossiping. As yet there had been no official announcement of the switch in destination, but a number of theories were being bandied about the lounge. Mr. Wirth was just telling the Gordon Smythes how he knew for definite they were bound for American Samoa when Felicity came bouncing in from the bow cabin. "Guess what?" she blurted, "Japan's declared war and we're heading back to Manila!"

There was consternation. "Oh my God, I knew it," her mother cried shrilly, "we're going to be trapped out here!"

"Be quiet, Cynthia," her husband barked. "Felicity, where the devil did you hear this?"

"Those two oilmen were telling me about it. There was shooting yesterday in New Guinea. Golly, Daddy, if we're stuck in Manila can I become a nurse with the Americans?"

"No you can't, you stupid girl!" her father snapped. "I say, Sir Ambrose," he called as the diplomat went by, "what d'you make of this rumour about the Japs declaring war?"

"I think that is exactly what it is, a rumour," Sir Ambrose replied calmly and carried on towards the bar.

Two cabins away Ruth Simms had her knitting out. The little girls and Ricky, bored by the endless cloud, were wandering the promenade passage restlessly. "At least it's smooth now," Ruth sighed thankfully to Maria Bianchi. "I'm hopeless in turbulence."

"Yes, me too," Maria agreed. She sounded preoccupied. Ruth tried another topic.

"I was speaking to that Prince Cherkassy again after breakfast. He's such a charming man. You know I believe you have an admirer there," she said archly. "He's talking of spending Christmas in Honolulu." She stopped suddenly, "Heaven's, Maria, what's the matter? Did I say something?"

Maria was staring at her with a look of dismay.

Slater locked the door of the rear men's washroom and took a copy of

The Adventures of Huckleberry Finn from his pocket. Switching on the shaving light he studied the radio message hand-printed in red ink on a yellow form. Four lines of regularly spaced groups of five letters, eight groups to a line.

His key was the following day's date. December 8. He wrote it beneath the signal. Adding 8 to the year – 41, gave him the page number to be used for decoding.

The first cipher letter was a K. Opening the book at page 49 he ran his finger along the letters till he came to K. It was the seventh letter of the second line. In the code therefore it stood for the seventh letter of the alphabet which was G. He wrote that down. The next code letter was F. In the book F was the sixteenth letter after the K, discounting every twelfth character for December, the twelfth month. That transcribed as P.

It was a simple variant on the one-time pad. Cumbersome but completely secure.

The third letter came out as M. He cursed. This was gibberish. Surely he had the key right? An idea struck him. He turned back a page and started over. This time the first transposition gave him a W. It was followed by an A and then an R. WAR. This was more promising. The signal had originated in Washington on the other side of the International Date Line. Over there it was still December 6th.

WAR JAPAN IMMINENT HOSTILITIES EXPECTED 48 HOURS X ENEMY FORCES BELIEVED PREPARING STRIKE WITHOUT WARNING ALL REPEAT ALL US PACIFIC POSSESSIONS YOUR ROUTE X POLITICAL SITUATION DICTATES THEY FIRE FIRST SHOT X STEP ON IT X KIM

He had just finished when someone rapped at the door outside. "Everythin' okay in there, sir?"

"Yeah, yeah, wait a minute, goddam you!" Blasted nosy steward. He read the complete message through quickly, committing it to memory. Then he burned the signal in the washbasin, flushing away the ash with the taps, and put the book back in his pocket.

Tad Gotto was waiting outside as he unlocked the door. "What the hell's your game, boy? Can't a guy use the john in peace, for Christsakes?"

"Sorry sir, I . . . I thought somebody press the call button. Sorry!" Tad bolted off.

"Now keep steady while I put in the hairpin. There!" Aft in G cabin, Georgiana held up her powder compact for Yu-Ling to see herself in the mirror, "Doesn't that look cute?"

"Yes, yes, now I see," the Chinese girl clapped a hand to her mouth as she burst into a fit of giggles. Her sleek black hair was caught up behind in a chic French knot. "*Oh ko*, now I am western-style lady, no?"

"You surely are," Georgiana was laughing too. "Right, next some colour." Rummaging in a crocodile skin vanity case, she produced a lipstick and deftly applied a dash of scarlet to the girl's mouth. "Press your lips together to smooth it over – like so," she demonstrated.

"Say, pretty smart, I like that!" The curtains parted and Bob Cashin entered from the corridor with César. Yu-Ling blushed and hid her face. "Aw c'mon, don't be shy now," he kidded her.

Georgiana leaned back in her seat and tucked her slim legs up under her. "So, Bob, what's the news? Max Munro still in charge up aloft?" Her tone was casual. César bristled.

"Major Slater doesn't seem too happy about it, I heard him sounding off on the subject at breakfast."

"That's plain dumb. Max is the best darn pilot flying."

The Simms children ran squealing past in the passage. "Darling," Georgiana stretched out a languid arm to César, "be an angel and fetch me my cigarettes. I must have left them in the lounge somewhere."

His dark eyes smouldered. "For you anything, *querida mia*."

Yu-Ling watched from beneath her lashes. *Ai-yah*, extraordinary the way *quai loh* took orders from their women so. If only she could do that with Minister Soong.

The journalist squatted down beside her on the seat in his rumpled suit. "Miss Chen, how's your uncle, the Professor, this morning? I hope the flight isn't proving too much for him."

A lump rose in Yu-Ling's throat. She shook her head, "He is sick long time now."

"Oh really, I'm sorry to hear that," he sounded concerned. Then a beady look came into his face, "What is it that's wrong with him exactly?"

"*Bob!*" Georgiana's voice cut in sharply. "That'll do, leave her be."

MIDDAY. The crew clung onto their stomachs as another jarring air pocket rattled the flight deck. Scott's watch was ended. Munro had taken over the yoke again, climbing relentlessly to fourteen thousand. The turbulence was vicious, invisible fists buffeting the aircraft, shaking and bouncing the wings as they flew through the cumulus tops. But the overcast was thinning, there were blue patches at last above the cloud. Another five hundred feet and like a whale emerging from the sea the Clipper broke through into clear air, skimming along between towering mountains of cu-nim with the sun showing through a thin haze.

Everyone sat up relieved and Davey Klein began to whistle '*We'll meet again*'.

"This is the best I can do, Kurt. You'd better get aft with your sextant while I try and hold her steady. Stewart, any luck with that radio?"

"Sorry, Skipper, still too much static."

"Don't call him that!" Thyssen snapped. "Ross is Skipper still."

"Balls, you're just jealous!"

"Listen, smart-ass, one more crack . . ."

"Knock it off!" Munro ordered sharply. "Kurt, get going, we haven't all day to hang around!"

Thyssen departed sulkily. Inside ten minutes he was back. "Okay, I got enough for a position line. Take us down again, I'll need to shoot another drift sight."

"Roger, hold onto your seats everyone."

The nose dipped and the cabin darkened as they sank down into the cloud. Rain beat on the windshield. Munro watched his instruments. The turbulence didn't bother him, this was nothing compared to the storm front over the South China Sea. At eight thousand feet the buffeting ceased and at three thousand they dropped through the base and saw grey waves below.

Kurt was still working his calculations. Chris Fry was sent aft into the auxiliary hold with the drift sight. "And try not to disturb Ross," Munro told him.

"Aye aye, Max."

They flew on smoothly just beneath the lowering cloud base while the flask was dropped. The ocean looked chill and uninviting without a sign of life anywhere, not even so much as a wandering gooney bird. Which was how he wanted it. This was still the Mandate. The last thing they needed was to be spotted by a Jap ship.

Chris returned to report seven degrees of starboard drift. That translated into a twelve to fifteen knot wind blowing on the port quarter which wasn't such good news. It meant they were being edged southwards off their chosen track and would have to crab into the wind to reach Wake. "How did the Skipper seem?"

But Chris shook his head, "Couldn't tell, he wasn't in his bunk. Guess he must've gone to the john."

"Funny, he wasn't there a minute ago," said Davey Klein.

So Ross was awake. Suppose he took it into his head to assume

339

command again? Maybe they ought to get Latouche up to see him?

Chuck Driscoll interrupted his thoughts from the engineer's station, "Max, okay to transfer fuel up from the reserve tanks?"

"Sure, Chuck, go ahead."

"Hey!" There was a cry from Shapiro in the co-pilot's seat. "Light water coming up. Looks like it could be breakers on a reef!"

Every head swung to stare out the windshield. Kurt snatched the binoculars from the rack. "Jesus Christ!" He flung them down again and scanned the chart for an instant. "You stupid jerk," he rounded on Munro, teeth bared, "I warned you this would happen. You know what that is down there? Bikini atoll. *You've landed us over the goddam Marshalls!*"

At that moment an engine began to cough.

"Son of a bitch, now what?" the Chief emerged from the starboard engine hatch mouthing profanities. "Must be an airlock somewhere in the plumbing. Gimme full rich on Two!" he instructed. Chuck was already complying, turning up the mixture control to the carburettor. The noise quietened and everyone relaxed.

A series of backfires shook a motor on the other wing.

"*Full rich again! Booster pump!*"

The engine continued popping and spluttering.

"Shit, there's another one going!" Shapiro swore.

"*Emergency rich on all!*"

"*All Emergency, aye, aye, Chief!*"

Number Two was coughing and gasping again like a man dying on his feet. Munro could feel the power draining away as he struggled to maintain height.

"Switch back to main wing tanks!" The Chief was watching the gauges over Chuck's shoulder, flow meters and rev counters were flickering insanely.

Clack, clack, Chuck's hands leaped to the switches.

All four engines were stuttering now. Bereft of power the Clipper was staggering in the air, the altimeter swinging back. "Christsakes, Chief, we don't have the height for this!"

A violent shuddering seemed to seize the whole airframe. The port wing made a sudden lurch as the outer prop blades slowed.

"We're losing One! We're losing Two!"

The engines cut out simultaneously.

"*Jesus Christ!*"

The silence was deafening. Paralysed with shock they stared at the heaving sea below, willing the plane to stay aloft. The only sounds the whistle of the slipstream against the windows.

340

Then everybody was acting at once.

"*Stand by for emergency ditching*! Stewart, get ready to send out an SOS, our position is Bikini atoll, five hundred miles south-west of Wake!" Munro held the aircraft steady, letting the nose drop a little to maintain airspeed for flight. A touch of right rudder pedal to line them up with the distant rim of surf. It looked impossibly far off, but it was their only hope. If he could stretch out the glide somehow and still retain enough control to bring them down somewhere within the reef. If . . . if . . .

"Chris, Davey, get below and help the stewards with the passengers!"

"Aye aye, skipper!"

"*Hold it*!" The Chief yelled.

Down on the lower deck the passengers' initial frozen horror as the sound of the engines died was broken by screams of panic. "Stay calm, everyone! Put on your life-vests!" Scott shouted at the people near her in the lounge. Mercifully lunch had been postponed thanks to the turbulence. "Back to your seats, strap yourselves in!"

Feet thudded overhead. The Chief flung himself down the stairs in his overalls, colliding with Major Slater and sending him flying. Without a pause he plunged forward into C cabin and began tearing aside the carpeting. Before the dismayed gaze of the passengers he uncovered a panel in the floor and jerked it open.

"Here, grab this!" he told a man roughly, thrusting a flash at him. Pulling out a wrench he set to work uncoupling the transfer valves.

The flying boat continued its inexorable swishing descent. Snatching a glance from the portholes Scott judged they had five minutes at the outside. All around people were scrabbling frantically beneath their seats for life-vests. Sir Ambrose Hope was removing his coat as calmly as if he were in his London club. "Don't worry about me, my dear, go and take care of the children," he admonished her gently when she tried to help.

Slater stumbled towards her making for the stairs. "Get back to your seat, Major." She barred his path. "There's nothing you can do!"

Her jerked her roughly out the way. "Take a look out the window, sister," he spat. "That's a Jap island down there!"

Fifteen hundred feet. They were sinking like a lead brick. But the atoll was clearer now, a fringe of scrub covered sand battered by surf with a wide lagoon beyond. Almost certainly there would be coral under the surface of the water, he would just have to take the risk.

And Japs? Suppose there was a military post?

He daren't wait any longer to send out the SOS. "Stewart . . ."

The Chief's voice boomed up from below, "Okay, start the pumps, then give her the gun!"

"Roger, booster pumps Emergency Full!" Chuck was ready.

Munro's hands were slippery with sweat. "Tony, you'll have to pull the switches, I daren't let her stall."

"Will do, Skipper."

"Ignition on! Starting order Two, Three, One, Four!"

"Two, Three, One, Four, aye aye!"

"Throttles 700! Start and boost!"

A convulsive backfire from the port inner engine followed by a ragged coughing as if it were tearing itself apart. Munro's arms tensed as he juggled the controls. The altimeter was teetering on eleven hundred feet. More bangings from the starboard wing.

The vibration slackened as first one then a second engine caught. Two engines! Hope surged back through them all. On two engines they could stay airborne. Two engines would carry them to Wake.

All four engines restarted. The blockage, whatever it was, had worked through.

Speed began picking up. Munro pulled back on the stick, the nose lifted and they soared effortlessly over the edge of the reef. For the first time since the start of the crisis he removed a hand from the yoke and wiped it on his trousers.

"Jeez," Davey Klein breathed, "I gotta take a piss again."

Shapiro lit a cigarette and inhaled with a deep sigh of satisfaction. "Funny how you never notice the noise – till it quits on you."

"Hey, I think I got the Wake beam!" Stewart jumped up from the radio desk to twist the ceiling dial of the rotatable loop antenna, "Yep, there it is, 270 degrees."

There was a sudden shout from the hold. Davey came bursting back in, "Someone find the doc, quick! It's the Skipper, he's hurt!"

XXVI

Ross came to in pain.

Shards of fire gnawed at the inside of his skull and a weight on his chest tortured breathing. Moaning, he opened his eyes. The world spun giddily and a bright light seared his retina. Distorted faces seemed to be bending over him. White? Yellow? He could not tell. Voices boomed in his ears like monstrous echoes in a cave, their words incomprehensible.

What had happened to him?

Into his mind came a picture of an atoll. A reef, sand, palm trees and . . .

He could remember looking down and seeing the plane. *Her plane.* Twisted and broken in the waters of the lagoon. Or had that been somewhere else? Another island far away? He struggled to recall, the images blurred and confused. *Amelia, was it your plane? Did we find you after all?*

"Forget it, you hear? There was no plane, we never saw anything!"

"But why, Major? I don't understand, why don't we go back?"

"There's nothing to go back for. She's dead, they're both dead. It never happened!"

But there was a plane! I saw it! Amelia, I betrayed you!

Mili. Mili. Darkness washing over him again. A shadow in black. Terror!

More faces loomed above him. A pain in his arm. Pain, pain.

"Alors, he is quiet now," Latouche withdrew the needle from Ross's arm and swabbed the place with surgical spirit.

Munro studied the bandaged figure lying strapped down in the bunk. "How bad is he, Doctor?"

The Frenchman placed the syringe in a small enamel bowl from the ship's medicine chest. He shook his head, "Without an X-ray impossible to say. I have done what I can, but there may be concussion, a fracture of the cranium . . ."

343

"There's a hospital on Wake. We can be there in less than two hours."

The Doctor began taking Ross's pulse. Slater watched him, his hands clenching and unclenching irritably. "What the hell was he doing back there anyway!"

Munro had no answer. They were all asking themselves the same question. Davey Klein had found Ross slumped among the baggage of the after hold, bleeding from a wound to the head. He must have become disoriented, blundered through the wrong hatch and fallen in the darkness.

"What was that about Mili? Sounded like he might've been trying to tell us something."

Slater's expression closed like a trap. "Guess he was delirious," he said quickly. "Right, Doc?"

Munro saw an indecipherable glance pass between them. They were hiding something. What?

Slater spoke again, "Someone should stay with him. I'll see if I can get the priest up."

Da-dit . . . da-dit . . . da-dit Shapiro was listening to the Wake RDF range. Stewart Whitely had switched the radio through to the pilots' earphones for the run down to the island. *Da-dit . . . da-dit* the N signal was coming in with a touch of background static interspersed with the identification code ZQZ. *Da-dit . . . da-dit . . . dit-da . . . dit-da* Equal signals AN . . . AN. Then the continuous note of the on course signal R-R-R-R-R-R . . .

He glanced out the window. The Clipper was on automatic, flying at five thousand feet in calm air. The overcast was breaking up at last, there was sun showing between the clouds, glinting warmly off blue seas below. Out on the wings the engines were running sweet and smooth now, no repetition of the trouble earlier, thank God. Even so the Chief and Chuck were watching the gauges like hawks.

R-R-R-R-R-R-R . . . the signal was growing stronger. The island ought to be in sight soon. Shapiro felt relieved. Everything would be okay once they reached Wake.

Balancing a tray, Tad Gotto made his way along the promenade passage. Reverend Jordan was sitting alone in an after cabin. "Father?" No response, the priest was asleep, eyes closed, head resting on the back of the seat.

344

"Father, please I gotta speak with you," Tad's whisper was urgent.

Jordan woke with a start. "What is it? What do you want?" he gasped agitated.

"*Ssh*," Tad beseeched him. "Father, I want you to see something." From his pocket he brought out the gilt button with the chrysanthemum flower.

"Where did you get this?"

"You know what it is?"

The priest gulped. Sweat beaded his forehead. "*Kempe-tai*, Japanese Secret Police, where . . . how . . .?"

"Four days ago in Hongkong. It was left near the plane at Kai Tak. Father, I haven't told you everything . . ."

There was a footfall behind. Gotto snatched his hand back hastily. Major Slater stood in the cabin doorway glowering. "What gives?" he said.

"Nothing, sir, just taking Reverend Father's glass, sir," Gotto beamed frantically. "Can I bring you anything, sir?"

"Yeah, some matches, damn you."

"Matches, yessir, comin' up right away," Tad hurried out.

Slater watched him go, chewing the stub of his cigar, then swung back to Jordan. "That gook gives me the creeps. We should've ditched the punk in Manila. You stay clear of him, you hear, Reverend? I don't trust him."

Munro stepped through the after hatch in the crew quarters into the rear baggage hold beyond and closed it behind him. The lights were burning and Chief Crow was squatting by the bulkhead his tools spread out on the floor.

"Did you catch any of that?"

The Indian shook his head, "Nope, too much noise in here. How bad is he?"

"Bad enough, fractured skull by the looks of it. The doc's given him another shot."

"Best thing for him, I guess."

"He also came to at one point, started muttering – about Mili."

The Chief's flat black eyes widened fractionally which was as far as he ever went in showing surprise. Methodically he continued unthreading the filter from a valve projecting from the deck and removed a metal strainer.

"He used the word '*betrayed*' – who or what wasn't clear."

345

The Chief blew through the valve strainer and replaced it. "Ain't hard to figure out," he grunted.

Munro sat down on a rolled-up rubber life raft. Passengers' luggage was piled all around, suitcases and hatboxes stuck with exotic labels – *Shanghai* – *Buenos Aires* – *P & O*. In a corner stood an expensive set of golf clubs, Georgiana's presumably.

"That atoll we almost landed on, Ross must've woke up and seen it out the window. Probably looked like Mili to him. No wonder he lost his bearings and stumbled in here."

"You reckon so, huh?" the Chief scratched his chin.

"Sure. Why what's the matter, you found something?"

"No, leastways nothing wrong exactly," the Chief was reassembling the valve on the floor as he spoke.

"Christsakes, don't play games with me, Chief. What's on your mind?"

The engineer tapped a pipe on the bulkhead with his thumbnail. "This here's the main rising feed from the sponson tanks. It leads up from the transfer unit beneath the lower deck."

"Is this where the trouble started?"

The Chief shrugged, "You saw me check the valve out, it's clean as a whistle. But I was thinking," he squinted up at Munro, "it wouldn't need much of a mechanic to shut off the tap an' disconnect the lead above. Only take a few seconds for the pump to suck in enough air to jam things up good."

"Wouldn't the pressure drop show on the gauges?"

"Not so long as he re-connects again right away. A flutter on the needle, nothing more."

Munro stared at the valve, a sudden sick taste in his mouth, "And there's no access to his hold except via the flight deck or with a steward's pass-key from below."

Three forty-one pm Wake came in sight.

Eons ago a submarine volcano erupting up from the Pacific floor had thrust its cone above the waters. In the millennia that followed, the remorseless action of wind and waves ground down the land leaving only a horseshoe-shaped atoll of three flat sandy islets round a shallow lagoon ringed by emerald reefs. A minuscule dot in the ocean four miles long by a mile wide, whose highest point was a bare twenty-one feet above sea level.

The atoll had been sighted first by Spanish explorers in 1586, finding no water they sailed away in disgust. Two centuries later an

346

English sea captain, Samuel Wake, fixed its position and bestowed his name upon the main islet. Another century passed before the atoll was formally claimed – by the United States of America in 1898 at the outbreak of the Spanish war.

The new owners displayed little interest in their possession however and Wake remained untouched, as it had for 350 years, until 1935 when Pan American Airways were surveying the Pacific for refuelling points on their new air route to the Far East. Wake with its protected lagoon was ideally situated between Midway and Guam. In May of that year a construction ship hove to off shore and work began on a flying boat base.

Civilisation had come to Wake Island at last.

For visitors the atoll became a pleasant break on their journey. There was a comfortable forty-five room hotel staffed by Chamorro boys from Guam, perfect empty beaches, swimming in the clear lagoon, fishing expeditions off the reefs, the tranquil atmosphere of a tropic paradise. Only two flights a week passed through, one east-bound, one west. Pan American had Wake to themselves.

Then in 1941 came the decision to garrison the island.

Passengers gazed excitedly from their windows as the Clipper banked low over the sea, lining up for the approach. Munro held the yoke steady, letting her down gradually. The shallow lagoon was full of jagged coral heads with only a narrow channel blasted clear for landing. Among the trees he could pick out clearly the Pan Am Inn on Peale, the northern islet, and the Marine Corps airstrip and contractors' camp on Wake, the largest.

"All clear to come in, Skipper," Stewart Whitely was talking to ground control on the R/T. "Wind five knots south west. Water depth in the lagoon is nine feet."

A myriad of terns rose screeching from the bush as the flying boat's shadow brushed overhead. Gun emplacements were visible now and sandbagged bunkers defending the shoreline. Out on the airstrip sunlight flashed off polished metal. "Holy smoke," came Davey Klein's voice, "I can see pursuit planes down there! When did they blow in?"

"*Flaps forty!*"

"*Flaps down forty, aye aye. Speed is one-zero-five.*"

"*Give me full low pitch!*"

Figures on the sand were waving greetings. Munro had the channel dead ahead now. There was the long white jetty with the wind sock swaying and the launch circling ready. He eased the yoke and throttles back a fraction, feeling the cushioning effect of the air squeezed between water and wing as they sank lower. The pale green surface of the lagoon rose to meet them, crystal clear. A swishing sound like a hand stroking the hull, a curtain of spray and the Clipper's keel settled smoothly on the water.

They had made it.

Dazzling sunlight dappled the cabins glinting off the green water. As the hatches were unlatched warm tropic air spilled into the plane bringing a smell of the sea and the shrill cries of terns. Splashing off the launch, laughing, bare-chested, brown-skinned Chamorro boys warped the Clipper alongside the jetty and made her fast.

Eager to be ashore the passengers gathered up their belongings and crowded towards the gangway. Waiting on the dock to greet them was a cheerfully informal crowd in shorts and bathing trunks. Everyone was caught up at once in holiday mood. As Hollington Soong appeared a tall thin American in Navy uniform stepped forward and snapped a salute, "Minister Soong? Commander Cunningham, Officer-in-Charge. Welcome to Wake Island, your Excellency."

The Minister looked up at the US flag rippling gently in the breeze above them. "Thank you, Commander," he beamed sweatily. "You have had no trouble here, yes? None at all? Excellent, excellent, that is very good."

WELCOME TO WAKE ISLAND PACIFIC OCEAN, Yu-Ling read on the sign at the head of the jetty, MIDWAY 1185 MILES GUAM 1508 MILES. *Ai-yah*. Truly this place was a speck in the midst of nowhere.

Brilliant coloured fish darted in the translucent lagoon. Overhead sea birds wheeled in the hot sun, their cries mingling with the murmur of surf on the reefs. Much of the atoll seemed to be covered with low scrubby trees and bush. Shading her eyes from the glare, she helped her uncle up a crushed coral path bordered with pretty shells to the single-storey hotel, two low wings either side of a central lobby. On the lawn outside squatted more birds, fat fluffy albatross chicks, comically unafraid.

Inside, the hotel was simple but comfortable with easy chairs, a games room and welcoming chilled drinks. Everything was relaxed and friendly in a way she much preferred to the grandeur of Manila. Their bedrooms were spotlessly clean, very western-style modern.

There were fans to cool the air and sun shades over the windows. "*Aiee*," the Professor sighed sinking onto his soft bed, "I am weary unto death by all gods."

"Rest now, Honourable Uncle," Yu-Ling helped him to lie down and settled the pillows comfortably, "and I will make *cha* for you, *heya*?" She unpacked their teapot and rang the bell for hot water.

He held the casket in one frail hand, his eyes watching her as she moved about the room in her *cheong-sam*. Sweet Third Niece so pretty so graceful, what would become of her in the Golden Country? What would become of them all? *Aiee, t'ung t'ien yu ming.*

"Did you call, Honourable Uncle, *heya*?"

"No, child, I spoke for myself only."

The hot water arrived. Yu-Ling infused the special blend of herbs she trusted no one else with and held the cup for her uncle while he drank. "*Oh ko*, that is better, Third Niece, much better," he told her gratefully.

"Thank you, Honourable Uncle, shall I prepare a pipe now?"

"No, no, not yet, later perhaps. Put my diary close and leave me to sleep a while."

Ai-yah, if only he could rest more, Yu-Ling thought worriedly, looking at his waxen skin. This journey was taxing his strength. How many more days had they said? Three, four? Perhaps she could ask the *quai loh* doctor to see him later.

She let herself quietly out.

Scott felt whacked after the long flight. It was the altitude that did it. Making and unmaking bunks was tiring work at eight thousand feet. None of them had had much sleep besides.

A swim was what she needed. It was pretty darn hot still in the sun and the lagoon was inviting. Changing swiftly into her costume she ran lightly down towards the striped umbrellas along the coral beach. Many of the other passengers and crew were already in the water enjoying themselves. By the tennis courts she bumped into Yu-Ling, alone and staring wistfully at the bathers splashing in the shallows.

"Hi, you coming on in? The swimming's great on Wake, beats even Waikiki."

"Oh, no thank you," the Chinese girl blushed at once, "I, I have no . . . no clothes."

"No swimsuit? Well, that's no problem, we can fix you up at the hotel. They keep a supply to lend guests, bathing caps too."

Yu-Ling's colour deepened. She hung her head. "Also I not know how you do this," she mumbled shyly.

"Then I'll teach you. It's easy and the water's so shallow here you won't even be out of your depth."

Eddie Wirth had stepped out onto the diving board in gaudy Hawaiian trunks. Holding his nose he made a clumsy leap and hit the water with a resounding splash. Both girls burst into giggles. A squealing Felicity Gordon Smythe ran past along the sand chased by Chris Fry. *Aiee*, Yu-Ling looked back from her to Scott, shocking the way *quai loh* women exposed their bodies in public in such skimpy costumes!

But then again, she thought, why not? Where is the harm? Besides I must learn to be as one of them now.

"Okay, Sallee," she flashed a mischievous grin, "you show me, *heya*?"

Down on the dock there were sounds of skylarking. Base mechanics were running a full service check on the flying boat, clambering over the wings happy at having some work to do. Most of their six month tours on the atoll were exercises in pure boredom. Munro left the Chief to superintend and went on up to the hotel.

The guest register read like a *Who's Who* of the war. Generals, admirals, politicians, diplomats and journalists had passed through this coral strand. Trunks and shorts were the order of the day here. Music was playing on the Victrola and waiters were serving drinks in long glasses.

Munro could have done with a swim too but first he had to check on Ross. He compromised with a barely cooling shower. Coming out through the lobby again, a cigarette slanting from his thin mouth, he spotted Sir Ambrose Hope settled into a lounger chair with a large gimlet at his elbow talking to Bob Cashin.

"Ah, Munro, afternoon," the Englishman greeted him as he approached. "Quite a flight that. Should have thrown the yellow chaps off our tail, what?"

"Hope so, Sir Ambrose. With luck by the time they figure out what's happened we'll be safe through to Pearl."

Cashin was looking at him quizzically through his spectacles, "You reckon the Japs were really aiming to hit us, a US civilian plane? That'd be war, wouldn't it?"

"Let's just say we were anxious to avoid an incident."

"I'd have thought flying across their Mandate was a sure way to cause one."

Sir Ambrose coughed and brushed a shred of pipe tobacco off his linen jacket. "Yes, well jolly good show anyway. Join us for a drink now? The barman here makes a first rate cocktail."

"Sorry, sir, too much to do. Actually I was wondering if you'd had any response yet on that inquiry to Hongkong?"

"Hongkong? Oh yes, you wanted information on a priest, let me see, what was his name?"

"Currie. Ronald Currie."

"That's right, I remember now," the old man nodded vigorously. Bob Cashin was listening with interest. "No, there hasn't been anything so far. Like me to stir 'em up again for you?"

"I don't want to put you to any trouble, sir. It might just be important though."

"Oh it's no trouble at all, glad of something to do. I'll send Playfair another signal, tell him to buck up."

"Thanks a lot, Sir Ambrose, I appreciate that."

He made for the porch pausing to put on his sun glasses.

"Hiya, Max."

He looked round at the sound of his name. Loitering just outside the door in a green sun visor and sneakers was Georgiana. At her side in immaculately tailored slacks stood César de Santa Cruz. Both carried golf clubs. They looked like a fashion plate for glamorous living. "Haven't seen you to speak to all day," she flashed him a dazzling smile. "We're off to hit some balls into the sea, want to come?"

Munro's stare was chilling. "I'm busy," he snapped bluntly.

She stiffened as if she had touched an electric wire. César's eyes blazed. He lunged forward, shoulders swinging, and the stinging backhander lashed Munro's face like a whip cut. "*Cabron*, stay away from my fiancée!"

Munro caught the Spaniard's wrist in a grip of iron. "Your precious fiancée is tricky as a sack of rattlesnakes. You want to pick a fight, pick one with her!"

Letting go he stalked away.

At the bottom of the path Tom Keswick, Pan Am's station manager, was waiting for him in his battered car. "What was that in aid of?"

"Nothing. The guy's bride-to-be was once a girlfriend of mine, that's all."

"Hell, Max, you'd better cool it, you know the company don't go for messing around with female passengers."

"Kick her off the flight then, it's fine by me."

They set off for the hospital. "Boy, you sure stuck your neck out this time, Max. Head office has been burning up the airwaves ever

351

since that signal you had sent from New Guinea. Even the State Department's gotten in on the act; seems you left one of their people stranded on Guam."

"Tough, I had a whole ship's company to consider."

"You took one hell of a risk even so." Dust rose in their track as they shot along the white coral road past the square masts of the RDF transmitter which had guided the Clipper in. "Striking across the Mandate, exceeding fuel margins. Okay so you pulled it off, but you ain't out of the woods yet."

Munro's face was still smarting from César's blow. "You telling me I'm to be grounded, Tom?"

"Hell, man, it's no joking matter!" the station manager gripped the wheel exasperated. "You're goddam lucky Ross *is* sick and the ship short-handed or I'd have been ordered to relieve you by now. There's guys in the company who'd give a month's pay to see you shafted, Max."

They drove out over the causeway linking Peale with the main islet. With its hotel and tennis courts and beach parasols the Pan Am base had the air of an exclusive country club. Here it was different; bulldozers and graders stood parked among the bush where roadways and store dumps were being carved out. Twenty million dollars was being spent here to beef up the atoll's defences. They passed the barracks of the Marine garrison and approached the white coral airstrip.

"See you got some new arrivals," Munro nodded towards the sleek snub-nosed fighters drawn up on the apron. "F4F–3s, Grumman Wildcats."

"Yep, squadron of twelve flew in off the USS Enterprise three days ago. Mighty fine sight, whole darn island turned out to greet 'em." Keswick chuckled, "A feller sure sleeps easier with those mean babes around."

Munro scanned the sky out the window. No sign of any patrols up. The whole base appeared deserted, only a token sentry at the gates. Of course, this was Sunday, the men were all off-duty.

Tom wanted to know more about the flight. What was the dope on this special cargo? Was it true the Japs had shot down a US bomber in New Guinea? How come Ross had been relieved? Munro answered perfunctorily.

The hospital was a cool wooden-frame building orientated so as to catch the breeze and screened against insects. Here the gangling young Navy doctor who examined Ross had good news for them.

"That's quite a knock your man sustained. He's definitely concussed, so far's we can tell though there's no fracture."

"Great, how long before he's fit to fly again?"

"Least a week. Only cure for concussion cases is plenty of bed rest."

They thanked him and moved over to the officers' club for a cold beer. The club was a frame tent with a wood deck and open sides to let the breeze through. Inside, a crowd was listening to a short-wave broadcast of a ball game, following the play on a board with a white marker sliding back and forth on a string across a painted gridiron. In one corner Major Devereux, the Marine commander, sat drinking with Slater.

"Hi, pull up a seat. How's Ross then?"

"Looks like he'll be staying with you awhile."

"That's too bad. We'll soon have him fit again, this place is a regular health resort," the Major was small and wiry with a neat moustache. "Slater here says you brought us a Chinese VIP this time, sure makes a change from Japs."

Slater cocked an eyebrow. "Last month we flew Ambassador Kurusu out to the States from Tokyo for the peace talks," Munro explained.

"Government made us hold the flight three days so's he could make the connection in Hongkong," Tom Keswick put in. "Threw the schedules all to blazes."

"Well, I guess nobody wants those talks to fail," Devereux said.

"Amen to that," Slater grunted.

"What's the situation here?" Munro asked.

"Improving fast. We could use more equipment, who couldn't, but at least we got air cover now. I guess right now we could handle anything short of a full scale invasion attempt."

"What's your state of readiness?" Slater asked.

"Still B–5, fifty percent men and machines on four hours notice."

"*Goal! Goal!*" There was a burst of cheering from the football gang as the white marker slid all the way home for a run to touchdown. Slater seemed restive. Rising abruptly, he motioned Munro to accompany him outside.

They walked down towards the beach past an unmanned bunker. Half buried in the coral at the edge of the sand lay a large ship's anchor, relic of a German vessel that had foundered here in a storm. Waves were pounding on the outer reef throwing up bursts of spray. Standing here one realised just how small the atoll was.

Slater took out a pack of cigars and offered one. "We're taking Ross with us when we pull out of here tomorrow," he said flatly.

"The hell we are, Major, he needs hospital care!"

"He'll have it Stateside. I can't risk him being captured if the Yellow-bellies take the island."

"Why, because he knows too much about what happened to Earhart?" Munro snarled back.

"*Jesus Christ, forget about Earhart!* How many times do I have to tell you, she has nothing to do with this mission!"

"You call Reverend Oliver's murder nothing, for Godsakes?"

"That wasn't my fault, dammit!"

"Then what are you scared of, Major? Is it to do with that radio message you had? What did it say?"

"Only that the Clipper's as much a target here as anywhere else on the route."

"Does Devereux know this?"

"That's not important, he knows enough." Slater stared out to sea. "See here, Pilot," he managed to control his temper, "there's no call for you and me to spar all the time. You did a good job getting us to this place, I'll admit. If we'd tried to make Guam . . ." He swung back, his expression taut, "But things are moving faster than any of us realise. That photograph . . ." Munro tensed. "Miss Delahaye told me you came up with it?"

"Did she just?" Munro felt a knot of anger harden in his stomach.

"That's right, she said you had the thing stashed in the mail sacks. So much for those yarns you spun us back in Manila, huh?"

"I told you the *truth*, Major, the photograph wasn't with me, it was in the mail hold. If you'd thought to *ask* instead of tearing my room apart I might've been more cooperative."

"Alright, keep your shirt on," Slater scowled at him. "Prickly bastard, ain't you? So what happened to it then?"

"The photograph disappeared from my jacket on New Guinea two nights ago. Most probably stolen by the same person who Georgiana claims pushed her over the rail of the yacht. Didn't she tell you *that*?"

They stood for a moment, the smoke of their cigars curling up into the air and the terns wheeling and shrieking overhead. "Yeah, as it happens she did," Slater said tersely. "And you and I both know who the son of a bitch is."

"Who, for Christsakes?"

"Shit, don't stall with me, Munro. That goddam gook steward of yours, that's who."

"Tad Gotto? Have you flipped? If it hadn't been for him we'd have lost the ship in the fire!"

"So, maybe he had his reasons. I spoke to your navigator a while

354

back, he says they caught him with a whole stack of stolen gear in his locker."

That sneaking bastard Thyssen, Munro might have guessed he'd go to Slater. "Those letters could've been dumped by anyone. And why should he want the photograph? What could it possibly signify for him?"

"He's a Jap, ain't he? *They* want it! Face facts, pilot, *your man's working for the enemy!*"

Yu-Ling was having a wonderful time. Scott had kitted her out in a sky blue one piece costume with a silver silhouette of a Clipper on the chest. She had felt almost naked at first though, conscious of every man's eyes on her body as she tripped down to the beach. *Ai-yah*, but it is only the *quai loh* fashion, she told herself firmly, Sallee goes so and she is not a whore, by the gods.

And she thought, looking around covertly at the other girls, my breasts are not so large as the English Miss Gordon Smythe's, but they are firmer. And this new Western hair style suits me too.

Scott led her out waist deep into the lagoon. The water felt deliciously cool against her skin and she was entranced by the tiny fish darting among the coral. "*Ai-yah*, no big ones, no . . .?" she mimed huge jaws with her hands.

"Sharks? Oh heavens no, not in the lagoon anyways. Only creatures you have to watch out for here are morays."

"Please, *morays*?"

"Kinda big eels, real whoppers, sometimes grow to six or seven feet. They live in holes in the outer reefs and their bite's worse than a shark's." Scott saw the Chinese girl's eyes widen in alarm and laughed. "Listen, don't worry I'm just kidding, it's perfectly safe here."

Her gaze strayed to the beach behind where the Simms children and Ricky Bianchi were playing noisily in the shallows. All at once a look of annoyance crossed her face, "Darn it, here comes Kurt!"

Thyssen knew he looked swell in trunks. Plenty of people had told him so. He'd gotten a good tan too this trip, which wasn't easy on account of his skin tending to peel.

Swaggering confidently along the sand, he saw the two girls out in the water and smirked to himself. He'd guessed Sally would be down here. Chucking his towel, he splashed in to join them. "Hi, water's great, huh?"

"Just a pity it's so crowded," Scott answered pointedly.

"Aw c'mon, Sally, let's be friends," he laid an arm on her shoulder. She pushed it off irritably. Yu-Ling looked at them puzzled.

"Scram, Kurt. We're having a swimming lesson."

"Swell, I was high school water polo captain. I'll show you some strokes." He reached out to take the Chinese girl by the waist, "You just lean back against me, honey."

The next instant he was choking underwater, Scott had ducked him hard from behind. "Keep your hands to yourself, you creep!" she hissed as he came up spluttering. "Now take off!"

"*Dew neh loh moh*, it makes no sense, by all the gods. The information was precise – *Sunday, Sunday!*"

"*Ai-yah*, Minister, maybe that fornicator Huang got it wrong. Or lied to us, *heya?*"

"No, no, no, Chungking confirmed everything. They have known for weeks what the Sea Devils were planning. Their message says the warning went out yesterday – *East Wind Rain!*"

"Maybe the operation was cancelled then. Fortunate for us, *heya?*"

"Peasant! Straw-head! It *must* be allowed to proceed, how else are we to bring the *quai loh* into the war?"

From the window of his room where he and Feng were arguing Hollington Soong could see the bathers returning up the path from the beach. His heart gave a little jig as he spotted Yu-Ling's scantily clad figure moving towards him. The child is truly exquisite, he thought scratching himself, without doubt a virgin still. Her maiden essence will restore my *yang* to vigour and *oh oh oh*, what a dowry she brings!

Yes, but not if the filthy Sea Devils kill us all!

He turned back to Feng. "Listen, we must get word to Chungking, find out what is happening. Quickly, *heya?*"

*　　*　　*

HONGKONG SIX PM. The sunset was a riot of angry hues, the violent-coloured cloudscapes seemed ominous almost, like the prelude to a typhoon.

By Shamshuipo police station the barrage balloon crew were winching down their elephantine charge for the night. Inside, sweating constables added yet more armfuls of files to the heaps that strewed the floor of Playfair's office and spilled out into the passageway.

The seizures were without parallel, their urgency unquestioned. The Governor himself had signed the order. Church halls, missionary societies, newspaper offices, public libraries, government departments had all been stripped. Personnel records, reports, newspaper cuttings, bundles of faded periodicals, anything that might yield a clue.

"Right," the Inspector addressed the half dozen British junior officers he had assembled, "get to work. I want everything checked. You're looking for references to an American missionary – Currie, first name Ronald, believed working in North China as late as last year."

"*Any* reference, sir?" one asked incredulously.

"Yes, damn you. What's the matter, are you deaf? Bring whatever you find over to me at the desk. All pictures of missionaries you come across go in that box there, we'll sort through them later. Now get cracking, this is a murder hunt!"

"Yes, sir."

They began delving into the files. Playfair watched them, tugging at his moustache, blaming himself for Harris's death. It was a long shot at best, most of the religious groups were based in Shanghai and kept their records there. It was the only lead they had.

XXVII

Tad Gotto took a stainless steel filleting knife from a drawer in the Clipper's galley and tested the point with his thumb. Carefully, using surgical tape from the First Aid box, he strapped it to the inside of his left wrist, blade uppermost, and stood for a moment listening. It was eight pm. Up in the wings Wake's mechanics were at work servicing the engines. Everyone else was ashore dining in the hotel.

He rummaged in a tool locker for the flashlight and screwdriver he'd used before and slipped them in his pockets. If his hunch was right though he might need the weapon too.

He set off aft through the saloon to the tail.

The rear rest-rooms were both empty. He checked each, then tried the door to the rear suite. It was locked, he used his pass key. Inside, the cabin smelled of incense. Minister Soong had been burning joss sticks during flight. Let into the bulkhead opposite the door was a small hatch, also locked, leading to the tail.

Tad took out the knife and held it ready.

He jerked the hatch open and shone the flash inside. The funnel-shaped space within sloped back ten feet into the tail, a bare unsound-proofed compartment seldom visited by flight crew. Control wires for elevators and rudder ran along the tapering sides, disappearing into the narrow tail cone. Gripping the knife tautly, Tad played the flash on the cables and up over the end-frames of the hull. Drops of oil glistened in the beam. Not a sign of anyone having been in here. He heaved a sigh of relief and closed the hatch again.

That left only the upper deck then.

Out in the passage again, he climbed the ladder to the baggage hold. Faint through the forward bulkhead came sounds of the mechanics in the control cabin. Working quickly, he cleared a space on the floor above where he judged the washroom to be. The decking was made up of aluminum section fastened directly to the fuselage frame. One was loose, the securing screws missing. He levered it up and pulled away a pad of sound-proofing material. Suddenly his heart began to pound.

Concealed in the cavity below was a cloth-bound Boeing maintenance manual for the flying boat's fuel system. With it, a small metal object. Tad's fingers trembled as he touched it – a valve handle.

On an impulse he stuffed both inside his uniform jacket. Hurriedly he replaced the deck panel. Lifting the after hatch, he scrambled back down the ladder again.

His feet touched the floor. He reached up to pull the hatch shut and turned. "Oh Jeez!" he froze shivering.

Standing by the rest-rooms, wearing a grim smile was Major Slater. Behind him two armed marines.

"I din't put them there! It's the truth, I swear to God!"

"Yeah? Then who did? One of your buddies in Manila?"

"I don't know. *I don't know*! I was trying to find out."

"Liar!" Slater's voice slashed him. "You hid 'em there. What for? So's you could cripple the plane for your yellow-bellied friends? Is that why you had the knife too?"

"No, it was for protection – I was looking for a stowaway!"

"Liar! You're a spy. A stinking lying Jap spy!"

"I'm not! I'm an *American*! Mister Munro, tell him I'm not a spy!"

The lines round Munro's mouth were harsh in the saloon lights. He'd have betted his life on Gotto's loyalty. He still couldn't believe the steward was a willing traitor. "I don't understand," he said patiently, "Tad, if you suspected something how come you didn't report it?"

"Oh God, Mister Munro, I wanted to honest, only I was scared nobody'd believe me!" Tad hung his head.

They made Tad turn out his pockets then and Slater grinned wolfishly at the sight of the *kempei-tai* button. "You're shit outta luck, spy. Sure, you just found this too. Next you'll be telling us it came out of a novelty cracker." Even Munro looked troubled now.

"Okay, let's go," the bigger of the two hefty marines said. Hot tears of shame came into Tad's eyes as they led him out along the jetty and across to one of the lockable store rooms behind the Pan Am hangar. "Ain't got no regular guardhouse here, bud," the marine apologised with heavy humour, opening the door. "So we fixed this up. Guess it'll do."

The cement cell was bare and windowless with a single skylight high in the ceiling. There was a cot with a blanket and nothing else. Tad gulped. He wished he were dead.

Munro put a hand on his shoulder, "I'll bring you over something to read. Keep your chin up, kid."

They shut the door and he heard the key turn in the lock. It hit him then that he was a prisoner. He threw himself down on the cot and wept.

Few people had witnessed Tad's arrest. At the Officers Club they were showing a movie – *Blood and Sand* with Tyrone Power and Linda Darnell. Normally the base was off-limits to passengers but tonight Pan Am had laid on a bus after dinner and the outdoor theatre was crowded.

Maria Bianchi volunteered to stay and keep an eye on the children. "You and Eliot go, it will do you good to relax," she told Ruth Simms.

"Well if you're sure, it would be nice. But only if you promise to let us do the same for you tomorrow on Midway."

"I promise, it'll probably be the same movie too. Enjoy yourselves."

She saw the bus off and went back into the lobby. Under the fans Bob Cashin, the Dutchman Van Cleef and several others were also spending the evening at the hotel. She joined them for a drink.

The talk was all about war as usual. "Obviously the Americans expect to be attacked soon," Van Cleef was telling the company. "Why else divert the flight? Everyone knows Guam would fall to the Japanese without hours of war being declared."

"I don't see that we're any better off here on Wake, old boy," Gordon Smythe countered.

"You are forgetting, my friend, we are not surrounded by enemy territory like Guam. The nearest Japanese islands are six hundred miles away. And Wake is well defended, to take it they must mount a big expedition."

The Englishman sniffed into his whisky glass. "A handful of fighter planes and a few marines, how much resistance could they put up? Personally I'll feel a lot happier when we reach Honolulu."

"Watch what you say about the US marines, feller," one of the oilmen told him. "Ain't no finer bunch of men and they'll kick the hell outta any slit-eyed bastards who do try to land here. Begging your pardon, ma'am," he added to Maria.

She smiled mechanically, thinking of the war she had witnessed. The fighting in the Shagnhai delta and later in the city itself. The bombing and shelling, people blown to pieces, burned alive in the streets. War. Yes, but in America they would be safe again, she and Ricky.

Major Slater was approaching the bar. At his side, chattering away volubly, was Hollington Soong. They were accompanied by Sir Ambrose Hope. Catching sight of her the Englishman bowed slightly.

"Let's hear your opinion, Minister," Bob Cashin called, "will the Japs attack before we make Hawaii?"

Soong's face went white. "What is that you say, Hawaii has been attacked?" he rolled his eyes in alarm.

There were laughs. "Not so far, Minister. Why, do you expect it to be?"

"*Ai-yah*, I know nothing about any attacks!" Soong declared, gesturing angrily. "We are at war with the dwarf bandits already. Alone, *heya*? You should show more respect."

"I'm sorry, Minister," Cashin's expression was all innocence, "no disrespect intended. Let's have Major Slater's view then."

Slater took the cigar out of his mouth. "I think you ask too many damn questions," he said tersely.

There was a moment's awkward silence. Sir Ambrose coughed, "What about the Philippines, will Japan strike there d'you think, Van Cleef?" he inquired switching the conversation.

"Undoubtedly, otherwise they leave their flanks open when they move against Malaya and the Netherlands East Indies."

"*Bueno*, let them come, they will get a thrashing!"

Everyone looked round. César de Santa Cruz had entered the lobby, his arm possessively at his fiancée's waist. Georgiana wore a sulky discontented look. "César's a fire-eater," she said, breaking away. "He can't wait to be at war and prove what a hero he is."

César ignored the sarcasm. "We are only a small nation, but we are not afraid to fight," he said. "*Si*, and we will win!" Snapping his fingers at a Chamorro waiter he ordered champagne served. "I give you a toast," he declared raising his glass, "*General MacArthur – and the defeat of Japan!*"

"*– the defeat of Japan.*" Sir Ambrose murmured with the others. He gazed round the circle of faces. Which of these present, he wondered, was the traitor?

A shirt-sleeved messenger tapped his shoulder, "Pardon me, Sir Ambrose, but there's a radio signal come in for you from Hongkong. It's flagged urgent."

Maria went to check on the children. Both little girls were fast asleep, Debbie clutching an ancient stuffed toy rabbit that was her favourite possession.

Slipping into her own room she found Ricky awake.

"It's hot, Moma, I can't sleep."

"Ssh, I know. Shall I read you another story?"

"Yes please, the one about the Elephant's Child."

"Alright, lie quiet then."

Switching on the bedside lamp she opened the book. "*In the High and Far-Off Times the Elephant, O Best Beloved, had no trunk . . .*

"God in heaven!" Munro stared at the diplomat shocked, "Lieutenant Harris? Why? Why him, poor bastard?"

"Hongkong aren't certain. According to Playfair's signal Harris had been ordered to follow up our request for information on Dr. Currie."

"*Currie*! Dammit, so maybe we were right, there is a connection there somewhere."

"Yes, but what though?" Sir Ambrose darted him a shrewd look, "That photograph perhaps? Slater says it's lost again."

Munro shook his head. "Not lost, *stolen*. Someone swiped it on New Guinea."

"You guys mind filling me in?" the Chief interrupted mildly. "First I heard about any darn photograph."

He and Munro were sharing a room as usual. Sir Ambrose had tapped on the door just as they were discussing what to do about Tad.

Munro sketched in the details. The Chief grunted, "This man Currie, he was in the snapshot along with Georgiana?"

"According to Jordan. He said Currie was dead, of enteric fever I think it was." Munro was silent for a moment, back once more in the dingy room above the Wanchai with the sheeted thing on the bed and the smell of death in the air. *Kokuryu-kai*, had the Black Dragon pursued them half across the Pacific?

Sir Ambrose frowned, "It would help if we could find out more about him; when exactly he died and where?"

"Playfair didn't come up with any information then?"

"Not a scrap so far, I'm afraid. He's wired the American consul in Shanghai, they may produce something. Otherwise it's as if the chap never existed."

"Seems to me like we oughta talk with the Reverend again," the Chief scratched his chin. He sat down on a bed and the springs squeaked in protest under his bulk.

"Yes, that's what I thought. Fellow's not in his room though and no one seems to have seen him."

"He's probably over at the movie," Munro stuck a cigarette in his mouth and reached for a box of matches on the dressing table next to the pile of comics he'd collected to take to Tad. His jaw hardened. "Major Slater's had one of our crew arrested, were you aware of that?" he asked Sir Ambrose abruptly.

The diplomat's manner sharpened, "No. Who?"

"Our junior steward, Tad Gotto."

"The *nisei*?"

"No, a nisei is a full blooded Japanese born in the US. Tad's father was an American officer. Unfortunately for him he takes after his mother."

"And Slater thinks he's a spy? Does he have proof?"

"He was caught just now trying to sabotage the ship." Munro shrugged. "Claims it's all a mistake."

"He's being set up," the Chief snorted from the bed, "by the same sneaking son of a bitch who planted that stolen mail in his locker on New Guinea."

"Is that right?" Sir Ambrose glanced at Munro.

"Your guess is as good as ours. Tad was always the proudest American anyone ever met. I'd have said he wouldn't betray his country no matter what."

The ceiling fan paddled the air steadily, whirling away the smoke of their cigarettes. Sir Ambrose's aristocratic features were shadowed sphinx-like in the light from the table lamp. "There *is* an enemy agent on this flight alright, but it's not your Tad Gotto. Last month London intercepted secret intelligence of an unnamed European recruited through the *German–Amerika Bund* to work for the Black Dragon. He's out to deliver this plane into Axis hands. And, gentlemen, *whoever he is we've got to stop him!*"

His hands were shaking, Munro saw.

". . . *So the Elephant's Child went home across Africa frisking and whisking his trunk.*"

Maria closed the book. Ricky was asleep. Gently she tucked in the sheets and kissed him tenderly, loving him. Soon, soon they would be in America, safe and secure for ever. And her son would grow up there free and unafraid.

So different from her own childhood.

It was a long time since she had thought back.

"*Shang hei tz! Yao ma shang hei tz!*" the peasant women used to shout, "*Children! Children for sale!*" Shanghai. Detestable Shanghai.

363

City of despair, of abject poverty and slavish wealth. Of the great stores and banks along the Bund, women in furs and corpses in the gutters. Limousines and rickshaws on the Avenue Foch. Chinese gangsters in shiny suits, sleek pimps and starving beggars, pickpockets, opium dealers, gold traders, touts, coolies, cripples. Shanghai, where millionaires jostled with drug addicts and sing-song girls. Dread last hope for every destitute western refugee in China.

Maria's mother had been one such. Daughter of a Polish general exiled to Siberia, she had arrived penniless from Vladivostok fleeing a typhoid epidemic which carried off a tenth of the city including her husband of three months. Faced with the prospect of starvation or the streets, she had placed her new-born baby with a Christian mission and sold herself in marriage to an elderly Mongolian tea merchant, enduring twelve years of hell before succumbing to the syphilis with which he had infected her.

Upon the Mongolian's own death two years later, his son's first act had been to terminate the arrangement with the convent. "Why, you are quite grown up," he declared when Maria was brought to him. To demonstrate which he violated her that same night, delighted to discover from her screams she was a virgin. Thereafter she was raped regularly and sometimes lent to friends before being sold for two thousand dollars to a Blood Alley whorehouse.

And this had been at the beginning of the Great Turmoil when war and revolution ravaged the world and in Russia the Red Terror swept a tidal wave of refugees eastward. Before long the streets of Shanghai were filled with girls in rags desperate to barter themselves for a meal.

But Maria had survived. Survived the brothels and the dance-halls, the filthy conditions, the disease and ill-treatment that killed nine out of ten before their thirtieth year. Yes, and gone on surviving and fighting and clawing her way up from the gutter. Using the only assets she had, her beauty and her brains. Finding a protector to buy her out. Mistress first to a customs officials, finally to a banker. Doing anything, suffering anything to acquire the money, the power, the influence to protect herself. Above all the money.

"This is Shanghai!" she had told the other girls, the ones who worked for her later. "The only way out of here is money! Forget the old men pawing, the drunks, the beatings, the degradation. Take their money. Whore for it, cheat for it, steal for it if you have to, but *make money!*"

A few succeeded. Most did not.

Meanwhile war again. The Japanese and the Chinese fighting in the delta. Slaughter and destruction and more, always more refugees pouring in till the city was choked with them and still they came.

But also luck. Marriage to my darling Tony Bianchi. Five blessed years of happiness when we opened the club and built it up to be the finest in all Shanghai, and best, best of everything the birth of our son.

But Tony's dead. Ricky's all I have left and now I'm taking him away from that rotten world to a new life for us both.

Nothing is going to stand in our way. Nothing.

Switching out the light and shutting the door quietly, she was walking back down the passage when she bumped into the Prince.

"Good, I want to talk with you." Gripping her arm he forced her out of a side door into the gloom of the garden. "So, you have considered my proposal long enough, what is your answer?"

She shook his hand off furiously. "You make me want to vomit! *That* is my answer."

"Ach, who are you to be so choosy? The madame of a whore-house! Instead you will be a princess."

"It was a nightclub not a whorehouse! You Russians and your phony titles, you're nothing but jokes!"

"*I am a Prince!*" Cherkassy spat through his teeth, a flush suffusing his hideous face. "So was my father, and his father before him. *Boyars*, noblemen for more than nine generations till the filthy bolsheviks raped Mother Russia!"

"And now you are just another penniless emigré," Maria sneered cuttingly. "It means *nothing*, do you understand that? In America your ancestry counts for nothing at all. They have archdukes driving cabs!"

"I will have money." He gave a harsh laugh, "*Your* money!" His eyes drilled her like a snake's. "You are no American. I know your kind, *viblyadoks*, stateless half-breeds selling themselves for *kopecs*, the vermin of every city in the east. You got a passport, how? By marriage? It must have been a trick. If the Americans learn you were owner of the Red Lips, how long before they send you back? Yes, and the boy too!"

Maria's hands slashed at his face, nails clawing, "If you so much as touch my son I swear I'll kill you!"

The Russian caught her arms easily and pushed her back against the wall. With callous indifference he smacked her hard. Once, twice. Across the breasts. The pain made her gasp. "See, that is what you get if you try to fight me!" he grunted as she tottered, clutching herself. "Now, listen to what I tell you; we are going to be *married*, under-stand?"

"*Never!*"

"Shut up! Or by *Kristos* I hit you again! We will be married, I shall

365

gain a rich wife and, more important, American citizenship." He gave another mirthless laugh, "Maybe we will go into business together on Hawaii, perhaps set up another club, eh? *Ha, ha!*"

If Maria could have killed him then she would have done.

. . . Lucky Strike – the only cigarette from which all trace of harsh tobacco tar has been removed. Smoke Luckies, the cigarette that's kind to your throat . . .

It was nine pm. Sir Ambrose had just left. Munro had opened the shutters to let the smoke out. Faint through the window above the noise of the surf came the tones of the radio in the hotel lobby. Down by the jetty lights still gleamed aboard the Clipper where the mechanics were finishing up.

"I'd give one hell of a lot to know what's in that cargo," he muttered savagely.

"Twenty-five hundred miles to Pearl. If the limeys are right that leaves the Japs plenty of time to hit us still."

"We could sit it out here till dusk tomorrow, then try for Midway overnight. The Navy's got a sea-plane base there, maybe we could drum up an escort at last."

"Sure, an' meantime Deveraux'll lend us a couple of his marines to stop this Jap agent cuttin' a fuel line or pouring water in an oil tank or any of his other damn tricks! We gotta find him, Max."

. . . This is KGMB Hawaii bringing you the best in entertainment this Saturday night. And now a news bullentin – in Washington talks are continuing through the week-end between State Department officials and envoys of the Japanese Government in efforts to bring peace to the Far East. Meantime controversy builds over Press disclosures of Administration contingency plans to send an expeditionary force to Europe. In a statement, Secretary of War Stimson said . . .

"Least they're still talking," the Chief sniffed. He was silent for a minute, pondering what had been discussed earlier, "This photo, guess you took it on account of Georgiana, huh? Must be kinda hard for you having her on the trip?"

Munro made a wry face, "It ain't my choice."

"How d'you rate that *hidalgo* of hers then?"

"César? The guy's loaded, they're well matched."

"And if he weren't around?"

"*Christ*, Chief, I don't know! Thought I was shot of her for good after the last time – seems it ain't that easy."

"She's a sparky dame. I always did like her."

. . . Turning now to foreign news – reports from Moscow say Soviet forces today launched a major counter-offensive to relieve the city . . .

Munro closed the shutters. "She's one heap of trouble so far as I'm concerned."

The engineer stood brooding. "From what I heard the German *Bund* is strong in Manila. Could be César is our man or your Dutch polo playing friend Van Cleef?" he glanced up questioningly.

"Maybe," Munro's expression was grim. "The traitor could just as easily be an American – one of us even." He moved towards the door, "Let's get those pass-keys from Pat before the movie winds up."

Ten minutes later the passage was quiet. Munro tapped softly on Prince Cherkassy's door. There was no response from inside. Slipping the lock with the key borrowed from Pat O'Byrne, he let himself in.

The room was identical to the other four he had tried. Neither of the twin beds had been used yet. Switching on the table lamp he began his search. The bathroom first, checking cupboard and waste basket as well as the contents of the toilet bag.

On a table by the window lay a few dollars worth of gaming chips from the Manila casino. Ignoring them, he turned to the clothes press, feeling in pockets, rifling through shirts and underwear. An oilskin pouch discovered in a drawer interested him briefly but yielded only a slim packet of contraceptives.

Another blank, he was wasting his time.

So far he had checked the Gordon Smythes, Ed Wirth and Van Cleef. None had yielded anything incriminating, unless you counted finding Chris Fry's necktie under the English girl's bed. He didn't enjoy this prying into people's rooms behind their backs but there was no other way.

The next room was number 18, Latouche's.

To his chagrin there was no sign of the Doctor's black bag. Only a plain leather valise in the cupboard and nothing else of interest.

Or rather *one* thing.

On a bedside table lay a book. He glanced at the title as he picked it up, *Les Eléments Actinide*. The author's name was giving underneath – *Maurice Latouche, Institute Curie, Paris*. It had been published three years ago.

Munro's French was conversational at best, certainly not up to the close study of a textbook. As he flipped the pages though, for the first time on the trip he began to have a glimmer of understanding of what could be at stake.

It scared him.

Then he saw the key.

Over in the opposite wing Chief Crow relocked the door of César's room and squinted at his watch. Nine forty, the bus would be returning soon. Time to check one or two more maybe.

Number 10 was occupied. Pausing outside he caught the fluted sing-song accents of Professor Chen. Next door would be his niece's, better skip both. Anyway they'd already decided to leave the Chinese out of it for the present. He moved along to number 12.

It was Reverend Jordan's room.

This one took him no time at all. The priest's few shabby possessions wouldn't have filled Georgiana Delahaye's Luis Vuiton hat-box. Which just showed what you got, the Chief thought sourly, for devoting your life to the service of your fellow men. No camera anywhere, Jordan must have it with him.

A well-thumbed prayer book by the beside was inscribed on the fly-leaf – *'Jesse' Jordan, from his brother in Christ, Francis John Buchan. Peking 1937.* It fell open at the story of the Last Supper and betrayal by Judas Iscariot. Very appropriate.

He let himself out again and came face to face with Scott in the corridor.

"I just heard about Tad," she gasped at him. "Those brutes!" her chest heaved. "Pat told me what you're doing, I came to help!"

"How about the movie, ain't it over?"

"Yes, but I got a ride back in a jeep, the bus with the others hasn't left yet. Have you found anything? We've got to clear him, Chief!"

"Everyone's clean as a scrubbed nun, dammit."

They stopped outside the next door, voices low. "Who's is this, d'you know?"

"Mrs. Bianchi's, I think. Her little boy'll be in there though, I'd try the one further down. Oh," Scott wrinkled her brow, "that's Kurt's."

They exchanged glances. The Chief's mouth tightened. "Let's take a look."

. . . Singapore – the British naval build-up continues. Battleships, an aircraft carrier and other heavy units have arrived in the Fleet base which is said to be impregnable to attack. British forces in the Far East have been placed on full alert and according to a report in Time magazine odds on war with Japan are now nine in ten . . .

Stewart Whitely had skipped the movie. Instead he was holed up in the tin-roofed company radio office with Earl Henry, the operator on duty, tapping out CQ calls, pulling in stations around the rim of the Pacific. Eavesdropping on traffic from points as far away as Sydney and the Aleutians.

"Load of bullshit," Henry yawned, flipping the switch to cut the broadcast off.

"You reckon so?" Stewart cocked his head.

"Sure, people've been saying war's on the way ever since I landed on this spit-kit island an' that's five months ago yesterday."

"Sounded to me like the shooting could start any time."

"Nuts to that." Henry removed the sponge-rubber earphones and rubbed his short ginger hair. He reached for a mug of coffee on the desk. "I stopped by the Navy station yesterday. They got copies of all the crypto systems in use through till June '42 aboard. Aircraft recognition, RDF frequencies, the whole bit. If war breaks out they'll be up for grabs by the Japs but there ain't been no order yet to strip ship. So the Navy ain't worried."

"Guess that makes sense," Stewart admitted. He pressed the receiver switch again and toyed idly with the tuning dial, listening to the cheep of morse bouncing off the Heaviside Layer. "Have you been picking up any signals on the lower marine band these past days?"

"I don't listen much on the low frequencies," Henry frowned over the rim of his mug. "What kind of signals?"

Belatedly Stewart recalled the oath of secrecy he had taken in the tunnel on Corregidor. He shook his head, "Nothing in particular, I just wondered, that's all."

Maybe the carriers had put back.

A horn beeped on the coral road outside. The bus was returning from the base.

Monogrammed shirts, hand-made shoes, Kurt Thyssen had expensive tastes alright. The Chief snorted to himself dourly as he searched the clothes press. Still how a man spent his pay was his own affair, it certainly wasn't treason.

Scott was checking the bathroom. "I think I heard the bus," he called to her. "Time to wrap up."

"Chief, come here a second."

He went through. "What's the matter? You found something?"

"I'm not sure. I dropped the washbag and while I was picking it up I

369

noticed this envelope taped underneath the lavatory cistern. See," she showed him, "it's full of cash."

The Chief thumbed through the contents. "Must be three or four thousand bucks," he muttered. That was a year's pay for a flying boat officer.

Scott was staring at the notes, her face pale. "Back in Manila, he tried to give me this gold watch," her voice faltered. "I don't understand, where does he get so much money?"

"*What the fuck d'you think you're doing?*"

They both whirled. Standing in the doorway was Kurt.

The big galvanised-iron Pan Am hangar stood by the shore at the head of a concrete slipway up which the flying boats could be hauled for dry-docking. The main doors were kept shut at night, more to keep birds out than anything else. This evening though there was a rifle-toting marine standing sentry duty outside. Munro watched him pacing up and down in the pool of light from the overhead lamp. It looked like there was only the one. Maybe with Tad locked up Slater wasn't too worried any more.

Coral dust scrunched under his shoes as he made his way cautiously round to the rear. The back of the hangar was in darkness. No sentry this end but the doors here were locked. He'd been expecting that though, without difficulty he located a window he could force. These buildings hadn't been constructed with security in mind. Prising away the fly mesh he climbed through.

Inside, the hangar's cavernous interior loomed vast and dark like the nave of a cathedral. Faint rays of illumination filtered down into the gloom from skylights in the roof. He crouched on the floor listening. In the stillness the smallest sounds seemed magnified. He could hear the surf outside and the scrape of the sentry's boots on the slipway.

From memory the cargo area lay over by the right hand wall. He groped his way slowly across the hangar's empty space, feeling in front of him like a blind man till his hands encountered a wire grill. Slater's footlockers should be here. He took out his flash, shielding the beam with his fingers while he risked a quick look. Yes, over in the far corner. Two box-like shapes beneath a canvas cover. The coffin wasn't with them. They must have left it aboard.

The gate was locked. Reaching for the top of the frame, he made a spring and pulled himself up. The wire grill rattled loudly as he scrambled over. Shit. Jumping down on the far side, he ducked behind some boxes, praying the sentry hadn't heard.

No sounds of alarm. He crept to the canvas sheet and threw it back. In the beam of the flashlight the steel caskets gleamed squat and strangely menacing. No identifying marks, just the number stencilled on the lids: 92.

He took the nearest.

Latouche's key fitted the padlock perfectly. His pulse quickened as he lifted the lid.

Underneath was a second lid made of a different dull grey metal that was oddly familiar. It had no hinges, instead it was secured at the corners by four heavy catches. Munro unlatched them and lifted the inner lid off, surprised momentarily by its weight.

He shone the flashlight inside.

The interior was lined with shock-absorbing rubber of the kind used to protect sensitive instruments and radio gear aboard the Clipper. Set in the midst of this in two rows were twelve flasks made out of the same metal as the lid.

Munro lifted one out.

It was about the size of a cocktail shaker, smooth and cylindrical in shape. Again he was struck by the weight of the thing. Laying down the flashlight, very gingerly he unscrewed the top. His fingers were sweating.

There was a hiss of a vacuum released as the top came off. A slim core slid into his palm, lustrous white in the flash beam and strangely warm to the touch. Even as he stared the surface sheen seemed to cloud, tarnishing in the air, oxidising to a purplish hue before his eyes.

Clack . . . Clack . . . Clack . . . Night became day.

With blinding suddenness the lights blazed on all about him. Doors slammed open, there were shouts and sounds of running feet. He jerked round, the flash flying from his grasp. It hit the floor and rolled clattering away across the concrete.

"*Hold it right there, Mac!*" A circle of gun barrels aimed at him through the wire.

Munro blinked in the glare, fingers clamped tight around the darkening metal slug. "Easy on those triggers, boys," he drawled, "you might cause an accident."

XXVIII

It was night again. Night was his special friend.

A just waning moon shone down on the atoll through a veil of scattered overcast. The birds were quiet, but out on the reefs the breakers kept up their unceasing murmur. Lights spangled the islets and the lagoon was smooth as ink around the pilings of the jetty.

Blackened like a spectre the Japanese picked his way sure-footed through the Clipper's holds. He felt almost at home in the great plane now. The thought brought a flash of anger. *By the Amida*, this mission had been bungled from start to finish! *Karma*, he told himself, the time is soon. Yes, very soon now.

Squirming through into the port wing stub, he located the hatch in the floor. It was fastened securely. After New Guinea the fool barbarians were taking more care. Stealthily he eased the catch. The mooring dock below was empty and silent. He dropped through.

He landed noiselessly in a pool of shadow cast by the wing and froze, even his breathing imperceptible. Water lapped quietly round the plane's hull. No other sounds. His eyes traversed slowly. Ahead a wooden ramp ran up to the long floodlit jetty. All was still but he sensed the presence of *gaijin* nearby.

His sword slung at his back, he flattened himself on his belly against the planking and slithered to the head of the jetty. A mooring post, a loose coil of rope, a pair of rubber fenders gave all the cover he needed as he blended effortlessly in their shadows. He paused, checking his surroundings. Up on the shore an automobile's headlights were cutting through the bush towards the hotel. Still no sign of soldiers. He reached for the sack at his waist.

A minute later he was moving again, along the side-pilings of the jetty. Hanging out over the water like a black-clad spider, clinging to the slimy piers by the sets of steel claws strapped to his hands and feet. Invisible in the shadow of the railing he swung himself along, pausing at intervals to press an ear against the beams.

All at once he tensed. Faint through the wood came the tread of booted feet. *Hai*, guards returning! Holding his breath he listened, timing the steps. Only one and still right up the far end, moving slowly. Plenty of time. He resumed his progress, checking more frequently now.

Klunk . . . klunk . . . The footsteps drew nearer, echoing on the planks. The Japanese crouched, shrinking in under the pilings. *K-lunk . . .* Silence. The rail creaked and the shadow of a helmet appeared outlined on the water below. The *gaijin* was leaning over. Had he seen something? Soundlessly the Japanese drew a honed steel dart from his sleeve. Its tip was needle-sharp, smeared with blowfish poison to cause paralysis within seconds, followed by death. A flick of the wrist and the knife would bury itself unerringly in the victim's throat choking his cry still-born. He braced himself against a cross-beam ready for the throw and the upward spring to catch the corpse before it fell.

The guard let out a yawn and straightened up. Shouldering his rifle again he moved off. As the sound of his feet faded the Japanese relaxed and slid the *shuriken* back into his sleeve. Stupid barbarian, he'd been a hair's breadth from the void!

He reached the shore without incident and vanished into the bush.

"Heaven and earth are ruthless, they treat the myriads of creatures like straw dogs."

Yu-Ling was reading to her uncle from the *Tao Te Ching*, the book of five thousand characters, and wishing she too could have gone to the movie.

Once in her life only she had glimpsed a Western-style film, when the nuns at the convent had arranged a special showing of Cecil B. de Mille's *The Ten Commandments*. The girls had been enthralled even though the Mother Superior had stationed herself by the projector to block out scenes considered unsuitable.

Joss. Honourable Uncle had wanted her to remain. It was her duty to obey.

"The sage too is ruthless, he treats the people like straw dogs."

She stole a glance at her uncle. The Professor lay on the bed, eyes closed, hands clasped beneath his silvery beard. His withered cheeks were the colour of old ivory, the breathing scarcely visible. The devil-box was under his pillow.

Ai-yah, he was asleep. Good. Setting down the book, she drew the coverlet up around him and tip-toed out to tap on the door of the room opposite.

"*Wey?*" Bodyguard Feng's voice answered.

"*Ai-yah,* I am going for a walk. Honourable Chen is resting, see he is not disturbed, *heya?*"

In Latouche's bathroom Munro turned on the shower.

The water was scalding. Deliberately so. Gasping under the steam, he soaped himself down and scrubbed violently all over. The hands especially. Rubbing the skin under the nails raw with the brush to remove every possible trace of contamination. Even then he still seemed to feel the eerie warmth from that lustrous metal slug on his fingers. *Jesus Christ,* what had he gotten into this time?

He towelled off and went back to the bedroom.

Latouche was waiting for him, his black bag open on the dressing table. "*Bon,* if you will please sit on the stool."

Wearing surgical gloves, the Doctor took an oiled filter-paper from a freshly opened pack and wiped the inside of Munro's right hand carefully with it. He did the same with the left, placed both swabs in a plastic specimen box and passed him two more, "For the inside of each nostril, *s'il vous plaît.*"

A houseboy brought a fresh set of clothes. Everything Munro had been wearing had been removed to the laundry, even down to his undershorts. He began to dress again, while Latouche set up what looked like a portable wireless on the table and attached to it a metal probe on the end of a lead.

"That's what you were using out on the river in New Guinea?"

"*Oui,* an ionization meter. It measures the amount of contamination present on the swabs." Latouche switched the unit on and held the probe slowly over one of the samples, watching the dial.

The door jerked open without a knock and Slater strode in. At the sight of Munro his eyes blazed, "You! Shit, I might've guessed," he spat. He swivelled to Latouche, taking in the ionizer and swabs. "Alright, what happened? I got a call over at the base there'd been an accident. Were the containers breached?"

Latouche switched off the probe with a shrug. "One flask ruptured and the contents exposed. Perhaps a few milligrams lost through oxidation, nothing more."

"Of the *enriched*? Godammit to hell, how? How'd this asshole get himself contaminated?"

The Doctor changed the swab he had tested for another and switched on the probe again. "*Alors,* he entered the hangar and opened a container. As to why, you must ask him."

Munro pulled on a clean shirt. "I was testing a theory."

Slater gaped at him, "*Jesus H Christ,* you sneak into a guarded building and bust open a top secret cargo and you expect us to wear *that*?"

"I don't give a solitary damn what you believe. I wanted to check if there was any danger to my passengers."

"The hell you did, flyboy! That cargo's worth more than your whole goddam plane and everything in it!"

Latouche interrupted. "There is no risk to the Clipper," he said with firmness.

"Stow it, Doc," Munro told him irritably. "You didn't put me through those tests just to pass the time."

Latouche removed the last of the swabs and disconnected the probe. His thin hawklike features concentrated on the American pilot. "There is no health risk to the Clipper," he repeated carefully, *"provided the samples are not removed from their flasks again."*

Voices sounded in the passage outside. Arguing. Scott and Kurt Thyssen. Munro reached for his pants and buttoned them on. "Look, Doc, I majored in physics, I know the periodic table. So suppose we all quit fencing and level with one another, huh?"

The shock in their faces was total.

"What else do you know, wise guy?" Slater's voice was low and menacing.

"Enough, Major. I found out tonight what you're carrying in those footlockers – and I'll hazard a damn good guess why!"

"You son of a bitch!" Slater's eyes slitted. His hands moved suddenly and a gun appeared from under his coat. "Just what the hell is your game, Munro? You'd better come clean. *Fast.*" The hammer cocked with a deliberate click. Munro's fists clenched. The muzzle was pointed directly at his belly.

There was a soft cough from Latouche. Stepping firmly between them, he pushed the pistol up. "Captain Munro is an ally, let us not turn him into an enemy. I suggest we talk, *oui*?"

Swiftly, purposefully the Japanese circled through the bush. His passage was noiseless, invisible, using every trick of moonlight and rustle of breeze to mask his movements. *Joei-on jitsu, the washing of sound and shadow,* but one facet of his endless training handed down from a feudal past so remote its origins were lost in myth.

Flaring his nostrils to test the air, he approached the west wing of the hotel down-wind through the garden. A wireless was playing somewhere and lights filtered through the shuttered windows, streaking the close turf. Cautiously he drew closer, *haragei* probing the shadows for hidden guards. But no, there were none. *I-ye*, truly the barbarians suspected nothing.

Or was it a trap? Even as the thought formed in his mind there came a clack of a screen door and the scuff of stealthy footsteps on the concrete path. *Namu Amida Butsu!* With the hiss of a striking snake the *katana* blade leapt from its scabbard, ready to kill.

A figure appeared, outlined sharply against the lights behind. A man, dark clothes, peering nervously this way and that. Worried. Searching.

The Japanese relaxed. Lifting his head, he gave a low double whistle.

Bless all gods, Yu-ling thought as she wandered down towards the beach, so lovely to stroll along the sand in the warm evening. No one around, stars glittering overhead and the air smelling fresh and clean. Taking off her shoes she paddled barefoot in the shallows at the edge of the lagoon, the soft ripples were deliciously cool as they tickled her toes. Away in the distance she could hear the boom of surf on the outer reefs. *Ai-yah*, such a peaceful place.

Only three more days now till they reached the Golden Country. *Oh ko*, what would become of them there?

This evening after dinner she had once more consulted the Oracle. Its response had been ominous: *K'un*, the earth hexagram with six in the sixth place – *dragons fight in the wilderness, a great battle ensues, the colour of their blood is yellow and black.*

Dragons again, *ai-yah*. With a shudder she turned back towards the lights of the hotel.

A flicker of movement in the dark caught her alarm suddenly and her heart skipped a beat. She strained to see into the shadows. *Oh ko*, nothing, a bird only. No danger here. Stupid to be nervous.

She hurried up the path. Jazz music floated down through the garden on the evening breeze, coming from the lobby. The other passengers must have returned from the movie. Yu-ling felt a renewed pang of envy.

A twig cracked close by. Again a stirring in the bushes. Instantly all her fears returned. Something, someone was creeping stealthily under the trees up ahead. She halted petrified as a dark figure stepped out onto the path. *Aiee*, who was this?

"Sssh, do not be afraid, little Jade Years," came a throaty whisper.

Yu-Ling's heart began to thump. *Ai-yah,* Minister Soong! He must have followed her down. Before she could make a move to escape he had caught her in a plump embrace.

"*Aiee,* let me go, please!" she squealed, struggling furiously. "Honourable Uncle is waiting. . ."

"*Ho, ho,* the old fool can keep, little maiden," he chuckled twisting her face towards him. "My turtle's head is impatient for your golden gully, by all the gods!"

Yu-Ling choked, disgusted at the slobbering wetness of the Minister's mouth. "Please! *Please no!*"

"Ungrateful little wench! But for me you and your fornicating uncle would still be trapped in Macao! You want to be sent back, *heya?*"

Grunting like a hog in rut, Soong forced her up against the tennis court fence. His great belly pinning her helpless, he clawed clumsily at the buttons of the *cheong-sam.* She felt cloth rip and fingers fumble inside, and cried out with pain as he pinched cruelly at her small breasts.

In desperation she bit down on his ear with all her strength.

"ARGHHH!" the Minister's screech pierced the night. "*Dew neh loh moh,* you filthy dung-infested Manchu whore!" he yelped obscenely clutching his wounded ear.

Yu-Ling pushed him off and fled up the path towards the hotel. "Say, what the heck gives?" a male American voice demanded as she blundered into him.

It was Bob Cashin.

Hollington Soong stumbled out of the bushes cursing vilely. At the sight of the journalist he pulled himself up with a jerk, flushing hotly in the dark. "*Ai-yah,* what are *you* doing here?"

"I heard cries," the journalist's glance took in the panting girl and her torn dress. "What's the matter, Miss Chen? Has this skunk been bothering you?"

Yu-Ling gulped. She nodded without speaking.

"Lies, lies! The dirty little baggage led me on, by all the gods!" Soong spluttered. "*Dew neh loh moh chow hi,* mind your own fornicating business!" he spat furiously at Cashin.

The journalist clenched his teeth, "You lousy son of a bitch! If you lay a finger on her again I'll personally bust your ass!"

Choking with rage and loss of face, the Minister stood glaring at them both. Mother-defiling *quai loh!*" he hissed savagely in Cantonese. "*Ai-yah,* your time is coming. Yes, yes, you will see! Soon you will find out, all of you! *East Wind Rain, heya?*"

377

Barging past them, he stormed off up to the hotel.

Munro went back up the passage to his own room. It was empty, no sign of the Chief. He threw himself down on the bed with a cigarette to think. Shit, what an evening! His guess had been right though, or most of it. He knew now what was at stake. And the risks, Jesus!

Slater had made him swear to secrecy. Never to reveal anything of what he'd been told tonight. "If Berlin and Tokyo crack this one the war's as good as lost."

"Which war, for Christsakes? – here in the Pacific or against Hitler?"

"The *world war,* asshole. Don't you listen to the newscasts? The whole goddam globe is set to ignite!"

Latouche's remark had been scariest of all. "It is a race, *mon ami,* with a prize of world victory. A race *les Boches* are leading."

He had told them then about the talk with Sir Ambrose.

"The British think there's an agent among the passengers. Someone working for the Nazis, a European or American."

"The Brits have Nazis on the brain, for God's sake. Sir Ambrose told us that story in Manila, it's horse shit. CIC double checked everyone on the flight and came up with zilch. Christ, you saw those gooks we shot up yesterday, it's Yellow-bellies we gotta watch for out here – like your man Gotto!"

Sweet Jesus, what to do about poor Tad?

He rolled over on the bed as the door opened. The Chief came in followed by Scott and Kurt Thyssen. All three were grim-faced. Wordlessly, the Chief showed him the envelope of money.

"Son of a gun, where'd you dig up this lot?"

"It's mine!" Kurt pushed forward impatiently. "Give it back. You've no right to go searching people's rooms!"

Munro got off the bed, still holding the envelope. He was frowning. "Feels like a heap of dough, Kurt. Care to tell us how come?"

"That's none of your bastard business!"

"Everything to do with this flight's my business," Munro's voice was granite. "Unless maybe you'd rather explain to Major Slater?"

Thyssen paled under his tan. Some of the truculence went out of him and he dropped his gaze. "I won it in Manila if you must know. At the government casino. Roulette."

"Gambling? *You* Kurt?" Scott's tone was derisive and even Munro managed a bleak smile. The Chief said nothing.

"When? This trip?"

378

Kurt nodded, "The first night. Scott wouldn't dance any more so I went to the Casino. I. . . I was lucky."

"Four thousand bucks, I'll say," the Chief rumbled. "What was your stake?"

"A hundred only." Kurt licked his lips, "Like I said it was my lucky night, the cards were with me."

"*Cards*?" Munro's gaze sharpened, "You said roulette a moment ago."

"I . . . I started with blackjack, then moved to the tables!" Kurt was sweating now. "Listen, what the hell is this? You think I stole it or something?"

"You lying son of a bitch!" Munro whirled on him suddenly, his voice savage. "You were never near that Casino or you'd know the pay-out's in *pesos* not dollars!" He saw a flash of fear in the navigator's eyes. "Who gave you the money? Was it the Japs? The truth, for Christsakes!"

"*The Japs*!" the blood drained from Kurt's face. He stared at them incredulously. "You think I'm working for the Japs? That's crazy. You can't be serious?"

"You'd better believe I'm serious. *Now where the devil did you get this cash*?" Munro's cold rage was frightening.

"I made it! That's the truth, I swear," Kurt gasped appalled. "On the black market in Hongkong. Trading US dollars for Chinese. The Chinks are desperate, they'll pay anything for greenbacks. It's a cinch."

"*It's also illegal*. And if the Brits catch on you'll be in jail."

"No, it's legit, I promise. It's against the law to deal in Hongkong currency or export it except through a bank, but *Chinese* dough's a different matter. Any US citizen can take out as much as he wants."

There was a pause. They all stared at him uncertainly. "So then what?" the Chief demanded. "How d'you get rid of the stuff?"

"No sweat, just take it along to the Central Bank in Manila. They give a real good rate for Nationalist dollars. And you know why?" Kurt was grinning now with relief. "The US government buys it all to finance the aid program. It's cheaper than going through the Chinese Finance Ministry. Ain't that a hoot?"

He smirked again and held out his hand. "Now can I have my dough back?"

In silence they watched him go out. "He's smart, okay," the Chief said grudgingly when the door had shut. "You gotta admit that."

Sure, if you believe him, Munro thought bitterly, disgusted at himself and at the whole wretched business. Jesus, who would be under suspicion next? This trip was fast turning into a nightmare.

Abruptly he picked up a pile of magazines from the bed. "I'm going to take these over to Tad."

"I'll come with you," Scott said.

They went out the back and through the garden on the west side. The big main hangar down by the shore was all lit up and there were more guards front and rear now with others inside too. ". . . and they've orders to shoot this time, so stay away if you know what's good for you," Slater had warned. Munro caught himself rubbing his hand as if he could still feel the warmth of the silvery metal on his flesh. The tests had showed negative. "No cause for concern," as the Doc put it. Whatever the hell that meant.

"Max," Scott muttered as they neared the stores block, "what happens when we leave? Are they going to keep Tad locked up here or let him fly out with us to Midway?"

He shook his head, "Slater wants to interrogate him again first thing tomorrow. I guess he'll decide then."

"Brutes!" Scott cried passionately, "How could . . ." They came round the corner of the block and blundered into someone in the gloom.

"Who's that?" Munro peered. "Oh, it's you Reverend. What are you doing out here?"

"They . . . they told me the Japanese boy was being held prisoner," the priest replied diffidently. "I thought perhaps a visit might . . ."

"That's swell of you, Reverend," Scott was touched. "Only Tad's not a Jap, please. He's an American, okay?"

The marine guard unlocked the storeroom door. Tad was sitting on the cot, looking small and lost in the bare narrow cell. He jumped up, pathetically grateful to see them.

"They gonna le'me out? Sir, you gotta make 'em le'me out!" he cried desperately.

"Sure, Tad, of course," Scott said, taking his hands, "of course they're going to let you go."

Tad looked from one to the other of them, unconvinced. "Don't leave me in dis place, Mister Munro! Promise you won't fly wit'out me, sir!" he begged, eyes huge with worry in his brown face.

His plea cut Munro to the quick. "Tad, we're all behind you and we'll get this straightened out, I promise," he said, despising himself for the triteness of the words. Jesus Christ, the kid was distraught, what else *could* he say?

Deep down he was certain Slater would never allow Gotto back on the flight. Can I blame him? No, not with what's at stake, he daren't take the risk. I'd do the same, I'd *have* to.

Tad stared at them mutely. "*He's here!*" the words burst from him. "Mister Munro, I kin *feel* it, sir!"

"Who's here? What're you talking about, Tad?"

The youth shivered like a whipped dog. "*Sakki* – the force of the killer." His expression crumpled. He slumped on the cot, tears coursing wetly down his cheeks. Scott knelt beside him and threw her arms about his shoulders, hugging him.

"Thanks, Reverend, for coming over. I appreciate that, so will the rest of the crew." Sick at heart, they made their way back to the hotel.

"I left him a prayer book, if only there was more one could do. He seems such a nice boy to . . . to be a spy?"

"Don't say that!" Scott burst at him furiously, "Tad's not a spy. He's not!"

"No, no of course not. I didn't mean to suggest . . ." Jordan gulped hastily, wiping his forehead. "It's all so dreadful; first Morris murdered, then those dreadful killings on Bataan, Father Carmichael and Dr. Bell . . ."

His words triggered Munro's memory. Something he'd been meaning to ask, "Reverend, that reminds me, Dr. Ronald Currie."

"Currie?" the priest stumbled and Munro caught his elbow.

"Yes, the fourth man in the photograph. Hongkong can't seem to find anything on him. You said he died of fever, was that right?"

"Enteric, yes," Jordan quavered. "What . . . what did you want to know for?"

"You saw him die?"

"No, he . . . he was in another prison. They told us it was enteric, but there was a rumour . . ."

"A rumour of what? That he was murdered?"

The priest gripped Munro's arm fiercely. His voice was a croak, "*Kokuryu-kai*. Black Dragon!"

"*Till the blue skies drive the dark clouds far away.*"

The Victrola was playing in the lobby. Davey Klein had found the current favourite in the hotel's collection. Chris Fry was dancing with Felicity. Over in the crowd by the bar Georgiana stood twirling a glass in a black sleeveless dress, looking sulky. As Munro entered with Scott their eyes met for a moment. Her lip curled and she turned away.

They joined a table with Sir Ambrose and Bob Cashin.

"Max," the journalist said seriously, "you oughta hear this. You too, I guess, Sally." He told them about the incident in the garden with Soong and Yu-Ling. "The girl's okay luckily. She's a plucky kid. Made me promise not to tell her uncle."

"I'll go see her," Scott said and hurried off.

Munro got up too. "I'll settle Soong right now. I don't care if he is a VIP."

"Mr. Munro," Sir Ambrose stopped him, "I most strongly advise you not to interfere."

"Godammit, sir, we're talking about a young girl, a child almost!"

"We are talking about Chinese," Sir Ambrose corrected him in a quiet voice. "There is face involved. Hollington Soong is a government minister, a powerful man in her country. The girl and her uncle will not thank you if you turn this into an incident."

Munro hesitated. "I don't like to see the slob get away with it."

"If you wish, I could indicate to him, *discreetly*, that further such behaviour will not be tolerated."

Munro took a deep breath. Hell, what was he going to do, throw the Minister off the flight? The Company would go mad. So would the State Department. "Yes, yes, I suppose that might be better. Thanks."

"Sir Ambrose is right," Bob Cashin said. "It's better not to meddle. Boy, was Soong mad, called me every filthy name under the sun. I just wish I'd laid one on him."

The journalist took a swig at his drink and regarded the others grimly a moment, "Soong said something else too, sounded like a threat almost: "*Ai-yah, your time is coming, East Wind Rain!*"

There was silence round the table.

Munro stared at him in shock, memories flooding back. Hongkong, Jimmy's Bar, Wei-Wei's warning – "*Ai-yah, Max, you fly Golden Country, no come back, East Wind Rain, heya?*"

And Wei-Wei was dead, murdered.

Cashin caught the look on his face. "Rings a bell, huh? Well, it did with me too – Simon Ho used the same words the night he died."

Sir Ambrose stirred in his chair. "*Higashi no kaze ame – East Wind Rain,*" he murmured half to himself.

Instantly the other two zeroed on him. "You recognise it? What's it signify?"

"Since November the words have been on the lips of every fifth columnist and pro-Japanese sympathiser from Singapore to Tokyo." A film seemed to come over the diplomat's deep-sunk eyes, "It's thought to be the signal for war with the West."

"Son of a bitch!" Cashin whispered quietly.

*"We'll meet again, don't know where, don't know when
but I know we'll meet again some sunny day."*

Tad hated the way the moon shone in through the skylight, bright
enough almost to read by. The pale beams gleaming on the whitewash
gave an eerie graveyard feeling to the cell. He had shifted the cot round
but still he couldn't sleep.

They were going to leave him behind in this place.

Through the wall he could hear the snores of the guards asleep in the
neighbouring cell. He crept to the door and studied the lock. It looked
quite flimsy. If only he had a tool of some kind maybe he could force
the bolt.

The cot. He pulled off the blanket and turned it over upside down.
The frame was braced at the ends with metal cross bars. They were
screwed down tight into the wood but Tad's stocky build held a lot of
muscular strength. Sweating and straining silently he managed to
wrench one free.

Elated, he straightened up. Now for the lock. Turning, all at once
he froze.

In the corner by the door a shadow moved.

For perhaps a half second Tad gaped at it, then he jerked round
staring up at the ceiling in terror.

The skylight was open. He had heard and seen nothing but it was
open and a dark shape was crawling through the aperture. Tad
watched, paralysed with fear, unable even to scream. It slid through
the hole in the roof without sound and lowered itself to the floor on a
thin rope.

It stood erect and faced him, hooded and masked, a figure out of a
carnival nightmare. Its eyes looked into his and held them like a snake's.

He knew then.

The *dojo* in Manila. The deadly swordmaster from Japan. From his
mother's homeland a legend come to life. In a flash of understanding
he saw how Mitsuji and the others had betrayed him. Used him and
when he wouldn't cooperate, made a scapegoat of him to shield the
real spy.

"*Kokuryu-kai, Black Dragon,*" he whispered and lifted the cross bar.

There was a flicker in the moonlight. The bar was twitched away
and his arm dropped numbed. He cringed for the killing blow but the
black-clad shadow did not stir. Only the eyes appeared to widen,
boring into Tad's, remote, impersonal, as if piercing to the very
depths of his being.

Slowly the hooded figure extended its arms, hands clasped, fingers linked in a strangely disturbing pattern. Sweat broke out on Tad's brow as he gazed mesmerized at the moonlight playing upon the mystic convolutions. Dimly he heard words chanted or was it only the murmur of the surf on the reefs? He knew he was witnessing a deadly magic, that he must look away at all costs but the will had been sucked from him.

The spell besieged his brain, lulling him to sleep. Slowly, inexorably he was being drawn down into the darkness. The cell, the atoll, Hawaii, the Clipper, all were fading, washed from his mind like an ebbing tide. He felt the blackness of the void closing in.

Oh, my beloved country! A great despair came over him. He had failed. His limbs buckled and with a sob he fell forward into nothingness.

QRK? QRK? QRK? QRK? The squeal of morse in his headphones woke Earl Henry from a doze. He was tuned in to the emergency frequency. Instinctively he glanced up at the clock on the wall. A quarter of one. Shit. Fumbling for a pencil he began scribbling down the letters. QRK? QRK? QRK? – *Can you hear me? Can you hear me? Can you hear me?* KKKKKKKKKK . . .

The rhythm was so faulty it was hard to tell dots from dashes. Either an ill-trained operator or else someone on unfamiliar equipment. Must be helluva close though, the signal was almost piercing his eardrums. Abruptly it switched to a stream of text, the same message repeated over . . . HIGASHI NO KAZE AME . . . What kind of garble was that?

CQ CQ CQ An answerback crackled urgently out of the ether. QTH? QTH? QTH? – *Where are you?* Rapid, accurate morse this time, a regular operator with a powerful long range transmitter. NISHI NO KAZE HARE QRK? QTH? QRU? . . .

The exchange lasted some three minutes, then ceased as suddenly as it had begun.

Almost at once the telephone on the desk buzzed sharply. Earl answered. It was his opposite number at the military listening post on the main island.

"Hey, what you fellers playing at over there?"

"You mean those signals just now? Hell, I thought it must be you people!"

"Godammit, we got better things to do nights. D'you get a bearing on 'em?"

"The answering station read due south, but that first guy sounded like he was sitting on the roof! If it wasn't you and it wasn't me, where *did* it come from?"

"How should I know, for Christsakes? Probably a Jap plane strayed off course calling for help. Forget it, none of our business anyway." The phone clicked off.

Earl picked up his headphones again. For a long time he listened, straining to catch another bleep of a transmitter through the mush of atmospherics. Nothing. Whatever it was had gone.

Across in the hotel Munro had given up trying to sleep. He slipped out of bed and pulled on pants and a shirt. Perhaps a turn in the fresh air would clear his brain. The other bed was empty, the Chief had elected to sleep aboard.

There was a solitary lamp burning in the lobby and a Chamorro boy snoring at the desk, who did not stir as Munro quietly opened the glass main doors. Outside, the breeze had stiffened, rustling the leaves of the scrubby trees. Some cloud too, moving up from the south. Suppose the weather socked them in tomorrow? That made another worry.

Automatically he headed down towards the lagoon. Everything was peaceful and quiet, the black surface of the water riffled gently by the wind, reflecting the lights on the jetty. Out the far end the Clipper lay like a beached whale, silent and still.

A marine sentry stopped him at the pier. A fresh-faced youngster about Chris Fry's age. "Gee, sir," he said shouldering his rifle again when Munro showed his identity, "guess you'll have to see the sergeant if you wanna go aboard. My orders are to let no one up here."

"That's okay, son, I was just checking. Mind you keep an eye on her for me."

"You bet, sir, mighty fine ship. Goodnight, sir."

Munro strolled on along the beach, the coral sand scrunching under his feet. Crabs scuttled for their holes and up in the bush an occasional bird squawked. Away in the distance more lights shimmered by the military base. Wake was changing. He could remember when there'd been nothing at all besides the hotel here.

Then he saw her, standing by a rock.

She made no move as he approached. It was almost as if she'd been expecting him. She was wearing the same black dress and her feet were bare.

"All on your own?" she greeted him finally. "What happened to the little blonde?"

"Can it, Dixie. Jealousy doesn't suit you."

She shivered as if she were cold and clutched her arms. "You got a cigarette, Max?"

He lit one and gave her it.

"You and Luckies," she blew the smoke out of the corner of her mouth. "You know after we broke up I told myself I'd never have another? I went back to Stuyvesants. This is the first Lucky I've smoked since."

They walked on side by side, not touching, not talking. Listening to the surf. The moon had come out from behind the cloud wrack bathing the atoll in silver. Georgiana slipped and Munro put out his hand to steady her.

"Don't," she pulled away.

"What's wrong?"

"I turn to jelly when you touch me. I can't stand it."

"Dixie . . ." he stopped.

She swung back, the moonlight shining full on her pale face. Tears were glittering in her eyes. "Damn you, Max Munro," she said fiercely. "Why d'you have to come back into my life?"

It was so much what he'd told himself he couldn't find an answer.

"I couldn't stand to go through that again."

"It wasn't all bad, Dixie."

"It gets to be in the end though, doesn't it, between you and me? We don't seem to be a able to look at each other without fighting." She stabbed at the sand with her toes.

"When I think of the men I've put through the wringer, I suppose I'm paying for it now."

"Don't talk like a fool. Nobody owes anyone in this life."

He reached out. She shuddered, "No, Max, no please!"

He held her by the shoulders. Her whole frame was taut, resisting. He pulled her head back, feeling the silky mane of hair in his fingers the way he used to and kissed her on the mouth. Her lips were stiff and shut. She turned away. "Don't."

Is it César?"

"He wants to make me happy. He's crazy about me."

"Godammit, you don't love him! Stop fighting it, Dixie."

"Oh God, Max!" Her voice was a whisper. She raised her face to him blindly, white arms slipping round his neck. This time he felt the open softness of her mouth seeking his, the slim back arching towards him, the twin pressures of her breasts. A surge of desire flooded

386

through his loins. They kissed again fiercely, their pent-up passion hungering for release.

"Dixie, Dixie, I love you too, dammit. *Oh Christ, how I love you!*"

★   ★   ★

All around the Pacific the night was quiet. Far off in peaceful Manila General MacArthur and his wife were retiring to bed at their luxury penthouse. Earlier the General had told newsmen he still expected war to come 'sometime after January 1st.'

Across the ocean in Hawaii, Pearl Harbour blazed with lights. All nine battleships of the Pacific Fleet were in port. Liberty crews swarmed ashore to Honolulu's bars and massage parlours mingling on the streets with soldiers and airmen from Schofield, Shafter and Hickam Field. The officers' clubs were crowded, so too was the Navy's new Bloch Recreation Center where musicians from the USS *Pennsylvania* won a contest for the best band in the fleet. As another packed evening ended at the Royal Hawaiian Hotel on Waikiki Beach, the legendary '*Pink Palace*,' the dance orchestra struck up *The Star-Spangled Banner*.

Round the world again in Washington, it had been a raw cold day, the wind whistling down Pennsylvania Avenue rattling the bare branches of the trees. Most government offices were closed for the weekend or operating on skeleton staff. At the White House President Roosevelt was hosting a dinner for thirty-four to be followed by a violin musical. Kim Delahaye was not present. Early that afternoon a government plane had flown him to Chicago for a top-secret meeting.

Guests noticed the President's manner was restive and distracted. Half-way through the meal he excused himself abruptly and left the table.

Shortly before nine thirty pm, a lieutenant commander from OP-20-GZ, handed in a locked pouch containing the latest digest of intercepts to the White House mailroom. In the oval study a coal fire was burning. The President was clipping stamps at his desk. Keeping vigil with him on the sofa was Harry Hopkins.

The decode contained the first thirteen sections of a fourteen part message from Tokyo to Japanese Ambassador Nomura intercepted by the Bainbridge Island listening station. Roosevelt read the type-script slowly, holding up one page at a time in his big hand. When he had done he passed them over to Hopkins.

"*This means war,*" he said quietly.

387

XXIX

MONDAY DECEMBER 8th. HONGKONG.

The grey hour before dawn. British and Canadian troops crouched in their trenches along the border. Royal Navy gunboats patrolled the seaward approaches. The garrison was braced for an attack.

Upstairs at Shamshuipo police station, windows were shuttered against the blackout. Papers and records lay in heaps on the floor; Inspector Playfair and his team were working through the night. The task was daunting. More than eight thousand Protestant priests currently based in China, two and a half thousand in Shanghai alone.

A skinny British officer staggered in with yet more bundles of yellowing newspapers. "*Shanghai Gazette* for 1935," he dumped them on the nearest table. "There's a load more outside."

"For God's sake," someone grumbled, "the Japs are massing at the frontier and we waste time reading newspapers."

Playfair looked up from a tray of photographs, his face lined with fatigue. "If the Black Dragon capture the Clipper's cargo more than just this Colony will be at risk," he remarked evenly.

Everyone stared at him.

The telephone on the Inspector's desk shrilled. Instantly. Urgently. Playfair picked it up and listened. "Right, I'll pass the word."

He replaced the receiver. "That was Fortress HQ. Enemy forces have commenced landings on the Malay coast. Gentlemen, we are at war with Japan."

There was a moment's stunned silence. A young man cheered uncertainly. Someone broke into a rousing chorus of *Rule Britannia*, soon the lot of them were singing.

Playfair got up from his desk. He crossed to the window and threw open the shutters. It was nearly light outside, a cool breeze coming off the sea. A rickshaw had pulled up in the street below. A man got out and walked towards the police station. Across the way, the barrage balloon swayed on its mooring.

"Alright, leave all this," Playfair told his officers. "They've hit the

American fleet too, apparently. Well, that's it, I suppose," he said tiredly. "What we've been waiting for. You'd better get along to your mobilisation posts."

There was a tap at the door. "Inspector Playfair?" a man poked his head round. Short, youngish with a homely face. He wore a turn-around collar, the accent was mid-West American.

"The name's Currie. Understand you're looking for my father, sir? *Dr. Ronald Currie.*"

★   ★   ★

Clackety-clack-clack-clack . . . "Six o'clock, Miss!"

On Wake Island Scott awoke with a start as a Chamorro boy's knuckles rattled the slatted bedroom door like a stick on a paling fence. Sunlight was filtering in through the shutters bringing with it the screeching chatter of the birds. Hopping out of bed, she sponged her face and slipped on her swimsuit.

Bugle notes sounded on the breeze calling the marines to reveille. Outside, the sands were rosy pink in the dawn and the rising sun splashed the lagoon with fiery red and gold. The air was warm already with the promise of a hot muggy day. Terns flapped away shrieking angrily as she ran down the beach. The water was cool and invigorating, transparent as glass. Diving in, she swam out to the end of the jetty where the Clipper lay.

Shoals of tiny fish darted away and the Stars and Stripes reflected silkily on the ripples as she breast-stroked beneath the flying boat's starboard wing. One of the nacelle hatches was open but there was no sign of the Chief about.

The sudden roar of aero engines made her look up. A plane's belly zoomed low overhead, the blue circle with the white star and the snouts of the .50 calibre guns showing plainly on the wing. The dawn patrol taking off from the marine base. Shading her eyes, Scott watched the stubby little fighters head out over the reefs and climb away south.

Up in the hotel Shapiro woke and turned over as Chris Fry slipped back into their shared bedroom, his hair tousled. "Morning, lover boy, have a good time?" he yawned. "How's Felicity?"

"Ssh, keep your *voice* down, for heavensakes!" Chris hissed

389

agitated. "Her Mom's out there. I almost got caught."

Shapiro gave a snort of laughter as he sat up and scratched the hair on his bare chest. "Boy, I can just see her face if she had!"

"It's no joking matter," the young Texan told him seriously, stripping off his shirt and going through into the bathroom. "She'd have me up before the Skipper and I'd be out on my ass for sure. We're both in enough trouble as it is."

"You mean Macao? Forget it, with Ross out the way no one's gonna bother with that any more. And don't worry about old Max," Shapiro put his arms behind his head, leaning back with a chuckle, "'cause he sneaked out from his room last night too."

"*Max* did?" Chris looked round from the basin. "You're kidding?"

"Honest injun. I was walking back from a crap game over at the base and there he was on the beach with the Delahaye babe. And they weren't playing pattycake neither."

"*Whee wheeww!*" Two Chamorro boys weeding the flower beds in front of the hotel whistled softly under their breath as Georgiana came out through the glass doors in a black one-piece bathing costume with a halter top that made them sweat with envy at all the long-legged, high-breasted womanhood of her. Carrying a driver and a new box of balls, she sauntered down to the water's edge, teed off with an expert pinch of sand and swished the air a few times to loosen up.

From the end of the beach Scott glimpsed the supple athletic figure poised for an instant at the top of her swing. The thin shaft winked smoothly in the sunlight and she heard the click of the ball as it shot up and out over the water like a black dot, vanishing with a splash a good two hundred yards out. Wow, some drive, she thought with admiration.

She watched as Georgiana repeated the stroke unhurriedly with the remainder of the box, each drive as clean and perfect as the first. A fraction of draw on one, then a fade to match, the waterspouts leaping up like gunshots at each smack. A tablecloth would have covered them all. Evidently the price of balls didn't bother her none.

The last one had plopped into the lagoon when there came a shout behind and César appeared hurrying down from the hotel in a blue polo shirt. Scott saw him catch her arm and begin speaking vigorously. It sounded like they were having a quarrel.

Well, that was their business, with a shrug Scott turned away and started up the path. She wanted to see Tad before breakfast. The time was six forty and Max had scheduled take-off for nine am.

Three miles away at the tip of the main island a small radio van stood under the trees by the airstrip. From it a six man US Army detachment maintained a communications link for the Air Corps. At ten minutes to seven the PFC on early shift had just begun warming up his equipment for the day.

He checked his aerial, switched on the main receiver and twirled the dial, seeking the frequency used by the nearest Air Corps base, Hickam Field, Oahu. Hawaii time was twenty-two hours behind Wake. It would be eight fifty am there, still Sunday December seventh.

Static crackled in his ears as he slipped on the headphones. Fragments of indistinguishable morse lost in a wash of atmospherics. He fine-tuned the frequency needle a fraction and reached for the key to begin tapping out his call sign.

Dit-dit-dah . . . dit-dah-dit . . . dah-dah-dit . . ." a burst of high speed morse slashed through the ether like a band saw, the operator running the letters together in his haste. *Dit-dah . . . dit-dit . . .* the rhythm blurred and jerky as if his hand were shaking with nerves or fright.

He scrabbled for his pad, scribbling down the letters as fast as they spattered over the airwaves. He sat up in his chair aghast as he read the frantic message. It was in plain English, uncoded, in violation of all military procedures.

"Oh Christ!" he gasped. "Son of a bitch, those goddam Japs!"

Tumbling out the van, he tore for the Command Post.

Across at the hotel Munro was shaving.

"Hey, fellers!" A door slammed and feet went running down the passage. "Hey, there's a war on!"

A moment later Stewart Whitely burst into the room without knocking. "Max, Max, it's started! We're at war. The Japs have attacked Pearl Harbour!"

"*What?*"

"A flash just came through on the radio. The Japs are bombing Pearl and Hickam Field!"

"Hawaii?" Munro stared at him in disbelief, "That's crazy. They must mean the Philippines?"

"No, it's Pearl. The bastards have launched a raid on the Pacific Fleet. It's for real, Max!"

"Well, I'll be godammed. So they finally did it."

He finished the last few strokes of the razor hurriedly, rinsed off and reached for his shirt. Stewart was still chattering away excitedly, "Boy, those Jap bastards really stuck their heads in the noose this time! The Navy had it all doped out. They tracked the Jap carriers clear across the ocean. Remember those signals we picked up the first day out? That was the strike force. Corregidor confirmed it. The Yellow-bellies steamed right into the trap."

"Let's hope," Munro was still struggling to take it all in. His mind raced, trying to figure what the news meant for them here, stuck in mid-ocean with the Jap fleet out. Suppose they hit Wake next or Midway? Jesus, what to do then?

Shapiro came tearing in with Chris Fry, breathless and shirtless. "Hey, Max, did you hear the news?"

"Steward just told me," Munro's voice was deliberately nonchalant. "Alright, quieten down. Go get dressed and round up the others. We'll meet in the lobby."

"Aye aye, Sir." They rushed off.

Munro ripped open the ship's briefcase. Among the metal log books and cargo manifests was an envelope marked Contingency File. He slit it with a thumbnail. Inside was a sheaf of instructions covering every emergency from Air Piracy to Outbreak of Plague. Under the heading War the advice was succinct – *evacuate all Pan American passengers and personnel to nearest place of safety*. Great, that was a big help.

The lobby was full of half-dressed passengers milling about the cane furniture, talking and jabbering at the tops of their voices. Pat O'Byrne was doing his best to calm things down. Over by the bar Slater and Bob Cashin were fiddling with the radio. At the sight of Munro everyone surged round speaking at once.

"Say, Captain, is it true we're at war?"

"What'll we do if Hawaii's invaded?"

"Are the Japs going to attack us here?"

"Hold it!" came a bellow from Slater. There was a hush, then faint and far away against a background of static they heard the tense voice of the radio announcer. ". . . *Webley Edwards speaking to you on KGMB. The island is under attack! I repeat the island is under attack! Japanese aircraft are bombing Oahu. Pearl Harbour, Hickam Field and Wheeler Field have all been hit. There is heavy gunfire over the fleet base. A number of enemy planes have been shot down. This is the real McCoy!*"

The voice faded out.

"Oh, my God," a man said. "It's war alright." A woman began to

392

sob. Most people seemed stunned. Sir Ambrose Hope moved to the bar and poured himself a glass of whisky.

"*East Wind Rain*," Bob Cashin croaked hoarsely, his face strained and white. "This was it all along. The peace talks were just a blind. Those godammed sneaking Yellow-bellies!"

"Yeah, they played us for suckers, okay," Slater snorted grimly, "the sons of bitches. We'll lick the hell outta them for this."

"I say, Captain, does that mean we're stuck here?" Gordon Smythe called out in pyjamas and dressing gown. "How will we reach San Francisco if the Nips take Hawaii?" There was a chorus of alarm. Ruth Simms clutched her children. Next to them Georgiana stood wearing a sweat shirt over her swimsuit, César's hand on her shoulder.

"We'll get you home, don't worry," Munro answered, pretending a confidence he didn't feel. "Maybe the Navy'll send planes to escort us in, I don't know. Right now though I suggest you all go finish dressing. We may be pulling out at short notice."

Thyssen pushed though the throng, his tie crooked and hair all anyhow. "What're we going to do, Max?" he muttered anxiously.

"Get down to the ship and warn the Chief to begin fuelling up. Take Shapiro and Fry with you. They can start on the loading schedule while you check out our flight plan to Midway."

"Hell though, suppose the Japs are bombing Midway too?"

"We'll worry about that when it happens," Munro snapped harshly. "Now shift your ass." The navigator flushed furiously and started to speak, then changed his mind and strode out. Shapiro and Fry followed.

Munro swivelled, "Stewart?"

"Here, Max."

"Stay by that set of yours, whatever you pick up could be vital. Send me word the moment anything develops."

"On my way," Whitely nodded. "Where'll you be?"

"Over at the base with Devereux. He may have some more on the situation. Pat," he turned to the purser as Stewart hastened off with Davey, "you're in charge here till I return. Keep everyone together, make sure they stay *inside* the hotel. Don't let people start wandering off. See they have their bags packed and get some breakfast inside them."

"*Skipper! Skipper!*" Everyone jerked round. Scott came rushing in from the rear. She was in uniform, her face shocked. She saw the crowd of people staring and pulled up short. "What . . . what's going on?"

Munro told her, "It's the Japs, they've declared war. They're bombing Hawaii."

"You're kidding?" She gaped at them incredulously as the words sunk in. "Oh no," she whispered. Then abruptly her face crumpled. "I've just been over at the stores. It's Tad, he's . . . he's . . . *Oh God, come quickly!*"

General Quarters was sounding from the tannoys on the base as Munro and Slater went out through the screen door and across to the store sheds at a run. A truck roared past in a cloud of dust, honking its horn, carrying a crew out to man the five inch naval guns of Battery B on Toki Point. The three marine guards were standing round the door of the cell, nervous and jumpy.

"Search me how the bastard done it, Major," the lanky corporal began blustering straightaway, "there was a man awake all night next door an' nobody heard nothin'."

Munro felt a hollow in his gut. "Open the goddam door."

"Yessir." The man fumbled with the keys. Munro snatched them from him impatiently and wrenched the door open.

"Oh shit, no," he choked.

The early morning sun slanting through the skylight cast bright bare patches against the whitewashed walls of the cell. Dust motes floated in the air like shafts of smoke. At the rear by the upended cot, the body of the steward hung limp from a cord looped over a roof beam, small and shrunken-looking.

"Well, I'll be a son of a bitch," Slater said behind him disgustedly. "The goddam Yellow-belly skipped out on us after all."

They all stared at the hanged corpse. It didn't look much like Tad any more. The thin cord had bitten deep into the swollen flesh of the neck and the purpled features were bloated grotesquely.

"He must've stood on the cot to reach the beam," the corporal pointed out cold-bloodedly. "Kicked it away with his foot when he had the noose on."

"How'd he get hold of the rope?" Slater snarled at him. "This place was supposed to've been cleaned out, by God."

"I dunno, sir. Guess maybe he brung it in with him. No one said nothin' about the guy killin' hisself, sir," the corporal added defensively.

"Makes one less of the slit-eyes to deal with," another of the guards muttered.

"Dammit!" Slater smacked fist into palm in anger, "Some fuck-up this has turned out. I wanted to question the skunk. He might've told us a lot."

394

Munro interrupted. "Cut him down," he said thickly through the nausea in his belly.

They all looked at him. No one moved. "I said cut him down. You got a knife?" he snapped at the corporal. "Well, cut the godammed rope."

Sheepishly one of the marines produced a clasp knife with a snap-button blade. The kind that was SOP equipment with enlisted men the world over. Munro and the corporal took the weight while he cut the cord. It was strange how heavy a corpse seemed even with two of them and one to lift the legs.

The other marine set the cot right side up again and they laid Tad on it. There were flecks of dried blood on his face around the mouth where he'd bitten through his tongue. A lousy way to go.

Munro fingered the end of the dark cord. It felt like no kind he'd met before, thin and supple, very tightly-plaited. Too soft for ordinary hemp. Silk maybe? Where had Tad gotten it? It hadn't been on him when he was searched.

Latouche arrived, summoned by Scott. The Frenchman glanced down at the body with pursed lips. "*Alors, un suicide.* You were expecting this?"

Slater shrugged. "He was a spy. Guess it's all the proof we need."

"*Shut up!*" Munro turned on him suddenly savage. "Shut up, you goddam son of a bitch. He was one of my crew."

Leaving them standing, he went outside. Scott was sobbing against a tree. She raised a tear-streaked face as he came over. "He *wasn't* a spy, Max, I know he wasn't!" she cried furiously. "He was a decent honest boy and they killed him, those brutes in there. They hounded him to it! God, I hope they rot in hell for what they've done!"

A car came skidding up the coral track from the hotel, slewing violently as it took the corner and braked to a halt. Tom Keswick, the company manager, leaned out. "Jesus Christ, Max, I've been searching all over for you. Major Devereux wants you down at the Command post – *urgent*."

Back at the hotel rumours were flying. San Francisco had been bombed. Japanese forces were occupying Oahu. The US Pacific Fleet had sortied to do battle with the attackers and had captured a Japanese carrier. There was no hard news which made the passengers jumpier.

"Nothing but darn hula music," snorted one of the oilmen crouched round the radio. "Maybe it was a hoax. You know like that Martian invasion story."

395

"No way, that was Webley Edwards, he wouldn't put out a fake. Sounded to me like the Yellow-bellies got creamed. Serve the bastards right, the nerve of them attacking our people."

"Maybe it weren't the Japs," Eddie Wirth suggested darkly. "Maybe they were Germans."

The others blinked at him. "You think Japs could pull a stunt like this? The hell they could. The Nazis are behind it, I tell you."

"German pilots in Jap kites, say that's smart," someone else said. "Just the kinda trick Hitler'd spring."

"Christ, then boy are we in trouble. Those Luftwaffe sons of bitches are hot."

The story spread fast. So did others equally far fetched. The nerves of many passengers were being stretched to breaking point.

"Fold up your nightgowns and bring them to me, quickly! Debbie, fetch the toothbrushes from the bathroom. Hurry, hurry! Where are your slippers?"

"I can't find them, Mummy."

"Try the closets, look under the beds. They must be *somewhere*."

The girls' room was in chaos. Clothes and toys lay scattered everywhere. Ruth Simms was scurrying around frantically, a housecoat over her slip, trying to cram things into suitcases.

"They're not there, Mummy," Debbie crawled out from under the bed. "They must be lost."

"They can't be. We've *got* to find them. And now look, you've got dirt all over your frock! You'll have to change. Take it off, oh God, oh God!" Ruth cried.

"Gee, it's only some dust, Mom."

"Take it *off*, I said! Do you want to make us miss the flight?" Ruth fetched the girl a slap. Both children burst into frightened tears. Their mother had never hit them before.

"Darling, darling, I'm sorry, I didn't mean it!" Ruth wailed, clutching them to her, sobbing. "Don't cry, please don't cry. Oh God, what's going to happen to us?"

The sounds of the children's tears carried across the passage to the Professor's room. Yu-Ling was wrapping up the porcelain teapot, trying to keep her hands steady. *Oh ko,* what would happen to them all?

"Honourable Uncle," she asked timidly, "will the Sea Devils attack here, you think? And how we get to the Golden Country now, *heya?*"

The old Mandarin's hands smoothed the silk covering of the casket. "When Tigers fight, the forest is shattered. *Joss.* Either the barbarians will protect us or they will not. There is nothing we can do but wait. *Joss.*"

Joss, always *joss*, Yu-Ling shut the suitcase with an angry snap. *Ai-yah*, she wasn't going to wait calmly to be raped or killed by the filthy Sea Devils. Maybe the *quai loh* journalist would tell her some news.

"Gee whiz, Mom, are we really at war?" Ricky Bianchi asked his mother as she knelt on the floor packing for them. He made a pistol with his finger and cocked thumb, "Pow! Pow! I'm gonna be a soldier."

"Ach, so you are going to fight the Japanese? That is good."

Mother and son jerked round. Prince Cherkassy was smiling sneeringly at them from the doorway, "Perhaps in Hawaii I could show you how to shoot a real gun, eh?"

"Wow, would you really? I'd like that."

Maria got up from the floor, her face taut. "Ricky," she said, "go see if they're serving breakfast yet."

The Russian patted the child's head as he went out. He shut the door. "A fine boy. Does he know yet about his new father?"

Maria Bianchi's eyes glittered with pure venom. "If you say one word to him, as God is my witness I'll kill you," she hissed.

Devereux's CP was alongside the air strip. Starter cartridges were sputtering as the car pulled up and hazy blue exhaust smoke rolled across the apron. A second pair of Wildcats trundled towards the runway, clouds of dust mushrooming from the downdraught of their props. Munro watched them climb away into the sun, wings wobbling as each pilot hand-cranked his landing gear up.

Everywhere there was frantic activity now. Four more of the tough little fighters stood nearby, cockpit covers thrown back, pilots in their seats suited-up ready for instant combat. Armourers swarmed over others loading hundred-pound bombs and fitting long belts of .50 machine gun ammunition into the wings. Along the edge of the strip, men stripped to the waist were digging slit trenches and foxholes and labouring to top off earth revetments protecting the aircraft on the ground.

397

The Wildcats were still climbing away when they heard the bugle call.

It was Morning Colours. Everyone on the base ceased what he was doing and came to attention facing the flagpole. As the long slow notes rang out the flag soared up the halyards and unfurled, whipping in the breeze. The last call died away and for a moment there was perfect stillness. Munro felt his throat tighten with emotion.

The time was eight o'clock. The US had been at war just two hours.

Officers and noncoms streamed in and out of Devereux's office. The orderly tent was beseiged by a mob of civilians clamouring for weapons. The Pan Am party fought their way through. The marine major greeted them grimly.

"It's for real this time, gentlemen." He showed them the latest dispatch from the CinCPAC – EXECUTE UNRESTRICTED AIR AND SUB-MARINE WARFARE AGAINST JAPAN. "If the Japs have hit Hawaii, I figure we can expect bombs to start dropping here pretty soon."

"Any dope on the battle yet?" Slater demanded.

"Your guess is as good as mine. Sounds to me though like they caught us flatfooted. Sunday morning was a smart time to pick."

"How about Midway?" Munro asked him.

"Nothing so far. Guess they're waiting for it like us." Devereux chewed his lip. "All this leaves you people kind of caught in the middle, huh?"

"Our radio operator got through to Hawaii Division momentarily," Tom Keswick told him. "They said for us to remain here till the situation clarifies. Then they went off the air." He gestured helplessly, "The Clipper base is right in Pearl City."

There was a sober silence.

"I figure our best bet's to hang on till nightfall," Munro said, "then try to make Midway under cover of dark. Once there we'll be within range of Navy escorts." The station manager nodded his agreement. "Meantime, what can we do to help?"

Devereux stepped to the door of the tent a moment. Through the flaps they could see the long barrels of a nearby five-inch battery training out over the reefs. Marines were manhandling shells into bunkers and filling sandbags. "Most of those guns are older than I am, but they still shoot and we'll make the Japs work to take this island. My main problem is I'm blind. I don't know what's out there. I've no radar and too few fighters to maintain effective patrols against attack."

"For reconnaissance you need a plane with plenty of range," Munro pushed back his white uniform cap. "We've got just the bird for you, Major, right here – the Clipper."

"I hope to hell you know what you're doing, Pilot, that's all. Your plane's our only ticket out of this sandpit."

"Godammit, d'you want us to sit around on our butts till the Japs arrive? You heard what Devereux said, he needs all the help he can get."

The marine sentry saluted as Tom Keswick's car dropped Munro at the jetty. Out on the flying boat's wings mechanics in white overalls were hauling up fuel bowsers and the smell of avgas drifted in through the flight deck windows as he briefed the crew.

"I want all the gear stripped out, the mail and the rest of the cargo ashore, passengers' baggage too. That should lighten the load by twenty thousand pounds."

"Hell, Max, ain't they going to give us any guns then?" Thyssen protested. "We'll be sitting ducks up there."

"What d'you think we are here, for Godsakes? Stripped down we'll have speed to outrun anything except carrier fighters. And if there is a flat-top waiting over the horizon, well then we're shit out of luck anyway.

"This is strictly a volunteer mission, I can't order you to come. Anyone who wants out had better speak up now."

He paused to let them take it in. The younger ones like Davey Klein and Chuck wore expressions of eagerness. Stewart Whitely looked scared. Only the Chief seemed unmoved. "How much gas you need, Max?" he asked, almost boredly.

"Enough for twelve hours flying minimum. I want gas to make Midway in an emergency if we have to."

The Indian nodded. "Three thousand gallons should cover it. C'mon, Chuck." They disappeared into the starboard wing.

Munro glanced round the others, "Any questions? Okay, Stewart, you stick on your set. The rest of you open up the holds and start shifting those mail sacks."

"Where d'you want us to put them, Max?"

"Christsakes, dump 'em on the beach, let someone else take care of it. *You're at war now!*"

Up at the Pan Am radio shack Earl Henry had joined the operator on duty, scanning the airwaves desperately for news of what was happening. Just before nine am they picked up a frantic signal from Guam. The island was under attack too.

"Enemy troops have landed in the bay!" they heard the Guam operator call. "Their warships are shelling us. They've hit the hotel, it's *burning!*"

Moments later came a final message, "The Japs are in the town, we're falling back! God bless America. This is Guam signing off."

The radio went silent.

Scott had gone back to the hotel. Tad was dead, there was no time to waste weeping. She dried her eyes and set about helping Pat O'Byrne organise the passengers.

The sight of the flying boat being unloaded had caused an uproar. Tom Keswick was forced to make an announcement in the lobby. "Everyone calm down now. Nobody's abandoning anyone. You'll all be flying out to Midway tonight just as soon as it's dark."

"Why are they taking off our bags then?" Gordon Smythe demanded plummily. "We've a right to know what's going on."

"The allowance for the flight will be fifteen pounds per person. Captain Munro's orders, we're evacuating the local staff with us."

"But I've some very expensive clothes in my cases," Cynthia Gordon Smythe shrilled. "You don't expect me to leave them here on the beach. What will I wear in America?"

"Forget about your clothes, lady, you'll be damn lucky to make it there at all," Bob Cashin told her caustically.

Out of the corner of her eye Scott saw a passenger slipping away out of the doors. "*Reverend!*" she hurried after him down the path. "Please, the Captain said for everybody to stay in the hotel."

The priest halted and turned to face her. Unlike the others he appeared perfectly calm. "I have to see to the Bishop," he explained quietly. "They mustn't leave the coffin lying in the sun."

In fact it was starting to cloud over.

Munro's gaze narrowed as he checked the weather. The hazy overcast which had been around since dawn was starting to thicken up in patches. Rain squalls would be hitting them soon.

He walked briskly back up towards the shore. It was ten o'clock and they had lightened the Clipper by almost five tons. By the end of the jetty a gang of Chamorros were carting away the stack of canvas mail sacks and assorted baggage dumped on the sand. Discarded among them, he recognised the couturier gown from Manila.

Tom Keswick had left the car for him. He drove up past the hotel and over the causeway onto the main island. Through the bush he could see men digging in along the outer shore, siting machine guns to sweep the reefs. In the marine camp look-outs were scanning the sky from atop the fifty foot water tank.

At the airstrip a flight of Wildcats was returning from patrol. Munro watched the pilots climb out. Young, confident, full of swagger, they looked like they could give a good account of themselves. Ground crews began refuelling from fifty-gallon drums as four more of the fighters sped down the runway, one behind the other.

Major Putnam, the soft-spoken commander, came over, aviator's goggles pushed up on his leather flying helmet. "No sign of bandits yet. Maybe we'll be lucky today."

"Guam's fallen, you heard that?"

"Yeah, just now. Poor bastards never had a chance."

They both squinted up at the sky. Intermittent banks of cloud hung low over the sea and a squall line was moving in from the south.

"Darn surf don't help any," Putnam muttered. "Japs'd be on top of us before we heard a thing. Sure wish those revetments were ready, any planes on the ground are sitting targets till then."

They moved towards the Command Post.

The squall was coming closer. It was half a mile away now, almost directly over the southern end of the atoll. "We're going to catch it in a minute," someone said. A flock of seabirds shot up suddenly from the south shore and wheeled away, their wings flashing sickle-shaped against the sun.

Devereux appeared at the door of the CP, calling to a noncom. He beckoned them into the tent.

"Hey," a voice cried by the squadron tent, "here come our B-17s."

Munro glanced back over his shoulder. His heart skipped a beat. A flight of twin-engine planes had dropped suddenly out of the cloud. He stared at them paralysed, too numbed for a second to react. This was it, the moment they'd been expecting ever since that first alarm. Soundlessly the planes came boring in, the drone of their engines swamped by the surf. They were at less than two thousand feet, he could see every detail, the rising sun emblem on the wings, the bomb doors opening . . .

"Look, their wheels are falling off!" a civilian shouted.

"The hell they are!" Putnam yelled. "Those aren't B-17s, they're Japs! They're dropping bombs!"

There was a crackle of fire as the .50 calibre machine guns along the beach opened up. "*Take cover!*" Devereux bellowed. "Air raid! Everyone take cover!"

The scream of the falling bombs shrilled in Munro's ears as he sprinted for an unfinished foxhole. He reached it and threw himself in just as an enormous blast slammed him to the ground. Stunned and deafened, he lay hugging the dirt while the earth heaved around him. Ear-splitting explosions rocked the atoll. Lumps of stone and coral rained down. The air was full of smoke and howling steel splinters. Sticks of bombs fell across the maintenance sheds tearing them to pieces. With a frightening *whoomph* a fuel dump vomited fire as twenty-five thousand gallons of avgas went up in a pillar of yellow flame.

Machine gun bullets and cannon shells kicked up the sand as the bombers' shadows flashed by overhead, so low Munro could see the rear gunners crouched behind their spitting weapons. Heavy concussions shook the ground. An ammunition truck careered past, the driver twisting and turning the wheel in a frantic attempt to avoid the bombs. Fifty yards short of a patch of bush it took a direct hit and disintegrated in a shattering blast. The hot breath of fire scorched Munro's face.

There was a momentary lull. Groggily he staggered to his feet, amazed to find himself uninjured. Fury filled him at the sight of the cratered airfield, the blazing buildings, the mangled bodies strewn over the ground. How dare they, he wanted to shout, how dare they attack an American possession?

Putnam stumbled up beside him, plastered with dust, his flying suit blood-spattered. "*Bastards!*" he yelled, shaking his fist impotently at the bombers as they swung off over the lagoon. "Dirty murdering goddam *bastards!*"

Miraculously none of the grounded Wildcats seemed to have been hit. The strip was still serviceable – just. Four pilots leapt out from a slit trench and raced across the apron to their machines.

Machine guns stuttered afresh. Sheets of flame sprouted from the fuselage of the nearest fighter as a second V-formation roared in strafing the field with tracer bullets. More bombs screamed down. Munro saw two of the pilots fall, then a third, their bodies torn to pieces by shrapnel. Zigzagging through a hail of metal, the last man somehow reached his plane and pulled himself up into the cockpit. Smoke puffed from the starter and the prop blades began to spin. An instant later a stack of incendiaries engulfed pilot and plane in a fireball.

Screams pierced the air. Dead and injured everywhere in the carnage. Crackling like Fourth of July fireworks ammunition aboard the burning planes was exploding in the heat. Ignoring the bullets,

Munro and Putnam dodged across the apron to help drag the wounded to safety.

The last of the attackers droned away, waggling its red splashed wings in a *banzai* victory signal. Dazed, the survivors picked themselves up. About them the base was a shambles of total destruction. Of eight Wildcats caught on the ground seven were flaming torches, another badly damaged. Every building had been wrecked or gutted. Fires raged out of control among the oil and gasoline stores. In less than twelve minutes the Japanese had knocked out sixty percent of Wake's air defence.

Munro stared across the lagoon. The Pan Am base was hidden beneath a pall of oily smoke.

XXX

Georgiana clawed herself upright. Alcohol fumes stung her throat. She'd been standing by the bar when the bombers struck. The floor was carpeted with smashed bottles leaking pools of raw spirit. Against the wall a Chamorro waiter crouched, fingers pressed to his ears.

Dimly among the confusion came shouts and thin screams. Passengers were stumbling about, bewildered. "Outside! Everybody outside and take cover!" someone shouted, choking on the smoke.

Shards of glass cracked underfoot. A figure groped towards her, blackened with dust.

"Georgiana, *querida*, you are not hurt?"

"No, no, I'm okay," she shook off his hand and stumbled through the shattered doorway. Black puffballs of AA drifted between the clouds. Thick oily smoke was boiling from a blazing fuel dump, darkening the sun. The planes were gone.

Yu-Ling emerged behind her, supporting the old mandarin with Scott. Reverend Jordan was staring up at the sky, his turn-around collar awry. The two Simms girls clung to their parents, sobbing with fright. Astonishingly there seemed to be no casualties.

At the back of the hotel the kitchen block was roofless, flames crackling greedily among the wreckage. It looked to have taken a direct hit. Soot-blackened men scrabbled through the rubble, bawling obscenities, dragging out screaming wounded. A patch of bush had been set alight, burning with an acrid stench. Fragments of charred ash drifted in the air and over all three islets of the atoll hung ominous palls of smoke.

"*Ricky!*" Maria Bianchi screamed. Her son was rushing round excitedly collecting up spent brass .50 calibre casings dropped by the raiders. "Come back here!" she seized him by the shirt, pulling him under a tree.

"God in hell!" an Army man hollered, gaping at the devastation. "How'd the sons of bitches get through? Where were our fighters and our anti-aircraft?"

Georgiana stared wildly towards the lagoon. A shaft of fear made her knees weak suddenly.

"*Querida, wait!* Where are you going? Do not be a fool!"

Ignoring him she tore down the beach, hair flying. At the pierhead a marine tried to bar her way. She dodged past him and ran onto the jetty. The planking was pockmarked with bullet holes and splinters. Men were yelling in the smoke, trying to douse flames spouting from ruptured fuel lines. A mechanic lay gritting his teeth, blood staining his shirt. Georgiana dashed past and flung herself down the gangway to the pontoon.

"Hold it, where you think you're goin', lady?" a bear-like growl demanded as she cannoned into someone. Hands gripped her shoulders, steadying her. Eyes streaming from the smoke, she blinked up into the flat, Choctaw face.

"Oh God, Chief," she cried clinging to him, "*Max, where's Max?*"

"Behind you, kid!" He spun her round. Leaping and bumping down the track from the main island, a powerful motor bike was roaring towards them in a cloud of sand.

The sheaves of the cargo derrick squealed.

"Okay, lower away. Slowly . . . slowly . . . Easy with it!" Shapiro called from the wing.

The stretcher hung swaying from the slings above the flying boat's hold as Chris Fry reached up to guide it through the hatch. Ross's bandaged face was grey against the sheet. Unmoving. The doctors had given him another shot of morphine.

It was eighty minutes since the attack. They were pulling out. Evacuating. No point now in recce flights.

"She's flyable, Max!" The Chief had been as amazed as Munro. "God knows how the jokers missed her but they did. Chuck an' I was nose-down in a storm drain when they came over firin' full blast an' we both figured she was lost for sure." His manner was rock steady as ever. "She took a dozen slug holes in the skin, they're being patched now. Engines an' fuel tanks all check out A-1. We can pull anchor just as soon as you give the word."

The steel footlockers had already been loaded, so too had the coffin. "If you're stuck for weight, Pilot, throw off a passenger," Slater had overridden Munro's objections ruthlessly. "That coffin's security cover for the mission, it goes along."

"Christsakes, who are you trying to fool? The Japs blasted the base to rags without putting hardly a mark on the Clipper or the hangar.

405

That wasn't luck, Major, those damn bombers knew damn well what they were about. It's a straight race now!"

"Stick to your job, Pilot. I'll figure strategy, you just get this bus outta here!"

The derrick swung back, slings hanging empty. Without ceremony it was dumped ashore with the piles of other gear. Everything that would come loose had been ripped out and thrown overboard to save weight. Down the beach Davey Klein was burning the ship's papers in an empty fuel drum.

A harassed Major Devereux stopped by. He gave Munro a message for CinCPAC. "See the Admiral gets it, Max. If you can. My main radio's knocked out. I've three planes left and half my guns are unmanned. Radar gear for Wake's been sitting on the dock in Hawaii this past month. I need fire-control sets, machine gun ammo, three and five-inch shells. Tell him we'll do our best to hold till the fleet gets here. We'll give the Yellow-bellies a fight even if we wind up eating fish and rice."

"I'll do my best for you. Good luck."

"You too, Max. So long."

Munro wondered who'd need it most.

"Thirty-six additional, Jesus Christ!"

The passengers were filing down the dock past the litter of abandoned equipment. Maria Bianchi clutching Ricky firmly by the hand, the Simms family tight-lipped and afraid, Hollington Soong, Van Cleef, Sir Ambrose Hope limping from a bruised knee, Latouche with his black bag. Behind followed Earl Henry and the other Pan Am staff, several bandaged from splinter wounds. Earl had been lucky, two of his buddies were dead. Scott and O'Byrne herded them all aboard urgently.

Everyone was tense, checking the sky.

"Godammit, Tom," Munro eyed the long line aghast, "that's three tons extra weight!"

"You think we'll make it off?" Tom Keswick gnawed a fingernail nervously.

Munro glanced out over the lagoon. Given a long enough run the Clipper could lift a house. But the coral-free channel on Wake was barely half a mile between the two arms of the atoll. Even with a normal load it was a bitch. He gave a brief shrug, "Only one way to find out."

406

"Is that the last o'them?"

Scott ran an eye down her lists. "Yes. *No!* No wait, Pat. We're missing someone! Reverend Jordan hasn't shown."

"Drat the fellow, what the devil's happened to him?" O'Byrne said exasperated. "You sure he didn't slip by you?"

"Yes, yes I checked everyone," Scott was scanning the beach. "He must have gotten left behind. I'll go find him."

Panting, she ran up the path to the hotel. "Reverend! Are you there? The flight's leaving *now!*"

There was no answer. The lobby was strewn with abandoned baggage. She tore through to the rear and met him hurrying across the sand from the hangar.

"Heavensakes, Reverend, what're you doing? Don't you know we're pulling out?"

"I . . . I forgot my prayer book in the steward's cell," he gasped. "Sorry."

"You almost missed the plane. C'mon, there's no time to lose!" Grabbing his arm she hustled him down to the jetty.

"Engine starting order – Two . . . three . . . one . . . four."

"Two . . . three . . . one . . . four, aye aye, Skipper." The Chief was standing by at the switches, *"Ready on engine two."*

Munro cracked the throttles open to seven hundred, watching the fuel-pressure gauge. He reached for the buttons on the overhead panel. *"Start and boost."*

"Number two turning!" Shapiro sang out from the co-pilot's seat as the port inboard prop clattered into life.

"Ready on three."

"Start and boost."

"Number three turning!"

"Stand by to cast off."

Down below Scott felt the rumble of the motors and sent up a silent prayer as the flying boat edged ponderously away from the dock. The passenger deck was crammed, every berth occupied. She and Pat were perched on jump seats in the galley. God alone knew how Max would ever get this load airborne. On a hook next to her hung the apron Tad used to wear. Tears welled suddenly in her eyes.

"Secure all doors and hatches." Running up each engine in turn to full rated power, Munro taxied the Clipper slowly out to the start of the channel and turned her into the wind. He snapped on the interphone button a moment, "Any bandits aloft, Chris?"

"Negative, Skipper," Chris Fry's voice came back from the astro-dome in the hold. "Nothing but birds."

"*Ready for take-off.*" Through the window Munro could see a forlorn knot of watchers on the dock. "*Flaps fifteen degrees.*"

"*Flaps fifteen, aye aye, sir.*"

Smoothly Munro advanced the throttle, keeping the power equal on all four engines. The deep bellow of the Cyclones filled the cockpit and the needles on the dials leapt into quivering life. The far shore looked horribly close.

"*Thirty knots . . . forty,*" Shapiro called out, "*. . . forty-five.*"

Spray was streaming from the sponsons. Back of the flight deck Slater was strapped in at the Captain's desk, swearing silently to himself. Everyone stared ahead. Five hundred yards now to the opposite beach. They could make out the marines in their gunpits gazing at them.

"*Sixty . . . seventy . . . eighty . . .!*" Shapiro's voice was sharp with nervous tension. Two hundred yards to go. One hundred and fifty. Sweat broke out on his brow, "Skipper!"

"ABORT!" Munro wrenched the throttles back. The engines' scream died away. With a surge the flying boat's hull settled in the water. Her speed fell off. Shapiro wiped his face. There were mutters of relief.

"Silence," Munro snapped curtly.

Down on the lower deck the passengers waited anxiously as they taxied back for a second try. "The wind has dropped on us," Van Cleef peered out a saloon window. "He will need a longer run."

Opposite him Georgiana and César sat stiffly, saying nothing to one another.

"*Flaps ten. Alright stand by.*" Again the engines roared out. Munro had hauled back as near in shore as he could. The Clipper drew fifty-two inches fully laden and he daren't risk grounding on a coral-head. Everyone aboard tensed as the Boeing surged forward.

"*Seventy knots . . . eighty . . . eighty-five . . . ninety. We're on the step!*" This is better, Skipper!"

Munro eased back on the yoke. The shore was rushing towards them, water drumming underneath the hull. He pulled back some more. The vibration continued undiminished. The nose stayed down. She wasn't going to lift.

"*Dammit!*" with a savage curse he shoved the stick forward, chopping the throttles again. "Dammit! Dammit!"

The others looked at him. "Christ, Max, what're we going to do?" Thyssen gulped.

Downstairs there was real fear now. Scott and Pat went up the aisles as they taxied back for a third attempt, trying to reassure.

"We'll never get off! There's too many of us!" Ruth Simms cried frantically. Her voice became a shriek. She was close to hysteria. Her husband gripped her hands trying to calm her. Scott ran for the First Aid box and found the Seconal pills.

"Give her these, they'll help."

Angrily Munro swung the nose round, sweeping back and forth across the channel in a series of S's. Without a breeze the glassy surface of the lagoon was acting like a suction against the hull stopping them from getting airborne.

"All clear back there still, Chris?"

"Aye aye, sir."

If the Japs caught them now, tanks filled to the brim with high-octane fuel . . .

Passengers began to look green as the flying boat rocked on the swell. The motion was worst in the rear cabin, where the four Chinese were squeezed in together. Hollington Soong plucked feverishly at his seat belt and flung himself into the lavatory retching. Yu-Ling clutched the gold crucifix at her neck and prayed.

They reached the start of the channel again. Grimly Munro eased her into the turn. Behind, the Chief was watching his gauges. The cowl flaps were wide open. Cylinder head temperatures entering the red. Manifold pressure two inches above the maximum.

The engines blared as Munro thrust the throttles forward once more, feeding them the power. With a deafening roar the Clipper ploughed across the lagoon. She reared up on the bow wave, picking up speed. "*Eighty knots . . . ninety . . .*" Shapiro was calling the odds again. The shore was rushing closer. ". . . *ninety five!*" She was riding clean but not yet flying. Pull back on the yoke. Still she wouldn't unstick. Barely two hundred yards to go. Kurt Thyssen gave a cry of fear behind.

In desperation Munro remembered a trick he had once used. He jerked the stick forward sharply, then back, jockeying the plane in a last effort to break the suction. Less than a hundred yards now. Again he rocked the yoke. And again . . .

With a burst of relief he felt her respond. The water was still drumming under the keel but the wing had her now. He gave her a touch of tail trim and eased back the stick further. The spray cut off suddenly as the hull broke away. She sagged. Sweating, he let her flatten a moment. Holding her inches from the surface, nursing her for vital seconds till the speed built. White sand flashed beneath. It was now or never. He drew the yoke hard into his stomach. Smoothly the great flying boat lifted into the air, winging over the islet scant feet above the bush. Cheers erupted on the flight deck. Shapiro was pounding his seat. They were airborne. The Clipper had made it.

Wearily triumphant, Munro pointed the nose west towards Midway. Behind them Wake burned. A few lonely figures waved.

★   ★   ★

And now the war was as wide as the whole world.

"*. . . first reports indicate . . . vessels sunk or damaged with heavy loss of life . . . this is NBC bringing you latest news of the Japanese attack . . .* Five thousand miles away in Chicago it was a cold winter evening. Snow lay on the sidewalks. In a drab suburban lecture room eight men, military and civilian, listened to the radio shocked.

"It can't be true, can it?" one scientist demanded in disbelief. "I mean the Japs attacking *us*? Surely they mean the British?"

"It's no mistake," a grizzled Navy captain answered him grimly. "Of all the *dumb* plays, a Sunday morning sneak attack with carriers! Hell, that's straight out of the war games manual. And we let them catch us with our pants down!"

The door opened and Kim Delahaye entered, his expression drawn. "I got through to the White House, spoke to Harry Hopkins. Things are looking bad, I'm afraid. Our forces have taken a heavy beating."

There was a moment's silence. "What about the Project?" someone asked. "How will this affect us here?"

Kim shook his head. "Nothing changes. The President's decision stands. The military will assume control as from today, development to go ahead with maximum speed."

There were murmurs of approval round the table.

"I disagree," a short, scowling scientist protested in the guttural consonants of Eastern Europe. "It is taking too great a risk. We need more time for research, much more."

"Time is something we just ran out of," one of his companions countered drily. An alert wiry man, early forties, he held a Nobel Prize for physics. "The red team have a lead on us already."

"Sure, sure, Lawrence, but it's all *theory* still. Take the separation problem, at least three different methods – centrifuge, diffusion, electromagnetic – we don't know which will work. *If any.* And the wrong choice could set us back months."

"No," Kim cut in. "The President and I have talked this over. Work will proceed on all three enrichment methods simultaneously."

The committee blinked at him. "But the cost?" a treasury official gasped horrified.

"There will be no limits on funding or resources," Kim gripped the arms of his chair. "The White House is convinced firstly that the weapon is feasible, second that whichever side brings it off ahead of the other will win the war. We cannot afford to fail. The only question is – how long?"

"Years," Dr. Lawrence answered promptly. "Years. And millions of dollars. No one knows yet how much material will be needed even. It may be many tons and we are working with *grams* in laboratories still. What news of the French supplies from China?"

Again silence. The Senator's face had gone grey and pinched. "The cargo was aboard the Pan Am Clipper en route to Pearl Harbour," he said quietly. "Nothing has been heard from the plane since the Japanese attack."

★   ★   ★

At four pm the Clipper reached the *Point of No Return*.

Munro had held her down tight at sea-level all day. Twenty-five feet from the wave tops. No more. She was heavy in the air, mushing along at a hundred and twenty knots. It made for a hell of a strain flying. A moment's lapse of concentration could send them crashing into the ocean but it lessened the chances of Jap attack planes spotting them.

The skies had stayed empty though.

Navigation was a worse problem. With Wake's RDF destroyed there was no beam to direct them outbound. Midway was not transmitting, presumably for fear of Jap bombers. They were flying twelve hundred miles across featureless water from one pinprick atoll to another with nothing to guide them but dead reckoning.

The horizon deepened to a band of indigo. The sun was sinking, sliding down into the ocean in a blaze of glory. Skimming the waves as dusk fell the Clipper crossed the invisible boundary of the International Date Line, the 180 degree meridian dividing East from West. Monday December eighth became Sunday the seventh again.

Munro's arms ached from the strain of holding the altitude. Handing over the controls to Thyssen, he let himself out through the after

411

hatch. It was time he checked on Ross.

Stripped of mail and cargo the empty hold echoed cavernously to the roar of the engines. The Bishop's coffin and the steel footlockers had been stowed aft in the baggage hold to maintain trim. Up in the astrodome Slater was standing observation duty for a spell, releasing a crewman. "Nothing but goddam seagulls," he growled lowering the binoculars a minute. "How're we doing?"

"Two thirds of the way – if our navigation's right."

"It'd better be, Pilot. This ain't no time for distress calls. Anything from Hawaii yet?"

"No, but we picked up a BBC news broadcast. Hongkong, Singapore, Manila have all been hit."

"Shit, the Yellow-bellies had everything worked out. Bastards!"

He found Latouche in the crew quarters. Jordan was there too. It gave him a moment's surprise. He'd forgotten about that arrangement.

"How is he, Doc?"

"The injection is wearing off, you may speak with him if you wish."

Latouche went out, closing the door. Jordan remained, his pale face watchful. Munro leaned over the bunk. "Skipper?"

The eyes opened and focused with an effort, "Mister?" he croaked.

"Yes. How you feeling?"

"I could use a drink of scotch."

Munro grinned, "I'll see if I can arrange it."

"Where the hell are we?"

"Six hours out from Wake heading for Midway. Skipper, you've had an accident. You fell down in the baggage hold. Can you remember what happened?"

A grimace of pain crossed Ross's features. He looked old and sick but some of the colour had returned to his cheeks. He swallowed painfully, "I was in here. Someone came through, I think . . . noises next door, thumps on the bulkhead. I went to check . . ." His voice trailed off. Jordan leaned closer to hear.

"Nothing more? Did you see anybody?"

The eyes closed, "I don't . . . remember. Only a . . . pain in my head."

Silence. Ross seemed to have relapsed into sleep. Munro was straightening up when abruptly a hand caught his own in a grip of iron. "*Mister*, Slater, is he with you still?"

"He's next door. You want to see him?"

"*Don't trust him!* He betrayed Amelia. We found her ship that time

412

on Mili. He made me swear not to tell . . ."

QRK? QRK? QRK? Stewart Whitely thumped on his bakelite key. *Can you hear me? Can you hear me?* The empty hiss of the ether sang in his ears mockingly. KHAZA PACIFIC CLIPPER TO KNBV MIDWAY ISLAND – *Come in please! Come in please!*

Nothing. He'd been trying two hours now. Midway was dead.

Darkness had come at last. A Pacific night studded with stars to the horizon. Safe from marauding fighters, they had climbed to six thousand feet on auto-pilot and opened up on the radio.

To no avail.

The cockpit curtains were drawn tight, shutting out the lights of the cabin, and the fluorescent instrument lamps turned down. Munro cupped his hands to the glass of the windshield and peered out into the dark. Wraiths of cloud smoked over the wings. Far below scattered cumulus showed like grey shadows against the empty blackness of the ocean.

"Tony, take the con, I'm going back."

"Sure, Skipper."

The lights of the cabin made him blink. Kurt Thyssen was marking up the chart. He had two star positions plotted – beautiful three-star fixes, the lines cutting almost at a point. With the ship totally dependent on celestial navigation he and Davey Klein had been taking observations together, checking each other's readings.

"Looks like no more than a half hour?"

Kurt fiddled with his slide-rule a moment. "Twenty-eight minutes." He shrugged, "If it's still there."

"The island can't move."

"The Japs could've taken it."

Across the cabin the Chief sat watching his instruments, impassively chewing on a stick of gum. Next to him Stewart was glued to the radio listening vainly. Alone at the rear desk, Slater snored, head pillowed on his arms.

Was it true what Ross had said? Had Earhart's flight been a spy mission gone tragically wrong? Had she and Noonan been abandoned on Mili – to be captured by the Japanese?

The answers would have to wait. Right now they had more urgent problems.

He tapped Whitely on the shoulder, "Still no joy from Midway?"

The radio operator pushed back the headphones. In the cabin lights his face was taught with worry. "I've tried all the frequencies, even the

413

emergency. Why don't they *answer*, for God's sake?"

"Take it easy, Stewart. We've an ETA now for twenty-one fifteen. Keep sending that out. On voice too if you can. We should be in range. At least let's not be shot down by our own side."

"Aye aye, Max," Stewart swallowed and drew the key towards him.

"Hey, Skipper!" Shapiro called back. "Looks like something burning up ahead. I think it's *Midway*!"

"Son of a bitch, the whole goddam island's on fire!

"No wonder the poor bastards didn't answer the radio!"

Everyone had crowded into the cockpit. Three thousand feet below flames laced the atoll. Billows of red and orange smoke shot with incandescent sparks towered up into the air in a spectacle of lurid beauty.

"Alright, back to your stations," Munro snapped. Reaching up to the overhead panel, he flipped two stitches. Red and green nav lamps sprang into life at the wing tips and from the inboard engine nacelles twin illuminated searchlights stabbed forward into the darkness. He punched the interphone button, "Purser?"

"Sir?"

"See all the passengers are strapped in, life vests on. Turn up the cabin lamps and open the blinds. I don't want anyone on the ground mistaking us for a Jap."

"Aye aye."

"You're going in?" Slater asked. "Dammit man, the yellow-bellies could be down there waiting for us. They could blow us outta the sky!"

"What else d'you suggest? That we hang around up here till we run out of gas? We've no goddam choice."

He eased the throttles back. The engine note changed pitch as they started their descent.

Eight hundred feet . . . five hundred . . . four hundred . . . Munro nursed the plane downwards. Everyone was silent, straining to make out the scene below. Stewart Whitely chewed his knuckles till the blood ran as he waited for a barrage of shells to explode around them. At this range no gunner could miss. Down on the atoll hangars and buildings could be seen blazing fiercely. The landing beams lit up the whirling props and cast weird shadows on the smoke. At two hundred feet Munro levelled off above the lagoon.

414

"Jesus, what a mess," Shapiro whistled. Munro's mouth tightened. The buoy lights of the landing channel were dark but in the glow of the flames small craft and debris could be seen drifting loose on the water.

"Looks like a clear patch out by the rim of the reef. What's the depth there?"

Shapiro flicked the pages of the flight manual. The lagoon was bigger than Wake's, almost four miles across. "Twelve feet maximum."

"We'll have to chance it. Give me low pitch."

They ran out over the ocean, dipped the port wing in shallow turn and came back in, sweeping low.

"Full flaps!"

"Auto-rich!"

A green lamp glowed on the instrument panel as Shapiro threw the solenoid switch. *"Ninety knots . . . eighty . . . seventy-five . . ."* he called off the speed. Seventy-five feet on the altimeter. Rate-of-descent forty feet a minute. Taking a slight tension on the yoke, Munro let her sink gently through the darkness, feeling for the surface. Thirty feet. Lights dazzled on the water. This was it. A bouncing jar rattled the hull. Damn! Misjudged the height a fraction. He chopped the power quickly and the Clipper surged to rest.

They were down on Midway.

Inner props spinning slowly, they taxied gingerly across the lagoon searching for the Pan Am jetty. Up in the nose Chris Fry scanned the water ahead for obstacles. A light showed coming to meet them. Stars and Stripes fluttering. The Pan Am launch.

"You were damn lucky to get here when you did! Jap warships just shelled the hell outta the airstrip. Half the hangars burned out an' a mess of planes lost."

"We were bombed on Wake. You been hit yet?"

"No, but we're expecting it. You guys better not hang around."

As the passengers disembarked at the dock by the light of torches, Midway ground crews milled round.

"What's the story on Pearl?"

"We ain't heard nothing. Don't you guys know anything *either*?"

The Chief and Munro sought out the boss mechanic. "What's the fuel situation here?"

"The sons of bitches hit the main underground tank. It's still burning. Some of the emergency dumps may've been luckier, we're checking now."

415

"Can you scrape up enough to get us to Hawaii?"

"Do our best. Trouble is it's all in fifty-gallon drums spread around the island. We'll have to haul 'em down on sand sleds an' hand pump the stuff aboard. That's gonna take time."

Fires from the Navy base cast a ruddy glow as the passengers stumbled up the sandy path from the jetty, weary and stiff from the long cramped flight. Midway's hotel was a copy of the one on Wake. The windows were blacked out, the glass taped against splinters. People crowded into the lobby, bombarding the stewards with questions. How long were they staying? Was it safe? Could they wire their families?

"What's the plan, Pat, you any idea?" Scott brushed a strand of hair out of her eyes harriedly. They were both dead on their feet. "Are we stopping over or what?"

"Skipper hasn't said, I don't think he knows yet. They can have rooms to freshen up and the hotel's organising a meal."

Morale revived over dinner. After their narrow escape on Wake there was a general air of camaraderie. Rumours abounded. Eddie Wirth told the Gordon Smythes he'd heard for a fact that the USS *Pennsylvania* had captured a brace of Jap carriers and was towing them back to Hawaii. Another story went round that the Russians had bombed Tokyo.

The hotel staff confirmed though that a bulletin had been picked up from KGMB. Governor Poindexter had proclaimed martial law in the Territory of Hawaii. Spirits sank. Perhaps the islands had been invaded?

"It makes me mad the dirty rats pulling a sneak attack like that without having the guts to declare war even!" Tom Keswick spluttered.

"Maybe they did, only we weren't told," Cashin suggested wryly.

"Hell, that ain't possible – is it?"

"Of course President Roosevelt was planning this," Van Cleef asserted. "He manoeuvred Japan into war deliberately. Letting them attack first was a stroke of genius. Now even the isolationists will have to support him."

César glanced sardonically at Georgiana. "I told you the Japs needed to be taught a lesson, eh, *querida*?"

"We don't know they have been yet," she snapped, irritated.

He scowled, "That is not very patriotic."

"Oh shut up!" she flared. "I don't need any lectures."

Across the dining room Yu-Ling helped her uncle swallow some *quai loh* soup. "Afterwards I make *cha, heya?*" She had packed all his cordials, the herb teas and the opium pipe in a small bag. All but one of her pretty *cheong-sams* had had to be left behind. *Joss.* But she had managed to squeeze in the *I-Ching*.

And the devil-box too. She shivered at the thought.

She tried to understand some of the chatter going on around them. "Excuse please, Honourable Minister," she asked politely, "this war between the Sea Devils and the Golden Country, who will win, *heya?*"

"*Dew neh loh moh,* how should I know? I'm not a fornicating *fung-sui,*" Hollington Soong snarled rudely. "Be quiet and mind your own business!"

Sun chou pai, dirty stink-wind coward! Yu-Ling retorted silently under her breath. *Ai-yah,* the Minister was more frightened than she was.

Down by the flying boat dock jittery marines stood guard while mechanics slipped and cursed, manhandling fuel drums in the gloom. Coughing on the fumes, Munro checked the luminous dial of his watch again impatiently. Eleven fifteen.

A bulky silhouette loomed up. "How's it going, Chief?" he asked.

"Eight hundred gallons pumped so far. The rest is on its way down. I figure one-thirty before we're through."

Munro glanced back over his shoulder. Across the atoll flames still flickered against the sky. "Try to speed it up. If the wind blows the sparks this way we've had it."

Slater appeared. He had been over to the Navy base. His manner was uneasy. "It's chaos. The CO's off directing the defences, they're expecting Japs to hit the beaches at first light. I spoke with some lieutenant claimed the Navy took a beating at Pearl."

"I don't buy that. Whitely says our intelligence people knew the Jap fleet was out."

"Sounds like someone screwed up, then."

Maria Bianchi slipped out into the garden through a side door. Ricky wanted to be read to and she'd left his book on the plane.

The night was an ominous red, heavy with the sour stink of burning oil. Tractors growled along the sand, towing sleds laden with fuel drums down to the jetty. In the distance men's shouts as they fought the fires mingled with the crackle of ammunition blazing in the hangars. Shanghai had been like this during the delta battles. Fear tightened in her throat at the memory.

All at once she stopped. Prince Cherkassy was standing under the trees at the end of the path, watching the fuel convoys. Before she could dodge away again he glanced round.

"Ach, so it is you," he said, squinting in the gloom. "Good, good." He moved towards her, rubbing his hands. Maria stood her ground.

"Leave me alone. I want nothing to do with you. *Nothing!*"

"Ach, you have spirit. I like that in my women." By the glow of the fires the Russian's disfigured face was hideous as he leered into hers. Abruptly he lowered his voice, "Listen, how much money have you on you, eh?"

"Money?" Maria clutched her purse, "None, none at all, I . . . Ahh!"

"Lying whore!" the Prince's hand smacked her viciously on the cheek. His eyes glittered, "Give it to me!"

A stab of dismay pierced her, "No!"

The Russian's laughter was chilling. "Think of it as a dowry – a downpayment."

"*Never!*"

He caught her in a vice-like grip. "Give it to me, all of it, or by *Kristos* . . ."

Desperately Maria fought as he wrenched open the purse. "Pig!" she hissed. "Let go of me or I'll scream!"

He jeered, "Scream then, whore. Tell the world who you are!"

Fury and despair rushed over Maria. Her whole life was crumbling in ruins, everything she'd slaved for torn from her grasp. Groping inside the purse, her hand touched something cold and hard. The pistol. In a burst of hatred she snatched it out and pressed the muzzle against the Russian's chest.

"Pig, this is all you'll get from me!" she squeezed the trigger.

"Jesus Christ, what was that?"

"It's the Japs! Up there in the trees!"

Pow! Pow! Pow! Pow! Shots split the night as jumpy sentries opened up all across the atoll. Tracer bursts laced the sky. Machine gun fire sprayed the dock. Mechanics and crew threw themselves flat while bullets zipped overhead, whanging off the fuel drums. A man yelped, nicked by a ricochet.

Risking his life, Slater ran bent double to the head of the jetty.

"What the goddam hell are you shooting at?" he yelled to a BAR team blazing wildly into the dark as fast as they could load the clips.

"Japs, sir! Japs in the bush! Must've landed the other side the island!"

BAM! BAM! BAM! an anti-aircraft gun boomed. Hot shrapnel rained down hissing into the lagoon. A flare burst overhead suddenly, flooding the atoll with eerie light.

"Cease firing!" Slater bellowed, "Hold your fire, godammit! You'll blow the whole dock apart, assholes!"

The shooting died away as suddenly as it had begun.

Spotlights snapped on near the hotel. "Hey, Major," a voice shouted, "there's a dead man up here!"

A bunch of people gathered round the Russian's corpse.

"Small calibre weapon, close range by the looks of it," Slater played his flashlight.

"It weren't none of my boys' fault," the marine sergeant said defensively. He swiped at a mosquito. "The guy dint have no business out here anyways."

"Godammit, don't your men know to challenge before they shoot?" Slater snarled at him. "They darn near killed everyone on the dock as well."

Sir Ambrose Hope joined them. The Midway manager went through the dead man's pockets, collecting his wallet and passport. "We'll have to file an acccident report," he said, straightening up. "I'll need statements from your men, Sergeant."

"Yessir," the sergeant answered woodenly.

"We don't know for sure it was an accident," Munro pointed out.

"Jesus Christ, stay out of this, Pilot," Slater told him. "Just get that plane of yours fuelled up before these screwballs shoot someone else!"

Two marines brought a stretcher. As the others moved off Sir Ambrose Hope paused a moment. Near where the body had lain something glittered in the sand. Bending stiffly he picked it up. A gold and jade earring. Now where had he seen that before?

Saying nothing, he slipped it in his pocket.

Hands trembling, Maria Bianchi tidied herself in the washroom. Amid all the shooting no one had seen her snatch up her purse and run for the hotel. The gun she had hurled away into the thickest patch of bush. There was nothing to connect her to the killing.

She checked her appearance in the mirror and went back into the lobby.

One am. Scott clanged the boarding bell twice. In nervous silence the passengers trooped down through the tropic night to the dock. Few words were spoken as they took their seats again. The flying boat's engines were already turning. Out on the lagoon the launch made a hasty inspection of the water and a green flare soared up.

With Midway's long run there was no problem lifting off this time. Nav lights were doused again and portholes sealed as they levelled out at five thousand feet and headed away over the ocean once more, leaving the burning atoll to dwindle behind. The air was calm, only stars pierced the blackness. Red-eyed with fatigue, the crew spelled one another at the controls while down below the passengers dozed fitfully.

"The Navy's undersea telegraph cable was still working when we left." Tom Keswick told Munro on a visit to the flight deck. "Midway promised to try to get a signal through. Oahu should be expecting us."

"So long as the Japs aren't too."

Steadily the Clipper flew on through the night. As the blush of dawn stained the eastern horizon they glimpsed the peaks of the Hawaiian mountains rising purple in the distance.

"Prettiest sight I seen all trip," the Chief said happily.

"Stewart, how's about trying the radio again?"

To their surprise the anwer-back was prompt. PROCEED LAND PEARL CITY CURRENT TEMPERATURE 74 DEGREES WIND 19 KNOTS SOUTH-WEST LIGHT SHOWERS 3000 FEET OFF DIAMOND HEAD X

"Well, I'll be damned," Munro scratched his head, "just like peace time. Guess things can't be too bad or they'd have diverted us to Hilo."

Lighting cigarettes, they flew on.

Scott appeared on the flight deck. "Hi, looks like we made it, huh?"

Munro heard chuckles and caught a whiff of familiar perfume. He glanced back. Georgiana had come up behind his seat. "What's this, Dixie?" he tried to growl. "Who let you in?"

"I got restless down there. I promise I won't get in anybody's way."

"Better not or we'll put you on engine cleaning duty."

The sun was warm as they neared Oahu. The deep blue of the ocean giving way to coral shallows, bright with the lighter colours of the sea. Beyond, the solid green hills, incredibly reassuring after the infinity of day and night in the Pacific.

"Don't see any patrol planes out," Slater had come forward to look.

"Maybe they watch this sector on radar."

Diamond Head was in sight now, a rainbow arching from clouds to the west of its rugged slopes. They could see the city of Honolulu gleaming in the sun and the rollers cresting in towards Waikiki Beach.

Munro switched on the seat belt sign to the lower deck. "Okay, landing stations!"

The sun slid along the wing as they banked out over Mamala Bay shedding altitude. The engine noise dropped to a steady purr. A touch of rudder and the Clipper drifted left, lining up for the approach to Pearl.

"*Oh my God!*" Georgiana gasped.

Down on the lower deck passengers stared from the portholes in stunned disbelief. Off Ford Island the battleships of the Pacific Fleet lay bomb-blasted, overturned, decks awash, blackened with oil from their ruptured tanks. Fires still smouldered among the crippled leviathans and in the debris of the shattered dry-docks, sending up thin plumes of smoke into the crystal clear sky. Skeletons of burned out aircraft strewed the aprons of Hickam Field and the Naval air station. It was Wake all over, magnified a thousand-fold.

"*Dew neh loh moh!*" Hollington Soong hissed appalled clutching his seat. "Impossible, by all gods! The Sea Devils could never . . ."

The cabin door crashed open. Bob Cashin burst in, his face chalk white, chest heaving. "You bastard!" he cried chokingly at the Minister. "Two-faced traitoring bastard! *You knew! You knew all along!*"

XXXI

MONDAY DECEMBER 8th. TERRITORY OF HAWAII. THREE PM. In downtown Honolulu's Federal Building the FBI field office was swamped. Hawaii's Japanese population numbered a hundred and seventy-five thousand, every one a potential fifth columnist. Special Agent Paul G. Emory had exactly twenty-five men under him. Ever since the attack they had been working round the clock, chasing up espionage reports, interrogating suspects.

"Hey, Boss!" a young field agent called above the hubbub. "RCA got some crazy on the phone wants to speak with you. A Brit calling from Hongkong or somewhere. Say its urgent to do with the Pan Am Clipper."

"*Hongkong?* Christsakes, we got enough worries of our own. Tell him to get lost." Emory had been without sleep for thirty-six hours. He was crushing out a cigarette viciously when the mention of the Clipper jarred his memory. "No, godammit, I'll take it!"

"Line three."

He stabbed the button, "Emory."

The voice of the female operator came over the line, "Sir, we have a person-to-person for you on the scrambler system from Hongkong. A Chief Inspector Playfair."

"Okay, I'll speak. Put him on."

"Yes, sir." There was a series of clicks and buzzes as the RCA scrambler was activated. "Reception is bad, sir," the operator warned. "Go ahead, Hongkong."

"Hello. Hello. Is that FBI, Honolulu?" the nasal English tones were all but inaudible against a background of whistling static.

"Yes," Emory bawled back, "this is FBI. What can I do for you?"

". . . must know . . . Pacific Clipper . . . arrived yet?"

"Hell, what is this? We're at war. I can't pass out that kinda dope."

"Yes, yes, I understand . . ." The static noise grew louder, ". . . Major Slater . . . extremely urgent . . . trying to reach you since yesterday."

"Slater? You want to speak to Slater?"

The connection improved momentarily. "Yes, it's vital you get a message to him at once. Can you do that?"

"Sure, I can reach him." Emory grabbed a pencil, "Okay, shoot."

"Have spoken to Doctor Currie's son here . . . says his father . . . alive . . ."

A whining and banging intervened on the line. Emory cupped a hand over his other ear to catch the words. "I can't hear, you'll have to speak up."

"Sorry," the Englishman's voice came back. "Spot of bother this end. Nips bombing us again . . . nuisance."

"Oh," Emory felt a sudden bond with the man five thousand miles away across the ocean. "The sons of bitches hit us yesterday too."

"Yes, yes we heard. Listen . . . not much time . . ."

"Sure I understand, go ahead."

"Currie is alive . . ." the din on the line increased again, drowning out Playfair's words. Emory fancied he could make out the thud of bombs. Jesus, those poor bastards. He strained to catch what was being said. *"Living Honolulu, Kaumalapau Church. Urgent you warn Slater . . . Reverend Jordan . . . murdered . . . Black Dragon . . ."*

"What's that? Can you repeat it?" he shouted.

"Jordan . . ." with an ear-splitting crack the line went dead.

Dreams come true, in Blue Hawaii . . .

Turquoise waters lapped the golden sands and a breeze rustled the palm trees that clustered about the coral pink bell towers of the Royal Hawaiian. Out on the reefs breakers rolled in towards majestic Diamond Head, but today there were no surfboards riding the waves or outrigger canoes. The beachboys with their ukes were gone and the fruit juice vendors. Instead soldiers were stringing barbed wire defences along the shoreline and where once sunbathers had lounged on Waikiki Beach the ugly snouts of machine guns leered out to sea.

War had come to Hawaii.

Horn honking, a taxi sped down Kalakaua Avenue and made a right opposite Seaside Street into the hotel grounds. On the rear seat César sprawled carelessly elegant in a Palm Bach suit, one finger only tapping restlessly.

Royal palms striped the driveway with their shadows, the gardens beneath were lush and beautiful. A Rolls Royce sat parked under the trees, yellow paintwork gleaming in the sun. Millionaire vacationers took suites here for the season, shipping limousines and chauffeurs across from the mainland. At the pillared porte-cochère a smartly uniformed porter stepped forward to whip open the cab door.

Inside the foyer Chinese bellhops stood ready to chop-chop mis-see's parcels like always. The block-long lobby with its huge tree fern hung with flowering orchids, its embroidered tapestries and coral pink ceilings, was near empty of guests. Most people were downtown at the Matson Line office clamouring for passages back to California.

"Good afternoon, Señor de Santa Cruz," the sallow-skinned *hapa-haole* desk clerk recognised César at once. The Spaniard had stayed here before. Several times. He was a lavish tipper. "What can I do for you, sir?"

"Miss Delahaye, is she back yet?"

The clerk ran a finger down the register, "Room 204. One moment, sir, I'll check for you." He dialled the number and listened a moment. "Sorry, sir," he replaced the receiver with a shrug, "still no reply."

"Tcha!" César's cat-handsome features turned sulky. Scowling, he stalked irritably out onto the wide terrace overlooking the bay.

Nombre de Dios, where was Georgiana?

Three floors up by an open window Max Munro heard the sound of the plane and paused in his shaving to squint at the sky. Jap reconnaissance sneaking a look most likely. Not many US aircraft left, Hickam Field and Wheeler had been just about wiped out by all accounts.

It was eight hours since *Pacific Clipper* had touched down amid the oil blackened waters of Pearl. Incredibly the terminal itself had escaped the raid undamaged. Pan Am staff were waiting at the landing stage with tots of whisky, everyone congratulating him on the plane's safe arrival.

The scene at Pearl was horrific. Wake had been bad, but this made you feel sick inside. Sick and angry. The smashed, fire-gutted battleships, the whaleboats full of sheeted bodies being ferried ashore, the stomach-turning stench from the inch thick layer of coagulated crude clinging to the wreckage. Outside the base it was as if the whole island had been militarized. Convoys of troop trucks bumper to bumper, road blocks with MPs sweating in the dust and heat, tanks dug in to cover intersections. Everyone jumpy as hell, scared the Japs would hit the beaches next.

Munro had been too tired to care. Leaving Slater to take Devereux's letter to CinCPAC, he had headed straight for the hotel and bed.

The plane droned on paralleling the coast, the sinking sun winking on its wings. He finished shaving and showered. On the palm of his

424

right hand was a small red patch that itched like a sunburn, except no one ever sunburned there. That was where he had touched Latouche's metal ingot.

Wrapping a towel round his waist, he went through into the bedroom.

The windows were open onto the balcony and a breeze ruffled the drapes. Clothes were strewed carelessly over the marble floor. He let his gaze travel to the bed and linger there. Drowned in sleep, Georgiana lay on her stomach, head buried in the pillows, flaming locks cascading over the sheets. Gently he touched her shoulder. She did not wake. His fingers travelled down her back, tracing the slender length of her spine.

She stirred finally and gave a yawn. From under the veil of hair the impossible green eyes surveyed him drowsily. "Mmn, I ache all over," she murmured huskily, "it's lovely."

Throwing off the sheet, she rolled over on her back and stretched voluptuously, muscles rippling along the silk-soft graceful limbs that looked fragile but in truth were taut and strong.

He felt himself hardening again at the sight of the pale nipples stiff on the perfect creamy skin of the full breasts that were even more beautiful now for their fullness than when he had first known her, and the swelling auburn triangle between the long white thighs.

She brushed the hair from her eyes. On one slim finger a stone glittered. She was wearing César's ring still. The lines deepened round Munro's mouth. "You're going to have to make your mind up, Dixie."

Her tongue licked out teasingly, "Maybe I like things fine the way they are."

"And if I don't?"

She watched him carefully, "That's your affair." She rubbed the diamond quickly on the pillow.

Munro's arm snapped out and he caught her by the wrist. "*Ow!* Damn you, Max, leave me alone!" she squealed as he forced her fingers open and ruthlessly wrenched the ring off, throwing it to the floor. "Give that here!"

She made a lunge to retrieve it and he grabbed her back, pinning her on the bed. Angrily she fought him, kicking, biting, nails scoring weals across his shoulders.

Ripping off the towel, he caught her hands again and stretched her out helpless. Desire flooded through him and he crushed his mouth on hers brutally. Georgiana struggled beneath, her fury mingled now with heat. Wanting to be overpowered and fighting it still. He cupped a breast and felt a shiver of arousal. Her back arched to meet him. Both their hands were wandering now, their bodies slippery with sweat, flesh electric.

"Oh God, Max," she whispered, biting his neck as he spread her, "you don't give a girl a chance, you bastard."

"Man, those Jap Zeros are hot!"

Out on the terrace a couple of Army pilots were regaling the bar with accounts of yesterday's battle.

"They can fly rings round any of our ships," the lieutenant was very young, a blond fuzz struggling to form a beard on his chin. "I caught up with one over Hickam, had him in my sights and was just squeezing the tit when the son of a bitch turns inside me like a bat and fills my tail full of lead!"

"He shot you down?"

"The hell he did! I put her into a spin and broke free. Temperature gauge is off the dial so I figure the coolant system's taken a hit and I better set her down quick, when godammit our own AA opens up! Zowie, the next thing I know there's flames spouting into the cockpit so I cracked the canopy and jumped. Came down in Honolulu Harbour with my pants scorched off. I'm putting in for a Purple Heart and the Silver Star!"

"Sounds like you were lucky," Bob Cashin said.

"Yea, a lot of our guys bought it yesterday," the other pilot, a major, wore a wound dressing on his hand. "They took out my crewman, but I got one of the bastards."

"Well, the Japs proved one thing," Shapiro swilled the ice in his glass and crunched some with his teeth, "battleships are finished, obsolete, it's carriers from now on."

"C'mon, those ships were sitting ducks. The Yellow-bellies couldn't miss," Chuck rejoined. "Anyway protection of the anchorage was the Army's job."

"Bullshit, the Navy was caught flat-footed. Now they're looking for someone to blame."

"I don't understand how the Japanese sneaked right across the ocean without being spotted," Chris Fry said.

Bob Cashin sniffed, "The whole thing stinks. The Chinese knew, they could've warned us easy. Chungking *wanted* us in this war."

The lieutenant nodded, "I heard they even knew in *Washington*."

"That's just a dumb rumour," the major rounded on him sharply. "Cut it out."

426

"There's a lot of guys believe it, all the same."

"Yeah, well cut it out. Rumour ain't fact."

Cashin was staring at them aghast. "*Jesus Christ,*" he whispered, "*it can't be true. They wouldn't have.*"

Back in the lobby the *hapa-haole* desk clerk looked up as another guest approached. "Reverend Jordan, sir, there was a message came in for you a while ago." He rummaged in the bank of pigeon holes behind him, "Here you are."

The priest tore open the envelope. As he scanned the note a muscle twitched spasmodically in his cheek. "When did this come?"

"Around two hours ago," the clerk glanced up at the clock. "The gentleman said not to disturb . . . Is something wrong, sir?"

Sweat beaded Jordan's brow. He stared blankly at the message, "No, I . . ." Crumpling the note in his fist, he hurried abruptly away.

Minister Soong had slept all afternoon. Waking with an appetite, he had sent out for a tray of *dim sum*. Tasty morsels of steamed dumplings and sliced pork liver and his favourite *chien chang go*, Thousand-layer sweet cake. He was musing on Yu-Ling. Bless all gods, the Princess is exquisite, truly a *ch'u-nu,* an unburst melon, he told himself greedily, feeling his *yang* stir and smacking his lips in anticipation. Her resistance on Wake had only stoked his desire. Today, finally, he would extract a promise from the old Manchu .

He rang the little handbell on his tray, "*Ai-yah,* Bodyguard Feng . . ."

"Da skirt come back, Miss," the pretty *wahine* opened Scott's door with a smile. "Da laundry pressin' it like you ask an' I wash out da blouse fo' you."

"Swell, that's sweet of you. *Mahalo, mahalo nui,*" Scott thanked her profusely. Now she could dress and slip out to the shops in Waikiki. The Company was making an emergency allocation of twenty dollars each towards replacing clothes left behind. Enough for some underwear and fresh stockings at least. Her lovely silk evening gown was gone for good though. Oh well, that was war.

Down in the flower-decked lobby, she ran into the Gordon Smythes talking worriedly together in their thin English jabber. Eddie Wirth was with them, wearing the beach shorts and gaudy *aloha* shirt he had travelled in. "Say, Miss Scott, do you know what's gonna happen to us? There's a rumour the military's taking over the Clipper and we're all being sent home by sea."

"We've just come from the Castle and Cooke office," Gordon Smythe added. "The place is packed. Every liner berth until March is booked up."

"Honest, I haven't heard anything, but I'm sure the Company will do it's best for you, whatever happens."

"And what about our luggage?" Cynthia Gordon Smythe demanded shrilly. "A thousand pounds it'll cost me to replace my wardrobe! And there's Felicity's too. When's the airline going to reimburse us, I want to know?"

"Maybe you'd rather still be on Wake?" Scott flashed in irritation. "Me, I'd be grateful, you might've lost your lives."

"Well, I never . . .!"

Leaving the Englishwoman fuming, Scott set out for the town.

The afternoon was soft and warm with a hint of fragrant ginger on the air and the marvellous honey coloured light that was unique to Hawaii. The sidewalks were more crowded than she had expected. Graceful, dusky-skinned *wahines* with flowers in their hair, cheeky grinning *kanaka* shoeshine boys, 'half Chinese, half Schofield', and anxious tourists worried about getting home. People queuing to stock up on supplies in case of further raids. Jeeps and Army trucks tearing past in the road and guards outside the sandbagged entrances to the banks. Many shops had their windows boarded up or taped against blast. Along the edge of the Ala Wei golf course shelters were being dug and there was a big crater at the intersection of Lewers Street and Kuhio which some said had been caused by a Jap bomb, others by an anti-aircraft shell. Everyone had their own story about the raid. The US had taken a knock, all agreed, but now the thing was to get back into the fight and show those damned Yellow-bellies, by God!

It was strangely exhilarating.

There were plenty of Japanese-Hawaiians on the streets still, hurrying about their business harassed and unhappy. Many had been arrested and there were frequent tales of sabotage. Outside the Waikiki Tavern Scott saw plainclothes men drag a nisei off the sidewalk and hustle him into a black van while a crowd of whites shouted abuse. Poor Tad, at least he'd been spared this.

She must do something about Tad.

She finished her purchases and caught a bus up to Kakaako, the Japanese section on the eastern side of Pearl Harbour. Scott had never been out here before. The little wooden cottages with their bougainvillea and vine-screened porches looked quaint and peaceful but there were police patrols on every corner. One of these directed her to the Gotto house. "Any slant-eyes give you trouble, lady, just holler," a burly plainclothes man added.

The cottage steps were set about with flowering plants, poinsettia, hibiscus, vanda orchids. There was no answer at first to Scott's knock. "Hi, is anyone home?" she persisted. "I'm from Pan American."

Still no response. She was starting back down the path when she heard sounds of the bolt being drawn. The door opened a crack. A tiny wizened woman in kimono and straw geta peered out at her fearfully.

"Mrs. Gotto?" Scott said with gentleness. "My name's Sally, I'm . . . I was a friend of Tad's. He was a brave boy. We were all proud to know him."

The woman stared at her. Slow tears began to trickle from the corners of her soft black eyes. Timidly she reached out to clasp the American girl's hands.

Downtown at the Federal Building, a trim brunette in a tailored suit knocked at a glass-panelled door. "Sir, Major Slater is here."

"Hi," the FBI man's paunch strained his shirt as he reached a hand across the file-cluttered desk. Cigarette butts overflowed the ashtrays and the air in the room was stale with smoke. "Paul Emory. Take a seat, Major. We've been searching all over for you."

"I was over at CinCPAC, whole damn place is chaos. Admirals running around like chickens with their heads cut off," Slater dropped into a chair and broke open a pack of cigars. "So where's the fire?"

"Hongkong came through on the scrambler line."

"*Hongkong?*" Slater ran his eyes over the message transcript Emory had passed him. "Shit, this is all?"

"Line went dead on us – like that," Emory snapped his fingers. "RCA reckon the Japs cut the submarine cable."

"How about radio? Can't the Signal Corps help?"

"We thought of that. I got onto a pal of mine at Shafter. He pulled some rank. They couldn't raise Hongkong either at first. Finally they managed to make contact via Singapore."

"And?"

"Seems a Jap bomb took out the building the limeys were in," Emory made a wry face but his eyes were hard. "Casualties were one hundred per cent. Your man's dead, Major, so where do we go from here?"

429

A mile towards Diamond Head, Reverend Jordan found a public phone booth on Kalakaua. Shutting the door, he put in a nickel and dialled a four-digit number.

It rang for a long while. At last there was a click. "*Ae,* Kaumalapau Church," a woman's voice answered with a Hawaiian accent.

"May I speak with Dr. Currie please?"

"Doctor 'im no here, suh."

"What time do you expect him back?"

"Doctor come back bimeby, mebbe four, fi' o'clock."

It was after four already. Jordan replaced the receiver. Frowning, he dialled a second number.

"*But they knew!* Soong, the State Department, Washington, the whole lying bunch. They *knew* the Japanese were going to hit us, they *knew* Hawaii was wide open and they did nothing. Not a goddam thing. It was a set-up, a dirty stinking trick to get us into the war."

"Bob," Sir Ambrose said quietly, "it doesn't do any good."

They were strolling in the shady cool of the hotel gardens, once the playground of Hawaiian royalty. A pink plumeria was in full bloom still, the air sweet with its rich scent. Somewhere off among the coconut groves they could hear the shouts of children running free on the short clean grass. Otherwise they were alone.

"Three thousand men!" Cashin screwed up his eyes behind his glasses. "Three thousand. That's how many they killed, *murdered.* I spoke to the Clipper's radio officer; they picked up signals from the Jap carrier force last week. US Intelligence tracked them clear across the Pacific. *Washington knew!*"

"Bob, it's no use."

"Like hell it ain't! They've got the press muzzled here but soon as we make California I'm going to contact every editor in the nation. I'll spread this story coast to coast. You watch!"

Sir Ambrose shook his head sadly, "They won't believe you, Bob, and if they did they wouldn't print it. There's a war on now. The country has to be united."

"Tell that to the guys aboard Arizona when she went up," Cashin was bitter. "It was their country too and I'm going to blow the whistle on the government that let them die.

"Bob," the diplomat's voice was harsh suddenly, "don't be a bloody fool. This isn't a *game* any longer."

Shrieks of laughter sounded up ahead. The two Simms girls appeared running down the path, fair plaits flying, pursued by Ricky

430

Bianchi. A troubled look came into Sir Ambrose's face. There was something else he had to see to. Reaching in his pocket, he felt for the jade and gold earring he had picked up on Midway.

Upstairs a telephone rang beside the bed. "Max?"

"Chief, where are you?"

"Down at Pearl. Listen, you'd better get over here."

"Why, what's up?"

"You'll see." The phone clicked.

Munro brushed away a lock of hair and kissed Georgiana on the nape of the neck, "Sweet dreams, Dixie." He rolled out of bed.

Downstairs he caught a taxi. The driver was a hatchet-faced old *haole*. "I'll drop you at the gates, Mister. I ain't gettin' trapped inside the base if the Yellow-bellies come back. I gotta family to consider."

They drove along King Street past the Palace, guarded by tanks behind its screen of banyan trees, past Hotel Street's tawdry bars and tattoo parlours all empty now, out onto the Moanalua Road. Beyond the town, pineapple plantations and canefields rose up the lush green foothills towards the peaks of the Koolau Range, saw-edged against the piercing blue Hawaiian sky.

The driver switched on his radio. ". . . *the attack yesterday on the Hawaiian Islands,*" a familiar voice was saying, "*has caused severe damage to American naval and military forces. Very many American lives have been lost . . . American ships have been reported torpedoed on the high seas between San Francisco and Honolulu . . .*"

"That's Roosevelt," the driver snorted, "declaring war in Congress this morning. This whole damn business is down to the Democrats. They've been tryin' every way to get us into war. Well, now they done it."

Four pm. Down at the Navy Yard a factory hooter sounded. Clocking-off time had been moved up an hour due to the curfew. Across the harbour in Pearl City arc lights blazed in the Pan Am hangar where shifts of mechanics were working against the clock to make *Pacific Clipper* ready for flight.

Atop the immense three-storey working platform beneath the port wing, a short muscular nisei waved to an overhead crane driver. "Okay, Joe."

The hoist chains tightened taking up the slack. Slowly, carefully, the 1600-horsepower Cyclone, minus its propeller, was eased out from the nacelle. Abe Shiso stood by watching critically. A Five Year Service pin shone proudly on his coveralls. Next March he hoped to sit his exams for foreman. The Company was the greatest thing in his life and he thought the Boeing flying boats the finest planes ever built.

"Hey, Abe," the supervisor shouted to him from the floor below, "can you stop on late tonight? We're short handed."

"Sure t'ing, Mr Griswold," the little engineer called back willingly. An ROTC boy and former Punahou tackle, he knew how vital the big Clippers were to the war effort now. Like almost all nisei on Hawaii he had been outraged by the Japanese attack on his homeland. This was one way he could demonstrate his loyalty.

The winch rolled back on its rails, positioning itself over the jigs ready to lower away. Abe checked his worksheet. One of the engine mounting bolts had stripped its thread being removed. He would have to draw a replacement from stores, maybe get a drink of juice while he was at it. Whistling cheerily, he descended to the ground.

In the darkness above the lights the Japanese tensed. For the past two hours he had watched this one patiently, studying his actions, gauging his strength.

Still whistling Abe walked to the rear of the enormous hangar. A nine foot high screen wall sectioned off the stores area. The door to the washrooms lay to one side. He opened it and entered the passage beyond.

Silently unseen, the Japanese kept pace, moving sure-footed among the open rafters. Stalking his prey with relentless, unblinking intent. Voices rose from below, mingling with the clatter of machine tools. *Gaijin* were all about, alert and hungry for vengeance. The slightest error would bring failure and death.

Karma. Death was the Way of the Warrior. Resolute acceptance of death the code of his *ryu*. The warrior must keep his spirit correct from morning till night, accustomed to the idea of death, resolved on death, considering himself as a dead man. Only thus could he become one with the Way.

Remember the Four Oaths, they had taught him, and put aside selfishness. Then you cannot fail.

Be swift with respect to the Way
Be useful to your lord
Be respectful to your parents
Pass beyond love and grief, exist only for the good.

From the pouch at his waist he took a grappling cord and attached it to a steel beam. His right hand gripped the weapon.

The washrooms were empty. Abe used the urinal, rinsed his hands and dried them on an oil-streaked towel. From the window he could see over the anchorage. Shit, some mess out there. *Nevada* aground off Waipo Point decks awash, *West Virginia* smouldering still in a lake of oil, *Arizona* a twisted wreck, torn apart by explosions that had killed a thousand of her crew. God damn those Tokyo bombers!

Yes, but they didn't sink our carriers, he reminded himself. Or bomb the fuel farm or the dockyards. That was dumb of them. We'll repair our fleet and teach the lousy bastards a lesson they won't forget. Yessir!

He went back into the passage.

The blow slammed into his ribcage with the force of a concrete block. Three ribs shattered like glass, splinters of bone piercing the lungs. Rivers of pain spurted through him. Gasping for breath, his chest afire, he reeled against the wall.

A dark form blocked his path. A figure swathed in black, hooded, faceless, inhuman, a creature from another world. Like monstrous wings its shadow loomed up the walls of the passage. The eyes were pits of stone, devoid of feeling. Fear enveloped him as a chill wind blowing.

Kami. Demons come to life. Legends from the past, nightmare tales from a homeland he had never known. A weapon gleamed in the dim light. The polished blade of a three foot hardwood pole. A *bokken*. Understanding came to him. Understanding and fury.

"Emperor lover, I gonna kill you!" he hissed and charged forward, fists flailing.

The shadow flickered. Swishing, the *bokken* cut the air in a two-handed vertical sweep. With crunching force the rounded pole smashed down on Abe's shoulder, pulverising the clavicle. Grunting from the shock, he staggered backwards, legs buckling. Another paralysing blow rammed into his kidneys. Sickening pain engulfed him. His vision blurred, heart hammering in his ribs, lungs labouring.

Ruthlessly the Japanese drove in again, *bokken* whirling for the *death-kata*.

Thunder boomed inside Abe's skull. There was a burst of searing light, then a crushing darkness as if earth and sky had slammed suddenly together squeezing him to nothingness. A terrible sound seemed to echo through the world, demons howling for his soul. America! he tried to shout, America! America!

Sayonara.

Eyes glittering, the Japanese stooped over his victim. He felt no

433

remorse at the killing. The youth had died bravely, fighting as a man should. His soul would be reborn. *Karma*. Thrusting the *bokken* through his belt, he seized the corpse by the arms and slung it effortlessly over his shoulder.

"Anyone know where Shiso got to?" the supervisor asked. "He said he was okay to work this shift."

"Probably changed his mind an' went home. That's Japs for you. Can't trust none of the bastards."

The supervisor sighed, "I figured Abe was different. Guess you're right though." He shook his head, disappointed.

It was clouding over as Munro walked briskly down through the base and the breeze carried a sour stench of burnt diesel. Seen from close to the carnage off Battleship Row opposite was horrific. The scale of the disaster had been catastrophic. Unbelievable. He counted at least four capital ships sunk, a dozen more damaged. One armoured behemoth looked to have capsized completely, her rusted bottom plates pointing to the sky.

East Wind Rain. The Japs had stolen first base alright. At one blow they had knocked out the world's mightiest fleet. Now the islands were bracing themselves for invasion.

And where did the Clipper fit in now?

A few drops of rain began to fall. He quickened his pace, hurrying for the rear entrance to the hangar. Through the door the service passage was in semi-darkness. All at once he stopped.

Something was wrong. A premonitory shiver passed up his spine, pricking his scalp. He experienced a sudden urgent feeling of being watched. Of danger near. The same sixth sense warning that had come to him once before – by the pool in Manila. *And minutes after he'd been fighting for his life*.

He reached for the switch, blinking as the lights snapped on.

To his left in the doorway of the washroom, a man stood staring at him. An oriental. *A nisei*. Broad-shouldered and stocky, flat yellow face shadowed beneath the brim of a baseball cap. He wore white overalls, a duffel bag slung over one shoulder.

"Who the hell are you?"

The figure regarded him unmoving. Black eyes slitted like chips of slate. Alien. Hostile. Munro felt his blood chill. "Who are you?" he repeated.

Footsteps echoed somewhere nearby. Abruptly the other seemed to relax a fraction. "Mechanic Shiso," his accent was guttural. Smiling, he tapped his chest, "Five year service Pan Amelican, okay, Joe?"

"Oh, Sorry I . . ."

"*Mister!*"

The whiplash crack of the voice made them both start. Munro whirled. Behind him in the passage, fully dressed, uniform cap hiding the bandage round his head, was Ross.

"Skipper! What the blazes are you doing here?"

Ross thrust out his jaw, the corners of his mouth creased in a scowl, "I'll ask the questions, damn you. You're not in charge here any longer, Mister. *I'm resuming command.*"

The blood drained from Munro's face. He felt as if he had just been kicked in the belly. It had never occurred to him they might jerk the captaincy back. "Does Erickson know this?" Walt Erickson was station manager Honolulu.

Ross snorted impatiently, "It was his idea to have the medics certify me fit again."

Of course, Erickson was an old buddy of Ross's. He'd do that much to help his friend. Munro could taste the bitterness of disappointment in his mouth, choking him.

"The military have been on. They want the ship ready to leave tonight. Our ETD is twenty hundred hours. Okay, Mister?"

"Aye aye, sir," Munro said thickly. Departure ten pm, that was less than six hours away. He glanced back to the washroom.

The doorway was empty. The nisei mechanic had vanished.

Outside in the drizzle, the Japanese jammed his cap further down to hide his face and joined the queues of dockworkers streaming out through the main gates.

By the Amida! He cursed himself for carelessness. For a moment there he had allowed control to slip. The *gaijin* flier had sensed his presence from the passage. Unwittingly he must be a *haragei* adept, such cases were rare but not impossible.

A threat to be neutralised. Yes, but to kill him now would risk alerting the *Amerikans. I-ye,* be careful then. Wait. His time would come. *Karma.*

"C'mon, hurry it up there, dammit!" a rain-soaked MP was shouting at the gate. He checked the dead mechanic's pass perfunctorily. Goddam gooks all looked alike. He waved him through.

Concealing his relief, the Japanese paused a moment outside the

435

gates to get his bearings. A broad highway, busy with traffic, ran past the perimeter wall of the base. The sidewalks were thronged with a mixture of races, Hawaiians, Orientals, whites, hurrying home before curfew. Directly opposite, sheltered by the branches of a massive cotton tree, was a fruit juice stand.

A jeep full of sailors came roaring round the corner as he crossed, the driver swerving deliberately to splash him. "Fuckin' Yellow-belly!" a voice shouted vengefully.

Filthy barbarians, he stifled his rage, Japanese forces would humble them. He looked back a moment through the gates at the shattered fleet and pride filled his heart again. *Oi, how great was the Imperial Navy!*

The stand was deserted, the owner putting up his shutters for the night. An Okinawan with broad features, high cheek bones and short bristly hair. "We jus' closin'. Wat you want, huh?"

"*Ohaiyo*," the Japanese answered, speaking softly in his own language. "Greetings from the Land of the Gods. I seek a friend . . ." He palmed something from his pocket and held it out for an instant. "*Higashi no kaze ame.*"

The Okinawan stiffened. "*Nishi no kaze hare,*" his gaze flicked down at the chrysanthemum button. The whites of his eyes flashed fear as he checked round hurriedly. He lowered his voice to a hiss,

"*They say the priest must die!*"

XXXII

Naked, Georgiana sat at the dressing table in Munro's room, brushing her hair. She had bathed and now the breeze from the open window was cool against her skin. Down below she could hear the surf rolling in on Diamond Head and the shrill cries of the gulls, wheeling and diving out over the reefs.

She turned her head, watching herself in the mirror. There was a bruise on her left shoulder. Max's. He had been rough with her that last time, frightening almost. She shivered at the memory, her nipples stiffening. The danger excited her, the instant of fear when she goaded him beyond control and all that smouldering violence erupted into savagery.

He was right though, she must make a choice.

Laying down the brush, she moved to the window. The beach was deserted. Not that she cared if anyone saw her. Her body was magnificent, she knew that. The sun was going down, sliding into the arms of the ocean. Time to return to her own floor. Max hadn't said when he'd be back. He never did. He was jealous of her, beat her even when she cheated on him, but he wouldn't run after her.

She began to pull on her stockings.

A wave of cloying scent hit her as she entered her bedroom. The place was filled with flowers. Orchids, lilies, great sprays of pink and white carnations. César naturally. He must have bought up the contents of the hotel florists, the kind of gesture he made from habit. He would have done the same for his mother. Irritably she began opening windows to let in fresh air.

There was a rattling at the door handle, "Georgiana, let me in. At once, *pronto!*"

She threw the door back. "Oh, it's you," she said coldly.

"*Nombre de Dios,*" he pushed into the room. "Where have you been?"

437

The emerald eyes flashed, "Since when do I have to account to you for my movements?"

"Since we became engaged," he shot back, "*querida.*"

Georgiana turned away with a defiant toss of her head. She glared at the flower-decked bureau. "Lilies, godammit, I hate lilies!" She seized an armful and dumped them over the balcony.

César's lip ncurled, "Quit showing off." Georgiana ignored him. Picking up a vase, she sent it crashing into the gardens below. César made no move to stop her. Fingers trembling, he took a cigarette from his gold and ruby case. He put it to his mouth but did not light it. "I know where you have been," he said, suddenly accusing. "You were with your pilot – *Munro.*"

She spun to confront him, furiously catching the wild hair back from her eyes. "*If you know, why ask?*"

A bush-jacketed Hawaiian waiter brought China tea and English muffins out to the Coconut Grove *lanai*. "*Mahala nui,*" he said as Maria Bianchi signed the check, "thank you."

"Ricky," Maria called, "Ricky, do you want your ice cream, darling?"

Ricky came running over. "Gee whizz, fudge topping! Say, Mom," he paused between sticky mouthfuls, "are we gonna stop in this place now?"

"I think so, darling, for a while anyhow. Do you think you'll like it here?" Maria watched him anxiously.

"Sure, it's swell. Uncle Eliot says the Japs could bomb us again. Boy, I hope they do, I wanna see it this time."

"Ssh, don't talk so," she gave him a quick hug, scared for him suddenly. Oh God, was there nowhere he would be safe from harm?

She glanced up to see a tall figure approaching. "Good afternoon, Sir Ambrose," she smiled, remembering his kindness in New Guinea. He looked lonely, she thought, and sad. "Would you care to take tea with us? If you can put up with a small boy eating ice cream, that is."

Sir Ambrose lowered himself stiffly into a cane chair, "I was a small boy once myself."

High on a cool balcony looking out towards Diamond Head, Professor Chen laid aside his ink brush.

After the bloody failure of the Boxer Rebellion, he re-read the characters he had inscribed, *China was humiliated by the victorious Western powers.*

438

Foreign troops looted and burned Peking, not sparing even the Forbidden City itself. Stripping off her jewels and finery and ordering her treasure buried in the remotest corner of the palace, the Empress Dowager fled with her court beyond the safety of the Great Wall.

One gem only Tz'u-hsi kept, the Great Jewel stolen from the Duke of Chou and now worn always next to her heart. For she believed that the living metal would indeed restore her lost youth as Jung-Lu had promised.

In vain had the Duke warned Tz'u-hsi of the jewel's malign power. Convinced he was concealing the source of the magic element and determined to prevent others learning of it, the ruthless Empress decreed his execution. Even as battles raged without the city walls, eunuchs dragged him from his cell. By ancient law a Manchu nobleman might die only by hanging with a silken rope, but the palace was in a chaos of panic and the killers had no time to spare for niceties – the eleventh Duke of Chou was thrown down a courtyard well.

Glutted with booty from their sack of the city the barbarian armies at length retreated. Backed by loyal forces, Tz'u-hsi regained the Dragon Throne once more and set in hand the restoration of her beloved palace. But her health was failing even as the Duke had foretold. Sores broke out upon her breasts and corruption multiplied within the Jade Body. Doctors were helpless. From Tibet the Dalai Lama sent sacred images blessed by his own hand, to no avail. At the Hour of the Goat in the seventh year following the Duke's murder, the Old Buddha turned her face to the South and surrendered her spirit.

Thus did the curst jewel betray her even as it had the Duke. After Tz'u-hsi's death the Mandate of Heaven was withdrawn and the Ch'ing dynasty driven from the throne forever.

In a chair at the foot of the day bed, Yu-Ling sat absorbed in a foreign-devil fashion magazine. There came a knock at the door. She jumped up.

It was Hollington Soong. He was alone.

"Greetings, Honourable Chen, do I disturb your rest?"

"I had hoped to settle here, but . . ." Maria set down her cup. Her fingers plucked at her shantung skirt. Its blue matched her eyes. "Sir Ambrose, do you think the Japanese will come back?"

Ricky had left them. The two were sitting alone on the *lanai* in the fading afternoon, listening to the mynah birds quarrelling raucously among the bougainvillea.

"I imagine they would get a very different reception this time," Sir Ambrose remarked drily. He lit up his pipe. "So you have left Shanghai for good then?"

"Yes," Maria assented firmly. "Yes, for ever."

439

"And the *Red Lips* Club?"

A glaze of shock spread across her once beautiful features. She gripped the arms of the seat to steady herself, her knuckles whitening. "You too! Who . . . how did you find out?"

"Hush, m'dear," Sir Ambrose said soothingly, "there is no cause to be afraid. I am not a blackmailer, nor did I learn your secret from Cherkassy."

"*Cherkassy!*" Maria shuddered at the name. She stared at him, "How did you know then – about the Red Lips?"

Sir Ambrose drew on his pipe, the scent of the tobacco wafting on the warm air. "You will not remember, m'dear, why should you?" A far away look came into his face, "The summer of 1913, twenty-eight years ago now. I was on my first tour of the East, you were the star of the show. The loveliest, most wonderful creature I had ever seen. Every night I would slip away from the dinner parties, the official receptions to listen to you sing. He smiled wistfully, "Shanghai's Nightingale, I called you."

"Nightingale," Maria's features softened, "I *do* remember. We danced . . . later you taught me the poem. How does it go?
Thou wast not born for death, Immortal Bird.
No hungry generations tread thee down;
The voice I hear this passing night was heard
In ancient days by emperor and clown," her tone became husky, she faltered.
"*Perhaps the self-same song that found a path*
Through the sad heart of Ruth, when sick for home,
She stood in tears amid the alien corn. . ." Sir Ambrose finished for her. His hand pressed hers and gently folded something into the palm. She looked down. A jade and gold earring.

Scott almost had an accident on her way back to the hotel.

The visit to Tad's mother had been harrowing. Mrs. Gotto had cried when Scott told her what a fine guy her son had been, respected by the whole crew. Pat O'Byrne had gotten Munro to have the log record 'killed in line of duty', with no mention of arrest or suicide, so there was that at least.

They had sipped aromatic tea in the spic-and-span cottage living room with its little Shinto shrine in the corner and Japanese language daily on the table. Tad's younger brother was out with the ROTC guarding the beaches. he didn't know yet about Tad's death, his mother said, weeping softly.

It was raining again when Scott left. Fat warm drops plopping down into the red sandy dust, turning it to mud and washing in the gutters. Half-soaked, she managed to scramble thankfully aboard a bus. The time was close on five pm, traffic downtown was heavy with people hurrying home before curfew. Rounding the corner by the Kalihi-Palama fish market, there was a squeal of tyres as the bus crammed on its brakes. A pedestrian had stepped out suddenly in front of them. Scott clung to the seat as they skidded across the wet road. Peering out the rain-splattered rear window, she had a momentary glimpse of the offender. It was Reverend Jordan.

He must be visiting a church in the area, she supposed.

Back at the Royal Hawaiian, she took the elevator upstairs. With ships not sailing and the hotel fully booked, she and Yu-Ling had agreed to share a room again. As she opened the door loud sobs greeted her. The Chinese girl was lying on the bed, crying her eyes out.

"What's wrong? Tell me what's wrong," Scott hugged her. "Yu-Ling, please let me help."

"Oh ko! Oh ko!" the girl raised a tear-stained face. Her shiny black hair was tied back in ribbon, she looked about thirteen. "Impossible to help, Sallee. It is my uncle's wish."

"Your uncle? Professor Chen? I don't understand, what's he done, for heavensakes?"

"Minister Soong has been to see him. He . . . he wants me for . . . for his *tse mui*, his concubine," Yu-Ling wailed, burying her small face in the pillow again. "And Honourable Uncle says *joss* I must accept!"

A soft amber glow lingered in the early evening sky as Georgiana stood on the Royal's terrace. Away out to sea beyond the dark slopes of Diamond Head crater, rain clouds were rolling in from Molokai on the south wind. Down on the beach the soldiers were putting up shelter tents by their gun positions.

The high lonely wail of a bird sent an involuntary shiver through her. Darkness was coming, and with it a sudden premonition of evil threatening. Hugging her arms about her, she turned back inside. Perhaps Max had returned.

The lobby was busy. Another car had drawn up underneath the porte-cochère of the main entrance. A frail *haole* was being helped down by the Hawaiian doorman. He wore an ancient linen suit with a turnaround collar. "Thank you, thank you," Georgiana heard him saying, "I'm looking for a colleague of mine staying in the hotel, a

441

Reverend Jordan. I had word from him to meet here."

Georgiana's pulse quickened. "I'm sorry, what did you say?" she interrupted. "You're wanting Jordan?"

"Yes, yes that's right," the old man turned towards her. "Are you a friend of his?" he held out a thin hand uncertainly. His lined, kindly face was sallowed from the tropics, the eyes milky. She realized he was blind.

CHINATOWN. A black sedan screeched to a halt in the driveway of the simple, coral built church. Slater and Emory leaped out and strode inside. It was cool and tranquil. An elderly Hawaiian was swabbing the vestry with a mop.

"We're looking for Dr. Currie. Is he here?" Slater demanded brusquely.

"No suh, Doc Currie wen' out."

"Dammit, did he say where he was headed?"

"Mebbe downtown somewheres," the old man leaned on his mop. "Dat's what I tell de other gen'men."

"Others? What others, for Christsakes?"

"De two gen'men askin' for de Doctor a whiles ago. Jap'nese, I tink dey was."

The two men stared at one another appalled for a second, then they were racing back to the car. The driver had the engine running already. "Sir, a flash just came in over the radio. It's the Clipper base. They got trouble!"

Out at Pearl Harbour, the Pan Am hangar was sealed ready for the night. The great doors had been rolled shut, coatings of black paint masked windows and skylights. Inside, beneath the hot arc lamps, repairs on the Clipper proceeded apace. Three fresh 1,600 horsepower engines had been installed and work started on the fourth. Aft at the stern, winches were hoisting a new rudder into position to replace the one holed in the attack.

The Chief and Chuck were working alongside the base mechanics. Ross had called in all the flight deck crew for duty. Up in the auxiliary holds, Munro was making a last check of safety gear, Chris Fry with him.

"Say, Max, looks like we need fresh batteries for the Gibson Girl."

Stowed among the life rafts was an emergency transceiver with a kite borne aerial and a range of around five hundred miles depending on the weather. Its nickname derived from its curved case.

"See the corrosion round those terminals? The humidity just eats into them."

Munro scraped away some of the white deposit with a finger nail. The metal underneath was green and pitted. "Where's Stewart? This is his baby."

"He and Davey went off somewhere with a guy from Navy Intelligence. Guess it's to do with those Jap transmissions we picked up."

Munro nodded. Maybe they were trying to figure why the warnings hadn't been passed on. He put the battery back in its case. "You'd better run this up to stores. Make them test it and give you a clean set. Don't accept this one back."

"Aye aye, Max. I won't let 'em snow me," the young Texan grinned.

Humming to himself, he ducked out the main hatch and sauntered round the work platforms to the rear of the hangar. The storeman received him with ill-grace. "Top shelf rear stack, you'll have to look out a replacement yourself. I've enough to do with these damn mechanics. And mind you keep your cotton-pickin' hands off everything else!"

"*Aloha* to you too, friend," Chris threaded his way through the stacks. Row upon row of metal shelving racked up to the roof with spares, everything a Clipper could need from two cent rivets to twenty thousand dollar stabilizers. Like the man said, the spare batteries were high on a top shelf. He reached for the ladder.

A dark drop fell on his hand.

He blinked at it and then at the floor. "*Oh my God!*" he whispered in horror.

At the foot of the ladder was a spreading pool of blood.

"So who in hell is he?" Slater demanded.

It had taken them exactly fourteen minutes from Chinatown using the siren all the way. The corpse had been brought down off the racks and carried into an empty cargo bay. The Clipper's crew stood round staring sickened at the half-clad body.

"It's Abe alright," a supervisor said thickly. "Abe Shiso, a mechanic with my division." He wiped his brow with a forearm, "Poor lad, I thought he'd run out on us."

"A *nisei*?" Slater snorted in disbelief. "You let a damn Jap work on this plane?"

The supervisor turned to him with a look of slow anger. "Abe was as fine a boy as any I know. He volunteered to stay late so you people could fly out tonight."

"Okay, keep your shirt on. What time did you see him last?"

"Sixteen hundred, just as the hooter sounded. Said he was fetching a spare bolt."

The FBI agent, Emory, squatted down on his hams to examine the injuries. "Skull's all bashed in, shoulder and ribs broken. Any of these blows could have killed. Looks like whoever did this took a sledge to him."

"What happened to his clothes?" said the Chief.

Munro felt a cold hand clutch at his heart. The figure in the washroom. Eyes like dark stones. "*Oh Jesus, it was him.*"

Attention zeroed. "What in hell are you talking about, Pilot?"

"The killer. I came in through the back and there was a guy in the washroom. A Japanese, wearing coveralls. He was acting odd, nervous. He had the deadest eyes I ever saw in a man."

"Which way did he go, for Christsakes?"

"I'm not sure. The Skipper came by just then." Munro tried to think, "He went outside. Yes, he went out through the rear."

A phone jangled on the wall. Ross answered, "Yes, he's here," he said curtly. "For you, Mister – a dame."

Munro took the receiver, "Yes?"

"Max?" Georgiana's voice sharp with urgency. "Max, listen you've got to get over here. I've found Dr. Currie. The one from the photograph. *He's with me now at the hotel!*"

"*Isogi! Isogi!* Faster, fool, or we will be too late!"

"So sorry, *Sensei*. Only . . . only we must take care. The curfew, *wakarimasu?*"

Six thirty pm. Dusk had come swiftly. Here on Hawaii was none of the drawn out twilight, the slow lengthening of shadows common to northern latitudes. With dramatic suddenness the sun plunged below the ocean rim and darkness descended over the islands like a veil of primitive terror.

The Okinawan had a van. He drove badly, nerves or inexperience, the Japanese had no way of telling. Weaving through the back streets, avoiding the avenues, he cut down from Chinatown into Waikiki and pulled up in an alley.

"That is the place?" the Japanese squinted through the smeared windshield. Across Kalakaua, looming fortress-like above the black

444

palm fronds, he could make out the ornate towers of the hotel.

"*So desu*," the other nodded, sweating. It had ceased raining. Buildings in the alley were closed up tight. "*Sensei,* please to make haste," he begged. "The patrols shoot on sight after dark, *neh*?"

"Silence! Tell me quickly, your network on the stinking island, does it operate a radio, *neh*?"

"A radio? Yes, yes there is one but . . ."

"Listen! The Clipper is being made ready again. The Amerikans intend to fly out the cargo tonight. Urgent we contact High Command – the contingency plan must be brought forward at once."

The Okinawan gulped frantically, sweat breaking out afresh on his face, "*Sensei*, it is too dangerous! The *Amerikans* have detector vans everywhere . . ." He choked as a curved blade leapt out of nowhere, the point nicking him a fraction below the left eye. Blood coursed down his cheek, he almost fainted.

"Curse the *Amerikans*! I care nothing for the *Amerikans* or their detectors! Listen, you filthy *eta*, if you fail in this, if you forget your duty, then by the Amida I will find you and flay the skin off your leper-ridden flesh. *Wakarimasu ka?*"

"*Hai, wakarimasu, Sensei,*" the man gasped weakly.

The hotel was unguarded. As he moved through the deserted gardens in the dark there was not a sentry to be seen anywhere. Incredible how casually the barbarians were still taking the war thirty-six hours after the attack.

The cloth soles of his *tabi* were soundless on the short grass beneath the palm trees. Blending effortlessly with the shadows, he approached the *lanai*, hands ready at his sides, fingers extended stiff as steel blades. The engineer's white coveralls were gone, rolled up and stuffed into a storm drain. Shrouded in black again, hooded and masked, he was once more invisible.

Pink-balconied walls gleamed ahead, windows and doors hung with heavy drapes. The blackout would make his task all the easier. Carefully, unhurried, he circled the hotel, noting entrances, apertures, paths of escape. *Haragei* probing the darkness extending his awareness. *Gaijin* down along the beach, but not a threat.

An eddy of breeze reached him as he crossed the terrace. Beneath the mask his nostrils dilated sharply. *Tobacco smoke.* His gaze raked the shadows. From the angle of a corner beneath one of the cupola towers came the half-hidden glow of a guilty cigarette. *Oi*, a soldier!

Motionless he watched, making certain there was only the one. His mouth drew back in a sneer, *gaijin* fool. Reaching into the pouch at his waist, he drew on a set of articulated steel claws.

The soldier took a last pull on the butt and ground it out beneath his heel. The Japanese darted forward. Soundlessly. The soldier glanced up and froze in terror at the nightmare apparition. His mouth opened to scream, as a hand lunged out of the dark. Razor-sharp talons ripped into his neck, tearing out his throat in a single swipe. Blood sprayed the air and the corpse slumped.

The Japanese caught the body deftly. Scooping it up, he darted to the bushes and concealed it among the leaves. In a moment he was back again, scanning the wall above swiftly.

Two floors up, Ricky Bianchi ducked back from the window scared.

It had been a game, hiding behind the drapes, pretending to be a sentry on look-out for Japs.

Only now they were here!

His mother had gone downstairs, but Aunt Ruth was across the corridor with the girls. He slipped out and rattled their door. Eliot Simms let him in. The girls were eating supper in bed. "Hi, Ricky. You wanna come join us?"

The boy stood by the door, eyes huge with fear.

"What's up, Ricky? Is something wrong?"

"*The Japs are here.*"

The room went quiet. Ruth Simms paled, "Now, Ricky, no more of your stories tonight. Come, sit on the bed by Debbie and have some pineapple."

"I saw a Jap – from the window. He was climbing up the wall."

"What's that?" Eliot Simms said sharply.

"A Jap came out of the bushes and climbed up the wall. He was all black, even his face."

One of the girls gave a little scream.

Eliot looked stern, "Ricky, that's enough nonsense. You're making this up. Now cut it out if you want to stay, huh?"

"I'm *not* making it up! I did see him," the boy repeated stubbornly.

"Stop him, Eliot! Stop him talking like that!" Ruth choked. Both girls had begun to cry now.

"*Ricky, go to your room!*"

"But it's true," the boy's voice rose shrilly. "*I saw him! I saw him!*"

Goodbye, Mama, I'm off to Yokohama!

446

Downstairs in the public rooms, the main lamps were doused, black satin sealed every window, the Egyptian ballroom had been turned into a movie theatre. In the Coconut Grove cocktail bar the radio was tuned to a West Coast station.

Goodbye, Mama . . .! The song's cheap bravado filtered through to the lobby where Georgiana and the priest were taking tea.

"I was worried, you see. My son wrote me from Hongkong that Jesse Jordan had died in China."

"Sounds like you two certainly got your wires crossed, Doctor. He was sure you'd been murdered by the Japs."

"Jesse said *I* was dead?" the priest's cup rattled in it's saucer. "I don't understand, why should the Japanese want to kill me?"

"Most likely I got it wrong and he meant somebody else."

César stalked past ostentatiously ignoring her and took a seat at the next table. Turning his back on them deliberately, he opened a newspaper and began to read. Georgiana watched him out the corner of her eye. He was listening, she could tell. She hoped he wasn't going to make trouble.

Stroking her hair, she changed the subject, "By the way, did you know we had our picture taken together in China once?"

"No, no I don't recall that."

"Peking in '36. On a trip to the Forbidden City along with Bishop Buchan."

The priest's sightless eyes gazed at Georgiana bewildered, "Miss Delahaye, there must be some mistake, I've never been to Peking in my life."

Goodbye, Mama, I'm off to Yokohama! . . . there was a round of clapping from the bar. A bellhop approached the table, "Doc Currie? Pardon me, suh, message from Rev'nd Jordan. He asks fo' you to please visit his room, suh."

"*But it's impossible!* Currie's dead. Jordan said so. Claimed the Black Dragon murdered him."

"Jordan was *wrong*. A message came through from Hongkong. Currie's alive and living here on the island. Only now the Japs are after him."

Emory had the FBI sedan waiting with a police cruiser for escort through the blackout. The town was dark as a pit. Not a light to be seen anywhere. Streetlamps, houses, neon signs on the juke joints, all dead.

The blue headlamp beams washed the deserted streets eerily. Every

447

building shuttered tight. Many people had evacuated up to the hills. Those left were huddled indoors, listening for the sound of the bombers coming back.

On Dillingham Boulevard they hit a roadblock. Sand filled fifty-gallon drums and a machine gun manned by jumpy reservists. A white spot snapped on. "*Halt!*" a bullhorn blared. "*Switch off your engine!*"

"Friends!" the driver yelled back. "FBI."

A helmeted figure poked the muzzle of an M1 carbine through the window. "Let's see some identity, bud. The rest of you too."

"Godammit, soldier, we're in a hurry," Slater snarled. "Why d'you think we got an escort, for Christsakes?"

"Piss on that, mister!" the PFC was young and scared, finger on the trigger. "Our orders is stop every vehicle. You could be Tojo for all I know!"

"Goddam Army," Slater was fuming as they drove on again. "They should've been this alert two days ago."

Munro was silent. Currie. Currie had been the fourth man in the photograph. He must hold the key.

If he was still alive.

Room 601. Georgiana pressed the bell. They waited but no response came. The door was unlocked. Inside the room was dark. "Reverend?" She tried the light switch. Nothing happened.

Dr. Currie touched her arm, "Is something wrong?"

"No, but the light doesn't seem to be working. Wait here a moment while I try the one in the bathroom."

She felt her way across the room, bumping her hip against the dressing table. The bathroom door was ajar. She fumbled for the switch. "Nope, this is out too. Must be the fuses."

A breeze stirred the drapes. Strange, Jordan must have left the windows open. She could hear radio music playing faintly somewhere. The door to the passage swung shut with a click, cutting off the light. Darkness was total now. She sensed a shadow brush past between her and the bed and felt a sudden unreasoning fear.

"Doctor Currie, you there still?" she called out.

ZZZIITTT!! A hissing noise split the air making her jump. There was a grunting gasp from over by the bed then silence. A hideous stench welled into the room. Her heart thudded in her chest.

"*Doctor?*" The only answer was her own harsh breathing. Her fear increased. She took an uncertain step towards the window. "Doctor Currie, are you okay?"

The drapes stirred again and parted. Dim light filtered momentarily through the chink. Terror surged in her throat.

Eyes gleamed into hers.

They seemed to hang in the darkness. Suspended without form or body, the pupils burning with a strange feral light. She had the impression they were staring right through her, focussed into the very depths of her being. There was no hatred in them or anger. They were relentless, implacable, pitiless beyond feeling, beyond good or evil, beyond humanity.

They were death.

With an inarticulate cry she stumbled backwards.

It saved her life.

The evil hiss stung her ears again. Something struck the window a violent blow, splintering the frame, shattering panes in an explosion of glass. Staggering aside, Georgiana found herself tangled in the heavy drapes. Another savage smash missed her head by inches, showering her with shards. Desperately, she struggled out of the loose folds. The curtain rail creaked. With a sudden loud crack the pole snapped, drapes and all came crashing down, burying the demon figure.

Wrenching open the windows, Georgiana staggered through onto the balcony. It was tiny. A trap. She could hear the roll of surf six floors down. God, what a drop! She glanced left. The hotel was built Moorish style on several levels topped by parapets and bell towers. Immediately below, a fall of only eight or ten feet, was a flat expanse of roof. She kicked off her gold sling-blacks and climbed onto the balustrade, grazing a knee in haste. Twisting round, she lowered herself down as far as she could and clung to the ledge gritting her teeth. Impossible to see down now. With a brief prayer she let go.

She landed with a thud that knocked her sprawling. Breathless she scrambled to her feet. The roof was some fifty yards across. On the far side another rise to the hotel's topmost level, three tiers of darkened windows like sightless eyes in the pale facade. Picking up her skirts, she ran like the wind.

Pools from the rain splashed underfoot. She made the far end. The lowest window balconies were out of reach. Nearby, fastened to the wall, was a narrow iron service ladder. She looked back frenziedly. Behind on the balcony, the silhouette of a black-clad figure was preparing to leap. Without stopping to think, Georgiana launched herself upwards. The rusted metal caught her skirt. She tore it free and gasping reached the top to collapse over the parapet as the moon came out.

"Help!" she cried. "HELLLP!!!"

Siren wailing, the FBI car screeched to a halt outside the porte-cochère. Munro and the others tumbled out and raced inside. The lobby was chaos, frightened guests milling about, state troopers toting helmets and guns.

Jordan was there, gaunt-faced, hands wringing, terrified.

"What's happened, for Christsakes?" Slater rapped.

The priest gulped. "J. . .Japanese," he stuttered faintly. "Another killing. A soldier out by the *lanai*."

"Have you seen Currie?"

"Currie? No, I . . ."

Munro caught sight of César, "Georgiana, where is she?"

The Spaniard's face twisted, "How should I know? Has the whore left you already, *gringo*!"

"Don't play games, man! Her life's at stake!"

César paled, "*Nombre de Dios,* she went upstairs – she had a message to go to the Father's room."

Jordan gaped at him aghast. "What are you saying? *I sent no message.*"

A cry echoed over the treetops. A woman's scream.

The wind whipped Georgiana's hair as she stumbled panting across the upper roof. Sheer drops on every side, trapped again. A hooded head appeared above the parapet. Terror rose to choke her like a wave. Her only chance was the bell cupola. A rococo tower rising at the far western corner. If she could barricade herself inside . . .

The elevator jerked to a halt at the sixth floor. Munro wrenched back the doors. A long corridor stretched both ways. Left or right? He chose right and sprinted down to the end, César at his heels. Opposite the entrance to a swank corner suite was a small unmarked door. He rattled the handle. Locked. No time to hunt up the floor boy. They put their shoulders to it and the catch gave, spilling them out onto the roof.

An enormous moon hung over the ocean beyond Diamond Head. Along Waikiki the coconut groves were black and solid like dark caves, not a light showing.

"HELP!" The cry was faint and far away.

Munro stared round wildly. *Where was she?* Nothing on this height. Suddenly César gripped his arm, pointing, "*Madre mia!* Up there!"

Sweat broke out on Munro's skin. High on top of the neighbouring roof was an ornamental bell tower. Right out on the lip of the ledge, clinging to one of the columns, was a slender figure. Clothes torn, pale limbs gleaming in the silvery moonlight.

"Oh Christ, Dixie!" he shouted, "DIXIE!"

They ran for the ladder.

The Japanese heard the shouts. Curse the *gaijin!* The mission was running overtime, the threat too great now. Pursuit was almost on him. To continue would risk compromising the main assault. He must break off.

By the Amida, he would teach the barbarians a lesson first. He reached for the sword at his back.

César gained the top of the ladder first and threw a leg over the parapet. Spectral moonlight bathed the roof. There was the cupola, Georgiana hidden from sight by the dome.

"*Querida!*" without pausing for breath, César darted for the opening at the base, Munro close behind.

A moving shadow sprang through the archway. Swathed in matt cloth, eyes only visible, glittering like stones from a narrow strip of flesh darkened with lampblack between the tight-fitting mask and hood. A blood-streaked blade gleamed terribly in its hand.

"*TENCHU!*" With the speed of a striking snake the creature leapt at them. It was on César before he could dodge, a horn-hard foot slamming outward in a flying scissor-kick. It caught the Spaniard full in the chest, fracturing a heart rib and smacking the air from his lungs. Staggering backward under the impact, César crumpled groaning to his knees.

Munro tensed in shock as the nightmare figure rushed at him like a bolt of black thunder. Moonlight flickered on the arcing blade and a split-second reflex instinct sent him diving aside for his life as the *katana* sang lethally in the darkness. He felt death miss him by a hairsbreadth and rolled desperately away across the asphalt.

Scrambling to his feet, he ducked again to avoid the return slash. The wind of the cut fanned his cheek. He reeled back and felt a low wall behind. *The parapet.* A ten floor sheer drop to the terrace below. Again the deadly blade hissed. He tripped and sprawled across the edge, clutching frantically at the stonework to stop himself falling as he sensed the black void below.

"*Amerikan!*" the Japanese spat venomously, lofting his weapon for the kill.

451

Twenty feet above, Georgiana clung paralysed to the cupola lip. Moonlight shafted on the two figures struggling by the roof edge. She glimpsed Munro spreadeagled over the parapet, the dark figure stooped over him like a bat. There was a flicker of steel and a cry.

"Max!" Now she was conscious of figures running onto the roof, flashlights jinking, the crack of shots . . .

Shimatta! The Japanese froze as a spot beam sliced through the darkness, transfixing him by the parapet. Shouts and whistles blown. Bullets whined and he felt a hot sear of pain in one shoulder. Abandoning his victim, he threw himself backwards, somersaulting for a pool of shadow beyond the cupola.

"*Hold your fire!*" Slater bellowed from below. "Godammit, don't shoot! I want the bastard alive!"

But the roof was empty. The Japanese had vanished as if he had never existed.

Munro's fingers clawed at the parapet edge to drag himself back. The stonework was old and crumbly. A piece cracked beneath him and with a surge of panic he felt himself starting to slide. His strength was exhausted, he couldn't cling on.

A face loomed over him, outlined against the night sky. César, blood streaking a cheek darkly. For a long second the two stared at one another. Rivals for the same woman. It would be so easy, each knew, for him to do nothing. To let his adversary fall.

The Spaniard gave a slight shrug, eloquent of everything that had passed between them. Grimacing painfully, he reached down an arm, "Up you come, *gringo*."

"He didn't grow wings, godammit," Slater stormed furious. "The bastard must be here somewhere."

The men with him peered over the edge. A straight drop, sixty feet. Recessed windows, no balconies. Down in the forecourt the white helmets of MPs bobbed in the darkness.

"Hey, you people see anything come down this side?"

"No! Say, what the hell goes on up there?"

"Shit knows. Think maybe we shot a yellow-belly."

"Well, for Christsakes!"

Ten feet below the parapet, squeezed up under the shutter overhang of a service window, the Japanese smiled grimly to himself. His left shoulder ached where the bullet had grazed it. Unimportant. He put the pain out of his mind. Lucky for him the fool *gaijin* had fired in haste. The gun flashes had dazzled their retinas for vital seconds giving him time to escape.

His muscles creaked with the effort of supporting his weight. *I-ye*, the soldiers would be on the alert still. Not till he was certain pursuit had moved away did he lower his legs to stand upright. Balancing on the narrow sill, he recoiled the plaited cord. Briefly he checked the cloth-wrapped bundle at his waist. Below and to his left he could make out the corner of the *porte-cochère* projecting from the main entrance.

Carefully he swung the weighted hook, paying out cord. Loosened, it shot up through the darkness to lodge in the guttering above. He tested the hold, took a firm grip and swung silently outward into the night.

Back in the priest's bedroom the lights had been fixed. A cop on the door was keeping people at bay. Slater pushed inside. "Oh shit!" he croaked, stopping short.

Behind him Munro felt his gorge rise. Splayed on the floor in a pool of blood and entrails lay the body of an elderly man, sliced almost in two by a diagonal slash from shoulder to groin.

The head was missing.

XXXIII

"*Minister Soong, Professor Chen, Yu-Ling . . .*"

Eight pm. Soldiers ringed the hotel, weapons cocked. A bus was drawn up under the porte-cochère. Scott stood at the steps with a masked flashlight. One by one, the passengers climbed aboard in the darkness.

Few spoke. The violence right here in the hotel had shaken them almost more than the bombing attacks. The once despised Japanese had become a race of supermen capable of anything.

And Currie's killer was still at large. A massive search underway even now.

Scott shuddered. But why? Why murder a blind priest, an old man, no possible threat to anyone?

"*Sir Ambrose Hope, Bob Cashin, Eddie Wirth, Van Cleef, Miss Delahaye . . .*" Stopping behind were all the Wake and Midway people, the Simms family, Maria Bianchi and Ricky. Their places would be taken by military personnel, VIPs with priority tickets. From now on all flights were subject to Army control.

Munro and Slater had gone ahead by car, taking Latouche and Jordan. The priest was in a state of shock.

Georgiana came last. Haggard from her brush with death. Long hair caught back, subdued glint of a jewelled evening sweater. A portrait by Sargent. César was at her side, his bandaged ribs sore.

"*Adios, querida.*"

"I don't understand. Aren't you coming with us?"

He shook his head, "Manila has been bombed. My country is at war now and I am a serving officer. They have promised me a passage on the next ship back to the war zone."

"Darling," she caught his hands impulsively, "I'm sorry it didn't work out. My fault, I guess. I don't seem to know my own dumb mind. I'd have made a rotten wife for you."

"*Ay, querida,* we had good times though, *si?*"

"Very good times," she brushed her lips against his a moment. Her eyes were wet with tears. A world was passing. The parties, dancing under the stars, enchanted Manila days, a way of life lost for ever, gone never to return.

She fumbled in her purse, "Your emeralds, I have the necklace still. Here, take them."

With a sad half smile he pushed her hands gently away, "*Te sienta bien,* it looks well on you." He bent to kiss her one last time, "Until we meet again, *querida.* Tell Munro . . . tell him to take good care of you. *Hasta la vista!*"

O'Byrne materialised at Scott's side in the gloom. "All set, girl? Let's be off then," he muttered.

They took their places in front. The escort jeep pulled onto the driveway, dimmed headlamps probing the shadows under the trees. The ghostly blue beams were invisible from the air it was said. Engine grinding in low gear, the bus followed.

On the back seat, Yu-Ling hugged her straw basket to her and shivered. *Oh ko,* everywhere spies and traitors. Wise the warnings of the *fung-sui* in Macao, *heya*? Yes, but only twelve more hours and they would be safe in the Golden Country. *Holy Mary, bless and preserve us. All gods save us from the Sea Devils.*

The moon went behind a cloud.

"*Aiee,* what was that?"

At her side the Professor stirred, "You spoke, Third Niece?"

"That sound, *heya*? Did you not hear it, Honourable Uncle?"

"*Ai-yah,* it was nothing," Minister Soong's unctuous voice came from across the aisle. "A branch brushing the roof. No need to worry, little Princess. Come, sit by me if you are afraid, eh?"

Yu-Ling pursed her lips and turned away.

The bus turned left out of the driveway onto Kalakaua, changing up a gear. Flattened on top of the roof, the Japanese tightened his grip as it swayed.

The priest was dead. His head committed to the deeps. *Karma.* All lives were forfeit to the *Kokuryu-kai.* The operation must proceed. Failure was unthinkable.

Cleave the enemy in two! I swear to be successful!

The wind whistled about him as the bus picked up speed. The humid night rushed past on black wings. A fierce laughter filled his heart. He was a *kami,* a demon of the void, riding the crest of death to the final battle.

Oi, ten thousand things could not touch him now!

PEARL CITY. With an echoing rumble the giant doors of the Pan Am hangar slid open, rolling back on their tracks to their fullest extent. Tractor motors growled, shouted commands volleyed in the blackness. Slowly the flying boat's lofty tail eased out onto the slipway.

Steel helmets glinted among the shadows. Marines in battle kit had sealed off the dock ready to shoot on sight anyone attempting to break past. Slater's orders. His authorization came from the very top. CinCPAC had checked with Washington. The White House confirmed:

Mission crucial to National Security. Priority over all other operations without exception. By personal direction of the President, counter-signed by the Joint Chiefs.

Every supervisor and mechanic on the base had been pulled in to search the ship. Interior panels removed, deck plates lifted, even galley fittings examined. Chief Crow and Chuck had personally checked the engine circuits and control cables.

Nothing. Not a sign of tampering anywhere.

"Okay! Keep her rolling!" the launch boss yelled. An inch at a time the tractor manoeuvred its monstrous load down the slipway to the water's edge. Ground crew in swim trunks splashed into the shallows securing warps to the flying boat's hull. Air hissed from the launch bogey's buoyancy tanks as the valves were opened. Restraining tackles were cast off. The bogey sank away. With an eddy of ripples the Clipper floated free.

Munro breathed again.

"It was *him,* Chief. I *know* it was."

"You said he was masked. Could've been anyone, leastways anyone Jap."

"You don't forget a guy you've fought. *Ever.* He was the one in Manila alright, and before that in Hongkong. He's been shadowing us ever since the beginning and he's out there still. *I can feel it.*"

"Slater's had the dock sealed off tighter'n a fly's ass. No way any damn Jap's gonna sneak aboard."

Munro swung his gaze across the blacked-out anchorage. Pinpoints of flame flickered on the darkened surface of the water. Cutting teams still trying to reach men entombed in the sunken battleships, poor bastards.

But why Currie? What was he to the Japanese?

"Slater can go to blazes. We're not pulling out of here till I've been over every inch of the ship myself."

Methodically, the Chief unwrapped a stick of gum and put it in his

456

mouth. "Ross won't be happy. This business has put the wind up him, that's for sure," he said.

A horn tooted up the dock. Blue headlamps approaching. The passengers were arriving.

As the bus drove in through the gates the Japanese shifted his hold, readying himself. *I-ye*, too risky to wait till it drew up, he must jump now. The vehicle slowed swaying to take a corner. He drew his sword and rose to a crouch. Selecting his spot unerringly in the darkness, he leapt outwards.

The lights were low in the Pan Am terminal building. Glancing nervously over his shoulder, Reverend Jordan stole out past the baggage area towards the exit door at the rear. Just as he touched the handle it jerked open suddenly. He recoiled with a start.

"Where the hell d'you think you're going, Reverend?" Slater spat suspiciously. Sir Ambrose was with him.

"The Bishop . . . I wanted to make certain . . ." the priest gulped.

"Godammit, I told you already the coffin's coming with us. Now get back where you belong, we haven't time to play nursemaid."

"Of course, I'm not important any more," Jordan retorted with bitterness. "Nobody matters so long as you get your precious cargo home!"

Slater rounded on him brutally, "You saw what happened to your buddy. Better do like you're told or you could wind up the same."

The priest flinched, patches of colour burning in his pallid cheeks. Wordless he turned away.

"Goddam missionary," Slater scowled after him, "he gets my goat every time."

"He is anxious," Sir Ambrose said, "small wonder."

Slater shrugged, "Tomorrow morning we'll be in the States. He'll be safe then."

A troubled look came into the Englishman's watery eyes, "He was so certain Currie was dead."

Scott was collecting tickets in the lounge when she saw the priest approaching. Poor man, he looked wretched. "Are you okay, Reverend? We'll be leaving in just a little while now."

Jordan allowed himself to be helped to a chair. He passed a shaky

457

hand across his eyes. "Thank you, thank you, it's just tiredness. I'll be fine once I get some rest," he answered faintly. "Only perhaps . . ." he faltered diffidently. "Might it be possible to have a berth in the stern tonight? I find it so hard to sleep . . . the engine noise."

Scott patted his shoulder comfortingly, "Of course, Reverend. I'll shift some of the army boys around and try and give you a cabin on your own."

The priest's eyes gleamed momentarily, "That would be most kind."

Beneath a parked vehicle a shadow stirred. It flowed invisible in the blackness to the base of the hangar wall and became still again.

A minute passed.

Footsteps sounded. Boots scraping asphalt. The dim outline of the sentry appeared, rifle slung at his back. He stopped. The intruder was directly in his field of vision now, motionless and inanimate as the wall against which he crouched. Even his breathing was imperceptible. The sentry continued to stare straight at him. He saw nothing. Heard nothing. With a yawn he hitched up his rifle sling and resumed his beat. His footsteps died away round the corner.

The Japanese relaxed. *I-ye, gaijin* everywhere!

Cordons thrown round the dock. Squads patrolling all approaches. Barbed wire. Machine guns. Dogs.

Hundreds against one.

He studied the lines of the building carefully. Reaching into the pouch at his waist, he slipped *shuko* claws on his hands and feet. The hangar was constructed of rough-cast concrete blocks. With a quick spring he began to climb, swarming up the wall in light agile movements, the steel spikes gripping the surface firmly.

In seconds he was out of sight, hidden by the pitch, claws restowed at his waist. Skylights sealed with blackout paint spaced the roof either side. He counted and crept soundlessly to the third from the end. The haft of his knife was chiselled like a jimmy. Working it under the rim, he levered.

The lid gave easily. Very cautiously he eased it up a fraction and peered in the crack.

Yoi! Directly below was the coffin with the cargo boxes alongside.

Munro took the bow anchor hold first. Lifting the bilge trap in the floor, he shone his flash into the keel space below. Chris Fry watched puzzled. "Gee, Max, the shore crews just got through inspecting ship."

"They don't have to make the flight."

He worked his way aft, testing the portholes in each compartment. Releasing a catch caused them to function as emergency exits in the event of a crash. All were firmly sealed, no sign of a forced entry. In the honeymoon suite the double bed was made up ready with clean linen sheets for Minister Soong's occupation. A new coffee table and easy chair had been installed to replace those jettisoned on Wake. A lifetime ago now. He wondered briefly how Devereux and his marines were making out.

Closing the door, he stood for a moment in the passage. The premonition was with him still, tugging at his mind like the throb of an old wound. He had a sudden vision of the black-garbed figure on the hotel roof, of a flashing blade and a headless corpse in the moonlight. Currie's killer had escaped. He was out there now in the darkness, watching, waiting. Somehow they were destined to meet again. Both knew it.

Nine forty-five pm. The cordon had been drawn tighter round the dock. Fuel lines snaked down to the water pulsating with the flow of 100-octane avgas being pumped into the flying boat's tanks. Mechanics stumbled in the darkness, cursing the blackout as they rolled a crane jib into position.

The cargo was loading.

Up in the main hold, Dr. Latouche opened his bag. With an electrician's screwdriver he undid four small screws set into the side of the first metal case near its base. Munro and Slater watched tautly as he removed a six inch plate. Inside, Munro glimpsed a tangle of wires and what seemed to be a clock.

From his bag Latouche took a flat block of marzipan-like substance and inserted it carefully in the recess. There was a click as he pressed a switch. "*Alors,*" he replaced the face plate, "she is armed now."

"Cyclonite," Slater grinned wolfishly at Munro, "plastic explosive. Inert as hell normally. You can even put a match to it, but stick in a detonator and pow! You were darn lucky she wasn't armed the other night, Pilot."

"Great stuff, why show me?"

"Just in case you get any more ideas about poking around. Anyone tampers with either of these babies now will blow the ship to kingdom-come. They can be set on timers for auto-destruct too if necessary."

Feet thumped on the roof. "*Hey, in there!*" Shapiro's voice called through the overhead hatch. "Douse the lights. We're bringing the Bishop aboard."

"*Easy!*" The winch sheaves whined. Slowly the teak casket was lowered through the hatch. Between them, Shapiro and Chuck lugged it through the crew quarters to the baggage hold.

"Stow it by the bulkhead," Munro told them. "We need weight in the tail." He waited while they lashed down the handles, the sense of ill-omen strong in him again. As if the coffin were symbolic of a curse afflicting the ship and all aboard her.

"Sure wish we'd left this one behind, Max," Shapiro muttered, reading his thoughts. "It's bad *joss*."

Bad *joss*. The whole trip was bedevilled by it seemingly.

Ten pm. The boarding bell rang.

The mechanics had finished topping off the tanks and withdrawn their hoses. A thick blackout curtain covered the main hatch. All passengers were being frisked on entry, their hand baggage searched. Bodyguard Feng was found to be carrying a gun.

"Preposterous!" Hollington Soong spluttered. "Of course he is armed. A person in my position must be protected."

"I'm sorry, Minister," Scott told him firmly. "No firearms permitted on board. Army regulations."

"I protest. We are travelling on diplomatic papers. You have no right to search us."

In the end they compromised. The gun would be held in the Captain's desk and returned on arrival.

The saloon interphone shrilled angrily. "What's holding us up?" Ross's voice rasped.

"We're still waiting two, Skipper, Captains Diller and Gorski from Wheeler. Purser's looking for them on the dock now."

"Call him back, dammit. Give them just three more minutes, then close the hatch."

"Aye aye, sir."

Everyone was nervous to be off.

Two young Air Corps men came stumbling inside as she put the phone down. "Gee, sorry, Miss, we got hung up in the blackout."

"That's okay. This way," she led them hurriedly to their places. Chris Fry stowed the last baggage in the overhead hold and darted aloft. O'Byrne shut the main hatch with a clunk and threw the latches. "All present and accounted for, Skipper," he reported on the interphone. "Thirty-six SOB."

"*Fasten lap belts please. No smoking,*" Scott passed down the cabins, checking everyone was strapped in. Aft of the main saloon, Georgiana Delahaye leaned back against the tan seat cushions looking pale, her eyes closed. Van Cleef and Bob Cashin were sharing the compartment.

"Say, Sally," the journalist stopped her, "what time do we make the Coast tomorrow?"

"Depends on the weather. The forecast is good. Our current ETA is scheduled for ten o'clock."

"Always provided the Japanese don't interfere," the Dutchman observed drily. He raised the edge of the blackout blind a moment to peer out at the darkened harbour. "Let us hope your forecast is right. I should not like to try this flight in daylight."

Slater and Latouche appeared from the upper deck. They made their way aft to where the Professor sat, thin and hunched, hands buried in the wide sleeves of his silk gown.

"You got that thing safe?" Slater asked him brusquely.

The old Mandarin's expression did not flicker. Silently he lifted his arms a fraction to reveal the yellow wrapping of the casket.

Yu-Ling's heart tensed. *Ai-yah, the devil-box!*

Up in the control cabin the rest of crew were taking their stations for departure. Munro went forward to the cockpit. Ross was already seated. "Where d'you think you're going?" he snapped.

"Don't you want me to fly the take-off with you?"

"*No, I do not want you to fly the take-off with me,*" Ross mimicked sneeringly. "Thyssen's acting as First on this flight. He'll take your place tonight and you can handle navigation."

There was an embarrassed silence on the deck. Munro's face was stone. Ross sat staring ahead of him rigidly. Finally Munro shrugged, "However you like it, Skipper."

"*Start one!*"

With a clatter and a roar the port inboard engine burst into life. A quiver ran through the flying boat as she began edging out from the dockside.

"*Control to Clipper. Run is clear. Over.*"

"*Roger Control. Commencing run. Over.*"

Up in the darkened cockpit, Thyssen scanned the water as the Clipper taxied slowly out into the channel. "There goes the signal." Half a mile ahead the green eye of the launch's directional-beam gun was winking in the blackness.

"Sure hope those Navy gunners have their triggers locked," Chuck Driscoll muttered.

"Hell, they couldn't hit us anyway," Shapiro said cheerfully.

"Oh yeah? Well, they shot down a slew of kites off the *Enterprise* last night, wise guy."

Chris Fry pushed back his cap, "Boy, will I be glad to see the old US of A."

The moon came out from behind the overcast, gleaming fitfully on the fleet anchorage. Off Ford Island the sunken, bomb-blasted hulks of the battleships reared like tombs amid the black waters, a graveyard of two thousand dead. For a moment the crew were silent, staring mutely at the spectacle.

Ross's hand closed on the red-topped throttles, easing them back. The engine noise sank away to a murmur as the Clipper wallowed on the swell.

"*Revolutions critical! Are we aborting?*" the Chief's voice cut through the flight deck.

Still as a statue Ross sat, his gaze riveted on the wreckage of the once mighty Pacific Fleet.

"*Skipper!* Are we going for it or not? We're liable to get a fanny full of shrapnel if we hang around out here much longer."

Ross stirred finally. With an angry movement he rammed the throttles forward. The engines' roar swelled to a thunderous peak. Cyclones bellowing, *Pacific Clipper* launched herself down the Pearl Harbour run, the foaming trail of her wake streaming behind like a comet's tail.

A lump in her throat, Maria Bianchi stood alone in the darkness, straining to catch the last throb of the flying boat's engines. Even before the passengers had pulled out, she and Ricky with the Simms had left by car for the safety of Red Hill Naval Reservation inland from Pearl. Tonight would be spent in a cramped air raid tunnel shared with fifty other families, but at least they would be secure from attack.

"*Thou wast not born for death . . .*" her fingers tightened on the jade earring. Strange the ways of fate. The war would last a long time, but afterwards who knew what life might bring? Sir Ambrose had promised to write.

"Maria!" Ruth's voice called from inside. "Maria, Ricky's asking for you." With a sigh she turned back. For now she had her son to cherish and he was all that mattered.

The Okinawan struck a match.

Shadows flared in the corners of the shack he used for a garage as he searched out a stub of candle. *I-ye,* too dangerous to risk a real light.

He pulled aside the heap of old sacks hiding the loose stone in the wall and dragged out a battered cloth suitcase. His heart was thudding as he carried it to the shelf and raised the lid.

Inside was a short-wave transceiver.

Using a dime store adapter, he plugged the power lead into the single overhead socket. An antenna coil connected to the rear of the set attached to a wire running up through a hole in the roof. Slipping on the earphones, he unlocked the bakelite key and checked his watch.

Three minutes to transmission time.

A rifle cracked in the distance. He tensed as a rattle of answering shots echoed round the harbour. Machine guns and light AA tracer lacing the sky. It lasted several moments, then ceased as suddenly as it had begun. Relief consumed him. Some frightened sentry firing at shadows.

It was time. He switched on the set and began to transmit – *dit-dit-dit-dit . . . dit-dit . . .*

. . . dit . . . dit-dah . . . Fort Shafter's monitoring station picked him up at the thirteenth letter. From an underground bunker, supersensitive receivers scanned every spectrum of the radio waves simultaneously. Within seven seconds a cathode ray display had identified the trace and plotted a bearing. Even as wire spools began recording the message for decipherment, cross-bearings were narrowing the search sector to a half mile triangle. Directions were flashed to waiting gonio vans ordering them to converge on the area. As the letter groups continued to splutter over the ether, the officer in charge got through to Emory in the FBI radio car.

"Looks like he's operating from Chinatown, in back of the harbour somewheres."

"Roger, Shafter, we're on our way."

dah-dah . . . dit . . . Methodically the Okinawan's finger tapped away at the key. The coded bleeps seemed to resound through the shack like hammer blows. He switched to receive and listened for the answerback.

Nothing. Just the empty swish of static.

He glanced at his watch again, the time was exact. *I-ye,* he dare not give up yet. Dare not disobey the Dragons!

"Here he comes again!"

"Sure it's the same guy?"

"You bet. Man, he whacks that key like he's using his foot. Keep

463

going, Mister Jap, just a little bit longer and we'll have you nailed!"

dah-dah-dit . . . The Okinawan's hands were clammy with sweat. Almost eleven minutes he had been transmitting now, easily enough time for the *gaijin* to have fixed him. Their trucks would be quartering the district even now, the technicians inside crouched over their receiver indicators, shouting directions to the driver.

In desperation he pulled out the plug containing the crystal, a thumb nail-sized piece of laminated quartz, and slotted in one tuned to a secondary frequency. *dit-dit-dit-dit* . . . he rapped the key frantically and switched back to receive again. *Acknowledge! Acknowledge! They must acknowledge!*

This was the last chance. The whole operation hung on it!

An MP waved a red lantern across the road. The FBI sedan screeched to a halt and Emory leapt out. One of the high-bellied gonio vans was pulled up nearby, engine running, its antenna directed down the block.

"We got the place targeted, sir. Round the corner in an alley. You want us to seal off the area?"

"No, it'll take too long and he may have a look-out, there's a risk we'd spook 'em. We'll go in now with what we've got. Call your men!"

dah-dah-dit . . . The Okinawan's fingers slithered on the key, running the letters into one another, blurring the groups in his urgent haste. He threw the receive switch, praying. *Acknowledge! Acknowledge!*

Oi! Was that a truck? *Gaijin* in the alley?

With a splintering crash the door flew open. Spotlights dazzled the shack as soldiers burst in weapons levelled. "Hold it right there, Yellow-belly!"

With a sob of terror, he snatched for the gun under the shelf. A blast of fire drowned Emory's frantic shout. The fusillade hurled the Okinawan backward against the shack wall in a bloody heap.

"Godammit, you trigger-happy apes!" the FBI man swore surveying the body. The headphones had fallen off. He picked them up and listened a moment.

dit-dit-dit-dah . . . *dit-dit-dit-dah* . . . *dit-dit-dit-dah* . . . morse crackled in his ears.

The answerback. High Command was acknowledging. The message had got through.

★   ★   ★

BERKLEY CALIFORNIA A light mist veiled the stars. Moisture dripped from the roof of the deserted railroad station. High on a gantry over the tracks a single red lamp burned. Muffled against the chill night air, the lone man waiting was thin and frail-seeming under a wide-brimmed hat.

Away in the darkness a whistle sounded mournfully. A door scraped and the station manager emerged. "That'll be her now," he grunted squinting at the man carefully. "Guess you'll be on gov'ment business, huh?" There was no response and he turned away sourly. *Eggheads.* He'd been warned not to ask questions. There was a war on now. Whatever it was had to be big to halt the *Overland Limited* on its thundering passage to the coast.

The rails began to sing. A second whistle sounded, closer. With deep pants of smoke the streamliner swept round the bend, riding lights doused, sparks showering from giant driving wheels as brakes locked on all along her length. The man stepped back a pace while the locomotive clanked past, slowing ponderously. The line of cars behind seemed endless. Steam hissed from massive cylinders, couplings jolted. With a grinding of steel the train rumbled to a stop.

Chinks of light showed at windows as passengers lifted their blackout blinds to see the reason for this unscheduled halt. The thin man threw away his cigarette with a nervy gesture and climbed hastily aboard the first car.

"Dis way, suh," a coloured steward led the way aft to a private stateroom and knocked at the door. "Yo' guest is here, Senator."

"Professor Oppenheimer," Kim Delahaye wrung his hand warmly. "It's good of you to come."

★ ★ ★

Midnight. A moon hung near the starboard wing, huge and yellow. A hunter's moon. The Clipper was flying at eight thousand feet through clear air in the region of the north east Trade winds. Honolulu lay four hundred miles behind with two thousand still to go before the California coast.

Thus far the flight had been uneventful.

Down on the passenger deck, the saloon was full of chatter and cigarette smoke. Sir Ambrose had invited Georgiana for a nightcap. Eddie Worth was there with Bob Cashin and the Gordon Smythes.

"Soon as ever I get back to Washington, I'm gonna enlist," he declared loudly, draining a second highball. "Yessir, this American's joining the war."

"I thought of becoming a nurse, in San Francisco perhaps where Chris is based," Felicity gushed, devouring a handful of cheese straws. "Do you think they'll let me, Miss Delahaye?"

"Humph," her mother sniffed, "it's high time you got over that young man."

"I guess they'll take every volunteer they can get," Georgiana said absently, brushing a thread from her sleeve. There were shadows round her eyes, she had barely touched her drink.

"Say, I got something here might interest you people," Wirth produced a packet from his pocket. "My snapshots of China. Wasn't going to leave these behind. How about this one, Miss Delahaye, mighty fine stone lions, huh?"

Her brow knitted, "Where . . . where did you take it?"

"Huh? Oh, Peking, the Forbidden City. You been there?"

"Yes, I . . ." she put a slim hand to her brow.

"My dear, are you feeling unwell?" Sir Ambrose said with fatherly concern.

Georgiana was staring at the picture, biting her lip.

"No, no it's just something I was trying to remember," she said slowly. The photograph trembled in her hand. She glanced up, "Has anyone seen Reverend Jordan?"

"He turned in already," Cashin told her. "Guess he's pretty cut up about his friend."

"Oh? Never mind, it's probably not important," she shook her head. Uncrossing her legs, she rose and kissed Sir Ambrose lightly on the forehead. "I'm whacked myself, think I'll get some sleep too. 'Night, everyone."

The Professor was in pain again. Latouche had been summoned. The Mandarin's breath wheezed in his chest, the pulse fluttery.

"A draught of the opium mixture then, if you must," the doctor's manner was grave, "only as weak as possible, *petite*."

Carefully, Yu-Ling measured out half a teaspoon of the tincture, any less would have no effect, and stirred it in a wineglass with water. Together she and Scott helped the old man to drink.

"*Aiee*, Third Niece," he sighed sinking back on the pillows, "truly it is simpler to die than to live and being born is the beginning of the end."

466

"Hush, please to rest now, Honourable Uncle," tenderly she smoothed the coverlet and tucked the cloth-wrapped box securely at his side.

When Scott looked in again the old man was fast asleep. She and Yu-Ling sat on the opposite berth whispering.

"But listen, in America a girl can't be made to marry someone. Certainly not a lecher old enough to be her *father* with heaven knows how many wives already."

"You not understand, Sallee, Chinese girl must all times be dutiful. Spirits of ancestors angry if disobey. Also Honourable Uncle may be dead soon, then what happen to me?"

"Darling, you have friends now. We'll . . ."

The curtains parted making them start. Bodyguard Feng leered in. He spoke abruptly in Cantonese to Yu-Ling. She flushed and hung her head.

"Gee, what was that about?" Scott asked as the curtains snapped shut again.

The Chinese girl wiped away a tear, "Minister Soong, he say I no talk to you any more," she answered miserably.

Alone at the bar, Sir Ambrose Hope nursed a glass of Dimple Haig. He let the last of the amber fluid trickle slowly down his throat, savouring the warm, peaty flavour. Reluctantly he set the drink down. Reaching inside his jacket he took out a leather pocket book and propelling pencil.

Buchan
Oliver
Carmichael
Currie
Jordan

He studied the list thoughtfully for several moments, then drew a box around the last name.

In the third cabin down Georgiana lay restless. Wirth's snapshot kept tugging at her mind. As the Clipper droned steadily through the night she tossed in her bunk, striving to recall images of that long ago trip with Kim.

Peking, the Forbidden City. A picnic in the water gardens, the scent of hyacinths and lilies, stone lions guarding an ancient bridge, missionaries with kindly faces . . .

Something was wrong, something vital. And the answer lay there, she knew.

If only she could remember.

The Chief passed a slip of paper across to Munro at the chart table:

Fuel consumed – 632 galls.

Fuel remaining – 2643 galls.

Present consumption by flowmeters – 199.1 galls/hr.

The time was just after one am. Ross had gone aft to write up the log, handing over the controls to Kurt and Shapiro. Light from the goose-necked lamp cast deep shadows on his weathered features as he sat hunched over his desk.

Whitely was standing up twisting the handle of the RDF loop aerial set into the ceiling. "*Skipper!*" his voice cracked suddenly, "I'm picking up signals ahead."

The cabin went quiet. Out on the wings the purr of the engines seemed much louder. "What frequency?" Ross rapped.

"Lower marine, 150 kilocycles."

The same as they had picked up over the South China Sea when the Japs had jumped them before.

"Think it's the Jap fleet?"

Whitely shook his head, taut with concentration, "Can't tell but it's code. And fast! Military, it has to be. *Ouch!*" he pushed the headphones back.

"What's the matter?"

"An answerback! Shit, the bastard almost burst my ears."

"What heading, for Christsakes?"

"He's too damn close to take a reading. Listen . . ." Stewart turned up the volume and an eerie whistling filled the cabin.

"Shit, what's that?"

"I'm not sure, could be an operator tuning his set or some kind of jamming signal."

"*Kurt, turn twenty degrees to port and take us up!*"

"Roger, turning two-zero." Thyssen yanked up the auto-pilot release levers and shoved the throttles forward. The engines throbbed under full-rated power as the flying boat's nose tilted sharply.

The high pitched howling noise cut off abruptly.

"He's gone," Stewart choked swallowing. His cheeks were pale. "Christ, it sounded like he was in the next room."

"Don't see any bogies," Kurt and Shapiro were peering nervously out the windshield.

"Mister, give me a fix on our position. Fry, get aloft in the dome. See if you can spot anything."

"Aye aye, sir." The Texan was back inside a minute. "Nothing but stars outside."

"Well stay up there and keep your eyes peeled."

"Yessir."

"Could be a freak skip from Hawaii," Davey Klein suggested hopefully.

"Yeah, or a Jap."

"Then we're all dead ducks," the Chief observed as placidly as if he were discussing a ball game.

Ross clenched his hands under the desk till the veins stood out. The pain in his head was back worse than ever. He needed a drink, badly.

Mili, Mili! Would he never be free of the memory?

Amelia, I failed you! I abandoned you!

Fear gnawed at him. Twisting round in his seat, he squinted back over the wing. From the rear of each engine a long blue exhaust flame stabbed, betraying their position like a beacon. The Clipper was racing eastward at two hundred knots, headed into the dawn where the enemy would be waiting for them with the rising sun. He knew it in his bones.

Nemesis.

The lower deck was quiet. Cabin lamps dimmed, passengers in their berths curtains drawn. In stockinged feet a figure stole down the carpeted passage from the stern. It paused at the entrance to the saloon, listening. No one sleeping here. From the stairs came an occasional murmur of the crew's voices.

Gliding between the tables to the forward bulkhead, the intruder studied the passenger instrument panel. Magnetic compass, altimeter, ASI. The Clipper's course, height and air speed relayed automatically from the cockpit overhead. His lips moved memorising the readings.

Noiselessly as it had come the figure retreated.

Yu-Ling woke trembling suddenly from a nightmare. *Oh ko*, in her dream she was back home in Macao being married to Hollington Soong grinning and licking his lips, plucking at her with his fingers. "*Stop! They can't make you do it!*" Sally Scott kept calling to her. *Ai-yah*, but she did not understand, Honourable Uncle must be obeyed.

The *fung sui* had led her to the altar and there, in place of the Cross, had been the hideous figure of the Empress-Dowager on her Dragon throne, cackling in glee and clutching to her bosom the devil-box glowing with evil light.

Then the vision faded and she was back lying in her bunk aboard the plane.

But the fear remained.

"*Skipper!*" Stewart's cry jerked the crew alert.

Night was almost done. The stars were dying, the eastern sky turning pearl at the approach of dawn. Up on the flight deck they had drawn back the blinds and cracked open a window to clear the stale air from the cockpit.

"Signals again. Loud like before!" Stewart was holding the headphones out from his ears. "Sounds as if the bastard's right on our tail!"

Instinctively everyone glanced from the portholes, quartering the still velvet sky for sign of an enemy.

"Astrodome, you got anything?"

"Uh uh, Skipper, all quiet astern," Fry's voice came back through the after hatch.

Ross drummed his fingers on the desk, "Mister, give me a chart fix. Kurt, what's our altitude?"

"Ten-three-fifty on zero-four-zero, Skipper."

"Take her up to eleven thousand."

"Gone dead again," Whitely said, listening into his headphones as they levelled off. "You want me to try raise San Francisco?"

"No, godammit, you'll give away our position. Probably just what the Japs are hoping for." Ross had come forward to the navigation table, "Mister, how much longer you going to be with that fix?"

"Coming up now," Bending over the table, Munro read off the distance with dividers and made a quick calculation on the slide rule. "Looks like we're bucking head winds," he showed Ross the result. "Twenty knots on the nose, maybe more. Another three hours at least."

Ross stared at the lines on the chart and his jaw tightened. It wasn't the fuel, the flying boat's tanks were brimming. With the load they were carrying they could make Seattle almost. It was the time factor. Sunrise had found them still five hundred miles short of the coast.

And the Japanese had struck Pearl at dawn.

There was a flash of suspicion in Ross's eyes. "I don't trust your figures, Mister. Your work's all over the shop lately." Abruptly he straightened, "*Kurt*, give me the wheel and get back here on navigation. See if you can find out where in hell we are."

"Roger, Skipper," Thyssen called with a smug tone that made Munro itch to belt him.

"Any orders for me, sir?" he said tightly.

"No, blast you!" Ross snarled scathingly. "Get out of my sight. Go down and check the passengers, it's all you're fit for."

Down in the galley, Scott woke from a doze. A buzzer was sounding on the steward's call button indicator. J Cabin's light was flashing. The Honeymoon Suite. Hollington Soong calling for attention. What did the skunk want this time?

By the saloon she met Munro coming down stairs, a cigarette slanting from his thin mouth. "Problems?" he flicked an eyebrow.

"Our VIP just woke up. Minister Soong wants his money's worth from the hired help."

"I'll walk up with you."

They knocked at the door to the suite. "*Enter!*" the Minister was sitting up in the double bed in hairnet and flowered silk pyjamas. Extra pillows were plumped about him. "*Ai-yah*, something is tapping at the window outside. It keeps me awake."

They both listened a minute, "I don't hear anything," Scott said, thinking of Yu-Ling and loathing him.

"It has stopped now, but before it was plain – *tap, tap, tap,*" Soong frowned at her accusingly from the bed. "Is there something wrong with the plane, *heya?*"

Munro raised one of the portside blinds a moment to look. They were skimming along in perfect calm. Down near the horizon Aldebaran still hung like a red eye among the Hyades. "Nothing out there that I can see."

They tried the tail cone. Freezing air rushed into the cabin as Scott unfastened the hatch and played her flash over the control wires. Soong shivered, buttoning his collar, watching them worriedly. He plainly had heard something. Munro's brow furrowed as he tried to figure a cause. "We've gained some altitude, it might be ice forming on the waste water outlets. I'll check the heads, see if there's a leak somewhere."

Up on the flight deck Kurt Thyssen let himself into the hold. The cavernous interior echoed to the deep-throated throb of the engines. Dimly he could make out the figure of Chris Fry perched up in the astrodome.

"That you, Kurt? Want to take a star shoot?"

"In a minute."

He picked his way through into the crew quarters. His flight bag lay under one of the bunks. Stuffed down into a side pocket was the Dale Carnegie book. His eyes gleamed as he opened it carefully. A block in the centre of the pages had been neatly cut out. Taped inside protected by cotton wool were four gold watches.

He fingered them gloatingly. Rolex Oysters, brand new, bought at a fire sale price off a Chinese merchant in Kowloon. Smuggled back through customs into the US they'd fetch an easy thousand bucks profit. Lucky for him those sapheads hadn't spotted them when they searched his room on Wake.

And that stuck-up tramp Sally Scott had actually turned one down as a gift. *Well, screw her.*

A thousand green. With the dough from his currency deals it had been another good trip. And it looked like old Ross was set to shaft Munro at the coming inquiry. At the rate the two of them were going the captaincy would be up for grabs.

He put the book away again. Might be a smart move to stash the bag till touchdown in case those interfering assholes started poking around again.

The baggage hold would be perfect, mixed up with the passengers' gear.

He unlocked the after hatch and switched on the light. No portholes here. The piled luggage cast deep patches of shadow against the bulkheads. Over by the rear, separate from the rest, lay a long box-like shape. The Bishop's coffin. He'd forgotten that was stowed in here. A shaft of foreboding stabbed him suddenly. Unaccountably, he felt afraid.

With an effort he pulled himself together. No sense letting his nerves get the better of him. Lashed to the side frames were several bulky items of emergency tackle. Furtively he stuffed the bag down between two rolled-up life rafts. The thing should be safe enough now.

There was a creak behind. He whipped round. "Who's there?" he croaked.

The silence screamed.

He took a pace forward. Another creak. He stopped dead, fear hitting him like a wall.

The coffin lid was moving.

At that moment, with a blinding suddenness, the lights went out all over the ship.

XXXIV

The Clipper lurched into a violent sidesheer, flinging Munro across the passage. Stumbling against the bulkhead opposite, he felt the plane level out and fumbled his way forwards to the saloon.

A flash dazzled his eyes. "Max, what happened?" Scott's voice sharp with urgency.

"We've still got engine power. Must be an auxiliary failure. Keep the passengers in their berths while I find out."

He swung up the stairs. The flight deck reeked of burnt rubber, ominous eddies of smoke swirled in the red glow of the emergency lamps. Ross was swearing obscenely up in the cockpit. By the radio station Stewart Whitely lay sprawled half out of his seat, clutching his head.

Munro pulled him up. Stewart winced, "Jesus, what was that, a lightning hit?"

"Call the Chief, dammit," Ross shouted back angrily. "How the hell am I supposed to keep this crate in the air without instruments?"

The lights flickered on. Sparks crackled angrily among the equipment on Stewart's desk and a valve popped. More smoke coiled up. The lights cut out again.

Ross cursed afresh. Davey Klein reached past Whitely and snapped out the main switches to all three sets. "Okay, now try!" he yelled.

This time the lights stayed on. "Mister, get aft," Ross commanded. "Find out what the trouble is and report."

The Clipper's electrical switchboard was located in the starboard auxiliary hold. Munro found the Chief sweating over a tangled mass of burned-out wiring.

"What hit us? Stewart said lightning."

"Lightning, my ass," the Indian snorted scraping burnt insulation with a screwdriver. "It's smooth as mother's milk out there. A lightning strike would've run up the trailing antenna and blown Stewart's valves but it don't knock out the lights. Some kinda power surge from the magnetoes jumped the fuses and fired the full load

473

straight down the line to the radio desk circuit."

"What's the damage?"

"Search me. There's four hundred different circuits to check." The Chief shot him a quick glance, "Only time I saw a mess like this before was when some joker on training wired a cable from the main lead across the fuse box."

"It was deliberate?"

The Chief shrugged massively.

Munro went back to the cabin.

"Main board looks like a shell hit it. The radio circuit's out, it'll be a while before the Chief can rig up a secondary."

"Tell him not to waste his time," Stewart said bitterly. He and Davey had the backs off their sets, bits of dismantled equipment strewed the desk. "This lot's nothing but a heap of junk. Even if we could replace the valves, the coils are melted solid."

"What the hell's responsible, Mister? Hasn't the Chief figured it yet?"

"He ain't sure, sir," Munro lied. This wasn't the moment to start a panic.

"Klein," Ross snarled over his shoulder, "go dig out the Gibson Girl. See what we can pick up on that."

Minutes later Davey was back. Empty-handed. "I can't find the thing, Skipper. It's not in with the life rafts. I looked all over and it's gone!"

They stared at him in dismay as the implication sank home. The same thought on all their minds. The Clipper was deaf and dumb, helpless prey for an enemy. And four hundred miles still to the coast.

Then Shapiro interrupted from the co-pilot's seat, *Where's Thyssen?*

Pat O'Byrne rapped urgently on the locked door of the rear men's room, "Who's that in there?"

"It's . . . it's me, Reverend Jordan," the priest sounded startled.

"Sorry, Father. Thought you might be Mr. Thyssen. You wouldn't have seen him. By any chance?"

"No, no I haven't."

Pat scuttled back to the saloon. Scott was there with Chris Fry, anxiety showing in their taut faces, "We checked every cabin, anchor room and tail cone too. There's not a trace of him down here."

"What's all the noise?" Slater appeared pulling on his jacket.

O'Byrne told him.

474

The shock registered, "Son of a bitch!" He made for the stairs. Stewart and Davey were bent over the wrecked innards of their radio sets. Up in the cockpit Shapiro had the controls alone. Ross was back at the desk, wiping his mouth guiltily. In the grey morning light his skin was pallid, slick with perspiration.

"What the hell gives? The purser says you've a man missing."

Ross's hands shook like an old man's. "The second officer's lost," he thrust the whisky bottle into the drawer and slammed it shut. "We're searching the ship."

"What d'you mean, *lost*? The guy must be on board somewhere. He can't just disappear, for Christsakes!" Slater took three strides to the after hatch and wrenched it open. In the main hold the cargo boxes were still as he'd left them. He whirled back scanning the windows, "How far are we from the coast?"

"Three, four hundred miles. Two hours at most."

"Then godammit, get on the horn, call up the Navy and have them vector an escort onto us."

Silence in the cabin. Whitely and Klein were listening blankly. Ross pulled himself to his feet. "Use your eyes, Major," he answered savagely, pointing to the wrecked sets. "We can't call anyone. *We're on our own!*"

Chuck Driscoll held the flash as Munro crawled out from the starboard wing. "Could be he fell overboard shooting a drift sight," the young engineer suggested.

"Sure, and shut the hatch behind him afterwards," Munro said cuttingly. He stood up, dusting himself off, "Sorry." They were all on edge. "We'll try the other side."

But the port hatch was securely fastened too. Kneeling inside the wing space among the safety gear, Munro peered through the glass. Far below the ocean lay like a wrinkled cobalt map unobscured by clouds. Often in the past they had sighted fishing boats from the abalone fleet this far out. Not today. This time the seas were empty.

The rack of drift bombs was untouched. No sign Kurt had been in here. But how did a man disappear on a plane like this?

The Clipper quivered in an air pocket. He reached up to steady himself on the overhead spar. All at once he concentrated. Something had flicked across his field of vision. A loose guy wire? A section of cable flapping against the hull?

A freezing blast from the two hundred knot slipstream filled the confined space as he unclipped the hatch. A picture flashed into his mind of Kurt tumbling helpless down through the screaming blue emptiness. All his life racing past him in those last endless seconds, eleven thousand feet to eternity.

Clinging on tight to the combing, he leaned out to look.

"What is it, Max? What'd you find?" Chuck called agitatedly, poking his head through.

"I'm not sure," with numbed hands he shut the hatch and squeezed back out into the cabin again. "Bring that flash with you a minute. I want to check in the baggage hold."

He snapped on the main light. The bulb flickered as if it were about to blow and shadows danced eerily among the stacked cases. The steady beat of the engines reverberated reassuringly through the gloom. There was another noise too, hard to make out. A low pitched hum he couldn't place. Something brushed his arm. He recoiled with a start. A loose securing strap dangling from the roof. His pulse rate eased.

Chuck Driscoll cleared his throat, "Kind of spooky here, Max."

Munro let the flashlight beam play along the inner skin of the hull, lingering on each spar. It took him a while to find it, even though he knew what he was searching for. Down at deck level, near the rear bulkhead portside, an air ventilator grill was let into the fuselage. From it trailed a thin wire.

He traced it with the flash across the decking, snaking round behind the suitcases. The thing was all but invisible to a casual inspection. Whoever had done it knew his business. At the far end of the bulkhead the wire disappeared. Polished wood reflected darkly in the beam. Brass handles and a nameplate.

Suddenly a load of things began to make sense.

Jesus, he thought, it couldn't be. It wasn't possible. But they had to find out. And there was only one way.

"Fetch me a screwdriver."

"What?" Chuck jumped.

"*A screwdriver. Quickly, dammit!*"

Someone was shaking Cashin's shoulder. "Bob! Bob! Wake up!"

"Okay, okay, gimme a chance," he propped himself on an elbow blinking. Georgiana was kneeling by the bunk fully dressed. "Miss Delahaye? Say, what time is it?"

"Almost seven. Look I need your help. Max is on duty upstairs, I can't get hold of him or Major Slater. Bob, are you *listening?*" she shook him again urgently.

476

"Sure, sure, go ahead. What's the problem?"

"Dr. Currie, the man murdered last night, Reverend Jordan said it was him with Bishop Buchan in Peking, right?"

"Yeah, Jordan was positive about it, I heard him tell Sir Ambrose on Wake. Why?"

But Georgiana had darted out of the cabin.

"What was all that about?" Eddie Wirth peered sleepy-eyed from between the curtains of the top berth.

"Hanged if I know," the journalist groped for his glasses. "But the dame's sure got the wind under her tail."

Georgiana's brain was racing as she hurried up the passage. Everything was coming back. A flood of memories unleashed suddenly like a channel unblocked . . .

. . . *after the picnic . . . Kim taking snapshots . . . a breeze whipping her hair . . . dear old Bishop Buchan and the others, among them . . .*

No, she must be wrong.

G cabin's curtains were drawn still but the berth was empty. No sign of the priest. On the unmade bunk lay his camera.

The case opened with a snap. She whistled in surprise. Boy, some toy for a penniless missionary! It was like no camera she had ever seen before. Most of the works seemed taken up by some kind of complex light meter with a calibrated gauge. Underneath was a bulky battery.

She found a switch at the back and pressed it. The needle on the gauge quivered briefly. She moved to shut it off again. Abruptly the instrument began emitting a series of sharp clicks. Startled she jerked back. The noise ceased. She tried again. The clicking returned, the needle swinging round on its gauge. The machine was reacting each time her hand passed in front of the lens aperture.

Not her hand, her wristwatch. The Cartier Tank watch César had given her. A watch with a *radium* dial.

Her eyes caught something else stuck right down in the back of the leather case. She worked it free with her fingernails. A yellowing photograph. Four men and a girl standing by an ancient stone bridge. The lion bridge of the Forbidden City! Her heart began to hammer as she recognised herself.

This must be it! The snap Kim had taken at the picnic. The same one Max had found in Hongkong in the room of the murdered priest.

Fingers trembling, she held the print under the light, studying the faces. Bishop Buchan and Reverend Oliver, Dr. Carmichael, she remembered him, and a fourth man . . .

A sound behind made her whirl. There in the curtains stood Reverend Jordan. His eyes glittered as he saw what she was holding.

477

Her hand flew to her mouth, "My God, *who are you?*"

Munro knelt by the cofffin and examined it carefully. The lid was plain and smooth, held down with brass screws. FRANCIS JOHN BUCHAN 1872–1941, the plate read.

He took up the screwdriver. "Max, for Christ's sake!" Chuck blurted.

"Just hold that flash steady." Clenching his jaw, he inserted the tip of the blade into the first screw and began to turn. Was it his imagination or had the humming sound increased?

The screw came free easily. So did the next. The back of his neck pricked at the thought of what he was doing. Clipped overhead against the bulkhead was a red extinguisher bottle. There was a fire axe with it. Stopping a moment, he reached it down and laid it ready on the deck beside him. Chuck watched astonished.

The last of the screws came away.

Taking the lid by both sides of the rim he tugged upwards. Nothing happened. Sweating he tried again harder. The lid remained firmly in place. Had he missed a screw? No, it must be fixed inside somehow.

He ran the blade of his pocket knife round under the rim of the lid. Near the head it met an obstruction. Something metallic. He worked at it for a moment. Every nerve in his body taut now. There was a sudden sharp click, the sound of a catch springing and he started back.

Hearts thudding they stared at the coffin. Stillness lay heavy as death in the hold. They could hear the swish of the slipstream against the skin of the hull outside. Munro swallowed painfully, his mouth dry. "Okay, stand clear." Holding the axe ready, he lifted away the lid. This time it came off easily.

"Oh shit!" Chuck choked.

The figure inside stared up at them with sightless blue eyes. Blond hair and a dark uniform. Kurt Thyssen, stone dead. Wedged between his legs was the Gibson Girl.

With a jerk of the wrist the priest pulled the berth's curtains shut.

Georgiana watched him transfixed. His eyes, she noticed for the first time, were cold as the grey sea, almost lashless. They reminded her of a snake's. "*Who are you?*" she whispered.

"Does it matter?" The feigned hoarseness had been dropped, in its place a ruthless self-confidence.

"This picture," she gazed in horror at the photograph, "it's why Dr. Currie had to die, isn't it? And Morris Oliver in Hongkong? The same reason you tried to kill me in New Guinea pushing me over the side of the yacht. Because we all of us should have known!"

He nodded calmly, "Your presence on the flight was unforeseen." He took a step towards her.

Georgiana backed to the window. "Stay away! Touch me and I'll scream the place down. My God, I was a fool! That first night in Manila when Max introduced us, you could hardly speak you were so shocked. You were terrified I might realise."

"But you didn't," the priest shrugged. The steady rhythm of the engines made their voices inaudible beyond the cabin.

"It was five years ago, why should I have done? And it wasn't as if I'd seen the photograph. Because this is the giveaway, the proof, isn't it?" she said bitterly, savagely. "If I'd once set eyes on this you'd have been finished. Bishop Buchan, Morris Oliver, Father Carmichael, all three dead now. And so's the fourth! Has been all along, hasn't he? The last man in the photograph. He's not Currie like you told us. That was just a trick, wasn't it? *He's Jesse Jordan – the man you claim to be!*"

"So you have tumbled to the truth finally," the pale gaze did not flicker. He stepped closer again, "Fortunately it is too late to interfere with our plans."

Then he struck her.

"Black Dragon. *Kokuryu-kai!*" Slater knotted his fists. "Their man didn't need to sneak aboard. The son of a bitch was hidden here all along. Riding with us right under our noses ever since China!"

Munro switched off the radio key. The humming sound ceased abruptly. The wavering light in the hold gave a macabre semblance of life to Kurt's features. A dark smear showed against the white shirt in the region of the heart. He touched it with his fingertips. Dried blood. The chest had a pulpy feel. The entire ribcage was stove in from a massive blow.

"*Bastards!*" Ross said thickly. His voice shook, "Bastards!"

The coffin's interior was lined with padded cotton. Cunningly concealed vents in the base provided air holes. The space inside was ample for one man and his equipment. Munro felt a wave of impotent rage engulf him. It was all so damn *obvious*. How could they have been so blind?

Everything fell into place. the crash of the bomber in New Guinea, the disappearance of its crew and the slaughter in the swamps, the

479

murder of Currie. From Hongkong to Honolulu the killings had dogged them every step of the way and *still* they hadn't guessed.

And now the killer was loose aboard!

Slater pointed to the Gibson Girl. "This is the emergency transmitter?"

"It's a homing signal. The key's locked down to give a fix on our position and the antenna runs out astern past the honeymoon suite. That was the tapping Soong heard."

"*A homing signal?*" Their faces drained as realisation hit them. "Can we use it to raise the Coast, for God's sake?"

"I'm trying, dammit!"

"Well hurry." Slater swung back to Ross, "We gotta find the guy did this and fast. Break out firearms and start with . . ."

A sudden scraping noise at the far end of the cavernous hold made them all whirl. The floor hatch was opening.

A figure appeared, silhouetted in the doorway by the passage lights below. Long hair and ivory skin. "*Dixie!*" Munro sprang to his feet as she stumbled through. Then he stopped dead.

At her back was Reverend Jordan.

"Ah, the chivalrous Mr. Munro. Major Slater too and Captain Ross. Good, good," the priest's laugh was chilling in the echoing hold. Shoving the girl before him, he climbed nimbly up and stood erect, throwing aside his jacket. The stubby barrel of a machine pistol gleamed evilly in his hand.

Jordan. And now too late they grasped the web of the conspiracy.

Slater stared at the priest like a dazed man refusing to accept the evidence of his eyes. Suddenly he seemed to recover. With a grunt he grabbed for his hip pocket. "*Drop it, Major!*" the weapon's snout lifted menacingly. "Unless you want your friends to die with you."

Slater froze. Slowly he drew his hand out. The gun fell to the deck with a metallic clunk. No one else moved. Munro licked the salt sweat from his lips, striving for calm. Georgiana was clinging to him. Blood smeared her cheek where Jordan had hit her. "Easy, Dixie," he said tightly.

"You, Captain, slide the gun towards me with your foot. *Slowly*, if you want anyone to live!"

Ross stared at the priest ashen. Trembling he did as ordered. "Murderer!" he croaked hoarsely.

Jordan's gaze flicked to the open coffin. He shrugged without emotion, "Fortunes of war, he chose the wrong moment to come in here."

"You'll fry for this," Slater spat at him. "You goddam traitor."

The priest's mouth tightened. "If I have killed it was in the cause of duty," he snapped, "*für Grösser Deutschland!* I owe no allegiance to your nation of degenerates."

Frustration and fury at his own stupidity squeezed in Slater's chest. The Brits had been right. Sir Ambrose warned the *Bund* had a man aboard. The Japs had been ahead from the start. How had they learned of the mission? How switched the priest's identity? And *Jesus Christ* what did they intend doing?

"We carried him with us. You and your pissing bishop. You played us for suckers all along. Well, you'll never get away with it, godammit. Never!"

Jordan laughed mockingly again, "We shall see." Abruptly his tone harshened. He motioned with the machine gun, "Enough talk. Forward into the control cabin all of you. Captain, lead the way. *Schnell!*"

Ross's mouth worked soundlessly. He turned to the hatch. The others followed, Chris first, then Slater and Georgiana. Munro brought up the rear. The screwdriver he had used to open the coffin with was in his right hand pocket. Not much of a weapon against a machine gun, but better than nothing.

As he stepped through into the cabin his blood ran cold.

The rest of the crew were frozen at their stations. Up in the cockpit Shapiro was sitting very still. Behind him, hooded and masked like some hideous apparition, loomed the Black Dragon warrior. In his fist gleamed a naked sword. Its razor-edged blade rested lightly against Shapiro's straining neck.

For a long minute no one spoke or moved.

Chuck was the first to recover. He made a wild grab for the rear desk where the pistols were stowed.

"*I-YEEE!!!*" The Japanese whirled, a blur of motion. The *katana* flashed in a hissing crescent and Chuck lurched back with a shriek, right arm slashed open elbow to shoulder. Blood spattered the cabin carpet. He collapsed retching.

Chief Crow's eyes blazed. Uttering a bull-like bellow he launched himself at the Japanese. "*No, Chief!*" Munro leapt between them, blocking the Indian's rush as the blade flashed again. The blood-streaked edge chopped to a quivering halt a fraction from his skull. Sweat poured off his body, his heart was pounding.

Very carefully both men backed off.

Down below, Scott peered out the galley porthole, praying for a glimpse of the California coast. Dawn was coming up fast, a deep red sun rising out of the eastern sea staining the sky with crimson fire. Far on the horizon floated a line of fleecy cloud tinged with bronze. It was going to be a beautiful day.

No sign of land yet. Safety was a bare three hundred miles off. Two more hours at most. So near and still so far.

A flash below caught her eye suddenly. Sunlight winking off burnished metal. Straining to see, she could just make out two dark spots moving against the wrinkled glass of the ocean. Their course put them on an intercept track with the Clipper. Her spirits soared. The Navy was here to escort them in.

Mesmerized, she watched the metal specks floating upwards through the cloudless air, growing gradually more distinct as they swiftly overhauled the lumbering flying boat. Single engine fighters with long predatory snouts and floats under the wings. Sea planes, probably launched off a ship. Handsome craft in deep maroon colours with a red belly stripe.

Soaring like a bird, the flight leader drew up level with the Clipper's stern. His port wing dipped momentarily.

A cry of anguish rose in Scott's throat. Flaring crimson against the silver fuselage was the Rising Sun of Nippon.

"*Attention, everyone!*" Jordan's voice crackled from the intercom. "*This aircraft is now under the protection of Axis forces of the Imperial Japanese navy. All passengers will remain in their seats and await further instructions.*"

*   *   *

SAN FRANCISCO. SIX FORTY-ONE AM. The wall maps told the story. Clusters of fat orange markers grouped menacingly off the coast like a dagger aimed at the California heartland.

Kim Delahaye surveyed the conference room appalled. "*You've lost her? but that's impossible!* There was to be an escort. The President ordered it."

The Presidio, San Francisco Headquarters Western Defense Command, was a madhouse. Squads of soldiers mounting weapons in hastily dug slit trenches, harassed messengers rushing in and out, doors slamming, telephones and buzzers shrilling, clerks banging away at typewriters, exhausted staff officers bawling for maps and plans. Everyone chain smoking, nerves on edge, talking at the tops of their voices. Rumours multiplying by the hour.

482

The war was only two days old. No one knew where the Japanese might strike next.

Kim felt his spirit twist inside him. Four thousand dead. The Pacific Fleet sunk, MacArthur's airforce wiped out on the ground. This wasn't how it was supposed to be. The President's plans had gone terribly awry. And now the Clipper . . .

"There's been no word from the plane? Nothing at all since departing Hawaii?" he choked.

The Navy captain on liaison looked unhappy, "A PBY from Almeda went up at dawn. They found no trace of the flying boat near the rendezvous point and no response to signals."

"Senator," a two-star general crushed out a cigar, "latest reports put the main Jap battle fleet less'n two hundred miles off the coast from Monterey. Bombs could be dropping down our throats any minute. We just don't have planes to spare for flying search missions. I'm sorry about your girl, sir, but the Clipper's on her own. *If she hasn't been shot down already.*"

Kim passed a hand across his brow, squeezing his eyes shut against the images. Summer days long ago, a laughing child running free across the lawns. A skinny-limbed twelve year old bareback on an arab colt. Innocent and shy in the white dress of her debutante dance. Flushed with the pride of her first tournament win . . . *Georgiana* . . . *Georgiana* . . .

He turned to the windows. Beyond the tree shaded slopes the waters of the bay were sluicing out under the great bridge, flecked with whitecaps. The tide was on the ebb.

★   ★   ★

"Oh God! Oh God!" Cynthia Gordon Smythe whimpered tearfully. "What's going to happen to us?"

Engines roaring at full throttle the giant airliner scudded over the ocean a bare two thousand feet from the wavetops, the seaplane fighters riding her wingtips like sharks driving a whale. Huddled together in their life vests on the floor between the cabins amidships, the passengers stared out in terrified disbelief at the sleek, deadly shapes alongside.

"Christ Almighty," Eddie Wirth gulped, "it ain't possible. Where'd they come from?"

"Short range kites. Flown off a ship most likely," an Air Corps lieutenant told the others grimly. "Means the Jap fleet must be here."

"*Ai-yah*, and where is the American Navy then?" Soong screeched from the rear ashen-faced, his jowls quivering. "We were promised protection. Now look what has happened. *Oh oh oh!*"

Cynthia gave a little cry. "It isn't *fair*, they shouldn't have let us fly if there was this danger," she sobbed accusingly.

"Chin up, Mummy," Felicity tried to cheer her. "Of course they won't hurt civilians, will they, Eddie?"

"It makes me mad how that priest made jackasses of us," Bob Cashin ground his teeth. "And all the time we were feeling so sorry for him, *goddam traitor*."

"If we could only rush the stairs somehow."

"Against a machine gun, are you crazy? They'd cut us down like ducks in a fairground. And what about the fighters?"

"Looks like some cloud ahead," Scott squinted out the window trying to see the sky. "Only a few scraps, but if it thickens we might have a chance to lose them."

"Forget it, sister," the second Air Corps man shook his head. "Unless you're bucking for a twenty mill enema. One squirt from those babies' cannon and we'll all be hitchiking to hell."

"*Ai-yah*, he is right," Hollington Soong agreed earnestly. "Stupid to resist without weapons. The Sea Devils want only the cargo. Give them that and they will leave us our lives, *heya?*"

Scott shuddered. What did the Japanese mean to do with them? She squeezed O'Byrne's arm fiercely, "Pat, we have to find a way out of this!"

The intercom crackled again. "*All passengers take their seats. I repeat, all passengers take their seats immediately. We shall shortly be landing on the sea. This will be your only warning.*"

Jordan cut the microphone off. "Not long to wait now, gentlemen," the sneer of triumph in his tone was undisguised.

Georgiana was kneeling on the floor at Chuck's side, her skirt bloodstained. He pushed her callously aside. "Brute," she flared. "He needs a doctor."

"Too bad, he will have to wait." Reaching for the ship's binoculars, the priest focused them ahead through the windshield.

"Think you're goddam smart, don't you?" Slater grated from the rear of the control cabin, clenching and unclenching his fists, longing to smash Jordan's face, obliterate him for his treachery, for fooling them so easily for so long. "Those signals you sent out will have been

484

picked up on the coast too. You'll have US Navy attack planes round your ears soon, by God."

The priest paid no attention. He glanced at Whitely, "The short range radio-telephone is on a separate circuit from the rest, I believe. It still functions, yes?"

Stewart gulped and nodded, too frightened to speak.

"Then connect me, *schnell*."

From the cockpit Munro eyed the seaplane flying alongside, so close he could make out the enemy pilot grinning at them across the intervening airspace, a white good luck scarf bound about his leather helmet. Arrogant bastard. He felt the sour taste of defeat in his mouth.

To his left Ross sat gripping the yoke grimly, gaze fixed on the empty horizon. The coast lay barely a hundred and fifty miles to the north-east. Forty minutes at full throttle. It might as well be the other side of the world.

Jordan was speaking Japanese over the R/T. Munro watched his reflection in the glass of the tachometer dial. No chance to go for that gun again. The man was ruthless. He had shown it.

And there was the Japanese. He could sense the swordsman's presence filling the cabin like an electrostatic storm field, the baleful glare boring into the back of his skull. Eight days he had travelled with them ever since Hongkong. Hidden in the coffin like an unquiet corpse. A phrase of Tad Gotto's came into his mind, *sakki – the force of the killer*. Munro felt a cold quiver in his belly. One false move on anyone's part and the *katana* blade would turn the cabin into an abattoir.

Time was running out. They had to act. In another few minutes it would be too late.

"*Portside bandit breaking off!*" Shapiro's voice cut across the cabin urgently. Every head snapped to the left hand windows.

With a smooth surge of power the lead seaplane pulled dextrously ahead, bright sun winking on the perspex cockpit hood. Dipping a wing, the pilot peeled gracefully away, swooping down towards the ocean. Instinctively Munro raked the sky, hoping against hope for sight of American aircraft blazing out from the coast to their rescue, but the blue was empty to the horizon. The other fighter still tucked in alongside to starboard, gunports leering.

Tossing the R/T at Stewart, Jordan came forward. "Follow him down, Captain, and remember no tricks," his face was hard, "or the lovely Miss Delahaye will be the first to die."

"*There, Captain!* There, where the water is stained!"

"Christsakes, d'you want to kill us all? This is open sea! We'll never make it!"

The crew gazed from the windows in dismay. Low beneath them long grey rollers surged relentlessly in a north-west swell backed by seven thousand miles of ocean weight. As far as the eye could see the heaving waste stretched barren of life.

The seaplane fighters were circling overhead. A quarter mile to starboard a patch of ominous red stood out stark against the background of water like a bleeding wound. Bobbing to one side was a dark object too small to make out clearly. Munro guessed it would be a radio buoy of some kind for the planes to home in on.

Sweat started along Ross's brow. Shakily he turned the flying boat into a slow descent. The altimeter unwound. Munro clicked on the seat belt warning switch for the passenger deck and pushed back his window. Salt air rushed into the cabin, smelling of kelp.

"*NO!*" A quiver ran through the airframe. The nose lifted as Ross rammed the throttles forward with a cry. "It's not possible, I tell you!" he cried frantically. "She'll dip a wing and capsize on us!"

"Skipper!" Munro grabbed for the controls. "The son of a bitch means it. Do like he says."

"I . . . I can't!" Ross sagged in his seat. With a sob he buried his face in his hands.

There was a vicious expletive from Jordan behind. "*You, take over!*" the steel muzzle of the machine gun ground savagely into Munro's neck. "Set us down on the water. *Now,* if you want the girl to live!"

Munro felt a surge of blinding rage. He could have killed him then with his bare hands. With a supreme effort he forced himself to act calmly. "Alright, for Christsakes, I hear you. Just take that bastard thing outta my ear."

Drawing up in a shallow turn, he let the flying boat fall away again into the wind, easing off the power for a long steady approach. Close to, the swells looked massive but the crests were smooth with long intervals between the troughs. He gauged the pattern, aiming to let the Clipper down as one crest rose beneath her, running with it as the ship slowed on the water.

"*Full flaps!*"

No answer. Ross was rigid in his seat now, locked on the ocean ahead, terror written in his face. Munro reached out to throw the solenoid switch, he would have to fly this one solo. A quick check of the instrument panel. Air speed one hundred ten. Too fast still. Seventy feet on the altimeter. Prop governors set to full low pitch –

2100 RPM.

"Close cowl flaps!"

"Aye aye, closing all!" the Chief operated the levers, his eyes on the synchronizers.

Fifty feet. Twenty. The waves rolled past under the nose. They were barely skimming the surface now. Ross was clutching the arms of his seat, his fingers clawing the leather. Levelling off, Munro eased the throttles open a touch and held her there waiting. The back of a long swell rose like a hill in the corner of his vision. Now for it! Drawing off the power, he let the Clipper sink into a stall. Water sizzled against the metal skin of the keel as they cut through a crest. Still airborne, they dipped into the trough beyond. Then, with a crunch that seemed to jar every rivet on the plane, they smacked head-on into a toppling swell.

The impact hurled the passengers against their seats. Loose fittings and hand luggage were catapulted to the floor. The flying boat's nose buried itself deep beneath the wave plunging everything into darkness. Cascades of water poured in through the ventilator grills. Screams of terror erupted.

They were going to drown! A bolt of panic shot through Scott as the portholes were blotted out. *The plane was sinking!* Then, miraculously, light returned. They were floating. Munro had judged the landing perfectly, cushioning the impact by the receding wave crest as it sucked away from the hull.

Wallowing in the swell the Clipper turned into the wind, engines ticking over to maintain stability. Passengers and crew stared in horror from the windows at the limitless ocean, praying, sobbing, wondering what their fate was to be.

"*Oh ko*", Yu-Ling trembled as she knelt by her uncle's bunk. "*Oh ko,* what to do? The Sea Devils will kill us all, *heya?*"

"*Joss,*" the old Mandarin calmed her, his voice fluttery. "*Joss.* Listen to heaven and follow fate."

With a supreme effort he placed her hands upon the casket at his breast. "The Great Jewel is in your keeping now. The Sea Devils must not have it. Remember your duty as a Manchu and a Princess of the Yellow Banner."

"Uncle, uncle," she wailed, grief and fear swamping her. "*Ai-yah*, I cannot leave you."

His eyes clouded, "*Joss.* The toll of my days is nearly spent. Weep not, Third Niece. As a daughter you have been to me."

More screams rang out along the deck. On the starboard quarter a patch of spume had begun to boil. A whirlpool was churning the face of the ocean. Froth and bubbles burst from the depths. Plumes of white spray geysered skywards.

The surface heaved and split. A monstrous shape thrust itself above the waves. Steel grey flanks, rust-streaked, streaming water. Rising, rising, roaring as it came like a giant beast. Yu-Ling pressed her anguished face to the glass. Into her fevered brain rushed the words of the old *fung-sui*:

"*The sun in the east is red with the blood of war and from the sea a dragon rises.*"

XXXV

"Isogi! Isogi!" The submarine's heavy bronze hatch cover clanged open with a rush of air. Feet pounded on the conning tower ladder as blue clad Japanese seamen swarmed up from below. With drilled haste multi-barrelled 25 mm AA guns were pulled from pressure-proof containers and slammed into bridge mountings. Ammunition parties panted up behind with clips of shells. Breeches snapped shut as the gunlayers sighted in. Rocking on the swell the American airliner lay broadside on to them, engines stopped, the seaplanes circling overhead like hawks.

"Hai! All clear astern!" lookouts were quartering the horizon. "All clear forward" Black exhaust plumes stained the air aft as the heavy diesels kicked in with a deep snort to begin recharging the batteries. "Main gun crew close up!" a klaxon blared imperatively. Another party splashed out along the drenched foredeck. In moments the heavy deck cannon was training round at maximum depression to cover the flying boat.

Carefully the commander made a 360 degree sweep with the binoculars. "Radio room," he unclipped a voice pipe. "Any transmissions in the vicinity?"

"Negative, *Captain-sama.*"

"Recall seaplanes! Boarding party away!"

Below the conning tower a massive pressurized hangar extended aft over the stern deck. At a curt command watertight doors hissed open. An inflatable boat was dragged out. The boarding party scrambled aboard and paddled madly for the Clipper.

"Schnell! Schnell!" At gun point Jordan herded Slater and Munro aft into the hold. He gestured violently at the nearer of the padlocked cases. "Hurry! That one first!"

Munro felt a cold sweat running down his back. Each box was a deadly bomb packed with explosive. The slightest attempt to force a lid would trigger the anti-handling switch and blow the ship to bits. In the half light of the hold Slater's expression was agonised, his mouth a lipless wound. What had Latouche called the mission? *A race – with a prize of world victory.* Jesus.

Stumbling to keep their balance on the heaving deck, they dragged the heavy crates through into the cabin. The Japanese stood guard by the stairs, sword swinging unsheathed. Beyond the portholes the submarine had edged in closer. They could see the officers on the conning tower watching them through binoculars, the alert gun crews. A boat had been launched. Munro counted six men, all armed with light weapons.

Somehow they must play for time. It was their only chance.

"Passengers, stay in your seats! No harm will come if orders are obeyed!" Jordan's voice boomed over the tannoy again.

Scott steadied herself against the saloon bulkhead, fighting spasms of nausea. With each swell of the waves the flying boat dipped and pitched sickeningly. Nearby the Gordon Smythes huddled miserably over vomit bags. There was no hysteria on the lower deck just a dull apathy. Already most of the passengers were too ill to care what happened to them.

"Pat, there's a boat coming. What're we going to do?"

Even as she spoke noises sounded outside the hull, splashes and thumps against the sponson, harsh accents jabbering. "Open up!" a fist pounded on the hatch. *"Isogi! Isogi!"*

Pat O'Byrne swallowed. "Do . . . d'you suppose we let them board?"

"We don't have much choice," Scott's voice sounded small and scared in her own ears.

"Doctor," Sir Ambrose Hope had staggered across the passage to Latouche. "The cargo," he gasped between retches. ". . . must not be allowed to . . . enemy hands."

Latouche nodded, resolute, "I know my duty, *mon ami.*"

The Englishman gripped his arm.

"Isogi! Isogi!" More shouts, angrier. Rifle butts began crashing against the lock.

Unclipping his belt, Pat picked his way forward over a mess of fallen hand baggage to the hatch. The other passengers watched with white, strained faces.

"KINJIRU!"

He froze petrified. The Japanese warrior had materialised at the top of the stairs, sword drawn. "Holy Mother of God . . ."

"KINJIRU!" a single bound carried the masked black figure to the lower deck. Pat cringed in terror as the blade jabbed at his throat. Hoisting his hands, he edged away. The others in the saloon sat holding their breath, too terrified to move or speak.

Wrenching back the handle, the Japanese pulled the hatch open. A wave slapped over the sponson and gusts of salt spray blew through, soaking the cabin. A Japanese officer pushed inside, pistol in hand, three seamen at his back. Short, squat men with round faces and shaved heads, their uniforms drenched. Long rifles with bayonets fixed. They gaped amazed at the black swordsman.

"Kokuryu-kai, neh?" Recovering, the officer bowed. *"Ohaiyo. Greetings, Sensei."*

The Japanese looked past them to the grey outline of the submarine, the Rising Sun emblem fluttering at the masthead. Pride surged through him. He could find no words. Against all odds he had won through, delivered the great plane into the hands of Nippon. Tears came to his eyes, he was ready to die.

"I-ye, be careful, fools!" the officer raged.

Slipping and cursing on the stair, the seamen struggled in vain to free the wedged steel locker. "It's no use, *Lieutenant-san,"* one gasped. "Fornicator is stuck."

"Bakomono! Idiot! Send for tools then. Cut the rail. Hurry! Do you want to wait all day for the *gaijin* to catch us on the surface?"

The radio-telephone crackled angrily. It was the submarine commander demanding to know the cause of the delay. The current had swung the Clipper's bow round and the main hatch with the dinghy alongside was no longer visible from the conning tower.

A saw was demanded. Ruthlessly the stair-rail was cut away. Grimacing beneath the weight, the seamen lowered the heavy case to the deck. Ropes were threaded through the handles and it was dragged to the hatchway.

"Wait!" The officer rounded on Slater. *"Kagi! Kagi!"* he demanded brusquely, prodding him in the chest.

"Take your hands off me, you yellow coolie!" Slater spat.

"I-ye!" a savage blow from one of the seamen behind knocked him to the deck. Munro and the Chief clenched their fists. Instantly bayonets were thrust at their bellies and they stiffened helpless.

491

"*Kagi wa!*" the officer repeated furiously. "*Doko ni imasu ka?*" he kicked the American with his seaboot.

"Where are the keys? He wants to unlock the box and remove the contents. It's too heavy to transport," Sir Ambrose translated hoarsely.

Munro's stomach turned over. Slater would refuse, he had to. And when the Japs tried to force the locks . . . his throat tightened. One hand strayed fractionally towards the screwdriver in his pocket, then froze as a bayonet jabbed at him menacingly. Scott was watching, scared, every muscle in her body tensed. The others too.

"*Messieurs!*" Munro tore his eyes from the deadly cargo as Latouche pushed forward. "The contents will spoil if exposed to water. Tell him that please," he said firmly addressing Sir Ambrose.

Clearing his throat, the Englishman translated. The others saw the officer hesitate, eyeing the doctor suspiciously. Latouche's manner remained steady, his gaze unwavering. "*Shimai!*" with a gesture of annoyance the lieutenant snapped his fingers at his men, rapping a string of commands. One sprang through the hatch to haul the inflatable up from the water onto the sponson. Using the ropes, the steel crate was heaved over the combing and inched down between the thwarts. A pair of men scrambled aboard.

"*I-ye!*" the Black Dragon warrior interrupted suddenly. Sheathing his sword at his back, he motioned one of the seamen insolently aside. "*Hai, Sensei!*" the man yielded at once, shaking, his fear apparent. Timing the swells, the others slid the boat off and began paddling for the submarine.

A roar of engines above jerked every head. Flashing in the sunlight, a seaplane swept past flaps extended to touch down expertly in the warship's lee. The enemy commander was taking no chances this close to the coast, summoning back his air cover to strike them below even as he hastened to seize the cargo.

Munro watched the plane taxi alongside the submarine. A derrick had been rigged ready to hoist it aboard. The dinghy was coming into sight, working slowly round under the flying boat's bows, low in the water, each wave almost swamping its occupants. Only five of the enemy left aboard now, four Japanese and Jordan. That lessened the odds slightly. If they could somehow seize a couple of weapons . . . *Forget it*, he told himself bitterly. That goddam deck cannon was a five incher at least. The Japs'd blow them to matchwood with the first shell. There wasn't a snowball's hope in hell of pulling anything unless they could somehow neutralize the sub first.

The sub. . . . all at once his pulse quickened. A plan was taking shape.

A thousand to one shot, but it might, it might just come off.

And if it didn't they were all dead anyway.

"*Yoi*," the officer stepped back from the hatch and motioned them to start bringing down the second cargo box. Taking a paper from his pocket, he read out a list of names. Passengers and crew listened in dismay.

Latouche, the Chens, Minister Soong and Slater were all to go aboard the submarine.

"But you can't!" Scott burst out. "Yu-Ling's just a child! Her uncle's sick . . ."

"*Wa!*" the lieutenant whirled on her furiously. His palm lashed out catching her a stinging slap across the face. "*Amerikan-zu* prisoner, no spik *Nippon-zin* officer!" he spat. "*Wakarimasu?*"

The Devil-box must be protected. Trembling, Yu-Ling took the silk-wrapped casket gently from the old Mandarin's feeble hands. She held it to her breast, feeling the burden of responsibility pressing on her spirit like a physical weight.

"*Ai-yah*, what are you doing, *heya?*" Hollington Soong caught her by the sleeve as she stumbled from the cabin. Bodyguard Feng was with him. The Minister's face was a sickly green. His eyes swelled at the sight of the casket in her arms. "*Oh ko*, I will take that," he gasped.

"No, no!" she pulled away. "Honourable Uncle made me swear!"

"Stupid stupid girl, with the jewel we can bargain for our lives, *heya?* The Sea Devils will free us in return for it!" He made a fresh attempt to snatch the casket from her. "*Ai-yah*, help me with the whore, Feng," he cursed.

"Please no . . . *Aiee!*" a squeal broke from her lips as she struggled with the two of them.

"Hey, what's this? Let her alone, you bastards!" Bob Cashin shouldered between them suddenly.

"*Dew neh loh moh!* Mind your own fornicating business!" Soong spat, trying to push him back. They jostled clumsily in the swaying passage. "*Ai-yah*, the Sea Devils will kill us all if she escapes!"

"*OI!*" a shout from the saloon spun them round. A Japanese seaman was advancing, rifle at the ready, the long-bladed bayonet thrusting like a spear.

Panic gripped Soong. His teeth chattered in his head, jowls shaking. "*Oh ko*; the girl has the jewel! This thief of a *quai loh* American is trying to steal it!"

"*Ikinasi!*" the seaman screamed at him. "*Ikinasi! Ima!* Get back!"

"*Ai-yah*, you don't understand, I am Honourable Soong, a friend *heya*?" the Minister babbled frantically.

The Clipper dipped into the trough of a steep swell. The deck tilted sharply, pitching him suddenly forward, arms outstretched. Instinctively the seaman jerked up his weapon. His teeth bared as he lunged.

"Oh shit," Cashin choked as the Minister flopped on the point of the bayonet like a speared fish. With a gasp of horror Yu-Ling turned and ran for the stern.

The last cargo box was the one Munro had opened on Wake. The burn on his palm tingled afresh as they returned to the hold.

"I gotta hunch Tojo's boys don't aim to make old men of us," the Chief grunted under his breath. "What d'you say we try an' take a coupla the sons of bitches with us."

"I'm on," Slater growled, eyeing the officer grimly. "Just leave sourpuss to me."

"*Shimatta!* No spik!" Impatiently the lieutenant prodded them in the back with his pistol. Together they dragged the crate through to the cabin. After the gloom of the hold it seemed dazzlingly bright, sunlight reflected off the waves shimmering on the bulkheads. Jordan was looking sickly green, his face sweat-bathed. The ship's motion was getting to him too. That might give them an edge. If it came to a fight every shred of advantage would count.

Munro glanced at his watch; almost nine am. Broad daylight and barely fifty miles from the coast. Where the hell were the Navy and Air Corps patrols? The dinghy was alongside the sub now. A derrick had been rigged to lift the steel locker on deck. Out to the south-west he could see the other seaplane was lining up to land.

Two seamen remaining on the passenger deck; Jordan, the lieutenant and one other up here. The boat would soon be back, the odds could only worsen. But the enemy were ruthless, any resistance would result in a massacre.

Abruptly Ross came to life. As the seaplane fighter swept down on the water he straightened in his seat like a man aroused from sleep. Throwing off his lap belt, he heaved himself up and lurched from the cockpit.

"*Ach*, what are you doing?" Jordan swung round, levelling the machine gun. "Stay where you were, dog!"

Ross swayed on his feet. He seemed not to have heard. "*Amelia*," he croaked. "Where is she? What have you done with her, you bastards?"

"Amelia Earhart?" The priest shrugged, "How should I know?"

494

Ross blinked at him, "The messages, the killings, Mili . . ."

"*Mili*," Jordan jeered. "Mili was nothing, a device to scare you and throw the fool British and Americans off the trail. It succeeded perfectly."

At Munro's side Slater stiffened. "I said that was a trick, godammit," he muttered angrily.

"Is she alive still? Tell me the *truth*!" Ross's voice cracked.

Georgiana had jumped to her feet, her face chalk white. "What happened on Mili? Where is Amelia?" she burst out. The two Japanese stood gripping their weapons, mouths agape, unable to follow what was being said.

"The Lockheed went down in the lagoon," Ross shivered reliving the memory. "The Japs captured them . . ."

"Bullshit!" Slater snapped. "We saw their signal fire. We could've beaten the Yellow-bellies to it, but you chickened out."

"We'd been spotted. The Japs had fighters out after us!"

"They wouldn't have fired on a Navy plane. Everyone knew there was a big search on. You lost your nerve, Ross!"

"You said there'd be another chance. That we'd be able to go back for them! You *promised*," Ross clenched his fists.

"I said we'd *try*, for Christsakes. it wasn't my mission, I was under orders. We both were. The politicians loused things up, said if we kept our mouths shut there was a chance of a deal with Tokyo. They were scared of stirring up a *war*."

"You *found* Amelia's plane?" Georgiana's voice was husky. "All this time you *knew* where she went down?"

The steel locker was on board the sub now, being carried off aft to the plane hangar. Munro gripped the screwdriver in his pants pocket. "Where is she, Jordan? Dead, murdered like Oliver and Currie? Or rotting in some stinking jail?"

The priest's face twisted, "You know the penalty for spies. Blame her precious *friends* who abandoned her!"

With an animal cry Ross leapt at him.

Two hundred yards out on the submarine's after deck, the Japanese warrior checked uneasily by the clamshell doors to the hangar. *I-ye*, something was amiss. he could sense it. *Haragei*.

Shading his eyes, he swept the water. The great plane rode bows on, wings outspread wide as a city block, props stilled. Figures moving in the cockpit. Impossible to tell who or what they were doing. Still the warning tugged at his mind. A hand strayed to his sword hilt.

495

Suddenly he tensed, every nerve straining. Above the sounds of wind and waves, the crack of a shot echoed across the water.

Namu Amida Butsu! If those bunglers had allowed the *Amerikans* to regain control . . .

He leapt for the dinghy.

The speed of Ross's attack caught Jordan off balance. Unable to use the gun he was trapped in a manic strangle hold. "Urgh, help me!" he choked.

With a hiss of fury the lieutenant's finger tightened on the trigger of his pistol. In the same instant Munro plunged the screwdriver into his ribs.

"*ARGHH!!*" The lieutenant's scream tore the cabin. His body jerked in spasm, the pistol exploding in his hand, as the stiletto blade buried itself agonisingly up to the hilt in his abdomen. The slug whanged off a spar and the gun flew from his grasp bouncing across the carpeted deck. Senseless with pain he clawed at his attacker. Munro tugged desperately at the tool's haft but the force of the blow had clamped it immovably in his victim's flesh. Steel gleamed, somehow the Japanese had managed to free the combat knife at his belt. The ship wallowed in a wave. Fighting for balance, Munro grabbed for the arm to ward off the blow as the short blade jabbed at his throat. In his pain and terror the man's strength was frightening. A hideous grimace distorted his features as he forced the point downwards.

A deafening blast exploded between them. White hot flame seared Munro's cheek, dazzling his vision, all but blinding him. The lieutenant's head swelled like a bursting melon and blew apart in a crimson gush. Slater had shot him at point blank range with his own pistol.

Blood-sprayed, Munro staggered free of the corpse. The Chief and Shapiro were struggling with the surviving seaman, trying to wrest his weapon from him. Boots pounded on the stairs. Two more Japanese came running up from below. "*Banzai!*"

The Chief let out a grunt of wrath. Seizing the seaman, he lifted him up and with a single heave of his great shoulders flung the man bodily at the stairs. All three Japanese went crashing down in a welter of limbs. "Assholes, I'll give you *banzai!*" Snatching up a rifle, he waded after them.

Ross had Jordan pinned against the chart table, hands around his throat. The priest's face was purple, the ligaments standing out on his neck like whipcords. He was fumbling frantically for the trigger guard of the machine gun. Munro's ears were still ringing from the shot. He knocked the weapon away. "Let him go, dammit!" he gasped, dragging Ross off. "We need the bastard alive!"

Sounds of fighting echoed through the lower deck. Guttural Japanese yelps, more shots and terrified screams from the passengers. Slater ran down to help. Another volley of gunfire, cordite fumes filled the aircraft. They heard the chief's voice calling for calm then he reappeared, breathing hard. "All secure, Max," he beamed. "Two of the slant-eyes got theirs an' the other's out cold. Shapiro took a nick in the leg. Doc's with him now."

Ross had slumped over the chart table exhausted. With a grunt he pulled himself together. He staggered to the cockpit. "*Stand by to start engines!*"

"*Dummköpfe!*" Jordan coughed, rubbing at his throat. "Idiots!" he glared savagely at them. "What do you hope to gain? That shooting will have been heard on the submarine. Surrender now and save your lives!"

"Shut up!" Munro flung a glance out the window. There was movement on the sub's deck. Figures swarming round the guns. The priest was right, the firing must've carried across. Any moment now shells could be falling round their ears. One shot in the fuel tanks and the Clipper would go up in a massive fireball. "Skipper, wait! Someone fetch Sir Ambrose – quickly!"

The others gaped at him. "What?"

"Sir Ambrose Hope, get him up here. Hurry, for Christsakes!"

Seizing Jordan by the collar, Munro forced him over to the R/T. "Right, *Spy*," he snarled grinding the Schmeisser into the priest's back viciously, "you're about to make the broadcast of your life!"

Sobbing in terror, Yu-Ling fled rearwards from the fighting. *Oh ko, oh ko,* Minister Soong was dead, betrayed by his greed! The Sea Devils would kill everyone. The evil of the devil-box was destroying them all! Stumbling against a bulkhead, she found herself clutching a ladder. Looking up she saw an open hatchway leading to a darkened hold. Without stopping to think, she began to climb.

"*Oi, Captain-sama,* shooting from the Yankee aircraft!"

"What is happening, can anyone see, *neh?*"

Binoculars raked the flying boat from the sub's bridge. "In the cockpit, fighting I think, *Captain-sama*. Shall I give the order to fire, *neh?*"

"Yes, no wait! There is still the other cargo. We must not risk damage to it."

Everyone watched tensely, gunlayers with fingers on firing buttons training their weapons to follow as the Clipper drifted with the current.

A voice pipe whistled shrilly. "*Oi, Captain-sama*, a signal on the radio-telephone. The Yankee plane calling us!"

"Tell 'em again!" Munro dug the machine pistol into Jordan's back again, ignoring his grunt of pain. "Repeat it. *There's been a fight, but you're still in control.* And no tricks! Sir Ambrose here understands Japanese."

The priest winced. He began to speak into the telephone. Halting sentences. The others waited sweating. "Make it good, damn you," Munro hissed. "Else your stinking allies out there are going to blast us all to hell!"

Almost at once there came an answering crackle from the sub. "They . . . they want to speak to Lieutenant Omuta," Sir Ambrose translated.

"Say they can't, he's been injured," Munro prodded Jordan again. "You have an urgent message for the commander. You suspect the Americans may have switched the cargo somehow. Imperative he open the case and check immediately!"

There was a gasp from Slater. He was peering from the cockpit windows, the dead officer's pistol stuck in his waistband. "Jesus," he whispered, his face agonised. "Jesus Christ, Pilot, you don't know what you're about!"

"Got any better ideas? That pig boat will blow us out of the water the second we try to start engines." Munro thrust the R/T receiver back at Jordan again. "*Tell them.* Or so help me I'll kill you where you sit!"

"*Isogi! Isogi!* Faster, dogs!" the Japanese screamed at the paddlers. Battling the current, the inflatable ploughed across the gap towards the flying boat. "*Isogi!*" Anxiety consumed him as he strove to see above the wave troughs. Suppose the cursed Yankees had retaken the plane, *neh*? They would have weapons now.

"*Hai*, steer to the left! We will board through the tail, take the *gaijin* by surprise."

Ross was growing frantic. "They didn't fall for it, Mister. Your plan's failed, I tell you. I'm going for take-off, it's our only chance!" He fumbled for the ignition switch.

"No, Skipper!" Munro restrained him urgently. "Touch those knobs and you've signed the death warrants of everyone aboard. The guns will open up the second they see the props begin to turn. They can't miss at this range!"

It had been almost four minutes. The crew crouched at their stations like athletes on the starting blocks, hands poised over the controls. Main batteries were on, props set ready in low pitch, all four engines primed for immediate take-off.

Jordan laughed softly. "Admit it, you have lost," he said contemptuously. "Surrender the plane now and spare innocent bloodshed. We want only the cargo. Hand it over and you will all be released to fly on to San Francisco."

"Shut your lying mouth!" Slater snarled. "I'll dump the goddam thing over the side before I let you shitheads have it."

"And risk thirty civilian deaths? I think not," Jordan jeered. He turned his back deliberately. The radio desk was close by. All at once without warning his hand leapt to the R/T button, "*Oi, Captain . . .*"

Slater whirled, pistol out, firing on reflex. The blast of the shots kicked the priest off his feet, spinning him around like a marionette and flinging him across Whitely's stool. His body slid to the floor and lay still. Stewart jerked away with a cry. No one else moved.

". . . *Nan desu ka? Nan desu ka? . . .*" the crackle of the radio-telephone sounded tinnily in the cabin. The operator's voice urgent, suspicious. The crew stared at each other appalled. "Christ, now what do we do?" Whitely blenched.

"*Take-Off positions!*" Munro and Ross were both in motion, reaching for the throttle levers, hitting the ignition switches. "*Raise flaps! Full Emergency Power on all engines!*"

"*Full Emergency, aye aye!*" The starter motor whirred. With a metallic clatter the long grey blades of the portside inboard prop spun into life. Munro threw a quick glance at the sub. Now the die was cast.

BRAANG!!! A waterspout leapt from the sea off the port wing. The sub had fired on the downward roll. BRAANG!! Spray lashed the windshield moments later as a second shell screamed overhead rocking the hull. Fear clutched at the crew's guts. A straddle. The gunners had the range now. The next shot would be a hit.

Streams of winking tracer hosed towards them. The AA automatic stuff joining in. They could feel bullets puncturing the fuselage whanging off the hull plates. The aircraft's nose was turning, increasing the angle.

"*Help! Help me someone, I'm hit!*" As the shells exploded about the ship the lower deck erupted in terrified panic.

"Everyone get down!" O'Byrne yelled above the din pulling Scott to the floor. A porthole shattered overhead, bullets whirring past like angry hornets. Eddie Wirth was rolling in the aisle, clutching his arm. Together they dragged him into one of the cabins. "*Doctor! Doctor!*" Latouche appeared, crouching double. The outboard engines were starting up now, the sound putting hope into their hearts. The Clipper coming alive, swinging slowly into the wind.

The thud of a third explosion rattled the portholes, different somehow. On the flight deck Georgiana gave a scream, "*The submarine . . .!*"

Munro twisted round. A puff of oily smoke had spouted from the pressure hangar abaft the sail. Orange tongues flicked along the deck. In an instant they had mushroomed, engulfing the seaplane moored alongside. Gouts of flame spurted up as fuel lines touched off, spraying the air with liquid fire. Suddenly the entire stern flashed alight. Figures could be seen running from the smoke, hurling themselves into the water clothes afire. Cordite charges and tracer erupted in the ready-use lockers. Signal flares blazed up in sheets of magnesium flame. The whole ship was an inferno.

"Holy son of a bitch!" Slater shouted, his face alight with devilish glee. "It worked, by God. They fell for it!"

Down below, Felicity Gordon Smythe let out a screech, "Oh my God, the boat's alongside!"

"*AIEEE!*" Caught in the backwash of the props the dinghy spun helplessly. With cries of terror the two seamen dived into the water as they were sucked in under the stern. "Fools! Cowards!" Balancing on the thwarts, the Japanese ripped the grappling cord from his waist. Smoke from the blazing submarine blotted out the sun. Dimly he could hear the cries of doomed men. Rage filled his heart. *Tenchu, punishment of heaven!* The tall *gaijin* pilot was behind this. Stupid, stupid to have let him live. Well, he would pay, by the Amida.

The great tail reared above him like a sail. He straightened up. Whirling the cord about his head, he let fly the hook.

"Skipper, Skipper, the rudder's sticking. The tail must've taken a hit!"

"Too bad, we'll have to chance it! Gimme ten degrees of flap."

Engines bellowing under full power, the Clipper switchbacked across the wave crests gathering momentum, every rivet and spar shaking under the strain. Deluges of spray crashing over the nose, forward vision impossible. Out to port the submarine lay wreathed in smoke, her guns fallen silent, bursts of tracer arcing into the air as more ammo belts exploded.

Their speed built, water rushing under the hull. She was on the step now, the buffeting of the ocean rollers eased, charging to meet the wind. Ross's eyes were glued to the airspeed indicator. He was holding the yoke steady, not trying to lift her yet. If one of these big swells bounced her aloft too soon she would stall. A slam down in these conditions would tear the bottom out of the hull.

Ninety knots . . . one hundred . . . and five . . . the nose was up riding high. This was it! Ross pulled back on the yoke. The Clipper lifted, sagged and lay on the air. Involuntarily Munro clenched his fists, willing her to stay aloft. Ross's knuckles were white on the control wheel. *One hundred and ten . . . fifteen . . .* the needle was creeping up. Relief rushed through them. They were airborne . . .

BRAANG!!! With an ear-splitting blast a giant fist slammed against the fuselage. A violent tremor ran through the flight deck. Instrument panels danced crazily on their rubber mountings and perspex splinters showered the cabin. Ross grunted like a man kicked in the stomach as the port wing slewed. With a hideous howling of motors the Clipper side-slipped towards the waves. The sub was firing again.

"Jesus Christ, we're *hit!*"

Black smoke was spewing from the port outboard engine. Ross clutched convulsively at the controls, standing on the rudder bar, pushing the yoke hard over, clawing desperately for height as the wing dropped. Part of the windshield his side had shattered and wind shrieked in the gap.

Munro wrenched back on the throttle furthest from him and rammed the other three levers forward against the stops. Behind, Chief Crow's big hands flicked across his flight panel in a blur, cutting fuel to the burning engine, closing the cowl flaps, reaching over to push the feathering pump button on his left. Switching on the selector valve, he pulled a black plunger to release a smothering charge of compressed CO_2 gas into the nacelle.

The surface was rising up at them like a wall. Munro braced himself for the crash. If the wingtip dug in now she would cartwheel end over end. Airspeed was quivering on one hundred and ten, Ross straining at the yoke white faced, grimacing with effort as he fought to hold the wounded ship steady. "*Stabilizer!*" he gasped. Munro grabbed for the trim wheel, rotating it back to its limit, the flying boat mushing in the air like a stricken beast.

More tracer winked past the nose. Rigid with fear the crew stared at the water, praying. Slater was gripping his seat, swearing in a vicious monologue. The Clipper seemed to hang on the edge of a stall, fighting for lift. The needles quivered in their gauges. With agonising slowness the port wing righted, they levelled out and began to climb.

Munro rolled the stabilizer wheel forward again. His palms were sweating, his mouth dry. But the sub was no longer in sight and the shooting had stopped. "We must be out of range," Stewart choked. "*Jesus*, that was a close one!"

The Chief vanished into the wing. Very deliberately Munro lit two cigarettes, surprised how steady his fingers were. He passed one to Ross and glanced back at the cabin. Georgiana was bent forward, head between her knees.

"Dixie, you okay?"

"I'm fine," she swallowed thickly. "God, for a minute there I thought we were dead."

"Son of a bitch, we *made* it though! We fooled the yellow bastards!" Slater crowed suddenly in disbelief. Davey Klein gave a nervous laugh. Then jubilation broke out all at once. The whole cabin was laughing, slapping one another on the back.

Only Ross stayed silent. Gingerly he took a hand from the yoke for a moment and touched the chest of his uniform jacket, very gently. The fingers came away wet with blood.

Gritting his teeth, the Japanese lay flattened on the starboard tail stabilizer, clinging with all his strength to the edge of the fin. The hurricane blast of the slipstream howled around him with numbing relentless force. A screaming flood of air crushing him against the duraluminum plating, helpless as an insect in a storm. His bruised eyes were squeezed shut against the wind. Forcing them open a fraction, he glimpsed the ocean surface receding below and a wave of nausea swept over him.

The air pressure increased, building to the limits of endurance. He had to fight for breath, the noise and turbulence deadening his brain. Move, he must move. To stay out here was death. Already the feeling was almost gone from his hands.

With a tremendous effort he willed himself to look down again. The Clipper was climbing strongly, the nightmare drop below increasing by the second. But the upward tilt of the nose momentarily lessened the appalling wind blast. Three swords length away along the ridge of the fuselage his streaming eyes could just pick out a hatch set into the hull. The emergency escape exit from the baggage hold. It opened inwards he knew. If he could somehow make that . . .

It was impossible.

Tears of frustration coursed down his face as he clawed in vain for a purchase on the smooth riveted fuselage. It was no use, if he let go the fin he would be swept away by the slipstream instantly. The hatch might as well be a hundred yards away instead of only ten feet.

Was this the end? Discordantly into his mind came fragments from the Hymn of the Dead:

Fallen on the sea, corpses in the water;
Fallen on the mountains, bodies covered with moss:
I shall die only for the Emperor,
I shall never look back.

Determination flooded through him again. *I-ye*, nothing impossible with spiritual strength! He glanced upwards. Overhead a thin wire aerial ran out from the tail fin to each wing root. Would that hold his weight? Only one way to find out.

The wind whipped at him with renewed ferocity as he straightened to his knees to reach up. He had to let go with one hand and lean out and for a hideous instant he felt himself slipping before his numbed fingers found the wire.

He pulled it down. The fixing seemed firm, with enough play to let him lie nearly flat. He would have to trust it. Grimly, hand over hand, he began to inch his way out towards the hatch. The Clipper was climbing still, on three engines, enormous wings flexing with the lift. He kept his eyes rigidly ahead, not daring to glance down again. *Eight feet to go . . . five . . .* The blood was singing in his ears, his arm muscles afire from the strain. *Two more feet only . . .*

He reached the hatch.

Forcing his chilled fingers into the slot of the catch, for a minute he hung there exhausted. The slipstream roared round him like an unseen enemy trying to drag him from the aircraft's back. Open the hatch! He must open the hatch. He pulled the lever.

It would not give. Vainly he tugged again. The catch was locked on the inside.

He felt panic rising. He knew he must break through or die, but his body was too spent to obey. The cold sapping his will.

In desperation he reached down into himself, invoking the *kuji goshin ho* – the nine syllable *jumon* mantra of protection of the *nin-po mikkyo*. The charged words of power that would summon the spirits of the cosmic deities to lend him strength. The indestructible energy and hardness of the *kongo* diamond thunderbolt and the twenty-seven skulls.

503

Rin-pyo-toh-sha-kai-jin-rets'-sai-zen, he screamed the mystic syllables into the teeth of the wind. Feeling the irresistible force of *kai* energy blazing up within him like a volcano spewing fire. And now in truth a thousand deaths were not enough for him.

With a strength greater than human he wrenched back the lever. The lock burst apart and the frame splintered like glass. The hatch dropped inwards and he fell through the gap into the darkness of the hold.

There was no pain in Ross's chest any more. only a great weariness spreading through his veins. Seven days and ten thousand miles they had come over the wide ocean. Men had died, fought battles, a fleet had been sunk, a world gone to war. Soon, soon for him it would be over.

It was taking all his skill and concentration to fly. The Clipper was struggling to hold two thousand feet, one engine dead, the other three straining to compensate. Number two was running hot already. Lesser damage included a leak in the fuel system somewhere. The Chief was below working on it.

A bar of cloud hung on the horizon. The Farallons coming up. A bleak clump of rocky pinnacles standing sentinel above the waves ten minutes from the coast. Back at the radio desk Whitely was trying to raise San Francisco on the R/T. Pretty soon they should be in range.

He eased the Number two throttle off a trifle. The rev counter sagged and the altimeter needle slipped back a hundred feet. His lips tightened, better to lose some height though than lose the engine. A red light winked on in the centre panel. The main reserve tank giving out.

Across the cockpit, Munro stirred uneasily in his seat and leaned forward to squint at the flow meters. The creases at the sides of his mouth deepened as if he did not like what he read. "Think I'll go take a look below, Skipper. See how the Chief's making out with that leak."

Where was Yu-Ling? As the Farallons slid by underneath Scott scoured the lower deck with growing anxiety.

Wind whistled through a dozen holes in the hull and the saloon was spattered with gore like a morgue. Three Japanese seamen had been killed with their own weapons, a fourth by a stray bullet from the submarine. Hollington Soong was dead, Shapiro and Eddie Wirth both wounded, Mrs Gordon Smythe under sedation. Weak with relief, the surviving passengers clustered together, laughing, joking, crying even. Unable almost to credit their narrow escape.

But Yu-Ling had disappeared. And the treasure casket with her.

There was a smell of avgas in the galley passage. the Chief had the deck plates up, working on the fuel pumps. Munro had joined him. Their expressions were sombre. Scott pushed in. "Max, I can't find Yu-Ling. You haven't seen her anywhere?"

"The little Chinese? She isn't with her uncle?"

"No, nor in any of the cabins. And the Professor's asking for her."

"Did you try the after cabin?" Bob Cashin spoke up, "She was with Minister Soong when he was killed. I last saw her running back towards the rear."

"The honeymoon suite? I looked there but I'll check again."

Munro's mouth became hard and tight all of a sudden. "I'll come with you," he said tersely.

The cloud line thickened and became a range of blue shadowed hills. Way off northwards a dark wedge of land thrust oceanwards like the tip of a spear. *Point Reyes,* where Sir Francis Drake had careened his flagship *Golden Hind* in 1579 and claimed the land for Queen Elizabeth.

Stewart was in contact now. San Francisco was standing by, attack planes scrambling to bring them in, Navy destroyers converging on the submarine's estimated position. Sunlight flashed in the distance on the waters of the bay. A dribble of moisture ran down the scarred windshield. The magnetic compass card swung as Ross put the wheel over, pointing the nose towards the Golden Gate.

The Chief reappeared, oil-stained and grim. His flat black eyes checked the gauges swiftly. Chuck sat up, wincing with pain from his slashed arm, "How we doing on the tanks?"

The Chief snorted. "Haemorrhaging fit to bust! That last shellin' sprayed her like a sieve. We'd better start for the deck, Skipper, 'fore the ole girl dies on us!"

Living as one already dead, I will repay chu-on to the Emperor.

Exhausted, the Japanese lay on the floor of the baggage hold, too weak for a minute to move. *Duty was all. Obedience life.* From his cradle the lesson had been instilled into him. Now the time was come to honour the vow. His own death was unimportant. The *gaijin* must not be permitted to escape.

505

Dragging himself up at length, he pushed the hatch shut. The darkness was total but he dared not risk a light. Much of the plane's emergency gear was stored here, he knew. Moving cautiously, working by touch, he located the big ten-seater inflatable life raft and cut the straps. The survival pack inside contained fuel tins for the fresh water still.

Abruptly he tensed, hand on sword hilt. *Haragei* was troubling him! This way and that his senses raked the blackness, alert for danger. The roar of the engines masked all noise. *I-ye*, nothing! Weariness playing tricks on his brain. That or the *karmi* of the dead *gaijin* in the coffin!

Seizing a bundle of life vests, he slashed them open and pulled out the kapok filling. Swiftly he made a pile under the baggage by the bulkhead, and drenched the lot in fuel. Shadows flickered against the roof as he struck a match.

There was a gasp behind. He spun about in sudden fury. Crouched in a corner, shivering with terror, was Yu-Ling.

Something was wrong, Munro could feel it.

Bodyguard Feng was in the rear suite, picking over his master's possessions. He whipped round startled as the two Americans entered.

"We're looking for Miss Chen, have you seen her?"

"*Heya?*" he gawped at them.

"Chen Yu-Ling, you savvy?" Munro demanded curtly.

"*Ai-yah, Chen Yu-Ling,*" Feng's mouth curled spitefully. "*Dew neh loh moh chow hi* on all fornicating Manchu whores!" he spat.

They went out. The Golden Gate was coming into sight. Ignoring the seat-belt sign, passengers were crowding the portside windows for a glimpse of the bridge. Munro stood for a moment in the passage frowning. The sense of threat was still present, stronger now like a cold shadow on his heart.

One of the engines on the starboard began to backfire angrily. A shiver ran through the aircraft's frame and the nose dipped. "Uh uh," Scott muttered, paling.

Munro stiffened. An acrid smell had caught in his nostrils. *Smoke!* He glanced up. Thin tendrils were leaking from the escape hatch overhead.

Oh Jesus. "Fire!" he yelled. "FIRE!!!"

"Gimme full rich on Number Four!"
"God damn those lousy Japs!"

506

The altimeter was showing nine hundred feet now. Pacific Clipper was sinking fast through the bright air, the green Marin County headlands raising to meet them below. *Airspeed below one twenty and falling!* Ross's arms felt leaden, every movement an effort now. Determinedly he shoved the nose down to avert a stall. Ahead he could see the twin towers of the bridge growing larger by the second, the blue bay beyond girdled with hills. Chief Crow switched the cross-feed pump to boost and pushed the mixture control lever forward. The starboard engine roared back to life. They breathed again.

Then came the screams.

Munro leapt for the ladder like a madman, slamming up the hatch with his fist and scrambling through, Scott on his heels. Flames were licking among the baggage. There was a sudden spurt of fire as a fuel can exploded. White smoke spewed into the hold. The rear bulkhead burst ablaze like a torch.

"Fire bottles!" Munro grabbed for the nearest extinguisher. The ship was awash with leaking avgas. If the flames reached the fuel lines they were done for.

A shriek rang against the roof. A cry of naked terror. Munro whirled and his heart leapt in his chest. Cowering by the open coffin was the girl Yu-Ling. A shadow loomed over her. Black clad, masked, sword unsheathed. *The Japanese.*

For an instant they faced one another amid the smoke. The burning plane forgotten momentarily. Hongkong, Manila, Honolulu and now here. It was as if all their previous encounters, the whole voyage even, had been leading up to this instant.

"*Tenchu! Punishment of Heaven!*" Flames flickered on the *katana*'s razored edge as the Japanese rushed at him. The blade hissed in the air like a spitting snake. Trapped against the hatch, Munro had no time to think. Jerking up the fire bottle, he squeezed the trigger. A stream of carbon dioxide gas blasted in the swordsman's face. He staggered in his tracks, choking. At Munro's feet lay an oar from a liferaft. Snatching it up, he aimed a wild blow at the hooded head.

"*Namu Amida!*" The sword rang. With a splintering crack the oar haft snapped in two like matchwood, the pieces spinning from Munro's hands. Stumbling back before the onslaught, he tripped and fell in the smoke. His head struck a metal spar. Winded and stunned, he struggled to recover his feet. By the red glare of the flames he saw the Japanese lofting his sword to kill. His eyes glittered "*Karma, Gaijin!*"

With a cry of horror Yu-Ling lurched forward. In her hands she clutched the jewel casket, lid lifted, holding it open against the black clad figure pinning Munro. *And from within a light streamed.*

A light such as Munro had never glimpsed before. An unearthly blue-white radiance, an iridescence welling forth from the heart of the great diamond like imprisoned moonlight. Refracted and magnified from a hundred crystal facets in a corona of incandescent splendour. Swelling and fading and swelling again, pulsing to the throb of some forbidden energy, the secret power of the source of all matter. *The Birthstone of the Dragon Empress. The Living Jewel of the Manchu Throne.*

★   ★   ★

"Here she comes, Senator!"

From the slopes of the Presidio, field glasses strained upwards at the airliner winging in from the north.

"Looks like one prop out," someone muttered.

"She's darned low. Those bridge towers are seven fifty feet."

White knuckled, the men watched as the great plane came on, growing larger by the minute, sinking lower in the calm bright air.

"Get her *up*, man, or you ain't gonna make it!"

"Oh shit, look at that!"

From the tail of the Clipper a plume of smoke had sprouted. "Jesus," a general whispered in disbelief, "Jesus, Senator, she's on fire!"

Kim's lip quivered.

★   ★   ★

Like men transfixed, Munro and the Japanese stared at the devil-box. The pale rays appeared to writhe and twist in the smoke, the gilding of the casket shimmering as if the dragon inlay had come to life.

Munro recovered fractionally soonest. A scything kick swept the legs of the Japanese from under him. He crashed down, cursing as the sword was jerked from his hand. Instinctively, he went for the knife in his sleeve, at the same time smashing a reverse strike to the American's kidney. Munro blocked with a forearm and chopped a left hook to his opponent's head. Abandoning the knife, the Japanese countered with elbow jabs and kicks. His fingers clawed for the face in a Tiger slash. Desperately Munro fought for the upperhand as they rolled among the baggage punching and gouging at one another, pitting his weight against his opponent's incredible strength.

With a bang the forward hatch to the crew quarters flew open. Chris Fry barrelled in clutching a pyrene extinguisher, Stewart and Davey Klein behind. At the inrush of air the flames leapt up roaring. Half the hold was engulfed. Scott staggered out of the smoke, beating at her clothes.

"*EII!!*" the Japanese gave a sudden furious bellow. His sword was gone, time slipping from him. With a violent heave he thrust Munro off and sprang clear, bounding for the hatchway amid the confusion.

A fusillade of backfiring shook the starboard wing again. It ran on for a second, then cut out sharply altogether. The plane sank like a stone under the drag of the windmilling propeller.

"*Chief, feather the bastard! Hurry, for God's sake!*"

"*Aye aye, feathering four!*" Chief Crow pulled out the safety clip and thumbed the red pump button. The whirling prop stilled as the blades turned edge on to the airstream. Her two good engines howling under the stress, the Clipper staggered on towards the bridge towers. A red mist swam before Ross's eyes as he fought to hold altitude. Smoke from the fire was wafting through the ship now. They could hear the panicked cries of the passengers below.

"*BANZAI!!!*"

The door from the hold exploded inwards as if struck by a shell. With a rending screech the Japanese erupted into the cabin like a demon from hell. Georgiana screamed once in pure horror as the black-robed, black-masked monster burst upon her, eyes blazing with chilling fury, talon hands reaching out to strike. Death Incarnate, the Slayer of the Apocalypse.

"*BANZAI!!*" The speed of his charge swept her aside like a boneless doll. With a throat-rasping yell the Japanese raced for the cockpit. Chief Crow was out of his seat, moving to block him, enormous arms grappling, but the onrush was too fast to stop. An outstretched fist drove into his belly with the impact of a spear thrust. The Indian let out a grunt of surprised pain and staggered back.

"*BANZAI!!* The Japanese plunged on past him. He reached the cockpit. Ross swivelled, his mouth opening in a soundless cry, lips drawn back, eyes straining in their sockets as he glimpsed the frightful apparition lunging for his unprotected throat. A quiver ran through the ship. The Clipper slewed and went into a stomach-wrenching dive.

In the same instant Munro came through the hatch and the Japanese whirled.

"We're going to die, we're going to die!" Cynthia Gordon Smythe screamed in a fresh paroxysm of fear. Down on the lower deck passengers clung to their seats. Smoke from the burning hold was billowing into the tail section. Slater had run aft. As the horizon tilted sickeningly he heard the sounds of fighting above and stumbled forwards into the saloon just as Munro and the Japanese toppled crashing down the stairs from the control cabin.

"Son of a bitch!" he croaked at the black-clad figure, barely recognizing his own voice. "I gonna kill you, Yellow-belly!" he tugged the pistol from his waistband.

The Japanese rolled clear of Munro. Cat-quick he was upright again, moving in. One foot lashed out and Slater felt a sear of hot agony shoot up his leg from instep to groin. The pain made him want to vomit. Vainly he tried to bring the gun up. Fingers like the jaws of a steel trap snapped shut on his wrist. Another tearing pain and the weapon fell from his nerveless hand as the joint broke.

Callously, the Japanese spun him clear. Panic stricken passengers were scrambling for the rear, but the *gaijin* pilot was on his feet again and two more *Amerikans* had appeared from the nose with rifles taken from the seamen. Ignoring Munro, in an instant, he vaulted a table to meet them. Surprised, the first checked and lunged clumsily with the bayonet. Side stepping, the Japanese caught the rifle by the foresight. Pivoting on his left foot, he snapped out a vicious heel stamp. The airman fell to the deck, screaming thinly, clutching his knee. Now the Japanese had a weapon.

The second airman worked his bolt frantically. The boom of the shot rocked the cabin as the Japanese knocked the muzzle up. Lunging forward right-handed, he slashed the bayonet blade brutally across the Amerikan's unprotected face. Kicking his legs away, he impaled him through the heart as he dropped.

In less than half a minute he had killed one man and disabled two.

Munro tore in, fists swinging. The black assassin spun, whirling the gun club fashion. A lurch of the plane threw him off balance and the rifle smashed into a table, shattering to pieces. The Japanese threw it down. Sweating, he blocked two punches before a third connected. *By the Amida!* His teeth ringing he reeled back a pace as another blow caught him on the temple. The *gaijin*'s strength was shocking.

"*EI!*" Switching tactics, he let out a great *kai*-yell, the energy releasing scream to dismay his opponent. Turning his head away, he dropped his left shoulder swiftly and thrust forward, striking with every ounce of force at his command. The body-smash of the *togakure-ryu*, first described four centuries ago and as valid now . . . *time the*

charge to your breathing, strike with the spirit tell the enemy is dead . . .
"*TENCHU!!*"

The impact hurled Munro backwards like a shot gun blast, the violence of the shock exploding the air from his chest leaving him gasping. Bewildered, he stumbled among the tables, ribcage afire, coughing unable almost to breath. It was as if he'd been hit by a truck. The pain was piercing. For a moment he thought a lung had collapsed.

Before he could recover a second stunning blow slammed into him. Limbs flailing, he staggered against the entrance hatchway like a drunk man. Every bone in his body ached as if it were fractured. *Jesus, what was this?*

Ruthlessly the Japanese bored in again, pouring out his reserves of energy prodigiously in a furious effort to finish. Munro saw him coming and knew he could not withstand another attack. Flouderingly, he struggled to regain his feet, grasping for a hold. His right hand fell on a lever, without thinking he pulled. There was a click and a sickening lurch behind. Freezing air blasted into the cabin as the hatch flew open, sucked back by the slipstream. Through the gap the southernmost tower of the bridge loomed hideously close, the supporting cables and vehicles on the traffic deck in plain sight now.

He saw his enemy's lips moving as if invoking a curse. The dark eyes blazed with a savagery bordering on madness. The bastard was trying to hex him. He was going to force him out the hatch!

Upstairs, Scott seized Yu-Ling by the arm and together they stumbled from the smoke-filled holds out through into the control cabin. The Clipper was still locked in a dive, Ross hunched over the controls struggling to pull out.

"*Skipper!*" Dropping hold of the Chinese girl, Scott scrambled into the cockpit. Ross was hauling back on the yoke with every muscle he possessed, his face a ghastly grey. To Scott's horror she saw the front of his shirt was soaked crimson. "Skipper, for God's sake, you're hurt!"

Ross clenched his teeth, sweat pouring from under his cap. "The props," he croaked. "Give me max low pitch. *Hurry!*"

The Japanese had Munro by the neck, fighting for a strangle-hold. The plane yawed, sending them lurching across the deck. For a hideous moment Munro thought they were going to plunge through together. The grip about his neck tightened, forcing him towards the opening. He could feel his heel on the hatch rim at his back.

Hatred boiled in his throat. Fury and hatred. They had come too far

511

to end this way. No damn Jap was going to throw him out his own plane! Like a cleansing fire the anger surged up within him leaving his mind suddenly clear and sharp, the stillness at the heart of a storm. The tendons of his body tingled as if charged with fire, the rage swelling and building into an irresistible wave. Wrenching himself free of the strangling hold, he let fly with a right cross packed with every last ounce of weight and strength behind it. In that split second it was as if the stricken flying boat came to his aid. A renewed coughing seized the port engine. The deck lurched sharply hurling the combatants together with savage momentum. All the energy of the Clipper's hull seemed to channel into Munro's frame, rushing through the bunched muscles of his arm, bursting forth from his fist with the violence of a dynamite charge. It caught the Japanese on the side of the jaw, lifting him six inches clear of the deck. Dazed, he stumbled back, his guard sagging.

One . . . Two . . . and again! Munro followed up. Hooks, jabs, uppercuts to the chin. Smashing blows battering his enemy, pulverizing, destroying. Blood roared in his ears. He was back in the ring again. *This was for Oliver in Hongkong! For Wei-wei, Thyssen and Tad Gotto! For the poor bastards who'd got theirs at Pearl and Hickam Field! For America!* All the pent up rage inside him, screwed down so long, bursting forth in a berserker's frenzy.

The black-clad figure tottered to its knees, arms raised in a vain attempt to ward off the rain of blows. Relentlessly Munro pressed in, denying him respite, punching with ruthless precision. Shoulder-jarring jabs to the jaw, temple, throat – no place here for the rules. It was a fight to the death. Kill or be killed.

Tokyo had started this, let them pay the consequences.

Uncorking a final uppercut, he let the Japanese fall and collapsed against the ruined centre table.

The hatch swung crazily in the slipstream, thudding against the hull. The Clipper was racing down on the bridge. The golden towers rose to meet them, vaster and nearer than was possible. He tensed instinctively for the crash. There were terrified cries from passengers up the deck as the cables scraped by under their wings. Then amazingly they were past and into clear air.

"Munro! Munro!" Sir Ambrose was groping his way unsteadily across the deck. He held a gun. Slater's.

Munro took it from him. His head was spinning. Sharp darts of pain lanced through his chest at every breath. "Okay, buster," he gasped, motioning to the Japanese. "On your feet. And make it slow."

The Japanese dragged himself upright. His mask was torn away, there was blood round his mouth, but the dark eyes were unyielding, hard as stone. Disregarding the gun, he stepped painfully to the hatch and squared his shoulders. Proud, resolute. The slipstream whipped his black robes as he glanced at Munro. "*Sayonara, Gaijin,*" white teeth flashed in momentary respect.

"*TENNO HAIKA BANZAI!!!*" the words were torn from his throat as he launched into space.

Munro slammed the hatch and ran for the stairs. The Clipper was flattening out over the water. Alcatraz prison island coming ahead. Ross was in his seat still, Scott beside him. "Max," she twisted round urgently, "quick, he's hurt bad."

"I'll make it," Ross's voice was a harsh whisper. There was a bloody froth now at his lips. "I can do it . . . one more time. . ." His hands moved on the throttles, easing them back slowly. "Give me . . . give me flaps fifteen."

Munro slipped into Scott's seat. "Aye aye, Skipper," he answered. "Flaps fifteen."

"*Prepare to land.*"

"*Ready to land, aye aye, Captain,*" Chief Crow's deep voice chimed in from behind.

"*Airspeed one hundred knots, Skipper.*"

Stewart Whitely appeared from the rear, exhausted and grimy. "Fire's out, thank God."

A line of white buoys flashed by on the blue water below. Ross eased the yoke gently back. There was a second's soft floating. A smooth hiss against the flying boat's keel. Light as a bird the Clipper settled on the surface.

Ross's head sagged forward on his chest. "Oh God," Scott knelt at his side, stricken.

Quietly Munro reached over and closed the throttles. Their way sank off.

Pacific Clipper was home.

Epilogue

"*Protactinium.*" Dr. Latouche closed the lid of the jewel casket carefully. His fingertips traced the gold inlaid dragon of the Ming dynasty. "Protactinium, a product of the uranium decay chain. This is the isotope 231, first isolated in China by the Duke of Chou at the turn of the century. A half life of thirty thousand years, its power has scarcely diminished. And so the Dragon Empress died." He sighed, "Professor Chen was the Duke's assistant. Only he now knows the location of the deposits in the north."

Battle-weary and scarred the *Pacific Clipper* lay tied up at the Pan American jetty. Today there were no welcoming crowds, no photographers or society journalists to greet her triumphant return. Instead marines in battle kit surrounded the dock and military vehicles waited to rush the cargo inland to a place of safety.

As Latouche stepped ashore Kim was there to greet him, "Doctor, welcome at last."

"Senator," the Frenchman bowed slightly. "An honour to meet you."

A derrick whirred overhead. The remaining cargo box was being swayed out. They turned to watch it lowered to the dockside. "It's we who should be honoured," the thin man, whose name was J. Robert Oppenheimer, answered with quiet earnestness. "You and your friends may just have saved the war."

Up on the flight deck the crew stood by silent while Ross's body was gently eased out from the cockpit seat. Scott choked as he was laid on the stretcher and covered with a sheet. "He . . . he understood, Chief," she wiped her eyes. "He accepted me at the end."

The Chief squeezed her shoulder, "Sure he did, kid."

A little knot of passengers were waiting by the gangway as the crew came out from the hatch. Bob Cashin, Sir Ambrose Hope, Van Cleef, the Gordon Smythes. Slater had his arm in a sling. "Godammit, Pilot," he grinned ruefully, "but you did a helluva job. We'd never have made it without you."

514

Shading his eyes, Munro gazed back past the forbidding presence of Alcatraz to the distant towers of the bridge. A coastguard cutter was heading out through the Narrows, Stars and Stripes snapping in the wind. "God help us if there are more like him," he said softly. "It could be a long war."

Georgiana slipped her hand into his arm. The breeze billowed her skirt and her lips were pale in the sunlight as he kissed her. "C'mon, Dixie," he said teasingly. "After all, you promised Kim you'd bring back a husband."

Yu-Ling gripped her uncle's hand. Around them the great city embraced the bay, tall buildings all prisms and crystal in the morning light, streets and waterfronts seething with life. The dawn haze had lifted, the air was clear and salt-sharp invigorating. Sparkling sea, white clouds sailing against a brilliant sky, the fresh sun gilding the slopes of the hills with its fire. Tears rolled down her cheeks. Never in her dreams had she imagined anywhere so beautiful. *Ai-yah*, indeed this was *Kum san – Land of the Golden Mountains*. Truly they had arrived.